BAD
REPUTATION

KRISTA & BECCA
RITCHIE

ALSO BY
KRISTA & BECCA RITCHIE

ADDICTED SERIES
Addicted to You
Ricochet
Addicted for Now
Thrive
Addicted After All

CALLOWAY SISTERS SERIES
Kiss the Sky
Hothouse Flower
Fuel the Fire
Long Way Down
Some Kind of Perfect

CIRCUS IS FAMILY SERIES
The Failed Audition
The Secret Ex-Boyfriend

LIKE US SERIES
Damaged Like Us
Lovers Like Us
Alphas Like Us
Tangled Like Us
Sinful Like Us
and more

STANDALONE ROMANCE
Love & Other Cursed Things

A NOTE FROM THE AUTHORS

Bad Reputation is a collector's edition of Willow & Garrison's story. It includes two novels, *Whatever It Takes* and *Wherever You Are*, in chronological order. For those that would like to read this book simultaneously with the Addicted/Calloway Sisters Series, there is a **reading guide in the back of the book**. If this is your first introduction into Willow & Garrison's story, we highly recommend either starting with *Whatever It Takes* or the *Addicted Series*. We structured this novel in a way that's best suited for readers who are already familiar with Willow & Garrison and the large cast of characters.

Bad Reputation is a New Adult romance. Even though the characters are 17 for much of the novel, we do not consider this book Young Adult. This book contains mature language and graphic sexual content and is recommended for readers 18+.

Also to note: Wakefield University is a fictional school set in London that has a high matriculation of International students and uses a semester-based curriculum. Since Willow is American, she uses many colloquial American terms for university (for example: referring to her room as a dorm) that UK students might not use.

CONTENT WARNING

This book contains graphic scenes of physical abuse from older brothers to a younger brother and verbal abuse that may be upsetting to some readers.

PART ONE

"It's the oldest story in the world.

One day you're 17 and planning for someday.

And then, quietly, and without you ever really noticing,

someday is today.

And then someday is yesterday.

And this is your life."

One Tree Hill

(SEASON 9, EPISODE 13)

WILLOW'S TUMBLR QUESTIONNAIRE

Rules: Complete the form by answering each section truthfully. Once you've finished, tag other users to complete the task. Begin by sourcing the person who tagged you.

Have you ever...

Been cheated on: never gave anyone the chance to
Kissed someone and regretted it: never been kissed (don't judge)

Drank hard liquor: a couple times. I didn't like the taste

Been drunk and thrown up: nope

Met someone who changed you: I met Loren Hale once (my only celebrity run-in). He was standing on my front doorstep (long story). Loren Hale left within like five minutes—but he actually spoke to me. He noticed my Mutants & Proud pin, and I mentioned liking X-Men Evolution (the cartoons). Then he made a comment about the comics and Lily Calloway. He called her his girlfriend, but they were and are still engaged if Celebrity Crush is right. It made me think that girls could read comics too—and the way he spoke, he presumed I already did. I never tried to read them until that moment, until he left and I thought yeah, I'm allowed to read these too.

I started New X-Men and related so much to Wallflower, a girl I really needed a year ago, when my dad divorced my mom. And I would've never read comic books and fallen in love with them if I didn't meet Loren Hale

Fallen out of love: I've never fallen in love to fall out of it

Found out who your true friends are: this is why I keep my circle small. Maggie is the truest friend there ever could be

Lost glasses: multiple times. My little sis sometimes takes them to be funny

Sex on the first date: ...idk maybe I'd do it? Thinking about it makes me nervous...

Been arrested: in a nightmare

Turned someone down: for what? Like dating?

Fallen for a friend: no. I don't like the guys at my school like that (you wouldn't either if you were me)

What was your...

Last drink: Fizz Life

Last phone call: umm, my Grandma Ida. She wanted to crochet me a scarf for next winter and needed to know what color yarn. I told her blue

Last text message: "I bought it! I bought it!" to Maggie, in relation to Understanding Comics by Scott McCloud—I've been saving up babysitting money to purchase the comic book. I read ANYTHING that Loren Hale recommends (my comic book guru), and he suggested this one not long ago on social media

More questions...

Do you have any pets: my dad hates pets, but when he moved out a year ago, my mom let Ellie get a hamster. It smells really bad

What did you do for your last birthday party: ate out at the Noodle House with just my mom, sister and Maggie. I don't like big parties, especially not ones about me

Name something you cannot wait for: A REBOOT OF NEW X-MEN (PLEASE HAPPEN!!! I'LL TAKE ANYTHING!!!) Also, for Maggie to meet Scarlet Witch (aka Elizabeth Olsen) one day.

What irritates you: being forced to speak up in large crowds

Nickname(s): none (I'm not that cool)

Relationship status: single

Favorite TV show: tie between Gravity Falls & X-Men: Evolution. I love them

High School: ready for it to expire

College: wish I could go. I'm working on it

Hair Color + Length: light brown, straight, and about to my chest?

Height: 5'5''

Your crush: TOM HIDDLESTON!!! (aka Loki)

Tattoos: my dad says no

Right or left-handed: Right

Any surgeries: nothing that serious

Any piercings: double lobe piercings on both ears, just four little studs, two bats and two stars

Favorite sport: sports? *runs and hides*

First vacation: never left Maine before, but when I was really little, we used to go to the coast, about 4+ hours from Caribou, and we went sailing one time. I can't really remember it, but my mom has pictures. Everyone seems happy

What do you like...

Hugs or kisses: hugs for now

Shorter or taller: taller than me. Even if it's only a little taller. That works too.

Older or younger: older but not too old—I couldn't do what Daisy Calloway does with her boyfriend, who's like seven or eight years older (I can't remember)

August

1

Willow Moore

"WE'RE NOT HAVING THIS CONVERSATION! IT'S ELLIE'S BIRTHDAY!" my mom shouts, the familiar octave present only when she's around my dad.

"Her birthday ended *twenty* minutes ago!" my dad yells. I haven't seen them endure each other's presence since the divorce. I invited him to my 17th birthday dinner back in March and he said he wouldn't come. His exact words: *not if your mom is there.* Now August, he's willing to stomach my mom for Ellie—his little bundle of princess joy.

I don't think I ever fit into what he wanted me to be. His words over the years have been etched into my head.

If you liked more girl things, you'd have more friends, Willow.

If you actually went to a party like a normal girl, you'd have more friends, Willow.

If you wore more makeup and made an effort, you'd have a boyfriend, Willow.

If you stopped watching superhero cartoons, you'd have a boyfriend, Willow. Every girl your age has one.

But mostly I hate that he left in the first place. I hate that he just walked out on my mom and broke my little sister's heart and tore through their lives, even if he'd already been tearing through mine.

He just said, "*I can't live with your mother.*" And as a teenager, I'm not privy to the details I guess, but the lack of them has only made hate fester more for him than it has for her.

I *hate* that his leaving caused my mom to cry every night for three months. I *hate* that Ellie asked repeatedly, *"When's daddy coming home?"* I *hate* that I was the one who had to say the truth over and over, and I had to watch tears roll down her cheeks every single time. I *hate* that he wasn't here to stomach their hurt—that he never woke up to it, never went to sleep to it, the way that I did. When I look at my dad, I only see the man who has hurt me by hurting the two people I love most.

"Willow?" Ellie whispers again, tugging on my wrist. I look down at my six-year-old sister, her eyes wide like saucers. And she mutters, "Can you tell them to stop?"

I fix her plastic crown that droops to the left. "Only if you wait here."

"I will. I promise." Then Ellie jumps onto my bed and plops down beside my laptop. I notice a Barbie doll in her hand. It must be new.

I leave her quickly, my bare feet on the old carpet, and I squeeze down the narrow stairs towards the kitchen.

"We're not talking about this here, Rob!"

His tone lowers to a heated growl. "Yes *we are*."

I stop short of the kitchen, able to peek beside the doorframe. The yellow linoleum floors are half littered with wrapping paper and pink balloons, the trashcan stacked with dirty paper plates. My mom hangs onto the kitchen sink, her knuckles whitening.

I only spot this much outward emotion from my mom when she's not noticing me or forgets I'm here. Though after the divorce, I've seen this side of her more often. On a normal day, she's sweet and subdued. Rarely heated. Almost never angry. She tries to bottle most dark sentiments, something I've learned to do.

As I creep from the corner, I gain a better view of my mom.

Just forty, she has kind eyes, a smooth pale complexion and rosy cheeks, but her usual put-together persona cracks beneath welling tears. She stands opposite a middle-aged man with light scruff, narrowed eyes, and a Miller Lite shirt. And I mentally take sides—I take *hers*, even if I'm supposed to remain nonpartisan.

I see him.

I see him hurting her.

I see him causing her these tears.

My mom who never asks more of me—when what I am is subsequently less.

I clutch onto the doorframe, watching as my dad crosses his arms over his burly chest.

He says to her, "We'll never finalize this fucking divorce if your lawyer keeps putting this off."

My mom inhales a shaky breath. Her nose flares and she fights tears again, straddling more sadness than rage.

No. Tell him to fuck off, Mom. Tell him you don't want him. I bite my tongue, hoping she'll stand up for herself.

"Please, Rob…" she cries. "Just come back home."

My stomach is queasy. I just want her to kick him out, to grow the strength to rip apart the thing that causes her pain. *Come on, Mom. You can do it.*

I wish I had the bravery to help her, but my feet cement to the floor, weighed like shackles of tar-filled balloons.

Through his teeth, he sneers, "I'd rather burn in fucking *hell* than be with a woman who spent over seventeen years repeatedly lying to me."

A chill races across my arms, and I swallow a lump.

"It has nothing to do with you, Rob." Her voice trembles, and then tears burst forth in a guttural cry. It pierces me through the chest, and I stagger one step. I'm blown back.

Meanwhile, *he* just stands there.

He just watches in disgust.

How could he—

"You abandoned *your son*," he says so passionately, so soulfully and hatefully that his face turns blood-red.

And I go utterly cold.

"Your fucking *son*," he repeats with glassy eyes. "The one that I knew nothing about!" He points a finger at his chest. Vibrating—he's vibrating in anger and pain.

I'm shaking with it too.

I don't understand…

My dad licks his lips and adds, "How does the fact that you saw the father of your son on *twelve* separate occasions for two decades, not affect me?"

No.

I rock back.

He's to blame.

Isn't he?

He has to be.

Tears crest my eyes as I try to block out the truth. No.

Think about it, Willow.

I don't want to. It's easy believing one way for so long, to put all of my emotions in this one drawer that makes the most sense. It *hurts* having someone yank open the drawer and dump out its contents, destroying what I know is real.

She's my ally.

She's my confidant and my friend.

She's my *mom*.

She wouldn't lie. She wouldn't *abandon* anyone. She's my mom… the person who spent five hours helping me with a science fair project in eighth grade—who took me to the midnight showing of *Avengers*, even though she had work early in the morning.

She's kind-hearted and loving. She's sweet-tempered and generous.

I can't imagine her abandoning a puppy, let alone an actual person…*her* person…

It's not real.

And then my mom says, with staggered breath, "I never saw his father after the day the baby was born…" I can't tell whether this is true or not. She plants her eyes on the ground in *shame*, never meeting my dad's gaze.

"You're lying again," he grits.

"I'm not!" she screams at the floor. "Those were checks from him, but it's been twenty-four years since I last saw him. He had his assistant fly out...and give the checks to me. Five years ago was the last one. I've told you this. Please, Rob—" She tries to grab onto his forearm, but he jerks away. She catches air and then grips the sink counter for support again.

I lean my weight on the doorframe, my glasses misted with tears, and I take them off with trembling hands and rub them on my green striped shirt. I try hard not to make a noise, but my nose runs...I wipe that with my arm—shaking.

Stop shaking, Willow. It's okay...

My chin quivers.

You've been on the wrong side of things all along. You fool.

I expected my dad to hurt me.

I never expected her to.

My father silently fumes before he bursts again. "And why'd he just give you checks?" He lets out an anguished laugh, hands on his waist. "You're telling me there was nothing attached to them? No stipulation?" He shakes his head in disbelief.

"I told you, he wanted me to keep quiet, out of pity, I don't know. He just kept sending them, and we needed the money for your car, the house—"

"You've got to be..." He yells at the top of his lungs, pissed and furious. I flinch, and then he grabs a nearby bowl of oranges. He tosses it violently at the wall.

I jump as the ceramic shatters all over the linoleum.

"He paid for *my* car, for *my* house?!" He points a finger at his chest again, a good distance still between him and my mom, as though it sickens him to even be near her.

"Please..."

"Did you cheat on me?" he suddenly asks, veins protruding from his neck. "Tell me the fucking truth, Emily!" He's crying.

I've never seen my dad shed a tear, not even from anger, not even when he said goodbye to me.

My mom rocks back a little, as though his words and voice have shoved her hard. At her extended silence, I want to press my back to the wall and slide down into a tight ball. I want to hide, but I can't unfreeze. I can't move.

"I didn't..." The way her voice trails off, it makes it so hard to believe her—but I still want to. I want to believe she didn't do this.

She didn't cheat on my dad. She didn't.

I believe it. I do. I want to be on her side.

My dad breathes heavily, his chest rising and falling, tears dripping. And then he asks, "Is she even my daughter?"

My throat swells closed. *She didn't cheat on my dad. He has it all wrong.*

Maybe I just really want her to confide in me. To tell me the truth. This force inside pushes me, and I round the corner. "Mom?" I sound small.

As I stare between my mom and dad, their rage and hurt and distress start to cage behind an opaque screen, one that bars me from entry.

I blink, wetness sopping my lashes.

I hate that they won't show me anything real right now—that I have to spy in order to see it.

My mom straightens up and rubs her cheeks with the back of her hand. "Go upstairs, honey." Her voice cracks.

"Who's my father?" I ask.

"Rob Moore is your father, and he's Ellie's too," she says adamantly. "It's not what you think—"

"I'm leaving," my father says, his tears dried up. Another glare plastered on his face.

He hardly acknowledges me.

He passes me to reach the doorway, and our bodies seem to lean away from each other, like pressing the wrong side of two magnets together, unable to near.

He has a clear aversion to me, and now I think I know why. He believes I'm not his child, even when I really am.

I listen to his footsteps all the way to the living room. Not long after, the door bangs closed, and my mom turns her back on me, beginning to clean a few dirtied glasses in the sink. She can't just act like nothing happened.

"Mom!" I shout.

"I'm done talking…" Her arms shake like mine, and maybe a year ago, I would've stayed quiet and just gathered these bare details and created my own horrific conclusion. I don't want to live with this half-picture anymore. I don't want to see through clouds, stained glass and opaque screens. I want transparency for my *own* life, and only she can give that to me.

"I'm not done." My voice is softer than I intend. She doesn't turn around. I take a deep, strong inhale. "Mom," I choke, "I'm *not* done."

She slowly spins around, her hand fisting a dishtowel, eyes blood-shot. She waits for me to speak this time.

I lick my lips and I ask, "Do I have a brother?" She lied about him. I'm not sure if I can trust her, and I'm not sure if I should love her—but I do love her, and I do still trust her. That can't vanish that quickly.

But right now, I resent her. For the first time, I truly do. And I hate it.

"Willow…" She shakes her head at me, struggling to reveal what she's kept secret for so long.

I wipe my burning eyes beneath my glasses. I shift my feet and accidentally step on a balloon. It pops loudly, and we both flinch.

My family tree has been set on fire, and I'm desperately trying to find *one* missing branch so I can make sense of myself again.

I need him.

Whoever he is. I need to know what he's like. How old he is. A name. A place. Maybe he understands things that I don't. Maybe he gets it.

"It was a long time ago," she says. "I was a teenager, about your age, a little younger when I was pregnant." She lets out a weak, broken laugh. "You can't even imagine…"

I watch her lean against the sink and stare off at the half-eaten vanilla cake, lopsided on the counter. "Is he still alive? Does he know—"

"Loren Hale," she says, her voice suddenly stoic and cold. "That's your brother."

My legs want to buckle, but I manage to stay upright, my mind whirling as pieces of a much larger puzzle fit in place. "He knew..." He came to *our* house about four years ago. She told me that she knew his father. And I realize, his visit wasn't random. He came and he left so quickly. "Did you tell him not to tell me?" I wonder.

Her lips press in a line, and I take her silence as affirmation.

"Oh my God," I mutter, my chin trembling again as I restrain a flood of tears. She kept him away from me. Why would she do that?

Loren Hale is my half-brother. All this time...we could've talked, had a relationship, been friends—seen each other. Instead there's just this black hole of *nothingness*, hollow and empty.

I feel empty.

"Can you just forget about it?" my mom asks me.

I shake my head in a daze. "No...I want to meet him." I need to tell him that I know the truth now. I want to regain this piece that I've lost.

"You can't," she says tiredly and brushes strands of her hair off her forehead. "The Hales are famous, Willow. The moment the media learns that Loren's related to you, they're going to harass our family. I've tried *so hard* to give you girls a normal life. You may decide to live in that world later on, but Ellie is young and she's not going to. Okay?"

I try to process this as quickly as I can. Hale Co. is what elevated Jonathan Hale's status to "wealthy billionaire" and his son to the heir. But their fame ultimately came through a salacious scandal that involved Lily Calloway, Loren's fiancée.

Soon after, the Calloway sisters and their men became public interest and fodder. They're all in at least three tabloids every day. Paparazzi follow them around Philadelphia, their hometown.

People love them and hate them.

I understand why my mom would want to protect us from that, but Loren Hale has only been this famous for a few years at most. She could've introduced me to him when he was just a rich kid in Philadelphia.

She never intended for me to meet him, to know him...

How can I believe anything she says?

"Willow," she pleads. "Let this go. Jonathan gave us a lot of money over the years. It's over, okay? No one can know that Loren's my…" Her face suddenly contorts. She can't say it.

My heart palpitates. "Your son," I whisper with burgeoning tears.

She shifts her body until I can't see her face. After a short silence, she says softly, "I was only sixteen, Willow."

She was so young.

And she's right, I can't imagine…

Jonathan Hale must've been so old too. I cringe at the picture—at the twisted, grotesque reality that I never knew I was a part of. I feel bad for her, but I worry that if I wade in grief then I'll never grow the strength to meet my brother. I'll flounder in her sadness and hold onto her hurt like I've done since the divorce.

"I'm leaving," I suddenly say—just realizing that these were my father's exact words minutes ago. She blinks back emotions again, and I'm already determining what I should pack. A duffel bag in my closet, some jeans and shirts, my backpack and my wallet.

I'm leaving.

I've never been this bold. I've never been this courageous. I've never felt this lost, but I know nothing's here in Caribou, Maine except pain, and I want to feel something better than this.

I'm leaving for Philadelphia.

"If he wasn't famous," she says slowly, "you wouldn't even think about meeting him." She throws this in my face.

That's not true, I want to believe wholeheartedly, but she roots doubt in my head.

"If he wasn't famous," I say softly, "then this would be a lot easier." I'd be able to call him on the phone. I'd be able to tell him in advance that I'm going to see him. I could even Skype him instead of travel all the way to Philadelphia.

None of that is possible when Loren Hale is an internationally recognized celebrity.

As I turn my back on my mom, as I head for the staircase, I know it's going to be a challenge even approaching him.

But I have to try.

I need to grab this branch before it burns. So I race upstairs, pack a bag, noticing Ellie sleeping on my bed. Five minutes later, I zip up my duffel and sling my faded JanSport backpack over my shoulder.

I hear my mom downstairs, cleaning, and I wonder if she'll try to convince me to stay. I wonder if she cares enough to keep me here.

Part of me wants her to fight for me out of love and fear.

Part of me wants her to let me go so I can be free.

I hesitate, Ellie's plastic crown halfway off her head, breath parting her lips as she sleeps. I crouch close to her and whisper in her ear, "I love you, little princess." I kiss her cheek lightly enough that she never wakes. I know she can survive just fine without me for a while.

She's the energy that keeps this house alive.

I'm just the shadow in the corner.

When I head down the narrow staircase, squeezing my duffel through, the sink shuts off, and my mom emerges in the living room. I slow down between her and the front door.

She dries her hands with a towel, poker-faced and more resilient. "I'm not paying for this," she says. "You're on your own now."

A tear slips down my cheek. "Okay." I guess she's hoping I'll become afraid, run out of money, and turn around. I want to be brave enough to stick it out, but I'm not sure if I'm wired that way.

She adds, "You're old enough to do what you want, and you're old enough to make your own mistakes."

I think about her around my age, pregnant and making some of the hardest choices she had to make. I suppose she would believe that I'm an adult now if she was forced to be one back then. But I'm scared, and I feel like a plastic doll headed for a toy car, unable to see outside of my Polly Pocket house. What lies beyond—I don't know.

"If you need me," she says, "you have to come home yourself." She works for the post office and has almost no vacation days— definitely not enough to chase me to Philadelphia. And I'm not asking her to.

I wish I could say that I'm full of bittersweet love, but I'm mostly dark and resentful. Most of me *hates*, and I can barely meet her eyes without feeling tricked and fooled and deceived.

I want to meet a different pair of eyes that hold greater truths and sentiments, and they're not hers.

I just nod, turn around, and open the front door, the sun already gone. The street lamps already turned on, and I unlock my gold '90s Honda. I jiggle the handle for it to open. The car used to be my Grandma Ida's, and I'm just grateful I have it, something that I can use to leave.

"Drive safe." I think I hear my mom.

I look back at the front door, but it's already closed. The lights are already off, and I wonder if she's happy that I'm going, if all this time I've been a bad memory for her.

Maybe just like Loren Hale has been.

THE CALLOWAY SISTERS & THEIR MEN – FAN PAGE

FOLLOWERS: 11K

Are you new here? Welcome! This is the fan page for all things Calloway Sisters & Their Men. It's not an "official" fan page and is in no way associated with the Calloways, Meadows, Cobalts or Hales. It's just run by a dedicated blogger (me, Olive!) who is in love with all things Calloway!

Don't know who they are? Let me give you a crash course...

There are four Calloway Sisters, but only the youngest three sisters have gained notoriety after a huge scandal. Headlines were *everywhere*. Even national news channels! It leaked that Lily Calloway is a sex addict, for real. It probably would have just breezed through the media if not for the fact that they're all heiresses. Their father owns Fizzle. So the Fizz Life or Diet Fizz you're drinking—yeah, the Calloway Sisters are heiresses of *that* soda fortune.

The Calloway Sisters (and their current ages):
Poppy Calloway (30)
Rose Calloway (26)
Lily Calloway (24)
Daisy Calloway (19)

That's right, their parents named them after flowers! How cute is that? So the biggest deal is that Rose, Lily, and Daisy all currently live together in a mansion (with their men) in Philadelphia. It's like a real-life episode of *Friends*! And you'll probably find a lot more fan pages about them, but I promise to bring the latest and best news about the Calloway sisters. So let's get to their men...

Dating
Daisy Calloway & Ryke Meadows (25) – the adventurous couple. Daisy is a former model and Ryke is a professional rock climber, but they're often caught riding motorcycles together!

Engaged
Lily Calloway & Loren Hale (24) – the geeky couple. Lily owns Superheroes & Scones, while Loren is the CEO of Hale Co. and Halway Comics.

Married
Rose Calloway & Connor Cobalt (26) – the genius couple. Rose owns Calloway Couture, a fashion company for the everyday working woman, and Connor is the CEO of Cobalt Inc.

Poppy Calloway & Sam Stokes (30) – the private couple. Both Poppy and Sam tend to remain out of the spotlight, but what we know is that Poppy is a stay-at-home mom and Sam works for Fizzle.

Children
Lily & Loren: Maximoff Hale (2 months old)

Rose & Connor: Jane Eleanor Cobalt (3 months old)
Poppy & Sam: Maria Stokes (7)

That's the basic run-down. Another important fact that you might want to know—Loren Hale and Ryke Meadows are half-brothers. They have the same dad: Jonathan Hale. There's been some terrible allegations in the press lately about Jonathan Hale. I'm not going to repeat them here because there has been *zero* proof, and like I said, they're *serious* allegations.

I'll have more information as it breaks. Until then, check out the photos and gifs page!

Love you like Loren loves Lily,
xo Olive

2

Garrison Abbey

"GARRISON, IT'S YOUR TURN." NATHAN PATRICK NODS TO ME, chewing on a toothpick with a wry smile. His combed red hair might as well be fucking brown from my vantage. Smoke from cigarettes and joints create a filmy haze in his family's den—the door open as people drunkenly pass in and out.

I suck a joint between two fingers before standing up and flipping my cards on the poker table, my two queens losing to Nathan's three kings.

Of ten people, three girls let out short cheers. Another two girls in only bras and panties smile but make no loud exclamation. One of them sits next to me: Rachel Barnes, a brunette with diamond earrings and Zeta Beta Zeta aspirations like her sister in college.

She's prescribing to her family's legacy—something I can't stomach without another crappy joint and bottle of vodka.

After overturning my cards, I lift off my black shirt, revealing whatever muscles lacrosse has granted me and a black skull tattoo on the crease of my forearm and bicep. In small font, my favorite lyrics from the *Interpol* song "Rest My Chemistry" outline the inked design.

I don't make eye contact with anyone. I remain standing and blow gray smoke up at the ceiling, my mind lulling and eyelids slowly closing. I'm almost always surrounded by people—friends and acquaintances from Dalton Academy—and even when I stand in a room with them, even when I'm physically here, I always mentally check out for a few seconds.

More if I can.

I always want to be alone, but then when I'm alone, I want to be with people. It's a fucking curse.

Whoever built my mind needs to redo the wires and find better balance because I'm leaning all over the place. I'm tilted and sideways and so fucked up—this isn't even half of it.

The weed is making you a paranoid shit.

I suck the joint one last time before passing it to Rachel, who hesitates before putting it between her lips. She takes one short drag and then coughs into her fist.

Nathan and two other guys give her a hard time. I don't come to her defense—since she's going to be in a sorority anyway. It's not like she's going to need to know how to smoke a joint.

"Your deal, Abbey," Nathan tells me, stretching over the table to pass me the deck of cards. I begin to shuffle.

A girl clears her throat loudly, sort of adjacent to me. "Hi, um…" She taps Rachel's shoulder. I'm not surprised. Rachel looks the most approachable.

Most of the guys are smoking and drinking, one even wears a gargoyle mask from a Halloween store, more stacked behind him on a leather chair. The other girls here have low-cut tank tops and nose piercings.

Rachel is the only one that looks like someone you'd take home to your parents. Though I've brought them all over to my house before. I don't discriminate.

I barely make out the girl's features among the smoke. All I can tell for certain: she's wearing overalls, like the saggy kind you'd put on to paint a house.

I frown. She can't live around here.

"Hi?" Rachel says uncertainly.

Not surprisingly, Nathan takes over, standing from his chair. "How'd you get in here?" He makes it seem like his party is invitation-only, when in fact most of Dalton Academy has been traipsing in and out all night.

"I…uh, the front door was open?"

"I mean the neighborhood. It's *gated*," he says.

The girl takes a step back, more towards me, but I stay still, as uncertain as her, as uncertain as everyone else. My eyelids are heavy, and it takes more control not to sink into my seat and just finish dealing slowly.

"The gate was open…someone was coming in, and I followed them through," she explains. "I'm just trying to find someone. I know he lives in this neighborhood, and I thought you'd be able to point out his house—"

Nathan snorts, and two of my other friends start snickering. "Let me guess—you want to see Loren Hale."

"Yeah," she says softly.

I grimace and turn my head away from her. *Fuck him*, I think. *Rich bastard.* I swallow spite and something else—because if I look around, I see thousand-dollar paintings, an antique globe that probably costs a fortune; I see Rachel's Cobalt diamond earrings, Henry's Rolex watch—my Balmain designer jeans that purposely appear worn.

We're all loaded.

Rich fucking kids. Fuck me.

I want to be alone right now.

But I want to be with people.

I don't know what I want to be.

"So…" the girl says. "Can you help me?" I have to strain my ears to hear her quiet voice.

Help her. All I have to do is point at the house literally down the street. I know the one. I've been around it with my friends *too* much. But something keeps me quiet. Something keeps me tight-lipped and blank-faced.

"Are you a weirdo stalker?" Carly asks. She lets out a short laugh. "Like, are you going to bring him a locket of your hair?"

"Carly," Rachel whispers and then ends up laughing with her.

The guys start in and laugh again.

They all stare at this girl. They all stare, and I keep my head down. I wish I had my hoodie. I wish I could just block everyone out for a second.

The cards slip from my hands, and I end up crouching to gather them, my reflexes fucking tortoise-slow from the weed.

"So you can't help me then?" the girl asks one last time, sounding meeker than when she first arrived—which is hard considering how shy she seems.

"Are you dumb?" Nathan laughs.

My face heats beneath the table, grabbing a king of clubs. I wonder if I was paying enough attention, if I would've made the same comment, the same way. I hope not—but I'm not a good person either.

I'm just as foul, and I wonder if I'm the only one that knows how cruel we all are. How fucked up we all seem.

If I am—I must be doubly cursed or something.

She's about to leave, but Nathan adds, "You want to play strip poker for the information?"

I glance back at the girl. Her lips part in hesitation, and she seems pallid and sweaty. I can barely make out the color of her hair. Light brown, I think, in a loose braid. These dorky black-rimmed glasses frame her small face, and she leans most of her weight on one foot—a nervous, slightly boyish posture that most cotillion, high society girls don't grow up with around here. Their moms would shit a rock if they did.

And she keeps anxiously reaching for her shoulder, like she's trying to grab a strap to a purse that's not there. Jesus Christ, she looks really out of place.

The more she waits to speak, the more I think she's considering playing strip poker with us.

And the joke would be on her. She'd get naked and Nathan would never give her the information. No one would, whether she won the right to it or not. They'd find that funny.

I collect the last of the cards and rise, my posture more assured than hers but I don't look like I took years of ballet like Rachel or like I listened in cotillion. I'm definitely not what my parents wanted me to be.

And I say aloud, to Nathan, "I'm not dealing another fucking person in, man. I've already started." And I start. Right now. Looking like a dick as I do so.

Before Nathan protests, the girl leaves, weaving between a sloppy drunken guy who spills beer on her shoulders. It's like watching Bambi lose its mother or something. And I can't help but feel like we were the ones that shot the deer.

What do I do about it? I finish dealing the cards and numbly begin the next hand.

AROUND 2:30 A.M., I FINALLY LEAVE NATHAN'S. I GRAB MY bike and *slowly* (so fucking slowly) ride down the dim street, lit only by lamps and the few houses that reside here. Instead of houses stacked closely together, each mansion has acres by itself, leaving the neighborhood mostly barren.

I bike past grass and a couple trees.

Not far down, I turn right onto Cider Creek Pass. I live in the same gated neighborhood as Nathan Patrick. As Loren Hale and the Calloway sisters. Ever since they moved in, paparazzi camp outside the gates, waiting for them to leave. It's pitiful—on whose part, I don't really know.

I take my palms off the handlebars and just peddle, trying not to think about those people.

There it is.

Floodlights illuminate my front yard, white rose bushes outlining a gray stone, out-of-place Victorian mansion. Like we're some kind of English royalty.

The minute I see my three older brothers on the stone front stairs—unevenly lounged and leaning against the iron railing—I think about riding away. My problem: I have nowhere else to really go.

"There he is." I hear the muffled voice of my oldest brother, Davis. He rises first, football in hand. "Where've you been?" he asks me straight. It's not concern on his face as much as annoyance.

I peddle onto the yard and then slowly climb off my bike, knocking it down without care. "Out," I say, wanting to climb the steps and bypass them into the house, but I gain five-feet before they all join me in the yard, silently saying *you're not going anywhere.*

We're all two years apart from the next. And somehow they all look the same: short haircut, collared shirts, khaki pants and Sperry boat shoes.

Davis is the twenty-three-year-old college graduate, striving for his MBA and a position at my father's million-dollar tech company. He sucks at computers, by the way. Can't even read code—but he's charismatic and a real "guy's guy" so whatever.

Hunter is the twenty-one-year-old athlete with anger issues that everyone blames on "pent-up testosterone" because he refuses to fuck or masturbate until lacrosse season ends. He's a dick—and I say this with zero brotherly affection. He destroyed that when I was a kid.

Mitchell is the nineteen-year-old pretty boy with less charm than Davis but more brains, so he's fucked. I'd like Mitchell more if he didn't act like Davis and Hunter rode golden chariots.

And me, Garrison Abbey, I'm the seventeen-year-old degenerate who skips class more often than he goes, who's yet to find a meaning in being *here*—in life. If I don't follow their footsteps, then I see nothing else I could do right, but I can't follow them and stomach it.

"Dude," Mitchell starts in. "Mom wanted this to be a *family* dinner." College summer break ended today, so they have to go back to the University of Pennsylvania.

"Sorry," I say dryly, scratching the back of my head with mock regret. "I guess I missed the part where we break bread, hold hands and sing hallelujah—maybe next time." I try to take a step forward, and Hunter puts his hand on my chest to stop me. I slap it off and back up immediately, my stomach knotting. "Don't touch me, man."

"Then don't make Mom cry, dipshit."

I stare at the night sky for a second and feel my eyes roll. I also feel Hunter let out an agitated breath and try to step closer to me, but I back up again, about to head for my bike.

"Hey." Davis grabs my shoulder and spins me around, his fingers digging in. He raises the football near my head like he's going to suggest a quick game. Instead he sniffs, and I turn and try to jerk away from him, my tousled hair falling in my eyes.

He grips harder.

"You smell like weed." His annoyance only grows, probably thinking how badly I'm hassling our parents. I'm not easy like my brothers. I don't know how to be and still retain a fucking *soul*.

"Really?" I feign surprise. My only real defense is dry sarcasm. "I thought I smelled like your girlfriend's p—"

Davis slaps the back of my head, and I almost fall forward. And then he shoves the football in my chest. "Like you'd know what pussy smells like." He messes my hair with a rough, irritated hand.

They treat me like a little kid. Like a little brother. I get that. I am one, but as I stand up and face Davis, Hunter, and Mitchell, I feel more like a toy they play with, one they've constantly broken.

I clutch the football. "You didn't really stay up to play football with me."

"Sure we did," Mitchell says with a shrug and looks to Davis and Hunter for confirmation. Neither says a word in agreement. Their hard gazes just drill into me.

I don't want to be here, so I drop the football and I turn around again and go grab my bike that lies sideways in the yard. Hunter chases after me, and I barely have my bike upright before he pushes me.

I drop the handlebars and stagger back. "What the fuck?" I sneer, my pulse quickening.

"We're playing football. You couldn't be here for dinner—you couldn't do *one* thing for Mom, then you're going to do this for us." And he adds (like Hunter always does), "You motherfucking cocksucker." It's his go-to insult, one I know I might've picked up and used before—and I hate that I have. Because it's lame as shit, among other things.

I grit my teeth and inhale once before I shrug stiffly.

Davis *throws* the football at my face. It hits my cheek before I can block it. The pain wells, but I stifle it by grabbing the football off the grass. The minute I straighten up, Hunter tackles me with his full weight. He's two inches taller, fifty pounds heavier, and the wind immediately escapes my lungs.

I choke and try to push him off, but Hunter grips my hair and whispers in my ear, "You think you're fucking cool? Get up, you pussy." He slaps my face twice and laughs, like it's funny.

When he stands off me with the football in hand, I slowly turn towards the grass, kneeling before I rise, my breath caged.

This is how brothers are, my mom always says. *They tease the youngest one. You just need thicker skin, Garrison.*

I wipe the bottom of my nose with the back of my hand and realize it's bleeding. Hunter is only a few feet from me, and I'm surprised he doesn't chuck the football in my eye.

"What? Are you going to cry?" he laughs.

I roll my eyes and just shake my head. I think this is his way of making me pay for whatever emotional hurt I caused Mom today, yesterday—whenever I became more of a nuisance than all of them.

And I'd like to think if I showed up for dinner, we wouldn't still be "playing football" like this. But they would've found some other reason to go hard. They always do.

"Tackle me," Hunter goads, arms outstretched. "Come on, pussy, let's see what you're made of."

I narrow my gaze, my eyes heated, my nose on fucking fire, and I just think, *I hate you. I really fucking hate you.*

Davis lets out a short laugh. *I hate you too.*

Then Mitchell. *Fuck you, Mitchell. Grow two feet and walk away from them.*

Have I even grown two feet yet? Do I even have a head? I blink slowly, wondering if I'm still blazed.

"What are you, dumb?" Hunter's smile fades, irritated, pissed. It's an ugly ass snarl that I've met all my life. I remember one moment as if it were yesterday. My parents ordered pizza for dinner, and Hunter called "dibs" on the last slice. He was seventeen, and my thirteen-year-old-self didn't know better.

I ate his so-called slice.

And then he wrestled me onto the floor, trying to force my finger down my throat so I'd throw it up. After his knee sat on my ribs for too long, I willfully stuck my finger down and vomited that last slice. He didn't want to eat it. He just wanted to deny me the one piece that should've been his. Because he called dibs.

Brothers, right?

Fucking brothers.

Hunter growls under his breath. "Come on!" I learned about a year ago to stop giving into their games. I'd avoid them or just *not* play whatever they wanted to play.

It doesn't always make things better, but it makes me feel like I stood up for something. Davis stares at me like I'm a little rebellious punk.

"It's football," he reminds me.

"Cool, you two play," I tell them, heading for my bike *again*. "I'm out of—" Hunter tackles me, wrestles me on *top* of my bike, the metal digging into my kidneys. I grimace and thrash beneath him, cursing and trying to throw him off.

He lays his weight into me, his usual insult ringing in my ears. He smacks my face a couple times, the blows harder, and then I gather the strength to shove him off and roll out beneath him. I cough once, digging my soles into the grass, and then I stand up enough to grab my backpack and run.

"Garrison!" Davis yells. "We're just playing!"

Fuck you.

I run faster, almost tripping as I reach the asphalt, and I look back once to see if they're following, but all three of my brothers stay behind in the yard. I gather speed towards the main street, off Cider Creek Pass.

Then I slow down, my pulse never slowing with me.

I rub my hands through my hair. "What the fuck," I whisper, hearing the sound of my shaking voice. *Are you going to cry?* Then I rub my throbbing cheek, the wetness apparent. "Stupid shit," I mumble softly and then rummage in my backpack.

I collect a cigarette and lighter, putting the end in my mouth. I suck in deeply, and then I look up and realize how far I've sprinted and then walked.

I'm at Loren Hale's house. It's a mansion, not as ostentatious as my family's. The lights are off, and the driveway is empty. I pace back and forth by the mailbox, smoking a cigarette.

I don't know why I linger. My friends and I—we've pranked their house since they first moved to this neighborhood, and at first, we were just curious. *Who the fuck are these people?* we all thought.

They're not famous because they did something revolutionary or because they acted, sang, and entertained their way into peoples' hearts.

They're famous because Loren's fiancée is a sex addict. The heiress of Fizzle—a soda empire—sucked a lot of cock.

You know, I *met* him—Loren.

He caught me after I shot paintballs at his house windows, and my friends—they just left me there, racing off with their own paintball guns, thinking he'd turn me into the police. Being loyal, I wouldn't have ratted them out.

But that night, Loren Hale let me go.

I don't get it.

I don't understand why he didn't turn me in. He seems like an ass. He's always glaring in tabloid photographs, not more than his half-brother, but still. He looks like a fucking dick—and he let me go.

I don't know why I do it now, but I reach into my backpack and grab a canister of metallic spray paint. With my heart banging into my ribcage, violently saying *no* with each beat, I spray the side of his mailbox. My nose flares, knowing it's bad.

Knowing I should stop.

But I don't.

The paint wets my fingers as I hold down the nozzle tighter, and on one side I write the word *Cock* and on the other, I write *Sucker.*

Maybe I should've just written *help* instead.

September

3

Garrison Abbey

SUPERHEROES & SCONES IS PACKED.

Slouched in a red vinyl booth, I listen to Nathan prattle off reasons why he can't stand this place—how it looks like Captain America took a shit on the walls, a red and blue and gray scheme. It's a dumb complaint. We're in a comic book store for Christ's sake.

I take a swig from a bottle wrapped tightly in a brown bag. *Shit.* Sharp vodka slides down my throat, inexpensive and probably a cousin of rubbing alcohol.

This is the best I could steal from the liquor cabinet. My parents only stock shitty vodka, and they'd notice if I took their prized Scotch and bourbon.

"Hey." Nathan waves a hand at my face, sitting next to me. "You here?"

I flip him off and then chug again, leaning against the window. Our friends John and Kyle are seated on the opposite side. Their faces begin to blur, which means today is better than yesterday.

I'm about to put the bottle back to my lips when noses suddenly press against the window, and girls *scream* bloody-murder outside.

"Christ," I curse before following their gazes across the store. Everyone here seems to freeze, comic books half open but eyes elsewhere. With their slack-jawed, wide-eyed expressions, you'd think an A-list movie star just made an appearance.

I'm not surprised by what I see.

Loren Hale and his half-brother, Ryke Meadows, just entered the main storeroom from the *employees' only* door. Nathan, John, and Kyle purposefully escalate their voices and mess with the sugar packets, tearing them open and spilling white granules all over the table.

I can't focus my gaze enough to make out Loren and Ryke's features. But I've read enough descriptions on Tumblr from *obsessed* girls (and probably guys, to be honest) to have their faces forever imprinted in my fucking head.

Loren Hale is all sharp-edged, his jawline like ice and his amber eyes daggered and so scary. He will murder you with them. He wears a lot of red Vans and V-neck shirts. He's so cool. His hair is shorter on the sides and longer on the top (guys take notes!)

How about no.

Ryke Meadows is all hard-edged, his scruffy jawline like stone and his brown eyes narrowed and so broody. He's an animal. Beware. I wouldn't be surprised if he was a werewolf in another life.

Tumblr girls are so weird.

And yeah, I read all of those in my free time. Internet culture is more entertaining than real life. Like right now, I immediately turn my head away from Loren. Because of what's in his arms.

A baby—*his* baby. The thing can't be more than two months old, and he's crying hysterically at all the noise and attention.

I glance back, only once, to see Lily Calloway taking her son out of Loren's arms. But he's too busy to really notice. He's glaring at Nathan, at *me,* and my friends, the table littered with sugar packets, their voices causing more havoc.

His amber eyes daggered.

He will murder you with them.

Part of me wants to glare back—to prove that he's not murdering me with anything. But my neck grows hot, my stomach unsettled, and I focus on my vodka instead.

Another swig, I think before taking one.

I can't even remember the last prank we did on Loren's house. We've done so many, even in the past month. Even when they had a fucking newborn in there—*stop.*

Drink.

I do.

Not long after, I feel Nathan press closer to my side. Loren squeezes into my end of the booth while his brother squeezes into the other.

Tumblr is right, I think. Despite both brothers having lean muscles, runner's builds, Ryke Meadows acts like the aggressive brute, his elbows on the table, the strong-hand that could literally drag any of us out of here if Loren Hale said so.

It always seems like Loren calls the shots though. He's the talker—his features murderous and cold.

"Hey there," Loren says with this irritated half-smile. It's iconic, his dry smile that says *you're a piece of shit and you know it.* I can't even replicate it. I don't think anyone can.

I hold his gaze this time. And I take the largest swig from my paper-bagged bottle. *I'm not scared of you,* I want to retort. I want him to feel it.

I'm not scared of you.

He tilts his head a little, unperturbed by me. His amber eyes are full of flashbacks, memories that contain all that I've done. The longer I stare, the more I see the paintballs I fired, blasting against the window—panic and shrieking from inside, from his soon-to-be wife.

Some people say that if you mess with Loren Hale's girlfriend, you're on his "metaphorical" kill list forever. That he has ways and means to do you in, to make life not worth living.

Too bad for him.

Because I'm already there.

He can't do me in. He can't touch me.

I miss a portion of the conversation, only hearing the part where Loren says, "I'm not going to lecture you."

I lean forward, not rolling over. "You can't kick us out. We have a right to be here like everyone else." I watch his narrowed eyes flit over my features. He recognizes me from that night—the night where he grabbed me and let me go.

He let me go. Who would even think to do that sort of thing? Who wouldn't turn someone like me in?

John adds, "Yeah, it's our first amendment right to be here."

Ryke Meadows rolls his eyes. "You all smell like cheap *fucking* vodka."

"Sorry," I retort, leaning back with a glare. "We'll buy better stuff next time."

"That's not what I…" Ryke lets out a frustrated growl, and I guess I'm tempted to provoke this "beast" and see him lash out. So I make a crude gesture with my hand and tongue, the vulgar gesture known to crawl beneath his skin. Less so when it's directed at him. More so when it's directed at a girl.

So I'm not really surprised when he doesn't launch himself at me. He just breathes through his nose and looks to his younger brother to deal with us.

Loren rests his forearms on the table, glancing between each of us with less threat in his eyes. "Come on," he says, "you all look no older than seventeen." He gestures to me. "Drinking underage is illegal, so you're not in a power position here."

I glare at the table. *No shit.* I've never been in a power position before. Not *once* in my life.

"What's your name?" Loren asks me.

"Fuck you," I retort, and I switch my V-shaped fingers to a middle finger. Flashes go off by the window near my head, causing white light to flicker in my vision. I wonder if I'll be in a tabloid like *Celebrity Crush* tomorrow.

Probably.

They'll call me the "unnamed delinquent"—predictable.

"How was that bourbon bath?" Kyle snickers. He high-fives Nathan across the table, and I'm reminded of a recent prank. It was John's idea. We filled a bucket with his family's liquor—stuff I would've rather drunk. His parents froze his bank account for raiding the cabinet, so it's not happening again any time soon.

When we had the liquor in the bucket, we tethered it to Loren's front door.

We heard it doused him *and* Ryke. "Two for one"—Nathan had said.

It's fucked up. Because they're both sober, and Loren Hale is known for his stint in rehab and difficulties recovering from alcohol addiction.

Ryke looks murderous at John. "You think it's funny?"

"Ryke," Loren says and shakes his head like *stand down*.

And I mutter, "Pussy." I think it's easier pushing him away. He keeps thinking he's going to change things with us—but he can't.

Nathan laughs. "Nice, Garrison."

I almost choke on the liquor. "Dude." I gape and nudge his side hard. My hood falls off my head.

They don't know our names, but now they fucking know *mine*. I look up, and Loren Hale is staring straight at me, his eyes full of sympathy—I don't get it.

I've *fucked* with him for months.

Hate me, I think. *Fucking hate me.*

"What are you looking at?" I practically spit. *Help me.*

"You," Loren says with hot malice.

I feel sick, my neck scorching now, and I lower my gaze to the table.

"Here's what's going to happen," Loren begins. "You all have two options." We stay quiet, waiting for him to say, *Jail. Jail. Jail.*

"You can stop the pranks," he continues, "never come around our house again. If you're that bored, I wouldn't mind hiring some of you to work here. If you don't want a job, I get it. You can have a discount on comics if that's your thing."

What?

I stare off in a fucking daze. Who is this guy?

Ryke says, "And I'd be willing to teach all of you to rock climb at the gym. But you can't drink."

"Sounds like so much fun," Nathan says with a dramatic eye roll, grade-F level sarcasm.

I tear a corner off the paper bag. "And the second option?" I ask.

Jail.

"You vandalize our house again or harass our girls, and we'll press charges," Loren threatens. *There it is.* "The minute we even see your goddamn pinky toe on our lawn, I'm calling the cops. Take it from someone who's been in jail, you don't want to be there. Even for a couple hours."

I let out a short laugh. "When were *you* in jail?" The guy grew up as a rich trust fund kid like the rest of us. His dad could've bailed him out before the cops even put on the cuffs.

He captures my gaze. "I doused some asshole's door with pig's blood." His voice is edged and chilling.

My face begins to fall.

"No way." Nathan gawks.

I straighten in my seat. "Yeah?" I ask, more curious. "Where's that asshole now?" *What'd he do to you?* I really want to ask.

Loren shakes his head and shrugs. "I don't know. That shit is long gone, man." His voice tries to soften, but his tone mostly cuts me inside out. "You're going to leave prep school and you're going to take your mistakes with you." He looks at my bottle. "You can stay here if you hand that over and don't cause any commotion. Otherwise, you have to go."

"We'll go," John says before I can decide. He nods to me. "Let's buy that six-pack and head to the elementary school playground."

I don't think I can drink anymore without puking. Not because I reached my limit—I just feel like I've digested something that doesn't go well with vodka or beer.

But I don't want to be alone right now.

So I rise with all of my friends. As I near Loren to exit, I look him over. I'm so fucking conflicted about everything—about who this guy is. About what he just offered. *Take it.*

And then I lose *all* of my friends. They're never going to back down. They have this stupid prank set up, one that involves gargoyle masks. They're not going to stop in favor of getting free comics or a rock climbing lesson.

I don't want to be alone.

But I don't want to be here either.

What escape do I really have?

I think short-term, and I shove the bottle in Loren's hands. "Here, you won't be such a pussy if you drink." If I push him away, then he'll make my decision for me. He'll revoke his offer.

He doesn't flinch. Doesn't even look mildly pissed. He just says, "If that's what you think." He tosses the bottle in the nearby trash.

I'm stunned for a second. I had my first beer at twelve. *You're a man now, kid,* Davis told me and rubbed my head. My dad laughed.

In this moment, Loren Hale looks and acts more like a man than I do, and I was holding a fucking handle of vodka. I have no fucking clue what's rolling around inside of me.

I can't look at him anymore. Rubbing my mouth with a shaking hand, I pull my hoodie back, and the door chimes as I push through, catching up to Nathan.

When I glance back at the store window, I see that girl—the one with the braid and worn overalls. I see her stand up and approach Loren Hale.

I nod to myself. *Good for her.* She finally found him. And she didn't need me to do it.

4

Willow Moore

"LOREN?" I ASK IN A SOFT, TIMID VOICE. I SCOOT AROUND RYKE Meadows.

Both brothers are so tall that I have to tilt my head back and look *up*. Maybe if they were shorter, I wouldn't be nervous. Maybe if they weren't famous. Maybe if I didn't know more about them than they know about me. Maybe if they weren't the current focus of every teenage girl in Superheroes & Scones.

If all of that changed, maybe it'd be easier.

My heart thuds harder and beats faster—their gazes suddenly zeroed in on me. Looking down while I look up. I can't really unmask their expressions. Ryke is stiff and unmoving while Loren shakes his head a little, his eyes flitting over my awkward frame.

I truly feel seventeen. I truly feel like Loren's *little* sister.

Please let him believe so too. I made it this far—I made it to him. It only took almost a month of scavenging Philadelphia for Loren Hale, and the closest I came before today was a house party that amounted to a beer-stained shirt and mortification.

It took me a solid five-minutes to even climb out of my car and enter that house, my first ever high school party, mind you.

I felt in the way. I never knew where to stand, where to scoot to, and even then, I bumped four or five elbows and shoulders. I left with my stomach twisted like a pretzel. And it solidified what I've always known: *Willow Moore is not meant for high school parties.* I'm just not built to live through them.

Fast forward to today: My bank account is creeping close to just $50, barely enough for another night in a Philadelphia motel. I've already spent five nights in my car to save money, and my last hope was staking out Superheroes & Scones. Which proved to be the winning strategy, even though I always thought it was a long shot.

But I've found *him*.

Loren Hale is standing right in front of me.

Now for the hardest part. I open my mouth and adjust my backpack on my shoulder with a sweaty palm. "Hi," I say. I lick my lips repeatedly. *Hi*—is that really all you have, Willow?

I had more planned, I think. I just—I'm looking at my brother. This is the second time I've met him, and I start to see a greater resemblance between us.

We have the same light brown hair. I subconsciously touch my nose.

We have the same slender nose—

Ryke's rough but sincere voice breaks my concentration. "Do you want an autograph or a picture or something?"

I try to meet his expression, but he raises his eyebrows at me like, *we can get anything for you.* Oh my God. I immediately look away and push my glasses up. "No…thanks." I cough a little to hide my nerves, but maybe that just makes it worse.

I'm used to seeing Ryke in video footage, yelling and throwing out F-bombs at paparazzi, trying to block cameras from his brother and girlfriend's way.

Seeing him now—with an unshaven jawline, crinkled brows, brooding eyes, and overwhelming masculine energy—it's like meeting a scruffy god in the flesh.

I'm surprised I haven't combusted into flames yet.

Ryke turns to Loren, probably wondering what to do with a crazy, awkward fan like me.

Say it, Willow. Tell him that you're his sister. Why is this so hard? I blow out a breath, prepared to let this truth out and desperately hoping Loren Hale will believe it.

I meet his amber eyes, our gazes locked for a strong, tense moment. And I say, "I'm—"

"My sister," he finishes.

The hairs rise on the back of my neck, a chill snaking down my spine and arms. My eyes burn as tears try to well.

Loren barely flinches. "Willow, right?"

My mouth keeps falling. All this time, I thought he's been looking at me like *who is this girl?* But he's been really looking at me in disbelief like *this is my half-sister, standing right here.* He's been piecing me together with the middle school girl he once met, so long ago. In Caribou, Maine.

"You…remember me?" is all I manage to say.

"Yeah." His lips rise, and my heart warms. "The day I met my birth mother is one I really can't forget."

"Oh…" That was the first time he met my mom? I mean, *our* mom. My eyes drop for a second. She really did abandon him then…

I take a quick glance at Ryke. His lips are parted in surprise, eyes a little wide as they go from me to Loren and back to me. I wonder if he knew anything about me. If he knew I existed out there, or if Loren just kept it to himself. Because my mom told him to leave Ellie and me alone.

"Do you want to talk over coffee?" Loren asks. I whip my head back to him, a chill never disappearing. *Coffee.* "Maybe in the break room?"

I nod over and over, and the tears just keep rising. I blow out another breath, my strained shoulders loosening.

He wants to talk. He's not going to kick me out. He's not going to tell me to *get lost, kid.* I feel like I'm reaching out to someone who's not only clasping my hand but drawing me closer, so I don't fall backwards on my own.

For the first time since I left home, I feel safe.

I'M IN THE BREAK ROOM OF SUPERHEROES & SCONES.

I can't believe *I'm* here—and yes, I'm slightly shaking. My arms tremble, and my legs have glued together. I wonder if the jitters are from the coffee Loren handed me, the only thing I've consumed today. Or maybe it's nerves—from being in the presence of a famous person for longer than one minute. Or from being related to *this* human being.

I cup the coffee mug, afraid to drink more and have a panic attack at Loren Hale's feet. *Please don't do that, Willow.*

He sits next to me on the bright blue couch. The break room is pretty typical: a microwave, small kitchenette, tables and chairs, a few racks of comic books, and a single bathroom.

Lily, her son, her bodyguard, and Ryke all disappeared upstairs to—well, I'm not exactly sure what leads upstairs. The point is: we're basically alone except for a couple of employees eating sandwiches at a back table, sitting beneath an *Iron Man* poster.

I think we can speak freely enough, but if Loren is cautious, I'll follow his lead and be cautious too.

"I…" I begin but realize I'm unsure of where to start.

Loren's confidence radiates and practically dwarfs what little I have in this moment. He keeps an arm on the back of the couch, rotated towards my body. "How'd you find out about me?" he asks, discovering a place to start.

Now I have to figure out how to explain everything. I tuck a piece of hair behind my ear, having trouble holding his gaze. "My parents divorced about a year ago."

"I'm sorry." He sounds a little cross, not towards me really, but maybe that's his normal tone of voice? Everything seems to come out harsh, but it doesn't always match his expression.

I guess if I looked at him, I'd have a better interpretation of this moment. *Willow Moore, that little turd, can't even look her own brother square in the eyes*—will definitely be my eulogy.

I shrug and push up my glasses that keep slipping down my nose. "Ellie had her sixth birthday about a month ago, and it was the first time my parents were together since the divorce."

The fight starts to flood me: the balloons littering the linoleum floor, the way my father passed me coldly and never looked back, the half-eaten cake and my mother gripping the counter. My chest tightens, and my eyes burn again.

"I heard them fighting in the kitchen," I nearly whisper, "about how my mom had a son, and she…abandoned you." I clutch my mug harder and finally look up.

He scratches his neck, appearing a little more uncomfortable than he has been. "I had my father, so it was okay." His throat bobs.

I wonder if Jonathan Hale is nice. Just based off tabloid rumors, I'd say *no*. (They're so awful I really hate to repeat them.) Disregarding those, all I have to go on is the fact that he slept with an underage girl—my mom, *our* mom—and got her pregnant.

He doesn't sound that awesome, but if he raised someone as cool as Loren Hale, then maybe he's not entirely bad.

When he swallows, he asks, "Did you confront her about it?" *Did I confront my mom about her abandoning you?*

I just picture my mom turning her back on me, trying to bury this. I see her never chasing me upstairs. Never chasing me outside. I see her in a new horrible light that I can't shake. It hurts…

"Yeah," I say softly, "right then. I asked her about it, and it took some screaming for her to really tell me the truth."

My voice nearly dies by the last word. I wipe my eyes beneath my glasses, hoping these tears won't overflow.

He angles closer to me, kind of like he wants to comfort me but still wants to give me personal space. I'm not a touchy-feely person. My mom wasn't ever that way, and I wonder—I wonder now if it was because of what happened when she was sixteen. Being kind of taken advantage of by Jonathan Hale… I mean, she didn't say that she said *no* to him. So I have to assume it was consensual.

But is it consent if she was underage? And the product of this event… is right in front of me.

My stomach knots, the coffee not settling well with these thoughts.

Then Loren says, "I'm sorry you had to find out like that."

My eyes *sear* now, tears welling as I realize full-force how much my mom kept him from seeing me. Loren wanted me to know about him.

"I ran away," I suddenly say, my voice cracking and tears leaking with the words. I'm crying in front of one of the most famous people alive in the world, and I don't even care anymore. I hate and resent her more than I ever wanted to, and it all *hurts*.

"You what?" His mouth drops a little, and concern overtakes the edge in his voice.

"I just…I was so mad." My breath staggers between tears. "I told my mom that I was going to find you, and she couldn't stop me. So…I hopped in my car and drove to Philadelphia."

He pinches the bridges of his nose, his eyes tightening closed. "You've been here for an entire month? Does Emily know—"

"She knows."

His reaction makes me feel like I made a mistake—and it's tearing a hole through me. With my mug between my knees, I cover my face in my hands, embarrassed now and heartbroken all over again and full of combatant emotions that cut.

He stands, and I don't have the heart to watch him walk around the break room. I just keep talking—trying to explain and justify why I'm here.

"She's waiting for me to run out of money," I clarify. "She doesn't have any vacation days left to leave work, so she can't come get me." I sound like the villain. My hard-working mother is left at home while I'm off chasing a long-lost brother, leaving her to worry.

If she worried so much, she would've called. A hot tear rolls down my cheek.

Loren plops back on the couch with a box of tissues. That's what he went to find? "How much money do you have left?" He hands me the box.

I take one tissue. "I'm not going back." It hits me now. I don't want to return home. My dad can't look me in the eyes. I expect after this, my mom will have trouble too.

"Willow," Loren says forcefully, "*how much money?*"

He's worried. My stomach has all but curdled. "Enough for a couple more nights at the motel," I lie.

His nose flares, upset. "I'll pay for a hotel tonight and tomorrow, and I can get you a plane ticket back to Maine."

Tears stream down my cheeks. "No, *no*," I cry. "Please don't make me go back. I just met you, and…" I hiccup and remove my glasses, wiping the fogged lenses with my striped blue and green shirt that peeks from my overalls.

I've never felt more alone or lost, and if I go home, these sentiments will only intensify. I can *see* it—all of it. An unbearable pressure mounts on my chest at this purposed future that may become real.

"Aren't you in high school?" he asks.

I don't speak, afraid that if I say *yes*, he'll grab his computer and book me the next flight to Maine.

He's more closed off towards me than before. He shakes his head a couple times. "Your mom is probably sick over this," he says to me.

"*Our* mom," I say, reminding him why I'm here to begin with. I set my glasses back on.

He's scrutinizing me a little more, his eyes flitting over my features.

I wipe beneath my nose. "And I don't care what she is." She can be sick. She can be angry. I feel just as hurt as her over this, and I'm acknowledging my own feelings for the first time in my life instead of burying them to make room for everyone else's.

He grimaces. "Willow—"

"She *lied* to me." I point to my chest. He has to understand how much this hurts. Doesn't he see? "I don't want to be around her ever again."

"How about I call Emily and see where her head is at?" His muscles seem to flex, and he scratches the back of his neck again. He offers me a single weak smile, but I realize that he's nervous…to talk to her, his mom.

She didn't want him. He should be so angry. He should hate her, shouldn't he? How does someone become a bigger person that way,

I wonder. How much time will it take because right now I feel like it'd be centuries before I grew a new pair of eyes, a new brain, and thought differently of my mom.

I just nod to Loren, not sure what other options there are. I tell him my mom's number, and after he types it in his phone, he stands. "I'll be quick. Are you hungry?"

I shake my head, holding the coffee mug again.

"Can you get her a muffin from the front?"

I look up and realize Loren has motioned to the employee underneath the *Iron Man* poster. I quickly wipe my wet cheeks, wondering how much this random person saw me break down. I'm never really that emotional in front of people.

"HEY." THE GRUFF VOICE PULLS MY ATTENTION UPWARDS. RYKE Meadows has entered the Superheroes & Scones breakroom with Maximoff Hale, his infant nephew that swats at his arm with a wide toothless smile.

"Hi…" I stiffen even more, watching him grab a couple comic books from a rack and then take a seat right in front of *me*, on the fuzzy white carpet.

Ryke rests his forearm on his bent knee—his whole demeanor confident and cool. He takes a quick glance at the closed bathroom door, the baby that tries to clutch a comic, and then me. Only as soon as we lock eyes, he doesn't look away.

I'm so nervous I may puke.

"You should eat." He nods to the muffin that's frozen in my anxious hand.

I swallow again and loosen my finger joints to pick at the muffin top and eat a small piece. The blueberry is overly sweet, but it's better than coffee.

It's quiet for a second, only the baby making noise. I'm not sure what to say, and maybe he's lost for words too. The tension here is different than it is with Loren and me.

We're both half-siblings to the same person. It's a common link, but trying to understand how we should be with each other—I think it's just complicated. With Lo, I can simply say, *you're my half-brother.* With Ryke, there's not really an easy definition.

Because Ryke isn't my brother. We just share one.

His brows harden in questioning. "What made you want to find him?"

"I learned the truth," I explain, glancing at my hands and the muffin more than a few times. "And I wanted to know him—not because he's famous or anything…" I pale. What if Ryke thinks I'm here to capitalize off his half-brother's fame and fortune?

Ryke scratches his unshaven jaw and nods to me again. "You know I'm his half-brother, right? We have the same fucking dad, so you and I aren't related."

"Yeah I know about you—or *of* you…or you know, whatever the correct terminology is…" I clear my throat and stare intently at the muffin, grateful that I didn't blurt out how I made a gif of Ryke tossing Daisy Calloway over his shoulder, using footage from the short-lived reality TV show.

He runs a hand through his thick, disheveled dark-brown hair. I really want to know what his palms look like. Which sounds *so weird* and creepy.

He rock climbs though, and Tumblr speculates whether his hands are really callused or cracked—which also sounds weird and creepy, but everyone's curiosities run rampant online. And it's hard not to be sucked into this all-consuming vortex that includes the Calloway sisters and their men.

"Your name's Willow?"

I nod in reply, but he says nothing more. He's trying to draw my gaze back to him. I sense it, and it takes me a couple long moments to stare into his brown eyes, hazel flecks around his pupils.

A piece of muffin goes down my throat densely, no matter how much I swallow.

He says, "I knew about my brother for a long fucking time—he didn't know about me, and it took me years to actually try to meet him. I could have, at any point in my life, but I just…I didn't."

I frown. "I didn't know that."

He almost smiles. "It's not on the fucking internet."

Right…this isn't public information.

His brows rise at me. "You being here at your age, wanting to turn your life upside down just to get to know your brother, it's fucking…" He shakes his head and lets out a breath. "I did it almost four, five years ago? I was in my twenties, and you here, now—it's just brave."

I wipe my eyes quickly beneath my glasses. "You don't think it's dumb?"

His brows furrow. "Fuck no. Meeting my brother was the best decision I've ever made."

I let this digest, and not long after, I breathe easier and peel the paper off the muffin, able to eat more.

His constant F-bombs remind me of a video compilation I've watched. Someone spliced together a lot of his "fucks"—and the video lasted around three minutes. It has over 16 million views and always makes me laugh when I watch it. Ryke seems badass in every frame.

Silence stretches, and Ryke tickles his nephew's foot. The baby has hold of the comic book and giggles.

"Loren knew about me, you know," I say softly. Ryke looks up at me, and I add, "All these years, he knew about me, and I didn't know about him." I'm not in the exact same situation that Ryke had been in. I was the one in the dark. Loren was the one with the knowledge.

Ryke glances at the bathroom door, then back to me. "I'm not sure how much I'm supposed to fucking tell you—but I don't want you thinking badly of my—*our* brother. I don't know what you've been through in your life, but he's been through a fucking lot. And what I do know…" He checks over his shoulder again and then to me. "…when Lo met his birth mom for the first time, he *wanted* a relationship with you and your sister. But Emily basically told him that she didn't want you two to know that you have a brother, and out of respect for her, Lo left you alone."

My chest tightens again. I figured as much, and then I fixate on something else he said. "So...does everyone call him Lo?" I try to straighten my glasses.

"Mostly." He watches Maximoff shake a comic book—oh, the baby actually slobbers on the corner, trying to gnaw on the pages of *Young Avengers.*

"I've been calling him Loren. Is that bad?"

He almost smiles again. "You're his fucking sister. I don't think he'll care either way."

I hesitate to ask something more, but I just let it out in one breath, "Do you think he's happy I'm here?"

His hardened eyes, like *stone*, nearly soften. "These relationships we have with each other—they're not fucking easy, but I wouldn't want to lose a single one. I think Lo feels the same."

"...is now a good time to be here?" I wonder. "Lily just had a baby—"

"Yes," he says deeply, strongly, full of heart. "Lo's the best I've ever seen him." It reminds me that Loren, or *Lo* (that'll take some getting used to), struggles with alcohol addiction, hereditary, on his father's side.

The worst part: I've actually watched him relapse. The paparazzi never missed a beat.

Suddenly, the bathroom door opens, Lo hugging Lily against his side. She's much shorter than him, and her limbs seem ganglier next to his defined biceps, all lean muscles. They stop at the rug, zeroed in on their baby Maximoff chewing the comic book.

"Close your eyes," Lily says quickly and then nearly jumps on Loren's back to shield his view of their son destroying *Young Avengers* right in sight.

"It's too late, Lil," Lo says. "I've seen it."

I smile as she climbs up his back. Lo holds her like he's going to take her for a piggyback ride, and her hands fit across his eyes.

"You didn't see anything!" Lily says.

I wish I could snapshot this and send it to Maggie. My smile fades…or is that wrong? I shouldn't want to publicize them anymore than they already are. That's not why I'm here.

Maximoff rips a page.

"Ryke," Lo groans. "I blame you for this."

"He's not even crying right now. I'm doing a fantastic fucking job."

"You gave him a comic book, and he can't even read yet."

"He's starting early then," Ryke says. "Maybe you should've given me his diaper bag or something."

I listen to them, but their banter isn't totally registering in my head anymore. I remember that Loren just talked to my mom, which means I could be receiving a one-way ticket to Maine soon.

Lily uncovers Lo's eyes. "We're in a store with *tons* of toys on the walls. You could've taken a Green Goblin action figure."

Lo chimes in, "Or Wolverine, Black Widow, Hulk, Spider-Man—"

"For fuck's sake, okay. I got it." Ryke retrieves the ripped and wet comic from Maximoff and then picks him up. The baby giggles, and both Loren and Lily look like proud parents, their smiles infectious.

I shouldn't be here, I think. They just had a baby. I try to remember what Ryke told me, but my gut is telling me not to impede on their lives too much.

"You should babysit more often," Lo tells his brother.

"Fucking hilarious." He hands the baby to Loren, and Lily slides to the floor.

I crumple the muffin paper, finished eating, and when I look up, Loren is suddenly focused on me. I have trouble reading his features.

"Your mom is going to fly out this weekend to talk with you. Until then, you can either stay with us in a guest room or at a hotel. I'll pay for the expense, no problem."

It's not a terrible verdict. My mom will probably reiterate what she's said this whole time: *if you stay here, you're on your own. You make your own mistakes now.*

"A hotel works," I tell him. "I don't want to impose any more than I already have."

His baby squirms in his arms, so much so that I can't take stock in his expression. Lily ends up taking Maximoff so Loren can continue talking with me.

"If you change your mind, the invite is always open." And then he asks, "How old are you, by the way?"

"Seventeen." It's not like I could hide it much longer.

"That's what I thought." He pauses. "You know, Daisy is pretty close to your age."

Daisy Calloway is nineteen—and Ryke's girlfriend, and also spontaneous, lively, and so much cooler than I'll ever be.

Ryke gives his brother a look that I can't decipher.

Loren adds, "She'd probably love showing you around Philly. Is this your first time here?"

Daisy Calloway? Showing *me* around? I don't think she'd be fond of me. I like books. I like scrolling through Tumblr and surfing the internet. I like *sitting* activities, and Daisy is always seen *moving*. She'd probably try to take me on a wild adventure, and I'd slow her down.

I nod. "Yeah, but..." I stand up since everyone else is, and I find comfort in my backpack, slinging it on my shoulder. "I'm not sure she'd like me. I mean, I don't ride motorcycles and...other stuff like that."

I purposefully evade Ryke Meadows since I'm speaking about *his* girlfriend. And he likes motorcycles. And he likes all that "other" stuff.

"Neither do I," Lily pipes in. "They're terrifying."

Ryke raises his brows at her. "You haven't even ridden one."

"*Because* they're terrifying."

I relax some. "Yeah, same. I've never been on one, but I'm scared too."

Lily smiles and then points a finger at Ryke. "Ha!" Maximoff coos in her arms, almost babbling in agreement with his mom.

Ryke rolls his eyes and then sets them on me. "Daisy won't care if you're not into bikes. She'd honestly do anything you want."

Maybe I don't know her well enough to judge.

"I'll take off work some days this week too," Loren tells me.

I remember what Ryke said again, about Loren wanting to see me, to build a relationship too. He's willing to forgo work, just for me. It's validation that this isn't a mistake. Not yet at least.

I inhale a stronger breath. "Okay then…where do we start?"

"How about lunch?"

Ryke and Lily chime in about how hungry they both are, but my glasses fog, my eyes burning with tears once more.

My chin trembles a little, and beneath my breath, I say, "Thank you."

He smiles, one that escalates with sincerity. "We have a lot of catching up to do."

5

Garrison Abbey

WITH A GROUPLOVE SONG BLASTING THROUGH MY HEADPHONES, I splice together roughly thirty-four clips on Final Cut, my Mac propped on my legs. I cut and duplicate four-seconds from *Princesses of Philly*.

Right now, I'm looking at Ryke Meadows on pause. He's staring at a mangled motorcycle on the sidewalk. I press play. *"What the f**k? Mother ****ing, piece of sh*t **** **** ******* kidding me."* I pause, trimming one-eighth of a second.

The clip is funnier if it's duplicated and overlayed with a song, so I add music on top of his bleeped out cursing and then add a two-second clip from an interview. *"What the f**k kind of question is that?"* He throws a pillow at the camera.

Nathan suddenly chucks a rubber gargoyle mask at me, hitting my laptop closed.

"Motherfucker," I swear, yanking my headphones to my neck.

"Dude," Hunter says—and no, this isn't my brother. It's one of my friends who pales in comparison to my brother's *greatness* and effervescent *beauty*.

"What?" I glare, lifting my computer screen back up. I set the mask beside me on the desk, the rolling chair squeaking as I shift.

Nathan's den is unusually quiet. No music playing out loud. No poker tournament or multiple conversations happening at once.

It's just a handful of my friends, with rubber masks, black clothes on, and a plan inside their heads. A plan that's put a feverish, crazed look on their faces. The adrenaline high of doing something illegal has already set in.

And I feel sick.

Maybe because Loren has talked to us, not just threatened us, but actually *talked* and it's hard—it's a lot fucking harder to see him as this impenetrable celebrity when he's humanized himself in more ways than one.

My neck heats, and I sweat underneath my hoodie. I can't stop picturing him and his kid, his *baby*.

And the plan tonight: we break into Loren's house. We scare the fuck out of everyone who lives there, and then we run away.

Infants are there. And I know one of the girls...one of the girls is messed up with PTSD or something. When Loren caught me with a paintball gun in hand, I remember one of them—either him or his brother—they said that to me. *My girlfriend has PTSD.* I think it's Ryke's girlfriend, and I'm not sure what this is going to do to her—but it can't be good.

I could voice this to my friends, but I hear their response: *it's only a prank. Grow some fucking balls, Garrison. You pussy.*

My skin crawls, and I'm about to put my headphones back on. The only thing keeping me from puking is this stupid fucking video. *Ryke Meadows and his "Fucks" – Part 2.* The first one I uploaded has over sixteen million views, so I figured a second one is due.

Someone else throws another gargoyle mask at me.

I block it with my arm. "What the fuck?"

"*Dude,*" Hunter emphasizes. "We're leaving in a second, and you're playing *Sims.*"

Nathan laughs after taking a shot of whiskey. "Did your virtual girlfriend cheat on you with the virtual pool boy?"

I flip them both off. They saw me playing *The Sims* one time, and they've never dropped it. I actually like that game—but if I even tried to admit it, they'd bring it up every minute of the day. And I'm avoiding that headache.

"Let's go." Kyle stands and puts his mask on. He thumps at his chest with his fists.

"You're a gargoyle, not a gorilla," Nathan tells him before sliding his own mask on his face.

"Same family." Kyle's muffled voice comes through. Not long after, everyone begins heading out. I stuff my laptop and headphones into my backpack but leave it and just carry the mask.

Each step I take, I feel worse, and excuses start blazing in my head. To get out of this, to leave. *I'm going to throw up.*

I wipe my forehead with my arm, the mask heavy in my hand. I close Nathan's front door behind me, and they laugh, practically *skipping* down his driveway to the road.

I'm the only one unmasked at this point.

As soon as my feet hit the asphalt, I just tighten up. I freeze in place. They're about five paces ahead of me when Nathan notices I'm missing. He turns around and gestures for me to follow. "Come on."

I shake my head tensely. "I can't," is the only excuse I can purge.

Nathan lifts his mask halfway up his head, tufts of red hair exposed. His eyes narrow at me, and he comes closer, our friends following. If I bail, there's a chance others may bail too—and this was Nathan's plan.

"Why are you being a little baby?" Nathan says loudly, so our friends hear.

"Just go without me," I tell them—the words spilling before I can take them back.

Nathan steps even closer to me. He's shorter and thinner than me, but still, my muscles flex and strain, my pulse accelerating and breath deepening.

"If you ditch us," Nathan sneers, "that's *it*—you know that, right?"

I glare. "Come on—"

"No, we're in this together. That was the *fucking* plan." Nathan gets in my face.

I shove him back, enough to give me space, and he's about to put his hands on me—I lose it and shift out of his path. "Seriously, don't fucking touch me!" I chuck the fucking mask at him.

"You're the one who hit *me*! God, what the hell is wrong with you, Abbey?"

I run a hand through my hair, the strands out of my eyes now. I'm shaking, and I can't say anything. I just walk back to his house, up his driveway, so I can grab my backpack and go home.

"Garrison!" Nathan shouts.

"Forget about him," Hunter says. "He's probably pissed he can't spend time with his fake friends on Tumblr."

I put a cigarette to my lips, shaking way too much to light it. My eyes burn, and I check over my shoulder once. Nathan is glaring at me, as though to say, *if you want to be my friend again, you're going to have a lot of making up to do.* He shakes his head, puts the mask over his face, and turns around, heading down the street with the rest of my friends.

I want to scream.

At myself. At them. At this stupid goddamn place.

But all I do is go inside, grab my backpack, and walk in the opposite direction of them, rounding the street corner to Cider Creek Pass.

6

Willow Moore

"FOR FUCK'S SAKE," RYKE SWEARS AFTER LAYING ON THE HORN.
I'm clutching my backpack strap and double-checking my seatbelt,
secured in the backseat.

Loren glances at me from the passenger seat for the twentieth
time, and I nod at him like *I'm okay.*

I've been in the car with them while paparazzi cars and vans
tail us, but never this badly. Cameramen caught an "unnamed girl"
climbing into the backseat of Ryke's silver Infinity, and the internet
has been going crazy with shadowy pictures of me.

I have Tumblr, Twitter, and *Celebrity Crush's* feed popped up on
my cellphone, and it's all everyone's talking about.

The number one speculation: *Ryke Meadows is cheating on Daisy Calloway.*

I've seen them together. In person. (I still can't believe it.) I
helped Daisy make enchiladas for the house, and Ryke entered the
kitchen to help too. I caught him stealing glimpses of his girlfriend,
as though just wanting one more mental image of her—and his lips
would always begin to rise in a smile.

Sure, I've always been a Raisy shipper, even if I can't relate much
to their adventurous spirits, but these small, hidden moments solidify
what I've always thought to be true.

Ryke Meadows loves Daisy Calloway.

So no, he'd *never* cheat on her. I don't believe it for a second, and
I can only hope the world does too. I don't want to interrupt or ruin
their lives by moving to Philly.

At a red light, Ryke angrily rolls down the driver's window and sticks his head out. "Don't cut me off!" he shouts at the nearest SUV, a camera pointing straight at him.

"What kind of precious cargo is in the backseat, Ryke?" the cameraman asks.

"I'm fucking serious. Don't pull out in front of me again like we're playing bumper *fucking* cars."

Loren cocks his head to Ryke. "Want me to drive?"

Ryke says nothing as he rolls the window back up.

"At least I don't have road rage."

"I'm a better driver than you—and don't *fucking* say it."

"You wrecked my car," Loren teases with a half-smile. "I've never been in an accident, so I'm a goddamn *great* driver."

Ryke rolls his eyes but stays quiet and taps the steering wheel, impatient for the light to change.

Loren glances at me again. "You doing okay?"

I tense more. "So is it usually this bad?"

"They're just out for blood today," Loren says. I notice his leg jostling a little, more edged than he's letting on. His phone is also in his hand, so I wonder if he's seen the speculations too. Then I spot the *Celebrity Crush* tabloid site on his screen.

I shift uncomfortably on the leather seat. "Maybe if Ryke kind of…keeps his distance from me, or acts like he doesn't care…" I trail off because Loren is almost near laughter. He has to rub his lips to keep it down.

"You're a fucking ass," Ryke tells Loren, though there seems to be affection in his voice, not hate.

I look cautiously between them. "What is it?"

Loren playfully puts a hand on the back of Ryke's headrest. "Telling Ryke to *not care* is beyond his superhuman capabilities. He's physically and mentally hardwired to *overly* care about people close to him."

I digest this and loosen my grip on my backpack. I'm slowly inching into their world, and I knew there'd be bad parts, like the constant gaze of cameras—but I don't think I ever calculated *these* parts: the loyalty from people who've just met me.

"Funny," Ryke says, hitting the gas pedal as the light turns green. "I don't remember ever being a fucking superhero."

Loren's smile fades, and he stares at his older brother for a long moment, like he wants to say something more. He ends up dropping his hand and swiveling towards me. "Stay close to me when we get out. They'll try to get in your face, and it'll be easier to walk inside the apartment complex if you're near me."

"They're going to ask who I am, right?" I nervously wipe my palms on my jeans.

"I'm going to lie, so you don't have to," Loren tells me. "Okay?"

I notice Ryke going rigid in the driver's seat, his eyes hardening through the rearview mirror. I don't know him well enough to understand why he's pissed. Maybe he's protective of Loren. Maybe he hates lies. Maybe it's the paparazzi in general.

All I know is that I'm about to make my debut in this media-crazed universe. And Loren Hale, my brother, is helping guide me.

"Okay," I nod.

"How many boxes are in the trunk?" Ryke asks.

"Just two. She only shipped my clothes and bedding." I said *she* instead of *Mom* to bypass the awkward tension of releasing her name into the atmosphere. I saw her not long ago. Our conversation at a local restaurant, Lucky's Diner, went something like this:

Mom: *If you stay here, you're on your own. I can't help you in Philadelphia.*

Me: *I know.*

Mom: **looks over her shoulder, expecting Loren Hale to jump out and frighten her by his presence**

Me: *He's not here. (He knew you didn't want to see him, ever.)*

Mom: **silence**

Me: *Can I still talk to Ellie?*

Mom: *When you call, I'll make sure to hand the phone to Ellie. *checks watch**

Me: *...do you want me to come home?*

Mom: ...*you would've been out of my house in a year's time anyway for college. Maybe this change now is for the best.*

Then she gave me the faintest of smiles, like a goodbye, like she'd already begun severing me from her mind and she was waiting for me to do the same. She's used to leaving children behind, I realized. Maybe she thought this was the natural course—that she should leave me behind too, in time.

Sometimes I wonder if it was all a ruse, if she just appeared detached so she could let me go more easily. If she spent the night crying on the plane. If she hopes my life will be better here than it was there.

I'd like to believe all of this because it makes me love her a little more and resent her a little less.

Leaving Ellie has turned out to be the hardest part of all. Without constant communication, I can't know how she'll fair. If I fool myself long enough, I can imagine that my absence won't have any real impact on her, but I know it will.

Ryke parks in front of a brick apartment complex, the lot nearly full with cars. I feel out of my element. Not only because four different vehicles park near us, doors opening and cameramen jumping out—but because I'm only seventeen and entering territory that college students step on.

Lo isn't happy about it.

I can see that now as he scans the twenty-something, backpack-clad students, strolling in the apartment complex. His brows pinch, and his eyes darken.

"I'll be okay," I tell him, having to raise my voice as paparazzi gather outside the car doors.

He shakes his head a couple times. "You should really be staying with us."

Six people live in his house: three Calloway sisters and their three significant others, all in their twenties. Along with two newborn babies, one is Loren's son.

There may be extra room in their mansion-sized house, but I don't feel like I'd fit in. In fact, I see myself *always* in the way.

I haven't even met Rose Calloway's husband, Connor Cobalt, yet. He could very well hate me. On the reality show, he came off as a conceited human being. I even made a gif set of him saying (with a straight face), *"Most people never reach the pinnacle of perfection. But I'm not most people, so think of it as an honor to meet me."*

He's a genius. A billionaire. And living in a bedroom down the hall from him sounds like a fantasyland not created for me.

"I don't want to complicate your life," I tell him honestly.

His brows rise at me, and he motions to a bearded cameraman by my window. "And I'm not complicating yours?"

The man meets Lo's gaze, and Lo flashes his iconic dry smile at him. Seeing that smile in person is more powerful than in photograph.

On impulse, I almost take a picture, but I control myself, flipping my phone in my hand. It's so easy to become part of the paparazzi without really knowing.

"I'm going to grab a fucking box and head inside. Do you have your keycard?" Ryke asks me.

I nod.

Loren seems reluctant to do this.

Ryke gives him a look that I can't read. "You can't force her to live with us," he reminds him.

"She's only *seventeen*," he whispers, running a frustrated hand through his hair, thicker on top, shorter on the sides. "She should be closer to the high school she's going to attend, not to Penn."

"I'm closer to UPenn," I say softly, "not Penn."

Both of the brothers swing their heads to the backseat, and I swear camera flashes go off like crazy. The windows are only slightly tinted, so I wonder how much the paparazzi catch.

I feel my cheeks heat, but the color drains, their eye contact more and more intimidating. "Do I have…something on my face?" My voice dies, and by their rising smiles, I immediately regret speaking. I shrink into place.

Ryke tells me, "The only people I've ever heard say UPenn are people who never attended the University of Pennsylvania." He pockets his car keys. "We all call it Penn. At least when we went there that's how it was. Who the fuck knows what students are calling it now."

He acts like he graduated decades ago, but he just turned twenty-six. I'm not that great at math, but I can subtract well enough to figure out that it's been four years since he graced *Penn's* campus.

Lo adds, "Most of the older faculty prefer calling it Penn over UPenn. It's just tradition and it sticks with some people when you're there."

"But Penn State…"

"Is called Penn State," Lo explains. "If you say, 'I go to Penn' around here, most people will assume it's not Penn State."

"And if they don't, who the fuck cares," Ryke finishes. He also flashes the middle finger to the cameraman outside my window. "He's too close to her."

"I'll get out and go around to her door," Lo tells him. "You pop the trunk and grab the first box." At this, both of them open their car doors and climb out. Flashes bombard them, along with a barrage of voices.

I unbuckle and scoot towards the door that Loren nears.

"Back up," Loren tells them before opening my door and letting me out. I squeeze between him and a camera lens.

"What's your name?!"

"How do you know Loren and Ryke?!"

"Who are you dating?!"

My shoulders curve forward at each incoming question, and I clutch my backpack strap, pulling it closer to my body.

Loren leaves my side to grab my second cardboard box, and I follow close by, as instructed. I trip a little over my feet and barely catch myself, avoiding a collision into Lo.

Do not fall, especially on your brother that you recently met.

Unfortunately, I'm most clumsy when I'm nervous.

It's a horrible attribute. I wouldn't wish it on my enemy, but then again, I doubt my enemies would ever feel nervous enough to be clumsy.

Ryke slams the trunk closed, and then we head towards the side-walk. A cameraman sprints in front of me and walks backwards as he films. "What's your name?!" he asks over the other paparazzi.

"She's my cousin," Loren lies with a dark glare. "So watch what you say and do." He stuffs a hand in his pocket, the action casual but somehow threatening.

About this time, we reach the sidewalk, a direct shot to the glass double doors of the apartment complex. Lo said they can't follow us inside. So I practically hold my breath in anticipation of ditching the eight—no, *twelve* cameramen that flank us.

And then, the weight on my shoulder goes from slightly heavy to very, very light—followed by a *crash* and a *crack!* I freeze in place and look down at the cement, wide-eyed at my backpack's contents.

Shit. The bottom of my backpack ripped.

And my laptop... I'm about to bend down to check it, but I notice other items that litter the sidewalk.

Like an extra T-shirt and shorts for overnight "crashing in my car" purposes. An extra pair of *panties*—these really childish looking blue pair with purple hearts.

Lots of highlighters, sticky notes, and pens.

What's most abundant: *tampons.* And not just one or two. There is an entire *box* of pink plastic-wrapped applicators. I know this because I bought a box recently, dumped it into my backpack, and thought nothing of it.

I tense up, locked in a shell-shocked state, most likely ghostly pale.

My heart plummets, leaving a hollow hole in its place. My bro-ther—a *new* brother—and his intimidating half-brother plant their gazes on me. And to make it worse: I'm surrounded by men with cameras who will no doubt post this on the internet.

I'm not ready to be a meme. Oh my God.

I can't move. I can't squat. I just stare like maybe this moment will rewind itself, and my jean backpack won't rip apart.

"Oh shit," one of the cameramen laughs.

I barely register Loren's murderous glare, plastered on the camera guy. He shrinks back a little and holds up a hand in surrender.

And then Ryke sets down his box. *What is he doing*—

No!

He starts collecting my tampons like they're pencils and not feminine products. I dazedly animate, like my legs belong to another girl—a higher force pulling the strings attached to my limbs. I kneel and quickly gather all the items, frantically stuffing them in my backpack's side pocket that's still intact.

Not a lot can fit there, so I bundle everything else in my arms. I decide to check the state of my laptop later, but upon glance, it seems okay.

"I can get that," I practically whisper to Ryke, gesturing to the tampons and two comic books in his clutch. I'm not sure he hears me, but I outstretch my free hand, showing him that I'll take it.

I struggle holding everything else, and I almost drop my laptop again.

"I'll carry this," he tells me. "You take that." He pockets the tampons and sets the comics on his cardboard box.

How can he be okay with pocketing my tampons? I'm about to refreeze and solidify all over again.

"Put your backpack on mine," Loren says, drawing my attention up to him. He pats the top of his box, and I rise, reluctantly letting go of my possessions, too afraid I'll spill them all.

"Thanks," I mutter, having trouble even *looking* at Ryke now.

"Does your cousin have a name?!" a camera guy shouts, his words dizzying me.

"Yeah." Loren uses one hand to hold the cardboard box, and the other sets on my shoulder, guiding me forward. "Her name is Willow Hale." He gives them one lasting dry smile before we enter the glass double doors.

As we ride up to the fourth floor in silence, I regain some consciousness that I typically lose in embarrassing moments. It's like a blackout, a fog, an out-of-body experience—my mind so stunned that it decides to abandon my body for a quick second.

I inhale, first and foremost. And then I look up. Ryke and Loren stand on either side of me, so tall that they make my 5'5" height feel short. I catch Ryke *glaring* at the space above my head, eyes narrowed on his brother.

Lo never looks towards Ryke as he says, "I had to lie. So you can stop glaring at me now. And in case you've forgotten, bro, I have the heart of Hades, so you shouldn't be surprised anyway."

"She's not a Hale, Lo."

Loren lets out a short, frustrated breath and meets his brother's darkened gaze. "Yeah? But I couldn't say she's a Moore and have press digging up her little sister's name. This is the better option for more than one reason. You know why?"

Ryke stays quiet and shakes his head, more like *this is wrong*.

"Now they think you're related too," Lo explains. "No tabloids are going to start rumors that you're hooking up…or whatever." Lo cringes at the idea.

I block out everything, internally dying and too overcome to concentrate on any other words or details. The elevator slows and beeps, and I nearly race off down the hall to my room: 458. I unlock the door with my keys—well, almost.

I drop them. I pick them up. And then I clumsily drop them again. It takes four tries before my joints work properly, and I turn the lock.

I have a very neat roommate, the tiny kitchen clean and pretty bare of appliances and food. Maya mentioned how she has a dining hall meal plan at Penn. The living room has a couple *Avengers* posters, *Battlestar Galactica* and *Final Fantasy*—plus stacks of anime on the coffee table.

Maya Ahn is cool. The Superheroes & Scones store manager had a roommate opening after her friend left for California, and it worked out in my favor.

I definitely can't afford the whole rent by myself, and I start working at Superheroes & Scones soon, thanks to Lily's kindness. Hopefully I'll be able to pay off the first month's rent that Lo loaned me.

The apartment splits off into two hallways; the left is hers, claimed by a Darth Vader poster on the door that says:

I WANT YOU FOR THE IMPERIAL FORCES!

The right is mine, unclaimed and bare. I open the door to a dorm-sized room, a simple built-in desk, a wooden dresser, a half-window, and a short single bed.

I take a seat on the slightly stained mattress, the wooden frame creaking. I hear footsteps as Ryke and Loren follow my shadow. I toss my phone from palm to palm, and it suddenly buzzes.

Maggie: Are you with Loren Hale right now?!?!?!

I balk. There's only one way my best friend from Maine could know this *that* quickly. I log onto the *Celebrity Crush* website.

"Oh my God," I mutter. A giant photograph of me snatching tampons off the sidewalk fills the landing page. Ryke has my panties on top of his box, and they've drawn a circle around them.

The headline:

Loren Hale's Cousin Has an Accident
in a Parking Lot!

I type back to Maggie: it's me...unfortunately.

Maggie: YOU'RE WITH LOREN HALE & RYKE MEADOWS!!!! WHAT IS UNFORTUNATE ABOUT THAT??? Also... why didn't you tell me you're his cousin? HELLO!

I knew that she might notice, but I doubt anyone else in Caribou will put two-and-two together and stir trouble for me. So I just text back: I just found out... please don't tell anyone. My mom doesn't want Ellie caught up in this.

Maggie: I won't tell a soul. Skype me soon... I need LOTS of details!

After her last text, I dazedly skim over the article, catching the part where they mention how my "visit looks like a permanent one"—and of course, they point out every single item I dropped.

"This place is small." Lo's voice emanates from the living room.

I set my phone on the mattress and stare at my hands, a little more numb and hollow than before the car ride here. I can't discern whether these feelings are from the severe lack of privacy...or just a normal bout of embarrassment.

"My first year dorm room was fucking smaller than this," Ryke retorts.

"She's not in college yet. She shouldn't live in a shoebox until she has to."

Ryke sighs heavily, their footsteps nearer. "I've already said what I've had to..." he trails off, and I sense them towering in the doorway, their hot gazes on my immobile body.

I can't look away from my palms.

A tense moment passes before I hear them set down the two cardboard boxes.

"Thanks," I say softly, unsure of what I'm feeling exactly. It's not every day that you grace the number one gossip site with your comfiest pair of panties and tampons strewn about. What a strange debut.

"Hey...Willow," Lo says, attempting to soften the sharp edge to his voice. "What happened back there—that'll be yesterday's news in an hour." He clears his throat when I don't respond. "You can think of it like an initiation? Welcome to the family..."

I choke on a laugh that twists my face into a cringe. I finally look up, and both Ryke and Loren wear sympathetic expressions.

Ryke more than Lo, which reminds me of the conversation in the car...about Lo's brother being *overly* caring.

I lick my dry lips, trying to form words when I usually keep everything in my head. It's a hard task to master, and I know I'm still very green at it. "I just…kind of hoped I'd be known for something other than the-girl-who-dropped…" *tampons.* I can't even say what they are. I wince at myself and glance at the scrap of worn jean material on top of a cardboard box. I can sew the bottom later.

"Like I said, it'll be yesterday's news," Lo tells me. "You'll be known for something else in a month's time…" My mind tunes him out the minute Ryke unpockets a handful of tampons, setting them on my dresser.

I go pale again.

"Ryke," Lo snaps, noticing where my attention lies. He whispers something to his brother, who's frowning.

Ryke whispers back, "They're just tampons. You're acting like she dropped a fucking dildo."

"Don't," Loren cringes.

Ryke rolls his eyes. "Lily, *your* fiancée, said she had a bad dream about her sex toys falling out of her luggage and paparazzi catching the incident at the airport—so I'm not the fucking weird one here."

Lo groans. "Why are you talking to *my* girlfriend about dildos?"

I don't know if I should find entertainment in this—if that makes me no better than *Celebrity Crush*—but I guiltily *and* eagerly listen along, wanting their back-and-forth to continue.

Ryke groans now. "We're fucking friends."

"*Hey*, can you at least watch how you say that? You're not friends that fuck."

"Why are you busting my balls?"

"You're the one who brought up Lily and goddamn sex toys. What the hell did you expect out of me?"

Ryke sighs and runs another hand through his hair. He meets my gaze as soon as his hand drops. "I hate that you feel embarrassed about this."

I shrug, unsure of what to say in reply. "You know…I'm a girl." It's difficult to say what I mean. I think I always sound more articulate in my head. "None of my friends talk about…periods or anything…"

Lo and Ryke exchange one look of knowing between each other. And then Lo dials a number on his phone and puts it on speaker.

Within the third ring, it clicks.

"Loren." An icy, female voice frosts the room. "This better be quick. I'm getting my nails done for the first time in *three* months." I think she even mutters, "I'm so sorry"—to her nails.

"God forbid I disturb you, your highness," Loren says.

"Wait—aren't you with your sister?" Rose Calloway, Lily's older sister, is one of the few people aware of the truth. I can hear her shift in her chair, as though straightening up. "Is everything okay?"

I've met Rose a few times. She usually does all the talking and I nod a lot. I like people that don't mind if I'm quiet, and since she's so loud, I thought she'd pressure me to be like her, to speak up and attack with confidence. She actually lets me say as much as I want and fills the rest of the silence with her own voice. I even think she likes it that way.

It makes me like her even more.

Ryke talks loudly so his voice is heard through the speakerphone. "She's upset. Her backpack tore while paparazzi were around us, and tampons fell out."

Every time he says *tampons*, so casually, my heart nosedives all over again.

"Willow," Rose says sternly. "Can you hear me?"

"It wasn't just one," I say under my breath. "It was an entire box…"

Lo puts his phone closer to his lips. "Did you get that?"

"Yes," Rose says. "Willow, most women have a period. We buy tampons or pads or other products. I personally like to be overprepared too. And if anyone—a cameraman, a peer, a stranger—makes you feel strange or uncomfortable for having seen you with them, then just know that they're *boys*, not men. They're *infantile*, little human beings that can't appreciate or respect a woman's body. And in no way should they even *touch* one." I begin to smile and she adds, "I have to go—*no* not yellow polish. I'm not a sunflower—"

She hangs up or maybe Lo does, either way—my shoulders have unconsciously lifted, my hands flat on my legs. I feel a little less numb, a little more awake.

I've never been given a motivational, encouraging speech in my life. The best part: knowing someone cares about me enough to give one. I realize that Ryke and Loren must've understood what Rose's response would be in this situation.

It's a bigger indication that they're all really close to each other.

"Thanks for calling Rose," I tell them.

They don't ask if I feel better, but I think they both can see that I am.

I stand up to check my laptop, which rests on a box. "You don't have to stay. I know I've taken up most of your time today already."

"We won't be that much longer," Lo says, "but I just...I need to tell you something. I just want to explain what happened. I know you probably read it online, but I think you should have our details."

I gather my laptop and then plop back down on the mattress. "Okay..." I think I know what this is about.

Someone broke into their house a few nights ago.

And I've been scared to broach the subject with Loren. It seems so personal, and I wasn't sure if I was allowed to bring it up since I lie on the fringes of their lives.

Ryke crosses his arms, casually leaning against the wall, unsurprised that Lo wants to talk about it with me.

Loren drags the desk chair closer to the bed and takes a seat, his elbows resting on his thighs and his hands clasped together. He stares at them for a long moment, just as I've stared at my own in dazed contemplation. The familiar action seems to bind us together, an invisible tether that's strung between siblings, here and there.

He lifts his head a fraction, just so our eyes lock. His gaze carries horrors and tribulations, I see. His gaze carries more than I've met. "Some guys around your age that live in our gated neighborhood," he begins, "they broke into our house. Everyone's fine." He adds that part quickly but his gaze falls back to his hands.

He looks haunted by the incident, and I glance over at Ryke, his brown eyes planted on the carpet with the same disturbed expression.

"This happened on Ryke's birthday?" I know it did. I read it in multiple articles. I push my glasses up, realizing my face is in a permanent wince.

"Yeah. I would've told you sooner, but...we've been trying to deal with a lot."

"It's okay," I say, just grateful he's telling me at all.

On September 19th, Ryke's birthday, I was at Lucky's Diner. Talking to my mom. Afterwards, I texted Lo that I was going to spend the night at a hotel and probably just hang out there the next day. He replied about three hours after I sent the message, a lot slower than normal.

Loren Hale: Okay, let me know if you need anything. I'm always here.

"They didn't steal anything," he explains. "They just came inside with masks to scare us, as a prank. It's not going to happen again, so I really don't want you to be afraid of coming around. The guys who did this, they *live* in our neighborhood. They're just rich pricks...or jerks."

My lips faintly rise. It's kind of funny when he tries to "censor" himself around me, like I'm a little kid. I've told him once that I don't mind when he curses, but he just shrugged. I don't know...I like more that he cares enough to try, even if it's not necessary.

And then my smile fades completely and my brows knot. "They live in your neighborhood?"

"Not for fucking long," Ryke says. He thinks I'm frightened by them being there—but that's not what's rolling around in my head.

If they live in that neighborhood, there's a good chance those are the same guys I saw at that party. The same ones causing trouble in Superheroes & Scones. "What do you mean, not for long?"

"We called the cops," Lo tells me. "We've let them off the hook a lot because...I know what a small charge can do to someone's future.

I didn't want to get them written up for putting dog shit on our front porch."

Ryke looks at his brother. "You did the right thing by waiting."

Loren nods a couple times, looking as though he's trying to believe it was the right course of action too.

"We fucking warned them," Ryke adds.

"Yeah." Loren nods again. "So we're pressing charges this time around." He motions to me. "I wanted to tell you sooner because I want to include you in my life, as much and as often as I can, okay?"

I smile. *Wow.* My eyes feel glassy, and I take a deep, strong breath and nod. "I'm glad."

"Good." Lo stands. "And you should know that some of these guys go to your new school. They shouldn't be there anymore, but some of their friends might be. And if they give you shit, you let me know."

I'm about to ask why they would "give me shit"—but then I realize...*I'm Willow Hale* to them. To everyone. To the world.

I'm the only relative of Loren Hale that will be walking the halls of Dalton Academy.

And Loren Hale possibly just sent their friends to jail.

THE CALLOWAY SISTERS & THEIR MEN — FAN PAGE

Big news! Loren Hale's cousin has moved into town. There's not much we know about Willow Hale—yet—but it will only be a short time before Redditors and paparazzi gather more information. Here's what we know so far:

She's seventeen.

That's it. Seriously! We don't even know where she came from. It's like she materialized from thin air. Maybe those conspiracy theories are right and Loren Hale's family all have superpowers. LOL!

But for real, Willow Hale is a mystery. Early reports were that she might have been Ryke's new girlfriend but that's been debunked now that we know Willow is a *Hale*. And not to mention Raisy is a ship that is clearly sailing into the sunset.

Until I get more information, check out the gif set of Willow's epic tampon fumble!

Love you like Loren loves Lily,
xo Olive

7

Garrison Abbey

I PACE OUTSIDE OF SUPERHEROES & SCONES AT 6 A.M., MY SHIT feelings causing me to linger. Only a few cars whiz by every minute, Philly beginning to wake—*why am I awake?*

It's Saturday. I should be in bed sleeping off these shit feelings—*I can't sleep.*

I stop and rest my arm on a parking meter for a second. An old gold Honda hugs the curb.

I parked my car a block away from here, needing the walk to think. Now that I'm outside the storefront, I'm still *thinking* apparently, and it's not helping.

Nothing is helping.

I tug my hood over my head, the morning air cold. Everyone at Dalton knows what happened at Loren's house, and most of them know that I was supposed to be there.

My mutual friends with Nathan—ones that weren't there that night—think I'm disloyal and a shit friend for welching. Believing that I could've helped them escape before Loren caught them.

I can't even hang out with the people that think Nathan is scum for what he did. I'm guilty by association. I passed Rachel in the hallway. She bristled at my presence and said, "You could've stopped your friends, you know. Why didn't you do anything?"

Some mornings, I wish I'd just gone ahead and done it with them. Because I know I could never be strong enough to convince all of my friends to turn around with me. No one gets that.

"Why are you here?" I mutter to myself under my breath. And then blinds begin to open from inside the store. I don't believe in signs or astrology or any of that, but this feels like something.

Move.

I walk away from the parking meter. Nearing the door. Why am I here?

Because I literally have nowhere else to go.

I have no friends. I have no life-altering aspirations. Every door feels shut except this one…the one that Loren Hale left open for me.

If this doesn't work out…I don't know what I'm going to do.

I eye the *closed* sign and then knock on the glass door. I lean over and see Lily Calloway through it. She looks startled, her green eyes widened at me.

Shit. I go still, more uncertain now. Her bald-headed bodyguard flanks her side, the burliest guy I've ever seen. His thick left arm could probably crush my windpipe.

She bites her nails, and I knock again, letting her know that I want to enter the store. I keep shifting, like I might bail and go home at any second.

Lily says something to her bodyguard, her gangly body looking even thinner while she stands next to him. She makes me less nervous for some reason.

He replies back, and then she approaches the door.

I tense as soon as she cracks the door and sticks her head out. I pull back my hoodie so she can see my face, and then I look over her shoulder. "Is Loren here?"

"No." That's all she gives me.

I deserve that.

I deserve even less, actually. I look at her bodyguard again. He crosses his arms and actually *glares* at me. I let out a pained noise, meaning it to be a laugh. "Forget it. This was a mistake." I go to turn around.

"Wait," she says quickly.

I hesitate, halfway turned.

"What do you want?"

How do I say this? I grit my teeth and try to purge my feelings, but all I say is, "Your boyfriend or fiancé or whatever... he offered me and my friends a job." I roll my eyes, realizing how this sounds after what happened. "It's fucking stupid anyway. Everything is."

I'm leaving.

The single thought sounds good, and I know how deep it actually goes.

"Lo told me about that." She swings the door wider open. "Do you want to come in?"

I hardly hear her. My lips part in shock, and my eyes burn. "What?" I breathe, looking between her and the opened door. I fully expected her to shut it in my face.

"If you want a job, you have to come into the store," she says nicely and even produces a smile. "Although..." Her eyes light up. "It'd be kinda cool if we had a superhero mascot out front. Do you want to be a mascot?"

"No." I shake my head in fog, barely registering anything she just said. How can she be this nice to me? She waves me in again, and I tentatively walk inside, my fists stuffed in my jean pockets. I don't think I've ever been this nervous.

Don't screw this up. I know. I know.

Her bodyguard blocks me about ten-feet into the store. "I need to pat you down."

Right.

I could have a weapon or some shit, looking for vengeance for them turning in my friends. I understand. I extend my arms, and the big guy pats my pockets and checks my hoodie. I hear some people talking softly by the cash register, but I don't look over there.

I scan the racks of comics, a cardboard cutout of a couple green-clad superheroes close by.

After Lily's bodyguard finds nothing on me, he nods to her in approval.

"So you want a job?" she asks.

My face twists, unable to detect any resentment on her features. She's what…twenty-four? She looks sixteen, to be honest—just really thin with a round face and rosy cheeks. Her brown hair is chopped at her shoulders, and she scratches her arm while she waits for me to speak.

I don't know what I feel, but it's all rising and hitting me fast. "You're not even going to ask me where I was that night? Or what happened?"

It's hard to believe Lily is a sex addict. The way she stares at me like *"oh right"*—slightly aloof but still approachable like a lost turtle—isn't someone I'd think would have a lot of sex.

Then again, one of my friends, Carly, has a tongue piercing and she's a virgin. So I don't know why I draw these conclusions, knowing they never add up anyway.

Lily pulls back her shoulders some and hesitantly asks, "Where were you?"

The question pummels me full-force, even if I was the one who basically asked it to myself. I look up at the ceiling and shake my head.

And it just rips out of me. "I'm not a good guy. I never told them to stop. I knew that they planned to break in and scare everyone, and I didn't do anything. I just let them leave." I choke on a laugh. "And now they're all looking at a year in prison. And I'm standing free."

She never even flinches. I watch her take in more than just my words, her eyes reddening. It's like she gets it. I don't know how… "What made you stay back?"

I stare at the carpet. "Everything your boyfriend said… fuck, I don't know. It just didn't feel right, scaring girls and babies… I know one of you has PTSD…"

She stiffens. "Wha…?"

"I didn't tell anyone," I say quickly, realizing this is private information. "I promise. I can't even remember who let it slip. Either Ryke or Loren shouted it at me. No one else was around." I drop my head, and my bed-head hair falls into my eyelashes. "I think… you should know that I planned to go with my friends."

I swallow a rock, struggling to force *tears* down.

Stop crying. I'm not crying, okay? I'm not. I just… I want to be someone else. I can't live with this anymore. And I don't even know what *this* is. Yeah I do…

This is me.

"I literally could not move my stupid feet," I say, my voice shaking. "And there's a part of me that wishes I was with them. That I got caught too."

She says softly, "You did the right thing."

I don't think I did. I look up at her. "Did I? I can't even say *I'm sorry* because it feels fucking stupid. Like…" I push my hair out of my eyes. "Like it's not enough, you know? It's not at all." It'll never be.

"This was enough," she says. "I promise, it was."

I try to let out a deep breath, and I try to believe what she's telling me. I don't think I can forgive myself, even if she's forgiven me.

I rub my reddened eyes with my arm and exhale again. I scan the store once more, grazing over the shelves and superhero posters along the wall.

I've never had a place that felt safe, but this one does. It feels like more than that.

"Here, I'll introduce you to Maya, the store manager," Lily says. "She'll have a better idea what positions need to be filled." She guides me towards the checkout counter.

I figure Maya must be the one with short black hair since she takes charge and shows the other girl the register.

"Hey," I say, nodding to the girls.

I startle the one with the loose braid. She bangs into the cash tray, overturning the plastic container. It lands on the floor, cash and coins spilling out. She freezes at first, blood rushing out of her skin, ashen and pale.

Shit.

"I'm *so* sorry," the girl says to Lily. She pushes up her black-rimmed glasses, and it hits me all at once.

I know you.

She seems to dodge my gaze, kneeling to gather all the fallen money. Maya stays at the computer, typing on the keyboard.

"I can help." I squat a little closer to this girl, hoping she raises her head and looks at me, just once. I want to know if she recognizes me too. If she knows who I am—if she hates me like almost everyone else.

Or maybe I just want her eyes to finally meet mine.

While I gather dollar bills, I keep glancing at her, watching as she picks up a few quarters and drops them in the same instant.

My lips rise, and I help her pick those up too. I can hear her breath shorten. And my fleeting smile fades.

Maybe she's scared of me.

I remember her from that party over a month ago.

The girl searching for Loren Hale.

I also remember her from a recent article.

The girl who turned out to be Loren Hale's cousin.

I still can't wrap my head around why she was asking which house Loren Hale lived in when she should've had his phone number. Maybe their parents are estranged from each other—I guess it's not an important detail anyway.

"Okay," Lily says hurriedly, "now you've met Willow and Willow you've met Garrison. Meet-and-greet has ended."

I haven't met her yet, not really. She won't look at me.

I rise to my feet at the same time as Willow, helping her fit the cash back into the register. "Are you new here?" I ask, kind of already knowing the answer based on Maya showing her the checkout counter.

Why won't you look at me?

"Yep," Lily says quickly. "Yep, everyone's new. Willow, can you get my purse from the break room?"

Willow shifts slightly, keeping at least two feet between us. "Sure." She tries to smooth down a stack of fives.

"I can do it," Maya says, scooting closer.

Willow abandons the register and heads for the break room. She has on those same faded overalls and a mustard-yellow shirt. When she walks, it's closed-off, tucked into herself—and a part of me understands that.

More than I ever thought I could.

She pauses midway to the door. "My backpack…"

I notice the old JanSport backpack, propped against the counter. "This?" I grab it and make my way to Willow.

She finally meets my gaze.

Her brown, doe-like eyes are inquisitive and nervous. I see recognition, her gaze flitting over my features, to place me correctly.

I stop about a foot away, and her chest rises in a large inhale.

Mine collapses in a deeper one.

I pass the backpack to Willow, our fingers brushing, and something tugs inside of me. I can't make sense of it. All I know: we've been bypassing each other for weeks, two separate strands of time—and in this second, we've finally touched.

"Thanks," she says, pulling the backpack over one shoulder. She holds onto the strap.

When she turns around, she trips over her feet, stumbling a bit before she collects herself and trudges forward.

I feel my lips pull up again, remembering the article. Where her backpack ripped open. She looked cute in the photograph—but the actual article was fucking stupid. It made me want to dump out the journalist's backpack or purse or whatever and highlight every item for the world to see.

"Garrison," Lily says as Willow disappears into the break room.

"Yeah?" I rotate to face one of the most famous people in the world. I think it'd dawn on me more if Lily Calloway didn't live in my neighborhood. If I didn't grow up surrounded by a similar kind of familial wealth.

It's just all ordinary for me.

"You can't," she says with a confident nod.

I frown. "I can't what?" I pull off my hoodie and then fix my hair with my hand.

"You can't...with her." She clears her throat. "I expect *profession-alism* in my establishment." She comically raises her chin, and I almost can't tell if she's being serious or not.

"Right..." I nod. "Yeah. I won't...with her." I don't really know what I'm agreeing to—my mind is halfway inside that break room.

Lily nods again. "Okay then. I have to go, but Maya will dole out duties and tasks. Please listen to her."

"I will," I say, wanting Lily to trust me. I know I have to prove myself.

She exits through the *employees' only* door. Leaving me alone with Maya.

The store manager pounds on the keyboard and lets out a frustrated breath. She never looks over at me, but she begins talking.

"You're the one who peed all over the tiles in the boys' bathroom."

I wince at the past memory. "No, that was my... friend." I'd like to say John drank too much alcohol and drunkenly missed the toilet, but he purposefully pissed on the floor.

Her lips purse, her glare set on the computer screen. "Then you're the one who rearranged all the action figures on the shelves into an orgy."

"Not me." I shake my head. *Kyle.*

Though her words are a punch to the gut—because I can deflect all day and know that these acts are partially mine to claim.

I never stopped my friends. I couldn't. And I'm not all innocent either.

"You're the one who put porn mags in front of every DC comic."

I shake my head harder. "That wasn't me." *Hunter*, not my brother but my friend.

She tenses and types faster on the keyboard. "Then you're the one who wrote on the bathroom wall with Sharpie: 'stop trying to invent the most revolutionary shit. It's already been done.' And then you drew a slice of pizza."

I rub my lips to keep from laughing. Her eyes flicker to me in my silence, narrowing and narrowing.

My mouth downturns, and I drop my hand. "Yeah, that was me." I gesture to her. "I can go clean it…"

She turns her attention back to the computer and says something in another language. I think Korean. I watch too many foreign YouTube videos that I can just barely detect the language. If I paid more attention, I might've been able to catch one or two words and understand her better.

That's not the point though. She purposefully wants me to *not* understand her right now. It's working. I shift uneasily, realizing how much trouble I've caused the store manager.

"I'm sorry," I finally apologize—what I should've started with. "I'm really sorry, and I'm going to try to make it up to you." I extend my arms. "Put me to work."

I expect her to direct me to the bathrooms, to go clean toilets. "I was going to put Willow on inventory today. You can start in the storage room with her—*blasted piece of technology!*" She bangs the side of the computer, frustrated.

"Hey, let me see." I head over to Maya, setting my hoodie on the counter.

She scoots to the side and points at the blue screen of death, pretty much the worst problem for Windows. "I've restarted it four times."

"It might be a hardware problem."

"How do we fix that?" She drums the counter with two fingers.

"You'd have to buy new equipment."

Her mouth falls. Before she freaks out, I add, "I'm going to reboot it in safe mode and then check the computer's memory. You didn't install any new drivers, did you?"

Maya shakes her head slowly. "No."

"Hey…" Willow emerges from the break room, hesitantly approaching us at the checkout counter. "What should I do?"

Maya is about to respond, but her phone rings, cutting her attention. She looks frazzled. "This is our indie distributor… I'll be back." She answers the phone and sprints into the break room.

I type in a couple commands and then wait for the computer to reboot. "I don't know if you remember me." I turn to look at Willow.

She stands closer to me than before, glancing at the blue screen and keeping her hands on the white countertop. "Sort of," she says softly.

My pulse kicks up a notch, and I motion to the computer. "I'm trying to get it working."

She nods and pushes up her glasses again. "Are you good at computers?"

"Sort of." My lips try to rise.

Hers almost do too, but she stays quiet, just watching the blue screen blink out while I discover the issue. I'm so used to loud, overpowering noises—my friends talking over one another—that the hushed quiet between us is different for me.

It beats the silence of being alone. Because I can feel her here, beside me, thinking.

After a minute or so, I speak. "Do you go to school around here?"

"I start at Dalton Academy on Monday."

Loren Hale's cousin is going to Dalton Academy. The preparatory school that Loren went to as a teenager.

My muscles tense, instantly scared for her—because there are a lot of people that dislike him, based on his reputation with their older brothers or friends-of-friends. Now that he's famous, there's a shit ton of jealousy in the mix too.

"I can show you around school," I offer, though I'm not sure how much this will help. It's not like I'm beloved right now either.

She stiffens. "You go there?"

"Yep." I bend down to check the hard drive after the memory check passes. The fan looks nasty with dust and cobwebs. I blow on it and realize that the thing probably overheated. I tinker with the equipment for another minute and let it cool off.

The front door chimes and about four more employees enter like they own the place, dispersing behind us towards the bakery and coffee makers.

Willow nearly hugs the counter. Like she's in the way, but she's not. She squeezes next to me, and then pauses. Realizing how close she is, she starts to back up. "Sorry."

"No worries," I tell her and gesture to the computer. "It's all fixed." The Windows screen pops up and asks for the administrator's password. I could login as "guest" but I test a few passwords, one being *Scott Summers* since the Cyclops cardboard cutout greets people when they enter the store.

It works. "Weak password," I mutter, opening Chrome.

"How can you tell?" Willow fixes her braid, her arm brushing mine. An electric current runs through my veins—the brief contact more innocent than what I'm used to. More pure. Maybe that's why it feels so different.

"A strong password doesn't duplicate characters and it has numbers." Anything less and an encryption program would take virtually three seconds to crack the password.

She gives me a cautious glance, a coffee machine grumbling to life behind us while feet clap against the floor.

"What?" I pop open Tumblr, about to type in my username.

"Do you break passcodes a lot?" Her cheeks pale again. "I mean, you don't have to answer that if you don't want to."

I want to hug her to my side for some reason. To comfort her maybe. She hangs her head a little and keeps glancing around at the employees, bustling behind us.

I don't wrap my arm around her or pull her closer though. She has that closed-off stance, which I take as a sign that she might not like me touching her at all.

"A few times, yeah," I tell her. "I have software that does it." It's not like I'm hacking into anything important. I've taken over my friends' Twitter accounts as a joke a few times—that's it. I could probably do a lot worse.

She doesn't say anything. She's dazedly staring straight at the Tumblr screen. "You okay?" I ask, typing my username: **ryumastersxx**

"No." She winces. "Yes, I'm good. Just…shocked that you'd like this and *this*." She points at the Tumblr logo and then my username.

My brows knot. "Wait, do *you* like *Street Fighter*?"

"You have a tattoo." She glances at my inked skull between my bicep and forearm.

"I don't know where we're going here."

"And you have a *ton* of friends—" Willow gets cut off as a college-aged employee walks behind her, nearly bumping into her side. I never move, so she ends up right against my waist, tucked close to me now.

"You okay?" I ask.

She nervously takes off her glasses and wipes the lenses. "I just never thought someone like you would like this stuff."

"Well I didn't think someone like you would be into an old video game."

After a short pause, she asks softly, "What's someone like me?"

I think about it for a second. "…a girl." I feel bad even saying it, and I realize that my perception of people isn't what it should be. Maybe no one's really is. We can't really know who people are until we meet them.

"I'm not the only girl who likes video games," she says. "And I'm definitely not the only one that likes Tumblr."

"That I know," I say, more than curious about how she uses Tumblr. Quickly, I reblog a couple gif sets from *Supernatural*. "What's your username?"

She fixes her glasses. "I can't say."

I raise my brows. "What is it, some secret?"

"Sort of."

"Sort of," I repeat with an uncommon, growing smile. "Can I get a hint?"

She gives me a knowing look. "So you can break into my account? No."

"What's your first pet's name?" I quip. "The city you were born in?"

She shakes her head at me like *not working*. I didn't think it would, but she's less nervous to meet my eyes. Hers are pretty: brown but a little hazel near her pupils.

"For the record," I tell her, "I don't have a ton of friends..." *at least not anymore.*

"It looked like you did," she mutters.

My stomach turns. I decide to change the subject back to the lighter one. "We could message each other if you share your username with me."

She thinks hard again. "You really want to know it?"

Do I want to know what she's like online? What kind of things she's into? Yeah, I do. "I wouldn't be asking again if I didn't."

"I'll tell it to you, but only if you fill out a questionnaire on Tumblr first."

I frown in confusion. "Why?"

She tucks a flyaway strand of hair behind her ear. "I've filled one out recently, and I don't like deleting things..."

It hits me. She doesn't want me to see her answers, at least not without jumping into the same boat she's floating in.

A questionnaire.

I try to stifle a laugh that almost escapes. It's probably one of those things you tag your friends in and they tag other people—I don't do those. Ever.

She begins to recoil from me, and I immediately want to punch myself in the face. *Shit.* I set a hand on hers, and she jumps.

"Sorry." I let go. "I'm not trying to be an ass. I just...you really want me to fill out a questionnaire?"

"Only if you want my username."

I give her a weak smile—I'm not good at smiling, to be honest. I can't remember the last time I was happy enough to reveal my teeth in one. Maybe never. I bet I was a morose, assholish baby. "Alright." I commit. "I'll do it."

She shows me a link to the questionnaire. I vaguely skim some of the questions, zoning in on really personal ones. If I end up doing this, it'll mean opening up to Willow…and Willow opening up to me.

What do you say, Garrison?

I say that I've never done that to anyone before.

This will be a first. And I'm surprised I have some of those left.

8

Willow Moore

GARRISON SAID HE'D FILL OUT THE QUESTIONNAIRE LATER. Maya came in and doled out duties for us before he could even start. Most of the day I spent checking inventory, and she made Garrison clean coffee machines, mop floors, and bus tables.

I don't see him when I exit Superheroes & Scones at 5 p.m.—though I can't stop thinking about him. He seems like trouble, like someone I'd stay a thousand feet away from in Caribou, Maine. If my suspicions are right, his friends were the ones that broke into Lo's house.

He seems characteristically *bad*.

I'm just scared he'd pressure me to do something I wouldn't want to do. I've never had friends like that, but he seems the type, doesn't he?

I approach my gold Honda on the curb, knowing that I'm judging him.

But I'm judging him off prior actions.

I can't make up my mind. In fact, my mind really hurts even trying to place Garrison in a category. Maybe I shouldn't try to place him at all.

I crawl into my car and then start the engine. It lets out a whiney noise. "No...come on." I turn the key again, and smoke suddenly plumes from the hood. "Crap." I climb out, and in haste to check beneath the hood, smoke rushes out, so hot that it burns my arm.

I drop the hood and it clatters down.

"Hey, Willow!" The concerned voice drives nerves throughout my body. Oh my God, Garrison is sprinting over to me, his hoodie wadded up in one hand and his car keys jangling in the other.

"Hey," I say, pressing my reddened arm to my chest, the sting lessening. I'm shifting so awkwardly that I probably look like I have to pee.

He wafts the smoke above the hood. "What happened?"

"I don't know… it's an old car." I cough as another gust of smoke rushes out towards me.

Garrison motions with his head to the curb. I follow him, vehicles speeding by on the city street.

"Do you know anything about cars?" I ask hopefully.

He shakes his head. "Just computers." He glances over at the corner street. "I can give you a ride to wherever you need to go. You can call a tow truck or get your cousin to come look at your car in the meantime."

Cousin? It takes me a moment to register what he means. Loren Hale, *my cousin*. Which means that Garrison read the debut article about me and my tampons.

I immobilize. *Don't think about it.*

"Willow?"

"Uh, yeah…yeah." I shake my head like I'm trying to rid all the cobwebs. "Thanks. A ride would be great." I'll call the tow truck later. So I end up feeding the meter with a few more quarters and then grab my backpack.

"This way." He nods towards the corner street. We walk a block until he stops by a black Mustang, black leather interior, and black custom rims. It has to be expensive. If it's not, it does a great job pretending to be.

"This is your car?"

He opens the passenger door for me. "Yeah…I live in the same neighborhood as Loren." An unspoken truth strains between us: *my old car is dying and spurting out smoke one block away.* After finding out that we share a few unique similarities, it's this economic difference that creates the most tension, both of us uncomfortable for different reasons.

"Was that your house that night of the party?" I ask before climbing in. Everything is clean, no stray water bottles or takeout wrappers beneath the seat. My car is a mess of receipts and paper napkins from Wendy's and Taco Bell.

I'm the slob, I realize. I sink further in the seat and hold my backpack on my lap, hugging it close to my chest.

He answers me when he's buckled. "Not my house. I live one street over." He turns to me. "Where do you live?"

"I should've told you that it's kind of out of the way—"

"It's fine. I have nowhere to be."

I nod and then give him the address. He plugs it into his phone and docks it on a stand, the GPS alive with directions.

"I thought you'd live with your cousin," he says, probably thinking I'd have Loren's type of wealth too. I guess he's learning differently today.

And I don't know why he keeps saying that—*your cousin*. He knows who Loren is. Maybe he doesn't like bringing up his name, not after the break-in.

"I didn't want to impose on him," I explain. "He has a baby."

"Yeah, I saw Maximoff's first baby picture along with the rest of the world." His voice is dry, not at all impressed with their celebrity status.

"You don't like *Princesses of Philly*, I take it." The reality show didn't make them famous or last long for a huge impact, not beyond some cool gifs, but it's easier mentioning PoPhilly than Lily's sex addiction.

He fixes the air vents, keeping the really cold air off me. Am I shaking?

"I've watched it, but it's not the show that bugs me." Garrison stops at a red light. "Every time I leave my neighborhood, paparazzi start shouting at my car like I might have a Calloway sister in my backseat. And the questions they ask are fucked up." He taps the steering wheel and then sets his aqua-blue eyes on me, a mixture of blue and light green—one of the most unique colors I've ever seen. "If you need a ride on Monday, let me know." He must note the surprise on my face because he adds, "I wake up early."

"It's out of your way," I remind him, though going to a new school with someone sounds a lot less anxiety-ridden than going alone.

But *Garrison?*

What if it's some joke? What if this is like *Never Been Kissed* and it'll end with him driving by and chucking eggs at me?

He says he's not popular, but he has all the makings of a popular high schooler: toned biceps that indicate his athleticism (i.e. he plays a sport), a face that'd be the lead in any CW show—or at least the little brother to the star (i.e. like Jeremy from *The Vampire Diaries*), and messy brown hair that sometimes touches his eyelashes—hair that says *I could be in a boy band, but I'm too cool for that shit.*

Not to mention his tattoo.

And his confident yet dark scowl…

I suddenly draw this conclusion: *I don't know Garrison Abbey.* Not enough to say whether or not he'd chuck eggs at me.

If I really believed he'd do that though, I would've never climbed in his car.

"I know it's out of the way," he says as the light turns green. "I also don't care. I usually try to waste three hours in the morning anyway."

Three hours? "You wake up at five a.m.?"

"Doesn't everyone," he says dryly, his fingers twitching a little. The car smells like citrus, not cigarettes, and there aren't any bottles of alcohol or beer anywhere, but I've seen him smoke and drink before. He switches topics. "Are you a junior?"

"No."

He frowns. "Sophomore?"

"Senior," I reply.

"You look younger."

"It's the braid," I mutter, shifting in my seat a little.

He glances at me once before focusing on the road. "The braid is cute."

I feel my lips lifting. *Do not smile like that.* It's this giddy smile that should never reveal itself to the person who put it there. "Okay," I suddenly say.

"Okay…yeah?" He knows that I'm accepting his offer to pick me up on Monday.

I nod. "How should we communicate?"

He switches lanes easily. "By letters probably," he banters. "I'd say two tin cans, but I don't think the string would reach from me to you."

"What about communicating in ones and zeroes?"

He feigns confusion. "What is that? Ones and zeroes…nah, I don't like those." He almost smiles, because after today, I know he likes the internet, maybe even more than me.

9

Willow Moore

I TUCK MY WHITE BLOUSE INTO MY NAVY-BLUE SKIRT, THE Dalton Academy uniform as uncomfortable as I feel. I check the clock on my wooden desk. *7:23 a.m.*

Garrison said he'd be outside my apartment complex at 7:30, and since we didn't exchange numbers, I should probably just go now and wait for him.

I grab my tattered backpack, wondering if this will be violation of some dress code. I've never attended private school before, and I would've gone to public school but Lo refused.

He said, *I'll pay for it. Don't worry about it. It's one of the best schools in the city.*

I told Loren that I'd pay him back. Every cent, and that was that.

In the elevator, I update ryumastersxx's blog, restraining a smile at his username. Ken Masters is one of the most popular *Street Fighter* characters, and his rival and best friend is named Ryu. Every time I've refreshed his page, gifs and edits are the only new content.

This time though…it's different.

Rules: Complete the form by answering each section truthfully. Once you've finished, tag other users to complete the task. Begin by sourcing the person who tagged you.

He did it. "Oh my God," I whisper, so caught off-guard that I forget to push the lobby button. I do and then eagerly and yet tentatively read his answers.

What was your...

Last drink: lightning bolt! + vodka

I'm suddenly scared to read the rest, but like a fiend or junkie, I just can't stop. I have to know more.

Last phone call: can't remember. Everyone just texts now

Last text message: "Fuck you." - sent to my middle brother. He's a dick.

Have you ever...

Been cheated on: not yet. Give it time and I'm sure it'll happen

Kissed someone and regretted it: I don't regret kissing

Drank hard liquor: no *sarcasm*

Been drunk and thrown up: only when drinking hunch punch that has too much fucking punch

Met someone who changed you: I guess one person. He's famous—so very few people would believe me if I said his name. He kind of gave me a hand when no one else did

Fallen out of love: I've fallen out of love with dill pickles. Fucking gross.

Found out who your true friends are: I think I just did

Lost glasses: don't wear them, but they look cute on this girl I just met.

I touch my cheeks that hurt from a smile that won't go away, but it disappears at the sight of the next topic.

Sex on the first date: do I really have to answer this? [w, if this makes you nervous, please skip over this]

W. I take a breath, wondering if I should glaze over his typed words, but if he's telling me to skip it, then maybe he knows the answer won't sit well with me. Or maybe he doesn't want to "come on strong"—it's not like he's hitting on me or anything.

This is just the start of a friendship, right?

I decide to look.

Already did it. It wasn't her first time either.

Either. Meaning he's had sex multiple times too.

And I haven't even been kissed…but it shouldn't matter. *Just the start of a friendship.*

Been arrested: not yet

Turned someone down: I don't know what this is implying. Turned someone down for a ride? For a smoke? What is this?

Fallen for a friend: sort of

Sort of. I don't know what *that* is implying!

More questions...

Do you have any pets: turtle named Abracadabra—it used to be my brother Mitchell's before he left for college.

What did you do for your last birthday party: smoked and watched Evil Dead with my friends - it was actually horrible (I had the spins all night and threw up)

Name something you cannot wait for: the end of senior year

What irritates you: being told what to do, what to wear, how to act

Nickname(s): Abbey

Relationship status: hiatus

Favorite TV show: Supernatural and American Horror Story

High School: sucks

College: probably sucks more

Hair Color + Length: brown, short but not that short idk

Height: 5'11''

Your crush: unknown entity ... not computable at this time

Tattoos: 2, one on the inside of my elbow, the other over my right shoulder blade (my mom started crying when she saw the first one, you destroyed your body!!)

Right or left-handed: Right

Any surgeries: broke my wrist pretty bad and my leg once. I had to have a couple pins put in - I was only about seven and then nine.

Any piercings: no I didn't want anyone trying to tug that shit out

Favorite sport: lacrosse. All my brothers played, and I'm not the worst at it but I probably hate it the most

First vacation: France. I was nine-months-old and can remember absolutely nothing

Currently...

What are you eating: cold slice of pizza

What are you drinking: that energy drink + vodka

What are you waiting for: a certain someone's username

Do you want kids: I already feel bad for these kids

Marriage: if I love her enough

Career: who the fuck knows bc I don't

What do you like...

Hugs or kisses: definitely kissing but I'd take both

Shorter or taller: girls? I don't really have a preference

Older or younger: probably younger or same age

I'm not tagging anyone else, but if you feel like doing this, knock yourself out. It's not as bad as it seems. And someone out there owes me a username -- see you in the morning if I haven't already.

"Are you getting off?"

"Huh?" I peel my attention off my cellphone. A college student with a backpack is waiting in the lobby.

She motions to the elevator. "Are you getting off here?"

"Oh yeah." I quickly step off and check the time, still five minutes early. I pocket my cell, surprised at how much information I received and then in the same breath, all the conundrums that he presented me with too.

I wonder if my questionnaire will read that way as well.

As soon as I walk outside, the September air cool, I notice a black Mustang parked on the curb. Garrison waits for me, leaning against the car with hands in his navy-blue slacks. His tie is loose around his neck, his white button-down fitting him perfectly.

In the Dalton Academy uniform, he looks more like a quintessential popular guy than the alternative black-hoodied one I'm used to seeing. He straightens up when he spots me, and I slow my pace a little.

No eggs are in his hand. I breathe easier. This is not a *Never Been Kissed* situation. He's just scanning me from head to toe like I did to him.

"Hey," he greets with a nod.

"You're early." I stop a couple feet away from him.

"So are you." His aqua-blue eyes land on my skirt and they never peel away.

"What...?" I wonder if I didn't iron the fabric enough.

"You're not wearing that right."

I pale. "What do you mean?" It's just a blue skirt, a belt attached with the same stiff canvas fabric and it forms a bow in the front.

"The bow is tied differently, and it shouldn't be lined in the middle of your body." He combs a hand through his hair.

I try to fix it, but I'm not exactly sure what it's supposed to look like. It's not like Dalton Academy gave me a manual on how to tie bows. I fumble with it, unsure and nervous.

Garrison takes *two* steps towards me, so close that his forehead almost brushes with mine when I look up. "Can I touch you?" he asks, his hands hovering by my hips.

My whole body heats, blazing from a moment in time. I'm barely able to nod. And then he takes the waistband of my skirt and shifts it to the right, the bow now resting on my hip and the zipper on my other one. It's not crazy to think the zipper was supposed to be in the back, is it?

He reties the bow, his knuckles brushing my waist more than once.

"Does the uniform matter a lot?" I ask.

"To most of the teachers, yeah. They'd make you stand up and retie the bow in the middle of the class."

I imagine all the eyes on me, and I wince, glad to be saved from that. When he finishes the bow, he tucks the edge of my blouse into my skirt, the corner astray. "I think you're good," he says with a couple nods. "I can take that." He gestures to my backpack.

I shake my head. "I'll hold onto it."

"Okay." He checks his watch—a charcoal-tinted one that appears expensive by the plate-size and band. "We'll make it on time."

About a minute later, we're in his Mustang and driving to Dalton Academy, back towards the ritzy neighborhoods and further away from Penn.

"My schedule is in the middle console if you want to compare," he tells me.

I open the middle console, take out a folded piece of paper, and then retrieve the crumpled one from my backpack.

I notice three similarities, which is a lot more than I expected.

"And?" he asks, glancing between the road and me.

"We're in the same British lit and Calculus class, and we have the same lunch period." I gauge his reaction, but he never smiles much, not even now.

He asks, "Are you good at British lit?"

"Sort of."

"Sort of…" He gives me a look. "What does that mean exactly? *Sort of.* Is it more of a yes or more of a no for you?"

"I guess…a yes."

He nods. "Good because I fucking suck at lit."

"I'm bad at Calculus."

He nearly smiles this time. "I'll help you if you help me."

I lean back. "You're good at math?"

"I like numbers more than words," he explains, "but I don't mind reading—just not classics. I fall asleep every time I flip a page." He fiddles with the windshield wipers as a sheet of rain suddenly falls from the sky.

"I like comic books mostly, but I pick up regular books from time to time." I hug my backpack closer, my skirt riding up a little. I try to tug that down. "Should I be worried…?"

He glances at me again, like he'd rather focus on me than the road, but the rain really steals his attention. "About what?"

"The people at Dalton. I know Loren called the cops on your… friends, and I'm just wondering if they're bitter towards him still."

Garrison tries to hide his expression, but I see him *cringe.*

"Oh God," I mutter, realizing it's bad.

"It's not just about that. Some of the guys there had brothers who went to school with Loren, and they hated him. That hate has passed down through siblings."

"Why'd they hate him?"

Garrison shrugs. "I don't know. It's probably just stupid shit, back and forth vandalism. My oldest brother killed a deer after hunting with his friends, and he put the head in some guy's pickup as a *joke*." He emphasizes the last word with more distaste.

My face contorts. People actually do that? "And they know I'm Loren's cousin?"

"Hey," he says, "if you're that worried, I can just tell some people you're with me."

I stiffen.

"Not like, with me, *with me*."

"So…you'll tell everyone that you're my friend?"

He shakes his head. "No, I have a lot of friends…" He stops short. "Or I *used* to. Anyway, that won't mean much to someone." He glances at me again. "I can just tell everyone you're my girl, and they'll probably back off."

"Your girl?" My brows jump.

He licks his lips and actually laughs into a small smile. "It's ambiguous. Not a girlfriend, but not just a friend. I don't own you or anything. It just lies somewhere between those two."

My shoulders loosen a little as I contemplate this. "It reminds me of the movie." I have to bite my tongue to keep from smiling. *My Girl*. A movie about best friends.

"What movie?" he asks.

"*My Girl*…you've never seen it?"

He shakes his head, and then he asks, "Are you okay with this? I can try to think of something else if you're not."

I contemplate it a little more. "So if someone asks you about me, you'll say to them…?"

"She's my girl." He says it with sincerity and threat, like *don't mess with her*. He takes a hand off the steering wheel and catches my gaze once. "Yeah?"

My arms heat, liking *my girl* more than I thought I would. Maybe because it's from him. "Yeah," I say, licking my lips. I realize they're a little cracked. "Are you sure they'll back off if I'm affiliated with you?"

"They'll probably just come harass me instead," he says with a dry smile. I don't think he's joking.

"Garrison—"

"I don't give a shit about any of the people at Dalton anymore, and I can take a few stupid comments and empty threats." He changes lanes and subjects. "I never asked where you're from."

"Maine," I say without thinking about my cover. *Willow Hale.*

"And you left your parents to be here?" He frowns.

I pick at a frayed strand on my backpack. "Yeah."

"How come?"

"I guess…" I start, trying to wrap my head around why I did this. Why I ultimately decided to plant roots here instead of return to Caribou. "I decided that I'd do whatever it takes to be the person I want to be and not what everyone else wants me to be, even if it means hurting some people I love along the way."

He stares far off as he drives. "Yeah…" He lets out a short breath. "I think I'm doing that too."

I relax more. "Willow bada boom thirty-three," I tell him.

He tilts his head at me. "Your username?"

"Yeah."

"I like it, Willow *bada boom*." He says it in *The Fifth Element* voice. My chest swells.

It's not every day you meet someone that understands the things you love, but somehow I've crossed paths with someone who really does.

10

Garrison Abbey

"READY?" I ASK WILLOW.

"Ready."

I open the door.

We step into the school, halls congested like most mornings. Instead of rushing to classrooms, friends huddle in groups by lockers or wander around, searching for a familiar face.

Willow walks in a diagonal line, almost inwards towards me. She avoids bumping into a few passing students.

"What's your locker number?" I ask while she adjusts the strap of her backpack.

I almost set my hand on her shoulder, but instead I just let her hover close by. As soon as she unfurls her schedule, she hands the paper to me.

It's a little damp, like her palms are sweating.

I'm not going to be a dick and mention it though.

I glance at the locker number with the code written out. "You're over here, further down."

She nods mechanically.

I understand the kind of nerves that just completely eviscerate you. Only I don't feel them on the first day of school, or the second, or even the last. They hit me when I bike near my house. When I drive by. When I'm feet from the mailbox and then the front door.

When I step inside. Knowing my brothers are there.

They're gone. They're at college, I have to keep reminding myself.

Thank God.

"Sorry," Willow apologizes in a whisper. I think towards me, but I realize that someone barely brushed against Willow's arm on the way to a locker.

The girl shoots Willow a weird look, probably unsure of what she said.

We move along, out of her sight.

"So there are vending machines in the middle of each hall," I tell her. "We can grab some waters before first period." I'll see her in second period, Calculus. Our first periods are different.

She'll be okay.

She left Maine all by herself, didn't she? Bravery exists somewhere inside of her. She just needs to remember that.

Two guys crash against my right shoulder with complete disregard. It knocks me into Willow. I catch onto her waist so we don't both slam into the floor.

Shit.

She stiffens but holds onto me for support too. Once we're stabilized, I take my hands off her and try to find the two assholes. I spin around.

"Really?" I snap, extending my arms at them, but as soon as they turn to face me, my arms drop immediately. One of the guys—he's a friend-of-a-friend who I've fallen out with.

He flips me off. "Watch it, Abbey," Pat Hayes snaps. Honestly, I expected worse than a shoulder-check and the middle finger.

"No thanks," I rebut and then walk forward, away from them. Willow keeps my pace. I glance at her. *You okay?*

She seems a little shaken.

The universe is basically saying: *Garrison Abbey, you're the shittiest welcome committee. Take a backseat and let someone who's actually well-liked show this sweet girl around.*

I don't want to hurt her.

Still, the thing I've always sucked at is leaving people when I should. I end up staying too long, too late. I'm not going to leave Willow alone, not now.

Maybe I should at least tell her I'm cursed.

I hear Pat huff angrily behind me, still enraged. He's captain of our crew team, an adversary of Dalton's lacrosse team. Our football team is shit, so all the country club sports are put on pedestals. Dalton's track, swimming, tennis, crew, lacrosse and equestrian teams are all top in the state.

Pat shouts, "You ran into me, Abbey!"

Bullshit.

I say loudly without turning around, "If that's what you think, then maybe don't have a fireside chat in the middle of the hall."

Pat shouts out a "fuck you" before a nearby teacher scolds him for his language. We're too far away from one another to keep combating. Thankfully.

Willow keeps muttering "sorry" every five seconds, and by the time we make it to her locker, I feel relieved for her. She wipes her forehead with the back of her arm. A strand of her hair is still stuck to her damp cheek.

I motion to her face. "Can I…you have something…?"

She's confused for a second and tentatively nods at me.

I pick the strand off and tuck it behind her ear.

She swallows once and stares at her feet and then her locker.

"Are you going to pass out on me?" I ask with concern, already trying to figure out the distance from her locker to the nurse's.

I think I could carry her there, no problem.

Willow shakes her head. "I'm not good at this…I forgot to warn you." Maybe she means that she's not good at being the new girl in a school full of strangers. Or maybe even more general: being surrounded by a lot of people at one time.

"You're doing alright."

She glances at her skirt. "How's the bow?"

My lips pull up a fraction. "Without a doubt, you have the best bow in the entire kingdom. If I were a princess, I'd even be jealous." I pass her schedule back as she begins to smile. "Fifteen, thirty-seven, twenty-seven."

I don't ask if she wants me to open it. I figure spinning the lock will be a nice distraction for a second.

While she turns the dial, I'm about to ask about her last school. I assume it was public and smaller than Dalton.

Just as I open my mouth, I spot someone familiar in the corner of my eye. Carly Jefferson. She whispers to a group of three girls, about fifteen lockers down from Willow's.

I'd like to think I'm more observant than paranoid. That this isn't all in my head. But I have this feeling. You know the feeling—the one where everything stills around you. Just for a moment. Where every crack and flaw that frames a photo suddenly magnifies ten *million* times over.

It's happening. Right now.

The hallway noises deaden in my mind. Leaving excruciating silence. Their furtive glances like sharp knives. Their smiles like snarls. Carly giggles and nudges her friend's side. A couple guys join the huddle of girls. They lean against lockers and smirk. Taking a front row seat to a show.

Wrong.

Everything is wrong.

"Willo—" I start and grab her arm to stop her from opening the locker.

The dial has already clicked, and the blue metal swings back.

It should be empty. But it's not.

Hundreds of tampons fall out, most in their wrapper. A handful have been torn open and soaked in what I hope is red dye.

She freezes.

I don't even know what to do. I go as still, as quiet as her.

And the hallway erupts in laughter.

Here's the truth: I've never been pranked at school. I've never been picked on by anyone but my brothers. I used to be well-liked. Even if I hated myself half the time.

I want to say something.

Do something.

Anything.

To stand up for the quieter person. For the first time in my life.

11

Willow Moore

MY INSTINCT IS TO RUN, BUT I HAVE NOWHERE TO ACTUALLY GO. I've already run away from Caribou, Maine. This is the place that I've run to.

My ribs tighten around my lungs with a hysteric thought and my new eulogy: *Willow Moore, that fool who ran away to have her locker filled with tampons and be publicly humiliated in a new school.*

It's not true. I can't let it be.

I ran away to build a relationship with my brother.

To become me without any apologies attached. None of these: "I'm sorry, Dad, I'm not as pretty or as popular as you hoped I'd be."

Garrison makes the first move. He kicks the tampons at a couple girls and guys, grouped several lockers away. When he swings his head to me, pieces of his hair fall to his eyelashes, and he says, "Blaze."

Blaze.

From *Streets of Rage,* an early nineties video game, she's one of the strongest female characters in a slew of men. While I don't have her judo skills or her physique, it's easy to pretend I'm her when someone pretends with me. And by saying her name, I know Garrison is trying to bolster my confidence.

On our trek from the parking lot to the school this morning, Garrison asked if I'd ever played *Streets of Rage.* When I said I did, he told me, *"So imagine you're Blaze and I'm Axel and this hallway—the one we're going to be walking down—is nothing we can't handle."*

"Axel," I whisper and brush the tampons out of my locker.

I remember the phone call from Rose Calloway—after I spilled tampons accidentally on the street. In front of the world.

I'm not going to be embarrassed. *Remember what Rose said.* I take a few deep breaths, my stomach twisting in knots.

It's harder than it sounds.

Garrison says, "Now I wish I had a crowbar." It's the go-to weapon in *Streets of Rage*.

My eyes widen behind my glasses.

"Kidding." He glares at the cluster of people, just now coming down from their laughing fit. "Sort of."

I quickly stuff my backpack into my now empty locker, slamming it shut. Just as I turn, I realize that Garrison has left my side. He's taken a few lengthy strides towards the group, all laughter faded.

I try to grip my backpack strap, only to meet air.

I stand stiffly, more in the middle of the hall. My uniform is as uncomfortable as I feel. I check the state of the bow, like a teacher will yell any second about its off-kilter state.

It looks okay though.

What doesn't look so great: the scene in front of me.

"That's not cool," Garrison tells the shorter girl with dirty blonde hair. I wonder if she'll have to take out her nose piercing before first period. This thought is trying to trounce the bolder, bigger one that screams, *these are his friends.*

He approaches them like he knows them. Like he's talked to them often. Like he's so familiar with who they are.

The shorter girl pushes out her chest and pulls back her shoulders to gain some height. "You know what's not cool? Betraying your best friends." Her eyes redden, and she takes an angrier step forward. The other girl clasps her shoulder. "You should be in there with John! You deserve jail time more than any one of them, and you know it!"

Her friend says, "Carly—"

"Leave me alone." She swats her hand off her shoulder and then points at Garrison again. I can't see his features, just the back of his head. He's unmoving. Even his fingers hang loosely, not curling into a fist. "You're a piece of shit, Abbey. You're a piece of shit—and you know it."

Garrison nears Carly a little more, and she goes still at his closeness. He hangs his head and whispers something to her. In seconds, she breaks down and bursts into tears.

"It's not fair!" she cries, sinking to the floor. I can only guess that she was close to John, maybe even in a relationship with him.

And I expect Garrison to swivel back towards me.

Am I being presumptuous? To assume that he'd come back?

Because he never does.

I watch him walk past his old friends. Away from me. I watch him disappear alone around a corner. I watch him vanish all together without another word. Without a goodbye.

The bell rings, and I'm left standing immobile in the middle of the hall. People pass around me like nothing occurred.

And I have two choices.

I can go to first period and forget about Garrison. I can act as though this intro to class never happened. Act like everyone else. *Forget about him, Willow Moore.*

Or I can go find him. I can step over my hurt feelings. The ones that say, *he left me,* and just make sure he's okay.

He approached them for me. To stand up for me.

That means something.

I make my decision.

I trace his footsteps down the hallway. I veer around the corner where I expect another hallway or a cluster of vending machines. Instead, I'm met with two bathrooms. Girls and boys.

"Oh God," I mutter.

I'm staring at the boy symbol. Just go in. This will be my first foray into this great unknown that is the boys' bathroom. I wish I didn't give a shit. I wish I could just push inside without a second thought or care.

It's just the boys' bathroom.

It's trivial, right?

Just go in.

I do this time.

I push the royal blue door with my shoulder. I'm met with one long row of sinks, two stalls, and three urinals. Not too shocking.

Garrison is sitting on the sink counter, a lit cigarette between his fingers. His head is hung, hair in his eyes, but as soon as I enter, he looks up. His bones seem to cement, joints unoiled. Frozen.

Maybe this wasn't a smart idea.

"I…" I gesture to the door I came from, as though that explains everything. It actually explains absolutely nothing.

Smoke wafts around his body, and it takes him a second to shift the hand that holds his cigarette. He casually sucks on it, quiet.

I like quiet.

I'm familiar with quiet more than I am loud. I walk further inside and rest my back on a locked, out-of-order stall.

He blows smoke up at the air vent. Then his aquamarine eyes study his cigarette, embers eating the paper. "Did you hear the bell?" He finally speaks.

"Yeah."

He nods a couple times, almost in realization, and then he takes another drag.

"Thanks for trying to help me," I say softly.

"I probably made it worse."

I cross my arms, feeling naked without my backpack. "They're your friends?"

"Were," he corrects. "They pretty much want nothing to do with me after…the thing." *The thing.* He takes a deeper drag of his cigarette. I know he must mean when his friends broke into Loren's house with gargoyle masks.

"What'd you say to Carly?"

He stares off past me, his gaze haunted. "I told her that she's right."

"What?" A weight bears down on me. And the room.

He puts out his cigarette in the sink basin. "I'm a piece of shit." He says it with such finality, as though he's accepted it for a long time.

I open my mouth to tell him that it's not true—that he's a great person. I pause.

I falter.

And I think. How much of Garrison Abbey do I really know? Not much.

Not yet.

I lick my dried lips and stare at the tiled floor. "You're better than your friends, you know?"

He says under his breath, "What an accomplishment." His pretty eyes land on me. "You don't have to cheer me up. It's a lost cause, honestly." He expels a deep breath and rubs his tired eyes with the heel of his palm. "You should go to class, Willow."

"Are you going?" I wonder.

"No." He pulls a carton of cigarettes out of his slacks. He undoes his navy tie and pops some of the buttons at the collar. Like the uniform has been slowly but surely choking him.

I unbutton some of mine at the collar and untuck my blouse. Feeling better. I don't brave a glance at him, but I do climb awkwardly onto the sink counter, right next to Garrison.

My legs are much shorter, and I push my glasses up before splaying my hands flat on my thighs.

"Do you smoke?" he asks me, staring down at my features. Our arms skim, and a thunderous sensation pounds inside of me, grasping tight of my lungs, reaching and stretching for my heart.

"Not a smoker," I tell him.

He doesn't offer me a cigarette, and I'm glad there's no pressure to join him. When he lights another one, he blows the smoke away from me.

We're utterly silent, but it's the kind that begins to slow my heartbeat. Silence and calmness, void of that aching loneliness.

After maybe five minutes or possibly ten or twenty, the door swings open, and in walks a five-foot-something student with short brown hair, expensive loafers and shock at the sight of me, a girl.

Garrison smiles in his next drag. He motions from the guy to me. "Barry, this is my girl, Willow."

My girl.

I begin to smile.

In context, it sounds just as Garrison described—somewhere between good friends and boyfriend-girlfriend.

Barry nods in recognition, at my name or the title Garrison has attached to it, I'm not sure. "Ohh..." He draws out the word, then he points at the cigarette. "Coach says you need to cut back for conditioning."

Garrison looks at me. "The lacrosse coach has this delusion that I can run a mile faster than my older brother. God forbid I fall behind Hunter Reagan Abbey." He spins the cigarette between his fingers. "Birthplace: Mt. Olympus. Age: Unidentifiable. Handsomest fucker there is." I can't tell if he's being sarcastic or just bitter.

Maybe both.

Before I can say something, Barry adds, "Cutting out cigarettes would help though."

Garrison gives him an irritated look. "Or I could just cut out lacrosse. How about that?"

Barry rolls his eyes. "Don't talk like that. You know we need you for state this year."

Garrison just takes another drag of his cigarette, more agitated. I remember his questionnaire answer about lacrosse being his favorite sport but hating it the most of his brothers. I wonder how deep that hate runs.

Barry briefly glances at me before disappearing into the stall.

Then Garrison hops off the counter and douses the cigarette in the faucet. "Calculus in ten."

Ten minutes? I check my watch, realizing it's almost time to go. I tuck in my blouse and button it higher while he fixes his tie.

I catch him glancing at me.

He catches me glancing at him.

His lips rise. I feel mine pull upward too. And I'm beginning to realize something.

I really like being in the company of Garrison Abbey.

12

Garrison Abbey

I SLUMP DOWN IN THE BACK STORAGE ROOM OF SUPERHEROES & Scones. I'm not on break. Not even fucking close. Unless this place gives breaks after only an hour stocking comics.

Unlikely.

I just needed to escape for a second. My fingers instinctively slip into my leather jacket for a cigarette, but I quickly ditch the attempt. I don't need to ruin the good thing I have going here by infusing Groot plushies with cigarette smoke.

I reach for my other pocket instead and slide out my phone.

A cardboard poster of Thor pokes my back. Pushing it away, I readjust and discover a bare patch of cement wall to lean against. Not like there's much. The fucking storage room is *crammed* with shelves of comics and merchandise, half of which is packed in boxes. It's easy to hide back here.

To get lost.

I log onto Tumblr and search for Willow's new username that she changed from *willowbadaboom33* and gave me ten minutes ago.

vegablaze33

It slightly matches mine. Vega is a character from *Street Fighter*. She told me that she usually dresses up as Vega for Halloween, so it has sentimental meaning.

What's terrible—what makes me hate myself more than she could even understand, more than she could know—is that I'm not even sure I would've befriended her if she came to Philly last year.

My group of friends—we'd been pretty tight since grade school. It would've been too hard to break away from that security. It's such bullshit.

I'm bullshit.

Because I already like her more than *any* shit friend I've ever had.

She dressed up as Vega, for Christ's sake.

I laugh and I smile. Just trying to picture it. I wish I'd been there. Right beside her, for every Halloween she had the balls to wear that costume. And I don't mean literal balls, but Vega is a dude.

What's worse: I think I'd return to my friends if it would be like it was. When I lost some of them to juvie and when the rest of my friends turned their backs on me, I lost *people*.

Not happiness. Just people. And that's what fucking hurts the most.

I'm not used to being alone. Having people near me, returning to what was, sounds comfortable and easier. Even if I wasn't really happy.

Willow's still a mystery to me. She's shy but brazen enough to enter a party where she knows absolutely no one, all to find her cousin. I can't even be without people that I don't really like and who don't really like me, and she could do that.

And she's wary of touch.

But she let me touch her.

I might be bad for Willow. I've been bad for everyone at some point, but I selfishly need something that will keep me riding down this road. I'm scared that Superheroes & Scones won't be enough over time, and I'll find a way to turn back around.

To return to people I've known practically all my life. To people who will never make me happy.

I'm just terrified. Of every single option in front of me. Even the good ones. Even the horrible ones.

To distract myself, I stick to Tumblr. Something I actually like. I scroll through her archive and find the questionnaire easily this time.

Here it goes.

What was your...

Last drink: Fizz Life

Last phone call: umm, my Grandma Ida. She wanted
to crochet me a scarf for next winter and needed
to know what color yarn. I told her blue

Last text message: "I bought it! I bought it!"
to Maggie, in relation to Understanding Comics
by Scott McCloud—I've been saving up babysitting
money to purchase the comic book. I read
ANYTHING that Loren Hale recommends (my comic
book guru), and he suggested this one not long
ago on social media

I didn't realize that she needed to save up money just for a comic
book. I just figured her parents were loaded since she's related to
Loren Hale.

My brows knot as I continue on.

Have you ever...

Been cheated on: never gave anyone the chance to

What does that mean? She's never dated? I don't know why that
surprises me. I just thought...Maine. She probably knew some guy
up there, right?

Kissed someone and regretted it: never been kissed
(don't judge)

Willow...

I reread this part about five times, not able to move on yet. My hand is frozen to my mouth for a second. I drop it after the shock lessens. I'm not judging. (I promise.) I'm just confused.

Why hasn't any guy kissed her before?

Did she not want them to?

Did no guys want to? That pulls at me because it fucking sucks and I'm still just...confused. Then again, it's not like a person *has* to be kissed by a certain age, right?

Drank hard liquor: a couple times. I didn't like the taste.

I'll remember that.

Been drunk and thrown up: nope

Good for you. It's not fun.

Met someone who changed you: I met Loren Hale once (my only celebrity run-in). He was standing on my front doorstep (long story). Loren Hale left within like five minutes—but he actually spoke to me. He noticed my Mutants & Proud pin, and I mentioned liking X-Men Evolution (the cartoons). Then he made a comment about the comics and Lily Calloway. He called her his girlfriend, but they were and are still engaged if Celebrity Crush is right. It made me think that girls could read comics too—and the way he spoke, he presumed I already did. I never tried to read them until that moment, until he left and I thought yeah, I'm allowed to read these too.

I started New X-Men and related so much to
Wallflower, a girl I really needed a year ago,
when my dad divorced my mom. And I would've never
read comic books and fallen in love with them if
I didn't meet Loren Hale

There's a lot to take in there. She only met Loren Hale once before moving to Philly—which makes a lot more sense. The pieces click together. Why she was searching for his house that one night at the party. Why she didn't have any way to contact him. Why she doesn't have as much money. Their families must have been estranged.

She *really* loves comics then…

Wallflower. I make a note to look that character up.

Her parents divorced a year ago. That's got to be fucking hard. Unless, it was a good thing. One of my old friends, Jesse—his parents split and his mom seemed much happier afterwards. Divorce isn't always that great and terrible monster some people believe it to be.

But that line *a girl I really needed a year ago* makes it seem like it may not have been a good change.

Shit.

Should I stop reading this? I skim the next question instinctively. I'm in way too deep.

Fallen out of love: I've never fallen in love to
fall out of it

Yeah well, in high school, love is for liars.

At least, that's how I feel.

Found out who your true friends are: this why I
keep my circle small. Maggie is the truest friend
there ever could be.

How small is *small?* And Maggie must be the girl she tagged in this questionnaire.

Lost glasses: multiple times. My little sis sometimes takes them to be funny.

That's not funny.

Sex on the first date: ...idk maybe I'd do it? Thinking about it makes me nervous...

The hairs on my neck bristle. I figured she was a virgin if she's never been kissed, but this causes a wave of panic. I reread that line over and over *idk maybe I'd do it?*

It makes *me* nervous that she'd even contemplate doing it if she's nervous about it.

Like, why?

And I know why. I know how guys are. I know sex.

I know what it feels like being pressured into something that you don't want to do. I mean, it's never happened to me with sex, but yeah…I know pressure.

idk maybe I'd do it. Thinking about it makes me nervous…

Shit.

Been arrested: in a nightmare

I actually laugh, my lips rising.

I glance at the storage room door to see if anyone heard, but it's just me here. No heavy footsteps or knocking yet.

Turned someone down: for what? Like dating?

Yeah, I didn't fucking get that question either.

Fallen for a friend: no. I don't like the guys at my school like that (you wouldn't either if you were me)

What the hell does that mean? I shift my weight on the ground, uncomfortable all of a sudden. And it takes me a moment to realize that I'm uncomfortable for *her*. Were they pricks? Were they aggressive? I'm just picturing assholes running around her school like uncaged gorillas.

More questions...

Do you have any pets: my dad hates pets, but when he moved out a year ago, my mom let Ellie get a hamster. It smells really bad

Hamsters are gross.

What did you do for your last birthday party: ate out at the Noodle House with just my mom, sister and Maggie. I don't like big parties, especially not ones about me

This one rips at me a little bit. Last time I had a small party—with only three people attending—was, well, never. I'd usually invite most everyone in my grade. Even when I was three and four and five, it'd be huge. I didn't want to be alone on that day—though I'd always sneak out early midway through.

Name something you cannot wait for: A REBOOT OF NEW X-MEN (PLEASE HAPPEN!!! I'LL TAKE ANYTHING!!!) Also, for Maggie to meet Scarlet Witch (aka Elizabeth Olsen) one day.

Again, she *really* likes comics.

What irritates you: being forced to speak up in large crowds

Yeah, that's not fun.

Nickname(s): none (I'm not that cool)

I shake my head. She doesn't even know how cool she really is.

Relationship status: single

I'm smiling, a full-blown smile that I haven't felt in years, honestly. I shake my head at myself. *You're in way too fucking deep, Abbey.*
I know.

Favorite TV show: tie between Gravity Falls & X-Men: Evolution. I love them

Never heard of either of them. I actually pop up the notepad on my phone and write down *Wallflower, Gravity Falls, X-Men: Evolution* so this all makes more sense.

High School: ready for it to expire

College: wish I could go. I'm working on it

Hair Color + Length: light brown, straight, and about to my chest?

Height: 5'5''

Your crush: TOM HIDDLESTON!!! (aka Loki)

Loki? Really, with the long black hair? I touch my forehead. My hair is a medium-whatever. I mess my hand through the strands as I continue reading.

Tattoos: my dad says no

Strict Dad? Why'd he let her move here then? She's not even out of high school.

Right or left-handed: Right

Any surgeries: nothing that serious

Any piercings: double lobe piercings on both ears, just four little studs, two bats and two stars

Yeah, I saw those.

Favorite sport: sports? *runs and hides*

Sometimes I feel like that too. At least with lacrosse.

First vacation: never left Maine before, but when I was really little, we used to go to the coast, about 4+ hours from Caribou, and we went sailing one time. I can't really remember it, but my mom has pictures. Everyone seems happy

What...

My knees fall, and my foot knocks over a cardboard cutout of Hawkeye. I pause for a second, but nothing else stirs, no one coming in here. I glance back at Tumblr.

She had never left Maine before.

Without having ever really traveled, she moved *here*. Away from her parents and sister.

These thoughts just crash into me, trying to process. Trying to understand. Because I see myself trying to do the same fucking thing, and I'm not sure I'd have the courage to step one foot out the door.

I stare at the wall, for about three minutes total. Just staring and *imagining* that giant leap into the unknown.

I don't know how...I can only feel fear.

Currently...

What are you eating: vanilla birthday cake that I made for my sister. I snuck downstairs for a slice & brought it back up

What the fuck. Why is she sneaking downstairs in her own house? Did they lock her up there? You know what, I don't like her family. It's a declaration I make in my head with limited facts from a Tumblr questionnaire. I get that. But I don't give two shits. I'm sticking by it.

What are you drinking: a flat can of Fizz Life

What are you waiting for: this birthday party to end

Seriously. What happened?

Do you want kids: idk I don't think about that

Marriage: I don't mind either way

Career: too soon to tell

What do you like...

Hugs or kisses: hugs for now

Has a guy ever even hugged her? It's my only thought. One that I'm sure will be plaguing me all night.

Shorter or taller: taller than me. Even if it's only a little taller. That works too.

Older or younger: older but not too old—I couldn't do what Daisy Calloway does with her boyfriend, who's like seven or eight years older (I can't remember).

And that concludes the questionnaire. She meant it when she said it was personal. I pull my knees up and rest my elbows on them, staring off at the ground.

Shit.

I thought the point of reading that was to get answers, but now I have a thousand more questions. My heart pounds harder, my pulse fast. My body has responded like I chugged a Lightning Bolt!

The door to the break room opens, and I immediately freeze, only now realizing that my legs have been jostling.

"Garrison? Are you in here?"

Lily Calloway.

Great. I'm about to get fired. I rub my temple and run my hands up to my hair, aggressively pulling at it for a second before taking a breath. And then, I slowly stand.

"Yeah?"

She keeps the door propped open, not edging further towards me. "The *Avengers vs. X-Men* issues need restocking, and they need more hands behind the counter."

She's not firing me?

I stare at her blankly for a second before nodding. "Yeah, fine."

She squints a little. "Are you okay?"

"Fine." I motion towards the door. "You going?"

She opens her mouth like she might say something, but then someone calls her from the break room. She turns back to me quickly. "Forget about the comics. Just go help up front." Her words drift as she rushes out to take care of something else.

I let out a breath of relief.

I still have this job.

And that has to count for something.

October

13

Willow Moore

"YOU'RE NOT DRESSING UP?" I ASK GARRISON.

Seated on my fuzzy blue rug, he plays *Street Fighter II* on an old Sega Genesis that he brought over in September. My dorm-sized room has more personality than just the bare built-in desk, wooden dresser, and short single bed from when I first moved in.

Daisy Calloway helped me decorate. She said she'd be my labor force, and I could direct her where to go, but I liked hearing what she thought. We both agreed to string lights over the ceiling, nail a yellow poster that says *Mutant & Proud* in the wall, and arrange my collection of comic books on my desk.

When I tucked in my white bedding, she tossed pale blue pillows on the mattress. The last one was a blue cupcake. It wasn't something we picked out in the store together. She said that she stitched it in her spare time—with Rose's assistance who's "the better sewer"—but it's my favorite pillow. Because Daisy made it just for me.

Sitting on my bed, I watch as Ryu (Garrison's character) attacks Blanka.

Ryu lands a punch, pushing Blanka back a couple inches.

"I don't know yet," Garrison says. His fingers nimbly fly over buttons, and as Blanka lies flat on his back, he pauses the game and rotates to face me.

A blonde wig is already tight on my head. I twist the hair in a single braid, the strands so long the braid reaches my thighs. This Halloween, I'm going with my staple costume, Vega from *Street Fighter*.

Garrison scrutinizes my hair and then his eyes fall to mine. "Are you sure you want me to come?"

My brother (it's actually starting to feel normal calling Loren Hale that) is hosting a Halloween party for the neighborhood. Garrison is technically already invited since he lives in the same neighborhood, but I asked him to come with me anyway.

This past month has been…difficult at Dalton Academy.

No one harasses me or stuffs my locker with things anymore, but I haven't made any friends either. Lots of behind-the-back whispers.

If someone even tries to talk to me, they only ever ask about Loren Hale. I always shut down at the start of those questions. If I discuss my time with Lo and Lily or any of her sisters, I feel like I'm betraying them.

But I finally have a nickname.

Wordless Willow.

Apparently not responding to someone paints a target on you. Though, my whole body was practically painted red before I even arrived at Dalton.

I haven't exactly told Lo any of this. I also don't plan to tell him today or tomorrow. Some things, I have to deal with on my own.

My current plan: focus on my classwork and not the *people* in my classes. I only have one semester after this one ends. I can make it.

"I want you there," I tell Garrison. *I'm not going to know many people besides Lo, Lily, her sisters, and their significant others.* "But if you don't want to go—"

"I do." He twirls a cigarette in his fingers. He won't smoke in my room. I've never told him, but he's the only reason school isn't unbearable. He's the reason there aren't more tampons in my locker—or worse. He made sure his old friends left me alone.

I've needed him.

If he wasn't here, I'm not sure I'd have the strength to stay.

Maybe I'd find it somewhere else, but he's kept me looking forward. At a better future. At a better place.

In our quiet, I hear the front door to the apartment opening, audible from my cracked bedroom door. Voices emanate from the hallway, and I'm sure my roommate (the only other person with a key) has stepped inside the living room.

Seconds later, my door swings further open, until Maya sticks her head inside. She wears a pink wig and plastic body armor. Her costume: Lightning from *Final Fantasy*.

"Hey," she says. "I'm heading out. You sure you don't want to come?" A smile creeps on her lips. "Your first college party could be a cosplay Halloween."

At seventeen, I might be living in an off-campus apartment near the University of Pennsylvania, but I've successfully avoided the college parties so far. Thinking about them brings on this whole new wave of anxiety that I didn't even know existed.

"It's tempting, but I have to go to Loren's neighborhood thing." *It's Lo, Willow.* Right. *Lo. Lo. Lo.*

"Yeah, I heard about that on Yik-Yak."

Garrison snorts from my rug. "Someone yakked about it?" He returns to the video game, eyes glued to the screen as he plays.

Maya squeezes a little further into my room but stays in the doorway. "I think the yak was something like 'my dream is to party with Loren Hale on his birthday'—not at all detailed." She casts sly glances from Garrison to me, back and forth, but she's not as worried as when I first brought him over.

As the Superheroes & Scones manager, she finds his attitude *troubling*. She was worried he'd steal the comics and sell them online.

The fact that I brought him to our apartment—that he's grown closer to me—made her a bit more protective and apprehensive too. I think she thought maybe this all might be a trick. Get close to the geek for other reasons.

Burn her. Make fun of her. Humiliate her.

Like classic teen movies. He'd try to change me, so that I'd become popular like him. Or he'd pull some cruel prank in the very end.

Neither has happened.

Outside of lacrosse, he spends nearly all his free time with me. He'll message me on Tumblr first. (We still haven't exchanged phone numbers.) Sometimes, he's already in the parking lot before he asks if he can come up. Sometimes I wonder if a tree was outside my apartment complex, if he'd climb it and knock on the window.

I think he would.

Garrison might not be up-to-date on comics like the other Superhero & Scones employees, but he has a geeky side that he's repressed and hidden from his friends.

He loves computers.

He *loves* video games. Retro things like Lion King on Sega and Pokémon. We spent three whole days playing Mario Party on N64, and if he asked, I'd waste another three weeks doing the same thing with him.

That doesn't *feel* like someone tricking me.

And so far, he's proven trustworthy at the store. No theft. No vandalism.

"Garrison," Maya says, catching his attention from the video game. "Just a heads up, I'll be quizzing you about Cable's history on your next shift. Two wrong answers"—she holds up two fingers—"and you have toilet duty."

"Shit," he mutters and mouths to me, *who's Cable?*

I try to restrain a smile. "I'll help you." Cable is in *X-Men* and has a complex history, tangled with Scott Summers, so it might go over his head at first, but he's caught on with other superheroes before.

Garrison swings his head back to Maya. "Should I take this *heads up* as you partially liking me?"

Maya wears a great poker face and then says something in Korean, knowing he can't understand. She grips the door, about to leave.

"One day I'm going to learn Korean!" Garrison calls after her. "And then what are you going to do about it?"

She pops her head back in. "That'll be the day." She slips out, just as quickly. Then she pops her head in one more time. "Friendly reminder: I'm to report back to Loren if anything R-rated is happening in Willow's room. I don't like being a spy, so don't make me be one."

I go rigid. "We're *just friends*," I emphasize for probably the millionth time to Maya, to Lily, to even Lo.

I haven't even hugged Garrison. I don't want to ruin what we have by turning it into something more. I can't imagine…I can't imagine losing his friendship.

Garrison nods in agreement. "She's just my girl."

I pale and then begin to smile impulsively. I hide it by busying myself with my hair.

Maya's eyes dart between us again, but they land on me. "Be sure to lock up after you leave. A lot of bodies will be roaming the halls tonight."

"I will."

She gives me the Vulcan Salute, and I return it before she disappears for good this time.

Garrison sets down his controller, pausing the game one more time. He rises from the rug, and I situate a mirror on my mattress. When it's settled, I remove my glasses, grab my eyeliner and mascara and tuck my legs under my butt.

I don't wear much makeup, except for costumes.

Garrison paces in front of my bed, running his fingers through his brown hair. At least that's what I think he's doing. Without my glasses, he appears mostly blurry. I can't see him all that well, and I'm debating about wearing contacts tonight. I don't like them, but my character for Halloween doesn't wear glasses like me.

"So…" Garrison draws the word out. "I have a question, and you don't have to answer if you don't want to."

I freeze, the mascara wand only halfway out of its tube. "What is it?"

"You know that questionnaire you made me take a month ago? I mean, you didn't *make me* take it. But you know…that one?"

How could I forget? It's what kind of started our friendship. When he told me that he read mine, he only mentioned how he was surprised that I hadn't traveled. He never explained his other feelings on it or if he had any.

And I didn't ask.

Maybe because I never probed him about his own questionnaire.

About why his relationship status was *hiatus*.

About what his tattoo looks like, the mysterious one over his right shoulder blade. He never takes off his shirt in front of me, so I've never spotted it.

Or what it meant when he answered *fallen for a friend* as "sort of"—a two-word combination that he's pointed out I use more than him.

We've both been sitting on these things. It's been easier to live without the full meanings; though I realize we're both curious about them. I'm just as interested in the reasoning behind the answer as much as Garrison.

It doesn't mean I'm not scared to find out.

"Yeah?" I say, unsure of the direction he's about to take us.

"In your questionnaire, you said that you didn't like any of the guys at your school and that people wouldn't either if they knew them." He faces me. "Why?"

I frown. "Have you been thinking about this for that long?" I drop my mascara on my bed.

He shrugs. "On and off, I guess." He turns his head like he's staring at the wall. I squint, but I can't make out anything else. "I didn't want to ask back then. I didn't want to pry or whatever. We were just getting to know one another. It's different...now."

We're better friends.

I pat my bed for my glasses. I can apply mascara if I put my face really close up to the mirror, if you're wondering. Garrison suddenly nudges my hand, my glasses in his clutch.

"Thanks." I put them on, the world ten thousand times clearer.

I also notice his downturned lips and worry creases in the corners of his eyes.

"They're just not the guys you would want to date," I try to explain. "Nothing terrible. Just...not my type."

He contemplates this and then rests his back against my dresser. "What's your type?"

"Not douchebags or guys who'd make fun of me…that's for sure."

His brows jump. "Did someone make fun of you?"

I stare at my hands. "I was mostly invisible. I don't even think they noticed that I left."

"I'd notice," he says, full of conviction, enough that I believe him.

"It's okay. I didn't want them to notice me anyway."

"Because they're not your type?"

"Exactly." It makes sense in my head. I've explained it to Maggie before, and she understood. Maybe you have to be there. In that school. Around those people. In my shoes. To truly feel what I feel. I let out a tense breath and ask, "What's your type?"

He shakes his head once. "I'm not sure." His eyes flit all over my room. Every time he's in here, he skims every item, every *thing*. Like the stuff propped on the back of my dresser: a copy of *Understanding Comics*, a Loki bobble head, ticket stubs to *Harry Potter and the Deathly Hallows Part 1 and 2*.

I wonder what his room looks like, but he says that he'd rather be here, away from home. I once asked him why and he said, *"My brothers are dicks. And they sometimes stop by the house so our maid can do their laundry."*

I didn't pry further, and I never beg to see his place, even if it's tempting to ask. He learns a little more about me when he steps foot in here. I don't see more of him.

Garrison plucks one of my old photographs off the dresser. It's of my thirteenth birthday at the mall, the photo taken right after I got my ears pierced for the first time. My mom is there, holding a tiny Ellie.

My dad couldn't make it.

Work stuff, he said.

"You also wrote about your little sister's birthday party." Garrison rests the frame back. "Why couldn't you go downstairs?" He sets his grave expression on me.

"It's not what you think," I say quickly, though I'm not sure exactly *what* he's thinking. "It's actually kind of funny."

"I hope so." He walks to my desk and sinks down in the chair. In all the times he's been in my room, he won't ever sit on my bed. Not once.

I've offered a couple times. Just to be nice. There's not a lot of comfortable seating in this cramped space. But he always chooses either the desk chair or the floor.

"It was a princess party," I start to explain. His brows knot the more I talk. "And Ellie wanted a real princess downstairs. She sees me as her kind of geeky older sister, so she asked if I could stay upstairs, and my mom hired another girl to be the elder princess."

A long wave of silence passes.

"So you couldn't go downstairs?" he asks like he's still confused.

"I wasn't...a princess..." I say slowly. "It makes more sense if you know my sister." I push up my glasses and stretch my mind to that vivid memory. "She took the theme of her party really seriously."

"Sounds like she was channeling a character from Cinderella."

I smile weakly. "She's six-years-old. She doesn't know any better."

"What about your mom? Does she know better?"

A sharp pang punctures my heart. I must wear a pained expression because he says, "Sorry"—and I shake my head like *it's alright*.

I haven't talked to my mom as much as I would like. Our conversations are so stilted anyway. She won't open up to me. She just says, *it's not your place. You're the child.* It's about *us*—doesn't she realize this?

I'd like to know why she goes quiet every time I utter Lo's name. Not just facts—I have some of those—but her feelings. He's her child. Why wouldn't she want to know him? Just a little more. And is she sad that I'm gone? Is she happy?

But I'm just the child.

"My mom," I say casually, "sided with the birthday girl. Which is only fair, it was her birthday."

Garrison does this thing where he groans without even opening his mouth, and I can hear the deep rumble in his throat.

"You don't agree?"

He shakes his head and retrieves a cigarette again. "It seems kind of fucked up."

I try to view the situation from his stance, and I think I can. I just don't want to.

"Can I ask you something now?" I wonder.

Garrison nods.

I open my mouth but struggle to broach *his* questionnaire. I actually pale again, and my neck heats. "Um…it's about one of your answers."

"Which one?" He doesn't sound surprised.

"Hiatus?" I quickly add, "Not that I care. I mean, I care out of… curiosity, but your relationship status can be whatever you want it to be." When I look up, the corners of his lips are lifting.

"I know what you meant." Still sitting, he rolls on the desk chair. Until he's positioned right across from me. "I've been on-and-off with this girl at Dalton who wants absolutely nothing to do with me now, so…" He shrugs like it is what it is. "There's my hiatus."

"Do you miss her?"

"Not like I probably should. And for the record, at the time, I thought—maybe if Frankie and my friends forgave me, I'd think about…"

"Going back to them?" *Leaving me.*

Would it be that easy for him? My heart sinks more, a pit in my stomach. This is why I never asked.

I can feel him watching me, and I turn towards my mirror, about to take off my glasses. His voice stops me. "It's different now. I'm different."

I can't imagine the person who he's described to me. The one who'd drink alcohol at playgrounds and destroy public property, just because he could. Who'd graffiti houses and knock over mailboxes with baseball bats.

He's said that he's always liked Sega, Pokémon, the Sims—and part of me believes that he was always *this person* on this desk chair, right in front of me. He just felt too much pressure to be a different guy in front of other people. He was too scared to be himself. With his friends gone, he has nothing to lose by being the real Garrison Abbey.

So he's let him free.

All I ask is, "What kind of name is Frankie?"

He almost smiles, glad that I'm not mad at him. "Nickname for Francesca."

"Of course, she has a cool nickname," I mumble. I don't know if he hears or not because I ask speedily, "What about your tattoo?"

He pulls off his hoodie, splaying it on the chair. Now just in a black tee. He stretches out his arm, about to show me the tattoo on his forearm, but I've seen that one before. It's a skull with lyrics to an Interpol song. I had to Google it.

"The one on your shoulder blade, I mean."

He goes a little rigid and then his arms fall to his sides. "That one is kind of an intense tattoo." He pauses. "My mom hasn't even seen it."

"Not even when you go swimming?"

"Honestly, I can't remember the last time I went swimming in my pool."

More silence spreads in a long moment. Neither of us moves or speaks.

We look at each other. We wonder. His brown eyelashes flit up, each time he peeks at me. Strands of his hair fall over his forehead, and he rests his forearms on his thighs, thinking.

I wait, just as calmly. Inspecting my mascara brush. Glancing at him.

He's never pushed me, and I won't push him to do anything or reveal more.

He licks his pink lips and then nods to himself once or twice. "How about"—he retrieves his phone from his pocket and then flips the cell in his hand a couple of times—"we make a trade. I don't know your Twitter username yet. You give me yours, I'll show you my tattoo."

As he processes his own declaration, his eyes flit to the wall, the ground and the window, more than a few times—almost nervously. His joints even stiffen more than usual.

"Are you sure?" I ask.

He raises his gaze and nods. "Yeah." He adds, "I want to see what Willow Hale tweets about."

Willow Hale.

He still has no idea that I'm not Lo's cousin. *I'm his half-sister.* Willow Moore. And I have no idea when I'll be able to trust Garrison enough to tell him the truth. It's not just my secret to keep. It involves *everyone.*

I know that I can't jump the gun on this, even if he's my friend.

"They're not that great of tweets," I warn him. "Mostly fandom stuff." I reach for my phone on my bed and then pause before logging into Twitter. "I was thinking about changing my username though."

"Oh no." He points at me. "You're one of those people who changes their usernames every day, aren't you?" He's nearly smiling as he says it, and he tilts his head at me. "How am I going to find my girl if you're *willowkicksass* one day and *vegalover* the next?"

"Ha ha." My cheeks hurt from my own smile. In the mirror, I notice an actual blush rising. "And you'd find me. It'd just take you a couple seconds...maybe even less." Not because he's good at computers.

But because he knows what I like.

"Probably." His knee brushes against mine, on accident. We both go still. My heavy breath is more audible than his.

So he scoots back his chair, giving me more room.

I clear my throat, my neck burning again. "The next username I make, I want to go public with it and promote Superheroes & Scones. Lily also keeps asking for my u.n. so she can tweet me." I hold my phone flat on my lap. "I won't change this one all the time like the others."

He sees the Twitter login screen. "Have you already picked it out?"

"Yeah, I wanted to do something like Lo. He has his name paired with his favorite mutant." His username: *lorenhellion*. "The problem is that *willowallflower* is already taken."

Garrison doesn't seem surprised when I say the word *wallflower*—instead he just points at my phone screen. "Make the double L's in 'wallflower' capital I's and it'll look the same on Twitter."

I type in the changes, and he's right. The I's show up more like L's, and this username is available. Before I accept the new username, I ask, "You know Wallflower?" She's not a well-known mutant, and she's not around for long in the comics.

"You mentioned her in your questionnaire."

I did?

"I looked her up," he explains off my confusion, "figured it couldn't hurt with Maya grilling me every shift." He spins some in his chair, pretty casual. "Do you like Wallflower with the blond guy or the brown-haired one?" He leans back.

I'm trying so hard not to smile like he's put his hands on my cheeks. Like he's kissed me. I just—this is surreal. That he's here, talking to me about my favorite mutants. He's not laughing. He's not calling me a little girl. He's not calling me dumb or silly. He's respecting the things I love.

He stares at the ceiling, trying to recall something. "I remember looking up their names." He swivels. "Shit." He thinks a second longer. "Elixir...and Wither?"

"Yeah, that's them. They're in a love triangle with Wallflower." I don't mention how their romances don't end very well, in case he wants to read the comics. "I like her with Wither, even if they're doomed from the start."

"Why are they doomed?"

I intake a breath as I say, "He can't touch her."

Garrison's chair goes still.

"Whatever or whoever he touches decays to dust." He also wears only black, but I don't mention this either.

Garrison blinks a few times, processing Wither's superpower. I think he mutters something about *being cursed* and then he asks, "What about Elixir?"

"He can heal people. He's an Omega-level, so his powers are even extraordinary among mutants." I pause. "He's also mean."

Garrison begins to smile. "I already hate him if you think he's mean." He suddenly brings his phone up to his chest, and he lifts his brows at me like he's doing something secret.

I take the time to log into my new username, and within the second, I get a new notification.

@garrisonwither: @willowallflower looks like it was time for a change for me too *gasp* we're matching

I look up at him, my mouth ajar. "…is…is this your real account?" He could've made a fake one just to tweet me.

Garrison nods, slipping his phone in his jeans pocket before he stands. "Yeah. It's my primary account. Favorite one." His voice is so honest that I trust him.

I have a matching Twitter account.

With a guy.

Maggie wouldn't believe me, even if I told her.

"So…" Garrison towers above me, his hands on the hem of his black shirt. He looks beyond hesitant.

He looks scared.

"You don't have to—"

"It's fine. Just don't freak about the bruises. Lacrosse gets rough and…" he trails off. "I tripped over some guy during last practice."

I swallow hard and just nod, but I wonder if this was the reason why he didn't want to take off his shirt. Or why he doesn't want to dress as Ryu or even Ken Masters for Halloween.

As he peels the fabric off his head, my eyes trace the lines of his lean, toned muscles. In a sharp inhale, his ribs are apparent, along with his tightened abs. Most of the bruises appear faded, but the dark, *dark* purple welt by his right ribcage seems brand new.

When he tosses his shirt aside, I say, "That looks bad."

He glances at the welt. "It's nothing."

"Garrison—"

"Don't!" Panic spikes his voice, and he raises his hands like I sprung up from the bed and tried to touch his ribs. I haven't even shifted.

He shuffles back, breathing heavily. Then he freezes and stares off for a second, attempting to calm down.

I hold up my hands to show him that I'm not coming at him.

He mutters a *sorry* but stays still.

My stomach twists. I'm just scared for him, of whoever did this to him. I'm not sure it's just lacrosse. "You said...you don't like your brothers, right?"

"It's nothing," he repeats, but he pauses and adds, "They play rough, but it's just brother stuff. Football. Wrestling. They don't mean it."

"What if your ribs are broken?"

"They aren't." I don't ask if he went to a doctor, and I can tell he wants to drop the subject. Especially as he turns his back to me. To show me the tattoo on his right shoulder blade.

It's another gothic skull, only its jaw is wide open, screaming. It's also inside the mouth of a wolf's head, which looks violent, saliva dripping off its teeth as it roars too.

You can't hear ink, and something about a silent scream guts me.

Everything about the tattoo is haunting. Everything about Garrison Abbey feels just the same. Like a boy you'd find lying on a tombstone, smoking a cigarette, a bundle of flowers on his chest. It makes no sense, but something deeper, something hidden, wants to crawl out. So I keep staring. I keep looking.

I'm not sure what I'm supposed to find. I'm not sure if I'll ever truly *see* what he's expressing, but I don't leave. Maybe later, I'll know. The pieces will add up and I'll see what he wants me to see.

Some things can't be forced out of people. I wouldn't want him to force things out of me.

Without even spinning back around, he picks up his shirt and tugs it on. He doesn't want me to see the welt again. When he plops down on the chair, he shrugs on his hoodie, and then our eyes meet.

"Have you ever been hugged by a guy?" he asks me, so suddenly. I shake my head. "No."

"Will you stand up for a second?" He adds, "If you want to."

I slowly rise, dressed in pants and a white blouse for my Vega costume. Then he stands from the chair, pushing it back into the dresser, away from us. He takes a step closer to me, until his chest is an inch from mine.

He mostly smells like citrus, spearmint and his pine car freshener. I once asked why he keeps his Mustang so clean. He never smokes inside, and the interior is always spotless, like a brand new car.

I don't like the smell of smoke lingering around all the time, he told me. *And I can't think straight if my car is dirty.*

Garrison, more than just a few inches taller than me, stares down at my features. I look up, my pulse quickening.

And he asks, "Can I hug you, Willow?"

I breathe deeply, pushing up my glasses. "I'm not that good at hugging."

"You don't have to be good at hugging. I'd still want to hug you."

"Why?" I whisper.

His aquamarine eyes skim my cheek, my neck, descending. "…because I think you may be the best friend I've ever had, and I've had a lot and spent a shit ton more days and months and years with them than the short time I've spent with you." His hand wavers by my hip, but he doesn't touch me. "I've never wanted to bolt out of your door. I've never wanted to leave you. This—it's a first for me." He nods to himself a couple times. "So you're the best—and I want to hug you, if you'll let me."

My lips part, speechless. Inside, I'm blown over.

Outside, I'm frozen in place.

When my brain functions again, I rewind and all I can wonder is whether this *feeling* of not wanting to leave my room—of not wanting to leave me—surprised him after he revealed his tattoo. After he was vulnerable in front of me.

Yes, my brain says. *Most likely.*

Can I drop my guard just the same? Can I express more emotion than I usually do? I don't think he's testing me, but maybe I need to test myself.

He watches me, waiting for a vocal response.

I open my mouth to say *you can hug me* but my tongue is dry and my throat closes.

His brows scrunch. "You nervous?"

I nod. "This would be a first...for me." *He knows that, Willow.* I cringe a little but try to wipe it away with a weak smile. "I'm not touchy-feely or anything like that."

Garrison's eyes soften like he's trying to understand me. "Would it be bad if I touched you?"

I can hardly look up at him, my gaze dropping to the floor. "Um..." I swallow. "I don't think so. It'll just be new, and sometimes new things are frightening." My heart thuds so hard and so fast.

"Willow," he murmurs.

I look up, our eyes lock, and he sets his hands on my shoulders. I hold in a breath. His palms—they slide *slowly* to my biceps, his skin heating my skin, and then they slip around me, to my back. He draws me tenderly to his chest.

My feet just barely cooperate and step closer.

Garrison leans his head down, his jaw skimming my cheek, his arms wrapped around me, and mine hang uncertainly.

He helps me. He lifts one of my hands and places it on his waist. I follow with the other. My touch is feather-light, but he doesn't seem to care.

Garrison pulls me tighter, his body warm and comforting. In comparison, mine is awkward and stiff. He holds the back of my head, and his breath tingles my ear as he whispers, "This okay?"

"Yeah," I breathe, so softly.

"You're shaking." He draws his head back, just a fraction, and I realize my arms and legs are trembling, out of anxiety.

"It's just a lot...not bad." I wish I could express my feelings better, but maybe that's the problem. So much has suddenly poured through me, so many foreign sentiments, that my system is basically overloading.

Willow Moore at approximately 115% capacity. Delete or reboot.

I don't want to delete anything with him.

Before he speaks, I ask, "Am I hurting you?" My hands are barely pressing on his ribs, but I just want to make sure.

"No." He pauses. "Am I hurting you?"

"No."

He nods a couple times again. Then he lets me go, his arms falling—then mine do too, but he never takes a step back. I worry about the second hug, now that the first has ended. I wonder if I'll grow used to this embrace in time.

"Will you alert me?" I ask him. "Next time you hug me again?"

"By plane banner and smoke in the sky."

"I don't think I'll be looking up."

He nearly smiles but feigns surprise. "You'd miss an aerial ad? No way."

His sarcasm isn't the mean kind. It pulls my lips higher.

Garrison never takes his eyes off me. "Willow," he says in a quiet, calm moment, "can I hug you again?"

My chest swells. "Yeah."

Garrison wraps his arms around me once more, and my arms almost stop trembling. His lips to my ear, he whispers, "How was that alert?"

"Perfect." I try to relax a little more.

He rubs my back, his hand soothing as it travels in a short up and down wave. And he says, "Thanks for inviting me."

I look up at him. "You were already invited to the party."

"Not by you."

This is the day, the very moment, that I realize how much Garrison Abbey is glad to be in my company. Mine.

Willow Moore from Maine.

You may not be such a fool after all.

14

Garrison Abbey

"SHIT." I CHECK OVER MY SHOULDER, NOTICING HANNAH'S MOM and her little five-year-old brother at Loren Hale's neighborhood Halloween party. Located in his overly decorated backyard. Before Mrs. Nash sees me, I pull my hood over my head.

I'm not in costume. Just my usual hoodie and dark jeans.

"What?" Willow asks, both of us loitering near the long snack table. She's filling her paper pumpkin-shaped plate with only a few kernels of caramel popcorn and two tiny bite-sized pretzels—you know the kind that people put in Chex Mix? Not like a giant soft pretzel at a movie theater.

"Just someone I know, or their mom, I mean. Not actually them." I shake my head like I'm being stupid about this. She won't talk to me. Would she? I wave Willow on. "It's whatever. Keep doing what you're doing."

"I'm done. So…" She pushes up her black-framed glasses. Even though they don't go with her Vega costume, I like that she wanted to be comfortable and keep them on. She tries grabbing the strap of her backpack. It's not there, by the way. So she catches air.

Willow notices me staring for a long or quick second—I'm not really sure which. "What…is it?" Her hand shakes, the paper plate rattling, and she clutches it with both to steady the thing. I spot her anxiety more than she'd probably like me to, but all I want to do is lessen it for her. I'm just not fucking sure how.

"You look pretty," I tell her the truth, "but you look pretty all days, so there's not really a difference here."

Willow pales. She does that instead of blush. "Um, thanks? You look pretty too." She winces. "I mean, you look handsome?"

I try to make this exchange as easy as possible. "Me? Nah. My dad says I need a haircut, and my eyes can't decide what color they want to be."

Her shoulders relax, and she peers close at my eyes. "I always just thought they were blue-green, which is aquamarine?"

"Maybe. I've never looked it up, which kinda shows the lack of interest I have in myself." I nod at her plate. "You really done?" I pick up my own plate. The food spread is intense. The tower of orange-frosted cupcakes alone could feed my entire lacrosse team.

"I don't have a big appetite when I'm nervous." She shrugs but stares off at the growing party, more and more teenagers, kids and parents arriving. Apples drift along the pool, water glowing orange from the lights. Torches illuminate the backyard as the sun descends.

I don't ask what she's nervous about when I'm positive it's just *this*. The party in general. The people. The *mingling*. I don't like it much either, but it doesn't bring me anxiety like her. I remember how her Tumblr questionnaire said she doesn't like large crowds.

She meant it.

I load my plate with the only thing that looks good to me. Cookies. Sugar, oatmeal—not a big fan of chocolate fudge—but I find the peanut butter ones, my favorite, and stack them high.

"I'm not really sure where to go," Willow mumbles, kind of to herself.

I stick a cookie in my mouth and point at an unoccupied haybale near the fence. "This way."

She walks beside me, passing the apple bobbing thing and a couple other games, and when we make it to the haybale she lets out a deep breath like *I made it*.

I'm not going to lie.

I want to hug her right now.

Instead though, I just sit next to Willow and chew my peanut butter cookie. I set a couple sugar cookies on her plate. "In case you're not as nervous later."

"Thanks." She starts to smile.

My lips rise too. I set a foot on the haybale and my arm on my knee. "If you could be doing anything in the world, what'd you be doing?" I ask her.

"Like a career?"

"No, just on any day, any time."

She nudges her popcorn around her plate. "I'd hang out in my room. Maybe watch a movie, read some comics, and surf the internet, nothing crazy. I know it sounds boring, but it's fun to me."

"It doesn't sound boring. Just laidback." I wonder how many people gave her shit for it—because my brothers give me shit for playing "girly" games like *Mario Party*. Which, honestly, is as much for girls as it is for boys. It's Nintendo.

"So I finished the fifth season of *Supernatural* last night..." she trails off as a blonde woman approaches us, a five-year-old clinging to her side. She's not really "in costume" like her Buzz Lightyear son. She just wears dangling ghost earrings and a tacky sweater.

"Shit," I mutter, too late to angle my body out of sight. I can't even force a fake smile.

Mrs. Nash greets me first. "Hi, Garrison."

Her daughter was my friend and part of the "*you should've been the bigger man and stood up to your friends and forced them to stop harassing people*" group. I agree, I should've done that. I should've done a lot of things that I never did, and I can't take it back.

I can't rewind time, and guess who has to live with *all* of this for the rest of their life?

Me.

It's my shit to bear.

And no matter which way people paint me, I'm still the lesser man. For ratting out my friends. Or for not convincing them to do the right thing.

"Hey," I say back, dropping my hood. I hang my head though, and my hair brushes my eyelashes.

"It was really nice of Loren to let you at his house."

"Yep," I agree. I would've never forgiven myself for what I'd done like he forgave me, but I'm not going to tell *her* that.

"You should find time to thank him tonight."

I see that she means well, but her coarse delivery rubs me wrong. I force a grating smile and say, "Yeah, I'll get on that." *Why do I say these things?*

"You're lucky you're not where your friends are, and frankly, the majority of this neighborhood thinks you should be there."

She wants me to express deep remorse, break down and maybe shed some tears, but I just—I just can't do that in front of her, in front of all these people. At this party. I can't. I know I probably should, but my defenses keep rising and rising. I don't know how to knock them down.

"Awesome," I say. "I'll be sure to pen that in my dairy tonight." I can't even look at Willow, but I sense her hesitation towards the entire situation.

I hate that my shit is making her more nervous.

So before Mrs. Nash can scold me some more, I add, "Is that all? Honestly, I don't have anything else to say about this."

"I'm so glad Hannah is no longer friends with you." *Ouch.* I just nod, and she focuses on someone else. "Willow, right?"

I sit straighter, lifting my head up because I don't want Mrs. Nash to attack her because of me.

"Yeah. I'm Willow."

I wait.

Mrs. Nash says, "Don't let him fool you. He's harassed your cousin Loren and his wife Lily for longer than he's probably told you. Just keep that in mind as he tries to make a friend out of you."

The sad part: it's all pretty much true.

Though I'm not fooling Willow. I'm not trying to, but she said that Loren told her everything that happened in the neighborhood. I never asked her to clarify which incidents, to tally off and see if he truly did recount everything to her. I didn't want to bring up my bad history.

Just as Mrs. Nash turns to leave, Willow speaks up. "He's a good person."

It gets to me. Like emotionally—it gets to me. I stay still, and I just intake that phrase that no one has ever really spoken about me.

He's a good person.

She said it so quietly that Mrs. Nash never heard. But I did. I watch Hannah's mom direct her son towards the table of food.

"Sorry," I apologize to Willow for that entire shitty conversation.

"She was rude."

"So was I," I say.

"Yeah, but…" She shrugs. "You see that you were. She doesn't see that she was. And I know it doesn't make it better, but it still matters in a way. I think, at least."

"Yeah…maybe." I'd like to believe that too.

She picks up one of the sugar cookies I gave her and takes a bite.

I feel my lips lift again. "So you finished the fifth season of *Supernatural* just last night and you didn't message me? I told you I wanted the play-by-play of your reactions. In gif form." She did it for season two, and honestly, it was the cutest thing anyone has ever sent me links to.

Most of my Tumblr posts are TV shows and movie gif sets I made, daily sarcasm, relating everyday events to pizza, and reblogs.

Her Tumblr posts are questionnaires, fan edits, fandom-related posts, and reactionary gifs as she live-updates watching episodes of TV. It bogs down my feed like crazy—and if you asked me my opinion about it before I met her, I'd say *it's dumb.*

It's not dumb. I hate that I thought it was dumb. It's really entertaining, especially when I've seen the show.

She swallows her cookie and tries to contain a wider smile. "It was 4 a.m."

I don't have the best sleep pattern, but I was actually asleep last night at that time. "Finishing the best season of *Supernatural* is the only good reason to wake me up at 4 a.m. Did we agree that the internet is the best form of communication?"

"We did, but our other option was two tin cans."

"Right." I smile at the memory. "What are your thoughts on a cellphone?"

I'm surprised when she shakes her head. *Rejected, Abbey.* Willow sets down her cookie. "I like seeing you on the internet. I mean we're not actually *seeing* each other."

"You mean my ones and zeroes aren't making contact with your ones and zeros? I thought they were dancing around each other. My ones know how to waltz but the zeros are just shit dancers. They like to step on other people's computer code."

Willow has this giddy smile that's a little infectious. "If my ones and zeroes could dance, they'd probably still choose to sit down."

I'd sit down with you. I don't say it because I'm literally sitting down with her. "What about bobbing for apples?" I ask. "No pressure, honestly."

"You say that a lot."

"What part?"

"*Honestly.*"

I hadn't noticed. Maybe I'm just scared people won't know what's sarcasm and what's sincere. "Hey, I wanted to mention something... don't take this the wrong way." Why am I broaching this now? *Don't scare her or make her feel bad.* I almost pause, but I let it out anyway— because I'm that guy. "That comic book character, the one we were talking about earlier, I looked him up again."

"Elixir?"

"No, the other one."

"Wither?"

"Yeah, him." I pause. "He kind of looks like me. For a cartoon."

"Comic," she corrects while color drains from her face. "...I like Wither, but I never said you *were* Wither."

"Yeah, I know. I just thought it was interesting." I feel like a dumbass, mostly because she can't meet my eyes. I'm about to change subjects completely and ask about her favorite part of *Supernatural* season five, but she points to the apple-bobbing tub.

"It's free. Do you still want to?"

I wonder if she was just waiting for the crowds to clear out around it.

"Yeah, definitely."

15

Willow Moore

THINGS I NEVER THOUGHT I'D BE DOING IN PHILADELPHIA: apple-bobbing at Loren Hale's neighborhood Halloween party.

Beads of water still roll down my cheeks, and Garrison, only a couple inches away, tenderly brushes the wet strands of hair off my forehead. Everything is blurry, and he must sense my unease, so he gently fits my glasses back on.

"Thanks." I concentrate on his blue-green eyes that dance across my features. He plucks a hair stuck to my cheek and tucks it behind my ear.

My everyday nerves try to subside, and giddiness flutters inside me like confetti falling from the sky. When his other hand skims my hip, I let out a small, nervous laugh. I prefer the giddiness over anxiety, but I can't really control which comes out first. I'm just not used to touching. Everything is so new.

"Is this okay?" he asks.

I push up my glasses, hoping I can reassure him that I like this so far. "Yeah." I nod more than once.

"Can I hold you?" Quickly, he adds, "Like put my arm around you?"

I waver between a bursting smile and apprehension. I want to be on the bursting smile side of things, and I trust Garrison more and more every day. "Yes."

Garrison's arm curves around my waist—

"Hey! You two!"

I instantly jolt and become a stiff board, my head swinging towards the exclamation, but I'd recognize that voice anywhere.

Lo, my brother Lo. The one dressed like a Slytherin. The one sitting on a cluster of haybales across the pool. The Lo that everyone thinks is my cousin. That Loren Hale—yeah, he sends a *seething* glare at Garrison, one that could set the universe on fire.

I hear the warning: *don't touch my little sister.*

We both immediately tear apart, an invisible wedge shoved between us until about ten-feet separates his body from mine. Garrison rakes a hand through the side of his hair before he lifts his hoodie back up.

Lily and Ryke are next to my brother, but I can only see their lips move. My hearing hasn't reached Superman levels. Nor my lip-reading skills because I have zero clue what they're saying.

Garrison rotates, his back turned to me, and his cellphone out. I (poorly) sewed a pocket in my Vega costume, and my phone vibrates once.

"Ca-Caw!" I look up as I take out my phone. Daisy Calloway sits on the rooftop with an antler headband. She calls down to her boyfriend who's currently dressed in plaid. "Ca-Caw!"

When Ryke sees her up on the roof, she smiles and says, "Hunt me."

I don't watch them for long.

I check my Twitter message notification.

From **@garrisonwither**

Going to the bathroom. I'll be back soon. If you're back on our haybale, save me a seat?

I reply with a *will do.* As I look up, he's already disappeared. So I head towards the haybale—but I stop dead in my tracks. *It's occupied.* I swing my head to the left and right, my eyes swerving like a frantic driver behind the wheel. Where do I sit? Most haybales are taken.

I'm not good at parties.

I just don't know what to do or how to fill the time. There's a hidden memo that says: *stay off your cell.* My phone actually takes away the nerves, but then I worry about being rude. And the anxiety returns. It's not a fun cycle.

"Sorry," I apologize to a family of pirates. They try to squeeze around me. I'm in the way. I apologize to two preteen girls dressed as angels. I knocked into one of their wings—or maybe I just barely brushed it? She didn't seem that upset. I don't even know if she noticed.

Willow Moore isn't a total failure at life.

I have something going for me.

I could go talk to Lily or Lo, but they look like they're having a sweet moment on their haybale, both squeezed close together, and their tiny son, dressed like a Gryffindor-to-be, is with them.

Likewise, Rose and Connor have their daughter in arm, and they stand so near one another, their lips moving too fast to keep up. Not that I'd approach them together. I think I could grow the courage to approach Rose *without* Connor.

I push up my glasses and mutter, "*Carpe Diem.*" I'm not a boy like any of the students at Welton Academy in *Dead Poets Society*, but I can Carpe Diem just like them.

I just need to...figure out where to go. I spin around, standing so close to the pool's edge that I back up and back up. Just what I need, to fall right in the—

I whack a torch.

Oh God.

I whacked a *flaming* torch staked into the grass. I go to grab the iron pole, and I fall with it onto a haybale. Where that awful neighborhood lady, Mrs. Nash, and her son sit. They spring from the hazardous area I just created, and I clumsily collapse onto the hay that begins to singe and burn and flame.

"Willow!" Lo yells.

I cough at the gust of smoke and try to stand, my cheek hot. I smack a flame off my skirt and just fall to the grass. So I can crawl away from the fire.

On my knees and hands, I quickly scuttle beyond the haybale that blazes.

Parents are already scooping water from the pool using plastic buckets and Solo cups. While they douse the flame, I stare wide-eyed, frozen in shock.

What just happened?

"Willow?" Lo squats beside me, his amber-colored eyes pinpointed with worry. He scans me to see if I'm singed. I think my confidence burned the most.

"I'm…" *sorry.* I blink a couple times, trying to push past this cold shock. As my horror meets his concern, I only hope that this flaming haybale isn't a metaphor for what I've brought Loren Hale. "I'm sorry," I whisper.

"She's in shock." I hear the icy voice of Rose Calloway. Dressed like Natalie Portman from *Black Swan*, she towers high above me. I notice Ryke and Daisy helping extinguish the fire while Lily and Connor hold their kids by the food table, distracting them from the mayhem.

I'm sorry.

I must mutter it again because Lo says, "I've done a hell of a lot worse."

I space out enough that he grows more worried. Suddenly, he scoops me in his arms.

Oh God.

Loren Hale is carrying me towards his house.

I'm being carried for the first time, and it's by my famous brother. My shock just quadrupled. Maggie, my only friend from Maine, would die in his arms.

As Loren Hale climbs the porch, Garrison is sprinting over from—well I can't really tell where he came from. Too many people are shifting around the backyard.

"Hey, what happened?" Garrison follows Lo as he brings me inside.

I don't hear Lo's response over the noise, but I can fill it in just fine: *Willow knocked over the torch and then almost lit herself on fire.*

Lo sets me on the kitchen counter, the house much quieter, and I hang my head, staring at my hands. I hear the faucet, and out of the corner of my eye, I see Rose wetting a washcloth.

"I'm fine," I mutter, but for some reason tears try to well, and I keep pushing my glasses up that slip down my nose. Only Rose, Garrison, and Loren are in the kitchen right now, but I don't release these kinds of emotions in front of people often. Even just three people seems like a lot.

Rose passes me the washcloth. "Here. This'll help."

I dab the coldness to my cheek and forehead.

Lo checks his phone. "Lily said it's not on fire anymore. See, it's not a problem."

I rub beneath my eye just as a tear threatens to fall. "I didn't mean to come into your life and set things on fire."

Lo can't help but laugh. "You think *this* is bad? Christ, Willow—I've set more metaphorical things on fire than this guy." He points at Garrison.

Garrison raises his brows in surprise. "Really?"

"Yeah, *really*." Lo, with his *sharp as ice* cheekbones and narrowed amber eyes, seems more frightening than the fire itself.

"It's true," Rose validates. "He's horrendous."

Lo flashes her a dry smile. "Says the girl dressed like a possessed ballerina."

"*Black Swan* is a *real* thing."

"Sure." Lo's gaze drifts back to me. "So what I'm saying is, you didn't ruin anything by being here, except a goddamn haybale that no one is going to miss. I'm just glad you didn't catch on fire. Because *you*—I would've missed."

My eyes fill with tears, but a different kind.

"Me too," Garrison chimes in.

"Me three," Rose proclaims.

I nod, more assured than before. *Okay.*

How I end up smiling, I can only attribute to these people, in this kitchen, who made me feel loved when I felt lost and alone.

Okay.

I smile. "Okay."

And for the first time in a long time, I've felt a part of a group.

A part of a family that I know is my own.

GARRISON DRIVES ME TO MY APARTMENT. AS HIS MUSTANG slows by the curb, I wonder if I should invite him in? We're not together, and I don't know if it'd come across as a suggestion.

"Thanks for letting me tag along with you to the party," he says first.

"Thanks for wanting to go with me at all." I take off my blonde wig and shake out my hair, a couple bobby pins were sticking into my scalp. "You're lucky that you left me for a while. I could've burned you." I'm not a smooth-talker, and in the quiet of his car, I feel more like a dork. *He knows you're a geeky dork.* And still, he wants to hang around me. That's something, isn't it?

He puts the car in park and rests his forearm on the steering wheel. We both sort of angle towards one another on our seats. I like how his hair always catches his eyelashes, and his eyes peek between the brown strands.

"About what Mrs. Nash said," he starts.

"It doesn't matter what she said." I wonder how long this has been eating at him.

"Yeah it does," he breathes. "Because…it's true, Willow. Loren can compare us all he wants and say that he did worse shit, but I did shit *to him*. I wrote on his mailbox. I put dog shit on his front porch—I even filled a bucket of…" He looks away from me, ashamed.

I know what he did.

Lo told me everything, and I told Garrison that he did. There must be a place inside of him that still feels *so guilty*. Or else he wouldn't feel the need to confess outright like this.

Garrison stares out the windshield, gathering his courage, as he says, "I filled a bucket up with liquor, so it'd pour on his head as he opened the front door. Knowing—*knowing*, he was an alcoholic and he was fighting to stay sober. I did that."

He doesn't add, *my friends were there.* I know they were, but he's not making excuses or shirking the blame. He's taking it all.

That's why he's a good person. Beneath what happened. Beneath his bad choices. He's a good person. I hope one day he can see this too.

"Lo forgave you," I remind him.

Garrison shakes his head, and softly, he mutters, "I can't forgive myself." He holds my gaze. "You shouldn't be around me, and I don't think I can be the better person and walk away from you, so you gotta do it for me. You have to tell me to stay away from you. You have to tell me to *never* come back here."

It's my turn. I shake my head vigorously. "No. I won't do that."

His eyes well. "Willow—"

"I'm not a fool." I remove my glasses, wiping the foggy lenses. "I'm just a girl from Maine who wants a friend from Philadelphia. You're my friend. I chose you as much as you chose me." I put my glasses back on to see how reddened his eyes have become. "You're the second friend I've ever had in my whole life, and I'm picky about my friendships. But I chose you."

This might be the most I've said in one sitting, my lungs filling with oxygen and threatening to burst.

Garrison tilts his head, his features twisting through so many emotions. "What kind of friendship requirements did I pass to be yours?"

"You're kind."

"I'm not."

"You're good."

"I'm not."

"You're honest."

He pauses.

"You make me feel safe."

He looks up at me, and the air tightens between us. Garrison extends his arm over the back of my seat, but he never drops it to my shoulders. He just keeps it there for a second, staring intently, thinking hard.

"Are you sure?" he asks.

"I'm sure." We're both trying to find our place in the world, at the same time. Sometimes it feels like we're floating, and we're not sure which way to land or if we even can. Before I ask if he wants to come in, his phone buzzes.

I notice the Caller ID says *Mitchell.* I think that's one of his brothers.

"I should take this. He's been calling me all night."

I get the hint, and I open the car door. Just as I close it, he rolls down the window and ducks his head so he can see me on the curb.

"Season six," he says, "want to watch it together next weekend? My house."

A *Supernatural* marathon with Garrison Abbey. His favorite show. At his house. The first invite I've ever gotten there.

"Definitely."

November

16

Garrison Abbey

Mom: Happy 18th Birthday! Do you want anything special for dinner tonight?

I BRIEFLY LOOK UP FROM MY CELLPHONE. ON A SUNDAY afternoon, the mall is packed with families. Babies cry in their strollers, and parents holler at wandering toddlers. I loiter next to a retro arcade called Galactica Arcadia and text my mom a simple reply.

Something like: I don't want anything for my birthday. Don't worry about it. I already have plans for tonight.

I basically just told my mom that my plans don't include her—which they don't. Guilt should strike me. My mom is *nice*.

Nice but completely...I shake my head, not wanting to touch any of this. Not wanting to spell out any more words relating to my parents.

While I wait for a certain someone to show up, I log into Tumblr and start digging through Willow's latest questionnaire. She tagged me in one, and I promised Willow the answers if she bobbed for apples during Halloween.

More than anything, I'm curious what questions she actually wants me to answer. It's different than the first one. Here, she's actively choosing which questionnaire I'll fill out. Whereas the first one, there was no initial intention that some guy from Philly would appear and ask for her username and yada, yada, whatever.

The past is already written, isn't it?

So here I am. In a noisy mall, filling out the new questionnaire with one hand stuffed in my leather jacket, the other gripping my cellphone.

Rules: Complete the form by answering each section truthfully. Once you've finished, tag other users to complete the task. Begin by sourcing the person who tagged you.

I source Willow using her new Tumblr account name: **@ vegablaze33**. Here we go...

Name: Garrison (It's an alright name, I guess.)

Age: 18 and surprisingly still alive

Zodiac Sign: Scorpio

Dream Home: anywhere but the suburbs.

Favorite Band: Interpol

Favorite TV Show: Supernatural. Sometimes American Horror Story.

I check my browser history for the next question.

What was your...

Last Google Search: porn. Jk, I was reading a tv recap for AHS.

Last person you told you loved: I can't think that far back.

Last time you felt jealous: not computable at
this time.

After Lily Calloway said that Superheroes & Scones needed a couple more staff members, Maya hired a new employee during the Halloween weekend. One of which goes to Dalton Academy. *Ace Davenport.* Never seen him in my life—though he said he heard of me.

I couldn't really tell if he hated or liked me. Maybe he's just indifferent, but the moment he saw Willow fumbling with a rack of comics, he crouched next to her and helped re-shelve them.

They exchanged smiles.

I had a flashback.

Of me doing something kind of similar. Helping Willow pick up fallen cash from the register. It was the beginning of our friendship.

My stomach roiled at the thought of the beginning of *theirs.* I stewed silently, and Maya must've seen my irritation. She gave me a look like, *don't do anything bad.* "He's *very* valuable to our team."

Valuable. "How?"

"He's a walking Marvel encyclopedia. He knows every character, every comic line, unlike other employees." *Unlike me.* I probably won't ever be Maya's favorite, not after making her job as store manager harder, but I won't stop trying to make it up to her.

I didn't even complain when she gave me toilet duty this week. And the bathrooms were so shitty. Pun intended.

I push Ace to the back of my brain and focus on the questionnaire again.

Last time you screwed up something important:
probably yesterday. Every day. Story of my life.

Currently...

What turns you on: girls with glasses.

My lips start to rise, a little surprised she asked this one.

What turns you off: anyone who's "mean" to girls with glasses.

Are you pissed at anyone: pick a brother.

Have you ever...

Been scared of the dark: never.

Cried in front of your parents: only when I was a baby

Kept a journal: nah

What do you like...

Love or Lust: only ever known lust.

Text or Call: text most of the time.

Nerds or Geeks: geeks, definitely.

Done. Not tagging anyone else, I slip my phone in my jeans pocket and then loosen my leather bracelet that digs into my wrist bone. A pack of cigarettes sits heavy in my leather jacket, but I can't really smoke inside the mall. Not to mention, I'm trying to curb the habit.

I retie my black Converse shoes for something to do, and when I look up, I see her.

Down the stretch of mall hallway, Willow spots me too, and she waves sheepishly—and her awkward smile causes my lips to curve higher than before. I skim her head-to-toe. Like I didn't just hang out with her yesterday at Superheroes & Scones.

She wears a mustard yellow shirt beneath saggy, faded overalls. Not especially trendy or something people would "like" on Instagram.

Just…geeky. No makeup, but she rarely ever wears much more than eyeliner. Her light brown hair is twisted in a sloppy braid. Flyaway pieces escape, and baby hairs stick up by her forehead.

It's nice to be around someone comfortable with who they are—and who they want to be—without bowing to peer pressure. In class last week, Rachel showed Willow a YouTube video of how to braid hair after critiquing all of her loose strands.

Willow thanked Rachel for the suggestions, but she never bothered with the "proper" technique.

Closer, Willow grabs tight of the strap to her JanSport backpack, always slightly tucked into herself. Overly aware of the strollers, the bumbling people, the sheer amount of bodies, and the many hands clutching Styrofoam coffee cups.

I see her mouth a few apologies for brushing arms with people, and she glances cautiously left and right. The crowds don't cause her to fall back. She pushes through anxiety to reach me and the arcade.

I'm appreciative…more than I can even express.

"Am I late?" She nudges up black-rimmed glasses and checks her phone.

I knot my laces and rise. "Nah. I'm just early." I gesture with my head to the arcade. "I had nothing better to do."

"Oh." Willow tries hard to stifle a smile. "Yeah…me too. Sort of."

"Sort of?" I hold the door open.

As she slips inside the nearly empty arcade, she says, "I got distracted this morning."

Ace Davenport. I frown and catch up to her side. "With what?" *That douchebag Marvel encyclopedia.*

"Lily let me feed Moffy dry cereal for the first time…I mean, he's allowed to eat solid foods, but it's the first time that I fed him. It's kind of cool that she trusts me with her baby."

And it's kind of fucking cool that Willow trusts me with anything related to Lily and Loren Hale, especially Maximoff Hale. Their son is like media fodder. *Celebrity Crush* eats up any and all information about their baby, who can't be older than five or six months now.

After Halloween, I already swore up and down to Willow that I'd *never* sell a single word to the tabloids. If I ever break this promise, she has full permission to spill any of my secrets to the world, my parents—whoever she wants. When I said that, we both paused in silence, remembering when I showed her my tattoos…and bruises.

In the end, I think she trusts me because I have no reason to speak to *Celebrity Crush* editors and reporters. I don't need the money. I'm not looking for fame or notoriety. I literally want to be left alone.

I'm also no longer surprised when Willow acts like she sits on the outskirts of the Hales when she's Loren's cousin. She mentioned her mom being estranged from everyone, and therefore, she was too.

"Would you babysit if they asked?" I wonder.

Willow nods with a growing smile. "I'm used to babies since Ellie is so much younger than me. I helped my mom a lot." She stares off for a second. "I can't even believe this is my life. I can hold Maximoff Hale—do you know how many people just want to touch his pinky?"

"About forty-five thousand."

She skids to a stop in the middle of the arcade. Retro machines line star-patterned carpet, and glow-in-the-dark moons and planets are glued to the ceiling. "You saw the poll?" she asks, color draining from her cheeks.

"The one on Twitter asking a *yes* or *no* question about Maximoff's pinky finger? No, never seen it," I tease.

Willow presses her lips together, hiding another giddy smile. Something flutters in my stomach—which is lame. But whatever. I don't care. I'll be lame with this girl.

We drift subconsciously towards the *Streets of Rage* machine.

"I didn't post that poll," she says more quietly, "but I definitely entered…and it's weird, right, that I'm so enamored by a baby just because he's famous?" She frowns in thought.

"Not weird. Not when the media makes the baby seem like American royalty."

Willow mutters, "Prince Moffy," with an awkward smile, not intending for me to see. When she notices me staring, she clears her throat and touches her lips. "Uhh...yeah."

"Hey, Prince Maximoff fanfic might *actually* be a thing when he's a teenager."

"I'd read it," Willow says and adds, "but in a...non-creepy way. I'm related to him. It's just like entertainment...like television. Sort of."

"Yeah, sort of," I agree, aching to stretch my arm over her shoulders, but I tense more. We stand side-by-side in front of the *Streets of Rage* control panel: red and blue joysticks and a couple buttons each. Nothing fancy or complicated.

I strain my ears to catch her muttering, "I'm talking too much."

"You're not talking too much, trust me," I assure Willow. "You could be quiet the whole day too, and that'd be okay. I just like being with you." I want to retract that last part because she stiffens a little more.

Tension winds between us.

"As friends," I add.

She eases more.

Just friends then. Right. *Just friends.* It's easier. I know that.

Willow lets out a breath and then meets my eyes. "Before we play...can I ask you to do something for me. I mean, it's okay if you say no. It won't hurt my feelings."

I nod, curious about where she's headed.

Willow sets the JanSport backpack at her sneakers and then unzips a pocket. Retrieving a phone, she clicks into the camera app. "So you know Maggie?"

"Your friend from Maine." *Her only friend.* Before I came along.

"Every day she asks me about Lo and Lily, sometimes even Connor and Rose, and Ryke and Daisy...and I can't answer her questions. She hasn't been answering my texts in two days, which isn't like her, and she unfollowed me on Twitter."

"Damn." I rest my elbow on the control panel.

"I know, it's bad."

I frown. "All because you wouldn't talk about your cousin and his friends?"

Willow flips the cellphone in her hand. "I used to tell Maggie everything. She has a right to be mad and upset that I'm...I'm shutting her out. I'd be sad too, and I want to share my life in Philly with her. I just can't share *that* side."

It clicks. "You want to share *me?*"

Willow pales again. "Not like *share you,* share you—"

I hold out my hand to stop her eyes from widening. "I know what you meant." I see how hard this is for her to ask. We may spend a lot of time in each other's company, but she still has no idea how I'll react to new situations or where our friendship boundaries lie.

New friendships come with a shit ton of untested waters, and half the fun is testing them—but then there's the risk of drowning the friendship altogether.

With a deep breath, Willow asks, "Can I take a selfie with you?"

I think I'll always remember this moment.

We haven't really taken each other's picture. Not even during Halloween. Not alone or together. I'm not opposed to photos either. People tag me in pictures on Facebook and Instagram all the time. Most of them are of me at parties with friends.

My father scolded me about a few that "future employers" would deem disrespectful and irresponsible. Underage drinking in one picture, and about six or seven show me giving rude gestures to the camera.

Without hesitation, I hold out my hand for her phone. "I have longer arms for a selfie."

She wavers. "So that's a...yes?" Seeing that it is—even before I answer—she hands me the phone.

"Yeah." I tweak the lighting settings, and then I raise the camera towards us. She stands on her tiptoes to be closer to me, the *Streets of Rage* machine a backdrop.

I dip my head towards hers, my hair brushing my eyelashes. We're not touching, but the *not touching* thing almost builds more tension.

A good kind.

Willow smiles that awkward smile, more horizontal like a line than upturned like a U. She looks happy, and I look like the delinquent everyone believes I am.

I snap several photos and then return the phone. "What are you telling her?"

Willow texts Maggie quickly. "*This is my friend Garrison. We're playing Streets of Rage. Wish you were here! Visit when you can.* You think that's enough?"

"Maybe add emojis. Hearts, sparkles, pizza."

Willow has this look like she wants to say something, but she's mulling over her words. Thinking about them. And then finally, she says, "You know, um, if we ever fight, now I know what emojis will bring you back." Avoiding my reaction, she slips the cellphone into her backpack.

"If we ever fought, it'd be my fault, and I'd be the one to send you pizza emojis and penguins, some turtles." She's smiling. "Maybe a raccoon."

"There's a raccoon emoji?" She braves a glance at me.

I have no idea. "I'll make one." I reach into my pocket for change, but Willow is already pulling out a Ziploc baggie filled with a ton of quarters.

"No," I instantly decline. "I'm paying." *It's a date.* I haven't announced this or anything, but in my mind, it's sort of a date. Kind of.

It could be.

Willow hesitates but then opens the baggie. "You can't pay."

I shift my weight and comb back the long pieces of my dark hair. "Why not?" *She doesn't want this to be a date, you idiot.*

"It's your birthday." She pops two quarters into the coin slots, one for player 1 and one for player 2.

I was the one who sent the Twitter message: Blaze, want to kick some ass today? Galactica Arcadia, noon-ish.

Willow replied: sure, Axel.

Now we face the game with the characters Blaze and Axel, prepared to wipe crime off a city street using crowbars and broken bottles.

I never meant this arcade outing to be a "birthday thing" but my date of birth is posted on all of my social medias. So she knows.

"Hey," I say before we start playing, "do you want to hang out after this? Nothing birthday-related. I just figured we could do that *Supernatural* marathon tonight, if you want to." I keep postponing on her, and she's too nice to bug me about it.

"Yeah," she says instantly. "Yeah, of course. Still at your house?"

I nod. "Still at my house." It's weird. I've never shied from bringing anyone over to my family's place, but I like keeping Willow to myself and far, *far* away from my parent's unwanted opinions.

17

Willow Moore

PLAYING VIDEO GAMES WITH GARRISON ABBEY IS LIKE SHARING one milkshake with two straws. I wear an uncontrollable smile that hurts my face. The kind of smile I've tried to suppress, but it's becoming fruitless the longer we play *Streets of Rage* in Galactica Arcadia.

I can only remember feeling this way one other time, when I imagined Tom Hiddleston (AKA Loki, Thor's brother and foe) running into me at Superheroes & Scones. He's never actually been to the comic book shop, but sometimes dreams are better than reality.

Except *this* reality. Right here and now, my cheeks are sore from the amount of times they've stretched towards my ears. We laugh. We curse when the game bosses arrive, and he helps me when I fumble with special combinations.

I may be better at everything comic-book-related, but Garrison is an absolute pro at gaming. I think he'd be able to work both joysticks and buttons with relative ease.

Time slips by fast, and when we run out of quarters, we come to a stop.

"New high score," Garrison reads the screen. We're second to someone who typed in the three initials: SUX.

"Not very clever, is it?" I say, pointing at the SUX scoreboard leader. It's the go-to initials for one-time players, really. Lots of machines probably have at least two *sux* in their records.

"I never really am that clever," Garrison tells me, catching me off guard.

"Wait…what?" My mouth falls. "This…is you?" I gesture to SUX, and as he nods, I want to collapse on the star-patterned carpet and bury my head. I just insulted him.

On his birthday.

What kind of friend am I?

My new eulogy: *that turd, Willow Moore, she's a "whatever" kind of friend. You should've left her while you had the chance.*

Garrison isn't looking at my downtrodden features. He's scrolling through letters to lock in the initials: GPW. I barely hear him say, "Garrison Plus Willow."

If he's not hurt over the comment, then I shouldn't agonize over it either, but for some reason, I zone in on *this* awkward part over every other great one. I wish I wouldn't do that. I rub my face beneath my glasses and then fit them on again.

"You okay?" he asks, not even noticing what threw me off. I'm making something out of nothing. Before I say *yeah*, his gaze travels to the glass entrance, and he curses, "Shit."

A scruffy older man lingers outside the arcade, his phone positioned towards us like he's using the camera. He must be playing the part of "coy paparazzi" today. I'm not sure if cameramen are allowed inside the mall or not, but I'm certain he's here because of me.

"I'll go to the bathroom," I say, "and when I come back, he'll probably be gone." I think I'm pretty boring compared to the Calloway sisters, and if I'm not with them or my brother, only one or two cameramen usually trail me during a whole week. It's not even a daily occurrence like it is for them.

"I'll wait here." Garrison keeps an eye on the older man.

I depart and find my way through the rows of arcade machines. The bathroom is lit with a neon sign that says *Relieve Yourself.* I grab the doorknob to the girl's bathroom.

"You're Loren Hale's cousin," someone says behind me, the male voice more accusatory than questioning.

I glance over my shoulder. A preppy guy waits outside the boy's bathroom. Collared shirt, khaki slacks, combed blond hair, twenty-something-years-old—he looks like a walking fraternity ad. Except for his face.

His angular features hold more contempt than I've ever personally met. *He knows Loren Hale. And he hates him.* It's the only conclusion that makes sense.

I instinctively shrink and refuse to answer the preppy guy. I just slip into the girl's bathroom. A sickening feeling descends to the bottom of my stomach.

"Nothing's going to happen," I mumble and reach for my backpack. I freeze.

I left my backpack with Garrison. *I have no phone.* "Okay," I whisper to myself and exhale a short breath. I'm making up something out of nothing again. That's what this is. At the sink, I remove my glasses and splash water on my face.

People say, *trust your gut.*

They also say, *step out of your comfort zone.*

So which one is this? Just a regular bout of anxiety or a real threat? How do I even determine the difference?

Using a paper towel, I wipe dripping water off my face, slip on my glasses, and look into the mirror. *That Willow Moore.* I've lost color in my cheeks, and my flyaway hairs stick to my forehead.

I swallow. "Step out of your comfort zone," I tell myself.

After tossing the paper towel, I exit, hoping the person has left. The minute I swing open the door, I'm met with *two* preppy twenty-somethings.

Hatred flames their eyes.

"That's definitely his cousin," the new guy says, looking from me to his cellphone screen. He must have found a picture of *Loren Hale's cousin!* from the internet.

I rush to leave, but the angular-faced guy physically blocks my path. I take a step backwards. "I'm just trying to leave," I say, much softer than I intend. "I don't know you."

"But we know Loren," the angular-faced guy says. "He slashed the tires of our car in college."

"Oh." *Oh my God.* "I'm sorry about that—"

He plucks my glasses right off my face.

I gasp and reach out for them, but I can't see. I catch air. My world is a blurry mess, especially with the dark lighting and the glow-in-the-dark shapes.

I hear the *crunch* beneath his shoe.

My heart nosedives. He...he just broke my glasses.

"You tell Loren that the public may love the person he's selling them, but everyone who *truly* knows Loren Hale still hates the fuck out of him."

I back up into the wall and reach out for the bathroom knob. I knock off a poster or something, and I go completely still.

They no longer speak. I listen for their footsteps, but it's hard to hear over the pinging of arcade machines. I think they left. *I hope they left.*

"Garrison," I say in a panicked breath. I meant to yell his name. So I try again. "Garrison." Slightly louder. Not loud enough. I crouch into a squat, feeling the carpet for my glasses. "Garrison!"

I touch the bent frame, broken in half, and the lenses are shattered. I prick my finger on the sharp glass and retract my hand.

"Willow!" Garrison must sprint because he's next to me in a hurried second. "What happened? What the hell?"

I can't see him. I can't see *anything* in here.

I start to ask, "Can I—"

He knows what I want. Garrison immediately catches my trembling hand and helps me to my feet. I edge closer to his frame, and his other palm rests on my waist. My heart beats so fast.

If I start picturing their faces, emotion threatens to well and glass my eyes. It's not even that I met real hatred for the first time. It's that they feel this boiling disgust towards someone I love.

Garrison keeps me close. "Do you have an extra pair of glasses in your backpack?"

"No, just in my room." My throat swells closed, but before he asks again, I start briefly explaining the encounter. He scans the arcade for signs of "preppy" guys, but he says it looks like they're gone.

Of course, I can't read his expression, but his body radiates with heat, angry and upset. Instead of hunting them down, thankfully he stays beside me.

My hand in his hand, he guides me out of the arcade. My backpack slung over his shoulder. (I ask to make sure he hasn't left it.) But I'm too nervous to ask if the cameraman is still looming.

"Escalator," Garrison says, pulling me back as I try to walk forward. His arm is wrapped securely around my waist.

Oh my God. Through everything that's happened, I still heat from the new touch. I can't help it. I'm stiffer than him. I'm unbending and hardly breathing properly.

Focus. I start to whisper, "I can't tell Loren what happ—"

"I hate *The Omen* too," Garrison cuts in, raising his voice. "There are so many better horror movies than that one."

I understand the hint. The older man with the camera phone—he must be right behind us. Riding down the escalator. Video-recording our conversation. Our every move.

I shudder. And this is just a taste of what Lily and her sisters deal with every day.

We both stay quiet until we reach the parking lot. Once inside his Mustang, Garrison locks the car doors. Lily dropped me off at the mall on her way to Superheroes & Scones, so my car is still at my brother's house.

The plan had always been to leave the mall in Garrison's car, but not…this soon. Not like this. I struggle with my seatbelt, unable to find the hole for the metal tip.

"Here." Garrison stretches over the middle console and helps, his hand on my hand. My nerves flutter. He guides the buckle, and I hear the *click*.

Secured.

Garrison places my backpack on my lap, and I hug the jean fabric to my chest. He pauses before starting the car. I feel him studying my features.

I replay what happened, and I go numb. My skin tingles as I try to submerge emotion like my mom taught me to do. *Don't let it out for other people to see. Bottle every last bit.*

He breaks the silence. "Did they touch you?"

I shake my head, the motion heavy. "Just my glasses." I swallow again. "I'm fine." *It could've been worse.* Partly, I think I'm in shock, throttled by the "could've beens" and the regret of not trusting my gut.

Garrison lets out a tense breath, his keys jangling like he's about to start up the ignition. He stops short. "What can I do to help?"

I open my mouth to speak, but I have no clue what to say.

"Will holding you make you feel worse or better?"

I shake my head again. Unsure. "I don't know." Tears threaten to rise, overwhelmed by everything: what happened, this moment, how nice he's being to me.

"You know I'm here for you," he tells me.

I nod and instinctively try to push up my glasses—which do not exist right now. "Thanks." We make a game plan to fetch my spare glasses at my place in Philly, and then we'll head to his house. I assure him that I'm not too shaken and that I still want to hang out.

He acts like his birthday means nothing to him, but he once mentioned that all his birthdays were spent with lots of friends. I imagine the crowds resembled the ones at Nathan's party—the one I crashed on my search for Lo.

Now Garrison is down to just one friend. Me. He has no extravagant party. No adoring crowds. He just has Willow Moore from Maine, and I hoped this would be a birthday he wishes to remember, not one he craves to forget.

I can't really replace his old friends, and I worry, in time, he'll only yearn for them more.

18

Willow Moore

"SO THIS IS MY ROOM." GARRISON SWINGS OPEN HIS DOOR. His house is abnormally large. Mansion-sized. A dream home. I'd get lost finding a bathroom if there weren't seven of them.

"Whoa." My eyes widen behind my spare glasses, vision impeccably clear. His bedroom quadruples my tiny dorm room.

With a curious gaze, I quickly sweep the area: king-sized bed, plain black comforter, a huge entertainment system against one wall (stereo speakers, multiple game consoles, flat-screen television), plush carpet, framed vintage Nintendo posters, and shelves and shelves of horror movies.

One thing is excruciatingly apparent: he is *neat*. And clean.

So clean, in fact, that I wonder if I should take off my shoes. Instead of asking, I notice that he keeps on his Converses, so I decide to leave on my sneakers.

Walking further inside, my head swerves left and right. Laptop propped on his sleek metal desk, the screen is black. No turtle, but I remember he said that Abracadabra first belonged to his brother Mitchell. Maybe the turtle's tank stays in Mitchell's room.

Garrison tosses a couple expensive black beanbags to the floor.

When he takes a seat, I plop down next to him and keep gazing at every wall and shelf.

He flips the remote in his hand and then glances at me. "What've you noticed?"

You have no pictures of your family. "You're not messy at all." No ashtray with cigarette butts. No scattered, half-opened DVD cases. No Fizz or Lightning Bolt! cans.

"That's because a maid cleans once a week," he explains.

I remember his spotless car, and I doubt the maid cleans his Mustang too. "Did she just come?"

Garrison contemplates this for a second. "No...I think she comes tomorrow."

If his room looks this picked-up after a whole week, then it proves he's neat. After two days, a pile of dirty clothes usually compounds on my desk chair.

At first I wonder if he's scared to be called neat, but after a while, I realize that maybe no one has ever pointed this out until now. Maybe he's never noticed his own trait.

Garrison switches on a DVD player for *Supernatural.* The title screen with Sam and Dean Winchester appears. I'm deeply aware that I'm currently in a boy's bedroom.

Alone. About to watch a television show.

We're just friends, I remind myself, still trying to relax and not sit so stiffly. Or else my stomach will start cramping.

More nervous than giddy, I interlace my fingers and unlace them. Unsure of where to put my hands. I try not to be suggestive.

After Garrison presses *play* on the episode I left off, he glances at me and shifts his arm close but then tenses. Pauses.

He ends up clutching his knee.

Someone knocks on the door—we both jump.

"Shit." Garrison hops to his feet, and he looks back at me with a *you alright?* expression. I nod, and he focuses on the incomer and opens the door.

For some reason, I expect his brothers, but the moment a stunning brunette woman appears, I remember they're away at college.

Standing on the other side of the doorway, his mom wears a pink dress that molds her hourglass figure. Diamonds cascade off her ears and neck, and her makeup, all pink shades, gives her a benevolent glow. Her straight hair is slightly curled on the ends, the kind of perfection I've only seen on *Real Housewives* shows. (Maybe she has a personal hairstylist.)

She's unquestionably beautiful, and if she wasn't a former model or beauty queen in her younger years, I bet people told her that she could easily be both.

Mrs. Abbey meets her youngest son's dour expression with a heavy sigh. "What did I do now?"

"Nothing," he snaps. "I'm just busy."

She peers into the room, at me, and offers a tiny smile before returning to Garrison. "If I knew you were bringing a boy over, I could've ordered pizza for you both."

Oh my God. She thinks I'm a boy? I stare down at my baggy overalls. *Don't change,* I try to remind myself. *Don't change because of his mom.*

"She's a *girl,*" Garrison emphasizes, and even though I only see the back of his head, I imagine his eyes narrowing a little. "And I already told you that I didn't need anything today."

Mrs. Abbey sighs again. "Why do you have to speak to me in that tone?"

Garrison shrugs. "Sorry." His voice is entirely dry, and I try to concentrate on my cellphone to give them privacy. It's hard not to overhear.

"You're acting like I've demolished your entire world, and all I wanted to do was say *hello, how was your day?*" She seems nice.

Garrison grips the door like he's seconds from slamming it closed. "It was really good. Now can I go?"

Mrs. Abbey's blue-green eyes flit to me, then back to him, and she tries to lower her voice. I still hear her say, "What happened to Rachel?"

He groans. "We've been over this. Rachel isn't my friend anymore." In my U.S. Government class, I heard Rachel vilifying Garrison. Saying things like, *he should've convinced Nathan and his friends to do the right thing. He's no better than them.*

She hates him.

"I just spoke to her mother yesterday," Mrs. Abbey explains. "She may forgive you if you just apologize and spend a little time—"

"*No*," Garrison cuts in. "I don't care about befriending Rachel again."

"She's a sweet girl," Mrs. Abbey continues. "I always thought she'd be a great influence on you, and if you go to the same college—"

"Mom," he groans and rests his hands on his head. "Just accept that your hopes and dreams of me marrying Zeta Beta Zeta royalty are over and *move on*. It's not like Rachel and I were ever a thing. You just made it all up in your mind because you're best friends with Rachel's mom."

"That's not true," she says, offended. "I just want what's best for you."

Garrison goes rigid, and eerie silence passes. A lump rises to my throat, but I stay quiet and respect their space.

Mrs. Abbey says softly, "You should apologize to Hunter."

Garrison drops his hands and stares at the floor.

"He graciously invited you to Penn for the weekend, and he told me that you cursed at him. Every single one of your brothers is making an effort to include you in their lives, and you keep pushing them away."

"You know why," he says, almost inaudibly.

She sighs for the third time. "Boys play rough. Your father is right; you need to stop being so sensitive."

My lips part at her response, and Garrison has completely shut down. He no longer speaks back.

"All I want and hope and pray," she says, "is that my four boys will be together as family. *Please* don't make this Thanksgiving uncomfortable by hiding yourself in your room. *Please*." She looks and sounds on the verge of tears.

My stomach knots at what she's asking him to do. By being around his brothers, he risks another bruise, possibly a broken bone—his safety. Yet, she acts like *he's* at fault for the strained sibling relationship.

In the aching silence, I find myself standing up and saying softly but loud enough, "I invited Garrison to Thanksgiving with me." I didn't really, but I suppose I just did.

His head whips towards me, surprise opening his mouth.

I approach but not too close, and Mrs. Abbey tries to place my appearance. I seem familiar to her because I've appeared on entertainment news sites. Which is just surreal in itself.

"I'm Willow," I greet with a sheepish wave.

Recognition floods her face. "Loren Hale's cousin." *Half-sister*, I mentally correct. She touches her heart. "I deeply apologize for what my son did to your cous—"

"Mom," Garrison interjects. "You don't have to go around making amends for me. We're already friends." He gestures between me and him.

Mrs. Abbey forces a kind smile, obviously peeved by Garrison's attitude. "So you'll be spending Thanksgiving with the Hales then?"

"Um…" I hadn't thought about this. Lo has already offered, but I've been contemplating returning to Maine to spend a little time with Ellie. I've been saving for a plane ticket. "I might actually visit my little sister in Maine, but Garrison is welcome to come."

Garrison knows about my strained relationship with my mom and my little sister. Maybe that's why he says, "Thanks, Willow, but I can't."

Did I do the wrong thing by interjecting? I just wanted to give him an escape if he needed one.

Mrs. Abbey radiates with joy. As though Garrison's rejection of my offer was an affirmation that he'll try to get along with his brothers.

I drift backwards as Mrs. Abbey tells us to "have fun"—not even worried that we'll hook up. No mention of "keep the door open" or "behave responsibly"—just, *have fun*. I wonder if it's because I don't look like anyone Garrison would ever hook up with. Or if she'd categorize hooking up as a teenage expectation for her sons, so she's okay with it happening.

If she had a daughter, maybe she'd be more protective. Maybe it'd be different.

Garrison shuts and locks the door.

I return to the beanbag, and not long after, he joins me and grabs the remote. He waits to press *play*. The air is heavy and weighted.

I stare at my hands when he says, "I'm cursed. I'm fucking *cursed*, and if I spend Thanksgiving with you, I'll ruin your time with your mom and your sister—or your relationship with Loren Hale. I can't do that to you."

It's better than you staying here, I think but struggle to say. I rewind to the beginning. "Your mom knows." It nearly steals my breath again. She knows that his brothers have physically hurt him before.

He's so quiet that I turn my head. He hangs his forearms on his knees, and his solemn gaze sinks into mine. "Hunter would bloody my nose. I'd tell my parents, and they'd just say *why didn't you fight back?* To them, I'm the youngest, so being picked on is just expected. My dad said that my brothers were trying to make me tough, but…" Garrison trails off and cements his gaze on the floor. "You remember the first questionnaire?"

"Yeah." It's impossible to forget.

"Remember my answer to *any surgeries?*" he asks, unable to meet my eyes.

"I think so. You said something about breaking your wrist and leg and needing pins."

Garrison nods. "I was seven and nine. First one, my dad actually saw. Hunter was pretending to be some wrestler in the driveway, and he kept trying moves on me. I was screaming for him to stop, but he body-slammed me into concrete. My wrist broke, and the bone tore clean through the skin."

I remove my glasses, the lenses misting. "And your dad just shrugged it off?"

"Boys will be boys," Garrison says flatly.

"And your leg?"

"I was nine, and Davis thought it'd be funny to duct tape my mouth, legs, and hands and toss me in the pool. I sunk and struggled to reach the surface. I ended up blacking out at the bottom, and I was told that his friend dove in, pulled me out, and basically punched my stomach until I coughed up water."

I don't understand...how did he break his leg? And how could *anyone* do that to another person?

Garrison rubs his forehead like the memory hurts. "I stood up shaking, and Davis said, 'Why are you being such a wuss?'. He laughed and then struck my leg with a lacrosse stick. Bone fractured."

Horrified, I shake my head over and over.

"To him and his friends, it was all a joke. They were older. I was younger. I told my mom what happened, and she thanked the boy for saving me more than she scolded Davis for nearly drowning me."

I fit on my glasses, my pulse speeding at the thought of Garrison spending Thanksgiving with his brothers. Brothers that would do all of that and parents that would never acknowledge the harm.

Garrison looks over at me. "It's in the past."

Is it? I'm so scared for him. "I'd rather you...I...will you..." Why are words so difficult for me right now? I wipe beneath my eyes. "Maine is pretty, and my mom won't mind extra company. Ellie will probably like you more than she likes me."

He shakes his head like it's not possible. "I'll be fine here."

"What if you tell Lo? He might help—"

"*No.* Please don't tell him," he says, panicked. "It's not that bad anymore, Willow. Ever since they went to college, it's been easier. Hell, ever since I could *drive* it's been better." Before I speak, he adds, "Why don't you tell Loren about what happened today?"

"What do you mean?"

"The guys who broke your glasses," he snaps, not at me but rather at their invisible presences.

For a moment, I'd forgotten all about that. "I can't..." Lo will freak out. "I can't make his life harder. He has so much to deal with already."

Garrison twists his leather bracelet. "I'm scared for you," he says exactly what I feel for him. "If those guys find out where you live, I'll…" He pushes his hair out of his face. "You can spend the night here if you ever need to, you know."

I'm speechless.

He recovers by explaining, "This is a gated neighborhood. No one can get in that shouldn't be in here, and where you live, that apartment or dorm or whatever, it's not like it has a lot of security."

"I'll be okay," I say quietly, but the offer starts expelling the heavy tension. We acknowledge that we're on each other's side when other people aren't or can't be. I relax more than I did, and he leans against his own beanbag too.

"Sam and Dean?" he asks, remote braced in his hand. Ready to watch two hunters fight supernatural entities.

I agree with a nod, and he plays the episode. We're more light-hearted, and we pause the show every now and then to check Tumblr.

We scoot closer and closer on our beanbags, and four-hours in, our arms are pressed together. I'm more lying down than sitting. He clicks *play* after we paused the show and makes funny commentary about Dean eating a hamburger.

Another hour passes, and my eyes droop. I yawn, the television screen blurring.

I only notice that I fell asleep when my eyes snap open. My cheek—my cheek is on his chest.

Oh. My.

God.

I fell asleep on Garrison. I've never ever been that comfortable around a guy to do that. I gently lift my head and first glance at the television.

Sam and his lush hair are freeze-framed. Garrison waited for me to watch the rest. I feel his arm wrapped comfortingly around my back, and he watches as I sit further up.

Actually, he sits up with me. "You okay?"

I push up my glasses.

Garrison licks his dry lips. "You know I wouldn't do anything…"

"Yeah, I know." *Just friends.* My heart sinks. Do I want him to do something? Partially, maybe, but not at the cost of what we have now. "I'm just surprised."

Garrison tenses. "At what?"

"That…that I'd fall asleep on you." I'm being painfully honest, but dropping all these walls with someone has almost felt cathartic in a way. "I've never done that before. With anyone else, I mean."

His lip quirks.

"What?" I ask, his rare expression stealing my breath.

"I like being your first." Garrison almost smiles. "Ones are my thing, remember?"

"And zeroes," I remind him about the other number in computer language.

"Fuck the zeroes." Garrison balances his remote on his kneecap, and I'm more aware that he's probably been with many girls like this. It may be my first, but it's far from his. Still, he's sweet and slow with me, and I don't understand why.

"Why are you so nice to me?" I ask.

It takes him aback. He's confused, but he answers as well as he can, "Because it'd be impossible for me to be a dick to you. Is that what you're asking?"

"You just…you care about what's too far for me, and not many do."

"That," Garrison says in realization. "Yeah…" He licks his lips again, and my shyness skyrockets, tucking my arms around myself. I'm more open than usual because he's been so vulnerable with me.

Garrison retracts his arm, but we're still breathlessly close. "I understand what it's like to be pushed out of personal boundaries, and I wouldn't do that to someone. I'm not gonna do that to you, *ever.*"

My chest swells, and my smile overwhelms my face. *Stop smiling.* I try to bury my face in my hand. God, I'm such a dork.

"Can I hug you?" he asks in a breath.

I nod without removing my hand, and instantly, his arms extend around my shoulders, his biceps flexing. I reciprocate, but my arms curve around his chest much looser and lighter. He squeezes like he's mastered the art of hugging long ago.

We're still sitting on the beanbags, but the position isn't awkward. He holds me against his body like that's where he wants me to be.

My heart thuds harder.

I feel so safe with him, and I see that he feels equally safe with me. Comforted. At ease. He only draws back when I descend into my head and overthink about my actions. My limbs stiffen, and he retracts his arms.

"You know," he says, "I didn't even realize how unhappy I was with all my huge birthday parties until now."

"What's so different?"

"You." He nearly smiles. "One real friend instead of a hundred horrible ones."

I'm about to reply, but my phone buzzes in my backpack. I give him a look like *one second* and I scoot forward and dig through the backpack's contents. I find my cell and gape at the time.

Two in the morning.

Maya has sent me four texts.

Maya: Are you okay? It's getting late, and don't you have school tomorrow?

Maya: Can you respond just to let me know you're in one piece?

Maya: Not cool, Willow. If you don't answer this in thirty minutes, I'm going to have to text Loren. It's my roommate duty

Maya: Just called him

Not to mention the missed calls and texts from my brother, Lily, Daisy, Rose, and even Ryke and Connor. Maybe my backpack muffled them or most happened while I was asleep.

"Oh no," I mutter.

"What?" Garrison straightens up and stands just as I do.

"I have to go." Lo has called me *ten* times and left seven texts, which range from slightly worried, asking about where I am, to full-on panicked, saying that he's five minutes away from calling the cops to find me.

And then this text:

Loren: If someone's taken Willow's phone—if you've hurt her, I'm going to wring your goddamn neck and shove your dick inside your body, you little shitty motherfucker. You'll be peeing out of your asshole.

"I can drive you to your apartment." Garrison grabs his hoodie.

"No that's okay." I sling my backpack on my shoulder. "I need to pick up my car from Lo's house, so I'll just drive myself home. I can walk to Lo's." Before he offers to walk with me, I add, "If Lo sees that I was with you, I think he might pop a blood vessel. I've never seen him this angry." I show the text to Garrison.

He reads it quickly. "I've seen that side of him already. I'm not scared."

"You're on good footing with him though and that took a while." I don't want to ruin his relationship with Lo either.

"Yeah, but you shouldn't lie to your cousin about where you've been. Not because of me. I don't have to walk with you, but just don't lie to him."

"Are you sure?" I ask before I leave. He wants me to be honest with Loren Hale. "If I tell Lo the truth about where I've been…" *He may hate you.*

"I'm sure."

19

Willow Moore

ON MY WALK TOWARDS LO'S HOUSE, I TEXT HIM AND MAYA, apologizing profusely and reassuring that I'm one-hundred percent okay. I also mention that I'm almost to his house, and as soon as my feet hit the front porch steps, the door bursts open.

Lo wears nothing but drawstring pants, the night air chilly, but maybe his anger heats him. His cheekbones cut sharp, and he has his cellphone cupped to his ear.

"She's here," he says to the person on the other line. "I don't know why yet. Just get your ass back home, bro." *Must be Ryke Meadows.* "I'll tell her. Okay, *okay*. Bye." He hangs up, and I stand uneasily on the porch—only an arm's length away from my half-brother.

Lo clutches his cell tight. "Ryke and Daisy have been driving around looking for you." He lets out a tense breath. "My brother said to tell you that he's 'fucking glad you're okay' and 'Daisy loves you.'"

My lips upturn at Daisy's comment to me. When I'm with all of them—Lo and Lily, Rose and Connor, Ryke and Daisy—I thought for sure, I'd gravitate towards someone like Lily. Comic book geek, resident introvert, and a lover of pop culture.

But when we're all together, Daisy keeps me the most company. She metaphorically opened her arms to me, and I walked straight into them. Life is unpredictable that way. Because I would've never predicted befriending Daisy Calloway of all the Calloway sisters.

We're the closest in age, but it's more than that. She never pressures me to fill the silence, and when I do talk, she always listens.

Even if it's about superheroes and comic books that she's never heard of before.

Just three days ago, Daisy invited me to pick apples with her at an orchard.

She climbed an apple tree in the spur of the moment, and she gave me a tug and boost to the lowest tree limb. Something I never thought I'd do. She's adventurous and spontaneous, but she likes the quiet more than most people would even believe.

We sat up there and just listened to the wind.

I love spending time with Daisy, and to hear that she loves me back floods me with warmth.

But at the sight of Lo's sharp exterior, my small smile fades quickly.

"It's cold out here," he says. "Come inside." His voice is like knives.

I follow Lo through the foyer. Soft voices emanate from the living room, reminding me that Lo lives with five other people and two infants. Everyone tries to stay hushed at night because of the two sleeping babies: Jane Cobalt and Maximoff Hale.

Lo veers into the living room, a typical set-up: long couch, loveseat, and a Queen Anne chair placed towards the television and fireplace. I've hung out here enough that I'm less and less uncomfortable every time I enter.

Tonight, however, I hug onto my backpack strap and hesitate on whether to sit or stand. We're also not alone.

Rose Calloway, Lily's older and fashionable sister, looms strictly by the window, her nightgown hidden with a silky black robe. And her brown hair is pulled in a tight pony. She looks simultaneously concerned and high-strung.

To add to the sheer intimidation, Connor Cobalt, her six-foot-four, dapper husband towers beside her. His confidence radiates like the rarest, most intoxicating cologne. Just like Lo, he wears drawstring pants—and his chiseled abs…holy crap. I can't believe those are real.

Maggie would faint on the spot if she saw Connor Cobalt in his nightly glory.

I suddenly think, *can he tell I'm staring at his abs?* Paling, I whip my head towards Lo. What if Rose saw me ogling her husband?

This is so embarrassing.

That Willow Moore should've never been unleashed into the world. I hate that eulogy, but it's staying for the moment.

Lo glances at me as he walks towards the kitchen door. I'm about to follow until he says, "Stay here for a second." He rubs the back of his neck. "I need a minute." He searches the room for only one person: a gangly girl in a muscle shirt (*his* muscle shirt) that covers her thighs.

Lily hovers by the staircase, her eyes big with questions and worry. For him, I realize. They both wear this soul-bearing empathy for one another that's almost hard to stare at straight-on.

"Lily," he calls out, his voice still sharp but urgent.

Without hesitation, she bounds towards him, entangling her arms around his waist, and together, they disappear into the kitchen. Leaving me alone with Connor and Rose, two people I rarely, if ever, talk to alone.

Sure, in group settings, they exist and persist—but I still don't know them personally the way that I've come to know Daisy, Lo, and Lily. Even though they live here too, they're constantly on the go—and with the little free time they do have, they make room for Lo, Lily, Ryke, and Daisy. Not really me. (I don't blame them. I'm not that chatty or the greatest of company.)

So most of my information about Connor and Rose derive from *Princesses of Philly* and tabloids and eavesdropping (I try not to overhear but it happens).

I've read their bios on Wikipedia handfuls of times and deduced that they're two intellectually superior human beings. I mean, they *both* graduated valedictorian of their prep schools and they competed in academic competitions all throughout college.

At this point in my life, I can barely pass Calculus.

I eye the closed kitchen door, worried about Lo. I strain my ears, but their voices aren't audible at all. *I upset him. This is my fault.*

It's all I can think now.

"Let me handle this, Richard," Rose says under her breath, but her voice escalates with each syllable. "You can take a backseat."

"Are you ill?" He touches her forehead, and she swats his hand away.

Rose glares a boiling glare and perches her hands on her hips. "That is the dumbest question you've asked me this week. I am standing right in front of you, *perfectly* healthy and coherent."

"Then why else have you forgotten that your husband, me—"

"I know you're my husband," she growls.

"—never takes the metaphorical backseat in your metaphorical vehicle," he finishes without pause. Without flinching either.

My eyes grow wide, stunned that I'm witnessing their rapid-fire back-and-forths up close and not on *Princesses of Philly*. I can't remember where Lily first dubbed these moments "nerd star" flirt-fighting. Maybe in the reality show or on social media.

I can't stop watching.

I'm hooked.

Maggie would love this. I almost retrieve my phone, but I know better than to film them and send the video to my friend. I keep my cell hidden in my backpack. Where it needs to stay.

"I've forgotten nothing," Rose spouts, heated whereas he's calm and cool. "I just put you in the backseat, Richard. Stay. There."

I forget that his middle name is actually Connor, and Richard is his real first name. Only Rose seems to constantly use it. Mostly as ammunition.

Connor grins. "The fact that you still believe you can order me around like a child is partially inane and partially amusing."

"You're *fully* aggravating—and stop grinning that way." Rose covers his mouth with her hand and growls into an annoyed groan.

It looks like he's grinning more, even beneath her palm.

She drops her hand. "Why can't you just let me drive the vehicle?"

"I will, but I'm not going to be relegated to the backseat. I'm sitting next to you in every metaphorical scenario, darling." He cups her cheek, and she lets him. Softly, he says a string of melodic-sounding French that I can't even begin to translate.

Rose raises her chin, treaties in her yellow-green eyes, and she whispers French in reply. She touches his hand on her cheek, and Connor brings them down, lacing their fingers together.

Then they spin towards me.

"Uh…" I gulp, not prepared to be the center of attention when it comes to the nerd stars.

"You should sit," Rose says coldly.

She's not really ever sweet-natured. I can tell she's not intending to be harsh when she approaches the Queen Anne chair and pats the cushion.

Rose is letting me sit in *her* chair? Lo and Ryke often tease her about that chair, but their words never dissuade her from taking a seat with crossed ankles.

Walking around furniture, I lower stiffly onto the regal chair, and then, nearly in unison, Rose and Connor sit on the adjacent couch. Rose looks a bit peeved by the synchronization, but she makes no mention of it.

Connor is staring through me. With his genius-level intellect, I question whether he can interpret my body language.

I hug my backpack on my lap and risk a glance at the kitchen door. No sound, no movement—*nothing.*

"Do you need anything?" Rose asks, making this less like an interrogation. "Coffee or a blanket?"

"No…thanks," I say, still a little uneasy.

Rose nods, her posture like a wooden board. "I can't sugarcoat anything, so if you can't handle bluntness, then I advise you to cover your ears or wait for Connor to spell out everything in his *nauseatingly* smooth voice."

"She means *pleasantly*," Connor says with a growing grin.

Rose drills a glare between his blue eyes. "I hate your voice."

"You love my voice," he rephrases.

I hope they continue to digress so I can leave this conversation without saying another word.

Rose unknowingly scoots closer to him, their eyes locked together in battle. "Is your name Rose Calloway—*no*, it's not. Therefore, you shouldn't translate my already intelligible words."

"I'm reading the subtext of your statements."

Rose snorts.

He continues, "Yes, you hate my voice, but you also love my voice. Tell me otherwise, and I'll stop."

"You'll stop chiming in?" She's disbelieving.

Connor arches a brow. "Only if I'm wrong, which I know I'm not."

Rose rolls her eyes and sighs. "How can I both love and hate your voice?" She doesn't deny the fact that she does.

"Because," he says, "you're a beautiful paradox."

Rose nearly smiles, but she seems to remember me, her game-face returning. Straightening up, she says, "Where was I?"

I shake my head. I'm just as lost.

"You want to be blunt with her," Connor reminds Rose. He's firmly on his wife's side, not about to come to my defense, if I even need one.

"Willow," Rose begins, "we all feel a semblance of responsibility for you, and while that may seem absurd since you're seventeen and clearly a young adult, we're still the people that'll take care of you if something were to go horribly awry in Philly."

I nod, hardly breathing.

Rose is about to swing a figurative axe. I see the power simmer through her. "Therefore," she says, "you *have* to think about us when you're out late at night. Alone. With too many fucking perverts that know your name when you have no idea who they are. Not to mention, the rabid, foaming-at-the-repulsive-mouth paparazzi." Rose lets out a single breath, on a hot streak. "We're all you have here, and we'd break our backs for you. Leave your phone on. Text. Call—whatever it takes."

The last three words ring in my head like a cliffhanger to a story about family and friendship and love. She's asking me to embrace them entirely, even when I don't fully know her beyond the media and the encouragements she's given me in the past—but I'm not here to be a burden or a nuisance.

I've already screwed that up. Yet, I still feel myself retracting. Wanting to distance myself so I'll never ever bother them again.

In the most tranquil voice, Connor says, "We also recognize your reluctance to integrate with the six of us."

They have?

"When we go out," he continues, "you decline our invites because you're afraid to be a hassle, and you refuse to move in because you're afraid to alter Lo's life."

I ruined that tonight. Before, I was a peaceful shadow. Now I've become trouble. Someone Lo probably wishes he could return.

I'm sorry, Lo.

Connor edges forward on the couch, as though reaching towards me with his calming eyes alone. "You have affected Loren Hale." It crushes me, tears welling, and before I apologize, he says, "You have brought your brother *love*, and with love comes an unbearable amount of worry that I used to believe made people weak."

Rose is watching her husband, eyes cast proudly and affectionately on him, and I'm caught in Connor's vortex of wisdom and reverence.

"Lo isn't weak," Connor tells me. "He's just trying to figure out how to love a sister and protect a sister at the same time, all without hurting you with his *imaginative* vocabulary."

Rose nods in agreement. "If someone knows how to slaughter with words, it's Loren Hale."

"And he's afraid to slaughter you," Connor finishes.

My lips part, and they wait for me to speak. "Maybe…maybe I should stay away."

Rose gapes. "*No.* That's not what we're trying to say. We want you *here*. With us." She nearly rises out of passion, but Connor tugs her down, seeing that I'm uncomfortable. Rose continues on in a fiery rant, "You are family. *We* are family, and family fucks up and can be the biggest pains in the asses—but we're also the very best when we're together. Not apart."

I want that.

I do.

It sounds beautiful, but I can't fuck Lo up. He has a baby and a wife, and he's a recovering addict. So is Lily.

I wipe my wet eyes beneath my glasses, and then I hear the front door swing open. I go very still. Rose cranes her neck over her shoulder as Ryke Meadows storms into the house. Not acknowledging us, he sets his focused eyes on the kitchen door, his features hard, jaw scruffy and dark brown hair messy. Somehow he knows that his brother lies behind the kitchen door.

He heads straight for him.

Ryke vanishes inside, the better sibling to Loren Hale between the two of us.

I slump in my seat, and then Daisy enters the living room. "Hey, guys," she greets with a bright smile that eviscerates the lingering tension.

I breathe easier.

Supermodel tall with brown hair, Daisy rounds the furniture to head towards me. I'm used to seeing Daisy with blonde hair on the reality show, and at one point afterwards, she dyed her hair an array of colors.

She told me that this is her natural color. The brown hue makes her seem younger in a way. Then again, in fashion ads, she looks *Rose's* age, all made-up with dark lipstick, smoky eyes, and sultry clothes. I'm not sure about the true facts or timeline, but Daisy quit modeling after she was thrown into the Paris riot a couple years ago (the one that started from an overly passionate rugby championship game).

Fans on Tumblr believe she quit modeling because of the thick scar that runs down her cheek to her jaw. I can't be sure what's fabricated and what's real, but she did once mention that modeling wasn't fun for her. It'd been her mom's idea to approach agencies.

Dressed in a pair of Ryke's track pants and a long-sleeved shirt that says *wilder than the wind*, Daisy sits on the armrest of the Queen Anne.

She mock gasps at me. "You're in one piece. It's a miracle." I smile at her theatrics while she looks to the ceiling and says, "Thank you, God."

Connor arches another brow. "No." That's all he says. *No.*

Daisy wags her brows at his brow. "Thank you, Connor, my savior. My one true love."

"Don't inflate his overinflated ego by comparing him to God," Rose says, tightening her ponytail.

"I'm hardly moved," Connor tells Rose. "She speaks falsehoods and lies. Her one true love is a barking dog."

Daisy only smiles, knowing Connor is referring to Ryke Meadows.

Just now, the kitchen door swings open, and silence blankets the living room.

Lo is the first one out, more assuredness in his step, but I cower, unable to make eye contact. I stare at my backpack and listen to the two other footsteps that belong to Lily and Ryke.

Out of my peripheral, I notice how Connor and Rose stand up with the others. Only Daisy remains seated next to me on the armrest. I can practically feel every pair of eyes boring into me, and I'm too timid to meet a single one.

"It's not like anyone died," Lo says, attempting to make a joke. His tone is too razor-sharp for one. No one speaks. No one even breathes. It's like the Grim Reaper plopped on the couch to watch us all, and we're all overly aware of its presence.

The quiet tension is killer.

"Jesus Christ," Lo says, "everyone, just calm down—and I shouldn't be the one saying that. Stop role-reversaling me."

"Reversaling isn't a word," Connor says, "and I'm always calm, darling."

Ryke Meadows rolls his eyes and mumbles under his breath while Lily bites her nails, catches herself, and stops.

"I'm sorry," I suddenly and softly apologize to everyone while we're all gathered. I stare at my feet but try hard to lift my gaze. "I fell asleep, Lo. I didn't see how late it was…I'm really sorry. I'll text where I am next time. I promise."

Everyone is looking at me. My cheeks heat, and I only look up when Lo says, "It's not okay, what happened, but it will be." He very briefly glances at his brother, and Ryke glances back with a nod like *you're doing fucking great, little brother*—and I wonder how much of what he said belonged to Ryke Meadows first.

Lo can't soften his features all that much, but he clears his throat before he speaks again. "Where were you?"

"The mall and then…Garrison Abbey's house."

Connor and Rose look more than perturbed. They're not fans of Garrison, for very good reasons. I don't risk reading anyone else's expression but my brother's.

Lo repeatedly rubs the back of his neck, and then he says, "Everyone, you all should leave while I talk to my sister alone." Lo quickly adds, "I can handle it. Alright? *Go*." He snaps at them and then shoos them away with two hands.

Rose combats, "We'll stay quiet." I think she must like to be in-the-know about everything.

Lo points at me. "Not your sister, Queen Rose. She's mine."

Surrendering, Rose huffs and then departs upstairs with Connor. Lily trots slowly and tentatively behind them. Lo looks regretful for shooing her away, but he stands by the decision, not calling her back to the living room.

Ryke waits for Daisy, and she nods to me like *everything will be okay* and then exits into the kitchen with her boyfriend.

Lo takes a seat on the couch, forearms on his thighs, and a moment passes before he collects his words. "You're just seventeen, and I get it." He stares off like he's imagining himself at that age. I wonder who he was back then. What he was up to. If he loved Lily all the same. "I get that you're old enough to do everything I'm doing now."

I make a choice and set my backpack on the ground. He just told his support system to leave, and if he's strong enough to do that, then maybe I can be strong enough to let go of a crutch.

One day, I want to feel safe and powerful without holding my backpack tight.

"I still can't drink alcohol. I'm not twenty-one yet."

Lo wears a bitter smile. "Trust me, from experience, you can still drink. It being illegal didn't stop me." He hangs his head for a second, then lifts his amber eyes to my brown. "Maybe I gave you the wrong impression."

My lips downturn. "About what?"

"About Garrison, for one," he says. "Christ, I *never* expected you two to be…" He cringes like it's painful to think about.

"Friends?"

He tries to relax at that title. "Yeah, *that*. I know guys like him. I *was* like him—it's why I'm nicer to Garrison than I am to most people—but that doesn't mean I approve of you hanging out at his place on a Sunday night. Or *any* night. No sleepovers." He pauses. "Can I make that rule?"

He's my brother, not my dad, but I see that he's just trying to protect me. "Yeah," I nod. "I like that rule." It means he cares.

Someone wants me home at a certain hour.

Someone wants me safe.

Lo hesitates and stares off again, his face a bit murderous, and I wonder if he's thinking about Garrison. Regretting giving him a hand.

"I'm glad you're nice to him," I say. "I think he needs that more than me."

Lo shakes his head once. "You're my priority."

It swells and breaks my heart. "Don't hate him because of me."

Lo runs his tongue over the bottom of his teeth, and he barely nods. It's hard to take that as an affirmation. "You should know something," he says almost inaudibly.

"What?"

"I'm petty." He flashes that iconic half-smile. "I hold grudges, and in past history, I'm not the good person. But goddamn, I'm trying to be." He lets out a deep breath. "It's hard, and I can't…I just can't promise anything, Willow."

I wipe my nose that runs before my eyes leak. "I understand."

We're all complex people with many layers and strings, and I can't sit here and pretend to know all of theirs. All of his. But in time, maybe I will see more.

Maybe I will know the kind of person they all were and maybe I'll be here to witness the kind of people we'll all be.

MY CAR WON'T START.

I'm trying to return to my apartment, but my gold Honda sits like a hunk of junk in Lo's driveway. Hood popped, Ryke tinkers with the contents while Connor points a flashlight towards the engine.

"You already checked the battery's water level," Connor says. It's not his first comment or probably his last. `

Ryke glowers. "What the fuck did I say two minutes ago?"

"I purposefully ignore you when you tell me to shut the fuck up, especially if you're wasting time *repeating* actions you've taken." Connor points the flashlight towards another part of the car and instructs him—much to Ryke's annoyance.

Our breath smokes the air, the November temperature dropping fast tonight, but we all put on coats and shoes. I cup a mug of hot chocolate thanks to Daisy. Lo is on the phone, sending work emails I think, but he's close by—and Lily and Rose stay indoors for warmth.

Daisy said Rose would probably be out here helping, but Jane started crying through the baby monitor.

"I can just drive her in Rose's car," Daisy suggests for the tenth time.

"No," all the guys say in unison. Because apparently she's a reckless driver, and I'm not even sure if she has her license beyond a motorcycle one.

"It might be a clogged fuel filter...fuck." Ryke winces, his finger caught in something, but he shakes it out.

Daisy's face contorts, a little concerned for him. He's a rock climber, after all—his hands are precious. "Maybe we should take the car into the shop tomorrow," she says. "We can let Willow spend the night. That's probably what Lo wants, too."

"No, it's okay," I interject. "I can call an Uber or something." I think everyone needs space from me for a while.

"That seems unwise," Connor tells me while shining the flashlight for Ryke. "It's late and people know who you are."

"Famous people take Ubers all the time in Los Angeles...I think. And I mean, I'm not famous like all of you. You know...?" I want to stop talking now. Thanks.

"We're not in LA. We're in Philadelphia," Connor says in a way that makes me feel dumb for making the comparison.

"Fuck off, Cobalt," Ryke says from beneath the car hood.

Daisy suddenly swings her head to the left, and I follow her gaze. Warm lamplight illuminates the neighborhood street, but darkness lies beyond.

She solidifies, eerily motionless. "Did you hear that?" she asks me.

I listen closely, but besides Ryke toying with the car's mechanisms, I can't hear much else. "Not really..."

Daisy breathes shallowly, her knuckles whitening on her mug of hot chocolate. "Something's out there," she says under her breath.

My own fear spikes, partly afraid of what she sees and partly afraid for *her*—I've never seen someone look so haunted before.

Connor watches her closely, and Ryke turns his head to Daisy. His brows furrow, intensely concerned.

"Do you hear that?" she asks again. "Something's...not right."

"Hey, sweetheart," Ryke says in a gentle tone, "you're fucking safe. Nothing's out there."

Daisy flinches, so abruptly—like someone threw something at her—and she drops the hot chocolate to shield her face. The mug shatters on cement, and no object flies her way. She's about to crouch, but Ryke immediately reaches her side.

"You're okay. I'm here." He wraps his arms around Daisy. "I'm fucking here, Dais." He hugs her tight, clutching her protectively to his chest, and his features simultaneously darken and harden.

I don't know what to do or say. I waver uneasily and just stay quiet. Daisy is immobilized by fear, and so Ryke effortlessly lifts her in his arms. Cradling her body, he carries her towards the house.

As he passes Lo, my half-brother asks him, "What the hell happened?"

Ryke doesn't answer. I think it might've been a rhetorical question. Lo knows everything that has happened to Daisy and why the dark would scare her. All I know is that Garrison and his friends didn't help with her fear.

Not when they shot paintballs at the windows, among other things.

Connor clicks off his flashlight and lowers the hood of the car. I wait to figure out what to do next while he towers above with supreme confidence.

In his presence, I feel small. I feel awkward.

I doubt he's ever felt either.

I push up my glasses and adjust my backpack straps. "I'll call an Uber."

"You'd choose the unwise option just to avoid us," he states aloud like it means little when it actually carries too much weight.

"I'm not…avoiding," I say, unable to even *look* at him.

Lo quickly finishes typing his email, about twenty feet away.

"To avoid: to keep away from or stop oneself from doing something," he defines. "You're stopping yourself from spending the night here, which is, in fact, *avoidance.*"

I clear a lump in my throat. "Do you always define words for people?"

"Only for people who need definitions."

Boom. Mic drop.

Maggie would love his burn towards me. She once tweeted: All I want for Christmas is for Connor Cobalt to insult me. Please and thank you. It's supposed to be an honor. At least, to the online community. For everyone off Twitter and Tumblr, I don't think they'd appreciate being called stupid, and I doubt he'd care.

I try to nudge my already pushed-up glasses. "Do you have... an extra car I could borrow?" I risk asking him, of everyone, but if someone else stood on this driveway, I'd definitely be asking them first.

Because Connor analyzes all of my words, all of my edgy movements, and my quick glances to Lo.

"We have many cars you could borrow," he says, "but Lo will want to ride with you."

"No, no, that's okay. Never mind."

He's so *un*surprised by my reaction. It's kind of unsettling.

Thankfully, Lo pockets his phone and approaches us. "So what'd we decide?" He appraises my Honda from afar, hood closed but still broken.

"I don't know. We couldn't fix it..." I trail off as a limousine pulls to the curb and then idles. Exhaust gurgles out.

Lo swings his head to Connor. "When did you call your driver?"

Connor Cobalt's limousine. It's nearly as famous as Lily's Wampa cap. Jane Cobalt was *born* in that limo. It's like this sacred relic. I'm stunned silent.

"The same time Ryke lifted the hood of her car," Connor answers.

My brother laughs into a small smile, and he pats his friend's shoulder. "Goddamn, you make life easier."

"It's what I'm here for." Connor spins his attention onto me. "I trust my driver. I've known him for years, so you'll be safe by yourself. I've already given him your address."

It takes me a solid minute to find words. "Thank you." I say my goodbyes to Lo, and he tells me to text him when I reach my apartment.

I dazedly enter the limo, the black leather seats perfectly intact and shined. A few water bottles sit unopened in a refrigerator section.

The limo rumbles to life, and the driver takes me home. I check my Twitter messages to find a new one from **@garrisonwither**.

How'd it go? You okay?

I message back: Strange...but good, I think.

I hope.

I lean back and look around this limo, and I imagine all of them here with me. Lily, Loren, Connor, Rose, Ryke, and Daisy—and I wonder how many places they've been. How many conversations they've had right here. Days and weeks and years ago.

I sit in a place that has held thousands of memories for infamous people—people that I can call family. I have trouble accepting this as reality. I feel like I'm part of someone's *Princesses of Philly* fan fiction.

But this is real life. My life. Canon.

December

20

Garrison Abbey

"PLEASE GO OUTSIDE, GARRISON," MY MOM BEGS FROM THE kitchen. The smell of freshly made Christmas cookies wafts through a ten-foot archway—straight into the nearby living room where I sit.

The ornately tufted furniture, including this taupe couch my ass is on, should honestly exist in *Downton Abbey*. Not Pennsylvania.

I don't pause or turn off my game console. "Maybe later," I say, more than disinterested.

During Thanksgiving last month, my mom guilted me into joining Davis, Hunter, and Mitchell for a "brotherly" dinner in the city. Unbeknownst to our parents, they really planned some Turkey Pub Crawl thing, and with my fake ID, I could accompany them.

On paper it sounds great. Bonding time! Brothers! Beer! But I'd rather cut off my big toe than be around Davis and Hunter when they're piss drunk.

I tried to leave when Davis started shoving my head with "brotherly" aggression, but Mitchell convinced me to hang around for a while longer. I should've bailed because at the next pub Hunter waved a hundred-dollar bill in the air. The consequence, of which, gave me a bruised kidney and dislocated shoulder. For a whole week, it hurt to piss.

I still hear my brother's stupid voice and see that pub and those fucking men.

"I'll give anyone a hundred bucks to fight my brother here," Hunter decreed, smacking my shoulder hard, cash between his fingers.

I jerked out of his hold. "No," I spit. "Fuck that."

Davis laughed and chugged his beer. Mitchell hung back, texting some girl he started dating.

Hunter raised his voice to announce, "He needs to become a man." He slapped my face hard enough to leave a handprint. "You're such a little cock-sucking pussy."

I shoved him towards a high-top table, and Hunter almost flipped a switch, his eyes flashing murderously. I raised a hand for him to stay put. *Don't touch me. Don't touch me.* My heavy pulse could've busted my eardrums.

Davis laughed more. "Why are you running away from him?" he asked me. "Push back."

Fuck that shit.

"Don't be a pussy."

If I pushed back, I would've ended up with two black eyes. Hunter outsized me, and he had Davis on his side.

"Going once!" Hunter hollered at the crowds, still waving the bill. "Twice!"

Two leather-clad biker guys—way older than us—exchanged a look and then hopped up from their bar stools.

"He's joking," I said, backing up towards the exit.

"I'm not," Hunter retorted. "Come on, Garrison. Fight back!"

"Be a man," Davis shouted, hands cupped around his mouth like he was cheering me on. Pumping me up. Encouraging me. To be a man.

Bullshit. I shouldn't have to bear my fists in a drunken brawl to be called a motherfucking *man.* They're the immature ones.

I kept backing up.

The bikers followed me. Step for step. Not slowing.

Not hesitating.

"I don't want to fight!" I screamed furiously and desperately, hoping someone—anyone—would hear me.

The bikers sped up to a sprint, and I spun around to run away. I fled the pub, reached the sidewalk, and was kicked in the lower back.

Right in my kidney. I fell to my hands. The man grabbed onto my arm, and my shoulder popped out as I fought against him. Freeing myself, I ran as far as I could and then spun back around to my parked car.

I offered to be the "designated driver" for that reason. I wanted an escape in case I needed one. My brothers found their own way home. Took a cab or something. And then they complained to our mom how I bailed on them.

I didn't tell anyone what really happened. Not even Willow, who was having a shit time in Maine already. Apparently, her little sister threw a tantrum about Willow moving away to Philly, and she refused to be in the same room with Willow the entire holiday.

Willow ate Thanksgiving dinner alone in her bedroom—but not totally alone. I Skyped her and ate my pumpkin pie at the same time.

In the living room on Christmas Eve, I pound harder on my game controller, crushing my score on *Street Fighter II*. My mom already guilted me into leaving my bedroom, but I'm not going to be guilted into any "brotherly" activities this time.

"Garrison." My mom says my name in a way that completely obliterates each syllable with disappointment.

I know how to fix it. How to make her happy. To vanquish her disappointment, I have to become more like my brothers, but I can't be them. I couldn't live with myself knowing I was just like Hunter or Davis or even Mitchell.

And that says a lot because I've barely been able to live with myself as is.

My mom appears in the archway, cupping a wine glass with lime seltzer. I try not to make eye contact, but she still lingers. "I know they'd love if you joined them."

They brought their lacrosse sticks from college, and they're playing in the yard, tossing the ball between the three of them.

"I'm busy," I say flatly, my stomach starting to knot. My character Ryu is knocked on his ass by Dee Jay. I lose the first round and try to concentrate on the second, but I'm overly aware of how many times I blink, trying to shake off my mom's presence and request.

I lose the second round.

In the short break, I grab the remote and turn up the volume, wishing she'd take the hint and leave me alone.

My mom struts over and snatches the remote from my hand. She turns off the TV.

I stare flabbergasted at her. Usually she stands passively off to the side and lets me be a spoiled, ungrateful shithead.

I angrily toss my controller aside and slouch back on the couch. I pull up my hood and wait for her to lecture or yell or whatever she's decided to suddenly do.

"Your brain is going to rot from these video games," she says like all moms do, but if life were different—if sports were perceived as "lesser" and video games were seen as something "more"—would I be the beloved son then?

"I have a brain?" I say, sarcasm thick. "No way."

Sadness softens her eyes, and she sweeps over my dry tone. "Your brothers are home only a few times out of the year. Why can't you at least visit with them?" It's the same question. The same fight.

The same request.

Over and over, it never changes. I don't think it ever will. "I don't like them," I tell her seriously.

"They're your *brothers*."

I lift my foot on the couch cushion, arm draped on my kneecap. It takes me the longest second to find words. I want to shut down, but if someone can help me, I think it'd be a parent. A mom.

"Mom, it doesn't…" I shake my head and meet the confusion on her face. "Just because we're brothers doesn't *absolve* them of all the shit they've done to me."

"They love you. I know they do. They tell me all the time." There she goes, defending them again. She fights tears and cups her drink with both palms. Like she's afraid her hands will shake and she'll drop the glass.

Love. Is how they treat me called *love*? I'm not making this up, right? They truly suck. It's not all on me. *It's not my fault.*

Is it?

I hate questioning myself. I used to do this as a little kid. Hell, I do it when anyone points out a bruise. *It's just what brothers do.* Now that I'm older, I'm starting to see it's not cool or right or something I want in my life.

It's why I avoid them.

"Garrison," she pleads.

I hang my head. "You know Thanksgiving?" *I'm going to puke.* I have to tell her though. I need to tell someone. I don't want this weight on my chest. "I only bailed on them because Hunter paid two guys a hundred bucks to fight me."

I brave a glance, and she only looks befuddled. Like she's trying to figure out a defense for her three sons. Like she's their trial lawyer.

"Were they drinking?" she asks quietly.

"Yeah, but…" *What does that fucking matter?!*

"I'm sure they were just playing around. You're too sensitive about things, Garrison."

"The man dislocated my shoulder," I say, my throat burning raw. "*Mom.*"

She sighs like I'm being unnaturally troublesome.

"I didn't want to fight," I say. "I didn't want to even be there—"

"Then maybe you should try to be happier when you're with them. They won't give you such a hard time."

I'll never win with her.

After a short pause, she adds, "Your father says you need thicker skin, and you know, he's right. The real world isn't kind either."

"Whatever." I shut down now and grab my controller. As she sees me about to play my game and ignore her, she lets out this wounded noise, between a sigh and a cry.

I stare blankly at the paused television screen.

She sniffs loudly. "I just…" Her voice breaks. I *always* make her cry in the end. "I just don't know what to do anymore, Garrison."

She acts like it's her fault that animosity exists between my brothers and me, but then when she has the chance to make it better, she puts it all on my shoulders. *Go spend time with them. Befriend them. Please.*

"You could've gone to jail. Just like your friends," she starts listing my terrible decisions, bad actions, awful characteristics. "You got tattoos without me knowing. You were found drinking vodka at school."

Once.

I was caught *once*, but I'd done it plenty more times.

"You've been in trouble for vandalizing, backtalking, and cutting class." She takes a pause to wipe a fallen tear. "But thank God you didn't break into Loren Hale's home that night. Watching your best friends get in trouble—I thought that was your wakeup call. But you're still skipping school. You still won't listen to me or your father. You won't speak to your brothers. Nothing has changed."

Everything has changed.

I'm certain that I'm not the same anymore. I feel overturned. Inside-out. I'm fighting against the person they want me to be and fighting *for* the person I am inside.

The fact that she can't even see this makes me wonder who she's even looking at. Does she even know me at all? Or is she still resenting the fourth son she was given?

I shrug and turn on my game.

With the biggest sigh, she retreats into the kitchen, and I numbly scroll through *Street Fighter II* characters. Every so often, I hear her sniffle like she's silently crying. I make no effort to comfort my mom, and it's fucked up.

I realize that, but a sick part of me wants her to feel as terrible as I do. How many times have I shown her bruises from Hunter's fists and lacrosse stick? How many times has she repeated my father's phrase, *get thicker skin?*

My skin could be superhumanly thick, and I'd still get bruises and broken bones. What then, Mom?

From the kitchen, I hear the sliding glass doors swoosh open and my oldest brother's voice.

"Mom, what happened?" Davis asks. "Why are you crying?"

Shit.

I quickly pause the game and shut off the television. My brothers must file into the kitchen, one-by-one, because they each say a few consoling words while my mom blubbers something about wanting me to be *with* the family this Christmas.

"He's with us, Mom." Davis comforts her easily.

While I stand, I catch a glimpse of my mom through the archway, dabbing her tear-streaked cheeks with a dishrag.

"We'll make sure he doesn't run off to his friends," Hunter says.

My nose flares, and I find myself waiting—to listen in. I should move. I should go. I know better.

"It's not like he has many friends left around," Mitchell says with a short, uneasy laugh. Like he's not sure if anyone else will love his joke.

Hunter does. "That's right." He laughs mockingly. "What does he have, like one friend?"

"You can't be surprised he lost them all," Davis says to our mom, I think. "If he's not on his computer, then he's on his cellphone or playing video games. The kid is socially inept."

I clench my teeth so hard that my jaw aches. This is what my family really thinks of me. A socially inept, lazy delinquent. Whatever.

"Mom, don't cry," Davis says.

"I'll get him to play two-on-two basketball with us," Hunter reassures her. "You can be sure of that."

I start high-tailing my ass towards the back staircase. I can lock myself in my bedroom or crawl out the window and sit on the roof.

For how big Hunter is, he's somehow deceivingly fast. Right as my foot touches the first stair, he fists the back of my hoodie and yanks me backwards.

My pulse explodes, and I spin frantically out of his hold. But my movement forces me back into the living room.

"Where are you going?" Hunter sneers.

"To the moon," I spit back, frozen by the couch. I'm afraid to try and pass his body to reach the stairs.

Davis and Mitchell linger behind me, their irritations bubbling. All three have the same short haircut, and they wear nearly the same clothes: Polo shirts and khakis.

My oldest brother takes a couple steps towards me. "Can you please be cooperative? For once?" He lowers his voice to a whisper. "Mom is in the kitchen *crying* because you won't spend time with us. Do you even care?"

I shake my head and blurt out, "I don't care." I come across like the biggest punk ass, and where Davis and Hunter grow red, Mitchell sighs like I'm digging my own grave.

"Come on, Garrison," he says.

I'm not going to be like *Mitchell*. I'm not going to pretend that Davis and Hunter shit gold. I hate them too much to embrace that illusion.

"Let's just go play basketball," Mitchell says and nods towards the backdoor.

I pull my fallen hood over my head. "I'm not going outside."

Davis rolls his eyes like I'm being unreasonably stubborn.

Hunter pokes my back. "You need the fucking sun."

I flinch away from him, and Hunter sidles to our other brothers.

Davis scans the living room furniture, the black television screen, and my game console and controllers. "We can play video games then."

A chill rakes my arms, uneasy and hesitant. "Yeah?" I wonder, watching Mitchell grab an Xbox controller and take a seat on the tufted chair. I was playing on the Sega Genesis console, but I have different ones hooked up to this television.

"Yeah." Davis raises his brows. "Mom wants us to hang out together."

Hunter collects the remote and switches on the television. *It's a trick*, my brain screams at me.

They seem nice all of a sudden. And they want to play video games. I could suggest N64 and go really classic with Mario Kart.

It sounds *almost* like fun, which is why I move towards the couch.

"Where are all the football games?" Davis asks, fiddling with a wooden box of Xbox games beneath the coffee table. I'm about to crouch and help him—*wrong move.*

Hands grab me around the waist and throw me to the couch. Laughter pierces my fucking ears, and weight crushes my back.

Hunter *sits* on me. I grit my teeth and try to rise, but Hunter is really heavy. He braces a hand on the back of my head, pushing my face into the slit of the cushion. It smells like moldy cheese, and my lip brushes something harry or furry or whatever the hell…

All I hear is laughter.

I try to push him, and he catches my arm with his other hand and stretches my limb hard across my shoulders. Imprisoning me.

"Get off!" My voice is muffled and lost in the cushion.

Hunter pushes my head more forcefully, extending my neck. *God, my neck hurts.* I try to kick out, and Hunter goads me, "So now you want to fight? Or are you still going to run away like a little bitch?"

"Fuck you!" I yell, my face hot.

"What was that?" he sneers and purposefully sits *on* my head now. "I can't hear you, Garrison. Speak up."

I can't breathe.

I can't breathe. I can't fucking breathe. I choke for air. *Stop. Stop. Stop!*

My pulse thrashes off course, and if I can just…*not panic*, for one second. I try to tame my fear. *I'm okay. I'm okay.* My heart rate slows a tiny fraction.

I gasp into the cushion. A little air fills my lungs. I think I can breathe.

"Are you playing video games now?" My mom's voice nears the living room, and Hunter slides off my back. I immediately lift my head and then sit up, gasping for more air.

"Yeah." Davis squats beside me and rubs my head playfully. Like we're best friends.

My mom smiles from the archway and gives me a look like *see, Garrison, they'd even be willing to play video games with you.*

I shut down again, numb inside.

She says that she'll be visiting Rachel's mom a few streets over and to call if we need anything.

With that, she leaves.

And Hunter wrenches me onto my stomach again. *Shit.*

"Get off, dude," I snap, shoving and kicking him as hard as I can. Hunter curses at me all the while, calling me names, shouting his usual commentary about me needing to grow up. Fight back. *Be a man.*

I almost roll onto the floor, but Davis grabs me by the neck. So painful that I concede like a wounded animal. Hunter pushes me again, my stomach thudding to the cushions, and then he plops hard on my back.

I wince.

"Move over." Davis passes Hunter a game controller, and he makes room. Davis sits on my upper back, his controller in hand. Their weight crushes me.

In more ways than one.

21

Garrison Abbey

Merry Christmas :) Meet up later to exchange gifts?

I SEND WILLOW A TWITTER MESSAGE AND DESCEND MY staircase. Already dressed, I'm scheduled for an afternoon shift at Superheroes & Scones, and I'm dying to get there. Holiday traffic has been crazy, but on Christmas Day, I actually expect it to be slow.

Either way, I'm ready for the distraction.

A second later, a notification buzzes my phone.

@willowallflower: Tonight?

It's a date. I almost hit send, but I shake my head and delete those words and retype: perfect.

We're not a couple. We're still just friends, and honestly, I can't lose Willow to anything else. I'm already cursed and shit at most things, including relationships. But—I don't know. Sometimes, I think about kissing Willow.

What it would feel like. Where I'd put my hands. How I'd make her comfortable. What she'd be thinking—since it'd be her first.

Her lips look soft.

Shit. Stop thinking about that stuff. *Just friends.*

Sometimes I even wonder if we could be more. After Christmas, this next stretch of high school will be our last. We're seniors, and she's getting more comfortable at Dalton. The timing seems better than it was.

Each step down the stairs, I feel more strongly about this. About her.

"Garrison, honey, can you come here?" my mom calls from the formal dining room.

I dip into the kitchen and pass through another archway that leads to the dining room. My mom, in a form-fitting red dress, sits next to my dad at a glossy oak table, decorated with a red winterberry centerpiece and Christmas garland.

I rarely see my dad. If he's not working, then he's at home with his face in an iPad or computer. Checking stocks, making business plans—or maybe he just surfs the internet. I wouldn't know, would I?

Today, though, he has no electronic nearby. In a powder blue button-down and expensive slacks, he's seated beside my mom. My dad has always looked a lot like a fifty-something Jeremy Irons. Not physically intimidating, but his resolute expression is less friendly than my mom's gentle one.

I have no idea what this is about. Ever since my mom joined this new church when I was ten, we don't open presents on Christmas Day. We attend church on Christmas morning, but it's always insanely packed, so we have to show up hours early just to secure a chair.

Because of that, we open gifts on Christmas Eve.

Even last night, I was reminded that I'm on the "naughty" list for my family. Good to my dad's word, he didn't allow anyone to give me a single gift. Punishment for vandalizing Loren Hale's mailbox and then squirting punch on some of Lo's roommates. His sister-in-law, Rose Calloway, was one of them.

I didn't fight the punishment because I deserved it.

Watching my three brothers open their gifts while I was left with nothing—that was the least of what could've happened.

"Take a seat." My dad points to the chair across from them.

I don't sit. My gaze falls to a white envelope on the table's glossy surface. I stuff my hands into my black hoodie. "What's this about?"

"Sit, please." He never raises his voice with me. Doesn't physically hit me. Doesn't do much of anything.

He's not a big force in my life like my mom. His million-dollar tech company leeches his time and energy, and this holiday, I only saw him smile once. When Davis asked him to throw a football outside.

He found the time to play a quick game with all three of my brothers.

I sat out, and maybe he's here to lecture or scold me. But what's with this envelope?

I teeter, stuck between sitting and standing, not knowing which to take. I decide to sit before he repeats the request.

Maybe this isn't about me. Maybe they've decided to split up or something. Uncertainty binds my lungs, and I'm not even sure how I'd feel about a divorce.

My mom slides the envelope closer to me. "This is your Christmas gift." She seems more nervous than excited.

I reluctantly pry the envelope off the table. Frowning, I haphazardly tear open the paper and find a sleek brochure inside.

FAUST BOARDING SCHOOL FOR YOUNG BOYS

I stare blankly at the photograph. A gothic New England building landscapes an upstate New York setting. Teenage guys in suits smile and hold books, some propped near a large stone statue. It looks like an Ivy League institution made for teenagers preparing for life at Yale, Princeton, and Harvard.

My stomach sinks the longer I stare.

"What is this?" I mutter under my breath, already knowing the answer in my heart.

"We've pulled you out of Dalton Academy," my dad says. "You're not excelling there, and after what happened to your friends…" He clears his throat. "Your mom and I think that Faust will provide the proper guidance you need to finish your senior year."

My brain flies a million miles a minute. Too many questions. I unleash one thing. "What about lacrosse?"

I grimace at my words. Seriously? Lacrosse.

I don't even *like* lacrosse. I pause, that sentiment not sitting right in my stomach. *I hate lacrosse.* I don't know if I really do. The thought of not playing feels strange. Feels wrong. I frown deeply. I'm not sure of anything anymore.

"Unfortunately, Faust doesn't have a lacrosse team," my dad tells me while giving my mom a look. This might've been a point of contention in their final decision.

My stomach cramps, and the brochure crinkles under my tight grip.

Mom scoots forward, hands outstretched towards me. "But Faust has a chess club and cross-country, tennis, and even swimming. You can be involved in plenty of other sports or an extracurricular."

I'll graduate at the end of May. I *barely* have any school left. It's not like I can just walk onto the cross-country team. It's not like I want to.

Why are we even discussing sports like this is actually happening? Who'd make their kid switch schools in the middle of their last year?

"This can't really be up for discussion," I say dryly.

"Of course it is," my mom says. "You can choose whichever sport you want. We won't make that decision for you."

"No," I snap. "*Not* sports. I'm talking about *this*." I wave the brochure that's battered between my fingers, no longer crisp and pristine. "Faust. I don't get a say?" I hear my own rebuttal before my parent's launch theirs.

You're rich. You've been given everything in life. You're complaining about a boarding school, you asshole. You spoiled, ungrateful brat.

Guilt tears up my insides. I feel like I have no room to complain. No room to scream or throw shit. No room to combat, even though I'm eighteen.

"No," my dad says, voice strict. "Your opinion doesn't matter. Not after you've made this year hell for your mom and me."

I owe them. That's what I feel. I owe them for the nice clothes. For this house. For the cash, the car, the food and electronics.

For putting up with a piece of shit like me.

I hang my head and listen to my dad continue on.

"You need to leave this neighborhood," he tells me. "The friends you grew up with, this atmosphere, it's all been toxic for you. Think of Faust as a fresh start. A new school, new city, new home." My dad lets out a breath like the weight of his troubles has finally lifted. "This is a good change, Garrison."

Months ago, maybe I would've agreed. *A new start.* Away from all my ex-friends. Away from my brothers. Away from this place. It would've seemed like a lifeline, but now I feel as though my parents are cutting the only rope that grounds me to soil, to earth.

I'm doing better.

I've made a real friend, something I've never had.

If I leave Philadelphia, I'll be leaving the one good thing in my life. *Willow.*

My throat swells. "There's nothing…" I swallow and start again, "Isn't there anything I can do or say to change this?"

"We've already withdrawn you from Dalton Academy," my dad explains. "You start Faust in January. You'll leave in a week for orientation and to move into the dorms. It's done."

A week.

A week.

The timeline rings shrilly in the pits of my ears.

After the shock wears off, I stuff the crumpled brochure into the envelope and wedge the thing in my pants pocket. "Is that it?" I wonder.

My mom and dad exchange a look, and then she sets her concern on me. "Are you sure you don't want to talk about it a little more?"

"What else is there to talk about?" I ask. "It's a done deal, right?" I stand from the dining room table. Not wanting to speak to them anymore. They've already proven how much power they have over my life.

Dazedly, I walk out of the dining room. Neither my mom nor my dad tries to call me back, and I snatch my blue Dalton Academy beanie off a coat rack and find gloves. I think about grabbing my skateboard from the garage, but I abandon the board and just walk.

Faster and faster.

Out the front door. Down the driveway. Past the mailbox.

I pick up speed until I jog towards Loren Hale's house. Cold rips through my lungs, and I welcome every bit of it.

Slowing to a stop, I see the red brick house and Christmas decorations. Nothing extravagant. Lights twinkle on a few trees and a wreath hangs on the front door.

As I veer up their driveway, I slip on the slick cement. My worn boots have god-awful traction, and before I face-plant, I grab onto a decorative, iron deer. My heart hammers.

Not just from almost falling.

I hope Willow is here. *She has to be.* One good thing has to happen today.

I need to talk to her. Face-to-face. Right now. Get this news off my chest.

I carefully climb the porch stairs. Crusted ice and snow covers the doormat, and I stand stiffly. Hesitantly. Not that many people in this house even *like* me. After my birthday—where Willow stayed at my house later than she intended—I can't even tell if I'm on Loren Hale's good side anymore.

And there's a *huge* chance I'll be met with anyone but Willow.

Everyone who lives here:

Lily Calloway

Rose Calloway

Daisy Calloway

Loren Hale

Connor Cobalt

Ryke Meadows

Maximoff Hale (six-months-old)

Jane Cobalt (seven-months-old)

So yeah—a lot of fucking people are inside.

Willow planned to stop by here for Christmas, so I hope she's made the drive already. No cars are in the driveway, but maybe she parked in the large garage.

I'm afraid I'll have to interact with Rose and Connor.

Loren and Lily—I don't mind as much. They're still celebrities, untouchable in a sense, but they've been cool towards me. Daisy is nice to Willow, but I don't really talk to her—and Ryke is whatever.

He says *fuck* a lot, and every time I meet his eyes, I remember all the videos I've spliced together with his *fucks* and uploaded to YouTube.

After scaring his girlfriend with paintballs, I wouldn't be surprised if he secretly despised me too.

I take out a cigarette, thinking about lighting it, but I just pinch the cig between gloved fingers. I reach for the buzzer.

As soon as my finger lands on the button, the door swings open. *Shit.*

Scorching yellow-green eyes pierce me, and I curse my luck. Rose Calloway, of everyone, has opened the door.

I stuff my fists in my black hoodie, and I watch her assess my Dalton Academy beanie. Why am I even wearing it? I'm not returning to that school. The fact sinks deeper and deeper and burns a hole in my stomach.

Rose doesn't personally know me. She probably has no idea how old I really am or that I regret *everything* I did to her and her sisters. We've shared space, maybe once, during Halloween. I didn't say anything to her directly, I don't think.

"Uh…" I stammer and glance at the thin, gangly girl trying to squeeze through the doorway. Lily, my boss at Superheroes & Scones. Right now, she's the only friendly face.

The tension unwinds in my shoulders when I spot her, but then Rose cracks the door and shifts her body into the space. Blocking Lily from escaping.

"Rose," Lily whines.

"I got here first," Rose says to her sister, but her glare remains fastened to me. Nerves rake my spine, and chills creep up my neck.

This might've been a terrible idea. I should've messaged Willow first.

I realize Rose is waiting for me to speak, so I clear my throat. "We haven't met." I outstretch my gloved hand. *Polite*, I congratulate myself. I'm doing alright.

"Yes, we have." Every word is frosted, and her grip tightens on the door.

I drop my hand.

"You and your friends sprayed red punch on my *infant* daughter and me with a water gun."

It was a joke. A fucked-up joke.

They're celebrities. Characters on television. In magazines. They weren't *real* to us. That changed for me, and I can't tell you the moment it did.

They're more than just famous. They're human. I should've seen this from the start—I'm at fault here. I know that.

I didn't break into their house because I knew there were babies and people inside, but that decision doesn't free me from all the other shit ones I made.

I don't know how to make amends for everything I've done. I'm not even sure I deserve forgiveness.

I'm not sure I want it.

But I have to say something. "It was stupid…I'm sorry…" I chew on my chapped lip. Did that sound sincere? Sickness churns inside of me. I am *so* fucking sorry.

Nothing I say will ever make it better.

So I think, *just get to the point, Garrison.* "Hey is Willow here?" I ask. "I know she's a distant cousin, or whatever…"

Please be here.

"She's coming around at two!" Lily tells me from inside.

"Lily," Rose chides, opening the door slightly. Lily's round face comes into view, and I notice how she tries to narrow her eyes at her older sister—but the glare looks goofier than menacing. Now that I think about it, I've never seen her chastise a single Superheroes & Scones employee.

"Willow and Garrison are co-workers," Lily explains to Rose.

And then Loren Hale appears. Hand on the door, he pries it from Rose's grip. The door slams into the wall. I can suddenly see everyone.

Daisy is sitting on her boyfriend's shoulders near the staircase, and she bends her head beneath the mistletoe, kissing him upside-down. They're in their own world. Thankfully not really noticing me.

Loren places a protective hand on his wife's waist, and she scoots near him. While he focuses on Lily, I wonder, *do you hate me like everyone else now?*

I wait for Loren to acknowledge my presence. Not afraid. Not afraid. *I'm not afraid.* His dark glare drives through me, and fear curdles my stomach. I can't even lie to myself. Can't even pretend like I don't care what he thinks of me.

I do care.

Loren's glower carries ten times the potency of Rose's—and her pierced eyes already make me want to run off this stupid porch.

Voice sharp like daggers, he says, "A co-worker doesn't show up on Christmas morning looking for another co-worker."

Dropping my gaze, I scrape the icy stoop with my boot. "Does this mat say *welcome* under here? I can't read it with all the snow."

"He's funny," Rose says in a way that makes it seem like I'm decidedly *not* funny. She looks one second away from seeking revenge for the punch I sprayed on her and her daughter.

"You're scary, no offense." I cough into my glove and check over my shoulder, hoping Willow will show up early. I can still wait for her here. I look back. "You're going to make me invite myself in, aren't you?"

"Yes."

My eyes flit to each of them. Rose looks fucking murderous. Loren glares like I'm the shit on his shoe he scraped off yesterday but then reappeared today.

Lily is literally the only one that smiles, but it's a weak, pitying smile. I don't deserve anything more than that.

Each one intimidates me in their own right, but I'm trying to form words. For Willow. I'm trying.

Open-mouthed, my breath smokes the cold air. "I just…I wanted to tell her that…" *I'm leaving.* I let out a weak laugh, my eyes burning. Whatever. It's all fucking over anyway, right? What's done is done. It's Christmas. I don't need to shit on their holidays too. "Never mind, it's fucking stupid…" I turn to leave.

Rose snatches my hoodie, and she physically tugs me backwards.

"What the fuck?" My heart lurches, and I spin around and quickly jerk from her hold, my pulse skipping. I frown deeply, not understanding Rose Calloway at all.

She should want me to leave. Not force me to stay.

"Are you asking her to prom?" Rose questions. "Because this is the most pathetic proposal I've ever seen. You need flowers, first of all."

"I'm not asking her to prom." My voice shakes. I can't help it. *Prom.* I won't even be at Dalton for prom. The cold realization ices me over more than the winter air. *Just let it out.* I lick my lips and say, "I came to tell her that I'm leaving, and I guess to tell you too." I nod to Lily.

No more Superheroes & Scones. Shit. I glance at Loren, but he still glares, so I avert my gaze to the ground.

"What do you mean?" Lily asks.

Rose stares off in the distance, over my shoulder. Not paying attention to me anymore. She must see something because she grabs a coat from inside and slips on a pair of boots in the doorway.

I focus on Lily. "My parents handed me my only Christmas present this morning: a white envelope." Bitterness dries out my voice. "I…*they* are withdrawing me from Dalton and sending me to this boarding school for 'proper guidance' to finish my senior year."

Rose passes me on the stoop. Honestly, I'm glad she's set her sight on someone other than me.

"Where is it?" Lily wonders.

"Upstate New York," I say. "Faust Boarding School for Young Boys."

Loren lets out a long laugh. Maybe he's happy I'll be out of his cousin's life, but maybe not. I don't know. His humor is too dry to read.

"Lo." Lily elbows his waist. "Don't be mean."

My brows furrow, not understanding either of them. "What?"

"Connor went to Faust," Loren explains, "and from the stories he's shared, you won't last a day." He flashes a half-smile.

"Great," I mutter and stare harder at the doormat. Coming here was a terrible idea. I just feel ten thousand times worse. I turn to leave, but his voice stops me.

"Hey," Loren calls out. "You want to see my si—cousin Willow, right?" He stumbles over his words, but I zone in on the Willow part. Hope floods me for a second. Will he really let me stay?

"Yeah." I nod over and over. "I just need to tell her about Faust. It won't take long."

Loren drapes his arms over his wife's shoulders, pulling her back against his chest.

I swear she kind of unconsciously grinds her ass against him, but I try not to pay attention. If Lily noticed that I noticed, I think she'd be embarrassed.

Loren appraises me head to toe. "Connor says that I'm too forgiving—that you'll probably bite my hand off if I extend it again."

I won't. I open my mouth to say the words, but a lump lodges in my throat. I feel sick.

Loren grimaces at me and then shakes his head. "Christ, I must be a masochist." He nods to me. "You want to wait for Willow, then you have to do it *outside*. You're not allowed in the house, got it?"

"Got it."

"He'll freeze," Lily combats.

"Then he freezes, Lil. It's his choice."

Lily pouts like he's being a dick.

Loren steals a kiss, and her cheeks flush bright red.

"You're deflecting," Lily notes.

"Me?" Loren feigns surprise. "Not me, love. I would *never*."

I clear my throat, and Loren's face contorts in a multitude of emotions. Landing on irritation. Lily starts advocating for me again—for maybe two or three full minutes—but it only makes Lo more and more pissed at *me*.

"I'll be fine," I suddenly say. Pulling my beanie further down, I warm my ears. "It's why God created fleece-lined pants, right?"

"Let's not give God credit for clothes," Connor says as he saunters up the porch steps. He barely glances at me—like I'm not worthy of that attention. His face is utterly unreadable, but when he leans towards Loren, he says loudly, "He's not coming in the house."

Connor wanted me to hear that.

Loren nods. "He'll be by the pool."

At this, Connor disappears further into the house. He looks back as Rose picks up her confident gait and reaches his side. Hand-in-hand, they're gone.

Lily detaches from her husband and races after them screeching, "What happened?!" Whatever that's about, I'll probably never know.

I'm lucky I've even been standing here this long.

Now it's just me and Loren Hale.

Do you hate me? I want to ask, but I'm afraid. I can admit that this time.

Another dry smile dimples his cheeks, but then he nods towards the outside. "I'll show you to the pool around back."

"I can find it myself."

"Just follow me." He shuts the door and then passes me on the stairs. His sharp glare could kill.

I trail after him. So much rams into my brain. I can hardly make sense of anything, and some of which, it's not my place to share.

Like the guys at the mall, the ones that fucked with Willow because they personally hate Loren Hale.

I have no idea what'll happen when I leave Willow alone at Dalton.

It makes me nauseous thinking about it.

I just realize I'm in the backyard, and Lo opens the pool gate.

I step inside. "I know you don't like me," I tell him, "but will you make sure that she's okay when I'm gone?"

Lo freezes mid-step to the snow-covered lounge chairs. "I already do now." His expression says, *combat me. Tell me I'm wrong if I really am.*

I nod a few times. "Okay."

"If you know something—"

"Forget it, dude. I'm being an idiot." I blink rapidly and stare up at the blue sky. "You hate me, right?"

I think I'm whiplashing him with my emotions, my swift detours, and he's having trouble following my frantic mental pacing. "What?"

"You *hate* me," I say, more forceful.

He laughs once. "Most of the goddamn *universe* is on my shit list." With that, he walks off to the backdoor. Leaving me conflicted and confused again.

I'm standing knee-deep in the unknown.

22

Willow Moore

I FIND GARRISON WAITING FOR ME BY LO'S COVERED POOL. Quickly, he stands off a lounge chair as I approach. The cold bites me through a puffy blue jacket and thin mittens, but I'd rather bear the winter with Garrison. A minute ago, I entered through the garage, and Lily said he was out back. And he had something important to tell me.

"Hi," I breathe softly, scanning his solemn features.

Garrison cracks a few knuckles, on edge. "You should sit." He brushes snow off another lounge chair for me.

My heart knots. Tension builds so rapidly, and for some reason, I feel like an avalanche looms in the horizon. I take a seat, and he sits on another lounge chair across from mine.

Garrison licks his lips and then says, "So...I saw your Tumblr post this morning."

Is that what he wants to talk about...or is he just sidetracking? "Oh yeah." I cup my cellphone in one of my mittens. Last night I made a post about *X-Men: Evolution*, the animated series. It was short and went something like:

Me: *sees Storm creating lightning and thunder*

Me: *Strike me down, beautiful eternal goddess!*

I nudge my glasses. "You didn't think it was lame?"

Garrison looks like he wants to smile but can't. "Have you checked your notifications lately?"

I slowly shake my head and remove a mitten. Fingers cold, I tap on my cellphone screen and pop open Tumblr.

I immediately smile. "You didn't..." *He did.* Garrison made gifs of Storm from *X-Men: Evolution* where she wields lightning with her mutant powers. And he tagged me in them.

There aren't many gifs of the X-Men animated series to begin with, and to have this—and know personally who made them, and that he made them for me—means more than he realizes.

"Merry Christmas," he says. "Really, though, that isn't the present I meant to give you."

My smile fades, remembering that I forgot my Christmas present for him in my Honda. "I left my gift for you in my car. I didn't know you'd be here right now, but I can go get it—"

"Don't worry about it," he says quickly. "I left mine for you at my house, too."

So he's not here to exchange gifts then. In the lingering silence, I fit my mitten back on, and Garrison hunches forward, winded by his thoughts alone.

"Can I tell you what I got you?" he asks. I think he must want to kill time before he unleashes the important news.

I nod tensely.

His blue-green eyes flit to my ears. "I know you always wear the star and the bat studs, but I thought you'd like something X-Men related."

My lips stretch into an uncontrollable smile. "You got me earrings?"

"Yeah." He pinches his fingers to try to describe them. "They're X-shaped, with a circle around them." *The X-Men symbol.*

A guy bought me a gift. A guy bought me *jewelry*. It's hard to believe. "It's perfect," I say without thinking.

Garrison tilts his head. "You haven't seen it yet."

I push up my glasses again. A nervous tic now. "I don't have to see it to know it's perfect." *Because you bought it for me.* "I made you something, so it's probably not as good, and it's sort of..."

His lips try desperately to lift. "What?"

"Dorky?" I cringe at myself. "It's a scrapbook." I just come right out and spoil it. Maggie would hate if I spoiled her about anything, and thankfully, she's been texting me again as I update her on my life with Garrison Abbey.

I have to constantly censor myself with my friend from Maine, so it's not as easy talking with Maggie as it is with Daisy Calloway. Recently, I've noticed that more and more.

"A scrapbook of what?" He takes off his beanie to rake his hair out of his eyes.

Sometimes (a lot of the time) his whole bad boy persona intimidates me. The tattoos, the skillful sarcasm, and the good looks, but he's *always* gentle with me. He has his mother's innate and natural beauty, I've realized, and of the pictures I've seen of his father, he has his hair and lean build.

"Um…it's hard to explain. I'll just have to show you later." My heart races at the sight of this person I really, really like. I can't imagine not crossing paths with him. Not becoming friends. I can't imagine my life without the company of Garrison Abbey.

He stares at me for a really long moment. His deep expression practically caresses my cheeks. My chest swells, and I find myself covering my face with my mitten-hands. I feel undone, and we're just sitting across from one another.

"Hey," he whispers, his voice low. Garrison stands and brushes off more snow beside me, and then he takes a seat next to me on the lounge chair. Our shoulders touch, but good nerves swarm me.

Nerves that shout, *"Carpe Diem, Willow Moore!"*

"I'm glad you're here," I suddenly say what I feel. Instantly, the bottom of my stomach plunges and I regret every single word.

His features contort, breaking and breaking. Then he rubs his face with his gloved hand.

I hold onto my knees. Lost for words. I can't look at him, but I feel him drop his hand and turn his head towards me, studying my anxious face and body.

"I'm leaving," he tells me abruptly.

"What?" My voice spikes, sounding strange. I feel even stranger. Like this out-of-body experience belongs to another Willow in an alternate dimension. Not me. Not here.

Not right now.

Garrison fists the beanie in a hand. "I'm leaving," he repeats, as though trying to make sense of this too. I dazedly hear his explanation about Faust, his parents, and being forced to finish his senior year at the boarding school in upstate New York.

The news pummels me. I jinxed myself. *Moments* ago I was thinking about how I can't imagine not sharing his company, and now he's leaving? I don't just need Garrison with me at Dalton Academy and Philly.

I *want* him.

And I've never wanted a friend like this. Never yearned for a person to be next to me. Never slept and smiled thinking about seeing them tomorrow.

The more he explains his fate, in a very dry but hollow voice, I slump forward. My stomach caves, and the avalanche begins to roar down the figurative mountain that is our lives. I shield my face with my hands, afraid that I'll start crying.

Crying is hard for me in front of anyone, and he needs encouragement. Strength. He needs, *it'll be okays*. Not a blubbering, dejected friend.

My throat and eyes burn.

"Willow," he whispers, his voice raspy.

I inhale deeply and wipe my running nose. "What about Superheroes & Scones? Maybe…maybe you can work the weekends."

"…maybe," he says, not entirely sure himself. "It's not like you'll be alone."

My face twists. "What do you mean?" I meet his reddened eyes.

"Ace Davenport? He's totally into you." His face is unreadable, and his voice is too flat to make sense of.

My gaze widens, and my face keeps twisting into a wince. "That's not funny." I think I might cry now. I quickly rub the corners of my eyes.

Garrison looks genuinely confused. "He always talks to you at work."

"To tell me how I stock the shelves incorrectly," I say. "And every day, after I help a customer with comic book suggestions, he makes a comment about how I'm a know-it-all, and that I'm really some poser trying to be cool." Ace is mean to me.

His nose flares, restraining hot emotion. "Why didn't you tell me he was a dick to you?"

"I thought you knew." I swallow the rock in my throat. "You always seemed irritated by him…"

Garrison stares up at the sky, tormented by this news too. "I knew this would happen," he mutters more to himself than to me.

I shake my head. "What would happen?"

He touches his chest. "I'm *cursed*…and I hung around you long enough, and I cursed you too." His voice breaks.

"I'll be okay," I try to assure him, rubbing my dripping nose as fast as possible. Pressure bears on my chest so hard that I feel physically sick. "*We'll* be okay."

His tortured gaze sweeps my face. "Then why are you crying?" A tear drips down his cheek at the sight of my leaking eyes. Water brims over my lower lids and scalds my skin.

"I'm scared," I say the truth so softly. I wipe my face again, and he rubs his bloodshot eyes.

Garrison lets out a staggered breath and then stands up. He extends a hand to me, and I put my palm in his palm. He pulls me to my feet, our boots knocking together.

Very tenderly, he asks, "Willow, can I hug you?"

I nod.

It might be our last hug for a really long while.

Garrison tucks a flyaway hair behind my ear, and then he wraps his arms around my body. I coil mine around his frame, my arms feather-light still, but his embrace carries warmth and extra pressure that dizzies my senses.

I hold tighter than before, my fingers gripping the fabric of his hoodie. *Don't go yet. Please don't go yet.* I'm picturing my life without him, and it's so much lonelier than before.

Garrison tilts and lowers his head to whisper against my ear. "You're still my girl."

And then, without a single pause, Garrison Abbey kisses my cheek. His lips leave a fiery imprint, and my body solidifies like hardened magma.

He drops his hand to mine. I'm too stunned to speak, too sad to say how much he means to me, and too heartbroken to wish for a real kiss.

"If Ace Davenport gives you shit, you'll tell me?" he asks, and he keeps talking as he sees me nod quickly. "You have my Twitter, Tumblr, and all that whatever, but…" He shoves his beanie in his back pocket. "I know we said we like the internet, but I'd really love your number."

He's asking for my phone number. It brings us closer in a different way than we both planned. "Yeah, of course."

After we exchange numbers and add each other to our contacts, he prepares to leave. Taking a few steps back, Garrison hesitates.

I wipe my fogged glasses and then set them back on my nose.

"It's not goodbye," he says to me, as though he can't bear that idea. "I'll come back here. I promise." He takes a few more steps backwards. "If not, then I guess I'll just have to find two cans and a string long enough to connect you to me."

My heart hurts, and just as he turns his back to me, I call out, "Garrison."

He glances over his shoulder.

I don't know what I planned to say. Maybe I just wanted to stop him. To see his face. I swallow hard and murmur, "Merry Christmas."

He hears my quiet voice. "Merry Christmas."

It's the saddest holiday of my life. I lost one of the most precious gifts I've ever been given. I lost my first friend from Philadelphia.

I lost him to New York. I lost him to Faust. To a boarding school and his parent's demands. I wonder if he'll return after he's graduated.

Maybe we'll grow apart. Our paths that kept crossing are beginning to diverge, and I'm really scared.

January

23

Garrison Abbey

CONNOR COBALT IS A GOD HERE. A SINGLE WEEK AT FAUST, and it's the first lesson I've learned.

The second: I'm in over my head. The guys here aren't just smart. They seem to *enjoy* learning. As if it's a gift given to them, and everyone supports the growth of knowledge. Translating whole passages from Caesar's Invasion is cool, and debating philosophy is just another pastime.

I know basic Latin.

Enough to chant out loud with the class, but put a sentence in front of my face and I won't be able to translate anything without a vocabulary list.

And yeah, I asked for a vocab list or a dictionary the other day. The amount of students staring at me for *that* was beyond embarrassing. And this is coming from someone who didn't give a shit if people thought I was stupid.

Here, it feels like the worst crime.

"So you have spoken to him?" my new roommate asks as I try to concentrate on translating a passage in *The Odyssey* from Latin to English. It's slow moving.

I wish this was Calculus—a language I actually am proficient at.

My roommate leans forward on his crimson bedspread, blond hair brushing his neck and brown eyes round and curious. He's asking if I've spoken to the legend himself: Richard Connor Cobalt.

The moment William learned that I'm from the same neighborhood as Connor, I've been bombarded with questions.

I promised to answer them later—which was my response for five whole days. Another five days dodging these questions seems unlikely since William has already spread the news to the entire boarding school.

It's whatever.

I'm just hoping the reasoning behind *why* I'm at Faust remains a secret. These guys don't seem like they'd take kindly to delinquents like me.

I curl my hand around the book, my other hand gripping a pencil tight. "I mean…not really. Kind of. I don't know," I say to William.

I heard Connor tell Loren that I'm not allowed in his house. That's about the extent of any conversation I've had with the guy.

I can't tell him that though. I'm trying to make friends here, and the students obviously worship Connor Cobalt. Letting them know I'm barred from entering his home for spraying his wife and baby with punch would be…fucked up.

It's all fucked up.

William frowns. "Well, have you seen him around? What is he like in real life?" he asks quickly. "Is he as tall as he seems on TV?"

"Yeah," I nod. "He's really tall." This is so dumb.

"Did he or his family mention anything about all the shit that's going down on social media?" William asks, eyes glittering for more knowledge.

"Which shit?" I ask. When it comes to Connor Cobalt, there's been a lot of shit recently. Especially concerning him and his wife. Yesterday, there were hundreds of pics online with Rose's hair dyed an ugly orange color. Tumblr created a meme and literally photoshopped foxes on her head. It was weird and stupid.

"The photos of Connor going down on his wife in a parking lot," William says. I saw those too. They were dark, taken outside while they were in a car. But you could make out his head and her legs around his shoulders. It was obvious what they were doing, and when they didn't deny it, social media went nuts.

"No one has said anything," I reply.

"Can you believe he did that and basically owned up to it like it was just another day?" William says in awe. "I mean, the guy is legendary. His wife is immortally beautiful and brilliant. He can give her head in a public parking lot and not even bat an eye. Are you sure no one has talked about it?"

"I'm sure," I snap. For the love of...why are we talking about Connor Cobalt? I run a hand through my hair. I want to physically eject myself from this conversation. Would it be rude to get up and leave the room? I've never really had a roommate—besides that couple times on family vacations I had to room with Mitchell, but I don't think that counts. This is all new for me.

Being at a new school.

New place.

I itch to grab my laptop and send Willow a Tumblr message. Anything to take me away from William's probing questions about a guy that hates me.

Thankfully, a knock sounds on the door.

Guys in black blazers and crimson ties (Faust's uniform) peek inside the room, grinning from ear-to-ear.

I recognize the freckled one from my Philosophy class. Tyson. He's the kind of guy who'll argue on the side that's wrong (like literally wrong) just to have a different point of view in the conversation. Sometimes he's so convincing, he almost makes me believe he's right. It wasn't a surprise when William told me he's president of the Debate Club.

Behind Tyson and the other guy, maddened footsteps cascade across the polished floor, hurrying towards something. More doors open, people leaving.

William rises from the bed, while I remain confused and motionless.

Tyson grins wider. "The Sophist's Speech is about to begin."

"Holy shit," William smiles wildly and reaches for his black blazer. Tyson and his friend leave as quickly as they came, while my roommate slows to the door, suddenly remembering me. "You coming, Garrison?"

I frown, still not understanding. "What's a sophist?"

He laughs. "Funny. You're funny." He nods to my blazer on the desk, even though I'm already wearing a hoodie. "Grab your jacket. You're not going to want to miss this."

ON OUR WAY TO THE COURTYARD, I QUICKLY WIKIPEDIA WHAT the hell a *sophist* is. Ten seconds later I have my answer. *A teacher in Ancient Greece.*

Another definition I found on the internet: *a person who reasons with clever but fallacious and deceptive arguments.* Seriously? I was supposed to know this?

My shoes crunch a light layer of snow, but I'm warm with the Faust blazer over my hoodie, crimson tie stuffed in my back pocket. Wind picks up as soon as we pass through arched oak double doors. I pull the hood up over my hair and follow William's quickened footsteps towards a large stone fountain, icicles hanging off the ornate moldings.

I expect to see a teacher heading this speech, but the person balancing on the ledge of the fountain is a student. Dressed in the same Faust blazer as most of the crowd, black hair slicked back, he commands the space without even saying a word. He can't be older than me if he's here, but for some reason he looks it.

A senior, probably.

"Who is that?" I whisper to William as we fall into the throngs of guys. Some of whom ran outside without grabbing a coat or blazer. They jump on the balls of their feet, looking more excited than cold.

"Gabriel Falls," William replies softly. "He was elected as our sophist for the term." Off my confused-as-fuck expression, William adds, "It's Faust tradition to have a senior give a sophist's speech." He grins. "Basically, it's bullshit that smells like roses. The best speech by far was Connor Cobalt's. The guy practically planted a garden with his words."

Traditions here are weird as hell. I'm used to the kind back at Dalton Academy. Which consisted of our lacrosse team drinking blue Gatorade before practice. Never the lemon-lime. And god-forbid someone even thinks to bring a Ziff on field.

I'm not even sure where the tradition started—or I guess, superstition—maybe it had something to do with the jocks hating Loren Hale when he went to Dalton. And you know, Ziff is a Fizzle product. It's a dumb name, by the way. *Ziff.* Fizz kind of spelled backwards. Whatever marketing "genius" came up with the name for the sports drink should be fired.

Thinking about Fizzle and Loren Hale and everything just reminds me of Willow. Can't see her. Can't work at Superheroes & Scones. It all blows.

"Gather 'round!" Gabriel calls out from his perch on the fountain. And then the guy starts speaking in Latin.

I can't with this.

Cold nips at my cheeks, and just as I'm about to bail, I see someone a few yards away. Shaved head and pale skin, he smokes a cigarette between fingerless gloves and leans against a tree. With his sleeves rolled up to his elbows, I distinguish black geometric tattoos on his forearms.

He's the first person I've seen that doesn't look like he was manufactured from a J.Crew catalogue. I leave William's side and slowly make my way to the tree.

Relief accompanies each step. No nerves. I've never been bad at making friends, and this guy kind of reminds me of ones back home.

He barely acknowledges me as I stop a few feet away, his gaze latched to the fountain. But I can only make out mumbled words from Gabriel's speech.

"Hey," I say and nod with my chin. "Could I borrow a smoke?" I eye the cigarette between his fingers.

His eyes finally flash to me. Like I exist. Casually, without even moving off the tree, he sticks the cigarette in his mouth, slides a hand in his blazer, and passes me a spare. Cold whips between us.

"Thanks, man," I say as he pulls out a lighter. "I'm Garrison."

"Sasha Anders. And I know who you are." He clicks the lighter with his thumb, and I lean in. After embers eat the paper, he adds, "No need to thank me."

I step back, blowing smoke off to the side. Wind chill bites at me more, and I hug my arm to my chest. This guy is wearing less than me, and he doesn't even have a single fucking goosebump.

He stares off towards the fountain and says, "That'll probably be your last cigarette at Faust. Enjoy it while you can." *Goddamn.*

I laugh under my breath, bitterness swimming in my gut. "Yeah? What makes you think that?" Maybe he's just messing with me. He can't seriously be like everyone else here? An asshole. An elitist prick who feels like he has the inability to lose.

He doesn't even look at me. Like I haven't even earned his full attention yet.

Eyes on the fountain, he says, "You walked over here. That was your first mistake." His gray, lifeless gaze flits to me for a millisecond. "We aren't the same, you and me." He looks to my tattoo, the inked Interpol lyrics peeking from my forearm, like he knows that's the reason I approached. He continues, "You could barely string four words together in Spanish class. You have no knowledge of Proust, Rembrandt, or Verdi. You're *inadequate*, but your biggest failure is your social ineptitude. The only mouse that would approach a snake is the one too stupid to realize he's in a pit of them." Sasha flicks his cigarette to the side, and it lands in the snow.

I saw that phrase in the common room, etched on a plaque and hung with other senior quotes.

The only mouse that would approach a snake is the one too daft to realize he's in a pit of them.

- Richard Connor Cobalt

Sasha gives me one last glance. "Don't look for friends, mouse. Find an exit." He pauses and his eyes dip to my fingers. "Enjoy the cigarette."

He walks off as Gabriel's speech ends. All the students disperse, and Sasha falls in line among the masses just the same.

Breath caged. My cigarette burns, ash falling to the snow. I don't know what to feel. I'm more used to the kinds of insults that try to tear me down in a single blow. *Pussy! Weak shit!*

What Sasha just did was the equivalent of taking a knife and slashing razor-thin cuts all over my skin—and then waiting for me to bleed out. Meticulous. Calculated cruelty.

I bite down and breathe out through my nose.

And what unnerves me the most—is that he knew I blew it in Spanish. He knows that I stumbled over those names in English, Art & Lit, and Music Theory. Yet, I don't have a single class with him.

It means people are talking about me. *Amazing.* Just amazing. I'm going to have a *great* time here.

I feel like utter shit, and there's only one person I even want to talk to right now.

Slipping out my cell, I walk towards the pond and try to FaceTime. The boarding school campus is an otherworldly atmosphere with frozen, barren waters and skeletal trees. Like I've been transported to Victorian England.

My breath smokes in the cold, and I ditch the cigarette in the snow.

The phone clicks, and Willow pops on-screen. She's crouched down next to a rack of *Inhumans* comics. She pushes her glasses up the bridge of her nose. "Oh, are you outside? Isn't it cold?" *God.* It's nice just hearing her voice. My stomach flips, and for a moment, I pretend I'm only a few blocks down the street.

"Yeah, but that's why I've got this…" I tug my hood down further, almost shrouding my eyes.

"Your fingers look purple," she says, concerned, and then one of the comics falls from its rack. She huffs. "Stupid broken rack."

"Is that *Inhumans*?" I wonder. "I thought Loren didn't want *Inhumans* stocked in the store. Didn't he call it a mediocre version of *X-Men*? And also a comic book line that's off-limits to all *X-Men* purists and if he can help it, off-limits to everyone?" He made that whole speech during last month's meeting.

"Yeah," Willow replies, grabbing tape and fashioning the broken rack back together. "But yesterday, Lily came in and told us Loren's bias over certain lines was not going to affect the store—since it's technically hers. And that *Inhumans* is a good series and needed to be stocked. So here I am…" She realigns the comics and slides them in. "…but I think there's a reason she put it on this crappy rack. Like maybe she subconsciously agrees with him." Willow nudges her glasses again and collapses on the ground. She straightens her phone so that I'm looking at her and not the comics.

"You okay?" I ask.

"Yeah." She pins her fallen employee nametag back to her shirt. "Honestly, I like *Inhumans*. And they're pretty cool on *Agents of Shield.*"

"I don't watch it," I remind her.

She nods, remembering. "*Supernatural* is better. It starts again soon."

"Yeah," I say, but I'm not even sure I'll have the time to watch *any* TV let alone my favorites.

Faust is a big time-suck, and on my free weekends, I'm planning to commute back to Philly for shifts at Superheroes & Scones. So I can at least have an excuse to see Willow. I'm just glad Lily Calloway agreed to let me keep working part-time.

I light a cigarette. If I'd known Sasha Anders was going to be a Grade-A tool-bag, I wouldn't have bothered pretending I had no smokes. Regret hammers me. And I usually don't regret social situations that turn sour. That shit flies off my shoulders. But being here—it's different.

"So..." she says. "How's the first week been? How's Faust and your roommates?"

I shrug. "Faust is..." I glance down at my cigarette. "Unusual. And my new roommate is...well, his name is William." I smile dryly. "Which bugs the shit out of me because every time someone says it, I just think about..."

You.

The names Willow and William are too similar to not be jarred by it. It fucking sucks.

Her cheeks ashen a little, and she glances down at her shoes.

"How's everything there?" I wonder, worried. "How's Dalton?" *My friends? Are they jerks to you while I'm gone?*

She shrugs now. "It's the same."

"The same?" I frown.

"I mean, not the same. You're not here," she says hurriedly. "It's really just boring and nothing goes on. Which is better than the alternative. More tampons in the locker would be rough."

"Yeah, definitely," I say. "Boring is better than tampon pranks." But I still feel badly that she's alone at Dalton. At least she's not completely alone. She has Loren and Lily, and she lives with Maya— who is pretty cool even if she hates my lack of comics knowledge.

"You'd tell me if something happened right?" I ask. "I know I can't really do anything being out here, but I'd want to know."

"Of course, I'd tell you." She pauses. "You'd tell me if something happened there, right?"

"Of course." Sasha Anders doesn't count. He technically didn't do anything to me, except call me a mouse. In the grand scheme of things, it was nothing. Really, it was kind of stupid. I've been through worse.

Silence eats at us for a second before she says, "Garrison."

"Yeah?"

"Can you go inside? I can see your fingers again and they look really purple."

"Yeah, okay." *She cares about me.* I think she does. I mean, that definitely means she does. Right? Someone on this planet actually cares about my well-being. That thought and feeling settles in my body like falling snow.

I drop my cigarette and turn towards the buildings. An employee distracts Willow for a second, asking if she'll swap workdays. I head inside and feel the rush of warmth. Classes in session, no one struts up and down the hallways. *Empty.*

I lean my shoulder against a staircase banister. Staying on the first floor, I realize I might be missing political science right now, but I don't care.

I focus on my phone and watch Willow return her attention to me. "So everyone loves Connor here," I tell her.

She smiles. "You need to tell me stories."

"I'd rather hear yours right now," I say honestly. "My whole day has been centered on Connor Cobalt, and I need a distraction. What's going on with you?"

"The media is getting kind of crazy," she says. "More so than usual. But luckily they're more focused on Ryke's surgery and Rose's new hair color than little ole me right now."

Ryke's liver transplant was heavily documented online. He gave a part of his liver to his dad, and I remember seeing the shaky video of Ryke being wheeled out of the hospital a few days ago.

I frown, thinking about something else. "I thought the media stopped hounding you when the novelty of you being Loren's cousin wore off. What's made them come back?"

"I think maybe Connor and Rose?" She shakes her head, not knowing either. "Paparazzi have been asking me why the two of them are suddenly so 'PDA-heavy' in public. I'm like the lowest person on the list of people connected to them, so they think I'll have looser lips or something. Even if I knew something though, I wouldn't say anything."

That, I know.

Willow has always been really careful around me when it comes to Loren Hale and his family. She won't talk about anything that isn't already public knowledge, and even then, I can tell she'd still rather be discussing something else. It's not new for her anymore, but it's still uncharted territory that she's trying to navigate by herself.

It's understandable.

She quickly changes the subject. "Make any new friends?"

"Nope. You?"

"Nope."

Good.

No, that's shitty of me to think. Really, I don't know how I fucking feel about her making friends, okay? Depends who they are, I guess.

The quiet weighs on us for a second, and then I say, "Hey, you know any Latin?"

"Um…just what's on the back of a dollar bill." Her eyes drop to my hand as I light a new cigarette. "Your fingers have returned to a normal color."

"A miracle." I blow out smoke.

Someone passes the abandoned hall and shakes their head at me. "No smoking inside, man."

I think he's just warning me, but then he stops a foot away and unfurls a small booklet. "I'm going to have to write you up."

"What?" I frown. *What the fuck?*

"It's against code of conduct rules."

"Are you like a hall monitor or something?" I say, confused. Aren't those only in movies?

"That's exactly what I am."

Fuck me.

Willow grimaces as I look back to the phone. "I'll let you go," she says quickly. "See you Saturday?"

"Saturday," I say into a nod and we hang up.

I wait while the hall monitor scribbles on the notepad, and Sasha Ander's words hound me. *Find an exit.*

It sounds like an easy task, but I've been searching for an exit my entire life and have yet to find it. Someone point the way. Anyone?

Please.

I'm waiting.

April

24

Garrison Abbey

BREAKING AND ENTERING WASN'T ON MY LIST OF THINGS TO do. Ever. But things change. I slide a paperclip through the keyhole of a deep navy door, scratches and dents marring the steel. Garbage stinks up the alleyway, and cigarette butts line the pavement.

Working at Superheroes & Scones gave me a lot of insight into this place. Like how the left alley door doesn't have any security cameras. Most of the employees smoke pot and suck face on this stoop. So I'm not even sweating as I take my time with the lock. The pitch-black night conceals me enough.

Honestly, I just need a place to sleep tonight. A warm floor. That's it.

Because I can't go back to Faust.

This morning the headmaster called me into his office—and I thought for sure he was going to just tell me I needed a tutor. Because I did nothing wrong. No vandalism. No cheating. No cursing. No cutting class—except for that one time with poly-sci.

I was on my best fucking behavior.

Bookshelves towered against every wall, and the place smelled like moldy paperbacks. I took a seat in front of his polished oak desk.

"Mr. Abbey," he said, "seeing as you're a new student, I've tasked myself with looking into how you're faring here at Faust." He barely blinked. "Unfortunately, your current academic standing isn't up to par with the other pupils."

Not a surprise. I shifted on my chair. "So who's my tutor…?" My voice trailed off as I saw the expression on his face. Pure fucking pity.

He sighed heavily. "I'm afraid, we're past that stage. With your current marks, you'd have to score well beyond one hundred percent on every final to even move the needle. This is the end of the road for you and your time here at Faust. You can pack your bags. A car is waiting to take you back to…" He glanced down at a sheet of paper. "Philadelphia."

It's official. I've flunked out of *two* prep schools.

Really, I was pulled out of Dalton before I even had the chance to flunk. But I was well on my way there.

The one silver-lining in all of this, Faust doesn't contact parents by phone. Not when most of the students have moms and dads sailing the globe on yachts or too damn busy to lift their own cell. So Faust does everything by mail.

Before coming to the comic book shop, I made a quick detour at my parent's house. Stopped by for point-two-seconds. Just long enough to swipe the letter from their mailbox. The one "notifying" them that I'm a loser.

The lock clicks. *Success.*

I push through the backdoor of Superheroes & Scones, and before the alarm can go off, I quickly type in the passcode. Yesterday, Lily switched the code, so Willow gave me the new one.

And yeah, I had to tell Willow I flunked. I couldn't lie to her.

I hate that she's kind of an accomplice to this whole "breaking and entering" thing. But the alternative was sneaking into her bedroom (she offered it as a place to crash) and I don't want to ruin us by being *that* guy. Willow doesn't deserve some loser crashing on her floor.

Quietly, I tiptoe through the deserted store. Not a soul or sound in the entire place. It feels like a comic book graveyard in the dark.

Dipping into the breakroom, I use a giant stuffed Millennium Falcon plushie as a pillow and lie on the hard ground.

I slide the letter out of my backpack and then flip open a lighter.

Flame to paper, I watch my future—or lack thereof—burn between my fingertips.

My parents aren't ever going to know I flunked. And if I have it my way, I'll never see them again.

Honestly, that's the only future I want.

25

Willow Moore

SOMEONE IS FOLLOWING ME.

I know I sound paranoid, and maybe it's because of the intense paparazzi onslaughts recently. Cameramen wait for me to leave Superheroes & Scones every single shift. Without fail. I even slipped out the backdoor (the one that smells like weed) and still had this mustached man shove a camera three inches from my face.

He could have broken my glasses. That was one of my fears at least.

He did scream so loud and so close that his voice drilled into my head. "Willow! Willow! Do you know anything about Connor & Rose?! Is their marriage fake?!"

The accusations against Connor Cobalt and Rose Calloway have been horrible lately. The media discovered Connor has slept with men, before he dated Rose, and now they think his relationship with Rose isn't real. Like he's using her to hide his sexuality.

Thankfully some fans realize that Connor can be attracted to men *while* also being attracted to women. That both things can be true: Connor sleeping with guys in the past and also loving and sleeping with Rose in the present.

It just sucks that some fans aren't louder than the media.

When the cameraman rushed me, I wasn't brazen enough to scream in his face, but I felt like yelling. A big part of me regrets not saying anything. Not sticking up for Rose and Connor when they've been so kind to me.

Especially Rose.

But I'm also kind of glad I didn't say anything. Opening my mouth probably would've made the situation worse. Anyway, Ryke and Lo are yelling enough for just about everyone these days.

I did write a few supportive Tumblr posts, and I reblogged cute Coballoway gifs from fan accounts. Garrison told me to send him the links, and he did the same.

I walk down the sidewalk towards my apartment building. With the parking deck under construction, I had to park a block away. A white Volvo slowly moves on the other side of the street and keeps pace with me.

That's weird, right?

Paparazzi have never really followed me to my apartment. They lose interest in me as soon as I climb into my Honda. They couldn't care less about abandoning Superheroes & Scones for Loren Hale's boring "cousin." I've been glad about that.

But this…

Changes things.

I tighten my hold on the backpack strap and quicken my pace. The apartment complex's front entrance is inches from my fingertips, and a man jumps out of the Volvo. "Willow! I'd like to ask you some questions!"

I flinch, my pulse spiking.

I don't know why, but he sounds more serious than the other paparazzi. Like a fancy news reporter. It makes me do a doubletake, and he quickly catches up to me.

"I'm with *Celebrity Crush*—"

Oh…no. Nope! Do not want to talk. *Celebrity Crush* has been known to spout off some of the worst and nastiest rumors about the Calloway sisters.

I mumble out an *I'm sorry* or maybe it was just unintelligible words. But I say something that my brain and mouth put together before bolting into the apartment complex. My hands shake as I dig for my cell. Just as I find it in the depths of my backpack, a text pings.

Garrison: made it to S&S. Thanks for the assist. Owe you like a million. Hey, did you know how comfortable the Millennium Falcon is? Who would've guessed?

I calm just reading his text. But my heart still thrashes against my ribcage, reminding me what I have to do.

I dial his number.

The line clicks. "Willow?"

"Lo, I have to tell you something."

IF I TOTAL ALL THE DAYS AND WEEKS THAT I'VE BEEN IN PHILLY since I left Maine, it's been around nine months, and I'd like to think that's a long time. Almost a whole year on my own. It makes me feel better knowing that I tried really, *really* hard to not be a burden on Lo. To not accept more from my brother than I absolutely have to.

If I felt safe enough to live in my apartment, I think I could have even lasted longer than those nine months. But after the paparazzi followed me home, Loren asked if I'd like to move into his mansion-sized house in a gated Philadelphia neighborhood.

The same neighborhood that Garrison grew up in.

I couldn't say *no* this time.

I really like the Calloway sisters, Ryke, and even Connor. They've accepted me into their lives without hesitation, and I know in the beginning that acceptance originated from their trust in Lo. But I hope that now it's because they also trust me.

"We should decorate and make this space more Willow-y," Daisy tells me, rolling around my new bedroom on a skateboard. All my stuff (which isn't much) sits in the middle of the room, still packed in a couple boxes and a suitcase.

I'm officially "moved in" thanks to Lo, Ryke, and Daisy's help this morning.

They had a few empty guest rooms on the east wing of the house, and Lo let me pick which one I'd like. He didn't seem pleased when

I chose the smallest of the three, but he didn't push me to choose differently.

I like how quaint this one feels. Just a bed, tin desk, and white wooden dresser. That's more than enough for me.

Daisy spins to face me as I unfold a box. She's always moving. It's kind of like watching a hummingbird flit around a space. "We could also paint the walls." She abandons the skateboard and plops on my bed. "There's a hardware store nearby, and we can buy some brushes and stuff."

I'm smiling so hard my cheeks hurt.

I have new roommates. Six adults and two babies to be exact. I'm living with the Calloway sisters and their men.

If you'd told me that's how all of this would have panned out months ago—I'd have said you were dead wrong. More surprising than that—I'm *comfortable* here. Not too nervous or skittish. I never thought I'd feel that way with people so famous and so much more interesting than me. I know it has to do with Lo. He made a lot of effort to welcome me and make my surroundings feel like home. He's my brother, but he *feels* like family now.

I follow Daisy's gaze to the walls and then I rip the tape off a box. "I have some posters in here too, and I love the new paint idea." We exchange a wider grin.

Daisy rests her feet on the skateboard, swaying them back and forth while she sits. "What color are we thinking? First one that comes to mind. Go!"

"Aquamarine," I blurt out, and then my face falls. Skin hot. Is it hot in here?

"Ooh, aquamarine. That also happens to be the eye color of a certain someone." She wags her brows. "Anything new you wanna share?"

I shake my head. "Nothing, really."

She sidles next to me with a pair of scissors, cutting open a different box. Her smile is softer and extinguishes the heat on my neck. "Nothing *nothing*. Or nothing *something*? Because I have this theory that nothing is just seven letters hiding an unspoken truth."

There are definitely unspoken truths when it comes to Garrison Abbey. But these truths aren't mine to release into the world. He's been so good about keeping *my* secrets from people—like anything I accidentally say to him about the Calloway sisters or Loren—that I wouldn't even think to share his.

And there are a lot of secrets at the moment.

Flunking out of Faust.

Lying to his parents about the boarding school.

Breaking into Superheroes & Scones and sleeping there at night.

I'm a little surprised I aided and abetted that last act, but he's my friend. And he needed my help. It's really that simple.

"The unspoken truth is…" I tell Daisy. "Besides you, Garrison is my only other friend, and so he pops up in my head a lot." I pale again. "Apparently, now with wall colors."

Daisy smiles. "Aquamarine would actually look really pretty. We can go to the paint store in a few—" She cuts herself off as her husky bounces into the room. "Hello there, Coconut." She squats down and scratches the dog's soft white fur.

A few months ago, around Daisy's 20th birthday, Ryke brought home the husky to help with her PTSD. Coconut is a certified service dog and also the cutest fluffy thing in this house.

"So are there house rules?" I wonder, pulling out a stack of hangers from the box. "It's just…I've never lived with three couples and two babies before. So I don't know how this works." Admitting my innocence causes my breath to shallow. I probably sound like a fool. Quickly, I look away before I can meet Daisy's gaze. If I can't see it, it won't be immortalized in my memory.

"Hey," she says sweetly.

I look up, and her eyes are kind and also vulnerable on me. Like she's trying to show me the sadder pieces and not just happy-go-lucky Daisy.

She tucks a piece of hair behind her ear. "I don't think many people have been in this living arrangement before."

We both look around the bare room. But it's not really the space we're feeling. It's the people, the fame, the wealth.

When our eyes meet again, Daisy says, "We're like unicorns here. Living out unique lives." She stares off in thought. "Not a lot of people will ever understand what we go through or even care, and that's partly why we've been drawing closer to each other, living together." She hugs her legs. "I wasn't always that close with Rose and Lily, but I really wanted to be."

"You weren't that close?"

And she goes on to tell me deeper things about her childhood, about being the sister left behind, and Daisy asks me more about my life in Maine.

We talk for hours and hours, and we forget about paint colors. It's a tomorrow project. Today, I just really like sharing her company. And I know I'm not going to regret moving in.

May

26

Willow Moore

INTERNAL FREAK-OUT STATUS: I'M ON A VACATION WITH THE Calloway sisters and their men.

Rose asked if I'd like to join their trip to the lake house.

Location: top-secret. No one online knows the destination. It's supposed to be a peaceful oasis away from the paparazzi. The fact that they're letting me in on this secret is a huge honor that I want to safekeep and protect.

The drive has been *long*. The kind that needs many pitstops and even driver rotations. Luckily, no has asked me to man the wheel. Not that I'm a bad driver. But both Jane Cobalt and Maximoff Hale are situated in car seats in the back, Connor sitting between the kids.

My nervous energy will most likely skyrocket with the responsibility of protecting the almost-one-year-old babies.

Right now, all that responsibility rests in Lily's hands, but she's undoubtably been the best driver so far. Her eyes barely even flit to the passenger seat where Rose texts on her phone.

"Is that Mom again?" Lily asks her sister.

Silence eats the car, and I wonder if whatever text Rose received is important. *Probably*. Very important people are in this vehicle. Like my brother. Lo sits next to me in one of the middle seats, an aisle between our chairs.

He gazes out the window, probably looking for the other car. Ryke and Daisy drove separately. The whole process of even leaving the neighborhood took security vehicles, diversions with an assist from bodyguards, and a lot of work before we even made it on our route.

It reminds me how secretive this trip really is.

I glance down at my cell, checking the ETA. We still have *hours* left. I wish I could text Garrison, but he handed me his cellphone this morning. It's currently stashed away in my backpack, squeezed between my shoes.

My stomach has been in a series of knots this entire car ride.

I may have…smuggled someone into this Escalade's trunk.

But he's blindfolded. (His suggestion.) He has *no* idea where we're headed, and he can't see a thing. I trust Garrison not to spill the location, but no one else in the car will trust him.

I know the blindfold might not help, but it's a last-ditch effort in case everything goes wrong and he's caught.

I haven't even been living with them long and I'm already doing something that could threaten their trust in me. My stomach tosses and turns, causing worse nausea than a normal bout of car sickness.

The alternative was worse. Leaving Garrison alone in Philly with nowhere to go. Lily installed extra security cameras at Superheroes & Scones, so Garrison can't sleep there anymore. If I don't help him, he'll have to return home where he could run into his brothers again. That's the last place I want him to be.

I'm his only friend.

Friends are supposed to smuggle each other in trunks.

That's just how it works, right?

Before I zipped him up in the duffel bag, I handed him a water bottle and a banana. He has nourishment and fluids. Still…

I'm freaking out a little bit.

It's impossible *not* to worry. He's in a *duffel bag* right now. Bumping along with the Escalade. And since his phone is in my backpack, Garrison has no way to communicate with me.

It's dangerous.

When we left this morning, I even shoved his cell back into his chest, knowing how risky this could be. What if he has heat stroke?

What if he doesn't get enough air? He could die inside luggage and I'm just sitting here with zero clue.

I told all of these things to Garrison.

But he just looked me in the eye and said, "You have to take my phone, Willow. Because if we get caught, you'll be in worse shit with your family if they know I had it." They'll think he snitched to someone about the lake house's location.

He was thinking about me.

I'm still thinking about him. I sort of hate that I agreed in the end. I mean, what's the probability that they'd even be angry if he had a phone? He's already blindfolded.

This was a *really* stupid idea.

"Rose?" Lily asks, since Rose still hasn't replied to her.

"She wants us at next week's luncheon," Rose replies, confirming that she's talking to their mom. "Which is *not* happening." I've heard about the fancy luncheons that the Calloway sisters go to just to visit with their parents. They don't sound fun.

A white Ferrari speeds up and drives next to our car; Coconut's head flops out of the open window. A big goofy smile on the husky's face. On the passenger side, Ryke clasps the top of the window frame.

Suddenly, Daisy steps on the gas, zipping off *fast*. The Ferrari must go from our speed (maybe forty?) to a hundred miles per hour in a second flat. My jaw is on the floor.

That is…terrifying.

And yet, I really love hanging out with Daisy.

"Uhh…" Lily gapes. "I'm not supposed to follow them, am I?"

Lo shakes his head. "No way. We're not driving off a cliff with Thelma and Louise."

Heat encases me, hot with worry. I dig through my backpack for a water bottle. "Do they know where they're going?"

Daisy said she planned to follow us, and I don't want her to end up in a ditch where we can't find her. Even the thought brings this wave of panicked sadness.

"Nope," Lo says. "I hope he gets lost." *Please no.*

"Knowing Ryke and Daisy, I'm sure that's their goal," Connor chimes in from the backseat.

I don't know if she'll receive it, but I quickly text Daisy. *Love you.* I wish I could text her the directions, but no one's allowed to share them over any electronic device. In case of hacks. Reminding her that I care is the best I can do. I wouldn't ever tell her to stop being who she is. Daredevil and all.

Leaning forward, I fiddle with the middle console air vents, trying to direct them towards the back. Even though I'm way too far away from the trunk.

But all I can think: if I'm feeling this heat, I just hope Garrison isn't suffering.

Please don't die in the trunk.

27

Garrison Abbey

I'VE DONE SOME STRANGE SHIT. DRUNK. HIGH. BUT BEING curled up in a duffel bag for *twelve* hours definitely is the strangest. And I'm stone-cold sober.

By hour three, I was rethinking the sober part.

I should've taken about five shots of vodka before Willow helped me into this bag. She volunteered to load the trunk just to make sure no one would throw their suitcases on me. Grateful doesn't even cut what I feel.

A blindfold covers my eyes, the fabric soft. I'm *fully* in the over-sized duffel with just an inch unzipped for air circulation. Every pitstop when it's clear the Escalade is emptied out of passengers, I readjust. Sometimes, I unzip the bag just so I can extend my legs. But I've only done that once so far. Not wanting to risk it.

She's putting a lot of fucking trust in me.

Bucket loads.

I'm not going to blow it.

But *fuck*, it's hot back here. My shirt suctions to my skin, sweat building. A water bottle pokes me in the spine, but I haven't taken a sip. I can hold my bladder as long as I don't consume liquids.

It's been a couple hours since the last pitstop where I stretched my legs, and I'm not about to do gymnastics with people in the car. Connor Cobalt's voice sounds the closest, which makes me think he's in the backseat.

That guy is way too perceptive not to notice something rustling around in the trunk. My legs ache, but it's better than ruining Willow's relationship with her family. I'm already putting that on a razor-thin line.

"You have two miles and then you turn right." Rose's voice is faint. *Front seat.* Maybe passenger side. It's been kind of a fun game trying to pinpoint the seating arrangements. At least it's taken my mind off of being in a duffel bag.

Fuck, my life is weird.

The car starts to meander around winding roads like we're driving on mountains. The movement churns my stomach. *Don't get car sick.* Dude, if I upchuck in this duffel bag and have to sit in my own puke, I might die. Literal death.

I breathe quietly through my nose and cinch my eyes close. I drift off for a couple minutes until Loren's voice shoots me awake.

"Hey!" Lo shouts. "Crazy Raisins!"

No clue what that's about. All I know is I haven't heard Ryke and Daisy's voices in the Escalade since we left Philly. I figure they must be in a different vehicle.

Rose yells, "Follow us, please! Daisy, you don't need to be driving in the dark!"

"How many times has she driven a car?" Connor questions calmly.

Recently, Willow asked me whether my Mustang would be faster than a Ferrari. I told her it depends on the models—but I'm not a car expert or anything. I don't think she meant to tell me more. I think she kind of slipped. But off my confusion about the question, since it was out of the blue, she kept going.

I know that Daisy's Ferrari is brand new. Two weeks new. I know it's also her first car, having only really driven motorcycles before.

Information I shouldn't have.

Information I won't share with a soul. I'd die first, I think.

Rose yells louder, "Daisy how many times have you driven any kind of car?!"

I strain my ears just to hear Daisy's reply from outside. "Cuatro!"

Four.

Holy shit.

"Bro, why are you riding in the deathmobile?!" Lo yells at his brother.

"We're fucking fine!" Ryke screams from outside.

If they're going to be fine, I have to believe I'm going to be okay. Because honestly, I can't tell what's a bigger risk.

Being in a car with Daisy Calloway or hiding out in this duffel bag.

Luckily, the choice has already been made for me.

THE ESCALADE IS PARKED FOR LONGER THAN JUST A PEE-BREAK. I can tell because they're all talking outside, too casually to be in a public space.

What I infer: we must have arrived at the lake house. I can almost taste freedom out of this suffocating duffel bag. Before that, though, I have to actually figure out a way to exit the trunk without being seen.

Easier said than done.

I stay quiet. Motionless. Listening to the sound of their conversation outside.

"Is anyone else scared of bears?" Lily's voice carries loudly. *Bears.* I have no clue where we are—but I'm guessing it's somewhere secluded in the woods. Shit, I don't really want to hypothesize when I'm not supposed to know the exact location.

"Moose are scarier," Willow says.

My lips inch up.

"There are moose here?!" Lily yells in fright. "Why didn't anyone tell me about the moose?! Lo, did you know about the moose?"

With her high-pitched tone, it sounds more comical than it should. My smile pulls higher, wishing I was out there. And then, my bladder suddenly rebels against me. Fuck, I have to piss. My legs ache, and I try to rub my hamstring without causing noise.

"No, no," Willow says swiftly to Lily, "I just meant in general. There were a lot of moose in Maine, but I've never been around here, so I wouldn't know."

"No moose," Connor declares.

Someone groans. Sounds deep like Ryke's voice. It's confirmed when I hear him say, "Can we please fucking ban the word moose from now on?"

"Agreed," Rose adds.

"I like a good moose in the morning," Loren pipes in just to be *that* guy and irritate the shit out of everyone. I'd give him a gold star.

I tune them out when my hamstring starts to fully cramp. *Motherfucker.* I grind down on my teeth and press the heels of my palms to my forehead. Might as well zip up this duffel bag and toss it into a hole. Bury me in the ground where I belong.

My insides twist, and I let out a tensed breath through my nose.

"We obviously need to go over the fucking rules about bears," Ryke says to something I missed. "Unless it's hunting season or the bear is attacking you, you can't shoot it."

"Says who?" Rose combats.

"The fucking law," Ryke replies. "I can't believe I camped with you, and we didn't talk about this. Look, I brought bear spray for everyone, so it's non-fucking-negotiable."

"Let's start unpacking before it gets dark." Connor's words ignite panic in every pore of my body. Unpacking involves popping this trunk. The one where I'm currently *stuffed* inside a duffel bag. I stop breathing. Stop moving.

I might as well be a corpse.

"You guys should look at the house first," Willow interjects. "I'll start unpacking."

She's got this, Abbey. Calm the fuck down.

"You're not here as manual labor," Loren refutes. "So you should explore the house with us."

Willow clears her throat uneasily. "I…" Her voice tapers off.

I wish I were out there helping her, but that'd just blow everything to shit. Guilt gnaws my insides. *You put her in this position*, my head screams at me.

I don't want to ruin her. Turn her into someone who lies to the people who love her. But I'm sinking, and I feel myself clinging to anything on shore. So I grip her fingers, and I'm terrified I'll pull her down with me.

I'm doing it right now.

I know.

I know.

Fuck, I know.

This was a bad idea.

Willow continues, more confident this time, "I was going to call my mom—I mean, *our* mom. Or…you know, whatever she is. I just needed a minute alone."

The quiet somehow sounds tense, and I'm not even out there.

A beat later, Loren replies, "Yeah, I didn't realize you were in contact with her, but…definitely, as long as you don't tell her the location of where you are—"

"No way. I'd never do that."

"I just had to make sure." He says something else, but cramping intensifies in my hamstring. It's worse than any cramp I've had in lacrosse, and I was that asshole drinking pickle juice on the side of a field trying to eliminate tight quads.

I think…I think I have to move.

Slowly and carefully, I reach down to my thigh, my fingers kneading the muscle. I have to angle a little to touch the spot. God, that feels better. I close my eyes as I continue massaging the muscle. My elbow collides with a hard suitcase and lets out a *thump*.

Pain blooms but it's dulled under my hysteria.

My heart jettisons from my body. Out of this car. Out of this planet.

Did anyone else hear that?

I listen harder. Voices are quiet, almost distant. I have no chance at distinguishing the words. I don't know if that's good or bad. And then...

The trunk beeps, indicating that the hood is lifting.

Oh fuck.

I suck in a breath, holding it. Not moving a muscle. *Please don't see the massive almost human-sized duffel bag in this car.*

"Garrison?"

Willow. I let out a breath of relief.

She whispers, "Can you...um...make sure your blindfold is on?" She adds quickly, "Don't reply. Lo is still on the stoop. I'm pretending I'm on the phone with my mom." She must have the cell to her ear. "I'm going to get you out of the trunk. Just hold tight, okay?"

28

Willow Moore

"ARE YOU ALRIGHT?" I WHISPER. "DO YOU NEED WATER? FOOD? Oh my God, your legs." I press my fingers to my lips. His calves are *swollen* the size of small melons.

Garrison rubs them as he sits on the edge of my mattress.

I've already snuck him inside the lake house, which took less maneuvering than I thought it would. All thanks to Ryke who wanted to give everyone a safety lesson with bear spray in the woods. They didn't question my phone call with my mom, so I stayed back to sneak Garrison up to my room.

Four stories, two-wrap-around porches, and giant maple trees *everywhere*, the lake house is a secluded majestic place. I feel a little badly that I blindfolded Garrison and he didn't get to see the outside. Because it truly is beautiful.

It's also *huge*.

Big enough that I have my own bedroom, and for this occasion— hiding a boy—I'm very appreciative of the size.

Garrison massages his calves. "I'm good, Willow." His voice is a whisper too. "Honestly, don't worry about me. You should go hang with your family. I'm cool to chill."

I wish we could be in each other's company for longer, and I hesitate to just abandon him here. "I'll bring up some snacks." My eyes flit to the en-suite bathroom. "If you use the bathroom when I'm not here just remember—"

"Not to flush," he finishes with a smile. "Got it. This isn't my first time being stashed away."

I pale. "Oh yeah. Of course. You've snuck into girls' bedrooms before." *Duh, Willow.* He was super popular before he met me.

"No. I mean, yes, I've done that. But not like this." He shakes his head. Eyes cinching. "I was referring to Superheroes & Scones. Although it was a stupid analogy. The place wasn't exactly packed with people when I was camping out there."

Worry pulls my face, remembering everyone I'm deceiving here.

He holds up a hand. "I promise, Willow. I'm not going to make a sound."

"I know. I believe you," I say softly. "I just want you to be comfortable." I don't want him to feel like a criminal I'm trying to hide away. Even though…that's exactly what I'm doing, isn't it? Hiding him.

He's not a bad person.

A tender smile touches his eyes. "Believe me, I'm the most comfortable I've been in a long time."

His words hoist my spirits, and we both quiet when the porch door creaks open. He nods me on with his chin. Silently saying, *go be with your family.*

What does it say about me, if I really just want to stay right here?

My feet, heavy like cement blocks, shuffle towards the door.

RAIN SLAMS ON THE DECK, THE PITCH-BLACK NIGHT CREATING an eerie feeling in the living room. The perfect atmosphere for a slumber party—which Rose Calloway has turned into a séance. Leather furniture is pushed against wide, floor-length windows to open up the space.

I cross my legs on a red bear-patterned rug and try to enjoy the evening. It's hard with the storm outside and my brain all the way back in my room.

My mind is on a 24/7 news cycle of Garrison Abbey. It's just…I haven't had much opportunity to check up on him. At least, not as much as I'd like. And I'm trying to stay in the moment and enjoy these gatherings. Many people would *kill* to play *light-as-a-feather, stiff-as-aboard* with the Calloway sisters.

I did just that.

The game ended with Ryke (who we were lifting) crashing down on Rose. Now we all sit in a circle, candles lit in the middle. It'd be scarier if we were trying to contact a demon or something. But Rose and her sisters just want to talk to their Old Aunt Margot, so it seems harmless.

That's what I'm telling myself.

A storm rages, thunder booming. It'd tag the mood as *dramatic* and *frightening*.

New eulogy: *that Willow Moore, what a chicken—afraid of some rain-drops.* Hugging my arms around my body, I watch the candles flicker.

Coconut howls from the kitchen, paws padding along the floorboards. Daisy goes rigid, and her head whips around the living room quickly. Like she's trying to mentally scan each nook and cranny.

I frown, worried that the dark, storm, and tiny bumps and bangs aren't good for her PTSD.

Ryke pulls Daisy closer to him, his lips beside her ear, whispering. She seems to relax a little at his words.

My lip nearly lifts, happy that she has someone like Ryke who cares. The thought makes me glance up towards the balconies.

Garrison.

I hope he's okay.

"Aunt Margot it is," Rose declares, pulling the attention back to herself. I think, maybe purposefully. That's just the kind of sister Rose is. She knows when to command the spotlight when others want to dip out of it. "Let's all hold hands." She extends her palm to me, and I take it.

Lily, Loren, Connor, Ryke, and Daisy complete the circle. The babies, Maximoff and Jane, are safe in their cribs upstairs.

"Close your eyes," Rose instructs.

My eyelids shut, darkness cocooning me.

"Aunt Margot," Rose begins the séance. "We're calling you, Aunt Margot." Rain hammers violently, the wind picking up. Goosebumps dot my arms. "We miss your beautiful, lost soul. Please come to us."

Lo chuckles, and it's practically contagious.

My lips threaten to rise, but I smooth them down.

Rose continues like Lo didn't ruin anything. "Fight through the barrier of the afterlife so that we may speak with you."

Craaaaaaaacccck!

I jump, my eyes shooting open.

Lily lets out a terrified, muffled squeal, her head hidden beneath a quilt.

"What the fuck was that?" Ryke asks. He glances out the floor-length window, maybe worried the lake house took damage from the storm.

"It's electrostatic discharge," Connor tells him. "Also known as lightning."

Lights flicker on and off until a bulb cracks and they all blink out. I think we might have just lost power. A chill snakes down my spine. Could this maybe not have happened during a séance? Coincidence, right?

"Ohmygod," Lily slurs in a panicked whisper.

"Old Aunt Margot?" Daisy calls out, the only one with her eyes still shut. "Can you hear us?" If I was just listening to her, I'd think she was having fun. Zero percent fear. But it's hard not to notice how her collarbones protrude like she's holding in a breath. Her knuckles whiten, gripped to her knees.

Whhhaaaaap!

Lily screams at the new noise, the one coming from upstairs. *Oh God, no.*

I shoot to my feet, my focus drilling on the staircase. I swear the sound originated from my bedroom, and maybe I'm just being overly paranoid, here, but Garrison is alone and there's a vicious thunderstorm outside.

Horrible images of tree limbs skewering windows and impaling *his* body ravage my mind. Gruesome *Final Destination* worthy fears that most likely aren't coming true, but it takes all of my energy not to run upstairs right now.

"What was that noise?" Lily asks. "Connor?"

Connor Cobalt stares at the ceiling. "An object fell."

"By a ghost?"

Unless the ghost's name is Garrison Abbey…it's no ghost.

Thuuuump! is accompanied by a long, sharp groan.

Garrison.

I don't even take account of the shocked, horrified faces around me. My ears ring, my focus tunneling as footsteps pad along the floorboards upstairs.

"Moffy." Lily bolts towards the staircase, towards her son's room, baby monitor in her clutch.

They think there's an intruder. Oh God. I mobilize, springing into action.

"Lily wait—" Lo runs after his wife, just as I sprint in the opposite direction. Footsteps gather behind me.

I'm being followed by Rose *and* Connor, but I don't stop. Not even as I hurriedly ascend another staircase on the west side of the lake house. Racing towards *my* bedroom and the source of the noise.

Without power, the second-floor hallway is encased in darkness. But even in the pitch-black, I know where I'm going. My pulse hammers in my ears. *Please be okay.*

Please be okay.

I land at my bedroom and turn the knob. Locked.

A glow from a cellphone flashlight abruptly illuminates the door—and me.

I squint from the sudden brightness. Connor holds up his cell from his six-foot-four height, and the glow bears down on me like I'm under the brightest spotlight.

Cover blown.

I don't care.

I don't care.

I only care about *him.*

I bang my palm against the wooden door. "Are you okay?" My voice cracks in worry.

"Is he in there?" Connor asks like he already knows who's on the other side. *How?* I instantly shake off my shock. I've been living with Connor Cobalt. He's perceptive.

Too much sometimes.

My mouth dries. Rose and Connor stand side-by-side, watching me.

"He didn't have anywhere else to go," I confess quickly, my chest concaving in heavy, petrified breaths. "I made sure to blindfold him here. I promise, he has *no* idea where this place is."

I've wrecked everything. They're never going to trust me again.

Rose raises her chin and takes my wrist, her touch more consoling than rough. She pulls me close to her, away from the door.

Connor reaches up to the top of the doorframe, a small key resting on the ledge. He uses it to unlock the door, and when he pushes it open, he points his flashlight cell at the room.

My stomach lurches.

Garrison sits on the edge of the quilted bed, a lamp shattered on the floor. *Blood.* I see blood. Spattered on the floor and trickling down the bottom of his heel. Garrison inspects his bare foot, a piece of glass lodged in the sole.

"Are you okay?" I ask and try to rush to his side.

Rose clasps my hand and tugs me back. "You're not wearing shoes either, Willow."

My stomach somersaults, but I stay put. Garrison avoids my gaze. Even with his head hung, I can see guilt caressing every inch of his frame. *It's okay,* I want scream and shout. He didn't mean to step on the glass. It's not his fault this secret is spilled.

Hair falls over his eyes. "I tried to turn the lamp back on. I ended up knocking it over, and I…" He winces and attempts to remove the shard of glass in near darkness.

"Don't," Connor warns. "Rose, can you get a first-aid kit and check on Jane?"

Rose is already heading to the door. "I'll be right back."

The room tenses now that it's just Garrison, Connor, and me. I scan the floor, wondering if I can Indiana Jones my way to Garrison without stepping on glass. Probably...*not*.

"One of you start explaining," Connor says casually, shoulder propped next to the doorframe and arms crossed.

Garrison mutters, "I hid in the trunk."

"He gave me his phone," I add quickly. "This entire time. He hasn't had it." I rummage through the pocket of my overalls—thank goodness they're deep. I hold up his cell. "See?" He can't contact anyone and leak the location of the lake house. I go further and explain how I snuck him into my room, while they thought I was talking to my mom.

Rose returns with the first-aid kit, her nearly one-year-old daughter in her arms, and a pair of shoes are on her feet. "I want to talk to Daisy and Lily," Rose says to her husband. Her piercing yellow-green eyes flit to me.

I've wrecked everything. "I'm so sorry, Rose—"

"I understand what it means to be loyal. But you shouldn't have kept this from us. If you wanted to bring your boyfriend along, we could've worked something out."

Boyfriend. Color drains from my face.

"Friend," I clarify. *Don't look at Garrison.*

"Would it make it better if we were dating?" Garrison asks.

My heart does a weird *thump thump* in my chest. Is he...no...I don't know. My face is numb.

Connor says, "It would make it exponentially worse."

Garrison's lips shut and his head falls again. I just want to hug him. And it's a weird feeling because I've never really *yearned* to touch anyone.

He's not alone in this. It was both of our choice to sneak him here. Guilt swims through me all the same. I waver uneasily by the doorframe. "Can I explain...I want to apologize to Daisy too...?"

Don't cry, Willow. I push back tears and emotion. But I feel horrible for causing her distress. For her thinking there was an intruder in the house, something that I know ramps up her panic.

This was supposed to be a safe place.

Thankfully, Rose nods. "Follow me."

We leave and find Lily and Daisy in Maximoff's room. Lily bends over the crib with a rattle, softly talking to the giggling baby. Daisy lies on the ground, her white husky curled up against her. She strokes her fur in long waves.

Rose shuts the door behind me, and Lily asks, "Is everyone okay?"

"Mostly," Rose says, then plants her gaze on me.

"I'm so sorry," I begin, water pooling in my eyes. Daisy lifts her head off Coconut's fur, confusion pleating her brows. And I just burst forth like a geyser. The truth flooding the bedroom floor.

I can't stop.

Not until I've outlined, in detail, how I smuggled Garrison to the lake house. Why he needed a place to stay in the first place, which means divulging the truth about him flunking out of Faust. By the time I finish the story, my eyes have glued to the ground, unable to stare them in the eyes.

"And I don't deserve your forgiveness," I add quickly. "Especially you, Daisy. So if you'd like Garrison and me to leave the lake house, I understand—"

"What, no," Daisy cuts me off abruptly. "I don't want that."

My heart thrashes, and I risk a glance. Daisy's on her feet, light touching her green eyes. She…she doesn't seem mad?

"You're not mad?"

She shakes her head. "You snuck a boy into a trunk of a car."

"Classic Gryffindor," Lily says under her breath.

Daisy continues, "You *blindfolded* him and took his phone just so that *we*"—she twirls her finger between her sisters—"could stay safe. Why would we be mad about that?"

I wipe at the corners of my eyes. "Because I should have told all of you."

"You're not the first person here to keep secrets," Lily says, rocking on the balls of her feet. "You fit right in."

Rose sends Lily a look. "Yes, but let's not make secrets a regular occurrence."

"Agreed," Lily nods.

Pressure lifts off my chest. "So Garrison can stay?" I ask.

Daisy plops on the edge of the bed. "He just spent twelve hours in a *duffel* bag." Her eyes ping to Rose. "You can't kick him out now."

Rose scoffs. "Why are you directing that to me? I agree wholeheartedly. He's earned his spot here."

Lily frowns like she's lost in thought. "How did he survive in that duffel bag anyway?" Before I can answer, she swings her head to me. "He must really like you."

Daisy crosses her legs and puts her chin to her fist. "Yes, let's talk about the one-and-only Garrison Abbey."

Oh no. "We're just friends," I reiterate. I feel like I'm probably going to be doing this for a while.

Lily squints. "You're going to prom with Declan, right?"

"Who's Declan?" Rose wonders accusingly, like she's a little perturbed she hasn't been told all the details. I like that she wants to hear about my life.

"He's a boy," I answer. "He's a regular customer at Superheroes & Scones."

Lily smiles, knowing about him since he frequents the shop so much.

"And he asked me to prom," I explain. "I said *yes*." Declan is nice. I met him at the comic book store. He was looking for classic *Star Trek* comics. We carry more *Star Wars*, so I had to go in the back to hunt for the issues.

He talks more than me. I just kind of listen.

"You don't seem excited about it," Rose notices.

"I am," I nod. "It's just…I'm nervous because we only really hang out at Superheroes & Scones. I don't have any classes with him at Dalton."

I've never actually been around Declan *at* school. I guess he could try to find me in the halls, but he never has before. I don't know what that means. "It's also the first time any boy has ever asked me out," I tell them. "I've never even been on a coffee date, so there are more nerves than excitement. That's all."

"It'll be spectacular," Daisy tells me assuredly. "And we'll help you get ready."

"Of course," Rose says like that's a known quantity in my prom prep.

Lily is still frowning. "Does Garrison know about Declan?"

"Yep," I say. "I told him. He said that Declan sounded like a starship trooper nerd."

Star Trek, I corrected him.

Aren't those the same thing? He feigned confusion. He's been working at Superheroes & Scones too long to get them mixed up.

All the Calloway sisters exchange a look that I can't decipher. Maybe they're thinking Garrison is jealous or that he's flirting. I've questioned it before, but I know the truth—we're *just* friends.

29

Garrison Abbey

GUILT HAS BEEN HAMMERING ME EVER SINCE WILLOW LEFT THE room. No…it's been that way since the lamp crash. No, since I was born. Maybe I came out of the womb with this sour, bitter feeling rumbling around inside me. Shame swims through my bloodstream, and it's going to stay that way until I bleed out.

Ryke sweeps up the broken glass, Loren lights candles around the bedroom, and Connor sits next to me with a first-aid kit.

"I can do that," I say when I see the tweezers in Connor's hand.

He passes them over. "You need stitches, and the nearest hospital is more than two hours away."

Let me bleed out, is my first thought.

The second: I'm not going to the hospital. I can't. There's no way I'm making this worse for Willow. The hospital will blow up this situation to catastrophic levels. I've already obliterated enough.

Ryke sweeps harder, pissed off. I'm not an idiot. He's angry at me for scaring his girlfriend. The one with PTSD.

I can't breathe.

I just grind my teeth back and forth, eyes clouding and burning. Connor's gaze sears every inch of me. "Can you stop watching me?" I snap.

"I could, but I'm waiting for you to answer me."

I inspect my foot, tweezers hovering above the glass. Under my breath, I mutter, "I'm not going to the hospital."

"What was that?" Connor's tone is calm, almost easy-going.

My nose flares, emotions bubbling to the surface. Unable to swallow them down, I shout, "I'm not going to the hospital!" I jab the tweezers towards the door. "I promised her I wouldn't ruin the relationships she's made with *any* of you—and if I go to the hospital, people will see you, take stupid pictures, and everyone will know whatever nowhere-ville state we're in. So *no*, I'm not going." I suck in a strained breath and focus back on my foot, jaw tight.

"Relax," Loren snaps. "We're not going to force you to do something you don't want, but I would like to know *why* you're here."

Ryke crouches to sweep the glass into a dustpan, his expression darkening. "If he's here to get laid—"

"What?" I wince. "No." I recoil at Lo's glare. "Not that I don't like Willow." *Jesus.* This is all going wrong.

Ryke joins in on glaring at me. *Great.* I have both of them wanting to rip out my jugular. But what am I supposed to say? I like Willow. If I could ask her out today, I would. But I'm too late.

I look to Connor as I admit, "Some starship trooper nerd asked her to prom, okay?"

And anyway, Connor told me this would be *exponentially worse* if I was dating Willow, so this starship trooper nerd should be a notch in the "you didn't fuck everything up" list. Except, I'd really just like to kick the starship trooper off the list entirely. He can go be in someone else's atmosphere and ask *them* to prom.

"Declan," Lo says the name that I'd like to never hear again. "You know who he is. Lily told me that he stops by Superheroes & Scones at least four times a week."

"To try to talk to Willow," I complain. "And what the fuck kind of name is Declan?"

"What the fuck kind of name is Garrison?" Lo retorts.

I roll my eyes and sigh. "Whatever."

Connor cuts in, "As amusing as all of this is, we're still no closer to answers, and I'd like them sometime in the next five minutes."

Ryke dumps the glass into a trash bag and then disappears into the bathroom. Lo kneels beside the bed and gestures for the tweezers.

I hesitate and then surrender them.

"Is there anything we can use to sew up the cut in there?" Lo nods to the first-aid kit.

That means we're not going to the hospital. *Thank you.* My shoulders drop and muscles ease.

"We can find an alternative if that's what he really wants," Connor says.

I nod. "That's what I want."

Ryke returns and hands me a cup of water. Connor passes me a packet of Advil. I'm unbothered by the physical pain, but something pushes through me at their kindness.

I don't deserve it. Not a single bit. Yet, here they are.

And it just barrels into me, the weight of the moment. I look between them, overwhelmed, and on the verge of tears. *Don't fucking cry, man.* I suck it down by asking a stupid question. "I thought you two hated each other?" I gesture from Ryke to Connor. Tabloids say they're at odds all the time.

Ryke answers, "We're good friends."

I stare at the carpet. Lost for words.

"What is it?" Connor asks.

I shake my head and tear open the Advil packet. "I was just thinking…I don't even know where I find the kind of friendship that you three have. My friends are dicks." I let out a short, pained laugh that scratches my throat. "I'm one too…"

A heavy beat pounds before someone speaks.

"We're all assholes," Lo tells me. "But one day, you'll meet an asshole that pushes you to be a better person. Those are the ones that stick with you."

I rub at my eyes once. *Don't fucking cry.* And then I toss back the pills with a swig of water.

"We're encroaching on my five-minute time limit," Connor tells me.

I don't even make a joke about him having time limits. Swallowing hard, I explain everything. Not even leaving out the part where I broke into Superheroes & Scones and slept in the breakroom for the past month. Failure is easy to admit

When I explain how I flunked out of Faust, my anger starts to boil. Eating me. I pull my hood over my head. "And you know, it's my parent's fault." My eyes burn as I look to Connor. He went to Faust. He must know how rigorous and fucking difficult it is. "Why'd they have to send me to a new school in the middle of the year? I know...I know I fucked up, but if I even want a high school diploma, I have to be *held back*. Do you even know what that feels like?" I'm an idiot for even asking.

Connor Cobalt is a genius. He's never felt *this* before.

"What about your friends?" Connor asks, ignoring my question. "They have houses, I presume."

"You mean all my friends that broke into your house to scare you? Those ones?" My stomach twists even thinking about them. How the judge sentenced them to a year each. *That could have been me.* Some days, I wish it were.

"No," Connor replies. "Your other friends."

"I don't have other friends. No one wants to be associated with the bad guy, not at Dalton and definitely not at Faust." I shrug. "I had nowhere to go, okay? I had Superheroes & Scones and Willow, that's it."

I. Am. A. Loser.

It might as well be tattooed on my fucking forehead.

But Willow is hands-down the most amazing person I've ever met—compassionate, brave, unique, shy—and she doesn't mind spending time with a loser like me, so that's something, I guess.

There's more to tell. More to get off my chest.

"I burned the letter that Faust sent my parents before they got it—the one that said I flunked. And you know..." My voice cracks, choked. "I've never been a good person. I don't even know what some of you see in me...because I'm shit."

"You're *not* shit," Lo tells me, forceful like that's already written in stone. Carved into marble. I don't know how he sees it so clearly. He adds, "You want this glass out of your foot?"

Lo is looking at me like I'm already a good guy. I don't get it. But I want to believe it. Someday. Somehow.

"Yeah," I release a deeper breath. "Yeah, I want it out."

30

Garrison Abbey

PULLED OUT OF DALTON.

Flunked out of Faust.

It's starting to feel like the worst kind of pattern, but I do have a third chance. "Your last chance, Garrison" as my mom so kindly put it. Confronting my parents about Faust was about as enjoyable as I thought it'd be. Spoiler Alert: it sucked.

My dad gave me the stern, *I'm disappointed in you* lecture. While my mom shared her disappointment by reminding me how my brothers were *never* this difficult. "You have so much potential, Garrison," she said. "You just don't *try*."

Right. It's all about trying.

My third chance comes in the form of yet another private school. Maybelwood preparatory.

I start in the fall. Maybe this will be it. Third time's the charm, right? I mean the school even has *Maybe* in its name. *Maybe* Maybelwood.

Luckily, I don't have to think about any of that right now.

It's still May.

School hasn't completely ended yet, even if this semester is over for me.

Walking down the neighborhood street, I step into a small pothole in the cracked cement. *Fuck me.* I don't fall. But my Italian black leather dress shoes are significantly scuffed. They cost about three grand.

This day is already going to shit.

But hey, I didn't drop the flowers. A bouquet of brightly-colored spring flowers is tight in my grip. Black slacks and white button-down complete my look for tonight's prom.

I check my watch.

Yeah, I feel like I'm running late even though it's still kinda early. But it's not like she *knows* I'm showing up to take her to prom. She probably needs time to get ready. Fuck, what if she rejects me? This?

What even is *this*?

Friends. *We're friends.*

I like her as more than a friend. I know that—but what if she doesn't like me in the same way? I mean, she was supposed to go to prom with the starship trooper nerd. I wasn't ever in the picture.

I force myself to just stop thinking, and I pick up my pace—but as I continue down the street and near the Hale's house, I see Connor Cobalt incoming like a fucking torpedo. He appears angled and aimed for the house across the street, not for me, but for some reason, I slow down anyway. I don't pass him.

With a quick glance, he takes in my clothes. The flowers. It's gotta be obvious what I'm doing, right?

"Where are you going?" he asks in a way that makes me even more certain he knows exactly where I'm going. Maybe this is like some Cobalt 4D chess. Hell, I just want someone to tell me I'm making the right decision here. That I shouldn't turn my ass around and hightail it back home.

I run a hand through my hair. Probably messing it up. Whatever.

"Some douchebag bailed on Willow, so I decided I'd ask her out…" I trail off, waiting for him to call me dumb.

His expression is blank. Typical.

The sun starts to set, casting warm glows around the street. "You have a couple hours before prom starts."

What does that mean?! Should I still ask her out? I wish he could drop his Connor Cobalt annoyingly accurate wisdom and just give me a fucking answer. Yes or No?

I point to him with the bouquet of flowers. "You know…people still talk about you at Faust. The upperclassmen said you had an answer for everything—that you were some kind of prodigy."

Please just tell me what to do.

Maybe he sees the desperation in my eyes. Because he says, "Here's my answer for you. Ask your friend to prom for no selfish reasons, no vain motives, nothing less than because you admire her and because you'd rather spend two minutes sitting beside her at a dance than five hours in the company of *anyone* else."

Friend.

I'm stuck on that word.

So he doesn't think I should ask her out as a date?

But he's not telling me to run away and ditch the plan altogether. That has to account for something. *Okay.* I can do this. She is my friend, regardless of the *other* feelings I feel for her. She's my friend.

Connor takes a step to the side and begins to head up the driveway. Not to the Hale House. But to the one *across* the street from it.

"Where are you going?" I ask him.

He turns to face me. "To set things straight."

Don't know what that means exactly, but I understand it anyway. I nod to him. "Good luck."

He smiles. "I appreciate the sentiment, but I don't need luck." *Damn.* He turns back around and heads up the driveway, reminding me that everything they said at Faust was kinda true. His confidence can't be fabricated.

I head across the street.

All emotions wrapped up into one goal. *Turn this night around for Willow.*

I reach the front door just as their garage door groans open. My stomach nosedives. She's leaving? For a split second, I imagine Lily probably whisking her out for a fun night to take her mind off prom. *I should have called.*

I run my hand through my hair again. It's totally messed up now.

Fuck it. I don't wait to see which car leaves the garage.

I knock on the door.

Please still be home.

No one answers.

I ring the doorbell.

I'm going to puke.

The door swings open. Rose stands on the other side, eyes piercing me in a pinpointed glare. I realize I didn't make the greatest impression by hiding in a duffel bag and crashing their whole lake house thing.

I fucked a lot of things, and Connor's already warned me that it'd be worse if Willow and I were dating. I can't expect them to be open to this idea of me taking her to prom.

Rose appraises me from head to toe, stopping for a long moment at the flowers in my hand. "You brought flowers," she says. "Who for? What are your intentions here?"

"I mean, obviously they're for Willow?" I say like a question. It's not a question. But I didn't expect an interrogation so early on.

"If it's so obvious, why do you seem so unsure?" she spits back.

Fuck. "No, they're *for* Willow," I say, confident this time. "That douchebag dumped her, and I'm here to take her to prom."

Rose tries her hardest not to smile—but she's failing. It makes me relax just a fraction, and I ask, "Is that cool?"

She opens her mouth, but she's cut off by a voice from inside. "Who is it?!" *Daisy.*

Rose gives me another harsh look, more in warning. "Don't fuck this up for her, or I will bury you in the backyard and let the squirrels shit on your corpse."

Jeeesus. I bypass that threat by focusing on the fact that she's opening the door wider. She's letting me inside. She's okay with this.

When I step into the foyer, I see Daisy hanging near the staircase. Her face brightens immediately when she sees me and the flowers and my formal attire. "Oh my God—"

"Go get her," Rose cuts her little sister off and shoos Daisy towards the living room.

I turn to look at Rose and...she's *beaming*.

Okay, maybe I didn't fuck this up.

"Where's Lo?" I wonder when it's just Rose and me.

"Determined not to go to the hospital." Rose explains quickly about his broken hand. Lily and Ryke are apparently in the garage, trying to get him to seek medical treatment. Knowing him, there's probably a slim chance he goes. But this is still good for me. I can at least see Willow without Lo chiming in.

I breathe easier again.

Until I see Willow round the corner.

Then my breath is gone. Behind her black-rimmed glasses, her eyes are a bit reddened like she's been crying. I want to run over to Declan's house tonight and strangle the guy for being a complete asshole. For hurting the sweetest girl on planet Earth. But I temper those feelings when Willow's eyes widen in pure shock. "Garrison?"

"That's me," I laugh. "In the flesh." This is it. I take a step forward. "These are for you."

She sheepishly takes the flowers from me like they're made of glass. "Wow...what are...is this...am I dreaming?"

"Not a dream," I say. "This is definitely real. At least, I hope so. I guess, I can't ignore the probability of some virtual reality. But— yeah, I just thought that since Declan turned out to be a Grade-A asshole, I'd take you to prom."

She puts her nose to the flowers, her smile lifting her lips. "Like a friend thing?"

My chest tightens. *Say no, not a friend thing.* But the happiness radiating from her is intoxicating, and if I say this is more like a date is that going to mess things up? Most likely...yeah. I mean, I'm the King of Fuck Ups. But I'm trying *so* damn hard not to fuck this up.

I nod. "Yeah, a friend thing."

Her smile doesn't wane. *Good.* Good. I made the right choice then. But why do I feel kinda like shit?

"Um..." Her cheeks flush in that giddy smile. "I should...get ready."

"Yeah, I figured. That's why I came early."

She smiles wider like I'm the sweetest person that ever existed. I don't see it. I never have, but I try to hold onto what she sees in me.

With Willow and Daisy gone, I'm left alone with Rose. Not the best feeling, but I can handle it. Even as she stares me down.

"So how are you getting there?" she asks *while* she pulls out her phone.

Seeing as how I'm grounded from using my car after the whole Faust shit, I only really have one option. And it's not the most romantic. "Willow has a car."

Rose looks up at me, horrified. "Her Honda?"

"Yeah."

"To prom." She says it like I'm unaware of our destination.

I'm fully aware.

"This was a last-minute kind of thing," I defend. "I mean, Declan dumped her *today*." Can we focus on the fact that he's the jerk?

"And he will rot in hell for eternity for it," she says coldly. Then she dials a number. "I'll take care of it."

"What does that mean?" For a second, I think she's plotting actual murder.

She puts the phone to her ear. "You're going to take Connor's limo." It's not a suggestion, and I'm fine with that. Anything to make this night the best it can be for Willow.

I just don't want to fuck it up.

WILLOW LOOKS STUNNING. LIKE OUT-OF-THIS-WORLD KIND OF beautiful, and Declan really needs to rethink his entire existence if he's dumping a girl like her. That sentiment was the *one* common ground Lo and I shared tonight. Yeah, he didn't make it to the hospital, so while Daisy, Lily, and Rose helped Willow get ready. Ryke and Lo were my company. We bonded for like point-two-seconds over the fact that Willow deserves a good night.

In the ballroom, her pale-yellow dress sweeps the floor, little pearls are somehow stuck into her braid like jewels (a product of Daisy's help, she told me), and most importantly, she seems to be having a good time. We smile. Laugh. The awkward limo ride is behind us as we drink some punch near the dance floor.

She told me a secret on the way here. One that I'm more *honored* to know than I am bitter to have been kept out of the loop of.

Loren Hale is her half-brother.

The world still thinks he's her cousin. I understand the need for all the secrecy. If everyone knew she was *that* closely related to him, it'd be a media frenzy. The thought of anyone invading Willow's space, like paparazzi and press, it would just send me. I hate it.

And yeah, it's big that she trusted me with the news.

I'm her friend.

She said that again in the limo. *Thanks for being my friend.*

It feels like the more we both say it, the more we put this weird kind of wedge between us. Like friendship has transformed into a legitimate third person that stands around and eavesdrops. The DJ switches to an old classic Green Day song that gets the crowd hyped.

I smile and turn to her. "Wanna dance?"

She pushes her glasses up the bridge of her nose. "Yeah, but I can't promise I'm any good at it."

"It's Green Day," I say. "It's more bouncing than dancing."

She looks around. Sure enough, most of the crowding is jumping and bouncing up and down to the beat of the song.

She nods a few times like she's gearing herself up.

I reach for her hand but stop. "Can I?"

"Hold my hand?"

"Yeah, dance partner." *Dance partner?* Jesus, that's lame.

She smiles, not seeming to notice my inward cringe. At myself, obviously. I'm being cringey. I don't know why. *Yeah, I do.* She nods, and Friendship the Person follows us onto the dancefloor.

It's awkward.

I don't know how to make it un-awkward.

I start dancing. Bopping to the beat. Keeping her hand in mine. *Don't intertwine your fingers*, a voice tells me in the back of my head. That's too much, right? Not friendship territory.

People are looking at me. Staring. Mostly because I'm *Garrison Abbey*—that kid who got pulled out of Dalton Academy. I recognize most of the faces, but I blur them from my mind. I just want to remember the good parts of tonight. Just her.

Willow and I are getting into the song. Head-banging. Singing some of the popular lyrics. Then she steps and slips on her dress, and I catch her arms to stop her from face-planting on the floor.

"Oh…" She breathes heavy. Her chest is up against my chest. My body stirs at the close contact.

Shit.

I pull away quickly, giving us space. "Sorry," I mutter.

"No, it's…" Her voice drifts off. *It's what?* I want to ask. We hold gazes for an extended moment; the awkward uncertainty becomes a sort of visceral, hot, yearning tension that I've never felt before. It fists my heart, my pulse thumping deeper. Just as I gain some courage, the DJ switches songs. A slow ballad begins playing, and part of the dancefloor clears for couples.

She stares at me for a long beat, waiting for a decision. *Don't ruin this for her.*

"We can still dance," I tell her.

"You sure?" She seems excited about it.

"Yeah, definitely." Staying on the dancefloor, I carefully and gently place my hands on her waist. Her eyes flit up to me. *She's nervous.*

I can tell she's as nervous as me.

My hands are at a respectable height a couple inches underneath her armpits, okay. Nowhere near the small of her back. Yet, I feel like I'm full-on hugging her even though I'm not. Lo would probably still murder me if he caught me touching his *sister*. Not that I'm scared of death by Loren Hale.

It's just that I don't want to push Willow.

Don't want to mess this up.

She eases a little as we sway to the song. I ease more too. We share soft smiles every other second. Even though it's May, the student council voted on a winter wonderland theme, so winter decorations sparkle from the ceiling. Glittery snowflakes and glistening silver tinsel. With the dozen life-sized ice sculptures and snow machine, it's obvious that Dalton Academy is well-funded. It's kind of magical.

It's prom.

In this gentle, wonderous moment, we sway and lock eyes, drifting into each other's gazes, and I'm swept into another reality. A reality where I deserve someone like her.

I think about tracking my hands down her ribs and then sliding them to the small of her back. I think about drawing her to my chest, my one hand slipping against the softness of her cheek. I think about her eyes closing as she leans in.

As I lean in.

I think about parting her lips with mine. Her soft exhale against my mouth. Her body sinking into me.

I think about all those things.

I act on none of them.

We dance. We drink punch. We talk. We laugh. We wedge a truth too deep.

Friends.

We're just friends.

And maybe that's all we'll ever be. Maybe.

August

31

Willow Moore

DALTON ACADEMY IS OFFICIALLY IN MY PAST. WHILE ALL THE seniors were ripping open their acceptance letters to Ivy Leagues and fancy private universities, they turned to me and asked where I was accepted.

With a weak, dying smile, I told them I never applied.

The shock and horror on their faces is forever engrained in my brain. But I'm happy with my decision to work at Superheroes & Scones for a while.

I'll save up money, so that when I'm ready for college, I can afford it myself. Lo offered to pay my tuition, but he's already financed my last year of high school *and* given me a place to stay. Coming to Philly wasn't about reconnecting with my brother for his wealth, and I have to be self-sufficient in order to prove that.

"Lily tried to slip me extra money in my paycheck," I whisper to Garrison in the storage room of Superheroes & Scones. I don't know why I'm whispering. It's after-hours, and we're the only ones here.

I'm supposed to be closing up, but Garrison stayed back to help me unpack the new *Spider-Man/Deadpool* issues that've been flying off the rack.

Garrison holds onto a plastic-wrapped comic, and his brows furrow. "Jesus. She wants you to go to college that badly?"

I shake my head. "She knows I want to go, and I think she feels guilty that I don't have the money for it yet. Anyway, I told her I wouldn't accept any bonus that the other employees aren't given."

Garrison smiles. "Knowing Lily, we may all have a 'surprise' holiday bonus next week." He makes air quotes with one hand.

"It's August," I say.

"Exactly." He places the comic on a stack, sorting the issues from oldest to newest. He's quiet for a second, unusually so, and I think maybe I said the wrong thing.

"Sorry," I apologize. "I shouldn't have brought up college…or lack thereof. For us both, I mean." I'm roasting.

He eyes me silently.

"It's just," I continue. "I know that it's a sensitive topic because of Maybelwood." When we returned from the lake house, Garrison finally approached his parents and confessed to flunking out of Faust.

They were angry, but they're also type-A's (as he put it), so they just went into immediate action and enrolled him in another school.

Maybelwood Preparatory. Also the same high school Ryke attended.

Garrison rarely talks about repeating his senior year, but I know his pride has been bruised. And I was the fool that just brought up college.

"Hey, Willow." Garrison leans over the edge of the box, two hands on the edge. We're a little closer now. I can smell his shampoo, a pine needle scent.

"Yeah?" I ask.

"No topics are too sensitive to talk about between us," he tells me. "Can we agree on that?"

I look him over, wondering if he likes discussing the tough parts with me—because there are so many untouchable, sensitive subjects in his life that we've been crossing together. "Yeah, definitely," I say, feeling relieved.

"Good." He smacks the side of the box and returns to sorting the stacks. "And I'm never going to college—so we can talk about it all you want. It's not a big deal."

I frown. "You don't want to go? Or you don't think you'll get in?"

"I don't want to go." His blue-green eyes hit mine. "You know when you think about something and it gives you this unsettling feeling, like you're a moment from breaking out into hives?"

Every day. "Yeah."

"It's like that. Times a billion. There's not a cell inside of me that wants to go. So I'm not going." His confidence in his decision radiates around the storage room. "Plus, there's an added benefit of getting to spend time with my girl."

My girl.

The room tenses at that term.

We glance uneasily at one another, then away. The air heavies. It didn't used to be like this. Not since *prom.*

We barely discuss what happened. How my date stood me up on the day of prom. My self-esteem leaped off a cliff into a major freefall.

That was until Garrison showed up.

He dressed in a suit and knocked on the door, ready to whisk me away and vanquish all the memories of ever being ditched.

We went as friends. That's what we both asserted *before* the limo, *during* the dance, and even *after* on the ride home. Friends.

There was no kiss.

No promise of anything to come.

Just friends.

It was a good night, but a little awkward. And tense. Like staring right at a purple elephant taking up the entire dancefloor. If I'm being truthful with myself, I *wanted* something more. Maybe not a kiss—I'm still not sure if I'm ready for that—but he could have put his hand on the small of my back or leaned in close. Instead, it felt like I was dancing with a friend.

Which is what we are. So I shouldn't be disappointed.

It's just…

He obviously didn't want to kiss me or else he would have asked like he did with hugging, right?

There was nothing standing in his way. No other boys. No school hundreds of miles up north. In fact, we're closer than we've ever been now that we live in the same neighborhood again. Plus, I confessed the biggest secret of all in the limo.

I'm not actually Loren Hale's cousin. I'm his half-sister.

"Whoa," Garrison said, but after the shock wore off, he smiled. Not mad that I lied. He was happy that I trusted him with the precious truth.

The opportunity to make a move was right there, wasn't it? But once that moment passed, awkwardness infiltrated tenfold.

And so the chance at prom came and flew by in May. Now August, we've skirted around the dance, but our friendship is solidly intact.

That's what matters.

But I can't deny the existence of this weird tension straining the room. I don't know what to do, so I just look at the first thing that catches my eye.

"Um..." I stammer before nodding to issue #6 where Spider-Man webbed Deadpool's mouth shut. "Could you hand me that? I haven't read it yet, and it looks like a good one."

"Yeah, sure." He grabs the comic from the stack and passes it over. Our fingers brush, and just as I'm about to pull away, Garrison takes my hand in his.

I drop the comic.

He drops my hand.

Oh God. "Sorry, I—" I have no words. I'm bending down to pick up the comic, and Garrison follows suit, until we're staring at each other from underneath a long wooden breakroom table that we drug into the storage area, just to sort comics.

"You don't have to be sorry." His own apologies skate across his features. *"I'm* sorry..." His nose flares.

We're both squatting, staring at one another. Unsaid things passing between us.

He shakes his head. "Dammit, I don't know why this is so hard. It's never been hard to talk to you." He rubs a hand through his hair. "But I fucked up."

"What?" I squeak.

"At prom. I fucked up," he says. "I should have asked you out then. It should have been prom. Not underneath…" He glances up, and I unfortunately follow suit. Wads of pink, white, and blue gum stick to the bottom of the table. *Ew.*

But my mind is wrapped around his other words. *I should have asked you out then.*

We meet each other's gazes.

My heart thrashes. "What are you saying?"

"Will you go out with me, Willow?" he asks. "And not just as friends. I want to be your boyfriend."

I didn't hear him right. I *must* be dreaming. This is about the same time I'd ask a friend to pinch me, but my friend is the one currently asking me out. So there's that.

"Um…" I stammer again.

Panic ascends his face. "You can say no."

I definitely do not want to say no. But still, I hesitate.

32

Garrison Abbey

WILLOW IS STARING AT ME LIKE I JUST TOLD HER WE'RE BOTH joining NASA together and heading on a one-way ticket to Jupiter. Maybe that sounds more realistic than the reality. Dating me.

I know I'm not a great catch, especially since I'm officially on my *third* prep school. But I just thought there's something between us.

Something more.

Unless I've been way off base.

Her mouth is ajar, eyes wide, startled like I'm a headlight that just blasted in front of her face. She hasn't said a word, and I figure she's probably questioning why we're even friends.

I fucked it all up.

"Hey, forget about it," I say quickly, salvaging what I can. "It's whatever. We can just be friends."

She reanimates abruptly. "No, I'd like you to be my...my um..."

"Boyfriend," I finish for her. My lips lift into a smile. *She'd like that.*

My excitement tapers off when she says, "Yes, that. But you should know some things before you officially ask me."

I can't help it, I'm smiling harder. "I thought I just officially asked you."

She pales a little, but her lips inch up. "Okay, true. But still, I need you to know what you're asking me."

Okay. No biggie. "Could we stand for this?" I ask. We're still squatting underneath the table. "My quads are killing me." Byproduct of Faust not having a lacrosse team, and now I'm getting ready to try out at Maybelwood's. Too much conditioning this morning.

Willow nods, and at the same time, we both rise. The box of comics is situated between us, and she skims her fingers over a cover like she's trying to take her time to gather words.

I wait. I can be patient.

A long beat passes before she lets out a tense breath. "I've never had a boyfriend before."

"I know."

"But it's more than that, I've never *kissed* a boy before." She stares at me, head-on. "And even though I like you—like *really* like you—and I want you to be my boyfriend, I still don't know if I'd be ready to kiss you right away."

Found the origin of her hesitation.

Honestly, I'm relieved. Because I figured this much out about Willow. It's not that big of a surprise. "I get that," I tell her. "I wouldn't want some label between us to flip a switch on what you're comfortable with either. We can be boyfriend and girlfriend without kissing."

"We can?" she asks like this scenario is unfounded and untested.

"One hundred percent," I say. "Honestly, I *really* want to kiss you. But I wouldn't pressure you. Whenever you're ready is good with me."

"What if I'm old and gray?" she asks.

I have a full-blown smile.

Quickly, she adds, "Not that I'm assuming we'd be together that long. Or even short." She presses a hand to her temple. "I don't know what I'm saying."

"I'm following," I tell her. "And I'm totally here for being senior citizens who only hug each other. It's not like some other dude would be making out with you or having sex with you—that I wouldn't be able to stand."

She nods slowly like she's almost in a daze. "Me too." She blinks. "I mean, I also wouldn't be able to stand some girl making out with you or…sex." She grips the edge of the cardboard box. "So you'd really be okay with waiting? Isn't intimacy like a foundation of a good relationship?"

"I mean, I'm not an expert," I say, "but I think we can have intimacy without kissing or sex."

Her eyes flit around me. "Like how?"

"Can I touch you?" I round the box to stand in front of Willow.

She nods once. I wrap my arms around her body and tuck her into my chest. My chin rests on the top of her head, and her arms kind of dangle at her sides. Her heart is a rapid, nervous organ inside her chest, thumping against me.

This tenderness doesn't exist in my life except right here.

"Willow," I whisper. "Can I be your boyfriend?" I ask again, this time better.

Her fingers slide against the belt loops of my pants. "Yeah. I'd like that." And then she adds, "So I'm your girlfriend? Does this mean I'm not your *girl* anymore?"

"No way." I close my eyes, letting my smile pull my cheeks. "You're still my girl, even more now."

September

33

Willow Moore

"SO I NEED TO TELL YOU ALL SOMETHING," I DECLARE TO TOO many people.

I don't love being the center of attention. Commanding a space like this is my own personal nightmare. Even if I'm just speaking to these six people in Lily and Lo's living room.

I count the heads: Lily and Lo, Ryke and Daisy, Connor and Rose.

The latter moved out of the house during the summer. They live in this regal mansion down the street, so it's not as if they're too far away.

Garrison stuffs his hands in his leather jacket, a backwards baseball cap covers his thick brown hair, and he watches me with silent encouragements in his aquamarine eyes.

Lo swings his head from Garrison to me and back to Garrison. My older brother's glare is slowly boiling. Eruption imminent.

And he doesn't even know why Garrison is here yet. Spilling this news might actually make it worse, but there's no going back.

I push up my black-rimmed glasses and take a steady breath. "I thought it'd be a good idea if Garrison was here too." I regret speaking the obvious detail. It causes an intense reaction.

Lo abruptly stands from the chair, and Lily clutches his leg like she's trying to keep him from confronting Garrison or maybe even chasing him out of the house.

"Is he part of your news?" Lo asks hesitantly.

Daisy suddenly wraps an arm around Ryke's waist, both seated on the couch. It's hard not to notice Lily and Daisy physically restraining their men.

Well, this is already going terribly.

"Yeah…" I grab onto the strap of my overalls, the motion a nervous tic.

Garrison slides closer to me, and his fingers thread through mine. My pulse accelerates, but I also breathe easier.

"Are you pregnant?" Lo asks me.

"What?" I choke.

"Yeah, *what?*" Garrison snaps, his face darkening. He motions to the entire room. "If anyone's knocking up anyone, it's one of you, and honestly, what the hell are you wearing?" He grimaces at Ryke.

"Underwear," Ryke says like it's just another day of being nearly naked in the living room.

"I see that, thanks," Garrison says dryly.

Do not look again, Willow. Do. Not. Look.

Since I've walked in, I've tried hard not to glance at Daisy's fiancé. (Yes, they're finally engaged!)

Me avoiding Ryke isn't just because he barely has a shred of fabric on, though that's a good reason. Mainly it's because his single piece of fabric happens to be a *tight* pair of boxer-briefs that, from a quick glimpse, look like they're five sizes too small.

Words might also be on the cotton.

I'm not about to do a double-take and stare hard enough to check.

Ryke is *intimidating.*

I thought since I've grown closer to Daisy, it'd lessen that intimidation, but it somehow amplified it. He's the fiancé to my best friend *and* the brother of my half-brother. Ryke and I don't have a personal relationship like I have with Lo or Daisy or even Lily who's my boss at Superheroes & Scones.

But I do live with him. He's around and helpful and not close to the aggressive jackass that the media likes to paint him as.

Still, Ryke Meadows is and will always be certified intimidating.

If I'm being honest with myself, most of the people in this room carry a hefty amount of intimidation with them. It makes this declaration that much harder.

I swallow a lump in my throat. "So, um…this didn't really go how we thought it would."

"Why are you saying *we* like he's a part of this?" Lo points an accusatory finger at Garrison.

"It's not what you're thinking," I stumble over my words. *This is going so,* so *badly.* "I'm a…" The word is stuck in the back of my throat. How do I do this? Help!

Garrison squeezes my hand, and thankfully, he finishes for me, "Virgin."

Lily peers over the couch at Garrison. "You're a virgin?"

Garrison groans. "No, *she's* a virgin. Good God, it's like tuning into five different radio stations at once when I come here. Don't you all ever get tired of each other?"

"I'm mostly tired of you," Lo refutes in his serrated tone. Even I flinch.

Garrison's lips downturn a fraction, and I can tell that missile struck him. "Whatever," he mutters.

I squeeze his hand this time.

Regret flashes in Lo's gaze for a quick second before he looks to me. "Your news can't be that you're a virgin and your friend isn't one, so what is it? Because I keep thinking you're leaving—"

"I'm not leaving," I say, confidently. "I don't have plans to move back to Maine. I promise I'd tell you if I was even thinking about it."

He nods slowly. "Is it…about something else with your parents?"

I shake my head quickly. There's no change on the parents front. My mom is standoffish whenever I call, and I haven't spoken to my dad since I moved to Philly.

"Then what?" Lo asks.

"We're together," I spit out and then lift up my hand that's interlaced with Garrison's. My heart wants to fly out of my ribcage. *Breathe, Willow.*

I realize I'm dating the same boy that vandalized their house. He was a part of a friend group that caused serious harm. I just hope they'll give Garrison a chance, so they can see what I see in him.

Lo's face is all scrunched up. Like he can't parse out what I just said. "What do you mean together?" he asks.

Connor gives a textbook definition of a boyfriend and girlfriend, and I make a mistake by looking at Ryke. His expression is ten times worse than Lo's.

Jaw set. Eyes flamed. Muscles in his biceps are ripped. He's a professional free-solo climber, ascending mountains with his bare hands. He could probably knock Garrison out with one blow.

Ryke fights with his fists, and Lo fights with his words. But I know Ryke wouldn't hit Garrison. I trust him enough in that regard, but I hate that it already looks like he's judged my boyfriend.

Written him off.

Whatever conversation I just tuned out, it ends with Lo glowering at Garrison. I have to fix this.

"It's only been a week," I explain quickly. "I know it's not a long time, but I really didn't want to sneak around, especially since I live with some of you."

Garrison watches me, still by my side. We feel like a team.

"We have rules," Lo starts.

"Have fun," Lily declares, her smile overwhelming. My lips start to lift.

"No, not have fun—what the hell, Lily?" Lo gawks at his wife.

"They're eighteen."

"Yeah, we're eighteen," Garrison echoes.

Lo glares. "Last I remember, you're still in high school." That's a low blow. I wince.

Garrison sighs heavily. "You're not her fucking father." This is true, and also a good point. I've tried hard not to burden Lo. I'm just his little sister.

"You're right," Lo says, "I'm her brother and the *first* person she should trust while she's in Philadelphia." He takes a step closer to

Garrison. "She's my responsibility, and while I trust you with a lot of things, I don't want you upstairs in her room past two a.m.—and two a.m. is more than I'd give any kid of mine." Another step. "And keep the door open."

Surprisingly, I relax at his words. Maybe Lo knows I'd want the rules.

Garrison said he'd be patient and wait for kissing and sex, but I'm more worried about me. That maybe I won't be able to say *no* when he asks me if I'm ready when I'm not. That things will go too fast and I won't know *how* to slow down. Everything is new for me.

The rules will help give me an excuse to stop things before I'm ready to move forward. I can blame curfew or my overprotective brother. It makes it easier to say *no* without feeling guilty about it.

I want this relationship to go at my pace. A slow pace. Even if it's a turtle crawl.

Me staying quiet is putting strain in the air. Both Lo *and* Ryke look five-seconds away from pushing Garrison out the door.

Before I can say anything, Garrison slowly unlaces his fingers from mine. My stomach drops, but he gives me this reassuring nod. "I'll text you, okay?"

I nod back. "Will you check my gifs before you go to bed? I want to post them, but I think one isn't working."

Garrison nearly smiles. "Yeah. I'll do it first thing." He acknowledges the rest of the room with a curt wave and then heads out the door.

"When? Where? How?" Lily blurts out.

Her excitement fuels my smile, and I feel my shoulder dropping in ease. "So you're all not upset?" I linger on Lo.

"You can do better," he tells me.

Daisy steps forward. "She knows Garrison in a way that none of us do, so we should really trust her instincts." *I love Daisy Calloway.* I've never felt what it's like to have a friend so unwaveringly in my corner until her. We exchange smiles.

"You know what I don't trust?" Lo says. "An eighteen-year-old horny motherfucking guy's instincts."

"Same," Ryke adds.

"That's why there are rules, right?" I say. "So nothing should go wrong?" I hang onto this. Or else their apprehension will start to seep into me. I'm heading into uncharted territories here, and I know I'll turn to people more experienced than me for advice. I just don't want their advice to make me *more* nervous.

Who am I kidding? Garrison Abbey, the practical reincarnation of *Jess* from *Gilmore Girls*, is my first boyfriend.

Repeat that a hundred times and maybe it'll seem true.

He is so out of my league.

Yeah…

I'm nervous.

34

Willow Moore

TACO NIGHT IS ALWAYS THE BEST NIGHT, AND LIVING WITH MY brother means it's a common occurrence.

I lean my hip against the bar midway between sprinkling cotija cheese and dolloping some guacamole onto my plate.

With greasy fingers, I text Garrison back. His parents are hosting some cocktail party at his house, so I invited him over for tacos.

I slide my phone in my overalls, and glance around the kitchen. Maximoff giggles from his highchair while Lo plays "airplane" with a spoonful of yogurt.

Lily stacks tortilla chips on a plate, creating a nacho tower. The house is quiet with Ryke and Daisy out camping for the night, and Rose and Connor are busy at their own place.

"Garrison's coming over," I tell them.

Lily immediately beams. "Oh perfect. It's a good night for..." Her voice tapers off at the look Lo is slipping her. "Tacos. It's a good night for tacos. What else did you think I was going to say?"

If I had to guess, she was going to say *it's a good night for a first kiss.* Lily made me pinky promise that I'd tell her when I had my first. She's very invested in blossoming love.

Lo's brows rise. "Every night is a good night for tacos, love." He turns to me. "And if he makes a move on you, his dick is going where it belongs. In the garbage."

It's not the first threat I've heard, so I barely react this time.

My phone buzzes.

Garrison: Hey, so I can't come over anymore. Parents are all over my ass about staying in and studying on a school night. I would argue with them but they've got friends over. Tomorrow?

I text back: Yeah definitely, tomorrow is perfect.

Lo and Lily watch me, and the air already tenses. I must wear disappointment all over my face.

But I brush it off quickly. "False alarm," I tell Lo. "He has to study."

Lo's face cinches, angrier at the prospect of Garrison *not* coming over. "He didn't seem to care about studying before he was dating you. Now he's ditching you to hit the goddamn books." He fake gasps. "Holy fuck, he's turning into a nerd." Lo accidentally whips the spoon around and yogurt flings off a little, splattering Maximoff's forehead.

The baby laughs so loud his face turns red.

"Listen up, Moffy." Lo wipes the yogurt off with a towel. "If you date a nerd, just remember that they'll love books over you."

"Not true," Lily interjects. "Rose and Connor love each other over their hardbacks."

Lo smiles bitterly. "The Queen and King are an exception." He looks to me, seriousness coating his brows. "Is Garrison okay?"

I still. "Why wouldn't he be?"

"Because it's a common line. Saying you have to study when something else is going on." He shrugs. "I can't even count the times I said it to our dad growing up." As soon as he finishes the sentence, he sees my expression and his face falls.

Our dad.

What…?

I don't understand. I'm…

Robert Moore is my dad…

Isn't he?

"Willow—"

"*Our* dad." I swallow hard. "What—what does that mean?"

"Fuck," Lo curses and drops the spoon in the sink. "Can you take a seat?"

I can't move.

He stares at me for a long moment. Maximoff lets out a small giggle. "Hey, Moffy," Lily whispers to her son. "Let's go watch some cartoons." She lifts him from his highchair and carries her baby out of the kitchen.

"I didn't find out until just recently," Lo says. "The day you told us you were dating Garrison. Right before you came over, that's when Ryke told me."

Ryke.

Ryke.

Oh…

I stagger towards the barstool, bracing the edge. Too much to process. I only think about one question. "How long did Ryke know?" I ask. "The whole time?"

Years?

Has he been keeping this from both of us?

Lo grimaces. "*No.* No way," he says. "He learned just last month. Our dad actually just found out last month, too." He laughs at that. "Bastard finally got the rug pulled out from under him."

Jonathan just discovered that I'm his daughter, which means something even worse. "My mom kept this secret," I whisper.

It's another horrible lie. Something she could have told me a year ago, at the very least, when I left Maine to come to Philly. Maybe she wasn't certain, but even then, she could have told me she had reservations about my birth father.

Instead, she stared at me point-blank and said, *"Robert Moore is your dad."*

I'm a Hale?

I grow cold all over and slide onto the barstool. Meeting Lo's eyes, I ask, "This…this doesn't change anything, does it?"

"Between us, no," he says. "You're still my little sister." He runs a hand along the back of his neck. "But now you have another big brother."

Oh.

My.

God.

Why didn't I think of that? Ryke Meadows is my half-brother. We're related. My jaw drops, my eyes grow wide. I can't even *think* of Ryke like that. He's Daisy's fiancé. He's Lo's half-brother. Ryke and I, we have no relation.

But now we do.

Lo zips to the refrigerator, filling up a glass of water. He slides it to me. "I'm more worried about our dad. He can be...harsh." He grimaces like that's not even the right word. "I'm being kind here." He exhales a sharp breath. "He's an asshole. A fucking dick. And Ryke will tell you to stay a million miles away from him."

I clutch the sides of the glass. "What do you say?"

"I love my dad," he confesses. "And even though he's done some horrible, messed-up shit, I know he loves me too." He laughs bitterly. "His love for his children is one of the few things that I don't ever second-guess. I get it, if you want to feel that again from a father...or maybe for the first time. It's your choice whether you want to actually see him, but if you do, just know that I'm going to protect you."

I think I need time to think it over.

Think it all over.

But I'm not sure I want to meet a "dad" that I'd need protection from. That sounds terrifying. Lo leaves me alone to drink my water.

I text Garrison: do you have time for a phone call?

His reply comes seconds later as the Caller ID lights up with his name. I spend the rest of the night filling him in. Saying the words out loud to Garrison makes it feel even more real.

February

35

Willow Moore

I'VE BEEN TASKED WITH "CAKE" PICKUP FOR DAISY'S BIRTHDAY. It also happens to be a joint bachelor/bachelorette party. My first I've ever attended, but I'm not covered in a nervous sweat or anything. It's supposed to be a super lowkey gathering at Connor and Rose's mansion. Just the core six, me and...my boyfriend.

A goofy smile expands across my face, just thinking the words. Garrison and I have been dating for months now—since September—but there still hasn't been a kiss. I'm more comfortable with his touches than I've ever been.

Handholding. Hugging. Lying on the same bed together.

It's been nice, and there've been a couple times I could've seen myself kissing Garrison. Like during the summer when fireworks lit the sky.

Yet, I was too chicken to make the first move. And he didn't attempt it.

I realize I'm the one who chose the tortoise-slow pace, and I might have to be the one to *initiate* a faster one. But I don't know how to go about that without descending in my head and becoming a mess of nerves.

Anyway, I'm trying to focus on good things. Birthdays. Bachelor/ bachelorette parties.

"I can't believe they ordered a dick cake." Garrison's eyes flit to the box on my lap. It indeed has a cake inside. Shaped like a giant penis.

Garrison's hand tightens on his Mustang's steering wheel, driving back from the bakery. His eyes meet mine briefly, and his brows rise. "It was a choice."

We're both near laughter. "Did you expect anything less from them?"

He shakes his head. "Not really." He glances from the box to me. "You want me to carry it in?"

"No, I can do it." Though that does cause a wave of anxiety, but I want to push through it for Daisy. It's her birthday after all. My eyes flit to the clock. We're running behind. Traffic near the bakery was a nightmare. Luckily, it's mostly cleared up now.

Garrison follows my gaze. "Hold on."

He accelerates, speeding all the way to the gated neighborhood.

"I DON'T KNOW IF I CAN EAT THAT," LILY SAYS, EYES NARROWED as Ryke cuts the head of the...dick cake.

The eight of us pack into Connor and Rose's enormous kitchen, fit with state-of-the-art appliances. I've chosen a nice alcove by the expensive toaster.

It's the furthest spot from Ryke.

Ever since I found out he's my brother, I've been avoiding him. I haven't even spoken about Jonathan Hale (AKA my dad) since my conversation with Lo.

Change is hard.

But this change feels monumental, and I know I'm taking the cowardly route by dodging the reality. But we can't all be Dorothy in the Land of Oz—brave and bold. At least, not all the time.

I've let this avoidance fester so long that anytime Ryke tries to talk to me, it's this big awkward mess. Ryke Meadows is like a brooding, teeth-bared wolf, unapproachable and protectively menacing, and that's just how I felt before he became my brother.

Now that we're related, I can barely step a pinky toe in his direction without cowering. It's ten times worse.

I never saw him filling this brotherly role in my life, and since I'm dating Garrison—that's *two* brothers I have with opinions on my very first relationship.

It's a lot.

Ryke looks to Lily and says, "It's just a fucking cake."

I push my glasses up the bridge of my nose. Garrison's shoulder presses right next to mine. It's nice that anytime I'm invited to something, he's automatically invited too. We're a pair now. And even though I never felt like a seventh wheel with the core six, him being with me brings this sense of completion. Like it was always meant to be *eight*.

Garrison leans casually against the refrigerator, an unlit cigarette peeking from the pocket of his leather jacket. His eyes are on me. Mine on him. It's hard to set them anywhere else when I feel the most comfort swallowed up in his orbit.

"Why'd you take so long?" Lo asks accusingly.

Garrison swings his head to my brother. "We pulled over to fuck," he says dryly.

Oh...*God*.

I am used to his sarcasm, but not in front of my brothers. Not like *this*.

Ryke's jaw hardens. Lo's sharpens.

I choke on a breath. "We...didn't."

"They know that," Garrison tells me.

Connor makes a pot of coffee. "It's as though you want them to hate you." *That actually might be true.* I think he feels undeserving of their kindness, so he pushes them away.

Garrison pauses before saying, "That's stupid."

"You said it, not me," Connor states.

"Who wants the head?" Daisy asks, raising a plate with a slice of cake. I give her an appreciative look for the interjection and then spin towards the freezer, grabbing a tub of vanilla ice cream.

"I'm trying to remember why I like you," Lo tells Garrison, ignoring Daisy, "but it's all clouded by an image of me stabbing you, so be lucky I'm not holding a goddamn knife right now."

Garrison almost smiles. "You still like me?"

I caught that too. My spirits lift.

Lo enunciates, "*Me* stabbing you to death. Value your own life for me, so you can at least be kind of frightened."

I focus on opening the tub of ice cream—helping out and distracting myself—and then I lean into Daisy's ear to whisper, "I'm so embarrassed."

Daisy hugs my side and says even softer, "They love you, you know?"

I glance to Ryke, but the second he turns towards me, I abruptly rotate back to Daisy. My brain is singing a song on a loop. It goes something like: *Ryke Meadows is your big brother. He's your brother. Older brother! He's Ryke Meadows and you've got him as a brother! HE'S YOUR BROTHERRRRR!*

My face flames and stomach churns.

I so clearly avoided his gaze, didn't I? There was nothing smooth about it. I refocus on the ice cream. Tasks are good. Tasks keep me away from thinking about how awkward I am.

After I stick a spoon into the ice cream, I notice Rose handing Lily a middle portion of the cake. Lily shakes her head. "I can't eat the shaft."

"Lil." Lo melds his body behind hers. "It's *cake*."

"It's a penis."

"No, love, *this* is a penis." He takes her hand and places it on his crotch.

"Lo!" A smile accompanies her squeal.

I'm used to the overly flirtatious antics and PDA, but I've been roasting since I showed up to this party. Today is on a different level. I sidle back to Garrison.

"Daisy!" Ryke calls out, standing near the dick cake. Swiftly, he scoops the chocolate cake into his palm and *chucks* the hunk at her face. It splats against her nose and mouth and eyes, pink frosting dropping off her chin.

Her smile stretches. "This means war," she warns.

"Come at me, Calloway."

Daisy digs her hand into the cake and throws a hunk at Ryke. It hits him square in the cheek.

The food fight erupts, Lily and Lo joining in. Connor and Rose sip coffee by the pot, hand-in-hand, and remain out of the battle.

I back up into Garrison's chest to avoid being pelted with a flying piece of cake. He wraps his arms over my collarbones, holding me.

Lo and Ryke are doing the most cake throwing, and one chunk finally pelts my shoulder, splattering my top with pink icing.

Garrison spins me around to face him. "You've got something on you," he says, lips inching up.

"That's because I was shielding *you.*"

His grin explodes. "And look at that, you did such a good job." He places his hands on either side of my shoulders, and slowly, we do this dance maneuver. I follow his lead until I realize we're just walking in a circle. Until *his* back is in the crossfire of cake.

He tells me, "Now it's my turn to shield you."

Warmth ascends. I block everyone else out.

He dips his finger into the icing on my shoulder and then draws on my cheek. I can feel the shape he creates. *A heart.*

My pulse slows down like it's drunk. Intoxicated.

I swipe some icing with my finger and reach up to his cheek. He dips his head so that I can reach. I draw a star on his fair skin.

We're a breath apart, his face closer to mine.

"Willow," he whispers so softly. "Can I kiss you?"

There is no hesitation. No question.

I know in my heart I'm ready.

"Yes," I breathe. I feel the sudden flare of anxiety that comes with doing something new, but it fades as his lips draw to mine.

I close my eyes.

He's soft and gentle, and his palms hold the small of my back, pressing me close. Eagerness zips through my veins. Pulsing in places that have never really been lit up by someone. I lean closer, and he matches the movement, pinning me to the cabinet. Sparks ignite throughout every inch of my body.

But then I remember I have hands.

Those pesky appendages are just dangling like noodles at my sides. My heartbeat speeds up in unease. *Where do I put these things?*

Garrison must sense my sudden apprehension, and he breaks from my lips for a millisecond. Just long enough for his eyes to caress mine.

Quickly, he just drops his hands off me and takes my palms in his. He guides them to the back of his head, and his baseball hat tumbles to the floor.

Oh…that's where they should go.

But he doesn't make me feel silly for not knowing. Instead, he presses a soft hand to my cheek and returns to my lips.

Our eyes close again, and he deepens the kiss, edging my mouth open. A soft noise catches in the back of my throat. One that I don't even know if *he* heard. But I cling harder to Garrison all the same. I follow his lead until he breaks away for breath. Forehead pressed to mine.

"That was my first kiss," I whisper to him.

He smiles. "I know." His eyes dance around me, trying to read my body language. I wouldn't even be able to translate it for him. "Did you like it?"

"Yes," I say, my body heating up from truth. "A lot. I think…I think we should do it again sometime."

"Definitely. But later," he agrees. "When we're not in a room with your brothers."

My brothers.

Oh shit.

I forgot about them. In fact, I forgot all about the other six people in the kitchen. I glance past Garrison's chest. Daisy and Ryke are lost in each other's eyes, swaying to invisible, nonexistent music. Cake stuck in their hair and covering their arms.

Lily and Lo are MIA.

Connor and Rose have migrated to the couch, backs turned to us. No one was watching us.

I'm not sure if that's the real truth, but I'm going to the grave believing it.

October

36

Garrison Abbey

WE'RE HUDDLED NEAR THE BACK OF CONNOR COBALT'S LIMO, my laptop propped open on the trunk. Water slowly trickles from a fountain in the yard. The Cobalt Estate is made for royalty. If their mansion could talk, it'd be calling all the other houses on the street "peasants."

Cold bites my bare skin. My costume for this lovely Halloween: a red T-shirt, red slacks, and a red-horned headband.

I'm the devil.

All thanks to Loren Hale.

Halloween happens to land on his birthday. And yeah, I phrased it like that because after knowing the guy for this long, I don't think the universe put his birthday *on* Halloween. It's definitely the other way around.

As a present to Lo, we've all let him decide our costumes for the night.

Willow tucks a piece of hair behind her ear.

A circular gold wreath hovers over her head. Knee-length white dress and matching wings round out the outfit. An angel to my devil. I'm shocked. Not that Lo would choose something pure and perfect for Willow, but because he picked *matching* costumes for us.

It looks like we're a couple.

We are.

But I didn't think Loren Hale wanted to announce the fact to the world. Not like *this*. He still glares at me anytime I get within three inches of her lips. I get it. He's overprotective of his sister, especially now that I'm dating her.

Willow and I are doing well, and that's all that matters to me.

She glances at the opened laptop, an email server popped up next to a hacking software. But we haven't been talking about that.

I'm stuck on news that recently came out. "I don't get it. The artists and creators of *The Fourth Degree* must have smoked one too many joints. None of it makes sense. I shouldn't have won."

Willow moves closer to me to whisper, "You deserved to win. Your superhero was the best." She says it like it's so simple.

A while ago, Lily and Lo gave every Superheroes & Scones employee a chance to create a new superhero in *The Fourth Degree* universe.

The Fourth Degree is a wildly popular comic book series from Halway Comics. Vic Whistler (Extent) is the main character, but they're diverging to new lines and opening up the entire world for more heroes, antiheroes, and villains.

The whole thing has been plaguing me ever since the winner was announced. I just…I don't see how I won out of *everyone* who works there. People were making flow charts for this shit. It was a big deal.

If Lily was the judge, maybe I'd think she was taking pity on me, but no one in the store has ever talked to Belinda and Jackson Howell, the artists and creators of *The Fourth Degree*. It's not like they could have played favorites.

Compared to the other employees, I shouldn't have won. I barely read comics. Barely know the lore. I'm doing better than when I first showed up, but I'm not a walking encyclopedia like most of them.

My throat is dry. "I don't know. Carter had a cool superhero."

Willow's face scrunches up. "His was basically a rip off of *X-Men*. And Maya was right when she called it a Walmart Pyro. You know, Maya even said if she had a vote, it would've been for Sorin-X. So it must be good. If you don't believe anyone else, you have to believe her taste at least."

Maya Ahn would have voted for my superhero…

Damn.

That hits me. Because Willow's old roommate is the last person to feed you bullshit, and she probably has the most comics knowledge at Superheroes & Scones. More than anyone.

Sorin-X.

My creation is going to be an actual superhero. Or…more like an *anti*hero. At least, that's how I pitched him. He has teleportation powers linked to the proximity of the girl he loves. He can't teleport more than four miles away from her. And he's a recovering alcoholic.

Lo never gave me shit for it, since it's kind of obvious I drew my inspiration from him. So that's something.

I tap my computer screen. "This shouldn't take me long. Maybe just tonight." Daisy's ex-friends have been finding ways to get her phone number, even after Daisy blocked them. They've been harassing her enough that she asked me for help. Hence, the laptop.

It sucks that the price of fame can be so cruel. Like past shitty friends coming back to make your life hell. Jealously eats people up in different ways, I guess. I wish that Daisy's ex-friends could find their chill, take a hint and stop texting her.

Willow pushes up her glasses. "It's nice that you're doing this for Daisy, but…are you sure you want to? Isn't it illegal?"

"Yeah, but is it *really* illegal if I'm doing it to help someone else?"

Willow ponders this for a second. "Um…that sounds like a trick question."

Damn, she really is an angel. I lean in to kiss the top of her nose.

"Mother of dragons!" Lo yells at the Cobalt's mansion.

We've been waiting for what feels like forever for Connor and Rose.

Dressed in a navy blue, silver, red Thor costume and a winged helmet, Daisy outstretches her plastic hammer towards Lily. "You stoleth thy lightsaber, you pesky fairy."

Lily looks even ganglier in her Tinker Bell costume, green tutu dress and wings. She whips out a blue plastic beam. "Prepare to meet thy doom, Thor." Lily and Daisy are grinning as the plastic weapons make contact.

Ryke gave Lily his lightsaber, and he also lent Daisy his blackish-brown robe. So now he's just dressed in a tunic and pants. I nudge Willow's shoulder and nod towards Ryke. "He still look like Anakin Skywalker to you?"

Willow grimaces and shakes her head. "Lo's going to be upset. *But* Daisy is pregnant, so maybe he'll understand that Ryke is trying to keep his pregnant wife warm." Willow beams at the words *pregnant* and *wife.*

Daisy went through hell and back trying to get pregnant, and Willow's happy for her best friend. Hell, I'm happy for Daisy. It's hard not to want joy for someone who brings so much joy to other people.

It's why I'm confused whenever anyone wants *me* to be happy. You know, why want that?

I point to my laptop screen, catching Willow's attention. "I'm going for it."

"I'll bail you out of jail if anything goes wrong," she says softly, smiling.

My lips lift.

"Devil!" Lo shouts at me from up the driveway.

I raise my gaze from the computer screen, unsurprised that I'm being given a nickname.

"You know what happens when an angel and a devil create a bodily union? The apocalypse." *Jesus* this *is why he gave us a couple costume.* "Do the right thing and don't end the world tonight."

"That's definitely not how that works," I say dryly.

Lo looks to Ryke. "Do you hear this guy?"

"Yeah. I guess he doesn't understand the fucking meaning of apocalypse. Want to spell it out for him?"

I cross my arms over my chest and give Ryke a look like, *why do you have to be on my case too?* Man, it royally sucks that Willow now has two brothers. One was enough since his name is Loren Hale. Adding Ryke into the mix is like throwing in barbed wire and explosives.

I'm not a fucking GI Joe doll. I'm not about to run through their obstacles with a smile and *yes, sir.*

It doesn't help that Ryke doesn't trust me. I see it in every inch of his *I fucking hate you* stance and his towering, broody ass glare.

"Apocalypse," Lo defines, "also known as the end of your godforsaken, puny little life by the powers that be."

"Also known as *me*," Ryke chimes in.

"And me," Lo finishes with a half-smile. "Welcome to hell."

I barely blink. "I've seen scarier."

Ryke's brows jump in surprise. "Who?"

"My brothers." I turn into my computer, a little shocked I even uttered those words. My abdomen tenses and I roll out my shoulders. Whatever.

Lo and Ryke have dropped the whole overly protective brother routine, and Willow nudges my shoe with hers. "Sorry about them," she whispers.

I shake my head. "It's good they care about you." If it were any other guy on the receiving end of their bullshit, I'd probably be applauding. Willow deserves people to care about her enough to grill whatever guy she's with. I'm just the lucky asshole who gets her.

"They're ten fucking minutes late now," Lo complains. As soon as he says the words, the front door opens. Rose struts out first in a long, light-blue draped dress with a gold belt, along with a platinum blonde wig.

Daenerys Targaryen. The Mother of Dragons from *Game of Thrones.* It's not my genre of choice, but I've been watching with Willow.

I glance to my girlfriend. Her smile has officially burst across her face. "It's perfect," she says softly. "I never thought I'd get to see Rose dressed up as Dany." Before I can say anything, she leans a hip against the limo and angles to me. "Are you nervous about the party?"

"The Halloween party?" I ask. Lo gave us bare details. It's in the Hamptons at some famous singer's house. He annoyingly forgot the singer's name. I know this is Willow's first "adult" Halloween party that'll include more than just chaste apple bobbing.

She nods.

"Not really," I tell her. "Are you?"

"Yeah, it's just…" She rubs her arm. "Their bodyguards aren't allowed in the mansion, and what if something happens?"

"Nothing's going to happen," I say, and I don't add that if anything *does* happen, it'll probably be to the people more famous than us. That'll just make her worry for Daisy. "What are you nervous about specifically, anyway?"

"People. Lots of people. Being touched or not knowing where to go. Getting lost…lots of things."

Fuck. "I'm not going to let anyone touch you." Even thinking about it is like drilling nails into my skull. Not happening. It's not fucking happening.

WILLOW AND DAISY ARE GONE.

They left us for the bathroom, and everyone thought they were "taking way too fucking long" so we all went on a search and rescue party.

It failed.

No surprise there. I told everyone we should have just stayed at the same spot they left us. The velvet-lined coffin. The probability of them returning was a million times higher than us finding them in this maze.

But this is what happens when you have Ryke and Lo together. They freak the fuck out. I don't have a sister, so maybe I'd be the same. I don't know.

I am worried.

Just a different kind of worried. I keep checking the doorway every five-seconds. On edge. Waiting impatiently for Willow. Her words from before keep cycling through my head. *Being touched.* She's scared about all the roaming hands and bodies, and it'd be impossible not to bump into people here.

Every room in this mansion is packed except for the kitchen. Maybe because it's the least decorated area in the house. Just tiny candles set along the granite countertops.

Lo, Ryke, Rose, and Connor all congregate near the kitchen bar, agreeing to the "wait it out" method. Connor is closest to me, watching me type on my laptop that's propped up on the stool.

He's dressed in an *almost* identical costume as Ryke. Except it's all white. White robe, white tunic, white pants. Like he's some ethereal fucking immortal. If he wasn't carrying the lightsaber, I'd just think Lo dressed him up as a god.

In reality, he's Luke Skywalker.

And right now, Luke fucking Skywalker is *hovering*. When six-foot-four Connor Cobalt hovers, it feels like you're under the shadow of the tallest high-rise. It's an intense, uncomfortable place to be. I'm trying to just ignore him, but he keeps watching my computer screen as I type.

I check the doorway again.

This time Daisy and Willow walk through it. I intake a breath, and before I can get a good look at my girlfriend, Ryke rushes to Daisy, blocking my view.

"Where the fuck did you go pee?" Ryke asks. "We've been looking for you two everywhere." He sets a hand on the top of Daisy's head, his cane in his other one. After Ryke married Daisy in Peru, he had a bad rock-climbing fall, and he needed surgery on his leg.

I don't even like to think about the climbing accident. I've had bad days—but almost losing Willow's brother…yeah, that ranks up there.

"To the moon and back," Daisy answers Ryke. He looks to Willow for a better answer.

"Just the first-floor bathroom. No one was by the coffin when we came back."

"Told you," I say to everyone. Immediately I regret it because I sound like a douchebag yelling out *told ya so!* I'm a dick.

"You're either *really* embodying this whole devil thing," Lo tells me, "or it's just in your soul." He's not even looking at me. He's raiding the house's pantry with Lily hanging on his waist, trying to pull him away with as much effort as she can muster. It's not much.

"Lo, you can't," she pleads.

Lo retrieves a box of Cheez-Its. "I *can*. Maybe they should've thought about snacks, huh?" He opens the brand-new box in front of her face.

Lily whispers, "Should we write an IOU?"

"Lil." He pops one in his mouth. "Think of it as their birthday present to me."

"It could be worse," Connor tells her, but he's still glancing at me and my computer. "He could have broken into the liquor cabinet and consumed a forty-thousand-dollar bottle of alcohol."

Ryke adds, "And had a bunch of Ninja Turtles chase after you down the street."

"See, love," Lo says to her. "My worst is over."

I almost snort. *That shit* actually *happened to him?* Jeez.

Lily smiles and holds out her hand. He pours Cheez-Its in her palm, his own smile spreading across his face.

Rose sips sparkling water and paces between the doorway, hawkeyed. She's been like that since we arrived at the party, even more so since Daisy and Willow got lost.

Honestly, I'm used to Rose being in complete battle mode. She's basically the Joan of Arc of the core six.

"No one fucking hit on you, did they?" Ryke asks Daisy. The sudden question slices my chest, and my focus zones in on Willow for a split-second.

She's sliding closer to me, and when she gives me a look like *I'm okay*, I return my gaze back to the computer screen and try to relax. Willow doesn't love attention drawn to her. Us being together and showing any kind of PDA is like a spotlight bearing down telling her brothers *look here!*

I'm trying my best to make sure that light isn't so bright.

So I pretend that I'm so fucking interested in code that I don't really notice her. But I slide my hand down her arm, her skin silky smooth, and my fingers lace firmly with hers.

I squeeze her hand, and I'm close enough to hear her breath shallow. *Fuck* that causes mine to shorten.

"I'm pregnant," Daisy reminds Ryke in a tone that basically says, *I couldn't possibly be hit on.*

"Yeah?" Ryke says. "Your sister thinks it wouldn't fucking matter if you were pregnant or not."

Willow clears her throat. "We were approached...Daisy handled it really fast though."

My head whips towards Willow. "What?" My stomach tosses, and it feels like the floor caves underneath me.

Ryke's jaw hardens. "What do you mean *approached?*"

Willow makes a soured face like she's grossed out. *Please tell me they didn't...*

Fuck. I can't even think it, but I know I have to ask it.

"Did someone touch you?" I ask under my breath, hopefully soft enough that not a lot of them hear. Preferably no one but Willow.

"No, no, like I said, Daisy handled it really fast. It was just... weird, I guess. He was old."

"Fucking fantastic," Ryke mutters.

I'd like to say I'm relieved, but I'm not. I hate that Willow had to go through anything that made her uncomfortable. I hate I wasn't there to at least call the guy a fucking creep or push him away.

"It does seem like there are more guys here than girls," Lily says, munching on Cheez-Its. I did notice that, but it's a statistic that I really don't care to be reminded of.

Lo nods to Willow. "You want to leave now?"

She shakes her head vigorously. "No. It wasn't that bad, honestly."

I don't know if she's just trying to be nice and not ruin the night. Worry mounts, and I kiss her on the cheek. Hand to the back of her soft neck, my lips move to her ear, and I whisper, "I'm sorry I wasn't there. Tell me everything that happened later?"

She nods and I pull her against my side, tucking her to my body.

"How many steps are left?" Connor asks me.

I shake my head, not following, and then I remember he's been watching me on my computer all night. I lick my lips and type one last line. "That's it," I say.

"That's it?" Daisy says eagerly, edging closer. She glances at the screen, full of computer code. Her brows scrunch together.

"Whoever they had hacking into your accounts will be met with porn spam when they try again. I also increased all your security passwords, and I've written them down for you." I dig into my pocket, pulling out a pack of cigarettes and a crumpled piece of paper. I hand the paper to Daisy. "I had to add a defense to all of your accounts, by the way. No one should be able to find your phone numbers unless you personally give it out."

Daisy releases a giant breath in relief.

I motion to Lily. "And your passcodes took me thirty-seconds to hack."

Lo gives her a look.

"Whaaa…" She crinkles her nose. "It's not anything familiar to anyone, I promise."

"It is though," I say. "Your favorite movie is *X-Men: First Class.* You said it in an interview, which is public knowledge. You can't use 2011xmen as your password—"

"Shhh!" she hushes me with bugged eyes and waves her hands like she's swatting flies. "Someone's going to overhear and get into my work email."

Besides the eight of us, there's no one in the kitchen.

"If you want, I'll help you change it tonight."

She nods repeatedly.

Connor closes his lightsaber and gestures from me to the laptop. "You taught yourself code?"

"Yeah."

"Why?" Connor asks like he's actually interested. But he can't be. I'm *me.*

"I like it." I shrug. "Code makes sense to me. Does there need to be another reason?"

Connor smiles. "There could be, but the reason you gave me is the best one."

37

Garrison Abbey

I COLLAPSE ON WILLOW'S BED, REELING FROM ONE WEIRD-ASS Halloween.

Willow places her halo headband on her dresser. "I still can't believe what happened," she breathes. "It's almost out of the movies."

Ryke and Lily disappeared from the group for a little bit, and when they came back, they were covered in white powder. Flour laced with *cocaine*. Apparently, a group of guys dressed as zombies flour-cocaine bombed them as they were leaving the bathroom.

"A movie we missed," I tell her.

We didn't see it happen.

She pauses. "Is it kind of bad that I wish it were filmed? Not just the flour-bomb. But the whole thing, I mean. And not for online or other people." She strolls to the bed, still wearing angel wings. "It's just, it'd be kind of nice to relive some of the good moments."

I nod, agreeing. My lips lift at that last part. "Tonight was good?"

"Yeah…besides the cocaine," she repeats. "And the emergency room." We all took Ryke and Lily to the hospital, just to get checked out.

Lily broke out into a rash, and Ryke's leg is bothering him. So they're still being admitted overnight for observation.

"So like ninety-percent *good?*" I ask.

"Ninety-nine." She smiles.

I don't want to bring up the guy she ran into then. The one who was gross towards her and Daisy. If she's not thinking about it, there's no point in rehashing something that would drop the "good" percentage.

"Come here," I say and lean forward, grabbing her wrist.

She slides onto the bed next to me. The house is empty. Everyone's still at the ER, and I can't remember who's babysitting Maximoff and the Cobalt kids, but the important part is that they're MIA.

Ever since our first kiss at Daisy's birthday, she's let me explore her body with my hands. But I've never touched her below the waistband of her panties or above the tops of her thighs. I'm careful to take things at her pace.

Don't get me wrong, I'm dying a hundred deaths waiting. Every particle inside me wants to rush through. To caress each inch of her flesh, map out her freckles and study her body so I know it expertly.

But I won't fuck everything up by pushing Willow too fast. I've fucked enough up in my life. I can't fuck up this.

My lips meet hers, and I guide her back down onto the mattress. Her angel wings crumple a little beneath her.

I cup her cheek and edge her lips open. My body stirs to find pleasure points in both of us. But most of the time, I finish in the bathroom.

I'm fine with that.

I just wish I could make her come. She's never had an orgasm in her life, other than from herself, and I, so fucking badly, want to give her that earth-shattering pleasure.

Her breath hitches as I suck on her bottom lip and then move to her neck. She's soft and hesitant and always in her head. Her hands lie next to her, not on me, because they're fisting her comforter tightly.

I suck harder on her neck, and her hips arc into me with need. I'm quick to rise on my knees, my bodyweight hoisting enough that she can't feel my erection. I don't want to pressure her into thinking she needs to get me off.

She doesn't.

I'm a fucking adult.

I'll be fine.

I barely pause, my hands sliding on top of her breasts. The fabric of her dress and bra soft under my palm. I knead her, and she lets out a raspy breath. I want to give her more.

And thank you *V-cut* dress for giving me easy access, so I graze my hand underneath her padded bra. Her nipple is already perked, and I continue massaging, my thumb brushing over the sensitive bud. Her breath staggers.

My dick throbs.

Hardening more.

With my other hand to her hips, I squeeze her flesh tightly. She squirms underneath me. *Fuck, how wet is she?* My head screams at me to check, to just slip my hand between her thighs and release these pent-up feelings that I can *physically* see coursing through her.

I clench my jaw, shutting down those thoughts.

"You okay?" I ask Willow in a whisper as my mouth glides to the other side of her neck. I press my fingers into the soft flesh of her ass, near the back of her thighs.

"Mmm," she breathes out her nose, already sinking into those cravings. And then just as suddenly, she goes rigid. Her entire body locked.

I lift up on my hands, enough that I can look her in the eyes. "What's wrong?" I ask, my gaze dancing around her body for more signs of discomfort.

"Nothing," she says so softly that I have to lean down a little to hear. "I just...I keep forgetting to touch you. It's not that I don't want to. It's that I get so lost in everything and—"

"You know where your hands are right now?" I ask her and look to her fingers, still tangled in the comforter.

"On the bed."

She doesn't get it, so I explain, "Willow, you're death-gripping the sheets like my dick is already inside you. It's fucking destroying me. In the best way."

Her lips lift slowly. "Really?"

"Really." Her shyness in bed is a literal turn-on. I never even predicated that.

She bites the bottom of her lip. "Should we get undressed?"

"It's up to you."

Her gaze flits to the top of my head, where my devil-horned headband pushes my thick hair back, keeping strands from falling into my eyes. "I like this." She touches a horn.

"Yeah?"

She nods, and then swallows hard. "We can stay dressed, if that's okay with you?"

"I'm good with that." Honestly, a little relieved too. My brothers came home from college to celebrate my dad's birthday last weekend. I'm still a little bruised and sore from their "brotherly roughhousing." Hunter elbowed me in the back when I tried to bail on dishwashing duty. I can still taste the bar of soap he shoved in my mouth.

I just don't want Willow to worry. I'll tell her about it another night.

She's quiet, still staring up at the devil horns on my head. I think she might be overthinking something else. So I just ask, "You okay?"

"Um...so I'm not ready to have sex," she whispers. "But I think I could do more tonight."

More.

Fuck. My muscles tense, head spinning. "Do you want me to make you come?"

She smiles. Like a fucking hundred-watt smile, brightening the whole room. "Yeah, I want that."

Fuck. Yes.

I roll onto my side, elbow propped up on the pillow and hand supporting my head. Willow moves like she's about to roll onto her side to face me. I press a hand to her belly. "Stay on your back," I tell her.

She relaxes where she is, but she turns her head to face me. I've come to know a lot about her. She likes instructions. It takes this immense pressure off her from feeling like she has to already know what to do.

"Can I touch your clit?" I ask her.

"Mmmhmm," she says, breathing through her nose again.

I smile and place a soft kiss on her lips. "That a yes?" I whisper against her mouth.

"Yes," she squeaks.

I pull back to stare at her beautiful brown eyes again. "Can I put my fingers inside you?"

She pauses, hesitates, and I sweep her frame, gauging her reaction. "Um…"

"That's fine," I tell her. "I don't need to be inside you to make you come."

Her mouth parts in arousal. "You can put them in me though," she says quickly. "I was just thinking that it might hurt. I've only ever had one inside."

One finger.

Fucking hell.

Blood rushes to my dick, begging me to ease into her. I grind down on teeth and bottle those urges. My hard-on strains against the fabric of my red pants, and I swallow down images of Willow fingering herself, which have definitely stormed my brain.

"Garrison," she smiles a little like she can see she's getting to me. "You okay?" She touches my jaw.

"*Fuck*," I groan and then stare down the length of her. "I want to make you come so goddamn badly."

"Then do it."

My mouth drops a second in shock and desire, and her glittering smile reaches her eyes.

"That a demand?" I ask.

Her smile falters. "No. Of course, you don't have to—"

Fuck. I kiss her again, stopping her from overthinking this to death. When I part from her lips, I say, "I'm going to make you come, but I'm only going to put one finger in you. How does that sound?"

She nods and relaxes more. I scoot closer to her, our legs tangled.

But I'm still lying on my side while she's on her back. I have a better view, and she has less chance of feeling my erection.

Our lips continue to explore each other, deepening, and while she loses herself to the moment, I skate my hand underneath the waistband of her panties.

Holy…

My fingers immediately dip into her wetness. Soaked. I skim the top of her swollen clit, and she shudders instantly. I barely rub her, and she breaks from my mouth with a soft cry. "*Garrison.*"

Fuckfuckfuck.

She buries her head into the crook of my chest, breath heavying as I make soft circular patterns over her sensitive flesh.

Moans breach her lips, and her eyes snap shut like her senses are overloading. Reboot and restore are not going to be in progress any time soon. Not until I give her the best orgasm of her fucking life.

I can't believe she's this sensitive with nothing inside of her.

It's blowing my mind.

I press my thumb more firmly onto her swollen bud.

Her thighs tremble, and she lets out a whimper.

"I have you," I say. "You're alright."

She starts thrusting against my hand. Arching her hips.

I don't think she even knows what she's doing because her eyes are closed, and she looks gone. But it's like her body is calling out for a release. Calling out for me to fill her completely with my length and bring her to that peak. It's like her body knows what it wants faster than her head.

But I'm listening to her head on this one.

Still, I watch her hips lift and lower in small throbbing waves. My body is set on blaze, and I ache to reach down my pants and release my one pent-up need.

I'm not there yet. But I've got to end her torment.

I slide a finger through her slick folds and inside her. Beyond tight, she immediately clenches around me. *Christ.*

Her legs vibrate, and her forehead presses harder into my chest. "Garrison. Ah…"

I pulse inside of her a couple times and continue circling her clit. It happens so fast. Her abdomen spasms and her cries bleed into the air. Her hand whips to my wrist to stop my movements. Too sensitive. Too gone.

She curls up on her side, even with my hand still against her heat. Like she's cocooning herself against me. My head is floating, a billion miles in the sky. So wrapped up in this girl.

Her flesh glistens with a light layer of sweat, and I brush back her hair so that I can see her face. "You okay?" I ask.

"Mmmhmm." Her breathing is still heavy.

I can't last much longer. I remove my hand from her panties, my fingers slick. "I'm going to the bathroom. I'll be right back. Promise—"

She catches my wrist to stop me.

Veins pulsate in my dick. "Willow," I whisper. "I have to go jack off."

"I know," she says, still out of breath. "You can do it here, though." Here?

"In your bed?" I lick my lips. "You sure?"

"Yeah. I want to…um…watch you."

I smile. "Seems fair." I just got to watch *her* orgasm. I lie on my side again.

She smiles back. "Do you need—"

"Don't offer it, if it's just because you think you have to," I say, stopping her. "I don't need you to touch me if you're not ready."

Hesitation fills her gaze. "You sure?"

"Yeah. This is enough." I didn't even think I'd be doing this tonight. I slide my pants to my ankles and kick them off. Just in my boxer-briefs, I slip my hand down the fabric, gripping my rock-hard dick. Unlike her, I don't close my eyes.

I keep them open and attached to Willow as I stroke myself.

She watches me with parted lips.

She looks at me like I'm an otherworldly thing too good for this Earth, but I'm lying next to her jacking off while literally wearing a devil's costume.

In my soul, I know, hell is where I'm from.

February

38

Willow Hale

ON ONE OF THE BEST DAYS OF MY LIFE, IT HAS TO BE POURING. Rain pelts the roof of the courthouse, and I guess it should feel ominous. But I couldn't be happier sitting in the first row beside Garrison and my dad.

My dad.

I've been referring to Jonathan Hale as my father for almost a year now. He reached out to me, *wanting* to have a relationship. Wanting to get to know me.

Our first real meeting as father and daughter was accompanied by Ryke and Lo, but it told me what I needed to know.

Jonathan Hale isn't perfect. Not in the slightest. But I've never had a parent fight to spend time with me. My mom let me run off to Philly like she was tossing feathers into the wind, and long before that, Robert Moore rejected me just on the assumption that I *might* not be his daughter. Maybe deep down he knew.

And he's here.

In the very back row.

He's the only part of the day that clouds the happiness. I don't peek over my shoulder again to check if he's still in the courtroom. I know he has to be.

Garrison holds my hand tightly, giving me encouraging nods. The fact that he's here with me through these giant moments in my life—it brings about this wave of comfort and longing. For a future. One that lasts forever with him.

Lily leans over Garrison, at the end of the first row with Lo, to whisper to me, "They're here."

Okay, I have to glance back this time. Sucking in a breath, I rotate a little. But four bodies block my view from Robert Moore.

Daisy, Ryke, Connor, and Rose walk down the aisle, and Daisy rings out her sopping wet hair, drenched from the storm. Her other hand rests atop her round belly, baby due any day now.

They came here just for me. It's an overwhelming feeling knowing that so many people care. This isn't a birth or a wedding. It's just one of those unique pivotal moments in my life that I didn't think would matter to other people.

But I see that it does.

My glasses mist, and I quickly rotate to face the front. Not wanting them to see me cry. I take my glasses off, wiping the lenses with my shirt.

When I turn back, they've already slipped into the second row. "Thanks for coming, everyone," I tell them.

"Wouldn't fucking miss it," Ryke says.

I put my glasses back on and hold his gaze, which has been easier these days. My relationship with Ryke isn't so awkward anymore. And I couldn't tell you the day that it changed. It was a slow, gradual process to accept that this intimidating force in my life is also my big brother.

"I meant to give you this." My hand shakes as I pass him an envelope. *Willow, you fool, stop shaking.* "You can open it now or later. I already gave Lo and Dad his."

"Are we doing presents already?" Lily asks.

Daisy stands. "I left Willow's in the car."

"No, it's alright," I tell her. "I can wait until later. The time just presented itself to give them theirs, so…"

Daisy gives me a smile. "I really want you to see it. I'll be right back, and I'll be really fast." She holds out her palm to Ryke, asking for the car keys. Daisy's enthusiasm is contagious, and I find myself grinning.

Rose and Lily stand like they're accompanying Daisy, and Ryke passes his wife the keys, despite the torrential downpour outside. Daisy jingles them in excitement before ambling out with Rose and Lily.

Just as they leave, Ryke tears open the envelope.

My heart beats faster. Gift-giving always has that effect. What if the recipient hates it? And then there's the worst scenario: the recipient hates a gift but pretends to love it, *and* it's so obvious that both parties partake in this quasi lie.

But luckily, I don't think Ryke would lie.

All worry washes away when Ryke pulls out a photograph. It was taken in a candid moment during Christmas at the mountain lake house. Lo, Ryke, and I sit on the patio around a fire. We're all drinking homemade, non-alcoholic Butterbeer that Lily and I concocted together.

All three of us are smiling.

Ryke doesn't say anything as he stares at the photo, but he has this faraway look like he's remembering that day. He flips it over.

I wrote on the back.

Ryke Meadows (Gryffindor), Loren Hale (Slytherin), Willow Hale (Gryffindor, like Neville Longbottom).

Thanks for caring about me, even before we were family.

I could have probably said more, but the photograph wasn't big enough. Anyway, I don't think there are enough words in the dictionary to describe what my brothers mean to me. What Ryke means to me.

He takes a deeper breath. "You changed your name?" he asks, his voice splitting.

Tears threaten to rise. "It's pending, but yeah." My eyes burn, fighting off the waterworks. "I just hope everything goes right."

I guess, there's still a possibility that things end poorly today. But I've tried not to believe that. I glance anxiously at the judge's bench. Empty. Once she arrives, all will either go smoothly or horribly.

Even though Jonathan Hale is my biological father, Robert Moore has legal claim, since he was my dad at the time of my birth. It's all really complicated, and I hate that there are hoops to be jumped through just so that Jonathan can be my dad on paper.

The biggest hurdle: Robert has to give consent to Jonathan.

I may be eighteen, but Jonathan wants me on his health insurance, and I'm willing to accept *some* financial help from him. Maybe not a lot. But I don't want to be drowning in debt when my dad actively wants to be involved. I figure it's easier accepting this than a twenty-grand medical bill from an accident or surgery or some unknown thing happening to me.

"I need to talk to you," Connor says, abruptly capturing everyone's attention.

His gaze isn't planted on me though. He's looking at Garrison.

My boyfriend frowns. "Me?"

"I am staring at you," Connor says, expressionless and calm.

Garrison turns to me for answers, just as puzzled as I am.

I shake my head. I don't know what this is about.

"Let's not drag this fucking out, Cobalt," Ryke says, but his brows are furrowed in confusion. I think that Connor might be the only one who's caught up to speed.

Connor says to Garrison, "I've been looking for a new investment, and I want to invest in you."

Garrison laughs like it's a joke. I want to whisper to him and tell him that I don't think it is, but his face quickly falls when he sees Connor is just waiting patiently for him.

"You're serious?" Garrison's brows shoot up. "You want to invest in *me*?" He pauses. "You do know who I am, right?"

"Garrison Abbey, proficient in tech and coding. You like Tumblr, gifs, hacking, Final Cut, classic video games, and the girl sitting next to you."

Wow…he's good.

Garrison shrugs off his leather jacket like he's hot with frustration. "I'm unreliable. I was kicked out of two high schools. I have no fucking plans to go to college—"

"You lack confidence, so I'll give you some right now. You're talented, self-motivated, and driven. If you don't see that in yourself, open your eyes and look at what you can do. All I'm asking is for you to create something, anything, and I'll back it."

Garrison blinks for a long beat. Stunned and shocked. "Why?"

"I value everything I just listed, and you need someone who believes in you. Create something brilliant, Garrison, or don't create anything at all. That's your choice."

Garrison stays quiet, processing. I'm doing the same. It's a lot to digest.

Lo says, "Take it, man. The god has spoken."

Connor grins.

Ryke groans. "Come on. He's a fucking six-foot-four human being with good hair."

"At least we've established one thing," Connor says. "Ryke loves my hair."

"I think you want to be fucking punched in a courthouse."

Connor's grin widens, but he plants his deep blue eyes back on Garrison.

My boyfriend's brows are furrowed, still thinking over the offer, and he keeps glancing at me. The second time he does, I realize why. It didn't really hit me until now, but if he accepts Connor's offer, we may not see each other that much anymore.

At least not for the next four years.

My stomach is already churning, but there's no desire to stop Garrison from this. Not for me. When he looks to me for the third time, I tell him, "Take it." Our eyes lock in a heady beat. "You can do *anything*, Garrison."

I truly, truly believe this.

Garrison looks back to Connor. "I'll have to stay in Philadelphia?"

"Yes," he says. "You've never done a start-up of any kind, and while you're creative, you need me to teach you about business."

Connor isn't the type to just blindly invest in a *person*. This isn't a normal job offer, and anyone receiving it would be jumping head-first at the chance. No questions asked.

Garrison angles towards me, confusion still pleating his forehead. His eyes carry raw, hard truths.

I've been accepted to Wakefield University, and I'll be leaving for London in August.

Different countries.

Different continents.

A whole ocean separating us. And I see that he wants to keep me close. I want him by my side, too. That was the plan when I chose this college. But he can't come to London and leave behind an opportunity as great and big as this one. Working at Cobalt Inc. is the road that will lead him in the right direction. I know it.

"Take it," I repeat, sucking in a tight breath. Pain lances me. "I just want the best for you." *This is the best.*

"The best for me is to be with you." His nose flares, restraining emotion. "I'm a better fucking person when I'm with you." He rubs his face a couple times, trying to stop himself from crying.

Our lives are about to split, fissure, and fracture by this one decision. But I think it'd break worse if he didn't choose the job. I think we'd both resent each other in the end.

I lean closer to him, a breath apart. "Don't be afraid," I whisper. "You can do anything on your own. I know you can." *But can I be without him?* The question rips through me, and my glasses fog up.

I take them off.

His reddened eyes meet mine, and he's a little fuzzy in my vision now, but it's not too bad. He clasps my hand, threading his fingers. "I love you," he says.

Tears crease my eyes.

"No matter where we are," he tells me. "You're always going to be my girl."

THE FUTURE FEELS DIFFERENT NOW THAT GARRISON AND I ARE planning to live apart. More somber and up in the air. But I try to push the reality behind me to focus on what's before me.

The courtroom quiets as Robert Moore approaches the bench. My dad and I already stand in front of it. I hold my arm to my chest, nervous that everyone is looking at me. *Because everyone is.*

I try not to glance at Robert. Not wanting to have my earth shattered today with a mental image of his expression.

The judge looks to him. "Since the means of Mr. Hale outweigh most, I wanted you here in person. I need to make sure you haven't been coerced, threatened, or swayed by financial means to give consent."

The court reporter's fingers move quickly, capturing the judge's words.

"This is what it's come to. I'm not surprised." Robert's words are a battleax to my heart.

He did raise me. Before the divorce, before things soured, he raised me.

"Are you in agreement surrendering your parental rights, Mr. Moore?" the judge asks.

I glance over at that.

Wrong move.

Robert shrugs. This nonchalant, *I don't give a shit* shrug. "All along, I think I knew that she wasn't my kid. It's not just about looks, but no one in my family needs glasses."

It feels like a hole is being chiseled through my chest. I'd have loved going the rest of my life not hearing Robert's opinion about me.

But he crosses his arms and keeps going. "She doesn't act like any kid of mine. She's practically mute half the time." *I can't breathe.* "She dresses more like a boy than a girl." *Please stop.* "She has no friends."

Feet clatter behind me, and I glance over to see Lily, Lo, Ryke, Daisy, Connor, Rose, and Garrison all standing to their feet. All silently saying *she's my friend.*

Tears stream down my cheeks. When my eyes land on Daisy, she mouths *my one friend* and makes a heart with her hands, smiling.

My best friend. Daisy Calloway. Her friendship is the rare, beautiful kind, and I'm never letting it go.

My smile matches hers, and I rub my wet face. I notice Lo's cheekbones sharpening like he's grinding his teeth. Ryke looks equally pissed. Just when I think they might explode in the courtroom, my dad's voice cuts in.

"Can I say something, Your Honor?" He raises his hand. His face is creased with severe, strict lines.

The judge nods. "Yes."

My dad narrows a malicious glare on Robert. The tension in the room seems to amp with that one look, setting ablaze any fake congeniality. "Don't ever insult my daughter again, you microscopic prick—"

"Alright, Mr. Hale—"

"In the seventeen years that she was with you—did you even talk to her?" my dad asks. "Did you know she's charismatic when you discuss things that interest her? Maybe you should've seen a goddamn movie with her—"

"Mr. Hale—"

"—instead of sitting around on your ass, you scum of this planet." He fixes his suit, as though a fistfight just ended with Robert Moore bloodied on the ground.

"Mr. Hale," the judge snaps, banging her gavel forcefully.

"I'm done," my dad says.

And I can breathe again.

Robert has taken five steps back like he's been physically pushed, and his beet-red face is coated in a sheen of sweat.

I think about something my dad said. How Robert should've seen a movie with me. In the first few weeks of even talking to each other, Jonathan Hale asked to watch a film of my choice. I picked *Doctor Strange*. And even though he hated the storyline and characters in the first five minutes, he still finished watching it with me.

"Let's continue," the judge declares. "Robert Moore, do you wish to give up your parental rights as Willow's father to Jonathan Hale?"

Without hesitation, he says, "Yes."

"Then the court recognizes Jonathan Hale as Willow's legal and biological father. Thank you all for coming today, and congratulations Willow." The judge's eyes flit heatedly to Robert before she leaves the courtroom.

I almost can't believe it. I'm…a Hale.

"Ca-Caw!" Daisy calls out to me, making the bird noise.

I laugh a tearful laugh as I turn around, and everyone in the room starts clapping. My heart has grown outside my body. Too big to fit inside me. Love. It's all just pure, unadulterated love.

Daisy squeezes out of the row, aimed for me. Robert passes her, leaving in a hurry and probably sensing my brothers' glares on his back. I make sure to watch this time.

I want *this* to be my final image of him.

Shuffling out of the courtroom with the realization that the daughter—the one he didn't really ever want—is loved. And I never needed him.

Daisy lands beside me at the first row and passes me an envelope. "This is for you, and I'm totally kicking myself because it would've been awesome if you had it before…all of that." She waves towards the judge's bench like it's already old news.

I carefully open the envelope. A simple silver pinky ring inside.

I immediately recognize the black square carved in the center. I gave her an identical pinky ring a long time ago when her ex-friends were harassing her.

I told Daisy, "*My favorite superhero wears this ring. It protects Tilly Stayzor from anyone outside of the Fourth Degree, basically her personal enemies. This ring is just a reminder that there are people who have your back. And we all need protection at some point. I want you to have mine.*"

She's still wearing that ring on her pinky, which means…she bought me a matching one. We're both crying. Tears flowing down my cheeks and hers.

We smile together as I fit the ring on my finger.

"We all need a little protection sometimes," she says, so she must remember what I told her. That crashes through me and I push back more raw sentiments. She adds, "And there are a lot of people who love you here."

I have to take my glasses off to wipe them. "This means…so much to me. Thank you." I fit my glasses on again.

"There's more," she says with a bigger smile.

More?

With a trembling hand, I inspect the envelope and take out a photograph. On the picture, a tiny little willow tree is freshly planted next to a cabin. The sign hung over the door says, *Green Willow.*

I immediately know what this is, and my eyes flood once again.

"You're now officially a girl's cabin at Camp Calloway," she tells me. "You didn't think I missed you, did you?" When Daisy started building her camp, she named cabins after her sisters. Pink Lily. Yellow Rose. Red Poppy.

I just never thought about myself in the equation.

Never would have assumed I'd be included.

I knew I was going to have monumental moments today, but I didn't expect for this to be one. Feeling Daisy's friendship and love and sisterhood wrap around me so tightly and protectively—I'll never forget it.

She holds out her palm for our friendship handshake, but I wrap my arms around her shoulder, light as can be since she's pregnant.

Daisy hugs me back.

Afterward, I search the courtroom for Garrison, and when our eyes meet, a bittersweet realization passes sadly between us.

London.

Philadelphia.

We're going to split apart. *Not yet.* We have some months left together before I leave for college, and I hang onto those like a lifeline.

August

39

Garrison Abbey

CANDLELIGHT BATHES WILLOW'S BEDROOM, ROSE AND VANILLA
scent strong. Music plays softly from a playlist. It feels like I'm living
a dream—and tomorrow I'll wake up in my tattered, damaged reality.

Until then, I'll stay here.

I'll never wake up.

Willow is tucked close in my arms, her heartbeat slowing as we
both let the night wash over us. I just took her virginity. Filled her in
ways I never have before.

It's been one of the best nights of my life, but it ends soon. And
I really haven't come to grips with that.

"What time is it?" Willow whispers, cocooned by my body. I have
the better view of the clock. It's that weird time period, what some
people call morning and other people call night. 3:10 a.m.

I know what she's really asking. "We have to leave in twenty-minutes."

Her suitcase is already downstairs beside the door. We've
even showered, dressed, and returned to bed, lying on top of the
comforter. I don't want Willow to leave my arms because there are
parts of me that wonder—maybe this is it.

This is the last time I get to hold her.

She's moving to London.

She's starting a life over there.

I'd be an idiot to think there's a good probability this can last. But
Christ, I want to believe it. I want to believe this is just a roadblock,
a setback—not the end.

Never the end.

I swallow hard and kiss the top of her head. We're quiet in the stillness of the room, letting the moment pass.

"Maybe I should stay," she starts.

"No." I rub at my dry, raw eyes. "Let's just head to the airport. We'll have more time in the car together." I need to get moving because the longer I lie here, I'll do something stupid. Like agree to her suggestion.

She wipes her nose with the back of her hand, and I see that she's been crying.

"Hey." I pull her into my chest. I need to be the strong one here. Even though I'm being ripped open. "We're not apart yet." I brush her tears with my thumb. "And when we are, I'll be all over you with my ones and zeroes."

Her lips lift in a quivering smile. "Me too."

We all drive to the airport together, the private plane sitting on the tarmac. Willow's not taking commercial this time because Lo wanted to say goodbye at the airport and not back home. Paparazzi aren't allowed here, and it gives Willow enough peace to talk to everyone.

Wind whips around us. The sun hasn't risen yet, but the airport lights illuminate the area. I watch as each of Willow's family hug her goodbye. Her dad, her brothers, Lily, Rose, and Connor. She bends down to put her arms around three-year-olds Maximoff and Jane. The toddlers sniff loudly, sad about their Aunt Willow and favorite babysitter leaving them. Nearly one-year-old twins, Charlie and Beckett smile as Willow kisses the tops of their heads.

When she moves to Daisy, it's harder.

Everyone falls hushed. In Daisy's arms is a six-month-old baby, Sullivan Meadows, who almost didn't make it into the world. Willow lets Sulli wrap her little fingers around her pinky, the one with the friendship ring. And Daisy and Willow break into sobs.

I stand off to the side, watching each goodbye through a sickness that tosses my stomach in awful knots. My throat swollen. My whole body tensed up in terrible ways.

Don't go! I want to scream.

Stay!

PLEASE!

My soul is fighting with myself.

I have loved her for longer than I have loved myself. I found her when living seemed like a worse choice than ending it all.

And now I'm losing her.

To London.

Fucking London.

Willow wipes at her wet tear-streaked cheeks, her olive-green shirt makes her warm, brown eyes glow even more in her sadness. Daisy backs away, crying and sniffing loudly, she walks into Ryke's arms.

And then Willow looks at me.

We're five-feet apart and that already feels like the biggest fucking distance in the world. *It's about to be a million times worse.*

Kill me.

Just fucking do it already.

I've been waiting all my life to die. She leaves, maybe I'm going to finally be ready. Maybe it's just time.

I can't tell her this. I can't tell her how hard this is going to be for me. Because if she stays for a loser like me, I'll never survive that.

Each step closer to her is a knife in my chest. It feels like my brothers are here. Standing off to the side, sliding in the blades.

One after the other.

Step. Cut. Step. Cut.

Step…

I'm bleeding out.

But I touch her. Hand to hers.

She's a mess of tears. She's *my* mess. "Willow." My voice cracks.

Her chin quakes. "I don't want to go. I change my mind—"

I bring her into my chest, tucking her close, hand on the back of her head. Tears stream down my jaw, but I face the plane, not her family.

I swallow the pain.

Swallow it down.

Down.

I pull back to look her in the eyes. It's somehow easier to speak. Maybe because she's right here. Like my brain knows she's not gone yet. "We're going to make this work," I tell her, trying to sound confident. "I'm going to text and Skype." I cup her wet cheeks between both my hands. "We're going to make this work, Willow. Because you're my girl, and that's not going to change."

Please...don't let that change.

She cries into my shirt, soaking the fabric. We stay like that until she has to board the plane. Until I have to watch her physically leave me.

I'm cut open on the ground.

Nothing without her.

PART TWO

"Broken souls are mended every day

by mended souls that were once broken."

Connor Cobalt

(FUEL THE FIRE)

40

Willow Hale

YESTERDAY I WAS A VIRGIN.

Today, I'm not.

And I know I'm not "supposed" to put this great big importance on my first time and virginity and all of that, but I didn't lose *it* until I was twenty. Having anyone touch me is a big deal. Having someone *inside* of me…is monumental. Like Thor crashing down during the climax of *Avengers: Infinity War*.

It was *that* big of a deal. To me. To him.

And now the guy who took my virginity is thousands of miles away in Philadelphia.

"Over here is the campus bookstore, which I checked does not carry comic books so it's already a complete fail," I say to my cell, video recording.

My head pounds from jetlag. It feels like I just stepped off the plane, and I've only thrown my bags in my dorm. I wanted to check out the campus before it got dark. As the sun begins to set, students meander into dining halls for dinner.

I focus my cell's camera on the campus bookstore sign.

Documenting my college experience at Wakefield University is my first order of business, while Garrison keeps me updated on his life back in Philly.

Long distance is not ideal. It's not my first choice. Or second. But until someone invents teleportation or I'm struck down by lightning and develop super-human speed like The Flash, we're stuck to modern technology.

"And over here…" I rotate my cell to rows of booths. "Are all the potential clubs that I'm probably not going to join—"

"HEADS UP!"

I turn. *No no no.* A frisbee is flying straight towards my face.

Ducking quickly, the frisbee sails over my head and across the quad to another guy's hands. My heart beats wildly, and my jaw slowly drops. Dumbfounded. Did I just outmaneuver a flying frisbee? Okay, my reflexes have definitely improved. I am certified-clumsy. Definitely not by choice. Maybe London is a good luck charm for me.

My lips lift into a bigger smile, and I turn to head back down the cobbled path—*oh shit,* my hip and elbow suddenly collide with a girl and her box, both coming out of nowhere.

She stumbles and manages not to faceplant from my elbow-knock. But the brown cardboard crashes to the ground, flaps opening, and I watch as condoms spill onto the cobblestone.

Shit.

"I'm *so* sorry." I quickly squat and start scooping up the condoms.

"No worries. We're both in one piece." Her English accent is noticeable. It hits me again—I am not in America anymore. Add in the fact that this is my new home. That I'm living here for four years instead of the usual three for UK undergrads because my degree requires blood, sweat, tears, and an extra year apparently.

It's all hardly sunk in.

I'm half expecting someone to pop out of the bushes with a big *Gotcha* sign.

I just…I hope moving here was the right decision.

The twenty-something girl in front of me blows a red curl off her lips and bends down to help with the condom spill. She's white, curvy and wears a Wakefield T-shirt—the letters WFU in a circular dark green and gold emblem.

I toss a huge handful of condoms into her box while I perspire everywhere. I am hot. Baking under embarrassment, and I'm aware that this is the most condoms I've ever touched.

When they lower me into a grave, my funeral eulogy will definitely be: *There was that young, innocent Willow Hale who ran head-first into a giant box of condoms and never revived.*

I must be staring too hard at the condoms because the girl says, "You can take some. That's what they're there for."

"Oh no, I'm a vir—" I stop myself. Because…

Willow, duh, you are a virgin *no* more.

The redhead narrows her eyes. "If you're a virgin, you could still use these." She's tossing a couple foiled packets in my direction. "You're in uni. It's better to be safe."

Except the only person I'd want to have sex with isn't here. But I don't have the energy or the time to explain my complicated relationship. Not that she'd even want to hear about it.

Box now full, we both stand, and I pocket three condoms in my faded jeans. She balances the box in one arm and holds out a free hand. "I'm Karla. The student warden…or I guess, what you'd know as an RA—over at Bishop Hall."

Bishop Hall. That's the name of my dorm building. I'm about to tell her that we live in the same place, thankful for such a serendipitous run-in, but Karla tilts her head and eyes my face more incredulously.

"You look familiar," she muses.

I pale and push up my glasses that slide down the bridge of my nose. Moving thousands of miles away was strategic in multiple ways. I thought, maybe, I could return to the shadows. Just for a bit.

No paparazzi.

Less people recognizing me.

I'm on the periphery of fame, and I'm settled with drifting out of it.

"I get that a lot," I say. "Um…I have to go." I jab a thumb towards nowhere. Technically, it's pointed to the middle of the quad. But without making any further eye contact, I actually just walk off in the opposite direction towards the bookstore.

It's a level 10 awkward departure.

My armpits sweat, and pressure slowly builds on my chest. What happens if I run into her again? It's likely, right? She lives in my hall.

And now she thinks I'm probably such a loser with zero social skills, and really I have no choice but to actively avoid her.

Less than an hour into my first day in London and I already have added someone on my *Person to Avoid Because of an Awkward First Impression* list. It's unfortunately a long list back in Philly.

I rehash my awkward departure on a loop like rewinding a car crash scene in a movie. What could I have done differently?

About a million things. A gazillion. Trillion.

My stomach sinks.

Shake it off, Willow. I find an empty bench behind the bookstore and sling my backpack on the wooden slates. After I take a seat, I turn to my phone, which has never stopped recording. *Shit.* I end the video and a notification from Garrison pops up. *New message!*

My breath quickens. Longing swells inside me, and then other unwanted sentiments start to infiltrate their way in. Regret. Guilt.

I wish he were here, but I have to settle with the 2D version of Garrison Abbey, which is better than nothing. The thought of him being completely gone from my life only brings a wave of panic and misery.

I click into his video message. A small pot of water is on screen, long noodles sticking halfway out, not fitting. *"My noodles are defective, Willow."*

I smile and my eyes water a little.

"And I know what you're going to say." He turns the camera to face himself. *"Break the noodles. But there has to be some Chef Boyardee rule against that."* He sighs deeply. His aquamarine eyes carrying a heaviness to them like he hasn't slept much. *"So basically, I'm a mess without you."*

"You're not a mess," I whisper to my phone. But he can't hear me.

He runs a hand through his thick, disheveled hair. The tattoos at his collarbone peek out of his plain black T-shirt. Small stars, shaped into a constellation. He has more tattoos, scattered around his body, while I have none. On paper, maybe it looks like we shouldn't be together.

He grew up in a mansion three times the size of my childhood home in Maine.

He was kicked out of two prep schools.

He was almost arrested for vandalizing, for drugs and for underage drinking, and if it weren't for the top shot lawyer his rich parents hired, he might have faced serious consequences at some time in his life.

Garrison Abbey is the kind of guy that wears a D.A.R.E. shirt ironically and hacks assholes' computers for fun. People flock to him because he's cool in this mysterious way. Like Jess from *Gilmore Girls*.

In Maine, most of the student body didn't even know my name. If it weren't for my connections to the Calloway sisters, I'd be considered painfully normal.

I still can't believe we ended up here. Together.

Okay, not together in the physical sense since he *is* thousands of miles away. But together as in we're boyfriend-girlfriend. It took a lot of cosmic happenings for that to come to fruition.

The video of Garrison attempting to cook spaghetti ends abruptly after he switches the stove off, giving up on it. I glance over my shoulder towards Bishop Hall. I don't think I can venture back to my dorm. I might run into Karla again, and I'm not sure I can take another awkward interaction.

As a last-minute distraction, I click into Tumblr on my cell.

My stomach lurches when I see a new post.

Oh no…

Garrison filled out a questionnaire that I didn't tag him in, and that *rarely* happens. He doesn't love questionnaires, but he does them because he knows I'm kind of obsessed. So it's odd that he did this, right? I don't know what it means.

I hold my breath like I can stop an impending impact and slowly read the post.

Name: Garrison

Zodiac Sign: Scorpio

Average Hours of Sleep: idk used to be about 7-8? It's less, so whatever.

Last Google Search: what time is it in London?

Relationship Status: </3

I…can't…breathe.

He put a broken heart as his relationship status. *Broken*. As in, I broke his heart? Or is it just fractured while I'm in London and he's in Philly?

My glasses suddenly fog and the emotion I've been burying suddenly rises tenfold. *Guilt*.

He took my virginity yesterday.

And I'm the one who left. Boarded a flight at 5 a.m. his time. Flew to a different continent and landed this evening. Put an ocean between us. Literally.

A sudden realization overcomes me…oh no. It was goodbye sex.

I had *goodbye* sex my first time.

Removing my glasses, I wipe them on my cotton shirt. My belly twists uncomfortably. New eulogy: *Here lies Willow Hale, the girl who fucked for the first time and then left*.

Maybe it wasn't even fucking. It was more like…love making. Sweet. Kind. And loving. It was perfect—except for the leaving part.

And I know Garrison doesn't blame me for leaving. Not like I blame myself. He held me after we slept together and told me that he still wanted me to go. Wanted me to pursue my dreams and take the hard path—the challenge.

Since I have such a big safety net in Philadelphia, I don't know if I can really thrive there until I learn to thrive on my own first. *London* is the challenge.

But it's also likely I will fail spectacularly, like a mega belly flop into a crowded pool.

I look back at the broken heart on Tumblr.

His words ring in my head. The ones he said to me before I boarded the plane. "*We're going to make this work. I'm going to text and Skype.*" He cupped my cheeks and both of us were crying. "*We're going to make this work, Willow. Because you're my girl, and that's not going to change.*"

We're going to make this work.

Broken hearts and all.

I try to believe it. Placing my tortoise-shell glasses back on, I keep reading his post.

Siblings: three older brothers. Be happy they're not yours.

Love or Lust: lust doesn't hurt.

He sounds sad, but not his usual sad. I reach for my phone to send him a silly gif from his favorite TV show—*Supernatural.* Just as my fingers slide over the screen, I notice the last question and answer.

Met a Celebrity: I think I might be becoming one...

It chills me for a second. How much my life has changed his.

Three years ago, I was no one. I was living in a sleepy town of Caribou, Maine, and my parents were getting divorced. My little sister Ellie was my only sibling, and I only had one friend.

Then I woke up one morning, and little did I know, but everything just...changed.

I found out that Ellie wasn't my only sibling.

I had a brother miles and miles away.

A *famous* brother.

Loren Hale has the kind of fame where he shows up on magazines and tabloids every week. The kind of fame where I had idolized him long before I even knew we were related. Imagine if someone like Chris Evans—Captain America himself—had a long-lost little sister. That sister being *me*. It was that impactful and unbelievable and really...

Three years later, it's still surreal.

Loren Hale changed everything.

For me and Garrison.

September

41

Garrison Abbey

SEVEN DAYS. SIX HOURS. AND THREE EXCRUCIATING MINUTES. But it's not like I'm counting how long it's been since Willow and I put an ocean between us.

I like numbers.

I like to code.

It's what I fucking do.

Even at two in the morning on a Friday night. My headphones are tossed aside on my mattress. Giving my ears a rest from wearing them in the office all day. Did I mention it was Friday?

Which means the asshole in the apartment next door is currently hosting some sort of first semester bash in his place. The walls thump from his shitty EDM music.

I can code with most music.

That's not what's really distracting me. It's the laughter and the high-pitched squeals and the frat-bro cheering that pulls my mind away from work.

"JARED!" a girl shrieks. Someone knocks into a shared wall and my *Silversun Pickups* poster falls off the hook and hits the floor.

Yeah, that's it.

I push away from my keyboard on my rolling chair and slide across the hardwood to my stereo setup. I crank it up. Full blast. And then I scroll through a playlist on my phone.

Fuck their EDM.

I put on my favorite band.

Interpol. The song "Evil" starts out slow and builds up, but it emits from my speaker so fucking loud that it's like I'm in a competition with my neighbor. Whose eardrums can we blast out first? Truth, I'd be fine getting a permanent migraine from listening to *Interpol.* It'd be worth it.

Barely a minute later, a knock slams on my door. "Hey!"

The guy says something else, but I can't make it out. Suddenly, the EDM music cuts off.

"HEY!" he screams, more clearly now. "Turn your shit down, man!" He bangs his fist at my door, and my pulse ratchets up.

She flashes in my head.

If Willow were here, she'd tell me to turn it down. Don't start a confrontation. Don't be that guy.

But she's not here.

I stand up.

The pounding on my door intensifies. "Fuck, can you hear me?!"

Striding over, each second there feels like someone is clenching my heart in their fist. *Pump. Pump.* Trying to wake the cold, lifeless organ.

The chorus starts as I put my hand on the knob. I've listened to this song a million-and-one times, but tonight it sounds different in my head. I should turn it off. But something is wrong with me. I feel it deep inside me like dark ink bleeding into paper, and Willow can't change me.

No one can.

I open the door.

My neighbor's angered brown eyes pierce me. Baseball cap turned backward. Penn shirt and khakis. He looks like he should be at the Alpha Omega Zeta house, not some apartment building in Center City.

"Yeah?" I ask, not needing to raise my voice over the music since we're close enough.

He holds out his hand. "I'm Jared, your neighbor. Sorry, man, I didn't get the chance to introduce myself yet."

I moved into this building the same time Willow left for Wakefield. I wanted a change. But it's been a week, and Jared and I have crossed paths a few times already. He's never said a word to me before. So this pseudo-fake-nice bullshit is just all for show.

"Cool," I say, but I don't shake his hand.

Jared pauses for a second and then drops his arm. "Hey, you think you can turn down your music? I'm kind of having a party. It's my girlfriend's birthday."

I glance towards his apartment and notice three girls and two guys wedged in his doorway, watching our interaction. I'm not even sure how many more people are inside his place.

"Then it looks like I'm giving your girlfriend a birthday present." I swing my head back to Jared. "Being introduced to *Interpol* is probably the best gift she's going to get tonight."

Jared laughs dryly, annoyance flashing in his eyes. "Look, we don't want to listen to your music."

"You're right, yours is so much better," I say, sarcasm on my lips. "It's been nothing but pure bliss for the past hour."

"Dude, I'm sorry." Jared holds up his hands in defense. "We didn't mean to be so loud. Maybe we can come to some sort of under-standing." His eyes scan me from my bare feet to my head. "You go to Penn? Come grab a beer with us. We've got plenty in the room."

Three years ago, I might have taken that offer.

Today, I just want to be alone.

"I don't want your beer. Just stop knocking into my walls—"

"Holy shit," a girl from the doorway exclaims loudly. Her friends huddle around her, staring at the cell in her clutch. "You're Garrison Abbey!"

Jared frowns, brows knotting. "Ana, am I supposed to know who that is?"

Ana glides over in heels, her blonde hair in a tight ponytail that looks honest-to-God painful. I don't know how girls do that. She puts a hand to Jared's chest. "Ignore my boyfriend. He isn't well-acquainted with entertainment news or *Celebrity Crush*."

I almost roll my eyes at the trash tabloid. Okay, I have picked up the magazine at the grocery checkout before. But it's certified crap.

Jared shakes his head. "Wait, he's been in *Celebrity Crush*?"

"Yeah, with the Calloway sisters," Ana says, pointing to me like I'm not *right* here.

Jared looks me up and down like he's trying to figure me out now. "So are you dating one of the Calloway sisters then?"

I almost laugh.

They're all married.

None of them to me. And if any of the Calloway sisters heard that question, they would most likely die in their own fit of laughter. Willow—she'd probably wrap her arms around me. I'd wrap mine around her. Just to say *this one is mine.*

"Oh my *God.*" Ana's face roasts a shade of red. "Please stop talking, Jared." To me, she says, "I'm so sorry. The second I have the chance, he's bingeing *Princesses of Philly.*" I haven't heard someone mention PoPhilly in a while. The short-lived reality show happened *years* ago. I wasn't in it. I didn't even know the Calloway sisters back then.

A docuseries featuring the sisters and their men is ongoing and more current, but *We Are Calloway* is critically acclaimed and covers serious topics like addiction and PTSD. Maybe too highbrow for this girl since she doesn't mention it.

I'm not in the mood to explain how I'm connected to the Calloways, but luckily I have Ana here willing to do it for me.

She's focused on her boyfriend. "You do know who Loren Hale is, right? If not, we can no longer date." She crosses her arms over her chest, like she's serious about this.

Jesus.

This is dumb.

It's like watching a fucking train wreck with *Interpol* still blaring in the background. Loren Hale should never be the decider for any relationship. If he were, mine would have ended before it even began.

Jared doesn't blink. "Everyone knows Loren Hale."

That's just not true, but okay.

"Prove it." Ana arches a brow.

"He owns Superheroes & Scones *and* Hale Co. I have his baby oil in my shower." Way too much information from my neighbor. And it's not specifically Loren's bottle of baby oil. The family-owned company manufactures baby products. Hale Co. is one of the most well-known brands in the country.

Jared looks to me. "Loren is also married to the sex addict Calloway sister."

My skin crawls with how Jared just described Lily Calloway. Like that's all she's fucking known for. Not the fact that she's the one who actually owns Superheroes & Scones. At one point in my life, I even worked *for* her.

Jared looks to me and continues on. "But I don't get it. How do you know Loren Hale?"

I open my mouth.

But Ana answers first. "He's dating Loren Hale's little sister."

And there it is.

I shouldn't be famous. I shouldn't be recognizable, especially when I'm not always around Loren or any of the Calloways. But it's happening. And there's only a small comfort in knowing that Ana at least took a few minutes to double check her phone before being able to recognize me.

It wasn't instant recognition.

Good.

"Huh," Jared muses.

"I'm going to turn my music down," I say before either of them can jump in. "Keep the banging to a minimum and we won't have problems."

"Wait, it's my birthday." Ana hooks her arm with Jared's. "Do you think you could like call Loren and have him wish me a *happy birthday*. Just really quick. It doesn't even need to be FaceTime. Hearing his voice would be the literal *best* birthday present ever. I'm a huge fan."

I glance to her boyfriend.

Jared's gaze is pleading. Practically saying, *come on, man, help me out.* Like he wants me to give him points with his girl so he can get a blow job later tonight.

I do have Loren Hale's number.

My gaze settles on Ana. "I already gave you your birthday present," I say. "Ask your boyfriend about it."

I shut the door on them.

Immediately, I go to my stereo, lowering the music to a tolerable level. My ears ring. My head throbs. I collapse on my mattress and stare up at a yellow stain on the ceiling. Seconds later, the EDM starts up next door again. But it's softer and no longer vibrates my walls and desk.

Willow did the right thing—leaving.

She can't make real connections here. Everyone eventually recognizes her as Loren Hale's sister, and in London, she has a chance to fall under the radar.

My phone vibrates.

It's now almost 3 a.m. Which means it's almost 8 a.m. in London.

Excitement thrums my veins, thinking it's her, but when I see the text, it's worse than a balloon pop. It's like someone shot a bullet at a blimp.

The person who texted me... It's my boss.

Connor Cobalt: Meeting tomorrow. 11 a.m. My office.

He attached a screenshot of the drug test I took my first day on the job.

It came back positive.

Fuck.

42

Garrison Abbey

HE SHOULDN'T HAVE GIVEN ME THIS JOB. IT'S WHAT I KNOW as I face the twenty-nine-year-old business titan. Connor Cobalt is the CEO of Cobalt Inc., a company that has a hand in just about everything you can think of. Magnets. Paints. *Diamonds.* The list goes on and on. One big company owning smaller subsidiaries.

So the day Connor looked at me and said he wanted me to create something for him—I should have rejected the offer. There's no way this is going any other direction than south. *Fast.*

I don't even look like I should be working here.

He fixes the cuffs to his thousand-dollar Armani suit.

I'm wearing black jeans and a hoodie. Though, he did tell me on the first day that I could wear whatever the fuck I wanted. So that's on him.

His blue eyes collide with mine as he reaches for his coffee. Intimidating is probably too delicate a word to describe this guy. He oozes *I'm fucking better than you* charisma. And don't ask me how it's charismatic. It should come across like he's an asshole, but it actually doesn't.

I don't get it.

Supreme confidence. That has to be it.

He sips his coffee. Silence lingering, and his eyes focus on me even harder.

It feels hot in here all of a sudden. I push up the sleeves of my hoodie.

"Garrison," Connor says after a tense beat. "I don't want to waste your time. I don't think you want to waste mine." He sets down the coffee cup and slides a printed piece of paper across the table. I recognize it instantly as the attachment he sent last night.

My *failed* drug test.

Awesome.

I read the small details quickly. The chart has a spike for increased levels of THC. *Marijuana.* I smoked a blunt a couple days before Willow left for London. If I'd known there was going to be a drug test at Cobalt Inc., I wouldn't have smoked—but this is my first corporate job.

The only other place I've worked is Superheroes & Scones, and the employees there were all nerds, geeks, or broken toys needing a home. No one even needs a reference to get hired at S&S.

"You're firing me," I assume.

Connor is a hard book to read. Face impassive. He could bluff his way out of any poker hand. It makes this interaction more uncomfortable. I shift in my seat.

"You really think I'd fire you over marijuana?" Connor asks, voice calm.

"I mean…maybe." I glance around the glass walls and the cubicles outside his office. Women walk around in pantsuits and pencil skirts. Men take phone calls and sit in meetings in boardrooms. Every wall is *glass.*

Like they want you to see how fucking important they are. I can't imagine any of his other employees smoking on their free time.

Connor leans back in his chair. "Garrison." He draws my attention back to him. "I don't care if you smoke, as long as it doesn't hinder your performance here."

My shoulders relax and I release a breath. "It won't," I say, almost hurried. It even surprises me. How much I want to keep this job. *It's the only thing I have right now.* "I don't usually smoke weed. I'm not a pot head or anything. It just helps me mellow out sometimes."

Connor nods like he already assumed this about me. "Company policy is to have you take a confirmation test to make sure the first drug test wasn't a false positive. But I'll take this conversation as proof that it wasn't." He passes another paper to me. "Because you failed the first, you're going to have to undergo random drug tests throughout your first year here."

Sounds fair. Shit, I'm just happy I still have a job.

He glances at the clock on his wall, then back to me. "Make no mistake, Garrison. If I find you're taking harder drugs like opiates or cocaine, you won't have a job here. This isn't *Wolf of Wall Street*. My employees are useless to me if their health is at risk."

"Noted." I don't mention how I've tried most drugs. Most I couldn't care less about. And I'm not around people who'd pressure me to do them anymore.

Connor puts his fingers to his temple. "Let's talk about your project."

I grimace. Honestly, I'd much rather talk about my failed drug test again. "It's going splendidly." My sarcasm is broken because it sure as hell wasn't supposed to come out during a meeting with my boss.

"You don't have an idea of what you're creating yet." Connor assumes correctly again.

"I mean, it's kind of difficult when you said I could create *anything*," I tell him. When it comes to tech development, that's a wide fucking spectrum, and I want to choose the right thing. It's just figuring out what it is.

"Take your time," Connor says. "You don't have a deadline."

That scares me even more. Because Connor Cobalt is the kind of guy where you *don't* want to waste his time. And he's giving me infinite quantities of it.

I'm also really aware that not a lot of people get this kind of opportunity. If it weren't for the fact that he's married to a Calloway sister—therefore has ties to my girlfriend—maybe I wouldn't be in this position right now. It feels like nepotism. But I'm not going to throw it away.

"What if I take years to even come up with an idea?" I ask. I can't believe he'd ignore his bottom line just for me. He's a business guy.

They tend to give a shit about money, and I'm currently on an eighty-thousand dollar salary with benefits.

"Then you take years," Connor says like it doesn't bother him. "But I don't think you will. And I'm always right."

He's always right.

A part of me wants to prove him wrong. And I don't know what that says about me.

LATER TONIGHT IN MY STUDIO APARTMENT, I TOSS A FROZEN pizza in the oven, sink onto my couch and scroll through Willow's videos she sent me. Re-watching them for the third time.

She's lounging on her bed in a baggie Superheroes & Scones T-shirt that has to be at least three years old—I recognize the design from a line of shirts when we first started working at S&S.

X-Men posters are taped to the walls above her head. She rubs at her eyes, her glasses already off for the night. Watching her makes me miss her more, but maybe I'm some sort of masochist because I can't stop. And I just want more.

"So my classes aren't that bad so far," she tells me. "Except for Intro to Marketing. *Ugh*..." She buries her face in a pillow. "They're making us do a *group* project." Her words are muffled, and she pops back up after a second. "I thought I had abandoned those at Dalton Academy. But *no*, they're in college too, and they are the literal worst."

"Agreed," I say to the video.

She brushes hair off her cheeks and her hazel eyes drift to the screen. She holds back tears. "Garrison." She says my name like she's mourning it. "Could you...could you call me when you get off work? Even if it's super early my time. It's nothing important. I just want to hear your voice."

My chest hurts like someone dropped a fifty-pound dumbbell on it.

I didn't call her. It was midnight by the time I left the office, and that's 5 a.m. her time. She's got a "hellishly" difficult morning class, and I promised myself that I wouldn't fuck with her studies. College isn't easy, and I'd hate myself if I distracted her.

My plan: call her during her break between classes tomorrow afternoon.

The oven beeps, my pizza done, and just as I rise off the couch, my phone lights up. Vibrates loudly. Her name is big across the screen. *WILLOW.*

I catch myself smiling. Selfishly, the first thing I feel is happiness. Like a tidal wave, it surges through me.

My lips downturn fast. And then worry follows close behind. I stand and click speakerphone. "Hey, Willow, isn't it early there?"

"It's six," she says into a yawn. "Did you watch my video?"

I could lie. But that's not something I ever want to do with her. "Yeah," I admit. "I was planning on calling during lunch, so you could sleep in."

She yawns again. "You're too nice, and also I'd rather talk to you than sleep."

Too nice is not something most people say about me. And the fact that she's willing to go without sleep for me is what I didn't want.

I lean against my kitchen counter, eyes transfixed on the screen, even though I can't see her. "Everything okay?"

"I just miss hearing your voice. In real time. Not like through a video clip. How was work?"

I tell her all about my failed drug test, and how Connor didn't even care that I smoked weed. When I end the story, Willow says, "He's right, you know. You're going to figure out what you want to create faster than you think."

Her confidence in me is like a drug. I close my eyes and grip the edge of the counter. It hurts to be away from someone you love so much. God, it fucking hurts.

"Garrison," Willow breathes. "Are you still there?"

I swallow a lump in my throat. "Yeah."

A beat passes before she says, "You remember the night we had sex."

I stop breathing. It's impossible to forget that night. Everything about it was incredible. And I've spent most nights remembering what it felt like to be inside of her. Afterwards, I always try not to think about when it'll happen again. Because likely—it's not going to be anytime soon.

We agreed I wouldn't fly out to visit until her second semester because if I'm up there *with* her, there's a chance the media will start hovering around Wakefield. *Give it some months. Let her settle in.*

I still believe that.

But the hornier part of me—that thinks with the wrong head—isn't fucking thrilled about it. Of course I want to touch her. I want to physically be with her.

I think about her words right now: *you remember the night we had sex.*

"I remember," I tell her. "It was a good night. The best night."

"So you're not upset about it?" she asks, worry in her voice. "You don't think it's *goodbye* sex, right?"

Jesus. "No, Willow. It wasn't *goodbye* sex." My pulse races. "If it were, we would have broken up. We're still together." *Fuck.* "Aren't we?"

"Yeah, I think so," Willow says, and I imagine her frowning.

We're on separate pages. Separate books. Shit, we're literally on different continents. I don't know how to jump back. "Willow, you're my girl."

"What about the broken heart?" she asks.

I rack my brain for a second, trying to figure out what she's talking about. "What...broken—" *Oh shit.* I pinch the bridge of my nose, remembering. "The questionnaire."

I can barely even explain what overcame me to want to fill one out. I was on Tumblr and scrolled past it, and it just reminded me of her. It was enough to quickly fill in the questions. But why did I have to answer with a broken heart?

I'm an idiot.

Willow says, "I just thought that since I left after we had sex, you were upset about it."

"Fuck no," I say strongly. "Willow, that was the best night of my life. I put the broken heart because we're in this shitty long distance thing and I just miss you."

She lets out a giant sigh of relief. "That makes more sense."

"Good." I pause and sniff the air. I smell something…burning.

Shit fuck shit. I forgot to take the pizza out of the oven. My joints unglue and I race to the oven. As soon as I pull down the oven door, dark gray smoke floods out at my face. I cough into my arm, and seconds later, the smoke detector lets out an angry wail.

"Garrison?" Willow sounds panicked.

"Burnt the pizza!" I yell over the alarm. "Call you later?"

"Yeah, go. I love you," she says quickly.

"Love you, too."

She hangs up, and I switch the oven off and try wafting the smoke away from the alarm with a dish towel. It's not working. I have to find… something that will reach the alarm. Fuck you, eight-foot ceilings.

Seriously.

A knock sounds on my door. "Garrison!" my neighbor yells. "Everything okay?!"

Jared and I haven't bumped into each other since his girlfriend's birthday, but the fact that I haven't deterred him either means he's a good guy or he just *really* wants my connections to Loren Hale so he can score points with Ana.

I can't tell which.

But I do open my door for him.

He glances past my shoulder.

"No problems here, man," I tell him. "Just burnt a pizza. You can go home." I'm about to close the door, but he puts his hand on it, stopping me with unwanted force.

I glare.

He's still looking past me at the oven. "Shit, that looks bad. Hold on a minute and I'll grab my broom." He leaves quickly, and I rub at my eyes. Against better judgment—or maybe worse judgment—I don't shut my door on him.

Jared is back in a flash and instead of passing me the broom, he walks right on into my apartment. I tense considerably. My space is *my* space, and I don't remember giving him an invitation. Oh wait, that's because I didn't.

I cross my arms over my chest and stay near the doorway, watching as Jared jams the end of the broom up at the alarm. It takes two *whacks* before it stops wailing.

"These smoke detectors are ridiculously sensitive in the building," Jared says. "Just a heads up."

"Good to know." I try not to sound pissed off or sarcastic or both.

Jared looks around my place like he's on an apartment tour. "Wow, you've got a sweet setup." He eyes the back wall with the desk and four monitors. Two servers. All the chords are neatly bundled and tucked at the floorboard. It took me days to put everything together and not have it look like a mess.

"You a gamer?" Jared wonders.

Probably not the kind he's thinking of. I don't play Call of Duty or Halo or even League of Legends. My true love is the classics on consoles like Sega and N64. But that's not why I have the computers.

"No," I tell him. "I'm a software engineer at Cobalt Inc."

Jared raises his brows. "Damn." He sounds impressed. "But I thought you said you were at Penn."

Never said that. He assumed it. Because I look my age—twenty. And this building is affordable and a short distance to campus. It adds up, I guess.

I shake my head. "I didn't go to college." I'm not ashamed about that. It's not for everyone. Definitely not for me.

Jared looks me up and down. "So you're like one of those geniuses from *The Social Network*?"

I almost laugh. I'm so far from a genius. I'm just good at what I do.

"Not really." I'm about to make up some excuse about work. Anything to get him out of my apartment, but he's already talking again.

"About the other night with Ana," he says into a cringe. "Sorry if she came on strong. She's just a huge fan of your family's."

"They're not my family," I correct him. They're Willow's. I'm just…adjacent to them.

He scratches the back of his neck. "Right, sorry."

"I have to work," I tell him.

"Oh, yeah. I'll get out of your hair." He picks up his broom. "If you have issues with your smoke detector again, you know where to find me." He leaves quickly. A weird feeling crawls under my skin, and I know it's from his sudden saccharine neighborly friendliness. It seems fake, but I really don't want to judge him.

I lock my door and then assess the kitchen. The smoke is almost all cleared out. Checking the pizza, my stomach grumbles and I let out an irritated breath.

Crispy and inedible. Pizza should be neither of those things.

I end up grabbing a Lightning Bolt! energy drink from the fridge and sink onto my desk chair. My computer is one of the few places I can just get completely lost in. Right now, that's all I want.

43

Willow Hale

"KEEP YOUR DOOR OPEN," LO SUGGESTED. "IT'LL BE EASIER TO make friends."

That was my brother's advice before I left Philly. Three weeks into the semester and I still haven't taken it. Laughter grows outside my closed door as students walk down the hallway. The air always buzzes on Friday afternoons, classes ending for the week. Plans for parties springing up.

Not that I've been invited to any.

Pencil midair and textbook layered with scribbles and notes, I almost stand from my desk chair and open the door. Almost.

But the laughter grows even louder. What if I disturb the conversation outside? I could ruin someone's joke, and then I'll be known as the girl in room 301 who's quiet and awkward and ruins fun. I'd be a literal buzzkill.

And what if they're all friends anyway? My experience is that tight-knit friend groups rarely allow interlopers. And if they do, the interloper has to bulldoze their way in.

I am not a bulldozer.

I am more like a slow-moving turtle. The only friend groups that will allow me are the ones with clear vacancies.

Before I can settle on a decision—door open or closed—a bright green flyer zips underneath it and slides across my floor. Curiosity spikes and I abandon my textbook to grab the flyer.

FALL INTO FILM BASH
BYOB. ROOFTOP OF BISHOP HALL.
THERE WILL BE SNACKS AND A SCREENING OF THE GOONIES.
FRIDAY, 10PM

Okay…so I've officially been invited to a party.

But the party is *tonight*. I'd need a good week to work myself up to it, or at least have Garrison to go with. There are a lot of reasons I probably shouldn't go. More reasons why I should. Maybe I just need a pep talk from my best friend. I check the clock and do the mental math to convert time zones. It's not too early in Philly, so I dial her number.

Daisy answers on the second ring. "Hey, I was just about to text you. The last pic you sent looked beyond delicious. It literally made my stomach grumble. So either it was fantastic or your photo-taking skills have become extraordinary. Or both. Probably both, right?" I can hear the smile through her words.

My lips already lift. "Bangers and mash *is* really good." Before moving here, I heard not-great things about the food in England, but so far I'm loving it.

I think it helps that Daisy and I made an agreement that I'd send pictures of each new meal, accompanied by a star-rating and review. Bangers and mash was a solid five-stars. *Yummy yummy yummy* was my official review. So it's a good thing I'm a business student and not a professional food critic.

"Hey wait, let's FaceTime." She hangs up quickly and calls back just as fast. When I click into it, her bright green eyes hit mine. Blonde hair splayed across her shoulders and a wide grin. It looks like she's sitting in her tree house, and her eight-month-old baby is curled up on her lap. Sullivan Meadows sleeps peacefully in a unicorn onesie, the hood complete with a glittery horn and all.

There's something about babies that makes me melt. Maybe it was because I grew up with a sister who was eleven years younger than me. I have fond memories of Ellie, and the fondest were definitely when she was young enough to not completely hate me.

Our relationship has been fractured ever since I left Maine, and the more I try to sew it back together, the more it just rips at the seams.

It's been months the last time my own sister even spoke to me, and her words were, *you chose your famous family. Go be with them.*

She won't let me have a relationship with her without severing ties with Loren, and it's unfair. I never felt like moving to Philadelphia was choosing Loren, my famous brother, over my little sister. I would have been gone in a year for college anyway. Moving to Philly, for me, was always about choosing to discover a part of my world that my mom kept secret from me.

Ellie never understood that. She still doesn't. And even though Loren is related to her too—he's her half-brother—I think there's too much resentment there for it to matter to her. I know I'll keep trying to rebuild what I broke, but I'm not sure if there's even a foundation left.

My dad doesn't speak to me. My mom will answer my texts weeks later, and my phone calls are always cut short on her end. I always think about the day I left Maine and the *what ifs*. What if I stayed? I would have never met Lo. Never would have had a relationship with my brother. But I would have kept one with my mom and little sister.

It's a horrible trade-off. One I can't dwell on because I've already chosen a path. This isn't like a comic book. I can't turn back time and see what the other universe has in store for me.

I stop thinking about Ellie and my mom just to focus on Daisy's baby again. My lips lift, joy replacing hurt because little Sulli is nothing short of a miracle.

My best friend went through hurdles and roadblocks and mountains just to have her baby girl, and so seeing Sulli is like a dream come to life.

"How is she doing?" I ask.

"Amazing," Daisy says, eyes lighting up. "She's a certified mermaid. It's officially official, she *loves* the water. I've never seen anything like it. She gets so excited when we take her to swim lessons. The trouble is pulling her *away* from the pool." Daisy crinkles her nose at the thought. "It's like destroying her favorite teddy bear."

I smile, loving these stories. Daisy and I are close in age. I'm twenty. She's just twenty-two, but we're on different trajectories. I'm starting college, and she's starting a family. Still, we make an effort to stay close and catch up. This is a friendship I don't want to lose, no matter how far away I am.

I've already lost one that I thought would never end. Maggie—my only friend from Maine—was supposed to be my forever-friend. But she stopped texting me. Stopped answering my calls. All because I refused to give her information about the Calloways and Loren.

You're related to him, she'd tell me. *Why can't you talk about him to your best friend?*

Because it never felt right. Because the closer I got to them, the more I didn't trust her to not spread it all over the internet.

So maybe I am to blame for that friendship ending. I couldn't give her trust. And she couldn't accept the fact that our friendship wouldn't include discussing Loren and the Calloway sisters.

"How's Ryke handling it?" I ask Daisy. The last time I saw him, he was having a nervous breakdown trying to get Sulli to stop crying. I've never seen someone *so* concerned over a baby's tears. Like he thought he might have broken her. All she needed was a good burp.

Daisy laughs. "I think he'd let her prune into a wrinkly baby just to avoid making her cry," she says. "Which is fine. I'm willing to play the not-so-nice cop role for my peanut butter cupcake." She kisses Sulli's forehead. The baby barely stirs. "But enough about me, Willow. How's Wakefield? How are your classes?"

I take a breath. "That's why I called."

I explain my dilemma and this party.

Daisy nods slowly. "Do whatever makes you feel comfortable."

"That'd be staying in my dorm for the rest of eternity."

"Then go. Have fun. Don't overthink it."

"What if I sit by myself all night and no one talks to me? There's a good chance I don't gain the courage to approach anyone." I can imagine it now. I'm the girl in the corner, eating popcorn and trying to dissolve into the chair.

"Then you'll have a stupendous, amazing time by yourself," Daisy cuts into my morbid thought. "You're an awesome person. All you need to do is believe it, Willow Hale." She wags her brows.

I touch my ring: a plain silver band with a black square in the middle. It's a friendship ring from one of my favorite superheroes in *The Fourth Degree*, Tilly Stazyor, and Daisy has an identical one.

My phone buzzes and a text pops up on top of the FaceTime screen.

Tess: SOS. Did you guys see the professor's email? We have to choose our product and email it to him by tonight.

Oh no.

Tess is a part of my group for that Intro to Marketing course. Last class, I briefly met my partners and we made plans to meet up next week to start our project. We have to create a print and online advertising strategy for a product, and it's worth half our grade.

"What's wrong?" Daisy asks, seeing the haunted look on my face. Another text pops up.

Salvatore: Emergency meeting. Where can I find you guys?

"I think I have to meet with my group tonight," I say. So there goes the party. "But maybe...maybe I'll invite them over here?"

Daisy nods and bites on the end of a Twizzler. "Yes, I like this idea."

Courage emblazons my bones. I am a Gryffindor for a reason, right? Like Neville Longbottom, I can put myself in situations that seem daunting and out-of-my-element. And I will succeed—if I can try to believe it.

So I text the group: My hall is pretty quiet. You all can meet at my dorm. 301. Bishop Hall.

Tess: Sweet. See you soon.
Sheetal: Brilliant!
Salvatore: I'll be there in twenty

Did I just invite people over? I did. Pride overcomes me, followed by an intense wave of worry. Shit, I don't even have snacks or sodas. How am I supposed to host people here? And my room—oh God. Two bras are on the floor and my hamper overflows. This is about the time I'd love to have some woodland creatures come help me. Yeah, if only my life were a Disney movie.

I CARRY A STACK OF FIZZ LIFE CANS AND REDIAL HIS NUMBER. Garrison just sent me a video and he looked different. He mumbled out words and had dark circles under his eyes.

I heard all about his pizza disaster and how his roommate has been acting oddly friendly. As a result, Garrison has been spending longer hours in the office just to avoid his apartment.

I worry he's not sleeping.

And we're both shitty at confronting insecurities head-on, I realize.

Running away and ignoring them is easier.

But I'm not going to ignore him. "Pick up…" I tell my phone. I only have a five-minute window before my groupmates start arriving. I make it back to my dorm when the call goes to voicemail. *Shit.* Struggling, I pocket my phone and fumble with my key. I lose balance and an aluminum soda can falls off the four-can stack. It rolls down the hall, and before I can chase after it, a guy places his shoe on top of the can, stopping it.

I take a quick note of the person who saved the soda. Dusty brown hair, squared jaw. Deep brown eyes and tanned, olive skin. He wears this navy tweed sports coat on top of a plain burgundy T-shirt, and it shouldn't match. But it does.

I also know this guy.

Salvatore Amadio. AKA one-fourth of my Intro to Marketing group. We only briefly met in class, but he's now five-feet in front of me. Bending down to snatch the Fizz Life off the floor.

"Thanks," I tell him.

He appraises the stack of cans in my arms. "Getting drinks?" His Italian accent is thick on the words.

He's from Naples but came to Wakefield for university. International students make up eighty-percent of the school, one of the main reasons I chose it over other colleges. Most people here are far away from their homes like me.

"Yep, can't have a group meeting without Fizz—*crap*." I drop the key and bend too quickly to pick it up. Another can falls off my tower and rolls down to Salvatore.

Okay, this is not going well.

"Sorry," I say.

He laughs. "Don't worry about it." He picks up the second can. "Here." He walks over and holds out his hand for the key. Am I that pathetic that I can't even open my own door? This is a new low. I must be frozen because Salvatore motions for the key again. "We'll switch. You take these." We somehow swap items. I'm carrying all four cans again.

He has my room key.

In seconds, the door is unlocked. I avoid his eyes as I go to my desk, setting down all the soda cans.

From an earlier assessment, I know that Salvatore is very good looking. The kind that would anoint him Prom King—even if he didn't go to that school—and I wouldn't be surprised if hundreds of girls slide into his DMs a day. While I can acknowledge his outward beauty, he is not my guy.

My guy is back in Philadelphia currently either passed out asleep or ignoring my calls. Both options concern me. But I can't worry about that right now—I'm hosting people in my dorm room. For the first time ever.

And right now I am alone with a boy in my room.

Who is not Garrison.

Before I become uncomfortable by the thought, a voice comes from my door.

"Hey, girl! Thanks for letting us use your place." Tess leans into the doorway with a beaming smile. She has tight black curls, dark brown skin, and wears camo cargo pants with a cute beige crop top.

What I've learned after one introduction to my group: I am the plain one. Tess, Salvatore, and Sheetal have trendy styles, where I look like I shop at Old Navy (because I do) in my faded jeans and worn T-shirt. It's not even a graphic tee because I don't love people reading my chest or abdomen or wherever the words would fall. It's literally *just* green. I'm okay with that though.

"Yeah, thanks, Willow," Salvatore says as he pops a can of Fizz Life.

Tess tosses her backpack on the floor beside my bed. "Not going to lie, when I saw Professor Flynn's email, I almost had a small panic attack. We're *so* far behind." Her American accent, I recognized when we first met, but I still asked where she's from. Atlanta. Born and raised.

Salvatore sits at my desk chair. "Where's Sheetal?"

"Took me ages to get a proper spot in the car park. Gutted, let me tell you." A tall Indian girl saunters into the room, tote on the crook of her arm. She's dressed in Calloway Couture's latest line: black trousers that just barely hover over the floor and an emerald-green silk top.

Tess grins. "I love how you say *proper* and *gutted*." She glides over and kisses Sheetal on the lips in greeting.

I've already gathered that they're a couple, but I don't know much more. On our first meeting, we just exchanged names and numbers and brief "where are you froms."

Salvatore is obviously curious because he asks, "When did you two start dating anyway?" He casually sets the open Fizz Life on my desk. My phone lets out a warning beep. Shit. It's dying. I walk around the bed to find my charger.

"Over the summer." Tess hooks an arm around her girlfriend.

"We met at orientation," Sheetal adds, her English accent thick.

"And you said you're from Liverpool." Salvatore notes like he's trying to remember our introductions from earlier this week.

"Is right." Sheetal smiles.

Salvatore looks to Tess. "You're from Georgia, the state not the country. And you..." He's definitely looking at me—or at least trying to—but I'm on my knees, the bed blocking me as I plug in my phone. "...I can't remember what you said."

I'm not surprised. I am unmemorable, and I never told any of them my last name. I don't think they've recognized me, so they could just not be into tabloids or celebrity gossip. It's a checkmark in the *yay I can still be just Willow* category. A major plus.

I pop up from the floor. "I'm from the States. Specifically, Pennsylvania. But I grew up in Maine."

Salvatore meets my eyes. "Yeah, that's right." He says it like he's suddenly remembered, and I'm not sure how I feel about that. On one hand, I'd like to drift into the sea of forgotten people, but on the other hand, I do want friends in London. Or at least acquaintances. Really, I only need *one* acquaintance. I'm not picky.

Sheetal shuts the door. "Now that your memory is sufficiently jogged, Salvatore. Let's get to work."

We start brainstorming different products that we could advertise for the project. Everything from shampoo to laptops. An hour later, we've made a snack run and have narrowed it down to three options. Whatever we choose will determine exactly *how* we're going to market it and what demographic we'll be marketing to, so it's the most important step.

Though, what's concerning me has nothing to do with this project—Garrison still hasn't texted or called me back. Not that

I've been checking. Okay, I have checked. Once or twice. *Maybe* five times.

I send him another quick text: Call me when you get this. I'm worried about you.

Footsteps from students running down the hall cut into our silence, all of us flipping through various magazines to grab more inspiration.

Tess stares longingly at the door. "I can't believe I'm doing this on a Friday night." She sighs. "Please wake me up."

Sheetal pinches her.

"Ouch...but thank you, babe," Tess says.

Sheetal smiles and tosses a pretzel in her mouth. "A third-year fella said that this project is *legendary* for business students. Mostly 'cause whichever student has the worst marketing plan ends up being a total whopper of the Fall semester."

A whopper?

Off my confused face, Tess clarifies, "They look like giant idiots."

Sheetal nods. "Last year, the worst in class created a toothpaste ad. Bright red paste for the holidays."

"Oh no." I grimace.

"It was a bloody disaster," Sheetal says. "Pun intended."

Salvatore crushes his Fizz Life can and stands up to throw it away. "Let's just choose from the three we have, they're not bad options."

I look at my notebook, our current options scribbled down.

An umbrella

Waterproof sandals

Fizz

"Let's eliminate Fizz," Tess suddenly says. "If we choose it, Professor Flynn might dock points because of Willow's connection to it."

Wait... *She knows?*

"Yes, go 'ed," Sheetal agrees. She doesn't seem surprised?

"Um..." I push my glasses up the bridge of my nose. "You all know who I am?"

Tess nods. "Your brother is Loren Hale, so that means your sister-in-law is Lily Calloway. Daughter of the CEO of Fizzle. It's all on Wikipedia." *Damn Wikipedia.*

"We also binged the *We Are Calloway* docuseries, like, a little towards the end of the summer," Sheetal says. "But Tess said not to bring it up to you."

Tess nods. "My mom is a director, and my dad is a location scout. As soon as anyone hears the films they made, I get asked a million questions. It's just kind of annoying. I thought it might be the same for you, so I didn't want to make it a big deal."

That's actually really sweet. I'm smiling, my cheeks hurting.

Besides the Calloway sisters and their men, there aren't many other celebrities in Philadelphia. It's not like LA or Hollywood where you can easily meet other people that go through the same public scrutiny. Paparazzi migrated to Philly *because* of the Calloways. Finding someone who gets it, even just a little, is a breath of fresh air.

"Thanks," I say to Tess.

"Don't worry about it," Tess says like it really is nothing.

I look to Salvatore, who's scrolling on his phone. I think he might be looking me up. When he catches me staring, he says, "You can Google me too. Salvatore Amadio." He spells out his full name.

Sheetal laughs. "Are we about to find out your deep, dark secrets, Salvatore?" But we all brandish our phones.

I do a quick Google search and learn that Salvatore Amadio is the son of two famous Italian actors. He was even in a movie as a baby, but he retired from child acting by the age of four.

Sheetal makes a dejected noise. "Well now I'm proper devoed, like. Me parents are in *finance*. An absolute snore. I have no famous family or long-lost siblings."

"You have *meeee*," Tess sing-songs and hugs her tight. Sheetal tries hard not to smile, but it's a lost cause when Tess kisses her playfully on the nose.

Salvatore pockets his phone. "It's not all great," he says to Sheetal but doesn't elaborate.

My cell suddenly vibrates in my palm, Garrison's name on the screen. *Finally.*

"I have to take this," I say quickly and then leave for the hall. It's empty, but I can hear muffled music coming from some of the dorm rooms.

When I click into the call, my worries just tumble forth. "Garrison, are you okay? Your last video looked like you hadn't slept in days. And I'm just now realizing that if you were sleeping I probably woke you up and you needed that sleep. I'm *so* sorry—"

"Willow," he cuts me off before I spiral. "I'm glad you called and texted and practically shot off a rocket flare."

Tears prick my eyes. "You are?"

"Yeah. And I'm in one piece. Like you said, I just haven't been getting sleep. I'm going to make sure I don't stay in the office past midnight."

"Promise?" I ask.

"Promise. What are you doing?"

"There's this group project thing."

"Right now?" Worry and concern breaches his voice. I know he's been worried about distracting me, but I'm making time for him in my life. That's what you're supposed to do for the people you love.

"Yeah, but I'm taking a break—hold on." My door suddenly opens, Salvatore, Sheetal and Tess slipping out of it.

Salvatore catches my gaze. "Hey, we chose the umbrella. We figured we'd just decide and call it an early night."

"I'm going to email the professor," Tess tells me, slinging her backpack over her shoulder.

"See ya, Willow," Sheetal adds before she leaves with Tess.

Salvatore stays for a second. Hands stuffed in his jacket. "We think we can advertise to the university students. Cool designs. Small and portable for class."

It's simple, but maybe that's the beauty of it. "I like it."

"Great." He walks backwards, eyes still on me. "See you in class, Willow Hale." He spins on his heels and heads toward the stairwell.

I don't understand flirting, but I know rom-coms and that definitely was straight out of the movies. Only it does the opposite of causing butterflies to flap in my belly. More like moths dying a slow and unnatural death.

I put my cell back to my ear. "Garrison, are you still there?"

44

Garrison Abbey

IT WAS UNMISTAKABLE. THE GUY'S VOICE ON THE OTHER END of the phone. But there were other voices too, and I'm not about to jump to conclusions like some jealous, paranoid boyfriend. I trust Willow, and she's allowed to have guy friends.

"Garrison, are you still there?" she asks me.

I lie on my bed in a black hoodie and jeans, staring up at the ugly, stained ceiling. "Yeah, still here."

"That was just my group for that project I was talking about."

Intro to Marketing. I remember. All the pieces clicking into place. "You can call me back when you're done."

"We just finished." I hear her shut the door. "I'm going to Skype you." She must be really worried about me, more than I even thought. Fuck.

I run my hand through my messy hair that touches my eyelashes. I don't want to scare her. And really, I'm coherent. Fine. I'm just burying myself in work, and that isn't *that* bad, all things considered.

Skype alerts me on my opened laptop, and I sit up, placing my computer on my lap, and click into her call.

I see my girlfriend, and I exhale. Willow is sitting on her bed, dorm room dimly lit, X-Men poster hung up behind her.

Her eyes flit around me quickly. "You're right, you are in one piece."

"It was touch and go there for a minute," I joke. A bad one.

She shakes her head, and so softly, she whispers, "Don't."

"Okay," I say. "You look good." Her olive-green shirt accentuates her warm brown, hazel-ish eyes that practically look like melting chocolate. Willow wore that same shirt on her last day in Philly.

I only remember because I went to the airport with her, and that image of Willow leaving is kind of engrained in my head.

"You're home," she realizes. "Isn't it only—"

"One p.m." I answer for her. "Connor sent me home." I don't mention that I fell asleep at my desk. "He thought the same thing as you. That I looked tired."

"He's looking out for you," Willow says.

I snort. "He's looking out for his company. I'm not his friend, Willow. I'm his employee."

She shakes her head like she doesn't believe that, but instead of carrying on, she asks if I've seen the latest episode of *Supernatural*. We talk about all the things we both love. TV. Pop culture. Video games. I'm suddenly wide-awake, just wanting to extend every second I can.

Willow glances at her clock and grimaces. "Holy—we've been talking for *three* hours, and I've sufficiently ruined your nap and the whole purpose of you getting rest." She buries her face in her palms with a long groan. "I'm the worst. I'm sorry." We're both beating ourselves up.

Her for distracting me.

Me for distracting her.

I don't know how to fix this.

"You're not even close to the worst," I tell her. "I enjoyed tonight—or today—or whatever you call it." Tonight for her. Still today for me.

She unburies her face and slowly braids her hair. "So do you want to… maybe… um…?" She takes a breath, her eyes soaking into me like she wants something. And then timidly, she slips off her overall straps and pulls off her green shirt, just in a blue cotton bra.

God.

Blood pulses in my dick, and my eyes trace her soft skin and the tops of her breasts. *Yeah, I want to.* Times a million.

I yank my hoodie and tee off my head. Tossing both on the floor. I adjust the computer, setting my laptop more on my mattress near my waist. I see myself in the screen—what she can see—and my whole body is almost in full view.

I focus on Willow, and I frown. "Hey, we don't have to do this if you're not into it, Willow."

Her shoulders are bowed in, and she's clutching her elbows. She pushes up her slipping glasses. "No, I want to. I really do. It just feels kind of…" She glances around her dorm room. "It's really quiet here."

"I can put on music."

She nods and rubs her arms.

I play an alternative rock playlist on my computer, so she'll hear the noise. "Better?"

"Yeah." Willow exhales. "I'm nervous." She shakes out her head. "I wish I weren't *this* nervous."

I know her well. I know that she's pretty shy and reserved. Our relationship moved *slow* from the start. Like the slowest I've ever had. And there wasn't one day where I wanted to press fast-forward and speed up. She's also the best I've ever had.

In everything.

"It's okay that you're nervous," I assure. "It's probably because we've never had Skype sex before."

I look her over, wishing I could be at her dorm a billion times more now. To ease her nerves, to make her feel good. Fuck, it'd be easier if I could just touch her…

She speaks so softly this time; I don't catch the next words over the music.

I hit the volume on my keyboard. "Say that again?"

"Does it turn you off?" she asks in the quietest whisper. "How nervous I am?"

I shake my head, almost smiling. "No." Honestly, I'm really smiling.

Her lips start to rise seeing my smile. "What?"

"Your insecurities are pretty cute. You always think you're so lame and meek, but you're like that daytime soap opera title."

Willow leans closer to the screen. "*General Hospital.*"

I push longer pieces of hair out of my face. "The other one."

"*As the World Turns.*" Willow grins a bit, knowing that's not the right one either. We both don't watch soaps, but we know our television.

"Damn, college is making you stupid," I say, sarcastic.

She laughs. "You say it."

I sweep her features. "*The Bold and the Beautiful.*"

Willow bites the corner of her lip, her smile appearing again.

"You're beautiful, Willow." I skim my girlfriend with hot desire that pricks my nerves and blankets my skin. My dick strains against my jeans. "I think you should get under your covers and watch me. You don't have to get naked or show me anything."

Her eyes widen. "You'd be okay with that?"

"Yeah. No question." I'm usually the one who takes the lead whenever we're in bed anyway. She prefers that, and I'd rather be in control.

Willow slips under her sheets, and the screen goes wonky as her computer falls to its side. After a second, she must prop the laptop on her lap—since the screen stabilizes. I have a clear view of her face, her cheeks flushed and glasses a bit smudged.

I stay in my camera frame for Willow, and I unzip my jeans and kick them off my legs. Left in black boxer-briefs, I palm my hard dick above the fabric. All the while, I watch her pleasure mount on-screen.

Her breath hitches. I strip off the last layer of clothing. Left buck-naked, and I spit in my hand and stroke my length.

My muscles contract. *Fuck.* Heat blisters across my body, and I look at my girlfriend, aroused flush creeping up her neck. And I imagine sinking my erection between her legs. I imagine Willow beneath me, trusting me—a girl who's delicate and shy at most touch, and I go slow and rock deep. My hardness filling her tight warmth that clenches around me.

I fist my shaft in an up-and-down motion and buck my hips up into my grip. "Fuck," I groan. I just want inside her. I just want to be in bed with her.

I just want more than this, and I know I have to be happy with the fantasy and our ocean-apart reality. Like maybe it'll be enough in the end.

I arch my hips into my clutch again.

Willow lets out a soft, aroused noise.

Fuckfuck. I watch as she adjusts her laptop. She's slipping further into her bed. Lying down. I think she props the laptop on the pillow next to her. I can't see below her breasts, but her arm seems to shift...

And move. Her lips part in a short breath. Her eyes shut for a beat longer.

Fuck, she's masturbating. My muscles flex, sweat glistening along my body, and pre-cum coats my hand.

Desire pulsates my veins like a coked-up drummer banging and banging. "Willow," I groan. "*Willow.*"

She gasps and squirms. I strain my ears to hear her whisper, "Garrison."

I'm an idiot and I reach out at the computer screen like I can touch her. This fucking 2D version is only half of my girl, and yeah, I'd rather be able to pull her underneath me right now.

She covers her face with her hand, nearing a peak. "I want you," she mumbles into a sharper breath. "I want you in..."

"I'm in you," I say in a tight, deep voice. I quicken the friction on my length. "I'm so fucking deep in you."

Willow moans.

My neck strains, blood bursting my veins, and I tilt my head back. "*Fuuuck,*" I grit down.

She quakes.

I hit a powerful climax, and an involuntary noise breaches her lips, this high-pitched whimper that reminds me she's completely let go. Out of her head, and I release into my palm. My body on fire as I pump out the tension.

Fuck.

She breathes hard with me, and I try to remind myself that even miles away, intimacy is still strung between us.

THE NEXT FEW WEEKS, WILLOW'S CLASSES GET HARDER, AND I back off calling my girlfriend until she can call me. I won't be her distraction. She's got shit going for her, and I've ruined enough. I'm not going to ruin her.

To not think about her, I just bury myself in work. It's the only thing that keeps me relatively sane. I'm averaging four to five hours of sleep. Which isn't too bad, all things considered.

And I haven't burnt another pizza. So improvement, right?

I grab my backpack off the bed. Normally on Saturday I'd be in the office, but Cobalt Inc. is having a party for the diamond division, and I really don't want to run into those pricks. They're the guys who pass me and "cough" out the word *nepotism*. They're not wrong. But it is annoying. Coughing words died in prep school. It's fucking lame—especially when thirty-year-old tools do it.

But I got a call, so I do have somewhere to be.

I'm babysitting.

I lock up my apartment and on the way to the stairwell, I pass the cracked door to the shared "smokers" balcony. I quit smoking a while ago, so I've never ventured out there. Voices are muffled from outside, but I can still clearly distinguish Ana's high-pitched drawl.

"What do you mean he's never around? Doesn't he live here?"

"I mean what I said, Ana. He isn't around much," Jared replies, freezing me cold. "Last time I saw him, I helped with his fire detector." I freeze. *They're talking about me.*

"That was *weeks* ago," Ana whines. "If we want to make headway into the inner-circle, you need to be nicer." I almost snort out a bitter-ass laugh. I knew it was all an act. It actually sucks to be right.

"Baby, I'm being as nice as I can be without getting on my knees and sucking him off."

"Maybe—"

"Ana," he snaps.

"I'm just saying, we have one chance to be *in* with the most famous people in the country. Can you not fuck it up?"

I can't with this shit. I leave, hurrying down the stairwell. I pull my hoodie over my head. My anger surging. I'm babysitting, I remind myself. I can't go into it with this type of anger. *Calm down.*

Breathe.

Breathe.

Fucking breathe.

SUPERHEROES & SCONES IS HARD TO WALK INTO THESE DAYS. Part coffee shop, part comic book store—it'll always remind me of Willow and all the time we spent working here. Stocking the shelves and serving coffees.

I was shit at the espresso machine. Shit at recommending comics. Shit at shelving the "popular" collectibles in the front and the older ones in the back.

But somehow, I was never fired, and that's kind of a success.

Lily walks out from the back, hearing the chimes of the front door. Her bodyguard lets me in and then locks the door behind me. After-hours, only soft lights illuminate the store, and it's eerily quiet. Like walking into a fucking morgue.

I hate being here.

It's the first time I've felt that in a really, *really* long time.

I hate thinking it.

"Garrison, thankyouthankyou for coming." Lily bounces a three-year-old in her arms and then sets him down. "I'm *so* sorry this is such late notice." I agreed to babysitting her toddler. It's something Willow used to do when she was here.

"It's not a problem." I nod to Maximoff Hale. "We're going to have a lot of fun, right?"

He stares up at me with big green eyes. "Will you watch Batman with me?"

Shit. I raise my brows at Lily. Her husband owns a comic book company called Halway Comics, but everyone in the world is aware that Loren Hale's true allegiance is to Marvel. He says *fuck DC* on practically every Instagram Live I've seen.

She cringes. "Moffy's love of Batman is not going anywhere, much to his dad's dismay."

"Cool," I say with a smile. It's amusing.

"Will you watch it with me?" Maximoff asks me again. "*Pleeeeeasssssee.*"

"Sure—"

He's already grabbing my hand and tugging me to the big TV near the collectible toys. Blinds are snapped shut over the windows and glass door for privacy. I'm introduced to a couple extra bodyguards that Lily is leaving with her son and me.

Both men stand near the entrance like silent shadows.

Lily runs around, grabbing keys. She calls out to me. "The fridge is stocked and you remember where the good snacks are?!"

"Break room, bottom cabinet," I mumble under my breath.

Lily doesn't hear me, but she's rushed and glances at the clock. "Thank you! I'll be back soon!"

She exits in a hurry, and her son stares up at me like I'm his total world for the next hour. Maybe because I am.

If Maximoff even knew how I came into his dad's life, would he hate me?

My stomach twists, and I try not to think about that. Moffy is a good kid. He just sits on a yellow beanbag and watches the movie, and when his favorite parts come on, he glances back to make sure I'm paying attention.

One hour and two bowls of popcorn later, the kid is out. Soft snores coming from his mouth. Finding an old *Ant-Man* fleece blanket on a shelf, I rip open the packaging and then cover Maximoff.

Babysitting duties accomplished. Yay me. I lean back against a bookcase, action figures on the shelves, and I scroll through Tumblr.

Willow hasn't answered a questionnaire since she left for Wakefield. Either she doesn't have time to do one or she's just not into them anymore. She reblogged a couple gif sets of that guy from *Gilmore Girls* that she says I remind her of, so that's a good thing, right? She's still thinking about me.

Shit, I need to stop dwelling on this. I run a hand through my hair and bury my head on my knees. I should be working and avoiding all thoughts about Willow. Seconds away from grabbing my backpack and fishing out my laptop, my cell rings.

She's Skyping.

My chest lightens, my lips lift. It's like someone switching on the lights in a dark room, and I know I need to figure out how to find that switch when she's not around. But it's just hard.

"Hey," she says, beaming when she sees me. Christmas morning can't even beat getting to talk to her.

Underneath my happiness is a gnawing sensation. Like something eating me from the inside-out. Termites in my basement, eroding the foundation. I don't know how to shake the feeling.

Focusing on Willow, I notice that she's sitting at her organized wooden desk. Pens and pencils stashed in a cup.

She must be Skyping from her computer, since I have view of most of her room, including her opened door. Students pass by in the hallway.

In another life, could that have been me? College. A dorm. Friends. In another life, I would have lived there and hated every second of it. But I hate being away, too.

I feel like I'm seventeen again, hating two polarizing things and not being able to find peace within the middle. Split apart. Trying to be sewn back together. It hurts. I hate that it hurts.

I meet Willow's eyes.

"Hey," I whisper back, trying not to wake Moffy. "You look pretty cheerful."

"So do you," she replies. "Or at least, more than last weekend."

Last weekend, I had two hours of sleep and downed four Lightning Bolts!—Willow told me that if I drank any more energy drinks she was sending Daisy to come check on me.

She scans my surroundings. "Are you at Superheroes & Scones?"

I nod and then flash the phone toward the sleeping toddler and then back to me.

She looks surprised. "You're babysitting?"

"It's hard to say *no* to Lily." Plus, I genuinely like her kid. Maximoff is sweet and probably the easiest toddler to look after—not that I have a lot of experience babysitting other people's offspring.

Willow nods like she gets it. "Lily has the best puppy dog eyes. They make you crumble."

I pull up the hood of my black jacket. "So hey, I… um, I came up with my project for Cobalt Inc., finally."

Her smile explodes. "Garrison!" she exclaims in a quiet voice, since Maximoff is sleeping. Her enthusiasm emits from the core. "That's amazing. And see, you didn't have anything to worry about."

I shrug. "I'm not going to tell Connor about it yet. He'll probably think it's stupid and pull the plug. I'll ask for forgiveness later or whatever." Which, I know, isn't something you should probably be doing when you're an employee of a multi-billion-dollar corporation.

But I'm too invested in this project to risk losing it. Plus, when I have a prototype, I can better sell the concept to Connor.

I think about not telling Willow the details either. So she doesn't have to keep this secret from her family, but in the end, I can't keep it from her, so I just say, "I want to create a video game based off Sorin-X." He's a character from *The Fourth Degree* comics, the same titles that Loren's company, Halway Comics, publishes.

I need the rights of these comics in order to adapt them into a video game, but I'll jump through that hurdle later.

Willow looks like she could hug me through the screen. But we can't touch, and that realization tunnels through me like a freight train at full speed. It's excruciating. I wish I just told her the news in person—whenever that would be.

"Garrison," she breathes deeply. "That's *perfect*. And you really are the best person to create it. I won't tell anyone, promise."

I nod, knowing she won't, and I quickly change subjects. "How's your project going?" I'd rather talk about Willow because the more I talk about the game, the more I'm probably going to curse the thing to hell. I can already see the project combusting in flames.

She grimaces. "I mean—it's a silly school project. It's not like yours." She pushes up her glasses that have fallen down her nose.

I'm about to tell her she's wrong. That her school is just as important and meaningful than a stupid video game, but someone stops in her doorway.

"Hey, Willow."

My jaw tenses.

It's *that* guy. The one I heard over the phone. I recognize his Italian accent.

He leans against the doorframe. In direct view of her webcam. He grabs her attention, and Willow turns her head to meet his gaze.

I glare. Yeah, I immediately hate this guy for no real reason other than he's showing up unannounced at my girlfriend's door.

Also: he looks like all the assholes in *every* prep school that I've ever attended. Khakis. Fluffy, styled hair. Sports coat. And I'm thoroughly ashamed to say that I attended *three* prep schools because I flunked out of two.

But it's whatever. I can't really read the expression on this guy's face because he's standing too far away from the camera.

That doesn't stop me from squinting at my screen.

"Hey, Salvatore," Willow greets. "Is it six already?"

"On the dot," Salvatore says. My brain starts processing more. This is the guy from Italy that Willow was telling me about. He's in her group for her marketing project. Willow also told me his name is spelled the same as Damon and Stefan Salvatore from *The Vampire Diaries,* even though they're not pronounced the same. She said it was kind of amusing, and at the time, I agreed.

I don't think it's amusing anymore.

"Shit," Willow says. "Time just slipped by. Can you give me a minute?"

"No problem. I'll be on the steps outside."

"Thank you," Willow calls out and then glances back to me. Apologies heavy her eyes. "Garrison—"

"It's not a big deal." I do my best to soften my glare. "Go." I don't even know what I'm telling her to *go* to. My chest is tight.

I don't want to be a possessive asshole. All I know is that I trust her. Don't trust him. Don't know him.

He looks like my brothers. No, he just dresses like a douchebag, like they do. But he's not them.

I swallow hard, my nose flaring. My insides twist, fighting with these feelings. I can't be the paranoid, controlling boyfriend who forbids her from talking to her own goddamn group partner.

I won't do it.

I don't even want to *appear* like I'm jealous or worried about him. She doesn't need that stress. I'm trying to be cool. Everything is cool.

Everything's fine.

She scratches at her arm. "I'm really sorry. This is when I wish I was Hermione and had a Time-Turner. But I am…sadly a mortal."

"A muggle," I rephrase for her, which is something I rarely do for *Harry Potter* references. She's usually correcting me.

She smiles, but it's a sadder, weaker one. "A muggle." She nods and then shakes her head, conflicted. Like she wishes she had time for me and school. Without me asking, she offers more details. "It's a group thing. We're going over to Barnaby's to come up with a slogan for the umbrella ad."

Barnaby's is Wakefield's popular bar. I know because Willow told me about how Tess and Sheetal took her there for an *Avengers* trivia night.

They came in second.

According to Willow, there were some trick questions relating to

Captain America that shouldn't have been included. Even coming in second, she had fun and she's making friends. It's a good thing.

She's happy.

I want that for her. That's all that should matter. We say our goodbyes, and just as I pocket my phone, Lily returns from her meeting. She rushes into Superheroes & Scones like she's been away from her child for a decade. Her 24/7 bodyguard stays near the door with the other two, and I can already hear fans coalescing outside.

My stomach knots. I'm going to have to push my way through those crowds. *Great.* I don't love people grabbing at me. I exhale a tense breath.

Lily skids to a stop when she sees her three-year-old curled up on the beanbag, cuddling the *Ant-Man* blanket.

Gathering my backpack, I avoid her gaze and rise to my feet.

"Garrison, thank you," she whispers so she doesn't wake him.

"It was nothing," I say. "See you." I head towards the door.

"Wait, Garrison." Lily catches up with me. "Do you want to come over for dinner? We're having spaghetti. I didn't make it, so it's edible." She smiles softly, and I see those pleading *puppy dog* eyes that Willow was talking about.

To me, it just looks like pity.

Lily knows I'm alone here in the city. My family might live in Philly, but I don't go see them unless it's a holiday and I'm coerced into it. I have no friends. All that's keeping me going is work. I should take her offer, but I don't want to get close to Lily and Loren or any of Willow's family.

I don't know how long our relationship is going to last. And if she breaks up with me, if this all ends, they'll choose her. Like they should. And I don't want to spend time with Lily and Loren just to lose them in the end.

I won't.

I can't.

"I have plans," I lie to Lily. "But thanks."

Without another glance back, I zip up my jacket and leave.

October

45

Willow Hale

"WHY ARE YOU TAKING PHOTOS OF THE CHIPS, WILLOW?"
Sheetal sips a beer and eyes my cell curiously. It hovers over a bowl
of chips—or *fries* as I call them. Barnaby's has great pub food, and
it's imperative that I send in my rating to Daisy.

"I promised my friend I'd document the food in London," I
explain. "And rate it."

Tess smiles and plucks a fry from the basket. "I'd give these fries
a solid two out of five. Needs more salt." She bites into it.

Sheetal reaches for the salt shaker. "You mean, *chips*."

Tess sticks out her tongue playfully. Sheetal tosses a fry at her, and
Tess laughs. Not long after, Sheetal asks, "You need another bevvie?"
She eyes her girlfriend's depleting beer.

"Not yet, babe," Tess says, smiling into a bite of fry.

They're an adorable couple, and I'm grateful that they keep asking
me to hang out. Even tonight, they could have left after we finished
the assignment for our ad, but instead they both ordered a pint.

In my experience, most people don't love the company of quiet
people like me. We don't bring enough to the conversation. We take
up space at your table when you could have someone louder and
more outwardly fun. And maybe that's just my insecurity because
Sheetal and Tess don't make me feel like an intruder. They actively
want me here, even if I'm quiet.

Someone bumps into our high-top table, and with my free hand,
I reach for the pitcher of beer before it spills.

"Sorry," the guy mumbles before stumbling over to the bar. Barnaby's is crowded, college students filled to the brim. We're lucky we arrived early and snagged one of the high-top tables.

I return to my phone. "So the *chips* are definitely five out of five." I text Daisy my review: Delicious. Pub food at its finest. My picture kind of sucks though. It's all grainy and the dim lighting doesn't do the chips any favors.

She quickly texts me back.

Daisy: They look superb! Wish you could mail them to me!!

Me too.

"Five out of five?" Tess snorts. "I'm going to need to taste test a few more to see what's up." She digs her hand back into the basket.

I pick up my beer stein and take a small sip, the top mostly foam. It's so strange being in a pub with students as young as eighteen, all legally drinking. "I can't believe I'm twenty and drinking in a bar," I say my thoughts out loud.

"I know, right?" Tess nods. "America needs to get with the program and lower the drinking age." She frowns. "Also, I'm just now realizing that by living here, my twenty-first birthday isn't going to be as epic."

"London has saved you from drinking the night away, getting bladdered, and smelling like a vomitorium," Sheetal notes. "You're welcome."

"Bladdered?" I ask.

"Piss drunk," Sheetal defines.

Tess grins and clinks her glass to Sheetal's.

It's another moment I wish Garrison were here. I don't feel like a third wheel or anything, but I want my new friends to meet him. He's so much a part of my life that it feels like I'm hiding something or omitting this essential thing.

I glance towards the bar. Salvatore leans a hip against it, bodies packed between him, but he's focused on a brunette with skin as pale as mine, wavy brown hair, and a deep blue velvet minidress.

"Speaking of ages," Sheetal says, capturing my attention. "I've been thinking about our little group." She waves around the table, but her eyes are on me. "Tess and I are nineteen. You and Salvatore are twenty. We're all the oldest in the class since we started Wakefield late, and I could see Professor Flynn grouping us off on purpose."

Tess nods. "It'd make sense, right? Our families are all well off, too."

I remember something. "He grouped all the Aussies together."

Sheetal lets out a breath. "Well, that probably confirms the theory. He's giving every group an advantage. Like a commonality somewhere. Being a fresher is hard enough, maybe the fella wants to ease some of the stresses on our first year."

"He *is* my nicest prof," I say.

"Mine, too," Tess agrees.

The music in the pub changes to a popular *Arctic Monkeys* song as I sip my beer. The liquid goes down bitter. Garrison loves this band.

"Oh no," Tess says. "You have that look, Willow."

"What look?" I ask and reach for a fry.

"Relationship trouble," Tess says. "Are you missing your boyfriend?" I only briefly told them about Garrison because the more I talk about him, the more I long for him to be beside me.

I'm waiting for the day where that doesn't happen. Where it doesn't hurt. But I'm also terrified if that day finally comes.

"I wish he were here," I admit. "Garrison and I have been through a lot together."

Salvatore comes back to our table and takes the opened seat beside me. He sets his whiskey down along with a basket of something fried-looking. "What are we talking about?" he asks.

"Willow's boyfriend," Sheetal says.

Salvatore swings his head to me. "The one in Philadelphia?"

"That would be the one." I point to the basket. "What's that?" I whip out my phone to take a pic. New food. New experiences. College success, but why do I feel so badly about it? My stomach twisting.

"Pork scratchings," Salvatore says.

"Or for us Americans, pork *rinds*," Tess adds and takes a couple.

"Do you have a pic of him?" Sheetal asks me.

I nod and scroll through my photos, landing on one where he's in his usual black hoodie. Only the hood is down, so you can see more of his face. Hair brushes his eyelashes. Messy like that. We're standing in front of a Groot cut-out in the movie theater, his arm around my waist.

The sinking in my stomach intensifies.

I understand now.

I'm at a pub. Trying new food. Drinking with new friends. Garrison is alone in Philadelphia. Either working himself to the point of exhaustion or in his apartment trying to fend off Jared, his fame-seeking neighbor. *Guilt*. It assaults me tenfold.

I pass the phone to Sheetal. Tess leans over her shoulder to see the screen, too.

"*Willow*, you like the bad boys," Tess says into a grin.

"What?" I frown. "How can you tell?" It's not like Garrison is wearing a sign that says *I've done some questionable things in my past*...right?

Tess and Sheetal laugh lightly.

"I couldn't tell," Tess admits, "but now we know."

Sheetal hands the cell back and smiles. "You and your lad look like a knockout together, of absolute cuteness."

"Thanks," I mumble and pocket it.

Salvatore looks me over in a slow appraisal like he's trying to figure me out. "How is he bad, exactly?"

"He's not," I counter. "He's a good guy. When he visits next semester, you all can meet him and see for yourselves."

"Looking forward to it." Salvatore takes a sip of whiskey. "He'll love me. I have the best first impressions."

Tess snorts. "Yeah, it's your second and third impressions you need to work on."

Salvatore smiles but nudges my shoulder when he sees I'm not doing the same. He grabs a couple of the pork scratchings and places them on a napkin in front of me. "Give us your Pennsylvania-Maine opinion."

"Whoa! YEAH!" A drunk college student starts screaming at the bar. "Chug! Chug!"

Bodies begin shifting and three people knock into our table. I'm not fast enough this time. The pitcher collapses sideways, and I jump up before beer soaks me.

These assholes don't apologize. Instead they face the bar, their bodies still close enough to ram into the table again.

"Hey! Watch where your arses are bumpin' into." Sheetal snaps at the rowdy guys.

They turn on her in an instant, and I just barely make out one of them say, "Daft twit."

"Hey." Salvatore walks in front of them. "Back off."

Tess tosses napkins on the spill, and I walk around the table to stand beside Salvatore. "Just give us some space," I tell the guys. I'm pretty nice about it, so I don't really expect their response.

"*Just give us some space.*" The taller one with blond curly hair mimics my American accent, only he over-emphasizes it like I'm an airhead.

"We don't want any trouble," Salvatore says.

"Wankers!" Sheetal yells at them.

Salvatore sighs heavily, but he's smiling up at the ceiling.

Tess laughs.

I'm trying my best not to grin. Lips pressed tightly together. Curly Blond pins his glare on me, as though my effort to suppress laughter is the serious crime.

Salvatore slides closer to me, and then puts an arm around my shoulder. It's sudden and all for show, but it still causes me to solidify to utter stone.

"I said *back off*," Salvatore tells him.

Sheetal eagle-eyes the Curly Blond and mumbles into her beer. "What a divvy."

He's about to reply when a server walks over. "We got a problem here, mates?" He looks between our group and the asshole, but unlike the four of us, all of the asshole's friends have left him and migrated back to the bar.

Curly Blond grinds on his teeth. "No. I was just leaving." He steps back.

The server sees the empty pitcher, plus the sopping wet napkins, and he gives us an apologetic look. "I'll grab some towels and bring you lads another round on the house."

He leaves and we all look between each other, seconds away from breaking into laughter.

Barnaby's is our spot. Officially.

And then it hits me. It was a silly, *normal* argument. That guy didn't recognize me. Didn't start a fight because he hated my brother. Didn't call me names because of my relation to the Calloway sisters. London and Wakefield are bringing me this overwhelming sense of normalcy, and I don't want to let it go.

But I don't want to let go of what's back home either.

Garrison.

My family.

I love them more than anyone here can understand.

46

Willow Hale

I HAVEN'T SPOKEN TO GARRISON IN WEEKS.

Days turned into nights. Nights turned into mornings. And time seems to seep like water between my fingers. Losing it all.

Our videos to each other have grown more infrequent and shorter. The ones I send, I'm rushed, frazzled running between classes.

His are more concerning. Heavy-lidded eyes and mumbled words before he dozes off.

I lie in bed, wide-awake. My eyes pin to the ceiling, little glow-in-the-dark stars pasted to the cement.

Call him again, my thoughts pull me. I snatch my phone and dial, but it rings to voicemail. Not surprising really. It's only 9 p.m. in Philly, and Garrison works until midnight. He's the type of person that zones completely into his work, loses time and sense of everything around him.

It's why he's so good at what he does, and I can't blame him for not answering. Not when there were plenty of calls I missed because I was in the library or dining hall or…Barnaby's.

I toss my phone aside.

A tree branch scrapes my window as the wind picks up outside. Rain pelts the glass and tries its best to soothe me to sleep.

But I'm too wired. Too longing.

Too much of a lot of things.

My fingers brush my lips. It's been so long since we've even kissed. Since he's held me. *Touched* me. Since I've run my fingers through his hair. Since he's wrapped his arms around me like I'm the only person he wants to embrace. To protect. To love.

I lean over and turn off my lamp, plunging my dorm room into darkness. Alone, with the sound of the rain shower, images of Garrison pop into my head. His hair that curls a little by his ears and his aquamarine eyes that always stare *through* me. Like he knows.

He knows.

What it's like to have people who are supposed to love you unconditionally but they don't. Who are supposed to protect you. But don't.

He'd touch my cheek and say, "It doesn't matter anymore. We're not seventeen. We don't need them. We always have each other."

I'd stand on my tip-toes and press my lips to his. Warmth underneath his palms as he slid them underneath my shirt. He's the only guy that ever touched me like that. Kissing. Hugging.

Anything. Everything.

My body hums, pulsing and clenching harder between my legs. Wanting him. Wanting more.

Ever since I moved to London, I dream up this one single memory when I want to get off alone. This one visual is enough to make me wet and come easily. So right now, I start to think about it again.

I think about the night I lost my virginity.

My hand dips down underneath the sheet. Underneath my pajama shorts. Under my panties. My fingers brush between my legs, breath hitching, and I feel the dampness.

Closing my eyes, I try to visualize every piece of that night. As if I'm back in my Philly bedroom.

Garrison thumbed my nipple, his mouth against the nape of my neck. Sucking a sensitive spot that quaked my sweaty limbs.

I remember the room. Bathed in candlelight, smelling of rose petals and vanilla. Soft music played in the background, and each touch between us felt tender, comfortable and wanted.

Our legs intertwined on the plush mattress. Fluffy blankets kicked aside.

He propped himself up on his elbow, and his hand traveled from my breast down the curve of my hip. Drinking in my bare body, and I soaked up his lean muscles that formed actual abs. Showing off his athleticism. I eyed his boxer-briefs, snug on his toned waist, and his dick pushed against the fabric.

Watching him made me calm down. I breathed and tried to stay out of my head.

Right now, I try not to remember how anxious I was. I don't want to warp the best moment into one of total nervous awkwardness.

Back in my London dorm, I rub my clit. *Remember, Willow.*

I remember how Garrison did this thing—something he usually did if we were tangled up and making out. He tried *really* hard (pun intended) not to grind his erection into me. Like he didn't want me to feel his hardness and pressure me to have sex if I wasn't ready.

Even then, when we agreed that night would be *the* night he'd actually enter me—he still hovered over my body. Like it was just instinct at that point.

I trembled, a little anxious. Also hot with temptation and anticipation. I craved him so badly. Arousal ate me up inside, pulsated between my legs. Blazed the back of my neck. Aching, *longing.*

His hand veered over to the soft flesh of my stomach. Shirt and jean shorts already on the floor, his fingers stopped at the hem of my panties.

"Is this okay?" he whispered in my ear.

"Yeah," I replied, voice raspy. He kissed my lips, urging them open slowly. I followed his lead, and his tongue slid sensually against mine.

I didn't know where to put my hands.

Don't remember.

But it's hard to forget how my palms made uncertain, awkward movements. Usually I would hold his shoulders. That night, I wasn't sure if I should touch his dick.

"Do you need me to…?" I started, but I didn't even know what I was offering. A blow job? A hand job? Another sort of job I was unaware of?

We hadn't even run all the bases together before that night. I've touched his dick—but I wouldn't call it a full-on gold-star worthy hand job, and I've never put him in my mouth before.

I'm always in my head. Anxious and nervous like I'm doing things wrong, and Garrison has been sweet in not pressuring me to go further. I'm just more relaxed with him touching me than the other way around, I guess. Usually, we just make out, grinding a lot, and he'll finger me until I come.

Back when we were in bed together, Garrison pressed his lips to mine again. More tenderly. "No, this is for you. Just relax, Willow."

His fingers skated below the fabric of my panties, his touch achingly slow, and when he brushed the sensitive spot, I let out an aroused breath.

I inhaled the vanilla scent around us and held his firm shoulders. He slipped into me, and I gave myself to Garrison. I trusted him.

I loved him—I *love* him.

He pulsed his fingers in me, filling me, and his thumb teased my clit. Torching my body and nerves. *His fingers would be replaced by something bigger and harder*, the thought lit me on fire and brewed excitement.

As I touch myself in London, I imagine he's here just like that night. About to fill me to the brim. His erection inside me. Rocking. Pleasing.

I remember how my breath staggered back. "Garrison," I moaned at the soft pressure of his fingers. Building more arousal.

He pressed his forehead to mine, rocking slightly. He needed friction. He wanted friction. He ached to be in me. I could see all of this in his eyes and shallow breath.

Pleasure mounted.

His bare chest was slick with sweat, and a deep noise rumbled inside his throat. A noise that drove home who he was. Masculine. Man. Mine. And I was his. *I am his.*

How? I wasn't even sure.

I was bookish and quiet.

He was rebellious and misunderstood. Guys like him usually didn't fall for girls like me. But here we were.

His movements grew faster, our lips skimming with hot breath, and he brushed his thumb over my clit. I crumbled against him in a crashing wave.

My toes curled and euphoria spotted my vision. My breath staggered, moans catching in my throat.

In London, I grip the twisted sheets and arch my hips. Wishing he were here, touching me. *He is*, I pretend.

"I've got you," Garrison breathed that night, lips to my ear.

I rolled down the blissful sensation. Eyes heavy lidded, I kissed the closest thing I could find—his forearm. A *very* pretty forearm.

When our eyes met, his overwhelming desire avalanched mine, covering me in so much need that I nearly quivered beneath him.

"You can do it now," I said softly.

He rubbed my thigh and searched my gaze. "You sure you're ready? I can get you off again—"

"I'm sure," I said, confident about this decision. My hands drifted to the ridges of his abs. "I want to feel you inside me."

Arousal pinned against his heady eyes. "Fuck."

We were both smiling. Excitement swelled around us like a ruthless, restless ocean, and we were both happy to let the riptide pull us under.

He rose off the bed and I watched as he made the trek to my dresser—where he knew I kept the emergency condoms. Just in case.

He was buck-naked like me. He was twenty like me. But tattoos inked his toned body and he moved with such ease and confidence. No longer looking like the jock that I pegged him as when I first met him. He was a bad boy. Misunderstood. *Mine*.

I pulsed just watching him, and I relaxed into my pillow. In quick movements, he had the foil packet and returned to me.

As soon as he was back on the bed, Garrison drank me in again, like I was the most beautiful creature to ever grace the universe.

"Willow." He said my name in a way that caused every inch of me to shudder. Like dipping a toe in a cold pool.

I glanced down at his length, his knees on the mattress as he ripped open the condom with his teeth. His dick was larger than anything that had ever been inside of me.

I leaned up, and he cupped my cheek and kissed me. I held his arms for comfort, wanting him close. He broke apart my legs with his knees. My heart beat rapidly.

I thought it might hurt a lot, and that was what I feared the most. Being scared and then making an awkward mess of things. But Garrison knew that already.

I'd told him before.

He whispered against my lips, "If it hurts too much, you tell me and I'll stop, okay? I'm fine with that."

His words were like magic. Vanquishing my nerves.

I nodded, and I rested my shoulders back to the mattress. My legs around him. Vulnerable and ready, *so ready.*

For the first time, I watched him sheath himself in front of me. More confidence radiating off every inch of him. It was contagious, fueling timid parts of me.

He climbed further over my body, his hand beside my cheek. He lowered his head, his lips fusing with my lips. His tongue tangling with mine, his breath melding with mine, his heart beating with mine.

I was swept up into hot sensations. Into the fiery moment, and his hand slid along my hips and then pressure welled between my legs.

A sharp pain came and went, replaced by an overwhelming fullness that dizzied and electrified. Sparking more need. More desire. More want.

"God, Willow," Garrison groaned like this is a very *good* place to be. I trembled underneath him, desiring more friction. His eyes soaked into mine. Concern wrapped in extreme craving. He was already moving his hips.

He was already rocking against me and watching him pump inside me—*oh my God.* I gasped, and he held my hand in his, lacing our fingers on the pillow. "This good?" he breathed.

I nodded, words lost in my throat. *So good.*

With that confirmation, he started thrusting harder. Working me up, sweat glistened on our skin, and a high-pitched noise escaped my lips, something else tickling my throat. "Ahh." I clutched onto his bicep, the one with the inked skull. I was riding a surge of pleasure, the end not even in sight. "*Garrison*...please don't stop."

"*Fuck*," he groaned, placing another kiss on my lips. He drove deeper in me and welled up sentiments pricked my eyes.

He let go of my hand and clutched my cheek. His pace and the fullness absolutely annihilating me. In the best way. Obviously worthy of a mental revisit.

I was lost beneath him.

He was lost above me.

We found each other between every staggered breath. Every racing heartbeat. Every aching need. Until we were both sweaty and overcome by an intense, passionate crash. Nerves firing. Breaths heaving. Bodies colliding with blissful pleasure after all those years of waiting.

In my dorm room, I ride the same wave. I reach a peak.

I cry out his name in a soft, aching whisper. He lights me on fire—even when he's miles away. But there's a difference.

I come down, and I roll on my side. No one else tangled in the sheets with me.

He's not here to pull me in his arms. He's not here to say *I love you.* He's not here so I can say *I love you* back.

He's not here to ask if I'm okay. To push the sweaty pieces of hair off my face. To kiss me one last time before we fall asleep.

So I fumble for my phone. And I try to call him again. "Please answer," I mutter alone in London. "Please answer."

It rings.

And rings.

"Please, Garrison." It stops ringing.

Beep.

"Voice-mailbox full," an automated voice replies.

I roll onto my back and hold my phone to my chest.

47

Garrison Abbey

HALLOWEEN.

Also known as Loren Hale's birthday. He already texted me about some "surprise" party he's throwing himself. Only it's a surprise for all his guests, not him—the guy with the birthday. It's so Loren Hale, you really can't make this shit up.

The elevator at Cobalt Inc. is slow as fuck today. Maybe it's broken? It goes down and down and down like the ticking of a clock, and I'm worried that I'm not ditching out of here early enough to avoid the party. I glance at the text again.

> **Loren Hale:** I'm picking you up at 9:45 p.m. for my birthday party. The outing is a surprise. No questions will be answered. Participation is not optional.

He's such an asshole, even in text. He didn't even ask where I'd be, so I assume Connor tells him I work until midnight. But joke is on him because I'm out of here at 9:30 p.m. tonight.

The elevator finally makes it to the lobby, and I pull out my phone to call an Uber. Just as I exit the revolving doors, shoes landing on the sidewalk, a black limo slows at the curb.

Fuck.

Second option: Avoid eye contact. Maybe I can get away with ignoring the limo. I focus on my cell and notice that the nearest Uber is ten minutes away. *Fuck* Halloween.

"Garrison Abbey!" Loren shouts from the limo. "Let's go! My birthday awaits!"

Don't be an asshole. I let out a breath of defeat and glance up. Half of his body hangs out of the limo's opened window. He holds out a hand like *come on.*

Trying not to seem too unenthusiastic, I pocket my phone, adjust my backpack on my shoulder, and approach the limo. Each footstep heavy.

Loren is about to open the limo door, but I grab onto the windowsill and shove it closed. Lo glares almost instantly like I just told his kid that Santa Clause isn't real. And in the next instant, his eyes soften considerably. Like he's trying to be nice—and that act is hard for him.

He opens his mouth, and I cut him off. "Thanks for the invite, but I decided I'm not going."

His amber eyes are really fucking hard to look at. They basically scream a million things. Disappointment. Confusion. I avoid them, preferring his ruthless glares to what he's showering me with right now. Seriously, I stare anywhere but at him.

The street.

The light pole.

The revolving doors I just left.

I can't hang out with them like we're friends.

I can't hang out with *him.* My girlfriend is his little sister. For fuck's sake, I vandalized his house three years ago. Did he suddenly have amnesia? He should be pushing me down on the curb. He should be kicking me and calling me a thousand different names. Not inviting me to *his* birthday party.

Jesus. It doesn't make sense.

I steal one glance back at him, and he's looking over my shoulder like he's trying to find someone. And then he tells me, "Because you have so many friends lined up inviting you places." In mock surprise, he puts his hand to his lips. "*Oh my God,* there's your bestie waving you down. He's so excited to see you."

Fuck him.

I glare.

He glares back, and then I think, *this is stupid.* He's just trying to piss me off to get me to go. He's a button-pusher, and the more I'm around him, the more he's learning mine.

I roll my eyes. "I have *work*, you fucking..." I let out an aggravated noise and scuff the sidewalk with my Converse. What the fuck am I doing?

"If the CEO of the company can take time off for my birthday, then so can his employee." Loren tries to open the car door again, but I lean my bodyweight against it.

His cheekbones sharpen.

"I'm serious." I take a deep breath. "I have to finish what I'm working on and..." I stare off. What else? God, I'm pathetic. I can't even come up with a decent excuse.

"Just let me out for a second. I won't force you in the limo." The edge is still in his voice, but there's no humor attached. He's serious.

I step back and pull the sleeves of my hoodie down over the tops of my hands, the wind picking up. Chillier tonight. Loren opens the door and climbs out of the car. No Halloween costume on, which kind of surprises me. Just a black crewneck T-shirt and dark jeans.

He's taller than me by a few inches, and I pull my hood back just to brush longer strands of my hair out of my face.

"I *want* you to come," Lo emphasizes.

I shake my head. Why? Because I'm Willow's boyfriend? Because he thinks I'm some loser without anyone to hang with on Halloween?

He stares right into me. "Jesus Christ, do I need to drop to my knees and beg?"

I blow out hot breath through my nose, and a bright flash in the distance catches my attention. We both turn our heads.

Paparazzi parallel parked down the street. Loren and the Calloway sisters attract them like moths to a flame, and they burn fucking bright. At least, I can get away from it. I can't even imagine having to *always* deal with the constant cameras.

We only have a minute before we're bombarded, and I don't want to be in *Celebrity Crush* tomorrow.

So I quickly say, "It's different." Loren swings his head to me, confusion lining his eyes. I continue on. "This is a boyfriend-girlfriend, couple thing. I'm the seventh wheel now that Willow is gone, and I see that it's a *pity* invite, man, so just *leave me alone.*"

He cocks his head. "Pity? Do you know who I am?" He touches his chest. "I have waded in self-pity too much to ever spare pity for other people. And you can ask Connor and Ryke in there." He points to the limo. "I don't aimlessly throw out invites like I'm a flower girl at a wedding. I have very few friends, and you're one of them."

What? No.

We're not friends. It may have been years since I spray-painted *Cock Sucker* on his mailbox, but it doesn't change the fact that I did those things. I don't deserve his friendship. I definitely don't deserve him trying so fucking hard to get me to go to his party.

I deserve *none* of it.

Me, being alone on Halloween is karma. It's penance for all my shitty deeds. That's where I deserve to be. Friendless and alone.

But he's here spending energy on me, and there's a part of me that wants to just get in the limo. That wants to give myself happiness and fun for maybe just one moment.

Loren tries to convince me again. "Willow would hate what we're about to do. You, on the other hand, will like what I have planned for my birthday. So I'm glad it's you and not her here." He flashes his iconic half-smile.

Okay.

Okay. *Okay.*

I breathe and then nod a few times.

A cameraman jogs closer, and Loren casts a scathing, threatening glare at him to stay back.

The guy cowers a few feet away, but he still shouts, "Where's Maximoff?!"

I glare now. Loren's kid is only *three*, and paparazzi harass him more in one week than I've been in my entire life. And anyway, I'm pretty sure that Maximoff and the rest of the Calloway sisters' kids are staying back with a babysitter. But like hell I'm telling this guy anything.

Loren ignores the cameraman like he's evaporated into thin air and his eyes ping to me.

"Let's go," I say.

Loren's lips curve upward and he slips around me to open the limo door.

What am I getting myself into?

OF COURSE, LOREN SURPRISES EVERYONE WITH A NIGHT AT THE Halloween Horror Fest, an annual October event at the nearest theme park. Mazes are decked out with decorations, and actors dressed as ghouls and zombies attempt to scare the guests.

Two out of ten on the "fright" factor. I swear I saw a vampire eating a pretzel on break. There's nothing terrifying about that.

Before we even make it to a maze, we stop at an iron café table in a safe zone where the actors aren't allowed to scare us.

Since I'm with the "core six"—as the internet affectionately calls Lily, Loren, Rose, Connor, Ryke and Daisy—bodyguards linger nearby in case they get a wave of unwanted attention. So far, only a few fans have stopped and asked for selfies and autographs. There'd probably be more if this place wasn't so disorienting with the fog, screams, and eerie music.

Mostly, I ignore everyone around me, including the automated cries that come from the nearby mazes.

Straw between my lips, I hold a soda with one hand and scroll through my phone. Willow should be asleep by now. She went to her first Wakefield Halloween party, and she texted me a bunch of drunk texts about an hour ago.

Willow: Garrrrisoon! Ur face is pretty. I miss ur face

Willow: ur my fav person ever

Me: Are you home?

Willow: Not yet. Still at house. I'll text pics. The decorations are... interesting

Whoever hosted just put out a bunch of fake spider webs and then a bowl of punch. That was it.

Willow: Lo would have a stroke if he saw

Me: Good thing he's not there

Willow: I miss ur face. Did I say that alrdey?

Me: You did. But I'm pretty sure I miss your face more

Willow: not possible

Me: I'm going to see your face soon

Willow: Soon *sparkly heart emoji*

Me: *praising hands emoji*

That was the last text. She's coming home for Winter Break, and it may still be over a month away, but I'm starting the countdown. Fuck, I've been counting down since she left.

A shriller scream blasts from one of the foggy mazes nearby. Our current spot resides closer to the main entrance, and I've already been briefed how this table is "home base" in case anyone gets lost.

Which—if I had to bet would be Lily. Scratch that, she's clinging to her husband so tight, there's no way she'd drift away from the pack.

Maybe I'd say Daisy, but she's going to be chilling at home base all night. Daisy's white husky is sprawled across her lap as she digs into a bag of cinnamon rolls that Lily and Loren brought back from a Cinnabon run.

I was kind of surprised Daisy even came along to this, considering she has PTSD, and this place should be hell for anyone who gets triggered by sudden, piercing noises. But maybe she just didn't want to miss out.

The night is special enough that the Calloway sisters brought costumes for everyone. Albeit, *simple* costumes, but they thought about that shit.

A flower crown rests on Daisy's blonde hair, an identical one on Ryke's head. Lily and Loren sport glittery alien antenna headbands, while Rose and Connor wear these regal golden crowns. I don't even think they're plastic. Like, legit crowns. The Cobalts have to be the most extra people I know, and honestly, I can't believe I work for one of them.

I fix my backwards baseball hat. It lights up to spell out the word *boo.*

Maybe my costume is a literal flashing hat so that Loren makes sure I don't ditch them, but I kind of like that it's loud but not *too* loud. The flopping antennas would have annoyed the fuck out of me.

I glance up from my phone just to see Connor and Rose still arguing over the route. The park map is spread over the table, and they both brandish Sharpies like there'll be a test at the end of this. *Fastest Through the Mazes* isn't a thing.

"What are you doing?" Rose snaps at her husband. "That is the worst path. You can't go from Texas Chainsaw Massacre to Nightmare on Elm Street."

"Why not?" He grins like he knows what she's about to say but wants to hear it anyway.

"We're not doing gore back-to-back." She gathers her hair on one shoulder and traces a line on the map. "It's better if we do The Ring maze in between."

A chainsaw roars, pretty close. Girls run away from the masked actor as he chases them. Legally, he can't touch them, so running away is the wrong way to go. From experience, the actors prey on the people who look like they're about to piss their pants.

I'm about to return to my phone, but Rose's voice grabs my attention again.

"Gore does not frighten me," Rose retorts. "If you don't believe me, give me a fucking knife and I'll stab you myself and you'll see how frightened I'll be." She motions to him for a knife.

Connor's attraction to her threat is clear in his eyes, like he could go down on her on the fucking table right now. Jesus, they're weird. His grin expands, and he steps closer to his wife.

Loren interjects, "Careful of her talons."

"She won't harm me," Connor says easily. "But I appreciate the concern."

"I will gut you, Richard," Rose threatens. Her chin rises as he nears again, towering above her. Confidence mixed with dominance.

"And?" he questions in a deep breath.

"And I will remove all of your organs slowly and painfully."

"Painfully," he muses. "You exaggerate."

Lily is grinning from ear-to-ear. She's obsessed with everyone being happy *in love*. I should know. She's asked me how Willow and I are doing about a hundred-and-one times. To the point where I think she'll be as devastated as me if we end up not working out.

Rose glowers. "Fear. Me. Richard. I will annihilate you in a murderous, bloody…" Her breath hitches as he steps nearer, their legs thread. She reaches back, palms hitting the iron table. He almost has her pinned.

"Fear what, Rose?" he breathes against her lips.

She says one word in French, and he says two more in the same language. Honestly, they look like they're about to kiss.

And this is where I'm definitely glancing back at my cell. Avoiding Instagram has been my mantra since I saw Salvatore Amadio. I don't need to look him up and have visuals of his entire life. So I'm not about to torture myself tonight with pics of his six pack abs or Porsche (not that I know he has either but with my luck, it's probable). Shit, stop thinking about Salvatore.

Tumblr, it is.

Willow hasn't reblogged anything in weeks. Her account is practically dead. Mine is almost the same, but I've got a couple gif sets from the latest season of *American Horror Story* on my feed. I haven't had time to make anything in a while.

No edits. No gifs. No videos spliced together. I want to blame it all on time, but deep down I know it's something else.

Something more.

Fuck it, I'm doing a questionnaire. I find the tag and click into the first one.

Current Location

I pop my head up just to see Daisy hoisting two cinnamon rolls in either hand. "My right bun is smaller than my left bun." She speaks to her husband.

Ryke is sitting beside her. Teetering back on the legs of his chair, he glances right at her boobs.

Her graphic tee says *boo-fucking-tastic*, and photographs of Daisy wearing that shirt have already spread over social media. To the point where the thing sold out on H&M in minutes.

Ryke focuses on Daisy's eyes. "Your buns look fucking perfect to me, Calloway."

The intense flirting is something I'm used to seeing from them, and it used to make me super happy. I think because Willow loves Daisy and Ryke, and seeing them together is a good thing—but now I just see two people in love. Who get to spend time together.

And I don't have that. My stomach twists in horrible knots, my soda not settling well.

I'm bitter, I realize.

I hate being this bitter.

Daisy licks the icing off the right cinnamon roll and breaks into a huge laugh. "You'll like this one."

"Why's that?"

"It's really wet."

Ryke casually uses two fingers to swipe some icing off the dough. Then he sucks them while staring too deeply into his wife. When he drops his hand, he says, "Not wet enough, sweetheart."

I grimace.

I see Loren seriously cringing.

Current Location: pretty sure this is some circle
of hell Dante hasn't invented yet

The kind made for bitter souls.

Daisy barely lowers her voice, teasing Ryke. "Will you still eat me?"

His *I want to fuck you* eyes answer her.

"Hey," Loren snaps.

Both of them casually turn their heads to him. Like this is just another day, and conversations about oral sex and cum are completely normal.

Lo adds, "Lily wants you to stop flirting."

Lily gapes. "I do not!"

Loren feigns surprise. "I could've sworn she said that you were making her nauseous."

Ryke raises his brows at me. "Sounds like you."

Mockingly, Loren touches his chest. "Never."

I almost snort.

Back to the questionnaire...

Height: 5'11''

Eye Color: I always thought they were bluish green.
My girlfriend calls them aquamarine sometimes. So
we'll go with that.

Why does every distraction I have make me think of her even more? Jesus...it's like running and hitting a brick wall and turning around and hitting another.

It's useless. I click out of Tumblr just as Loren is snapping his fingers in my face. "You. Garrison. Follow. Now."

I pocket my phone. "What, you forget how sentences work?"

Rose and Connor have already gathered their maps, Lily's hand is in Lo's, and Ryke walks away from the table, leaving Daisy in the safe zone.

Guess we really are heading out.

Loren drives a glare into me. "Says the guy who uses internet shorthand like brb and tbh." His half-smile meets me, but it doesn't scare me.

I just glare back.

He adds, "ICYM, I'm a sarcastic prick. Move your ass that way." He points in the direction of the first maze.

The Exorcist themed one.

Park security lets us discreetly skip to the front of the line. The perks of being around super famous people, I guess. It happens all without alerting the massive crowds that we've cut. Loren says it's for our safety. Waiting for hours in the roped off sections with park-goers is a sure way to cause stampedes and hysteria. They'll want autographs. Selfies.

We need to blend.

I'm not used to the constant scrutiny as much as them, but I can understand not wanting to be approached.

Ahead of Loren, I enter *The Exorcist* maze that's decorated like a little house. Pitch black. I can barely see in front of my face. Demonic cackling echoes around us, and the rest of our group walks in a single-file line.

"OhGodOhGod," Lily mutters.

I glance back to see her wide-eyed expression, and she's grabbing onto the back of Loren's shirt, so much that the collar is tight around Lo's neck.

Willow and I never went to one of these fright night things together. She's not into the scary shit as much as me, but I can imagine her here. I'd have my arms around her. She'd be pressed up to my side—

Shit, stop thinking.

Quickly, I look back ahead.

We enter the bedroom area, and a mechanical version of Regan MacNeil sits on the bed. Her head spins three-sixty degrees. It looks like whoever built the robot did a pretty damn good job.

"Cool," I say, impressed by the production quality. Even speakers are set up that narrate the exorcism from the movie.

"Lil," Loren says behind me. "Look up. It's not that bad."

I scan the area, trying to ignore them and focus on the rooms. There's so much detail, like how potted plants are overturned and furniture floats mid-air, as though a possessed being rattles the whole room.

Very cool.

"I'll have nightmares forever!" Lily shrieks.

From even further behind me, I hear Rose scream shortly in fright and then reprimand the actor, "You did that on purpose!"

I almost laugh. There's something about being with these people that make shitty days seem…I don't know. I shouldn't like their company.

I shouldn't want it.

Or ask for it. Or God forbid, *need* it. Because they've already done way too much for me, and they're not mine. They're Willow's.

I don't look behind me again, but I think I must be walking through the maze faster because Lily and Loren's voice drifts off. I enter one of the last rooms where fake puke flies onto the wall. I stand there for a couple long moments and literally the robot turns to me and grins. Wait…not a robot. This one is *definitely* an actress. She starts crawling on the bed towards me like she means to scare me.

I smile.

I don't know why.

Maybe because she thinks *this* is frightening. I've been afraid before—really scared—but not from green-puking demons. This is nothing.

She stops and tries to make another "freaky grin face" but I'm over it. I keep walking. Right on out of the maze. Cold air hits me just as I hear a shrill scream inside the maze.

I'm betting that's Lily. My lips lift into a bigger smile, just taking in the moment. I'm doing something on a random night, and it's not even bad. It's kind of fun.

One of the bodyguards nears me and stations next to my side. Like I'm important or something, but I realize in less than a second that he's blocking my body from onlookers. Girls laugh loudly around the maze's exit and steal glances at me.

Maybe they want my autograph or for me to divulge details about the core six—the latter is most likely.

I shouldn't ask the bodyguard, but I do. "Hey, how do you know I don't want to be approached by people?"

The bodyguards don't block Lily all the time. Definitely not Ryke or Lo.

"Loren informed us that you don't want the attention," he says. "Has that changed, sir?"

I shake my head. No. It hasn't.

I'm smiling more now, and then I spot Lo. He exits the building, carrying Lily piggyback-style. She's burying her face in the crook of his neck like she can't even take a peek without pissing her pants.

My brows knot. "It wasn't even that scary."

Loren holds her thighs. "She's scared of her own shadow when I shut off the lights at night."

"That was one time!" Lily protests without lifting her head up.

Loren and I both laugh, and then he says to Lily, "We're out of the maze now. You want down, love?"

Slowly, she lifts her head up enough to rest her chin on his shoulder and then glances around the park. People are laughing or power-walking away from the maze's exit. No one is bloody or dying on the ground.

"Can I stay here for one more maze?" Lily asks. "Then I'll drop down."

Loren nods, and Rose suddenly exits with Connor, both undeterred by the horror element. Connor honestly looks like he just stepped out of his weekly phone conferences with oversea

investors. Same casual *I own the world* confidence radiates off him…
and his wife.

The golden crowns make this twice as noticeable.

I glance at Loren, and he looks upset. Like maybe the whole
goal was to rattle the unshakeable. Nine mazes are left, and I know
Connor well enough as my boss—and I'm pretty sure you could put
him in a thousand mazes and he'd still exit each one with assuredness
and ease.

Rose narrows her eyes at Loren. Probably understanding his
ulterior motive.

Loren cringes. "Stop staring at me. I know you like my face, but
my face doesn't like you."

Rose's yellow-green gaze pierces him. "You're a *child*, Loren."

They're bickering is non-stop whenever I'm around them. At
first, I thought it was a fluke. Nope. It happens… All. The. Time. For
no other reason than they just seem to not get along.

Loren mimes wiping a tear with his fist to his cheek, surprisingly
able to hold Lily with one hand. "Go cry about it in your lair."

"Go dry hump a bed of nails." At this, she flips her hair over her
shoulder and marches ahead in five-inch heels. Her husband is the
only person that follows her, able to keep pace with his wife. Their
fingers thread together, holding hands.

Don't think about Willow.

I'm not…

I'm *trying* not to.

I swallow a lump in my throat as we all follow the King and
Queen—as the internet refers to them. With all the bodyguards
trailing us, it's starting to feel like they're actually American royalty.

The more we walk, the more my mind circumnavigates back to
Willow. Despite the skeleton-painted guys shrieking at the guests
and chainsaws revving, I know she'd want to be here. She loves her
family, and missing out on a group experience would bum her out.

There are pros and cons to being away, and this right now, is her
con. Even if I'm having a decent…pretty good time.

So yeah, I feel kind of shitty about that.

I hate that we're on two separate continents. We're stretched thin for time as it is. And I'm not a mind reader. I don't know what she's thinking all the time, and especially now that she's around college guys like Salvatore Amadio, she has to be beginning to understand that I'm not a great person. Bottom barrel. I'm shit, and once she realizes that completely, she'll want it to be over. And how can I blame her?

I glance back at Ryke and Loren. Her brothers. They talk to her every week, and I wonder if she's brought me up. I'm not going to ask though.

Should I?

I feel like that's prying.

They're her brothers, not mine. They're not unbiased or anything. Not that I need someone on my side. I think everyone should be on Willow's.

Swiftly, I look back again. This time not discreet enough.

"If you have something to fucking say, just say it," Ryke says. His tone is softer than his words. "We don't bite."

"I do," Loren adds with a bitter smile. "But count yourself lucky, I won't bite you."

I don't believe that.

But I do believe that if he lashed out at me, I'd probably deserve it.

I slow down just to walk beside them. Taking a deep breath, I just let it all out. "You both talk to Willow a lot—I'm sure about me—and you can probably gauge her feelings, right? Honestly, I don't need a ten-page-long synopsis or diagram or anything, but I just want to know the *percentage* you two think Willow will want to break up with me in the next few years."

I must be a masochist to want to know. But I do.

Ryke's brows furrow. "Don't you two fucking talk to each other?"

"Yeah, but do you even know what it's like being in a long-distance relationship? I can only say *I love you* so fucking much. It's not the same as..." I take off the blinking baseball hat, hot all of a sudden. "It's just harder."

I want to hold her. I want to *be* with her. How do you do that if you're physically separated from someone? And that physical part of a relationship—she could get it so much easier from a guy like Salvatore.

But even thinking of my girl with another guy—*God, stop.*

I focus on the question I asked: *What percentage do they think Willow will want to break up with me?*

"Zero percent," Loren says, not even really hesitating.

I jerk back. "Zero percent?" I glance at Ryke. "Is he good at math?"

"Am I good at math," Loren repeats like I'm a toddler. "I can count to ten. One, two, my sister is too good for you, four, five, you both will survive."

I take that in, focusing on the important part. "You realize you didn't reach ten, right?"

Loren swings his head to Ryke.

Ryke flips me off. Two middle fingers.

It's his go-to move, and really, I earned it. I'm nearly smiling. "What percentage?" I ask Ryke.

"Zero," he says, "but I don't know what you'll fucking do." *Wait... what?*

I frown. "Why would you think that I'd want to break up with her? I'm *worried* about her breaking up with me."

"That broken heart fucking thing," Ryke says.

Shiiiiiit.

My mouth falls in realization. I filled out that questionnaire months ago, but maybe it's been in the back of their minds. "You saw my Tumblr questionnaire?" Frustration surges. "How? You don't even *use* Tumblr. You're internet inept!"

"Fuck you."

Loren interjects, "It's true."

Ryke glowers at Lo. "I know how to use Facebook."

"Facebook is stupid, man," I say. "It's like the ugly stepchild of Tumblr." But right now, I'm not feeling great things about Tumblr either. It's easier liking the internet when it isn't cruel to you, and I've seen Willow and her family pressed underneath the weight of it. Like everything, I just think maybe there are good and bad parts of it.

Ryke wears a confused *I don't know what you're talking about* expression like I just spoke an intergalactic language. Loren laughs.

"Honestly," I say, "did you stumble on it or something?"

"Or something," Loren replies. *Fuuuuck*. That could only mean one thing.

I glare at the sky. "Daisy showed you?"

Ryke scowls. "Leave her fucking out of it."

"Whatever," I say into a big breath. "Look, it doesn't matter. I don't feel *great* about where I left things with Willow when she was in Philly."

Loren drills me with one of his iconic glares, a hell of a lot sharper than Ryke's. Which only confirms my suspicions.

"Great. She told you." *That we had sex.*

"Yep," Loren says.

Ryke adds, "And don't you dare fucking yell at her about it. We're her brothers."

That hurts. "I'd never…I wouldn't yell at Willow for anything…" I'm not that guy.

Ryke's eyes soften.

Loren is still glaring.

"If you're that fucking worried," Ryke says, "there's a solution right in front of your face."

"What?" I ask.

"Visit Willow," Ryke suggests. "Go to London. You don't have to fucking move there. Just see her for a week or two weeks."

Loren nods. "You'll both feel better."

They must not know that Willow and I have an agreement that I won't visit her until next semester. I worry about being the needy boyfriend, the one that doesn't give her space to succeed on her own.

Anyway, she'll be back in Philly for Winter Break, so if I fly out before then, I will, one-hundred-percent, seem like the overbearing one.

So the best I can say is something noncommittal. Because that's how I feel right now.

"Yeah. Maybe."

TEN MINUTES LATER, WE'RE HEADED TOWARDS THE SECOND maze, up on a steep hill. The entrance arch is decorated with flashing bulbs like a carnival. Creepy music that I recognize echoes. It's *American Horror Story* themed. I'm not sure the others understand the references or if they've even seen season four, but excitement surges as we approach.

Suddenly, a rumble of chainsaws revs from the hill, and an abrupt wave of clowns rush towards us. But that's not the immediate threat. I turn around to see a taller, thinner clown with makeup stretching from cheek-to-cheek, gripping a fake sword, and approaching Ryke.

It's even faster than the chainsaws.

The clown screeches in Ryke's ear.

Ryke whips around, without even thinking or pausing or assessing the situation, he *slams* a fist into the clown's jaw.

Holy shit.

"Fuck," Ryke curses, realizing what he just did. He raises his hands like he comes in peace. But, kid you not, the clown stumbles back and falls on his ass.

Note to self: *do not get accidentally sucker punched by Ryke Meadows.*

I take out my phone. This needs to be recorded.

For Willow. Not for anyone else. Definitely not for the internet.

Connor and Rose start nearing us, probably to do damage control, but the damage is seriously already done. There is a rule about touching the actors. *Don't.*

A few clowns on the hill yell, "Security!" like their friend is dying on the cement. Another heavier-set clown charges Ryke for vengeance.

I'm near laughter.

I probably should be helping, but I consider my presence here helpful towards one person. Willow. She's not going to miss this.

Lily clutches onto Loren's back, and Connor increases his pace and *sprints* to Ryke.

Connor extends a hand to the heavier clown. "It was an accident," he says in a calm business-tone. "My friend reacts before he thinks."

The clown suddenly stops but his lip still curls, pissed at Ryke.

"The clowns look mad," Lily whispers to Lo, but I'm close enough to hear. "Like *real* anger."

Connor must hear, too, because he replies, "That's generally the sentiment that appears after someone is punched."

Ryke doesn't hear, since he's busy apologizing profusely. "I'm so fucking sorry."

The bodyguards surround us, and they take over, trying to deescalate the situation with the clowns. Creating barriers between us and them. Bystanders have their phones out like me.

Loren spins around like he's trying to count heads.

His eyes land on mine.

I nod. I'm here. I'm alive. Willow gets to see this. Tonight isn't so bad. Rose even holds a can of pepper spray, aimed like she's about to douse any clown that approaches her. *Classic* Rose. I make sure to get a video of that for Willow.

The security team talks with the park staff, and within minutes the verdict comes in.

Ryke is being banned from the *entire* park. Not just the scare zones and mazes. It's actually kind of hilarious.

A minute later, the clowns disperse, and Loren sets Lily on her feet. We all huddle together. I pull the strings on my hoodie.

Ryke removes his flower crown, just to run a hand through his hair. "I'll go wait in the fucking car. You all just go on without me." He sets his flower crown back.

It's tilted to the side. Off-center like it might fall.

Connor, standing closest to Ryke, is the one who straightens the crown for him. It's weird. Sometimes it seems like those two despise each other, and then there are moments like this. It confuses the hell out of me.

"No," Loren tells his brother. "You're not waiting in the car like you were cast out."

"It's fine, Lo."

"The park did technically banish him," Connor cuts in.

"Then the park banished *all* of us." Loren touches his chest theatrically. "I'm not leaving Ryke behind." Ryke opens his mouth to protest, but Loren says strongly, "It's Halloween. I call the shots, and I say we go to Queen Rose's place and watch *Poltergeist* on surround sound."

"Can we order pizza?" I ask suddenly, catching myself by surprise. I want this. To spend time with these people. They make me feel good.

"And there'll be *pizza*," Loren says certainly, his gaze latching onto Ryke, trying harder to convince him. Guilt crests Ryke's eyes, not wanting to crash Loren's birthday.

"And ding-dongs," Lily adds.

Lo tries not to smile. "And ding-dongs. And surly-faced brothers named Ryke Meadows. Yeah?"

Ryke hesitates. We've only been through one maze, but it was fun while it lasted, and the clown-fight might go down in history. I can't wait to show Willow the video. Hopefully, it won't make her miss home even more. But maybe she'll be glad I'm here to record it for her.

I hold onto that.

With a nod, Ryke concedes. "Okay."

I'm going to spend a night watching *Poltergeist* and eating pizza with Willow's family, and I'm finally starting not to feel guilty about it. Maybe it's because I want to be happy, even if I don't deserve it. *Just enjoy it.* I think I will.

Just today.

December

48

Willow Hale

AS SOON AS MY PLANE LANDS ON THE TARMAC, A TEXT FROM Garrison pings my phone. Nervous, giddy butterflies invade my belly. Countdown to seeing my boyfriend: *minutes away*. It somehow doesn't even feel real.

I click into my cell, the plane rumbling to a halt and the other passengers grabbing suitcases from overhead.

Garrison: Waiting at baggage for you.

He's waiting for me. I take a deep breath, excitement trouncing nerves.

And then my phone rings.

But it's not Garrison.

"Hey?" I answer quietly, crammed in a window seat and hugging my backpack on my lap.

"Did you land yet?" Ryke asks.

In the background, I hear Lo retort, "She already did. I'm telling you the flight tracker says so."

Ryke growls back to him, "Let me ask our fucking sister, Lo."

Our sister.

It still rings through me like a soft padded hammer to a bell, even after two years of knowing Ryke is also my brother.

I can feel a smile on my lips. Palm sweaty, I adjust my grip on my phone and stare out at the tarmac. "Yep, I've landed."

I'm back.

"We're waiting in the car," Ryke tells me.

Lo chimes in, "Paparazzi won't hound you that way. Garrison should be at baggage."

"Yeah, he texted already."

"Great," Lo says. "Can't wait to see you." He mumbles something to Ryke about a honking asshole nearby, and after a few *see you soons*, we hang up.

I'm thankful there'll be less chaos when I reach baggage claim. Lo and Ryke would definitely bring a stampede of adoring fans.

They wanted me to fly on the family private jet, but I chose commercial, wedged in the back near the growling engines.

I still have a difficult time accepting the perks of being a Hale. Garrison says it's because I only learned that Jonathan Hale is my birth father two years ago—when I was eighteen.

It means that Lo is my full sibling. Same mom and same dad. And Ryke is my half-brother.

But my relationship with Jonathan Hale is new. Fresh. And it comes with a load of baggage.

Ryke hates Jonathan.

Lo loves Jonathan.

I'm caught in the middle. Not knowing how I should feel about a man who was rumored to have molested Loren. A rumor that was false and caused Lo to relapse years ago. What I do know: Jonathan isn't all good, even if that rumor was wrong.

But Jonathan is kind to me. He makes an effort to get to know me and my interests. We talk on the phone sometimes about comics, and he asks how my school is going. Rob Moore, the man I grew up thinking was my birth father, never even pretended to care about me. And he was right all along—I was never his daughter.

Not really.

So maybe he had a right to hate my existence.

It'd be so easy just to put all my hate into Rob, while putting all my love and trust into Jonathan. But Ryke says our dad is manipulative.

He says to not trust him.

To not fully love him.

I don't know what to think.

I'm paying for my first semester of college on my own, but I'm also taking some of Jonathan's money for the rest of the tuition. That's all I want to take.

So I don't fly private. I budget. I'm not going to pretend that I'm wealthy because it's not my money, and I don't want to be so far indebted to him that I can't find my way out.

"Thank you for flying with us," a flight attendant tells me as I exit the plane. I shake off all thoughts of my dad, each step towards baggage claim reminding me of the man on the other side.

Garrison.

Do I even remember what he smells like? I wonder if he changed shampoos while I've been gone. If he will look more tired and gaunt in person, or if that was just the trick of the cellphone screen.

Maybe the circles under his eyes aren't as dark. Maybe he's better…I hope so.

I follow the signs and descend two different escalators. My palms sweat and my heartbeat thumps wildly with each passing second. But then the baggage carousels come into view.

Whipping my head around, I try to find him in the crowds.

And then I freeze.

People move around me, passing to the nearest carousel, but my eyes are on *him.*

Garrison stands near carousel four, his gaze already pinned to me, a bundle of pink orchids in his hand. But he's just as frozen and rooted to place. Unmoving.

We just stare at one another like we're processing the fact that we're here.

In the same room.

Almost in breathing distance.

"Hi," I say, but he's too far away to hear me. But he sees me.

He sees.

Hi, he mouths back. I read his lips.

Tears prick my eyes, and I walk.

I jog.

I run.

My backpack almost slips off my shoulder, but I catch it at my elbow. He meets me halfway. We practically collide into one another, but it's like reuniting a missing puzzle piece. Arms fitting around bodies. Heads leaning to the correct side on instinct. His chest against my body, warmth blazes through me—a hug so powerful that I tremble from his touch.

Our lips meet like they can't stand to be away for a second longer. And I forget where I am. In public. In an *airport*. The only thing that matters is him.

My fingers slide up the back of his neck, threading his soft hair. His hand cups my cheek strongly, protectively. My head is lighter than air. Urges pulse through me, hungry for so much more. Touch. Talking. I want everything all at once.

I break from his lips first, lightheaded.

"Garrison," I say in slight disbelief.

He's here. I'm here. *We're together.*

He hugs me again, tighter this time. My forehead presses into his chest. His shirt smells like fresh laundry detergent and orchids. Different but the same.

Our chests are flush together. His heartbeat thumps and thumps, the embrace like a comforting return home.

But he feels thinner than I remember, yet still bigger than me.

"Willow," Garrison says quietly and tenderly as if we're the only people in the airport. We break apart a little, his eyes flitting around me like he doesn't want to stop staring. "You still look twenty." He tilts his head, longer pieces of his hair falling over his brows. He pushes it back. "I could have sworn that fifty years passed since you left."

I laugh and brush tears from my eyes. "You don't look twenty anymore," I say.

He's twenty-one now, and I wasn't here for his November birthday. Guilt tries to crash against me.

He shrugs. "How does twenty-one look on me? Gray hair. Wrinkles. I'm practically Gandalf, right?" I missed hearing his dry wit out loud. In person.

My cheeks hurt from smiling. "Gandalf is two-thousand years old. Maybe dock some years on that one."

He smiles. "Okay, yeah. Dumbledore, then."

"One-hundred-and-fifty years old," I say.

"Look at that." He grins. "I'm already a hundred. I'm in my prime."

"You're too pretty to be anyone other than you," I murmur.

But the dark circles weren't a trick of the screen. And his hoodie looks baggier on his body. Has he even been eating? Worry infiltrates, but neither of us stops touching.

My hands are still hooked around his neck. His still on my waist. Like if we completely break apart, some magical force may rip us away again.

Garrison takes a deep breath. "You're prettier than me," he says. "But also…" His eyes sweep my body. "Have you been eating Willow?"

I almost laugh, we're both worried about each other. I think it's been that way since I left. "I could say the same about you."

"I asked you first."

"I've just been busy and stressed with school." *And being away.* But I don't add that part.

He opens his mouth to reply but a man with a professional-quality Canon camera skirts over to us. "Willow!" he yells. "Where are your brothers?!"

Garrison slides his hand into mine, and he exchanges a look with me like *yeah, nothing has changed.* "Welcome back to Philly." Sarcasm drips from his voice.

Can't say I missed this part.

Garrison reaches into his hoodie pocket and pulls out a balled up baseball cap. He passes it to me along with the bundle of orchids. I gratefully put the cap on and shield my eyes.

"Willow!" Paparazzi approaches as we start walking towards carousel six. "Look here!"

There's only one person I want to look at.

One person I can't take my eyes off of.

Garrison glances back at me, and then he squeezes my hand. I feel it. Palm against palm. That simple pressure lights up my world. It's strange—how something so simple can mean so much.

His hand in mine.

I will never take that for granted again.

49

Garrison Abbey

AFTER A LONG CAR RIDE, WILLOW AND I ARE DROPPED OFF AT my apartment. Alone again. Tomorrow we'll be back surrounded by her family.

We're spending the holidays at their lake house in the mountains, which will be filled with a lot of screaming babies and crazy antics. But I'm honest-to-God looking forward to it. Because Willow is here.

I'm not going to be the seventh-fucking-wheel in the core six anymore, and I won't have to video-record anything. We can whisper to each other. We can laugh together.

Willow wheels her suitcase into my apartment as I flick on the lights. She never saw it in person. I moved in after she left, so she's soaking up the surroundings.

"It's strange," she says. "I feel like I've been here before, even though…I haven't. Obviously."

I get it. I've never been to her dorm in London. But I can picture every piece of furniture there. Mostly because I watched the videos she sent me about a million times.

"You're here now," I tell her. "Want anything to drink?" I pop open my fridge.

Only Lightning Bolt!, Fizz Life, a bottle of vodka and a couple six packs on the shelves. I do have a tub of hummus.

Willow notices the contents—or lack thereof. Her brows furrow. "What have you been eating?"

"The food of gods." I swing open my freezer, packed with five frozen pizzas.

She laughs.

"Also Cobalt Inc. has a pretty awesome cafeteria. They have everything: prime rib, sushi, and a thousand different vegan options." I nod to the fridge. "Pick your poison."

"The vodka, definitely," she says, which causes a chill to rake my skin. That would have been the very *last* thing I would have thought she'd choose. How much has she changed in four months?

My hand solidifies on the top of the fridge door.

Willow's lips slowly rise. "Garrison, that was a joke." She points to the soda. "I'll take the Fizz Life...or the beer. Either is good." That's what I thought she'd say but...

"Are you sure?" I question. I don't want her to feel like she can't change or grow. Like I'm stifling her. "If you want vodka—"

She puts her hands to my chest and electricity practically shoots through my veins. "Garrison." Her eyes fill mine, and whatever she was going to say, it just gets lost from her gaze to mine.

The air stills.

She curls her fingers over my jeans' waistband. I hold her cheek and lean down, our lips connecting. I kiss her strongly, pulling her closer. Heating my blood. We stumble out of the kitchen, never breaking apart.

Willow fumbles with the button to my pants, her chest rising and falling in quickened breath. I run my hand up underneath her shirt. Bare skin warm under my touch, but she still shivers.

Like this is the first time all over again.

"Willow," I breathe.

She slowly unzips my pants, so fucking slowly. Like it's a metaphor for how slow we've always been *physically* together. It almost makes me smile, but I nod her on like it's okay.

She inhales, trying to rid anxiety, I think. While we're lip-locked again, my hands roaming up her shirt, the backs of her calves hit my couch. I spin her towards my bed, and I walk her backwards and meet her eyes.

"You sure you want to do this tonight?" I whisper, cupping her cheek. "You can say *no*—"

"I *really* want to," she says and then stops unzipping me. "Don't you?" Fear springs in her eyes. Like maybe I wouldn't want to touch her.

Like maybe I've grown less interested.

Never. Impossible.

"No question. Of course I do." I kiss her again, fully and deeply. Reminding Willow that she's all I want. Her limbs seem to slacken in relief.

And I back my girlfriend up to my mattress. She plops on the edge just as she tugs my pants down, also slowly. I can practically hear her thoughts: *is this the right thing to do right now? Should I be taking off my shirt first or...*

I help her tug down my pants, showing that there's not a right or wrong way. There's just our way.

Willow smiles up at me, but as soon as my jeans bunch to my knees, her breath catches in *shock*.

She gawks at my thigh, then reaches out to trace the new ink. "When did you get this?" she asks softly.

I step out of my jeans. "Two months ago." I couldn't muster the nerve to tell Willow about it, so I figured she'd see the tattoo in person. It'd be better that way.

Willow seems to hold her breath. Unblinking, her gaze bears on the tattoo. An inked skeleton hand brushes fingers with a smaller hand like they're trying to hold on. Hang on. I didn't really plan on getting a tattoo, but I walked into a shop and sat down and came out with this.

"You don't like it," I assume.

She shakes her head. "It's beautiful but...also really sad." Her brown eyes rise to mine. "You're not dead yet, you know that, right?"

Do I?

How many skeletons will I tattoo on my body before I agree with her? Don't know.

I hold my wrist out to her, palm up. We've done this enough that she gets it. She places two fingers to my pulse.

Our eyes don't break. "Garrison Abbey, you are definitely *alive.*"

Only around you.

"It's a miracle," I say into a bigger smile. "Fire off the cannons. Light the torches. Let's celebrate." I lean close to kiss Willow.

Her mouth soft against mine.

I hold her face and gently urge apart her lips, my tongue slowly meeting hers while we both crawl onto the bed. Carefully, I rest my knee between her legs, and I grip the hem of her shirt, pulling the fabric off her head.

Her light brown hair messy around her face. Flush staining her cheeks.

After I shed my hoodie and tee, I dip my head back down. Returning to her lips. Willow hangs onto my shoulders, and I feel her heart quickening against my chest.

I know the more assertive I am, the more she sinks into the moment, and I easily take charge and unbutton her jeans, snap off her bra—desire and craving coats her eyes.

I yank her pants off her ankles and toss the clothes to the floor. Gray sheets beneath our bodies, our legs thread again. My waist aligned with her hips as I hover over her frame.

"Garrison," she whispers, *wanting.* Her fingers skate down my biceps like they skim the surface of a lake. Light touch that annihilates my senses and fists my dick.

Fuck. I knead her small breast, nipples hard beneath my thumb.

Her hips instinctively rise into me.

A guttural noise rumbles in my lungs. *Holy fuck.* My knees push apart her legs so I fit between them, and I suck the nape of her neck, finding a sensitive spot that shakes her limbs.

She quakes and lets out an aroused cry.

Blood pumps in my veins. *I want inside her.* Closer.

We both claw at each other for *closer*. Her fingertips gripping my ribs, and my hand descending to her panties.

I cup her warm heat, the fabric already soaked.

She trembles. "*Garrison.*"

My dick throbs.

Her palm travels down. She lightly touches the outline of my erection that presses against my black boxer-briefs.

I groan against her lips, "*Fuck.*"

She smiles, and with a heavy breath, I smile back. We stare at one another for a second, and very gently, I slip off her fogged glasses.

Willow breathes in, watching me reach over and place them on the nightstand. She holds onto me, and I lean back and whisper what I feel balled up in me. "I love you, Willow."

Tears well up in her eyes. "I love you too."

I brush the wet corners of her eyes, and then I pull off my boxer-briefs. Her hand goes back to my erection, and I slip aside the cotton fabric of her panties. Not removing them, just pushing them out of the way.

While we look at one another, I slide two fingers into her tight warmth.

Her smile vanishes to make room for a pleasured *O*. She half-gasps, half-moans, like she can't figure out how to inhale.

I soak up her arousal, my muscles tightening. Sweat already building. Her hand is still on my length. Not moving.

It brings me back to the past. To us together—how her hands always freeze in place—it's still the same. It hasn't changed. She focuses more on where my hands roam, the pleasure that wraps around her, and she forgets to move altogether.

It's the cutest thing, but I know it's also what makes her nervous. Thinking she's not getting me off, but whenever she remembers to shift her hands, she moves her palms in tiny increments. So light and teasing—the start-stop-start-stop drives my body to a fucking edge.

The best kind.

I pulse my fingers in Willow and rub her clit. My other hand gliding down her leg to her ass. Soft noises eject between her parted lips, sweat glistening on her bare body. She drinks in my naked form, the way my muscles flex above her—I'm not grinding my dick into Willow.

Not yet.

I'm not sure if she wants to go there tonight. I don't want to assume, even if I'd *love* nothing more than to thrust into her. But I've only had sex one time with Willow.

A cry breaches her, and she turns her head into the pillow. "Garrison. *Garrison*, oh my God," she cries, as I hit a point and I pulse faster. Her legs twitch, and she clenches around my fingers.

God.

Her hand reanimates, rubbing my dick again. *Fuuuck.* I grit my teeth, arousal spinning my head. The blistering, soul-affirming feeling mounts pleasure upon pleasure.

I force myself not to rock against her heat.

She turns her head, her hand paused again, and her eyes find mine. "Can we...can you...will you..." Her breath staggers like she's been on a ten-mile race. Sheepishly, she glances down at my rock-solid erection.

She contracts around my fingers again. *Fuuck.*

I tense with desire. "You want me inside you?"

Willow nods strongly, cheeks flushed. "Right now."

It takes a lot of energy to remove my hand and not get her off again. But I want my length inside her, too. I want everything with my girlfriend.

I reach for the nightstand drawer. For a condom, and she cranes her neck, feeling my movements.

"You don't need to..." she tells me.

She isn't wearing glasses, so she can't see much. "I'm getting a condom," I explain.

"We don't need one." Her voice is so soft that I dip my head closer to hear her next words. "I'm on birth control."

I frown. Okay, she wasn't on birth control when she boarded a plane to London. I'm trying not to think dumbass things. Like why she'd take birth control once we were split apart.

Lots of girls take birth control for more reasons than just to prevent pregnancy. Like acne and stuff, right? Maybe to help with cramps, I don't know.

Willow can't see my complete confusion. But maybe she can feel my body tense, because she rushes to clarify, "I asked Daisy if it was a good idea since you and I had sex before we left and it would probably happen again, and she said, *totally.* So I thought…I thought it'd be good to prepare for next time."

I'm an idiot.

I let out a breath. Easing a lot more. "That makes sense." I come back fully to Willow. "It is good." My hand encases her cheek. "No condom then?"

She nods.

I place another kiss against her lips and spread her legs wider around my waist. My pelvis aligned with hers.

She pants some and clutches my biceps.

I have her in my grasp. "Tell me if it hurts," I say, my voice low.

This is only the second time she's had sex.

The second time a man has been inside her.

Me.

"I will," she murmurs, instinctively touching her nose. To push up glasses that aren't there.

I peel a sweaty piece of hair off her forehead, tucking the strand behind her ear. And then I grip my shaft, and slowly, I press the head near her entry. Watching her reaction.

She clasps my arms tighter.

I slide inside Willow—*fucking*…she's so tight and wet, the pressure and warmth sending a rush through me. Head spinning. Nerves firing.

Willow shudders a little, but she hangs onto me. I hold her hip and sink deeper and *deeper.*

She lets out a strangled moan, head tilting back. "God," she cries softly.

I fill her completely, and I rock between her legs, slowly at first. Long movements, until the friction flames, and my body blisters for more. Ravenous, hungry—ready to eke out every ounce of pleasure from her and drive it into me. Months apart. Months without a single touch.

I thrust deeper, my ass flexing. Gasps escape her parted lips that can't close, struggling for breath, and my muscles contract—*fuck*.

Fuck.

I fuck Willow. Veins igniting, muscles on fire. My hands on her hips, I sit up some on my knees and pound into her—and her palms fall off my shoulders and find my wrists, clutching me for support.

"*Garrison*," she cries in a sharp moan, her eyelids fluttering.

I lower back, our mouths meeting. I kiss her as deeply as I rock in, and she pulls at my hair. I lift her leg higher on my waist.

Every thrust is filled with an emotional current that ravishes both of us. Like we've both been asleep and we're slowly recharging, coming back to life.

My forehead presses to hers. "I love you." I breathe it out a few more times. Rocking, *rocking*, and her love swims inside her eyes.

I lose time. I lose sense of space. It's just her and me. The world around us is gone until we both ride into pure bliss.

"Ahhh," she cries into my shoulder, and I hold her while her toes curl, her back arches. A groan barrels through me, and I milk out a climax that seizes my tendons in a vice.

We kiss and kiss, my lips stinging against hers—it's going to take heaven and Earth to pull me away from Willow.

I just want this to last. Longer.

Much longer.

How much time is left?

SITTING SIDE-BY-SIDE IN BED, NAKED, WRAPPED UP IN THE
sheets, and eating semi-warm pizza, I stroke her head while she picks
off the mushrooms and puts them on my plate.

"I could have made the cheese," I tell her.

"Supreme is better." She licks her finger. "I like the olives."

This, right here, feels normal. Pizza in bed, like the degenerate
I am. Can't even eat at a table. Being together at night should be
happening all the time, not just once every four months.

Okay, so maybe it's *not* normal, I guess.

This, right here, is rare. I hate that.

"How do you think we're doing?" She hands me the plate with
the mushrooms. "With this whole long distance thing?"

Terrible.

I shrug. "I miss you, but I think that's supposed to happen. Right?"

Her knees knock into mine. "Is it supposed to hurt this badly?"
Her voice cracks.

I kiss the top of her head. "I don't know."

She leans her cheek against my shoulder. "Maybe I should...
should I just...I could transfer to Pe—"

"No." I stop her before she says *Penn*. "You'll be harassed every
day by paparazzi."

"Then NYU, it's not too far a commute from Cobalt Inc.," she
mutters.

"No," I say, my chest on fire. I'd love to agree with her. To say *sure.
Yes. Please fucking come home.* But I couldn't live with myself. I couldn't
wake up with her in my bed, knowing she's sacrificed something for
my shitty existence.

I'm not meant to be fully happy. I've known that since I was little
and my brothers were shoving me to the ground.

I'm cursed. It's just the way it is. She doesn't need to share in this
damn thing.

Willow pushes her glasses up with her wrist.

"Wakefield is your dream," I say. "You have friends there. You have
a life. Don't start over for me. That's the *last* thing I want, Willow."

"Okay." She breathes heavily. "But you'll come out next semester like you promised? I want you to meet my friends and see my dorm and the campus."

"I promise. I'm there."

She exhales and takes a small bite from her pizza. "Something cool kind of happened."

"That's perfect because I'm in need of some cool. Working at Cobalt Inc. is literally the antithesis of cool. Most of those guys are pencil-pushing pricks."

Her lips rise. "Well, it's probably not *that* cool. Your expectations should lower a smidge."

"Lowered." I wave her on.

"Okay, so you know how second-year students usually room *off-campus?*" Willow sits up a bit more to meet my gaze. "I didn't think anyone would ever ask me to be their roommate. But Sheetal, Tess, and Salvatore *asked.*" She smiles, almost blushing. "They're getting this four-bedroom flat in the city and needed to find a fourth. Pretty cool, right?"

Happiness radiates off her. She has real friends in London, and that's big for Willow. I want to be the kind of person that's happy for her happiness.

But I hear the name *Salvatore* and my blood turns to tar. She's going to be living with him next year. The guy with the awesome accent and *Vampire-Diaries*-adjacent name and stylish haircut. The one who could've raided my brothers' closet.

He's going to be living with my girlfriend while I'm thousands of miles away.

Great.

Awesome.

So fucking happy about it.

I want to mention my feelings, but they're insignificant. Because Salvatore is *just* her friend, and she's going to say that to me. And I'm not about to ruin this good, *happy* thing in her life because I'm the paranoid motherfucker.

So I layer on a smile. "That sounds awesome. A lot of fun."

I must do a shit job because she's shaking her head like she can hear the sarcasm that I seriously can't control.

"I shouldn't have brought it up. I'm sorry." She sets her plate on her lap and winces, her head hanging. "I wasn't thinking. It's anything but cool. You're living alone, and I didn't mean to rub it in that I'm…"

Shit.

"Hey." I lift her chin, so she'll look at me. "I'm not upset that you have friends and I don't. I'm happy you feel included in London and not ostracized or whatever."

"You have friends," she argues with tears in her eyes.

I'm saying all the wrong things.

"You're right. I have you," I say quickly. She is my only friend.

My words don't help. She's shaking her head.

I cup her cheek in my hand. "You can't worry about me. You have to just live your life in London, Willow." Am I pushing her away? I don't know. I don't know what the fuck I'm doing. My insides twist, and speaking is starting to hurt.

Her tears spill over my fingers, but I don't stop holding her. She says, "You know what I learned in the four months we've been apart?"

A lump lodges in my throat.

"I'm unable to not worry about you," she says in a tight breath.

Something sits on my chest. Heavy. I want it off. *Off.* "I love you," I say. "But you have to, Willow. Because you're not going to be happy if you're just constantly worried that I'm not having a good time here in Philly." I want to say that I'll make friends, but I'm not planning on reaching out to random people and accidentally grabbing a fame-leeching parasite.

I want to say that I don't need any friends, but I don't want to lie. I hate being alone.

Hell, I also hate having friends.

Like I said, I'm cursed.

She sniffs. "Lo told me something like that."

Of course he did. "What'd he say?"

"That I have to let you get used to the long-distance. That I can't do anything to make you feel better."

Loren Hale. *Jesus.* I wonder if he even knows how much he gets me. Like he's taken a road trip in my head and come out the other side. I don't understand it.

"He's right," I say. "You sacrificing shit for me isn't going to make me happy or feel better."

"Then what will make you happy?"

I don't know.

I should have a better answer to that question. But there's one thing I know. She can't suppress her happiness because she feels guilty. I can't be poison in her life.

And then I hear her brother's worry in my head. *I don't know what you'll fucking do.* Lo and Ryke thought I'd break up with her. Now I understand why.

But I won't.

I won't.

I still believe we're good for one another, even a continent away. She *is* the thing that makes me happy. But it's on me—because I need to find something else that can push me through a day. Not someone. Some*thing.*

I desperately need something to get me through the next three-and-a-half years.

50

Garrison Abbey

WHAT THE FUCK WAS I THINKING?

I must be out of my mind. Watching Willow leave to board a plane and fly back to London must have really fucked with my head.

Because there's no other explanation as to why I accepted the invitation to return home.

It's the weekend before New Years, and I should have hung up when I heard my mom's voice, but instead, I listened to her pleas, *begging* me to just come home.

For a second. For a minute. To spend time with family. The family that I keep distancing myself from like the miscreant troublemaker that I am.

So I went home.

And during a ham dinner, I've been listening to stories about Mitchell's grad school. How Hunter is coaching lacrosse at Penn, and Davis has put his MBA to use, snagging a six-figure promotion at our father's loaded tech company.

"Garrison." Dad diverts the attention to me. He scoops the last portion of potatoes onto his plate. "How's Cobalt Inc. going?"

Davis wears a look of surprise. "You haven't quit yet?"

"Nope." I bite back a harsher retort.

Hunter laughs. "They haven't fired you?"

"Nope." But no one is more surprised about that than me.

"Connor Cobalt wouldn't fire him," Davis adds. "Not as long as he's dating Willow Hale, right?" He nods to me. "Keep that on lock, man."

I'm not dating Willow for my job. My skin crawls even letting that thought cross my mind. Sitting here turns my stomach. I stab at a piece of ham on my plate, not planning to force the thing down.

Our mom stands. "Garrison, stop playing with your food." She waits for me to set my fork down and hand her the plate, so she can clear the table. She doesn't always do the dishes. Most of the time we have *staff* wash them.

Did I mention my family is rich? Yeah, I think I did.

My brows scrunch at my mom. "It's already dead," I say dryly.

She sighs out like I'm being unreasonably difficult. "Please, Garrison."

I'm about to do as told, but Hunter kicks my shins from underneath the table. *Hard.* I drop my fork, the utensil clattering on the lip of the plate.

Fuck.

Dull plain plumes, and Hunter gives me a harsh look like *don't be a shit.*

My jaw clenches, my pulse starting to race.

Mom places a hand on my shoulder. "It's fine, sweetheart." Yeah, she knows my brother kicked me, but all she does is smile at Hunter with the shake of her head.

Boys will be boys, she used to tell me as a kid, blowing on my cut kneecaps after being shoved in asphalt. *You have to pick yourself up and fight back.*

Right.

She collects the dirty plates around the table. Including mine.

Hunter narrows his assholish eyes on me. He jerks his head from me to our mom like, *help her.*

I glare.

He has two feet.

I haven't stepped into this house for months. They're lucky I'm here right now.

"Garrison," Davis snaps out loud. "Help Mom."

Our mom waves me off. "No, you boys go relax and catch up. It's been so long since you've all seen each other."

Shit.

My heart rate ratchets up. "I'm actually going to head out," I say. "I've got an early morning."

Our dad makes a noise of disapproval. "Connor Cobalt surely isn't making you work during the holiday." True—I do have off—but that doesn't mean I'm actually going to take it. I still planned to go into the office. Because I love my job.

Because it's keeping me going.

Hunter pushes out of his chair and treks over to mine. "Come on, Garrison."

Relax, I tell myself, and I stand up. Hunter slings an arm around my shoulder and pats my chest. Once he starts pulling me to the door, he tightens his arm into a fucking *headlock*.

"Stop, man," I choke. I'm stumbling to catch up with my own goddamn head, and I try to pry off his stupid arm.

"That's all you've got?" Hunter goads.

I attempt to elbow his ribs—he slams a fist in my kidney. I cough.

Davis laughs. "Still can't get out of it?"

Acid drips down my throat. I didn't realize I was supposed to become a fucking wrestler.

Hunter laughs with our older brother, then he looks over at Mitchell, who's busy grabbing his Columbia coat from the hook. Acting like he sees nothing.

Hunter messes my hair with his knuckles, digging hard. Burning my scalp.

Davis snatches his coat while I'm still struggling to remove Hunter's bicep from my windpipe.

I don't have time to reach for mine. Because Hunter forgoes his own winter jacket. Front door open, he exits into the cold night in a preppy sweater and collared shirt—forcing me outside with him.

I almost slip on the fucking icy steps, and he's *still* crushing my windpipe. So by the time Hunter lets go and pushes me into the two-inches of snow with only my thin hoodie—I'm livid.

I land on my knees and hand. Body shaking, anger barely warming me in the chill. Picking myself up, my chest rises and falls heavily and my breath smokes the air.

"Come on," Hunter says like I'm a three-year-old kid crying over spilled milk.

I'm not crying.

"Fuck you," I sneer.

Davis tosses a football in the air. "He's just playing around, Garrison. Lighten up. It's the holiday."

I swallow hard. *Cool.* "I'm grabbing my coat—"

Hunter blocks me, his chest puffed out against mine. "What do you call this?" He fists my hoodie.

I slap his hand off me. "Don't touch me." My heartbeat hammers my ribcage.

He laughs. "Come on." When he sees I'm serious, he shakes his head. "Don't be such a pussy. You don't need a fucking coat." He spreads his arms out to illustrate that it's not cold, and how he's also without a winter jacket.

My speeding pulse is now in my throat. I tear my eyes off him, and I lift my gaze to Mitchell, who zips up his teal Columbia jacket—he looks away from me.

Not doing a fucking thing, per usual. It's hard to blame him, but it's easy to hate him.

Davis pats my back.

I tense more. We're adults, and I still can't figure out a good exit strategy from "bro time" with my brothers.

"Boundaries are the edge of the property." Davis points the football between all of us, his younger brothers. "Two-on-two. Mitch and Hunter versus Garrison and me. Tackling is fair game. You okay with that Garrison?"

Hunter smirks. "Or are you going to pussy out like you always do?"

I stare at my brothers. Davis. Hunter. Mitchell. All in their mid-to-late twenties now. And I'm not seventeen anymore.

I'm not a kid.

But they're still bigger and taller than me. Still treating me like the rope in a game of tug-of-war. Something to pull to achieve whatever the fuck they're after.

I rub my frozen hands. "No tackling."

Hunter rolls his eyes. "Seriously?"

"Yeah, he asked." I point at Davis. "I'm telling you *no* fucking tackling."

Davis gestures to me with the football. "How about light tackling?"

Really. "How about none?"

"Learn to compromise, man," Davis tells me like he's the wise older brother here. "It'll solve a lot of problems for you in life." He squeezes my shoulder. "Light tackling is fair game."

Hunter jumps up and down and cracks his knuckles.

Bile rises in my esophagus. Being here. Outside. Alone with them. Why did I put myself in this situation?

It's on me.

They're my family.

It's still on me.

I don't want to see them again… But they're my family.

It's still on me.

I war with my thoughts, unable to decide where to place blame other than myself. It's all I can think, even as Davis tosses me the football.

Run, I think. Move your fucking feet or drop the ball—something. Anything. But I'm frozen, and Hunter sprints towards me. He goes in for the tackle.

His full weight rams into my chest, his elbow driving in my ribcage, and I land with a violent *thump* on my ass. *God, motherfucker!*

I wince through my teeth, my tailbone searing, the snow not bracing impact with the hard ground. Tears sting my eyes—but I refuse to fucking cry in front of them.

Hunter pushes his knee in my stomach on his way to a stance. I cough hoarsely, and he grabs the ball from my loosened clutch. Far too easily for his liking.

Anger surges in his eyes. "Why do you have to give up? It *sucks* playing with you, man. You're worse than a fucking girl."

Say hello to my misogynistic brother. I try to catch my breath and glare up at him. "Then don't play with me." I cough again. "I'm fine with that."

He growls in frustration and swings his head to Davis.

Davis gives me a look. "You're too sensitive. Stop being weak shit. Get up." He gestures for me to rise.

I am weak shit. I feel it.

Sucking in a pained breath, I rise off my shrieking body that screams for me to *run away*. Flee. Flee.

Flee.

My hands are numb from the snow. My stomach is in knots. Like I might actually puke in a second. I stare right at Mitchell.

My twenty-three-year-old brother hangs back. Behind both Hunter and Davis, and I think, *can you please…*

Help me.

Mitchell stuffs his hands in his jacket. And he drops his gaze to the snow.

Right.

I rub my nose that drips from the cold.

"We'll be defense," Hunter says, tossing the ball to Davis.

Not again. "Look, as fun as this was," I say sarcastically, still trying to catch my breath, "I have work tomorrow—"

"Don't be like that," Davis says.

"Like what?" I snap, my pulse accelerating again.

He shakes his head, pissed.

Hunter cuts in, "You're such a little bitch."

"I'm not doing anything!"

"Exactly!" Hunter yells. "Just be a fucking *man*, you cocksucker. Stop pitching these tantrums."

I let out a short, bitter laugh. "I'm pitching a tantrum? Look in the mirror."

Hunter fumes, his jaw locking. He breathes hard, literal smoke coming out of his nose thanks to the cold air.

I glare back, against better judgment.

Davis pats the football. "Let's just play. Garrison sprint."

I have no choice. Because Hunter charges for me—already planning on tackling and Davis hasn't even thrown the ball for me to catch yet.

I run towards the neighboring house. Feeling the weight of my brother on my heels. Encroaching my space. Closer, and closer. Coming for me.

The ball soars through the crisp night air, and I don't care about it. I don't want it. Yet, I'm reaching up for the stupid fucking thing.

My fault.

Hunter tackles me from behind. My chest meets a blanket of hard snow, wind knocking right out of my lungs. I inhale but can't exhale.

He laughs, happy that I finally gave in. "Barely better." He messes my hair.

I'm about to stand, and he playfully pushes my head.

I shove his hand away as he tries again. "Stop, man."

He shoves harder.

"Hunter—"

He forces my face into the ground. Making me eat snow. Cold burns my lips, and I shut my eyes.

Davis laughs.

I struggle out from Hunter's hold, trying to rip his hand off my fucking head.

Mitchell just stays quiet. Just stands there.

I manage to turn over on my back, my face stinging raw. Hunter pins my shoulders and pulls my right arm in a lock. Like we've suddenly switched from football to wrestling. "Come on, get out of my hold."

Davis stands over us. "You got this, Garrison. Just try."

Just try. Why didn't I think of that? What a genius. "He has a million pounds on me."

"Don't make excuses," Davis says. "Or else you'll always be flat on your ass."

Hunter laughs, wrenching my arm harder. *Motherfuc*—I wince again, the brittle air drying my lungs.

I writhe under my brother. Trying to escape. He's cement. I'm being crushed to death, breath comes shorter. "Get off," I say, panicked.

He slaps my face. "Fight me, man." He slaps harder. "Come on, grow some balls."

My cheek sears. I push at his chest and scream between my teeth to force him off.

Unable to move him.

I can't move him.

I picture myself easily sliding out from under Hunter. I picture myself straddling him. I picture two of my fists repeatedly slamming into his face. Until my brother is bloodied beneath me—but my fight or flight response is screaming *fly the hell out of here.*

"Take a breath," Davis coaches. "Think about your next move. Stop flailing."

Hunter looks over at Davis, and they laugh like this is all in good fun. Always at my expense.

"I'm done," I choke out.

Hunter eases up some, enough that I gain control of my left arm.

"Swing," Davis says.

I stupidly try to sit up and swing.

Hunter clasps my fist and shoves me down. The back of my head hits snow. His knuckles land in my stomach. In my ribs, over and over. I heave for breath and try to curl into a fetal position.

Fuck.

"Stop," I gasp, clawing at the snow to get the fuck out.

Hunter drags me back, about to put me in another hold, and I kick his chest.

"GET THE FUCK OFF ME!" I yell into the deadened air. Somewhere down the street, I think I hear Christmas music.

I don't want to hear it.

I don't want to hear it.

Please don't let these bastards ruin Christmas music for me. Please let me keep something. I thrash and must connect with Hunter's dick because he backs off a little, clutching his crotch. Davis kicks snow in my face before I can get up.

I cough and wipe it out of my eyes. My whole face scalds painfully. My throat feels raw, but I can't tell if that's from screaming or the cold.

Staggering to my feet, I rise without another blow. Mitchell picks up the football off the snow and throws the thing in a clean arch to Davis. He catches the ball like we're still playing.

While they're distracted, I do what I've done since I was a teenager.

I stumble to my feet and I bolt.

"GARRISON!" Davis yells.

I don't look back, my feet carrying me to my car in the driveway. I'm shaking, and I fumble with the keys before I unlock the door.

Slipping inside the Mustang, I turn on the ignition. Heat almost immediately blasts from the vents. Great car, thank you. Exhaust gurgles from the pipes.

My hands are still quaking. My teeth clanking together, but I glance through my rearview and start to back out.

I almost think Hunter might stand at the end of the driveaway just to fuck with me and block me in. But the three of them don't move off the yard. And I start to get it.

Why they always let me go...

Because when I run away, I seem like the petulant child. Like the overly sensitive son who can't handle playing rough with his brothers.

Fuck that.

Fuck them.

I leave anyway.

SHE CAN TELL SOMETHING IS WRONG.

I never told Willow that I was having dinner at my parent's mansion. Even now, I don't tell her about what just happened with my brothers—how Hunter repeatedly nailed me in the ribs.

Part of me is ashamed. Shame is strong, even years later when I know my brothers are complete shit and it can't be all my fault. Right?

But she can sense that something's off—just over the phone. Elevators to my apartment complex are out of order, so I take the stairs. Slowly, one of my arms hovering around my battered ribs.

With the other hand, I press my cell to my ear, my boots making wet puddles on the concrete steps.

"Garrison." Worry coats her voice. "Can you please talk to me?"

"I'm talking," I say tightly, pain in every movement.

"No, you're *breathing*," she refutes. "Really weirdly."

"Then I don't want to talk." It hurts to breathe, and my fingers itch for a cigarette. Which makes no sense—I can barely breathe but I want to smoke. Sounds like me.

I reach for a pack in my jacket. I started smoking again a couple weeks ago. Just to stay awake during the later hours at work. Now, I light a cigarette because it calms my nerves.

My fingers shake while I put the cigarette between my lips. I stop in the stairwell, my shoulder bracing my phone to my ear.

Willow stops talking, but I hear the familiar pounding of a keypad like she's typing on a computer. She's back in her dorm room in London. She flew out there a couple days ago so that she could celebrate New Years with her friends from school. She invited me.

But I declined because I feel like that's her world.

Not mine.

Mine is here.

Apparently getting ragged on by my brothers. Oh, and I got this special text from my dad five minutes ago.

Dad: your brothers are just trying to make a man out of you. You're lucky to have them. I only had a sister. If you'd just stop and listen maybe you'd learn a thing or two.

Thanks, Dad.

I suck on my cigarette, and one more level up the stairs, I reach my floor. Slowly pushing through the heavy door and into the hallway.

"Do you have your passport ready?" Willow suddenly asks.

I cough on the smoke. "What?"

"Your passport," Willow says.

"I heard you—"

"Garrison!" Jared yells at me, just as the heavy door clanks shut behind me. He's leaning against the wall next to my door. He's been waiting for me?

"Shit," I curse. My hand hangs, cigarette burning between my fingers.

"Jared?" Willow guesses.

"Can I call you back?"

"No," she says. "I'll stay on the line. Don't hang up on me."

I clutch the phone, almost about to break down because *that* gets me for a second. Someone cares. She cares. Okay. *Okay.*

I take a deeper breath and walk forward to confront my asshole of a neighbor. "Jared," I say. "I don't have time." I put the cigarette back between my lips, and with my free hand, I fish out my keys from my pocket. Trying not to shake.

"Hey, man, yeah." Jared nods and scratches his neck. "I just wanted to invite you to—"

"Just fuck off," I growl out, my words mumbled through my cigarette.

"Look, this party is going to be lit. Maybe you can invite some of your friends, too. Promise, they won't want to miss this."

My anger surges like a geyser. My door clicks, unlocked. I pluck my cigarette from lips and turn on Jared. "How do you not understand this? I don't want to go to your party. I don't want you standing beside my fucking door."

"Come on." Jared reaches out to put a hand on my shoulder.

I jerk back. "Don't touch me."

He raises his hands in surrender. "Dude, I'm just trying to be a friend."

My nose flares. "We're not friends. Read my lips when I say *we'll never be fucking friends*. Ever. You know why I disconnected my smoke detector? So you couldn't offer your stupid broom again. You want to get down on your knees and suck me off, as your girlfriend propositioned?"

He turns red. "I…" He scratches his head. "She was joking." Jared reads my features. "You're really that pissed? Come on, man. You're famous. I'd *kill* to have what you have." He lets out a short laugh. "You know how easy you've got it?"

I glare, unblinking.

Rage and resentment infiltrates his eyes. He thinks he knows me, and I wonder if that jealous bitterness towards me has been there all along, hidden somehow.

"Stay the fuck away from me." I unlock my door and slam it closed.

That felt good.

That shouldn't have felt that good. I take a larger drag and blow smoke upwards. My hand trembles.

"Garrison." Willow's voice comes from the cell in my other fist. I press it back to my ear.

"Sorry," I mutter, involuntary tears squeeze out of my eyes. *Fuck.* I wipe my wet face with the heel of my palm.

"How soon can you make it to the airport?" she asks. "Because I can get you on the next flight to London."

I'm already heading to my closet. Grabbing a duffel bag. "Book it."

51

Willow Hale

IT'S BEEN ALMOST A FULL 24-HOURS SINCE I BOOKED
Garrison's flight to London. A delay from a snowstorm held up the
plane in Philly all night, and he didn't actually leave the airport until
noon today. The sun has already set, and my nerves have gone from
worry to catastrophic levels.

Thank God for the flight tracker app. I've been obsessively
watching the plane cross the ocean, and now it's only a couple
minutes from landing.

Sitting on the steps to Bishop Hall, the wind picks up and howls.
Music blasts from speakers on the snowy quad. A party starts to gain
momentum, people dancing and passing around cans of cheap beer.
Most of the parties here have been at houses or pubs, but apparently
Wakefield always has one themed party on the quad at the end of
every year.

Tonight, the theme is "celestial" and everyone is wearing white,
but I'm in a green puffer jacket and jeans. I don't even care that I
stick out like a neon sign. My stomach knots, unable to join in the
festivities.

I don't know what happened last night, but Garrison doesn't
sound that upset unless something is going on with his family or the
paparazzi or maybe his ex-high-school friends paid him a visit. My
mind has been racing through the horrible possibilities.

I was even tempted to text Connor about Garrison's job to make
sure he wasn't fired. But unless it's a group text, I don't really have

a texting friendship with Connor Cobalt. And anyway, I'd much rather learn what's going on from Garrison, not run around him for information.

So I'm waiting.

"Willow!" Tess plops down on the stair beside me, beer in hand. She wears this fluffy, white fur coat that contrasts her rich brown skin. Glitter dots her cheeks. She looks gorgeous, truly fitting the celestial theme. Tess frowns when she sees my green jacket. "Do you have nothing white to wear? We can go to my closet."

I tuck a flyaway strand of hair behind my ear. "Thanks, but I'm not doing the party tonight. I'm actually waiting for Garrison to get here."

Tess's grin lights up her face. "Wait, we're going to meet the boyfriend tonight!" Her knees bounce in excitement and she claps her hands, even with a beer in one.

"I mean…maybe," I say.

At this point, I'm not sure what will happen. Garrison could arrive in London and then just hop on a plane back to Philly. He didn't want me going to the airport to pick him up. His words: *I'm already inconveniencing you enough. Please just let me get a cab, Willow.*

Normally, I would have argued with him, but his voice was so… broken. I don't want to push him.

Tess sips her beer. "Well, I'll be excited to see him even from a distance. I can tell you love him a lot, and I may be biased, but I think you have great taste in people."

I match her smile.

Sheetal steps over in furry boots and a sleek white jumpsuit. "What are you two grinning about?"

"Tess was just saying that I have great taste in people," I say.

Sheetal narrows her eyes at her girlfriend. "I love how you find a proper way to compliment yourself inside a compliment to someone else. Bloody brilliant."

Tess smiles wider. "Say that again, but…" She tugs Sheetal onto her lap. "Now."

Sheetal's eyes fall into Tess's. "You're bloody brilliant." Their lips meet in a tender kiss, and I look away as the music changes to an EDM song that I recognize. It's one of Lo's favorites.

I let out a tense breath.

Sheetal breaks from Tess and frowns. "What's wrong, Willow?"

"Nothing, really," I mutter.

They both exchange concerned glances, and then Sheetal says, "You should be celebratin' like the boss champ you are. We all made the highest marks on our project. And second semester will be even better. Nowhere to go but up."

We did *very* well on our marketing project. It was a strange coincidence that we chose an umbrella for our marketing project, and then a month later Netflix dropped the trailer to their new show *The Umbrella Academy*. I'd already read the comics that the show's based on, and it seemed like a great opportunity to capitalize on the timing.

So we tied in some of our marketing around the show—and put in a budget of what it would cost to cross-promote with the studio and the actors. Of course, it was all a theoretical scenario. But I was able to put my old teenage skills in editing fan videos to good use, splicing the trailer into an ad. It was fun.

And it worked. The professor was impressed that we thought about our demographic: the superhero-obsessed generation.

Garrison and I already celebrated over Christmas. We read the comics together side-by-side while drinking champagne straight from the bottle.

Cold slices my exposed cheeks, and I zip my jacket higher, trying to block the wind. I shake my head. "I am excited about school," I tell Sheetal. "I'm just worried about my boyfriend."

Tess wraps an arm around Sheetal and explains, "Garrison is coming in tonight."

"Tonight?" Sheetal's brows rise.

I shrug. "It was a spontaneous thing."

"I'll say." Sheetal smiles, her excitement just as palpable as her girlfriend's. "We're finally meeting *the* boyfriend."

Tess nods. "That's what I said."

"Great minds—" Sheetal can't get the rest of the words out because Tess kisses her again.

My phone pings with a text. My stomach has butterflies, drunk on concern. Flapping around in my belly with an intoxicated, sluggish rhythm.

Garrison: Just got in the cab. Be there in twenty.

I just need him to be okay. *Please* be okay.
That's all I can hope.

52

Garrison Abbey

AN EXCRUCIATING DELAY, AN EIGHT-HOUR FLIGHT, AND twenty-minute cab ride later, I've finally arrived at Wakefield. The snow-blanketed quad in front of Bishop Hall is filled with inflatable jumping houses that little kids have for birthday parties. Music thumps the cobblestone path.

Willow warned me that since this is the one and only party on the quad it's a bit extravagant, but it feels more like some strange carnival. People dressed in all white, some have angel wings on their backs.

College is weird, man.

I tip back a small travel bottle of vodka to my mouth. The liquor slides easy down my throat. In first class, they were handing me these almost every fucking hour.

Okay, I asked for them.

It's been a shitty day. A shitty year.

A shitty life.

Each step towards the brick building is heavy. A couple of people shoot me weird looks, eyeing my clothes. Red T-shirt. Black hoodie jacket. Dark pants. If I came here to blend, I'm failing at critical levels.

My small duffel is slung on my shoulder. Cold wind bites my face, and I press my phone to my ear. No gloves. Forgot those on my hurried course to the airport. My fingers sear from the chill.

Willow picks up on the first ring. "Are you here?" she asks, urgency to her words.

"Yeah, present." I spin around, trying to find her. But everything suddenly blurs. My head tilts. Sickness rises in my throat. Shit.

"I'm waiting in front of the building," she says. "You can't miss me. I'm in green."

She didn't dress up for this party. She's been waiting for me. I don't know why that makes me feel like worse shit.

I rub my eyes. An angel passes me, laughing shrilly with her friends. I blink hard. *Jesus.* Where am I? I down the rest of the vodka and toss the little bottle off to the side. It lands in a deeper patch of snow.

"Garrison," Willow says, still on the other line. "I think I see you. Turn to your left."

I turn in a circle again.

"Your left," Willow repeats.

I stop, close my eyes, take a breath. Open them, but as I follow her instructions, she says, "I'm coming to you. Don't move."

Finally, I see her. Green puffy winter jacket. Glasses perched on her nose. Hair blowing in the wind. She's pocketing her cell so she can walk faster.

People wave to her like they know her. And I realize…she's popular here. Has a bunch of friends. Is loved and wanted. She brushes them off with a perfunctory smile, her course on me.

What the fuck am I doing here?

What the fuck am I doing to her?

My chest blazes in pain. I stumble back, almost falling onto my ass, but someone catches me by the arm.

I jolt, the touch pushing me to panic, and I shove at the person on instinct.

"Whoa!" The guy steps back, eyes confused and angry. "Just trying to help, man."

His voice. His accent is so familiar. And then I really look at him. Windswept hair and wide jaw. White sports coat, white pants and angel wings on his back. *You've got to be shitting me.*

"Salvatore." Willow jogs over, out of breath as she lands next to her friend. She waves to me. "This is—"

"Her boyfriend," I say. It doesn't come out right, though. I feel like a jerk.

Salvatore looks between us and he nods slowly, connecting the dots. I don't know what she's told him about me, but the way he's appraising me like I'm *exactly* what he pictured has me on edge.

"What are you looking at?" I snap at him.

"Garrison," Willow says and reaches for my hand, but I pull away. My focus is on Salvatore. All my rage pooling into this one goddamn thing.

Salvatore narrows his eyes at me. "Are you drunk?"

I wave my arms around. "Look around, *Salvatore*. We're at a college party. Everyone is drunk." I hate his name. It's cooler than mine. It still reminds me of that vampire TV show that Willow and I used to watch together. Gif sets that we'd send to each other.

It's like the universe is mocking me.

Here he is.

In fucking angel wings.

I mean, come on.

"Garrison," Willow says, but she doesn't try to reach for me again. "Let's just go inside." She hugs her arms to her chest.

Salvatore shakes his head and under his breath, but loud enough for me to hear, he says, "I don't think you should be alone with him, Willow."

"Fuck you, man," I growl. "I'm her boyfriend. Who are you again?" My voice accidentally grows louder, and people close by stop their conversations to watch us. Willow takes a step back as if she can physically avoid the attention.

My whole body tenses like my brother just slammed a fist into my gut again.

The world around me spins. I touch my pocket, hoping for a cigarette, but I think I ran out in the cab.

"I'm her friend," Salvatore refutes.

"Salvatore, you don't understand," Willow says quickly, sticking up for me.

"I understand that he's drunk and obviously angry and you shouldn't be near him right now," he says. That really rubs me the wrong way. Him dictating who she can even talk to. I don't care if it comes from a place of concern. Willow and I have been through more together than he'll ever know.

"Hey, she can make her own decisions," I snap and move towards my girl. She lets out a breath of relief.

But then Salvatore says something. I think *hold on*. He puts his hands on my shoulders to stop me from walking to Willow. It's a light touch, but it feels like someone descended fifty tons onto me. And I just swing.

My fist connects with Salvatore's cheek. Hard enough that he goes down on the ground.

Some other guy with jet-black hair is pushing me back like I might go in for a kick to the stomach. I wouldn't. I don't…I don't even know why I punched him.

My head throbs now.

My knuckles burn.

"Garrison!" Willow yells, but I can't see her.

"Get off!" I say to the guy trying to push me back. "Get the fuck off!" I hold up my hands, showing him I'm not going to start in on Salvatore.

He steps back.

People begin to clear a path, and I notice Salvatore rising to his feet, his angel wings bent from the fall. Willow stands near but her eyes flit around the crowds, searching for me. Two girls flank her sides and whisper to her. Their lips move hurriedly. I recognize them instantly: Sheetal and Tess.

Sheetal's hands gesticulate angrily and she waves them in my direction.

I can imagine what they're saying to Willow. *Don't go with Garrison. He's jealous, dangerous.*

Willow's gaze finally finds mine. Her brown eyes sink with pure concern. She's not scared or hurt or mad at me.

She should be.

I'm not a good guy.

Hasn't tonight proven that?

I take a step back and glance towards the street. Maybe I can catch a cab...

"Garrison." Willow's voice draws me in; she's already moving towards me, despite her friends' protests. She reaches my side and almost tries to touch my hand again, but she stops herself short. In a whisper, she breathes, "Can I hold your hand?"

"No." My answer is quick and caustic.

It knocks her back. But she blinks and nods. "Okay." She crosses her arms over her chest like she's cold.

"I'm going to go," I tell her.

She shakes her head adamantly. Hurt and confusion bunching her brows. "No. You're not leaving."

I can feel the cellphones whipped out, recording us. I don't even know if they realize who we are, or if they're just doing it for the internet. People are cruel like that.

One of the worst nights of my life will be out there for public consumption. For their entertainment. Hell, I used to be one of them. Feeding the gluttonous, cannibalistic internet at someone else's expense.

I can't tell if it's the cold, but it's harder to breathe all of a sudden. The wind stabs my lungs.

I lean closer to her.

The music picks up near the party.

"Willow," I whisper. "I think we should..." *Break up.* I can't even force out those words without my eyes reddening. Pain searing. It's selfish of me not to end this.

I know that.

She glares as tears run down her cheek. "Don't you dare. I *love* you, Garrison."

"I love you, too." I'll always love her. I stuff my chilled, burning hands into my pockets. "It's why I have to go."

We stand in the middle of her college campus. Phones pointed at us. And I feel like I've grabbed a shovel and buried us both under.

"You're not breaking up with me," Willow says in defiance. Like it can't be done. "I won't let you."

I don't deserve her. *I don't deserve her.* God, I don't. But I'm ruining her. My eyes sear, cold stinging the water that threatens to spill. "Willow—"

"You want to go," she says. "I heard you. So we're going to get in a cab and drive to the airport and you're going to fly home. But I'm coming with you to the airport. You don't have to talk. We can just *sit*. And then when you're back in Philly and sober, you'll call me. You'll tell me what's wrong."

I don't know if I will.

But I nod.

"I love you," she says again. Wrapping her arms around herself because I won't let her touch me. If she touches me, she'll know I bruised...or broke my ribs. Or rather, my brother broke them.

Maybe she already knows. It's probably on her list of possibilities. Still I can't bring myself to mention what happened. It doesn't excuse me punching her friend. It doesn't excuse how I ruined tonight.

Yeah, I should let her go. Reject her offer. But I feel like the inked skeleton, fingers slipping from the one thing still alive in its hand.

And I hold on.

I'm holding on.

But I don't know where we go from here.

January

53

Garrison Abbey

HEADING INTO THE FIRST DAY OF THE NEW YEAR, I TRY TO BE positive. *Don't fuck it up, Abbey.*

It's only been 48-hours since everything went down in London. But it's honestly felt like a millennium. Officially, I think I spent less than two hours in the country before flying back to Philly. It's pathetic on multiple levels, and embarrassed doesn't even cut it.

The only upside: it didn't end up on the internet. The students at Wakefield haven't really recognized Willow or just simply don't care. It's another big reason she needs to stay out there for school.

"I can come visit next week," Willow says, her soft voice echoing through my car speakers. I swivel the steering wheel and turn down a crowded street, traffic almost bumper-to-bumper.

Willow never got mad at me for punching her friend Salvatore. She wasn't even disappointed in me or sad. It makes me feel worse because she has every right to hate me.

She said that she understood I'm going through something. Her understanding is like air, helping me breathe. But I'm not sure I deserve my girlfriend's kind heart and empathy. I'm the bad boyfriend fucking with her perfect friends and her perfect London life.

I can't let her go.

I can't lose Willow, even if I'm the thing tarnishing the perfect world she's building.

She never even pushed me to reveal more of what happened in Philly. I've never pushed her past her limits either.

We've always been careful with each other, and that's something I appreciate. Because I don't want to lie, and I think if she asked point-blank—*did you see your brothers?*—I would've come up with some shitty excuse. Anything but admit that I was stupid enough to go home during the holidays, knowing they were there.

What she did ask: *Are you ready to talk about it?*

What I said: *Not yet.*

The moment she finds out I saw my brothers again, she's going to send in the cavalry to check up on me. Daisy. Ryke. Maybe even Lo. I don't need them to bombard me, especially when no one but Willow even knows that my brothers have hit me before.

I want to keep it that way.

"Garrison, did you hear me?" Willow asks over the phone.

I stop at a red light, hands tight on the steering wheel. "You don't need to visit. I'm fine, Willow." I take another breath, about to tell her something that might put her on edge. But *this*, I do want to be honest about. "I'm actually headed to my house. I have to apologize to my mom for bolting and pick up a hard drive on my old computer." It's got some stuff on it that I made back in prep school. It might be useful for the video game I'm creating.

"Wait—you're going home?" Willow's voice spikes with alarm.

"Yeah, but just for a second," I say quickly. "Davis, Hunter, and Mitchell already all left yesterday. They didn't want to spend New Year's Eve with my parents." I pull up to the gate at the neighborhood entrance. "So I'm not going to run into them. It's alright."

A security guard recognizes me and immediately presses a button to let me in. I wait as the gates slide open.

"Why don't you let Daisy pick it up for you?" Willow suggests.

Sweat builds, I lower the blasting heat and unzip my hooded jacket. "Because Daisy will ask questions. And like I said, my brothers aren't home." *It's safe.*

The line is quiet.

A lump lodges in my throat, but I want to say more… *I miss you. I'm sorry I fucked up.*

I love you.

Driving forward, all I say is, "You still there?"

"Yeah." She sounds concerned, but with a big breath, she layers on resolve. "Can you call me when you leave?"

I feel like I've already been calling Willow too much. We talk all night. Which is her entire morning.

Currently it's 9 a.m. for me, and I know she's not in class now. But Winter Break is almost over, and her business courses will be starting back up soon. This break is when she should be hanging with her college friends.

"I'll text you," I say.

"Right when you leave."

"Right when I leave," I agree.

We say *I love yous* and *goodbyes* as I park in the empty but plowed driveway of my parent's mansion. No other cars. It confirms what I already know: my brothers are gone.

I'll be quick.

Leaving my Mustang running, exhaust gurgling and visible in the cold morning, I take lengthy, fast steps up the front porch. The January chill barely touches me as I fumble for a house key. How my parents let me keep one—I don't know. They love me, I guess. Still after everything I put them through.

I unlock and enter. "Mom!" I call out in the posh foyer.

No one answers. Veering into the kitchen, I skid to a stop and locate my mom through the window. Towards the east side of the pool, she wears a pink pea coat and Burberry scarf, and while she's bent down, she shears thorns off rose bushes that surround a locked greenhouse.

I watch her brush snow off red petals. She's pretty meticulous about gardening. Don't get me wrong, we have gardeners, but no one except my mom is allowed to touch the flowers around the greenhouse and the plants inside.

It's her "calming" thing or whatever.

Maybe she needs calming after seeing me.

Great.

And this conversation is going to be happening *outside*. In the frigid ass cold. I'm not boiling hot anymore, and so I pull up my hood while I exit through the backdoor. My shoes slide on the icy patio, and I extend my arms for balance.

"Mom!" I call out again and catch myself from a face-plant.

Fuck, I hate the outdoors.

She lifts her head, brunette hair glossy and twisted in an intricate updo with diamond pins, and even though she looks like a rich housewife who'd have her fourth glass of pinot grigio by noon, I've never seen her drink more than a couple seltzers, and she's not too hands off or too overbearing. When my brothers and I played lacrosse in high school, she actually watched us and didn't just socialize with her PTA friends. She'd film the end for our dad who'd miss the action because of work.

So I'm not surprised that when she sees me now a genuine smile overtakes her face. "Garrison." She rises to her feet, brushing gloved hands on tweed pants. "What a surprise. Come here, sweetie."

I near the garden. "I just wanted to—" Words die in my throat as I see shadows through the frosted greenhouse windows. *People are in there.*

What if my brothers are home?

No.

No.

Fuck no...

"Garrison, what's wrong?" She touches my shoulder but I'm like the ice on the ground. Frozen. Only difference is that I break easier.

I need to go.

I need to *go.*

But I can't fucking move.

The greenhouse door swings open, and my pulse stops dead as Davis, Hunter, and Mitchell pool out together.

My oldest brother sets a glare on me. "Nice of you to show up when all the work is done," Davis says.

I feel my face crunch in confusion. "What are you talking about?"

"The greenhouse," Mitchell explains. "You didn't hear mom talk about how she needed help rearranging the plants and lights? You were at that dinner the other night."

I don't remember. Heat gathers again. Sweat caking my body and stifling me, but I can't unfreeze enough to unzip my jacket.

Our mom looks between them. "Boys, that conversation happened after your brother already left."

"Like he always does," Hunter adds, digging the knife in my back.

I drag my gaze across the snow.

Our mom lets out a sigh and says, "Be nice."

"He doesn't make it easy," Hunter snaps.

Likewise.

I swallow the retort and clear my throat to ask, "How did you all even get here? I didn't see your cars?"

"Uber," Davis says. "We were all still a little hungover from last night."

Right.

"We actually still need some help with the heaters and lights," Mitchell says to me. "You want to pitch in?" He nods towards the greenhouse and his eyes soften on me.

I think that Mitchell really believes he's giving me a lifeline to be in good graces with our parents and our brothers.

It's sad.

Because what I really need is for him to stick up for me. To keep our two older brothers from beating on me. But even if Mitchell tried now, he'd be twenty-one years too late.

"I left my car running," I say. "I wasn't staying long."

My mom squeezes my shoulder. "I'll shut it off for you." She holds out a palm so I can pass her the keys. "Go spend some time with your brothers."

I want to say *no.*

Deep in my gut, I don't want to be here, but it feels impossible to leave in this moment.

I nod tensely, and my brothers disappear back into the greenhouse while I search my pockets for car keys. My mom waits for me, patient.

I'm hot and I end up pulling off my jacket. Doing a piss-poor job, half my T-shirt rides up my waist in the process. As I clutch the keys and wad up my jacket, I look over at my mom.

Her eyes are unblinking and zeroed in on my bare abdomen. At the fresh welts that mar my cold skin. Ones from Hunter after he tackled me outside, the holiday dinner from hell. It wasn't even the first bad one I've had.

We're both motionless, except for our gazes that meet. Truths exposed and raw, and it's not like she hasn't known or seen before.

This just feels different. Maybe because I'm older. Maybe because she has the ability to protect me right here, right now, and I'm twenty-one and suffering under the belief that she won't.

She never has before.

My keys are cold in my hand.

She reaches out to stroke my cheek, and I stare down at the snow. Her soft touch feels as painful as the thorns she cut.

I glance at the greenhouse, then to my mom.

"Just give them a chance," she says in a pleading whisper.

I want to shake my head, but I can't. "They're not going to change."

She lets out this tiny breath and rubs my arm, and in her pitying gaze, I know that she's not waiting for them to change. She's always been waiting for *me* to change—to grow thicker skin. To be less sensitive.

More of a man, right?

I could make her a PowerPoint with all the evidence of their fucked-up deeds and she'll still claim I left the majority of their brotherly love off the slides.

I stick my arms back into my jacket sleeves, and once I shake off the snow from my hood, our eyes lock for another beat. *Protect me, Mom.*

Please.

I drop the car keys in her palm. Giving her my escape.

She has a choice to make, and she doesn't even hesitate. I watch her leave for the driveway. To shut off my running Mustang.

As soon as I walk into that greenhouse, I know for certain that I'm doomed.

IT HURTS TO BREATHE. PAIN SPLINTERS UP MY SIDE WITH EACH inhale.

How do I reach my apartment? I have no clue—the whole drive is a blur. Like a dusty Sega game, the TV screen crackling with static. But I remember the greenhouse.

I remember pushing Davis so hard that he fell into a stack of ceramic pots. They shattered. Dirt spilled. The door was finally clear.

And I left to the sound of my dad yelling at me. For destroying my mom's precious basil plants. They could've been parsley or spinach for all I know.

I didn't get a good look.

I didn't care, and I guess that's my fault, right?

Stupid, clumsy me.

Once I'm inside my Philly apartment, I hold onto my ribs and search my kitchen cupboards. Banging each one open. Trying to find some pain pills. When I was a teenager, one of my friends in the neighborhood dealt pills and gave me oxy. Her therapist would write her all kinds of prescriptions.

All I have now is ibuprofen.

With one hand, I place the bottle on the counter and twist the cap off, having perfected the one-handed twist on "child-proof" caps years ago. It pops. I purposefully knock the bottle and the pills spill on the granite countertop. I scoop a handful, not even counting and toss them back into my mouth.

As soon as they go down, I cough.

Sharp pain erupts in my ribs. They're broken.

I know they're broken.

Sinking onto my desk chair, I try to forget what happened. Maybe I can see the events from Hunter's fucked-up vantage. He just…he threw a bag of potting soil to me. It was heavy. I didn't see it coming. The bag slammed into my gut and knocked the wind out of my lungs.

I doubled over. Coughing. And the bag—it landed on a gardening hoe and tore open. Soil littered the floor.

Davis slapped me on the back of the head.

I tried to put distance between us, but I walked closer to Hunter. He shoved another bag at my back. As if I had hands connected to my spine to grab the damn thing.

He knew what he was doing.

The brunt force plowed me into a wooden shelf, and the corner jammed into my ribcage. I can still hear the *crack* in my ears. I can still feel my feet slipping beneath me and my legs buckling before I dropped to the ground.

"Come on, get up," Davis said. "Don't be such a pussy."

I blink back the images, and my fingers tremble as I type on my cell. I'm keeping my promise to Willow.

I text: *Made it back home. All good.*

I know—I'm not telling her the whole truth.

But she doesn't need to worry. I don't need to be the tumor in her life. Especially because this was the last time I'm *ever* confronting my brothers.

Before I left the greenhouse, I did something I never do.

I told them, "I'm never seeing you again." I choked out the seething words, and Hunter and Davis laughed. Like I'm some joke.

Mitchell got quiet. He looked between them and me, and his eyes fell to the floor in a daze.

I don't think any of them really believe me.

But it's true. I'm never going to see them again. Not even when I'm dead. I'd rather spend eternity in hell than come back as a ghost to haunt their asses. I refuse to let them have power over me anymore. The only problem…I forgot to grab my hard drive.

My stomach churns. It's either my hard drive or seeing them again. Fuck the hard drive, then.

I lean back, close my eyes, and wait to go numb.

54

Garrison Abbey

THE NEXT TWO DAYS ARE A BIGGER BLUR. I BURY MYSELF IN WORK and barely leave my desk at Cobalt Inc. Cans of Lightning Bolt! are piled in a tiny trashcan, and despite the fact that my ass hasn't left this chair for eight hours, my space is pretty organized.

I can't think if there's shit everywhere.

Suddenly, a Styrofoam container appears next to my keyboard. I stop typing to pull out two twenties from my pocket and hand the cash to the white guy standing beside my desk. Combed back auburn hair and an expensive suit, Keith looks like he's auditioning for the role of Douchebag #3.

He's a little older than me and an intern in the Cobalt magnets division. We have a deal going. He grabs food from the cafeteria three times a day for me, just so I don't have to leave my desk, and he upcharges me for ten-dollar sushi.

It's worth it.

And he should be walking away right now.

But he's still here.

I point to my headphones. They're noise-cancelling, so I can't hear him past the soft beat of my music. I can't even read his lips that well, but I see his brows furrow in frustration. Okay, I don't want to lose my personal Uber Eats because I ignored him on a random Thursday.

I yank my headphones to my neck.

"Abbey," he says. "This is the last time I'm doing this." He points to the Styrofoam. I grab it and open the lid, making sure he didn't spit on the tuna rolls. As far as I can tell, the sushi looks perfect.

I put the container in my mini-fridge under my desk. "Why is this the last time? Do you want more money?" I could go up to fifty, I think.

"No," Keith snaps. "I'm getting shit from the guys in my office. They're calling me your bitch." That's really not a surprise. I'm not well-liked here.

For one, I have ties to Connor, and I refuse to give these pricks an "in" with the boss. No secrets about Connor are coming from my mouth, despite numerous requests for weird shit. Like his favorite liquor and what time of day he's "least" likely to reject their proposal. Do I look like I'm a walking *Connor Cobalt Wiki*?

Secondly, I'm one of the only people who runs their own division alone in Cobalt Inc.

Connor said he'd officially title my division when I've presented my prototype. Right now, I'm keeping everything a secret—even the concept. Less pressure that way, and Connor doesn't seem to care about it.

The guys in the company—they care.

It's favoritism. Nepotism. All wrapped in one fugly looking package.

To Keith, I shrug. "I mean, them calling you my bitch is kind of a lame insult, man. Aren't we all Connor Cobalt's bitches at this point?"

Keith shakes his head and then slowly stops, rethinking. "Yeah, but you're not Connor Cobalt. You're what…twenty-three?"

"Twenty-one," I correct, probably not helping my case. "And just tell those guys to fuck off. You're making almost a hundred dollars a day off me because I'm too lazy to move my ass."

Connor doesn't do free internships, but Keith can't be earning what his senior coworkers take home.

"Exactly," Keith says. "You're lazy. You're young. You're *you*. I can't be seen with you, Abbey." He motions between us. "This partnership is over."

I roll my eyes as he walks off. There goes that one.

Focusing back on my computer, I put my headphones on and try to fix a bug in the code. I'm building the foundation of the game before I even work in the mechanics of design and more complex gameplay. It's harder not having a team of programmers, but I prefer to do it alone. At least, right now at this stage, I don't need a bunch of people in my space.

Another body arrives near my cubicle, and without even turning my head, I recognize the poised *I own this world* posture and Cartier wristwatch from my peripheral.

Connor Cobalt is gracing me with his presence, which doesn't happen every day. He gives me room to breathe and work and so far I've appreciated that.

I keep my eyes on the computer, some strands of hair falling in my face, but I keep typing. Maybe if I ignore him, he'll just vanish.

"Garrison," Connor says. I can hear his calm, assertive tone even over my noise-cancelling headphones.

I don't blink, my focus zoned in on the computer.

He waves a hand in front of the screen. Finally, I glance up at him, still typing like I'm *supremely* busy. Then I peek at his side.

Lily Calloway is here. And she looks about as out-of-place at Cobalt Inc. as I do. A casual long-sleeve black shirt and overcoat hangs baggie on her gangly frame. I don't even think she's wearing actual pants—just leggings.

There's only a handful of reasons she could be here, and I'm going to go with the most obvious. It's January 3rd, and *everyone* in this building knows what that means. It's Connor Cobalt's 30th birthday, and if you want to be on Connor's good side, you act like today is just any other ordinary day.

No fanfare. No wishing your boss happy birthday. Definitely no cake or gifts.

Apparently, Connor isn't that hyped on celebrating his age, but I'm sure his wife and sisters-in-law are planning something for him.

And all of this has absolutely *nothing* to do with me.

I return my gaze to Connor and click a button on my keyboard, turning off my music. "What do you want?" I don't know why, but those words come out a lot harsher than I intend. My muscles twitch.

"You're done for the day," Connor says, ignoring my tone. "I need you to come with us."

What?

My fingers still move over my keyboard, finishing up some last lines of code that I needed to plug in. I swing my head to Lily, trusting her more. "Is this work related?"

"Umm…" She mumbles and then shrugs.

Jesus. She's no help. And I bet she's in on this plan to kidnap me from my work.

"Will you come with us if it isn't?" Connor asks.

"No." I don't even hesitate. It's just the way it is. They're not my friends, and I can pretend all day long that they give a shit about me. But they don't. They care about Willow, and I'm an extension of her. Willow and I aren't in a great place right now, and the probability of us not working out has skyrocketed.

I'm trying to avoid a situation where I form these bonds with people and then have them all ripped away. I've been through the loss of friends before—and it's fucking painful. And I didn't even like those assholes.

It'd be infinitely worse when you actually enjoy hanging out with your friends. And I like Lily. I like Lo. I had fun at the Fright Night during Halloween. Having a good time with them scares the shit out of me. Because it's just another thing I could lose.

So…no. Whatever they're up to, it's a big capital *Fuck No* from me.

Connor doesn't miss a beat. "Then it's work related," he says. "Grab your things."

Seriously?

I wrench my headphones back to my neck with a deeper sigh. Abandoning my work. It looks like Connor's not going to let me bail on this. Plus, I'd prefer to keep my job.

To Lily, I say, "Just tell me where we're going and why."

"Ryke's house—or cottage."

I don't get why they call it a cottage. It looks like a fucking house. She adds, "It's a surprise party for Connor."

The word *surprise* jumps out at me. I'm living in a parallel universe where words don't mean the same thing. I glance at my boss. "How is this a surprise birthday if you know? And why the hell do you want me to go?"

"Surprising me is so rare that everyone uses the term loosely." He points at my computer. "You're here at six in the morning and you leave at midnight. *Seven* days a week. While I appreciate your work ethic, as your friend, it's disconcerting."

I inhale a tight breath. *Friend.* There's that word again. "You're my boss, not my friend."

"I'm both," Connor says easily, "and since you seem to be lacking in the friend department lately, I wouldn't turn my back on one, especially friendships as valuable as mine."

Believe me, I know how valuable his friendship is. The employees here can't stop reminding me about it.

Lily pipes in, "Having no friends isn't a bad thing."

I pinch my eyes. "Can you both just shut up?" It's hard to think with them in my ear. Another day spent with the famous couples: Lily and Lo, Connor and Rose, Ryke and Daisy. I should reject this forced invite, but for the sake of my job and my current sanity, there's only one real choice.

I roll back the chair and grab my backpack from underneath the desk. Lily glances at my ripped jeans, but she doesn't say anything about it.

Standing, I still have to crane my neck to look at my boss. The guy is six-four, and I swear the universe is playing right into his hand. People refer to Connor as some otherworldly being like an immortal god. He might as well be tall enough to touch the sky.

I sling the backpack over my shoulder. "If I go," I say to Connor. "You have to stop calling me your friend. We're not, okay?" I need him to understand this. I don't want him as a friend. If we're not, there won't be more collateral damage when I lose Willow.

Before Connor can reply, I look to Lily. "And I have friends…" I pause. *That's not completely true.* "One friend. She's just not here."

Willow.

My only friend.

Casually, like I didn't just offer this grand stipulation, Connor checks his watch. "Most people would be on their knees to be my friend. This just illustrates your lack of judgment."

Maybe.

I nod. "Thanks, boss." Sarcasm bleeds from my lips.

"Follow me." Connor motions to Lily and me. He saunters ahead with calm, reassuring authority. Most people love it. For some people, the arrogant superiority grates on them. After working months for Connor, I'm landing somewhere in between.

We pass a copy machine, Lily step-by-step beside me. I whisper to her, "Just so you know, you're my favorite boss." I've only ever had two. Connor and Lily.

She smiles wide, and a good feeling floods my chest.

I miss those days at Superheroes & Scones.

But I can't have them back.

THE CALLOWAY SISTERS & THEIR MEN – FAN PAGE

FOLLOWERS: 75K

It's that time! With every new year, I'm dedicated to updating you on the basics of the Calloway Sisters & Their Men. Take this as a bit of a "where are they now" post.

The Stokes
Poppy Calloway (33) & Sam Stokes (33)
Daughter: Maria (10)
Update: Not much to note about the Stokes. Like we said, this Calloway sister stays out of the media. Poppy and her husband have decided not to take part in the docuseries *We Are Calloway.*

The Cobalts
Rose Calloway (29) & Connor Cobalt (30)
Daughter: Jane (3)
Sons: Charlie & Beckett (1-year-old twins)
Update: Calloway Couture and Cobalt Inc. are both thriving, but the real news comes with a rumor that Rose might be pregnant with her fourth child!! #AlreadyPredictingBabyNames

The Hales
Lily Calloway (27) & Loren Hale (28)
Son: Maximoff (3)
Update: Maximoff might just be the cutest baby alive. We have no new baby news, but there are rumors

that the Sorin-X movie is coming along. It will be the first big movie franchise for Halway Comics.

The Meadows
Daisy Calloway (22) & Ryke Meadows (29)
Daughter: Sullivan (11-months-old)
Update: We don't see much of Daisy and Sulli out and about, and unfortunately Sulli hasn't been on *We Are Calloway*. So bummed! Especially since the Meadows baby might be the most sought after for pics. Everyone wants to see Ryke Meadows dad moments. But he's the face of Ziff, the sports drink, so we are blessed with those abs.

The Unofficial Calloway Sister
Willow Hale (20) & Her Boyfriend – Garrison Abbey (21)
Update: They're still dating even though she's all the way in London for college. We've seen a little of Garrison in the background of *We Are Calloway*. But unless you're following Willow on Instagram, she's been pretty MIA online. It's possible they might not even be together anymore, despite Lily's reassurance. We'll keep tabs, and if anyone has any connections to people at Wakefield University that want to drop some tips, hit me up in my DMs.

Don't forget today is Connor Cobalt's birthday! Be sure to tweet him and wish him a happy birthday. And check out this gif set below of him and Rose in Paris!!

Love you like Loren loves Lily,
xo Olive

55

Garrison Abbey

THREE-YEAR-OLD JANE COBALT TOSSES A HANDFUL OF CONFETTI from a little pink bucket. "Happy Birthday, Daddy!"

All of their children are front and center in Ryke and Daisy's quaint "cottage"—it's definitely not a mansion or as regal as the Cobalt Estate. But it's four-bedrooms. Not a shoebox either. The outside is all gray stone with a stone-stacked chimney like they live on a pastoral English countryside and not in a Philly suburb.

The décor is like Urban Outfitters threw up in here. Boho chic or whatever. I'm not an interior designer.

One-year-old fraternal twins, Charlie and Beckett Cobalt have their own buckets of confetti, and three-year-old Maximoff Hale makes confetti angels on the hardwood, little legs and arms moving about. Daisy kneels on the ground beside her almost-one-year-old daughter, helping Sulli throw the strips of colorful paper.

Ryke, Loren, and Rose stand off to the side, letting their kids "surprise" Connor.

I feel like I'm intruding.

But they wanted me around. So I'm here.

Still, I need air for a second. I slip out before anyone notices me and head towards the first-floor bathroom. I've been here enough with Willow to know where it is. Gold balloons litter the ground, and I push aside a black streamer, hanging from the ceiling. They went all out for a not-really-surprise "surprise" party.

I lock the bathroom door and immediately splash water on my face. Taking out my phone, I check my messages.

None.

I'm about to text Willow, but loud laughter echoes from the living room. I want to be around them. I shouldn't want that.

Get it together. You're already here.

I swallow hard and wipe water off my face before returning to the living room. The first thing I notice is the life-sized cardboard cutout of Connor standing in the middle of the hall.

Jesus…

They really went there.

Like he doesn't already have an ego the size of a galaxy? I tilt my head, examining more. It looks so much like Connor. One of them must have bought the cutout on a celebrity site. I've seen them before. The only reason I even check out those sites is to make sure Willow and I don't have our faces on T-shirts. We're not that famous, and honestly, I hope it never happens.

I prefer the periphery where people don't have a life-sized cardboard version of me in their bedroom. It creeps me out, but I see how Lily and everyone else are laughing about it. How they try to turn this into something fun. Because it's better than dwelling on the shitty aspects of fame. It's not all bad. And I guess, it's kind of a good gift.

Which reminds me: I didn't get Connor anything. And I'm at his birthday party.

Well, whatever. He knows I didn't actually want to come.

I head to the kitchen, passing a banner that reads *Happy 30ᵗʰ Birthday, Connor!* The only other people that pack the place besides the "core six" are their children. I'm literally the interloper.

Awesome.

Jane Cobalt giggles on the ground, covered in confetti. A photo of this child just smiling in celebratory streamers would be worth thousands of dollars, sold to any magazine in New York.

She's just a baby. I feel bad for her and Moffy. What kind of life are they going to have under this invasive microscope? Their parents got twenty-some years of peace before the spotlight roasted them.

They get *nothing.*

Sucks.

I shrug the thought off and slip further in the sunny kitchen, sunshine streaming through windows.

Loren pops a chip into his mouth, a jar of salsa next to him. His wife has her legs around his waist and arms around his neck in a piggyback. Lily is thin and bony and can't weigh much. He hands her a chip over his shoulder, and he's really the only person I care to greet right now.

"Hey," I nod to him and then hop up on the kitchen counter. I catch sight of a tiny potted basil plant next to the sink, and my chest tightens.

"You made it," Lo says, not surprised that I was invited.

I focus back on him. "Yeah."

He scoops a hunk of chunky salsa. "Was groveling involved to get your ass here?"

"Some."

"Good." Lo tosses another chip in his mouth. "I can't be the only one begging you to show up to birthday parties. As King Connor would say, it's *unseemly.*" He tilts his head. "How's my sister?"

I'm about to tell Lo that Willow is doing great, as far as I know. She never told any of them about how I punched her college friend or the fact that I visited her in London for all of two hours.

Can this stay between us? I asked her. I was ashamed. Still am.

She agreed.

But before I can say anything to Loren, his wife cuts in. "Lo," Lily says softly, but loud enough to pull his attention.

"Hmm?" He swishes around the salsa with a chip. His other hand is planted on Lily's leg. She's still on his back.

Their embrace just makes me ache to hold Willow. My heart physically clenches, and I knock my head back against the cupboard.

Come on, Garrison.

"Do you think Connor might be Batman or Superman?"

Lo drops her instantly.

She lands on her ass. "Lo!"

My lip twitches, almost smiling. God, I want to.

There are some things you don't bring up in front of Loren Hale. DC comic book characters might actually be number one on the list.

He waves a chip at his wife. "There are a goddamn *thousand* superheroes, and you chose two that I can't stand?"

"They make the most sense."

"They make about as much sense as calling Connor the Swamp Thing."

I almost laugh.

Lily picks herself off the floor. "That's just silly. Swamp Thing isn't even *close* to being Batman and Superman."

Willow would love this conversation. Comics remind me of her. She's the only reason I started reading them in the first place, and she still loves superheroes more than me. *I'll tell her about this.* It'll be a light thing after a lot of heavy shit.

Lo's glare sharpens and intensifies. "Please let me know where I can find my other wife. This one in front of me is a sellout."

Lily touches her heart and hurt cinches her brows. "I'm not a sellout. I just happen to not be an elitist about the whole Marvel versus DC thing, and I can appreciate *all* superheroes equally."

"You think they're all made *equally*?" Lo asks passionately. "Do you want to talk Green Lantern? We can talk Green Lantern."

"Okay, okay," Lily immediately concedes. "So I have my favorites, just like you." She's moved close, fingers in his belt loops, and she gazes up at her husband like the whole conversation is a giant turn-on. Lo wraps his arm around his wife.

I lean forward and grab a couple chips from the bag. Trying not to wish for Willow to be here.

Lo declares, "My best friend is *not* Batman or Superman." *Best friend.* That'd be Connor. It's weird hearing him say that out loud. Not that I don't know the fact. But because Connor is my boss. Loren is Willow's brother. Our connections to one another are too fucking tangled at this point.

"Then what is he?" Lily asks.

"Connor Cobalt," Lo answers without a pause. "He's Connor fucking Cobalt, and whatever powers he has, they're all his own."

I narrow my eyes, watching their exchange. Connor doesn't surround himself with people who only blow smoke up his ass, otherwise Ryke Meadows wouldn't be in this room. But pure admiration comes from Lo.

For me, I remember being a seventeen-year-old kid who vandalized a house. I remember the guy who gave me the handout when I needed it but didn't deserve it.

I don't know—Loren Hale is the one who has powers to me.

Lily's gaze drifts to a *Celebrity Crush* tabloid on the counter behind Lo, and her smile fades. "What is..." She seizes the tabloid.

I crane my head, trying to read the headline.

[POLL] Which Calloway sister has the cutest baby?

That's fucked up.

And the poll won't blow over well with Ryke, Daisy, Connor, or Rose either.

They're all insanely protective of their kids. Like they should be. Parents should protect *all* of their children. Not just the ones they like the most.

Shit, if I had a baby right now, I'd be gutted every time their name was in print. *I* can't even handle media attention. How could I expect my kid to deal with that?

And why the fuck am I thinking about a baby?

I'm twenty-one.

Willow and I are in the rockiest place we've ever stepped foot in. We may not make it to *tomorrow*. Babies are an unquantifiable part of my relationship. The more I think about the foggy future, my stomach knots.

Pain suddenly flares in my ribs as I focus more on the injury.

So I turn my attention.

Lo rips the tabloid out of Lily's hands.

"They polled our babies by cuteness," Lily explains. "They can't do that."

Lo's brows bunch. "They can do whatever they want."

"I just wish there were *some* ethical limitations," Lily says while Lo flips to the right page. Lily tries to stop him, pushing his hands. "Don't! What if Moffy is ranked the ugliest." She lowers her voice. "We'll know and we'll feel bad and it'll give him a complex."

I look around for Maximoff. The three-year-old is playing patty-cake with Jane on the carpet.

"That's not going to happen," Lo says. "We have an *adorable* baby."

"So do Rose and Daisy."

"You don't have to look," Lo tells Lily.

But I'm positive he can't help himself. I chew another chip and watch this go down.

I don't even know what I would do in their position. Maybe burn it. Stop the temptation.

While Lo reads through the article, Lily slides towards me and we chat about movies. I think it's helping distract her from the tabloid, but I haven't seen as many films as she's mentioning. Ever since Willow left, I haven't had the energy to go to the theater.

After a few minutes, Lo finishes reading the article and drifts back to us with chips and salsa in hand. "Little 'puff," he calls out to Lily.

Puff is just in reference to Hufflepuff, her *Harry Potter* house. Willow made me take the sorting quiz too, and I'm Gryffindor like my girlfriend.

I almost smile remembering how Willow spent an hour explaining *our* house to me and the history behind it. She said Gryffindors are brave, and I get why she's meant for this house—she's the most courageous person I've ever met. But I'm not sure I fit the mold. Really, of any house or secret club or thing.

Lo stands behind Lily and rests his chin on her shoulder. His eyes flit to me and then back to her. "What are we talking about?"

"Nothing," Lily says too fast and spins around to face her husband.

Lo stuffs the chip bag underneath his arm. "Nothing?"

"That's what I said," she snaps.

"Christ, when'd you get so sassy?"

Lily crinkles her nose, trying to put on a "tough" face. But she fails. Lo sticks his chip between his teeth, freeing up his hand, and he pinches her nose.

Lily playfully pounds her fist into his arm.

Lo feigns a wince and mumbles, "Ouch, love." He tilts his head back and the chip falls into his mouth.

Their love is an all-consuming thing when you're in the room with them, and my all-consuming love is thousands of miles away.

3,539 to be exact.

Why am I even here again?

To watch them flirt. To be the seventh-fucking-wheel.

So I blurt out, "We were talking about *Justice League 2*." The movie isn't coming out any time soon—the release now up in the air (which Lily and I were discussing)—but the mention of the DC property is enough to receive a Grade A grimace and glare from Loren.

Seeing him drop his own wife on the ground for talking about DC should have probably made me hesitate. But maybe I have a death-sentence.

Murder me.

It'd be easier being dead.

Lo flashes a half-smile. "Why don't you go talk about that down the street, turn right, approach a mailbox that says *Abbey*, walk up the driveway, slam the door—goodbye." He waves curtly.

Bile rises to my throat. If he even knew what walking up to my family's home means…

But maybe that's where I deserve to be. Pressure sits heavy on my chest, and I spin an unlit cigarette between my fingers. Ryke would probably shit a brick if I smoked in here, but I could leave.

That's what Lo wants anyway.

Anger and something worse pounds against me. "You want me to go home?" I snap and then grind down on my teeth.

Home.

Let me go home and break another rib.

Let me go home and give my mom a chance to save me. Only to push me in a snake pit all over again.

Lo holds my gaze. "I want you to not speak about what-shall-not-be-named inside my brother's house, and if you can't handle that, then yeah, you can go home."

"Lo!" Lily chastises in shock, jaw dropped.

Loren pushes her chin up, closing her mouth. He almost smiles. "Lily." He mock pouts.

She pokes his chest. "You're not being nice."

"Because I'm not nice."

I release a tensed breath. He's just being a normal, raging asshole. I have to remember that Lo doesn't know anything about my home. I don't think he'd poke at this part of my life if he had any idea about what goes on there.

Lily slides her hand to Lo's cheeks and she's looking at him with intense *fuck me* eyes, so I focus elsewhere. The ceiling. The floor. My phone.

No new texts.

Willow's probably asleep.

I waver between staying here and jumping off the counter and leaving. But even with Lo practically painting neon arrows towards my house, I like it here. My other option is sitting alone in my apartment.

Being alone sounds horrible.

I've never enjoyed my own company. It's mainly why I spent my prep school years with *terrible* friends because surrounding myself with people (even shitty ones) was better than being left with my own fucking self.

Instantly, I decide to stay. I'll grab a drink—soda because Ryke doesn't have alcohol in his house—and maybe eat some cake and then leave.

The cupboards are behind my head, and I reach up for a cup.

"Garrison," Lo says with enough worry that I turn quickly.

My head smacks into the cupboard. "Shit," I curse and rub the throbbing spot. Lo stares at me with a strange amount of concern. I don't get it. "What?"

He asks softly, "Where did those bruises come from?"

Oh…shit.

Shit.

Fuck.

My mouth falls, and I shake my head. I don't…how did…

God, my hoodie and shirt must have risen when I reached for the cupboard. *Fuckfuckfuck.*

FUCK!

I dizzy, my head whirling, knowing there's no hiding this. I haven't prepared for anyone beyond Willow to know about my home life.

I glance to Lily, the only other person in the kitchen. I have zero sisters, and there's something soft and kind about Lily. It makes me want to simultaneously open up but also step back, and I don't know how to handle telling her the truth.

Lo is different.

I guess he reminds me of me. It's easier to go head-to-head with someone who wants to rip me open than someone who wants to hug me. I don't want a hug.

His question jackhammers my brain. Pounding and pounding. *Where did those bruises come from?* I look back to Lo and lean into my usual excuse. "Lacrosse. Drop it."

Lily suddenly swings her head to the living room. "Oh look— Moffy." She quickly moves to leave. Lo pinches her shoulder, and they talk under their breaths before she disappears.

It's obvious she left on purpose. Because of me. Maybe they can tell I'm lying.

I stay seated on the counter, legs hanging off, and Lo slides closer to my spot. His sharp-edged gaze drills in on me.

"Honestly, it's lacrosse," I say.

"It's been Christmas break," Lo refutes, his tone serrated. "When were you playing lacrosse?" *Never. Not since prep school.*

Air is hard to intake. Emotion that I hate to confront is compressing my lungs. "I don't know...I just was...I was." Lies die in my throat. My mouth dry.

I end up staring at a patch of sunlight on the floor. Hair hangs over my eyes, and I remember that I'm still wearing headphones around my neck. I touch the sides, the familiarity suddenly calming me. "Let me be."

I'm seconds away from pulling the headphones over my ears like a real dick. Anything to avoid this conversation.

Suddenly, Lo hands me the salsa and then digs a hand in the bag of chips, passing me one.

I stare blankly at him. "What is this?"

I don't get it. What is he fucking doing? The pressure on my chest has intensified. Smothering me.

"Chips and salsa," Lo says. "If you don't like them, we can't be friends anymore." He pops one in his mouth.

"We're friends?" I ask incredulously. A part of me still thinks the invite here was out of pity, and because I'm just Willow's boyfriend.

"Jesus Christ, do I need to make friendship bracelets for you to believe it?"

"Fuck you," I snap. Hesitantly, I dip the chip into salsa.

"Don't be pissy because I'm prettier. It's just a fact you're going to have to get used to."

I swallow the chip and the lump that's wedged in my throat. "I thought the tall one was supposed to be the prettiest." If Connor knew I called him *the tall one*, I don't think he'd love it. Too generic for the mighty god. That's why I like doing it though.

Lo starts to smile. "Shh, we don't like to tell him the truth. It ruins his allure."

I nod, my shoulders sinking forward. Into myself. *Disappear.*

Lo sweeps me in this causal way. "So what are your brothers like? You have three, right?"

Easy enough question.

"Yeah," I answer. "Mitchell, Hunter, and Davis. We're all two years apart from one another."

Me: twenty-one.

Them: twenty-three, twenty-five, and twenty-seven.

A long, tense pause strains the air, and I stare at the small scar on the inside of my pointer-finger. When I was nine, Hunter made me fish in the garbage for a *Sports Illustrated* magazine I threw away. He was pissed because he never got a chance to read it.

I sliced my finger open on a tuna can.

"Which one's the worst?" Lo asks.

It drives deep into me.

Which one's the worst. His voice is strict and sharp, sounding protective before he even knows the real issue. But he must sense the problem is with my brothers. I'm sure I mentioned them briefly before, and I couldn't have said nice things.

I look Lo up and down. "I know what you're trying to do."

"Am I right?" He motions to my ribs. "Did one of your shitty fucking brothers do that?"

My nose flares. My throat swells. I try to swallow again. I barely can. No one but Willow has ever confronted me outright. And it's like submerging my whole body into ice water. I don't know how to breathe with this type of pain. I want *out.* Out. I glance left and right, searching for some sort of escape.

It's not a physical place I want to be.

Take it away. Take this fucking pain away.

My mouth dries more. "They're just messing around." My voice is barely a whisper. But I think he hears because his jaw clenches.

Anger flares in his amber eyes.

I don't know why I defend my brothers or regurgitate my mom and dad's words. It feels easier to agree with my parents than to say what I know is true.

Silence stretches for an uncomfortable beat and then Lo says, "Can I see it again?"

I glance to the living room.

Everyone sits on couches, most aren't facing the kitchen, and their attention cements to the little kids. Not aware of our conversation or they're purposefully giving us privacy.

I rotate back to Lo, and I realize he's being really patient.

Patience isn't a quality I'd shelve under his name. That gets me for a second. So I take a breath and grip the bottom of my hoodie.

I lift the black fabric, just enough to reveal the deep purple bruise that spiders up my ribcage. I'd love to say that it looks worse than it feels. But that'd be another lie. Instead of concentrating on my own fucked-up body, I watch Lo.

His cheekbones sharpen. And he looks visibly ill.

Pale.

He skims me quickly, trying to take it all in before I shut him out, and he peers around at my back. I haven't looked there yet, but I'm betting faint bruises exist from where Davis's shins connected with my spine.

"*Get up.*" I hear his voice in my head. Not just from this week. But from so many years. Colliding together. "*You're weak shit.*"

"Let me check out your other side," Lo whispers, tearing me from my own head.

My hands shake as I lift the other side of my hoodie. *Fuck.* I inhale, and I see another black-and-blue welt along my abdomen. But this one is fading.

"I'm the little brother," I say, so soft that he tilts his head to hear. "They just pick on me. It's what older brothers do."

Stop it.

Stop defending them.

I can't. I can't. Why can't I?

My limbs tremble. I'm shaking harder like an earthquake rumbles beneath me and I can't stop it.

Lo stares at me, straight-on. His face all sharp lines. "Your ribs are fractured."

A hot tear rolls down my cheek. "Yeah, I know." I wipe harshly. *Stop crying.*

"It's happened before?"

I shrug, muscles tensed. "Whenever I see them, they like to play rough, so whatever…"

"Which brother?" Fury flames his voice.

I lift my head. *Don't cry. Don't fucking cry.* My chin quakes. "All of them."

My voice splinters.

Lo blinks something back, his eyes reddened, and so softly, so quietly, he tells me, "I'm not going to let them hurt you anymore."

Fuck.

Those words just collide into me. I try to cover my shattering face. Palms to my eyes. I slide off the counter, attempting to stand, but my legs buckle underneath me.

Fuck.

My back slips down the cabinets until my ass hits the floor, and I bury my forehead into my bent knees.

I'm not going to let them hurt you anymore.

His first instinct is to protect me. No hesitation, no second thought that maybe I don't deserve protection.

Maybe I am the sensitive little brother. Having Loren Hale know about my issues at home is this giant, scary thing. It's why I'm trembling, and I can't fucking stop. My ears ring.

Lo is seven years older than me. One year older than Davis, my eldest brother. And there are days…weeks, months that I wished I had Willow's family instead of my own. But I can't trade them in—that's not how blood works, right?

And I'm just stuck here, wanting out. *God, I want out.* I sniff hard and wipe my nose with the sleeve of my hoodie.

Without lifting my head, I sense Lo kneeling beside me. "Does Willow know?" he asks.

I nod, still looking down. Strands of hair stick to my wet eyelashes. I'm afraid they'll blame her for withholding information. They shouldn't.

It's all on me. I've been evading the whole truth. Omitted shit. And she's been here for me so much already.

I choke out, "It's not her fault…for not telling anyone. She thought it stopped. It did…for a while, but when I went back for Christmas break, they were all there…" I blink back the most recent encounter, spilt soil and a collision into wooden shelves. I shudder and exhale a sharp breath. "Forget it. Forget I said anything."

Lo's voice grows even quieter. "Will you stay at my place, at least until Willow comes back?"

My body solidifies. He's not serious. Does he even know what he's offering? I'm…*me*. And Willow isn't coming back to Philly anytime soon. She just completed her *first* semester at Wakefield.

"That's *years*."

"So?"

I glance up from my knees. Unblinking. My eyes sting, and Lo stares at me with assured intensity, like he means every word he's saying.

I don't think he understands the enormity of his offer. I'm the kid that vandalized his house three years ago. I shouldn't be *living* in his home. But here he is, passing out second and third and fourth chances like they grow endlessly on trees.

But I know Loren Hale better now than I did three years ago. In reality, second chances don't exist with him. You hurt him and he cuts you off at the knees. Why I'm the exception to that, I don't know.

Maybe I never will.

I have to think about this logically. Where I go will affect the one person I love most in this world. I think about my girl.

"Willow could break up with me by then," I remind Lo. After the shit I pulled in London, I'm sure that day is coming.

"You'd still be a part of this family." He gestures in a circle. "I wouldn't kick you out because of it."

I'm bowled over again. It's harder to breathe, but for a different reason. My eyes burn, and I impulsively shove against his offer. "I have an apartment in Philly."

"You live alone." He pauses and then gives me a once-over. "I'm going to be blunt like my brother. You look like shit. You're a little gaunt, and man, you smell like you've been spraying cologne instead of showering."

"I've been busy," I snap, not wanting that pity. "I have a job, and it's the only thing that keeps me from…"

"From what?"

I shrug, and then it just pours out of me. "From feeling like a stupid loser. Like I have no purpose, alright?" I hold back tears. "I have something outside of *waiting* for a girl. I have something… and I need to put time in it. I shouldn't even be *here*. I should be working—"

"Hear me out," Lo cuts me off just as my voice cracks. "I have this little kid who's a big pain in my ass because he keeps begging for a sibling. Every day I have to hear, 'but Jane has two brothers' and if he just saw you in the house, he'd be happy. But most importantly, you'd save my goddamn eardrums."

I let out a short laugh. "The important things."

"Damn right."

I pinch my eyes. "Stop *crying*," I mutter under my breath. *Why can't I stop?*

"I get it."

"Do you?" I snap.

"Your brothers call you a pussy for crying? They tell you you're not a real man—*suck it up, Garrison. What are you, a little pussy, a little girl?* What kind of goddamn man are you?"

My mouth falls open, shock stinging me. I almost look around for Ryke. There's *no way* Ryke could have said that shit to Lo. But I can't locate Lo's older brother because the cabinets block my view from the living room.

Lo follows my gaze, and he must register who I'm trying to find.

"It wasn't my brother who told me to just *stop fucking crying*." His jaw tightens.

I frown. "Who?"

"My father."

I ice over. Jonathan Hale is Willow's dad, too. And she didn't grow up with the man, but he's a part of her life now.

Regardless of that, I hear what Lo is saying. All this time, I've been the exception to Lo's cut-throat attitude.

Neither of us knew each other's histories, but I think deep down, we both always sensed that parts of us were the same.

The broken parts.

Maybe he's just healed before I've gotten the chance to. Maybe I won't be able to. Maybe this is it for me, you know? I'm going to live forever with this thing inside of me, bearing down on all that I am. And it fucking hurts. It just hurts.

I keep rubbing at my face, the tears not ceasing. *Please, just stop.* My body is warring with what I want. *Stop crying. Stop crying. Goddammit, stop fucking crying.*

My sleeves are soaked, and Lo scoots nearer. "You'll be okay," he breathes. "You won't see it today, maybe not even tomorrow, but one day, you'll wake up and you'll want to live."

I choke back a sob. What he's saying seems more like a dream not made for me. I shut my eyes and open them. "Are you sure?"

"I'm goddamn sure. Look at me…"

It takes me a second to raise my head, hair still falling over my eyes, shielding me like armor.

Lo says deeply, "One day at a time. Can you do that with me?"

My throat swells. Lights in the kitchen are harsh on my sensitive, swollen eyes. *One day at time.* I'd reject that fantasy under different stipulations. I'm not made to be by myself. Not wired that way.

And that's okay, I think.

Because he's not just saying *one day at a time.* It's one day at a time with him.

With someone.

Not alone.

Okay.

Okay.

Quiet stretches around us, Loren just sitting by and waiting for me to collect my thoughts. I can do this. I can accept something good for my life. Nodding repeatedly, I finally make my decision. But I still have one last thing left that connects me to my family. One thing left to claim and then I can cut ties completely.

I glance to Lo. "…will you do something for me, if I move in with you?" My stomach twists, not wanting to ask too much, but needing this.

"Yeah."

My face scrunches at his lack of hesitation. "You don't even know what it is."

"Doesn't matter."

"I want you to kill someone," I deadpan. It's a bad attempt at humor. But he's the one who's blindly trusting me. No questions asked.

Lo glares. "You joke, but have you met me?"

I narrow my eyes. Look, I don't know what he's capable of. Just like I don't try to think about what I could do. I take a breath before speaking, not wanting my explanation to come out dry and sarcastic. "Two days ago, I told my brothers that I'd never see them again. I don't know whether they believed me. They rarely take anything I say seriously, but I told them. I just don't want to talk or see them ever." I swallow hard, my throat raw. "So two days ago…I also left my parent's house in a hurry and accidentally forgot one of my hard drives there."

"You want me to get it for you?"

"Yeah…but just don't…" I take a deep breath.

"Don't what?"

"Don't hurt them. Alright. I know it sounds stupid as fuck, but they're still my brothers. Even if I never see them again, I just don't…just *don't* do it." There've been plenty of times where I've wished Hunter dead.

Where I envisioned my fist pounding his face.

But at the end of it all, I don't want a single living soul to feel the pain that I've felt.

Not even them.

I just want it to stop.

"I won't," he says, and after everything, I believe him. "Give me your phone. I'll go get your hard drive now."

I pass him my cell.

"What about your parents?" Lo asks. "Do they know?"

Goosebumps crawl along my arms, cold all of a sudden, but it's easier to talk. "I've told my mom, but she just says it's *boys being boys*..." I pause. "And my dad likes Davis the best. They don't care about anything except making money, and ever since I got a job with Cobalt Inc., they stopped hounding me about 'doing something with my life.' If I never checked in, never returned their calls, they'd just think I was too busy for them, and they'd probably be *proud*."

"Huh," he says, frowning. "They sound like dicks."

I choke out a laugh. "Yeah, they are."

He scrolls through my contacts. I have shit emojis next to each of my brother's names, which Lo can definitely see. His lips pull down, and I'm just glad that I didn't have to paint vivid portraits of all the crap they've done over the years for Lo to believe me.

He just did.

With our backs to the cabinets, he presses the phone to his ear, so I can't hear. It's better that way.

Lo's eyes flit to me. "Will they answer?"

I nod. "And miss an opportunity to pick on me?"

He glares off in the distance. My knees bounce a little, watching him. Waiting.

Someone must answer because Lo says, "This is Loren Hale, from down the street." He pauses and then says, "Garrison left his hard drive at your parent's place. He really needs it soon. Can you swing by and drop it in my mailbox?"

That's a good idea—better. That way Lo doesn't even have to confront them. Weight releases off my taut shoulders in an instant. Pressure evaporating from my chest, and I breathe easier and lean back with less tension.

Lo cups a hand over the cell and looks to me. "Where's the thing?"

"Basement table."

He puts the phone back to his ear. "Basement table." There's a long silence, and I don't know if one of my brothers is talking or if it's just dead quiet on the line.

Truth: I don't care.

I'm just glad I'm not the one with the phone in my hand.

"Do you want to say something?" Lo asks my brother.

I pick at the ripped hole in my jeans. They want to talk to me? My stomach twists again. *Stop.*

"Yep," Lo says on the phone, grinding his teeth. Like he tries not to lash out. He'd probably eviscerate my brothers with his words if I wasn't sitting here. But I think he's trying to be nonconfrontational... for me.

That means something.

Lo's eyes redden, and his glare intensifies on the cupboards. "Sure." He hangs up and lets out a heavy breath he'd been caging. He tosses me the phone.

"What'd he say?" I ask.

"He'll drop it in my mailbox. He's sorry, and he thinks you never speaking to all of them is a good idea." Lo shakes his head, confusion cinching his brows. Maybe he's wondering how easily my brother could let me go. But I get it.

I know.

"You called Mitchell, didn't you?" It's the only thing that makes sense. I remember the look Mitchell had in the greenhouse, right before I left. How he was staring faraway. Like something clicked in his head.

He's sorry.

I rub my dripping nose.

Letting me go is Mitchell's way of protecting me from our other two brothers.

"What is he—the nice one?" Lo asks.

"Mitchell could've stopped them," I mutter. He's closest in age to me. Two years older. "He never did. Does that make him nice?" I shake my head. "…I don't know. I never stopped my friends from breaking into your house. I never stopped *myself* from pranking you. We're all the same. We're all *shit*." He needs to remember who he's inviting into his home. I'm not a good guy. Doesn't he remember?

Lo leans forward, and with utter conviction, he says, "This guy in front of me isn't shit, and I'll still be here when you finally believe it too."

I inhale like I haven't taken a full breath in all my life.

I was wrong about my family—how I can't trade them in.

They may be blood, but they're not mine anymore.

I can choose my family. Lo gave me that option.

And I choose this one.

56

Willow Hale

"LO TOLD ME I COULD PICK ANY ROOM IN THE HOUSE THAT I wanted with one exception," Garrison explains as he folds clothes into a new dresser. I watch him on Skype. Boxes surround him, and computer monitors and cords litter the queen-sized bed.

Before he officially accepted Lo's offer, he called to ask if the whole thing was a bad idea. He wanted to make sure that I was on board.

My boyfriend moving into my brother's house.

In Garrison's words: *"If you become unhappy in our relationship and this makes it harder for you to break up with me—then I won't do it."*

He's always thinking about me, in most everything. Even in some strange reality where I'd break up with him, he thinks about me. By the way, that's a reality that I refuse to believe will ever come true.

During the same phone call, Garrison spilled everything about his brothers. How they hurt him during the holidays and then again in the greenhouse. How his mom did nothing.

It gutted me, but I tried to stay strong over the line for him. Towards the end, we were both crying. I wish I could've been there.

With him.

His drunken anger in London made more sense, and guilt gnawed at me for not flying home with him that night. Garrison said he wouldn't have wanted me to, but I'll regret it forever.

"I regret a lot," I told him on the phone, wiping at my tears. "I could've confronted your mom or told Lo sooner—"

"No," Garrison forced out. "We were teenagers."

"I'm not a teenager anymore."

I could hear his tears and cracking voice. "What happened isn't on you, Willow. You left everything you knew to come to Philly. And you came here to meet your brother. Saving me wasn't your job. It's *mine*. And you know how many times I wanted to confront *your* mom but never did?"

He's been pissed about how easily she's erased me from her life.

"She's thousands of miles away in Maine," I said in quiet protest. "Your mom lives down the street."

"So what? I could've flown there. I have money."

I felt terrible for making this about me. "I'm sorry." I grimaced at the apology, hearing my best friend Daisy telling me not to apologize for my feelings. Even though it's hard. I sniffed back emotion and loosened my grip on the phone. "Sometimes I think that I'm a nonentity in so many people's lives—shy, timid Willow Hale," I whispered, "and I'm afraid of being a nonentity in yours." He's my guy, my only love, and it's terrifying to think that I could be this invisible shadow to the person who's been my everything.

"You've never been a nonentity to me, Willow," Garrison breathed. "From the first time we touched, you became my world and safe place. I'm so in love with you that my heart feels like it's being ripped to shreds just knowing you're sad, and I'm stuck here, sitting on this crappy floor. Wishing I could hug you."

I was sitting on the floor too. I told him that.

We laughed softly. Sadly.

I hugged my arm around my body, pretending that Garrison was with me. "Don't push me too far away that I can't ever reach you again, okay?"

"Okay." We listened to our breath over the line for a while. It sounds creepier than cute, but it felt…calming. To hear him ease and our tears dry.

So that was *the* phone call.

A big one.

All I can do is think about *now*.

How he's moving into my brother's house, and we're currently on a Skype call.

This move is a great thing for him. He'll be surrounded by people who care about him and love him. Happy doesn't even come close to what I'm feeling.

I've been grinning so much these past couple days that my cheeks hurt.

"Which room did you pick?" I ask Garrison. Back on Skype, I squint at my computer screen, trying to decipher which room he chose in the big eight-bedroom Hale house.

At one time, over half of the rooms were occupied. Way back when Lily, Loren, Ryke, Daisy, Connor, Rose, and I all lived under the same roof. Hard to believe that happened at all—but it did.

Now that it's just Lily and Loren and their three-year-old son, it must be a quieter house.

"I almost picked Ryke and Daisy's old room," Garrison tells me. "But then Lo said that I wasn't allowed because it's the smallest guest room in the house and I'm not permitted to do that to myself out of guilt."

Sounds like Lo.

Garrison starts untangling his wad of cords. "And I thought about your old room, but it'd be too weird. So I chose the guest room at the end of the hall, three doors down from Maximoff's. You remember it? It's the one with the paisley wallpaper."

I nod, still smiling. "Is that the one Lo says gives him a migraine every time he goes inside?"

Garrison laughs, a real heartfelt laugh. "That'd be the one." He glances at the screen, our eyes meeting for a beat.

I push up my glasses. "I wish I were there to help you move in."

I almost bought a ticket, but Garrison told me not to miss my first week of classes for him. That we'd Skype instead.

"You are here," Garrison reminds me. His positivity is palpable, and it runs through me like a drug. "Pick a wall for my poster." He travels around the room with his laptop.

"By the window," I say.

He smiles wide. "We are two minds in one. Who knew, I was thinking the same exact thing." The way he says it—he definitely wasn't.

"Uh-huh. Sure." I match his smile. It's contagious.

"I love your choice," he says. "That's exactly where it's going and I'm going to think about you every time I look at it."

My chest swells, and I wish I had that reminder in my room. I glance at the photograph of us on my nightstand. We're both lounging on the dock at the lake house, the sun setting, and he's kissing my cheek.

Garrison places the laptop on the dresser, the spot that lets me see most of his room. He grabs a hoodie from a box and tosses the clothing in a trash bag. He already told me he's throwing away every hoodie he owns. *New start. New look.* "How's school?" he asks.

I'm about to answer but the door opens abruptly. "Uncle Garrison!" The dark-haired toddler rushes in and belly flops onto Garrison's bed.

"Heyheyhey!" Lo calls out from the doorway. "What'd we say about knocking?"

Maximoff picks himself up from the mattress and turns to his dad. "I have to knocks before I enters," he slurs the words a little.

"Try again, bud," Lo says and then gives Garrison an apologetic look.

Garrison is full-on grinning.

Maximoff goes outside and knocks on the door. I hear Lo say, "And now what do you ask?"

"UNCLE GARRISON?!" Maximoff screams at the top of his lungs. "CAN I COME PLAY WITH YOU?!"

Garrison laughs. "Yeah, kid, come on in."

Maximoff just started calling Garrison his uncle. Even though they're not related. He'd be his actual uncle if Garrison and I got married, but we haven't really discussed that possibility. It can't be on Garrison's radar if he's thinking I'm going to break up with him.

I wouldn't.

The door opens and Maximoff bounds back inside. "Can I—can I help you unpack?" he asks with these big green eyes that are so Lily—it's impossible not to fall prey to them.

Garrison nods.

Lo notices the laptop screen. "Is that my sister?" Lo asks me, brows raised.

"I'm here in the…not-so-flesh," I say.

"Just a bunch of ones and zeroes," Garrison adds, and while standing behind Lo, my boyfriend winks at me. It's sexy enough that I blush.

Lo frowns and looks over his shoulder. "Are you two flirting in nerd?"

"Man, we're not nerds," Garrison snaps. "Aren't the nerd stars a few houses down the street?" Lily affectionately refers to Connor and Rose as the "nerd stars" but the Cobalts are so far from what you'd picture a stereotypical nerd. If anything, I fit the bill the most. Glasses, comic-book loving introvert.

Lo touches his chest. "Forgive me, you two are flirting in geek."

Garrison raises his brows. "That's you and your wife." Lily and Lo are the superhero-obsessed ones, sometimes even more than me.

Maximoff picks up a pillow and tosses it at his dad. Lo dodges it like it's nothing, his focus on Garrison. "Christ, you and words. Fine, you're flirting in computer shit or whatever you youths calls it."

"Binary," Garrison says.

"What?" Lo's brows knot.

"It's a binary numer—you know what, never mind."

"Good, I was thinking this was going to turn into a lesson," Lo smiles his half-smile. "You do know I dropped out of college."

"You tell us every chance you can get," I say lightly.

Lo turns back to the computer. "My sister with the jokes." He cracks another smile. "London is going well then?"

"Yeah, really well."

Lo's phone rings and he excuses himself to answer the call. Just as he leaves, I hear him say, "Hey, Dad."

My stomach twists, unsettled all of a sudden.

Maximoff rips the tape off one of the smaller boxes, helping Garrison. It's a good distraction for him, and I need a second to myself so that I don't look like I'm about to puke.

Because I'm hiding something from Garrison. From my brothers. And if I can, I'd like to take this to my grave.

It's about that night in London when Garrison visited.

After he flew home and I stayed back, I did some damage control. Students filmed Garrison punching Salvatore, and I saw the look on Garrison's face. If that footage leaked online, he would've been prime fodder for the media. We both have been memes before, and it's only ever easy when you're emotionally and mentally prepared to handle it.

It'd destroy him, and since Connor Cobalt—the usual damage control expert—wasn't around, I had to think of different resources. I couldn't call Lo or Ryke without alerting them that Garrison was drunk, and he made me promise not to say anything.

So there was only one person left.

My dad.

Jonathan Hale.

I did what I swore I would never do after he cut me a check for school.

I asked him for more money.

He gave me a hundred grand. He knew what it was for and wanted to help. Though, he called it "pennies" which I found…a little insulting. A hundred grand is a fortune to me. And it was enough to put my plan into action.

Sheetal had filmed the whole fight, and I was able to identify everyone with cameras who recorded Garrison. Luckily, Tess knew most of the students at Bishop Hall that night. So I gave them cash in exchange for the footage. They deleted their videos from the cloud and cells.

I, *Willow Hale*, paid people off with Jonathan Hale's money.

Ryke has constantly warned me about our dad. I know he doesn't give things without something in return. Allegiance. Time. I'm not sure what he'll ask for, but I never wanted to feel indebted to him. Now…it's all I feel. And what happens when he comes to collect?

Or worse, what happens if Lo, Ryke, or Garrison find out?

They can't. *They can't.*

I practically carve those words into stone.

August

57

Willow Hale

"WHAT'D YOU SAY?!" I TRY TO YELL OVER THE THUMPING BASS, a phone pressed to one ear while I plug the other ear with my finger.

I still can't hear my best friend over the flat party. Beer pong cheering, thumps of drunken bodies, and house music cranked to head-splitting levels—I'm in a noisy tunnel of collegiate pandemonium. Who throws ragers on a Wednesday at seven p.m.?

My roommates, apparently.

A little earlier, Sheetal popped her head in my room. "We're having a proper get-together, like. Need anything, a bevvie or a ciggy?" The party was already underway.

It was nice of her to remember that I'm here. I'm not invisible to my friends-turned-new-roommates: Sheetal, Tess, and Salvatore.

But I would've preferred an hour's notice, and if I'm being really honest with myself, I would've wanted a full day's preparation knowing we're hosting a *house* party.

After declining drinks and cigarettes, I keep thinking it'll die down, but it's only grown. I keep hearing the main door open. More bodies piling in. More voices amassing.

"Hold on a sec!" I raise my voice over the music and speak into my phone. "I'm gonna find a quieter spot, Daisy!" I scan the small room, more cramped than my old dorm. A light blue comforter is wrinkled on a twin-sized bed, hugged against a white wall.

Most of my crap is still in a few cardboard boxes. But I've had some time to tack up a few X-Men posters and unbox photos of my brothers, the Calloway sisters, and of course, my boyfriend. I did put my *Gravity Falls* Funko Pop! collectibles on the dresser. No room for a desk.

Still, I'm lucky that I have all this space to myself, and I only share a bathroom and common area.

I eye the tiny closet.

Bingo.

I snatch the laptop off my bed before heading to the closet. It's not a walk-in. So I bend down and sit beneath hanging overalls and plain T-shirts. Wedged under the clothes, I pry my fingers under the doorframe and scoot the door towards me until it's pretty much shut.

Darkness.

And finally, some muffled quiet.

I let out a sigh.

So this is sort of what Harry Potter must've felt like. I bet he had more room under the Dursley's staircase.

I push up my drooping glasses. "Can you hear me?" I ask Daisy and open my laptop, the bright screen illuminating the closet with a blue tint.

"A ton better," Daisy tells me. "Where'd you go?"

"The closet. Maybe Skype will be louder." I'm about to ask if she has time to video-chat, but she's already dialing me on Skype.

My lip twitches in a smile, one I haven't felt much tonight. I click into her Skype call, and her radiant, photogenic face pops on screen.

"Hey there." She bites on a red Twizzler, blonde hair hanging against a crop top that says, *yeehaw!* "If Garrison wasn't coming, I'd totally fly out there and whisk you away from the madness." She tucks her long legs to her chest. "We'd ride off into the sunset away from the loud and into the quiet."

I touch my silver pinky ring, and through the computer screen, I see the identical one on her finger. My lips keep rising. "Sounds nice." I fix my glasses again. "I'm not bothering you too much, am I? I know the summer just ended, but camp stuff has to still be eating your time." She's the founder of Camp Calloway, and she's spent so much energy building this adventurous getaway for kids in the mountains.

"Camp stuff has been dying down, and I like catching up with you." She twiddles with a frayed string on her crop top, not able to sit still. "I don't want you to think...that you can't call or anything."

Daisy has a baby now, a husband, a new career, and an ocean is between us.

Sometimes it scares me too that we might drift apart, but I know, deep in my heart, that she's the friend I'll have forever. Not just because she's married to Ryke, my half-brother.

It's what she said: if she were here, she'd help me escape the party, not try to pull me deeper into it.

Daisy loves the quiet as much as me.

"I don't think that," I say softly. "I'll always call when I can."

She's about to smile, but she flinches as screaming *blasts* on my end. Screaming that usually accompanies sports games.

"I hate beer pong," I murmur under my breath.

"You can ride it out with me until Garrison gets there," Daisy suggests. "I'm just at the cottage for lunch." The cottage is her quaint stone house at the end of the cul-de-sac, down the street from Lily and Rose in Philly.

My shoulders loosen, less tensed. She doesn't pressure me to go "mingle" and try to have fun with strangers. I know who I am, and I know it's not my cup of tea. Daisy never makes me drink the anxiety-inducing concoction.

"Thanks, Daisy." I try to stretch my leg in the cramped closet, the laptop swaying on my thighs. I lift my neck, and overalls smack my face. I push them aside. "I'm hoping this party is just a first-week 'welcome back to college' celebratory thing."

Bass intensifies and vibrates the floor beneath me.

Let this be a one-time occurrence.

Please.

I'm not made for house parties. I might've found college friends in London, but I'm still the same girl who lurks in corners of comic book shops and tries not to bump into shelves or strangers. I don't want to be in anyone's way, even with my roommates.

I'm an introvert at the core, and after one big group outing, I feel like I need to recharge alone for a whole week.

Staying in and watching Netflix sounds better than hitting the bars or inviting people to throw back shots and chitchat.

The latter is…exhausting.

"Are your roommates partiers?" Daisy wonders.

"I don't think they are. I'd go with them out to Barnaby's, but that wasn't every weekend." I frown, thinking. "It was…chill. Just the three of us, and if they ever went bar hopping afterwards or met up with larger groups, I usually declined." I pause. "Tess is super popular though. She knows almost everyone on campus, and Sheetal loves staying out late. So does Salvatore…" Oh no…

Could I have really misjudged what it'd be like to room with them?

"You're probably right," Daisy consoles. "It could just be a welcome back party."

"CHUG! CHUG! CHUG!" The chanting sounds close, like a foot away.

I focus on my computer. "I can't even tell them to keep it down—I'll ruin their good time and be the stuck-up roommate." It feels unfair to ask everyone to be quiet. I'm just one person. "And I already felt badly because I didn't warn them that Garrison is coming tonight."

"They still don't like him?" Daisy asks into a bite of Twizzler.

I shake my head.

I officially moved into the flat only a few days ago, and I wanted Garrison to see where I live, even if that means running into my roommates. He's in a much better place since he's been living with Lo for eight months now. But the last time Tess and Sheetal saw my boyfriend, he was swinging a fist at Salvatore.

"We just don't talk about Garrison," I explain to Daisy. "I think they're trying to be supportive, but…it's also like we're avoiding the awkwardness of what happened."

I thought about not rooming with them after the winter party, but they hugged me and said they still wanted me here, no matter what.

Garrison was also happy they didn't abandon me over his actions, but living with college friends feels different than living with the Calloway sisters. It's starting to feel like a challenging game boss on a new console that I've never played before.

"Your roommates might warm up to him tonight. I have a theory that the worst first impressions can be the mark of a really great person," Daisy says optimistically. "So hey, there's hope yet." She swigs a water. "Are you escaping the party with Garrison once he gets there?"

I frown, realizing everything is all messed up. "That wasn't the initial plan."

"Do you plan on *ravishing* each other to the bone?" Daisy teases with the wag of her brows.

My neck reddens. "Um…sort of."

"Willow," she gasps into a bigger smile. "What's '*sort of*' mean here?"

"I want to give him a blow job tonight—the first one I've ever given. And I've already been nervous about it."

"Nervous about what?" Rose asks icily, and on the screen, I see Daisy looking off to the side, like her sister just entered the cottage.

"Hey, Daisy," Lily greets.

Make that *sisters*. Plural.

I'm just glad they walked in and not my older brothers. After a few minutes of catch-up, Lily and Rose join Daisy on a couch with boxes of Thai take-out. They fit into the Skype box, so they're visible and ready to take part in my awkward dilemma.

I'm in a closet.

Avoiding a flat party in my own flat.

And discussing blow jobs. "I already Googled how to give one, and it's not a lot of help. They just talk about being confident. I'm more worried about the mechanics of a blow job. I want to be sure I'm not awkwardly going down on him or hurting him."

"You don't have to give him a blow job," Daisy reminds me. "I don't love giving them that much."

Lily blushes a little as she says, "I think they're fun." Quieter, she adds, "It's hot." Her shoulders rise as she nods to herself.

"At times, definitely," Rose agrees, popping open a container of what she said is Pad Kee Mao. "Other times, it's a pain in the ass, and I avoid."

"I want to try," I say more confidently. "Just to see if I like it or not. Garrison won't pressure me, one way or the other, he never has."

"You should practice," Rose coaches.

"With...like a banana?" I look around the closet for something phallic.

"Just wing it," Daisy suggests.

Rose cringes at those words.

Daisy mock gasps and says dramatically, "The disgust."

Lily laughs.

My heart does a weird nosedive. I miss them. Being around them. *Living* with them. Even if they've all moved into separate houses, they live on the same street from one another.

And Rose raises a hand to both of her sisters before scooting closer to the screen. "Willow, I was a lot like you."

"You were?" Fearless, fierce Rose Calloway, who makes men shrivel and quake. I know her better than when I first moved to Philly. She's not just a face on a Forbes magazine or the star of the short-lived *Princesses of Philly* to me. She's complicated and complex, and so I'm not too shocked.

"Nervous about giving a Grade F blow job, yes." Rose loves to succeed.

"What made you feel better?"

Rose takes a breath as she says, "Connor. He was patient and made me feel..." She rolls her eyes. "Like we were practicing together and that I had nothing to prove but everything to gain. So you don't need to practice alone beforehand. You can practice *with* Garrison."

Lily pops open a can of Fizz. "That's good advice, Rose."

"I know."

We laugh.

Daisy nods. "See, even if it's awkward, it's awkward with someone who makes you feel comfortable, therefore the awkwardness is nullified, and all shall prevail." She extends her arms theatrically.

"For…" I trail off, my thoughts dying as music grows ten octaves louder. Like my door has just opened…

I stiffen.

Oh no.

"What's wrong?" Rose asks, straightening up.

"Willow?" Daisy and Lily say at the same time.

"I forgot to lock my door," I whisper and strain my ears. Floor-boards creak, accompanied by giggling. "I think someone's in my room."

"Kick those motherfuckers out," Rose snaps, yellow-green eyes pierced like she's two-seconds from crawling through my laptop screen and fighting them for me.

"What's going on?"

Oh, *shit*.

That voice, that question—it's coming from *their* end. I watch their heads swerve at the sound of Loren Hale.

My brother.

And he's not alone. He stands behind the couch with Ryke Meadows. Both of my brothers bend over to peer at the Skype session.

"Willow?" Ryke's face darkens. "What the fuck is happening?"

Daisy explains everything quickly. *Thank you.* I use the time to listen to the intruders. The music dies down, and I'm guessing they shut my door.

My pulse speeds.

Okay.

You can handle this, Willow. They're just partiers. They probably don't know that this room belongs to a semi-famous person. I'm on the periphery of fame.

They won't steal your things.

Just…let it pass.

"Willow," Lo says sharply, grabbing my attention.

"Yeah?" I nudge up my glasses for the umpteenth time

"Are they gone?"

I shake my head. "I hear…" I cringe. *No, no.* "…slurping."

Daisy's mouth falls. "They're making out."

"Abort," Lily says. "*Abort.*"

Nervous heat pricks me at the thought of a confrontation. "I can't…"

"Go tell them to get the fuck out of your room," Ryke says harshly. I'm not him. I'm not Rose or Lo.

The hot-tempered triad (Lily coined the term) could resolve this fast and efficiently.

My face contorts at the sound of my bed squeaking and *mmms.* I look up at the darkness of my closet. "Just my luck," I mutter to myself, "two strangers are desecrating my bed when Garrison is supposed to be here soon—and how can I give him a blow job for the first time on the same place where strangers just touched?" *Wait.* I freeze.

I didn't just say that out loud. In front of my brothers.

To Lo, Ryke asks, "Did she just fucking say she's giving Garrison a blow job for the first time?"

I did.

Lo shoots him a look. "Thanks for repeating that. Like I didn't need to bleach my brain before."

"I thought she's already had sex with him," Ryke says in confusion.

"Huh." Lo's brows scrunch. "Does that mean you're still a vir—"

"No," I say quickly.

Cremate me, please. I hide behind my hanging overalls.

Rose snaps, "Blow jobs don't have to come before sex."

I'm shriveling like a withering flower, and the Calloway sisters tell them to stay out of it, coming to my defense.

It's easier to focus on the strangers making out on my bed now. I want to escape the embarrassment of Lo and Ryke knowing I'm planning to give Garrison a blow job.

538 **KRISTA & BECCA RITCHIE**

I tuck my laptop to my chest. "I'm going out there."

"Good," Lo says.

"We're here," Rose reminds me.

Daisy makes a heart shape with her hands.

They all watch me like this is a college-aged flick that they're very much invested in, and quietly, I push the door open.

"Right *there*, Mattie. *God*," she moans, not even hearing me crawl out of the closet.

I stand up. "Oh." I shield my face with a hand, blocking out the scene of a twenty-something dude going down on a girl in a miniskirt and floral crop top.

Should've stopped them sooner, Willow.

This is my penance. My dues that I must pay. "Um," I start to say.

She gasps at the sight of me. "Mattie. Mattie!" Bed squeaks as they shift.

"Can you please leave?" My cheeks are hot. "This is my room."

"Were you hiding in the closet watching us?" Mattie accuses heatedly, slurring some of his words, American accent and drunk-self clear.

"The fucking *nerve* of that asshole," Rose says loudly on the computer, which is faced towards my body. Not the strangers.

I drop my hand from my face.

They're staring at the computer with confusion. So they definitely heard Rose.

I try to play it off as nothing. "Uh...no," I tell them. "I was in the closet to block out the party. It was loud."

"You don't owe them a fucking explanation," Ryke growls.

Mattie makes a noise of shock. "Is that Ryke Meadows?"

I should've muted the video chat.

The girl fixes her askew skirt as she stands, ignoring her hookup buddy or boyfriend or whoever.

Mattie squints, trying to place me. "You're that girl." He sways as he rises off my bed. "What's her name, Dina?" he asks the brunette.

"You know the dorky one with the glasses? She rarely talks and she's always hanging around the hot blonde Calloway?"

I'm standing right here.

I don't back up. Trying to hold my ground.

"I don't know," Dina says, putting her hair into a ponytail. "She asked us to leave, let's go."

"Thank you," I say too softly. I'm not sure anyone can hear.

Mattie holds out a hand. "Wait, hold on."

I shake my head. "The party is out there." I motion to the door, laptop in my other grip.

"Come on, don't be like that," Mattie says, sounding kind. He offers me an amicable smile. "I'm even wearing the underwear Ryke, Lo, and Connor modeled for charity this summer."

Dina snorts like *yeah right*. Like he's lying, and then she exits the room.

Leaving me alone with him.

He watches the door click shut.

My heart rate speeds. "Um...could you please go? I'm kind of busy."

Mattie smiles back at me. "Do you have time for a drin—"

"Open your fucking ears!" Lo yells so loud, my speakers crackle. "She told you a hundred goddamn times to get out of her room. So get the fuck out before I make your life a *living* hell—you'll wish all I did was break your dick in two." His voice is dripping in acid.

Mattie looks...scared, just from hearing Lo. He doesn't even see the venomous glare attached.

"I...uh," Mattie stammers. "Is that...?" Befuddlement crosses his face, and I step forward and sort of corral him out, all without touching him.

I'm lucky that he doesn't put a hand on me.

"Wait..." He gawks, dazedly leaving my room.

I shut and lock the door.

"Thanks," I tell everyone on the computer. "I have this now." They voice encouragements and "stay safes" before I close the laptop.

Anxious heat still clings to me, even though the guy is gone.

It's in these moments that I wish I took up meditation. Daisy suggested it. She's been doing twenty-minute sessions in her treehouse every morning with Sulli. It's apparently good to refocus the mind. I need some intense refocusing.

A message pings my phone.

Garrison: Landed. In cab. See you soon *pizza emoji* *smiley face emoji* *heart emoji*

My anticipation ratchets up, and I quickly text him the apartment building's door code. I was going to meet him at the airport, but he said he'd meet me here. He knows I get anxiety at airports, but I wish I braved it for him tonight.

It would've been better than staying behind at this party. But just thinking about confronting the airport crowds made me break out in a nervous sweat for two hours.

I let out a tense breath and rest my back on the thumping wall. Music still blasting. Chants of "chug, chug, chug!" still happening.

And then I eye the smashed pillows and crumpled comforter. Gross.

Strip the bed, Willow.

I move my feet and do just that.

58

Garrison Abbey

ONCE I'M IN THE APARTMENT COMPLEX, I HEAR CLUB MUSIC and drunken laughter, and I'm thinking there's no way that's my girl's place.

A house party?

On a Wednesday?

It sounds like Willow's worst nightmare. Yet, I stroll up to the ajar door where the noise booms out. Weekend-duffel slung on my shoulder, I double-check the apartment number.

This is her flat.

What if she likes parties now? I'd like to believe she hasn't changed so much that I don't know her anymore. We saw each other a decent amount this summer.

I push into the rowdy, packed apartment. About fifty students here. Already hammered. Guys are wobbling and spilling their shit on furniture. Beer. Liquor. Fizz.

I glance back at the door. Can't believe that was literally half-opened.

Any stalker or creep could just prance right on through. This is a serial killer's wet dream and the way idiots die at the start of horror flicks, before the movie title even appears.

Thinking about someone killing Willow makes me nauseous. I rub a hand over my mouth, and stepping forward, my black Converse crunches a beer can.

"Drink it! Drink it!" college students shout as a guy sucks a shot off a girl's belly button, lying on the beer pong table.

Not even one more foot forward and a familiar face confronts me. Salvatore Amadio, AKA the vampire-knockoff that I knocked out, blocks my path.

Awesome.

Here we go already.

Two button-down preppy dudes flank him. A pen is in Salvatore's mouth like he'd been scoring some drinking game, and a glass of whiskey is in his hand. His plaid pants would look douchey on just about anyone, so I try not to judge him for it.

"Hey, man," I greet. "Sorry about…" I motion to my cheek, even though I hit *his* cheek before.

He glares.

I'm so great at making friends. God, it's weird to think that at one point, I was extremely popular.

I nod. "Right. Look, you know which one is Willow's room?" I dig my hand in a pocket for my phone. Planning to text her anyway.

Salvatore takes the pen out of his mouth with arrogance, like he's the big man on campus. "You're not welcome here."

He's got to be shitting me. "My girlfriend lives here."

"Exactly." He has these annoying overprotective eyes. Like he's still trying to protect Willow from me, and it's just…

I let out an irritated laugh. "Wow, you must be *so* concerned about the safety of your roommate. Leaving the front door *wide open* for anyone and their creep cousin to stroll through, that's real smart shit right there—"

"A creep like you." He steps forward, about to physically push me out, and I move backwards on instinct, away from his hands.

My pulse jacks up. "I'm not looking for a fight, man." I stop in the doorway. Refusing to be kicked out.

Taller than me, Salvatore grips the frame above my head. "You're lucky I'm not decking you in the face after you sucker-punched me."

Sucker-punch.

Fuck, I don't think I'd call it that. I'm not that strong. Or at least, I wasn't. Now that I live with Lo, I have access to his home gym and he practically pulls me down there every night to do reps with him.

In Lo's words: *exercise is good for people like us.*

Sometimes it does pull me out of bad moods.

"Appreciate it," I tell Salvatore, "but I'm here to see Willow. She knows I'm coming."

"She didn't tell me about it."

Yeah.

I know.

Willow told me she was working herself up to it, and I don't blame her for not wanting to get into drama with her new roommates.

Agitation gathers. "I didn't realize my girlfriend needed to send you personal memos every time she breathes."

He shoves my chest, hard and quick.

I stumble out, tripping over my feet, and he slams the door in my face.

Me and my fucking mouth. My pulse is in my throat now that he touched me. I'm not a fighter.

I flee, but he doesn't know that.

Swallowing my heart rate, I try to call Willow.

The line rings out, and I send a text: I'm here. Salvatore locked me out.

Yeah, I'm throwing the douchebag under the proverbial bus. He can eat shit.

My phone vibrates.

Lo: You there yet? There's a party at Willow's flat. Make sure this prick named Mattie isn't in her room or around her.

What the fuck is happening?

Worry mounts, and I pound a fist on the door. "WILLOW! WILLOW!"

The door swings open.

And this time, it's her. Glasses slip down her nose, beer spilt on her plain blue tee and jeans. "I'm so sorry. I didn't hear your call over this...?" She winces at the party behind her and looks uncomfortable, shoulders bowed in and head ducked.

I come inside and shut the front door behind me. "You didn't know they were throwing a party?"

She shakes her head.

Fuck.

She rubs her arm. "How was the flight?" She says something else, but I can't hear her soft voice over the noise.

"What?" I lean into Willow, a hand on her waist.

She takes a breath and whispers in my ear, "Do you need to a shower, after all the traveling?"

"Yeah, that'd be good." I eye the glares from Salvatore and his guy friends.

She follows my gaze and shoots them a look like, *stop*. The force dies as the front door whooshes open behind us and more students file in with cases of beer.

Willow tries to step out of the way, but she bumps into another girl. "Sorry," she whispers, and I clasp her hand. Drawing her into my chest.

She clutches onto my waist and calms more.

My mouth brushes her ear. "Where's the bathroom?"

"Down that hall." She points to the left.

I wrap an arm around her frame, and Willow leans into me while I guide her through the party. Once we're in the small bathroom, I lock the door.

We'll probably get shit for occupying the only bathroom here, but I don't care. This is Willow's apartment too.

"This isn't how I wanted you to see my new place," Willow says softly. "With people that I don't even *know*."

I drop my duffel on the bathmat. "Like this Mattie guy?"

Her eyes bug, then realization washes over. "Lo told you?"

"Not much." I push hair out of my eyes. "Can you fill me in here?"

She does. The whole story. It takes probably ten minutes, and we're both leaning against the sink cabinets, my arm around her hips.

It's a lot to digest. "If you see Mattie, point him out to me?"

With two arms, Willow hugs me around the waist while we stand side by side, her touch still feather-light. "You don't…you wouldn't want to confront him…right?"

"I'd just like to keep an eye on him. Know your enemies and all that."

She relaxes. "If I see him, I'll let you know."

I skim her more now.

Willow wets her lips and looks nervously at the tiled floor but also, she's smiling. "You're thinking about the other part of the story, aren't you?"

I smile back. She's so cute. "The blow job part."

She talks to me, not the floor. "I thought about omitting that, but I figured it might be better to just tell you, so we can…practice."

Have I imagined Willow sucking me off? *Yeah.*

But I'd be okay with never getting head if that's what she preferred. It's not necessary inside our living, breathing soul-deep connection.

"Let's practice." I pull my shirt off my head.

"Um…do I…?" She's about to drop to her knees, but I catch her waist and pull her against my body.

Cupping her cheek, I tenderly, slowly draw her lips to mine. We kiss, consuming this trembling affection that pumps blood. Heady and electric.

Her fingers curl around the waistband of my jeans. I taste her eagerness and desire, and I track kisses down her neck. Her body bows into me. Closer, her breath shallowing.

Christ.

My dick stirs, and I trail my hand between her shoulder blades. I feel wetness from *beer*, and I pull back to ask, "Did you drink a beer?"

Willow glances at her stained clothes. "No, when you texted, I rushed to the door so fast that I knocked into someone's Guinness."

I hold her face. My heart is beating double-time for this girl. "You want to take a shower with me?"

Her lips part, then eyes widen on the tub-shower. "I, uh…"

"You can say *no*." I press my lips to her forehead. "No pressure, Willow."

She thinks quietly, her hand now in mine. She doesn't let go, and I feel her fingers tighten around mine. "Okay."

"You sure?"

"I want to," Willow says, sounding assured. She fumbles with the buttons to *my* jeans, and I undo hers. Unzipping, I see the star pattern of her panties.

I dive my hand down to her ass, and she shuts her eyes, craving. Wanting. The same physical and emotional current runs through my veins. We shed each other to just aching skin, and I kiss her deeply while I reach out and crank on the faucet.

Water pours through the tub before I flick a switch. Heat cascades from the showerhead.

She takes off her glasses, setting them on the toilet lid, and we step in together. I help Willow so she doesn't fall. Close-up, she can see somewhat without glasses, but further away, it's all blurry.

I sling the shower curtain, closing us into the small space.

Vapor cocoons us, water drenching bodies and hair. I push mine out of my eyes, and I can see Willow descending into her head. Naked and vulnerable. Her shoulders turn in.

I bring her closer to me and hold my girlfriend for a second. Hugging her to my chest. I feel her speeding heart.

"You can bail at any time," I remind Willow.

"I don't want to," she murmurs. "I want this. I'm trying not to think too much and just…*feel*." She looks up into me and goes for the kiss.

I smile against her lips, and my hand roams along the curves and valleys of her soft skin. Parting her mouth with my tongue, I deepen the kiss, drawing a gentle moan from her body. *Fuck.* I harden.

She glances down, feeling me.

I let out a rough noise between my teeth. "Fuck, I want you."

Willow smiles. "You do?"

I whisper against her mouth, "More than air." I comb her wet hair off her cheeks. "You're beautiful, Willow Hale. Inside, outside, online, offline."

"You know, you are too."

"Nah. Not as much as you."

She loosens her arms, and her knees do this weird jerky thing. Like she almost drops down, but she stops herself too suddenly.

I put a hand to her shoulder. "You'll be at a good height if you kneel."

Willow, more confidently, lowers to her knees. My build blocks most of the water spray, so she's not being drowned. She rests an uncertain hand on my ass. "I might not be any good at this."

"You don't have to be good." I hold the back of her head, more tenderly. "We're in this together."

Her lips rise, excitement flickering in her brown eyes.

I palm my erection, and I drink in Willow's body and emotion before taking her hand in mine and showing her what I like. Wrapping her hand around the base of my shaft.

She opens her mouth. Tentative. I arch my hips forward since she's not moving her body or hand.

"Wider," I instruct. "Wrap your lips around your teeth."

She does, uncertain.

I nod to her. "That's it." Her lips glide against my hardness, taking me in her mouth, and the sensitivity shoots up my spine. *Christ, that feels...* "Fuck."

She pulls back. "Did I hurt you?"

"No, no. That felt amazing."

Willow brightens, and she tries again. My muscles pull taut, just watching my erection fit between her lips.

Fuuuck. My hand tightens on the back of her head. "Willow," I groan, and her free hand descends between her spread knees. Touching herself.

I light up. On fire.

Her teeth suddenly scratch my flesh. I try to stifle a wince, but she sees and pulls back. "Sorry, did I—"

"It's okay." If I wasn't so pent-up and if I didn't want to please her so badly, I'd probably coach her to try again.

But I descend to my knees. "Will you stand up?" I ask.

Her face falls. "It was that bad?"

Shit. "It wasn't close to bad. I just want you too much."

Her breath comes short and aching, and she kisses my cheek before standing. I drape her leg over my shoulder, our gazes diving deep, and I skim my lips against the inside of her thigh before I suck her clit. Kissing her heat.

"Ahh, *I*…oh my God." She clenches my wet hair. Body rattling and twitching in arousal.

She tastes like bliss. An ecstasy I want to drown into, and she taps my shoulder, alerting me that she wants to come with me inside of her.

We've fucked enough that I know that *tap*, and I drop her foot gently and then lift her at the thighs.

Breath jettisons from her mouth. "Garrison," she cries in want.

Our lips are parted and skim, as though to kiss, but we can't catch our breathes. Tension pulled, and I bring her back to the tiled wall.

She buries her head in my shoulder. "Please."

I push into my girl. Slow, carefully, and she gasps into a shudder. Her body trembling against me. My eyes almost roll back. God, the sensation, the warmth, her wetness—it's overwhelming.

Holding her, I rock, thrusting my hips, and the friction ignites between us. Steam making it hard to breathe, and the raps on the door and drunken complaints to "hurry up" are distant.

It's just me and her.

It's been us for a while, and I'm not letting her go. Against better judgment. Against all odds. I'm not leaving this girl.

She hangs onto me, and I fill her up, in and out. Muscles burning for more and longer, but we reach that peak together.

Once I feel her contract around me, it's over. I come, groaning out her name, and she cries into my neck. Pleasured cries.

Slowly, we come down, and we end up sinking to the bottom of the tub. Water raining on us, Willow is more tucked into herself, forearms covering her chest. Head bowed down. Sometimes after sex, she gets like this. More cerebral and closed-off.

But she's across my lap, sort of between my legs, and I have my arms wrapped around her frame, holding her in the position she feels most comfortable.

She nestles her head closer to my chest.

"You replaying it?" I ask against her ear.

She nods.

"Well, just so you know, Willow Hale," I breathe, "I loved it and I love you."

Willow smiles, then looks up at me. "I loved it too."

I nod, already knowing. But it feels good hearing that she's not second-guessing anything. After a few minutes, letting our heart rates descend together, we rise, and I wash her hair. She scrubs shampoo through mine. We laugh and joke, and everything feels about normal.

Except we're not in Philly.

London.

I'm here just for now. By the time we exit and dry off, we realize the music isn't on and the chatter is gone.

"The party must be over," Willow says, knotting a towel around her body. Black-rimmed glasses back on.

I could wear clean clothes from my duffel, but I think she'd feel more comfortable if we both went out in towels. So I tie a towel at my waist.

"I'll check." I open the door, and I see a graveyard of college debauchery. Spilt alcohol, bottles, cans, and cups—so many fucking cups. "Yep, it's over." I don't see Tess or Sheetal, but I'm guessing they're in their room or maybe they went out to a bar.

I grab my duffel, and when we exit into the common area, I roll my eyes at the sight of *Salvatore.*

Willow pales, holding breath.

At least the douche is cleaning his mess, plucking bottles off the kitchen counter and shoving them in a trash bag.

We exchange a glare but no words.

He makes a show of looking from her towel to mine. He zeroes in on my tattoos. Then to my girlfriend, he says, "If you need anything, Willow, just call me."

Don't be a dick.

Don't be a dick.

I bite down on my teeth.

"I'll be fine," Willow says softly and turns more to me. "That's my room." She motions to a door past the kitchen. Her phone suddenly rings, and I can't see who calls but concern cinches her brows. "I have to take this—" She leaves quickly for her room.

Not even glancing at me.

Something is wrong.

I'm about to follow when Salvatore says, "She's been acting strange ever since December."

My jaw tics, hating how he's acting like they're BFFs and I'm no one. "Yeah?"

Bottles clink as more fill the bag. "Her whole mood changes when she gets these phone calls." His eyes hit mine. "I thought it was you that was calling."

Not me.

I'm officially freaking the fuck out.

59

Willow Hale

I STARE AT MY BEDROOM WALL AND LISTEN, HAND TO MY TOWEL on my chest and phone to my ear. "All I'm saying is that the further you get into school, the more important internships are, Willow," my dad tells me.

Normally, I wouldn't have picked up his call after epic sex (definitely one of the best) and while Garrison just got here. But I missed the last two times my dad has called.

And I made a promise not to miss the third. I thought I could swiftly tell him that I'd call back later, but I've been standing here for a solid two minutes and have yet to find a space to speak up.

Garrison is leaning on the shut door in only a towel, arms crossed. He knows who called since I mouthed, *my dad.*

My boyfriend looks supremely sexy, and as I turn towards him, I have trouble not staring at his whole being. Not just his abs and lean muscles, the towel riding low, but the ink that represents him too well and the wet strands of hair that brush his ears. The corner of his lip that wants to lift in a slight smile.

His aquamarine eyes that hold our youth and early days spent together. The friendship that became an emotional lifeline and physical bond.

My heart swells.

I look away as my dad continues, "And you don't want to be in shitty fucking low-level jobs or with the Wall Street assholes who'd see you as pus—" He stops himself before saying something crude.

Something I think he'd say in front of Ryke and Lo. But not me. He clears his throat. "I'm just saying, there are plenty of CEOs or even low levels who don't appreciate women."

I think about my mom.

She was sixteen when she slept with Jonathan. He was *much* older. Was he one of those people?

If I asked Ryke, he'd tell me unequivocally *yes*. Lo would probably hesitate before also agreeing. But maybe our dad has changed.

He obviously sees the horrible side of some people in corporate power positions. My hand sweats on my cell. I open my mouth to reply, but he cuts me off again.

"So there's Harold Johnson and Patrick Nubell, both friends of the family. I'm going to give them a call. They'll have internships waiting for you next summer—"

"Dad," I say, finally interrupting him. "I'm fine. I don't need an internship." At least, I don't want him setting one up for me.

"What kind of goddamn business school are you going to? They should be teaching you that you *need* an internship. It's a fucking requirement." He mumbles something that I can't hear before saying, "This isn't negotiable, Willow. You have to have one, and you should be intelligent enough to take advantage of family connections."

I push up my glasses. "I'll be okay finding one myself."

"I can find you better ones," he says with a tight laugh. "You're so stubborn. Just like your brothers. Rejecting me on principle rather than being smart about this."

"I just want to do it on my own," I mutter. This is one of the first times I've felt his disappointment. It's a tsunami, crashing into me, especially after all that he's given me.

This is why you didn't want to take his money, Willow. I know. I know.

But now I'm stuck.

I can feel the heat of Garrison's confusion behind me. But I don't confront it yet.

"I used to be a CEO of a Fortune 500 company, Willow. You don't discard the connections I have out of a need to show that you're a big girl. But I can compromise. I won't call them myself. I'll email you their contacts. Your name will get you through the door."

I can't even say much else; someone must call him because he abruptly tells me he has to go and to have a good night.

We hang up.

Goosebumps dot my skin, and I shiver. Garrison comes closer, his softened eyes asking if he can touch me.

I nod, and he rubs my cold arm. I've decided that my dad isn't a great person when he's meddling in my life.

Garrison's voice is a whisper as he says, "What the hell is going on Willow?"

My mouth dries.

"Your dad is trying to get you an internship?" He shakes his head, brows furrowed.

"He's paying for my second year," I remind Garrison, and I step out of his embrace to approach the dresser. I tug out a drawer. *Empty.*

I forgot most of my clothes are still in boxes.

And technically, my dad is paying for every semester here on out. College is expensive, and my years working at Superheroes & Scones don't even make a dent in tuition. Garrison offered to cover it, but I can't take money from my boyfriend.

"You always knew he would pay for it," Garrison says, taking a seat on the stripped bed. Not questioning the wadded-up comforter since I told him about Mattie and Dina. "But that didn't stop you from telling your dad to keep out of your career. You said those words a year ago, Willow. You said: *I'm making the decisions.* I was there when both of your brothers backed you up and shut that shit down."

That was a long time ago.

That was before December.

"Things have changed." I don't dig into a cardboard box for panties or a shirt. I want to face Garrison, so I stay standing.

"Something happened." He frowns deeply again. "Willow…" He rises off the mattress and comes forward.

I stiffen. My joints freezing up.

Hurt flashes in his eyes. I'm the one with secrets now. And they eat at me, slowly gnawing from the inside-out.

Concern infiltrates his face. "I'm not leaving until you tell me what happened. I can stand here all night."

"It may take longer than all night," I say softly.

His face breaks. "All week. All month. *Willow*—"

"I'm fine. It's fine," I say quickly. I need to tell him something. Maybe the *vague* truth will work without causing damage. "Recently, I took more of his money."

Garrison shakes his head like that doesn't make sense. "If you needed money, you could have come to me..." He stops short and then rubs his lips. "Shit." He's putting as many pieces together as he can. "There's a reason you didn't. Probably the same reason you're not telling me anything now."

He's smart and he's right.

I take another breath. "My brothers also don't know I took his money," I say. "I'd like to keep it that way."

He rests a hand on his head. "I live with Lo."

I force down emotion, my eyes burning. Telling him might hurt him. I shouldn't be asking him to do this for me—to keep a secret from Lo. Everything is going horribly wrong.

"Willow, if you're in trouble—"

"I'm not," I say, confident about this. "My dad just wants to get me an internship. It's harmless."

"For now," Garrison says. "You don't know what he's capable of."

"I think I do." And then, I think about my mom again. What does it say about me that I'm talking to Jonathan instead of her? In her mind, did I choose the monster?

I shudder.

Garrison walks closer, and this time, I let him put his hands on my bare shoulders. "Willow," he says. "You can tell me anything. Don't be afraid of hurting me with the truth. I can take it. I'm way better than last year."

My body grows cold. "Last year," I whisper, remembering.

"Last year, I punched your friend," Garrison says, "I started smoking again—fuck, I'm still smoking. I barely slept. I couldn't figure out how to go home without being…" He takes a tight breath. "You know it got bad for a while there, but I'm better now. I'm home by dinnertime because there's this kid that gets super upset if I'm not at the table."

Maximoff.

My heart ascends, and I blink back the welling tears.

He continues, "Waking up every morning, knowing you wouldn't be next to me, used to be gut-wrenching. Now it's bearable." *It's not supposed to hurt.* I know that he's not telling me he's moving on from me. Just that it's no longer this soul-sucking pain. It's what I've wanted for him. To be happy, somehow.

He keeps his hands on my shoulders, distancing ourselves so that we can stare head-on, but I keep breaking the gaze to look at the floor.

"I'm saying this now," Garrison breathes, "because I want you to know that I'm doing better. And you don't need to tell me anything *right now*, but I'm going to be someone you can confide in again. I promise you that."

I wipe at my eyes, water leaking. "You'll be mad at me," I say softly.

"I don't think that's possible."

When we were seventeen, I felt like all we did was confide in each other, and I want that now. I have to be honest and open. So I say, "There was footage of your fight last December. I paid the students to delete it."

He's frozen. Like a statue.

I broke him.

Tears spill down my cheeks, uncontrollable. "Garrison…" I choke on his name and touch his chest.

"You took money from Jonathan," he says, his voice tight. "Because of me." He shakes his head. "And now you feel indebted to the bastard?"

I don't feel it.

"I *am* indebted to him. It was a lot of money." I cringe after I say the words. *Way to drive that knife in further.*

"Hey, no." Garrison touches my cheek. "It's good. Your honesty—it's good, Willow. I'm glad you told me."

My chest rises and falls like I've run a marathon. "I just have to play along with whatever he wants until school ends," I tell Garrison. "Then I can reinstate my boundaries and things will go back to how they were." I have to believe that.

He grinds down on his teeth, jaw clenched, but his words are firm. "I'm here for you. Whatever you want."

"Ryke and Lo," I say again.

"Shouldn't know," he agrees. "They'll blow this up into an unimaginable degree, and I think you want a relationship with your dad after this."

I do.

Something less complicated. But I want one. I've already lost one father. I've lost a lot of family like Garrison, and I'm not ready to put another name on that list.

"Thank you," I tell Garrison.

"You're my girl," he says. "I've got your back. Always." He kisses my forehead, cementing this fact, and when we part to get dressed, I scan the dresser and go cold again.

"I…I swear I had photos here." I sweep my hand over the dresser, only the Funko Pop! collectibles remain.

Garrison comes closer. "You sure?"

"I'm *positive*." Anxious heat cakes my body, and I gape at the door. "The party…" Strangers were here.

"Shit," he curses, blinking long and hard. Our eyes meet in sad realization.

They're gone.

My family photos are gone. Stolen. I don't even need to confirm. "People probably came into my room when we were in the shower."

"I'm sorry." He wraps an arm around my shoulder. "I should've thought about how you can't lock your bedroom on the outside."

I shrug. "It's okay. I'll print more." I frown though. "I guess we need to be more mindful of our fame." I look up at him. "I had photos of us too, and they're gone." Whoever stole the pictures— they were also interested in me and Garrison. Not just the famous Calloway sisters and their men.

His chest rises in a big breath. "Yeah. I forget sometimes that we've made it onto fan sites."

"Me too." Our fame has been a slow crawl, from small notoriety to something bigger, and I'm only afraid of it mushrooming out of control. Where there's no breathing room or escape.

December

60

Garrison Abbey

"I THINK US BEING TOGETHER—LIKE SEXUALLY AND NOT JUST seventeen-year-old chaste friends—is starting to finally click with your brothers," I say on the porch of the lake house. It's this huge place that the Calloway sisters and their husbands all share and use every Christmas and other holidays and generally when they want to escape Philly and the paparazzi.

I pinch a cigarette and blow smoke up in the air, my skin freezing from fingerless gloves.

It's fucking cold as hell, and I'm still reeling from my invite here. Without even knowing if Willow could fly down for the holidays, Lo asked if I wanted to join them at the lake.

Sure, I've been living with him for almost a year now, but he could have easily left me in Philly.

Willow is bundled in a pale blue ski jacket and sits on the wooden table. She pushes up her glasses with a gloved finger. "They've known that we've been sleeping together for a while."

"Yeah, but we've been separated the majority of that time. It hasn't been in their face. Now that we're with them and also together, it's *right there*." I raise a hand to her beautiful, rosy-cheeked face.

She smiles, a giddy nervous one that lifts her carriage, like this is the first interaction we've ever had and she's bracing herself. It's magical.

It makes me smile back, and after a quiet moment that I hang onto, I say, "Honestly, I think Ryke was glaring at me this morning."

She leans closer, hands on her thighs. "He glares at everyone."

I bounce on my toes, trying to circulate blood in the cold. "This was different. His eyes said *you're sleeping with my sister. Fuck you.*"

Willow laughs. "There was no fuck you in his eyes." Her lips start to fall. "Well, if there was it *wasn't* directed at you."

She touches my shoulders, and I stop bouncing. My cigarette burns between my fingers. Even though she doesn't smoke, she joins me on most of my smoke breaks. I'm going to try and quit again—I'm going to.

Just not right now.

I think she might say something super positive, but instead her brows furrow. "I'm usually the one overthinking everything," she murmurs. "This is…different."

I nod. "I'm getting a taste of inside your head, Willow, and honestly, gotta say, I don't like it."

Her lips quirk. "They're probably not thinking about us having sex. One, that'd be weird if they zeroed in on that. Two, I'm sure they're more likely questioning whether we're going to stay together." Her eyes don't have those questions. They hold this powerful confidence.

"You don't believe we'll break up," I say, putting the cigarette back between my lips.

She shakes her head. "We've rode out the bumpy parts."

"Are the bumpy parts named Salvatore Amadio?" I wonder.

Since August, I haven't been back to London. My one weekend at their flat was enough of a hurricane between me and Mr. Dickbag. AKA vampire-knockoff. AKA Salvatore.

Willow has had a pretty rough time living at the flat. I always thought she had this perfect thing going on in London, and it doesn't make me feel better knowing it's been shitty recently.

The apartment parties are sometimes as bad as three times a week, even after she politely had a "roommate meeting" and told them house parties aren't her thing.

She was probably too polite. I wasn't there, but she rehashed the conversation. She said they sometimes remember to lower the volume of the music. But that's about it.

She still loves Tess and Sheetal, just not as roommates, and I know she'd GTFO like yesterday. But she signed a lease, and she's stuck there till May.

I don't have to love Salvatore, but I have to find a way to tolerate him while he's still her roommate. I'm trying to get there.

"Maybe one Salvatore bump," Willow says softly.

After I blow smoke up in the air, I step closer and her gloved hands wrap around me. The backdoor slides open, and Daisy's white husky bounds out, sprinting down the stairs and descending the snowy hill towards the dock.

Coconut's fur matches the white landscape, blending in with the scenery.

"Nutty!" Ryke yells and follows the husky. Heading down the deck stairs, he nods to Willow and me, and I swear there's another stern glare.

I whisper to Willow, "I'm not imagining it."

"That's his *normal* face," Willow says.

"Jesus Christ, who left the door open?" Lo's voice filters outside, and he appears in the doorway. He looks between Willow and me.

"Ryke," I answer, not caring about throwing him under the bus. He, technically, was the one who left the door open anyway.

Lo leans outside, only in a pair of drawstring pants and a short sleeve T-shirt. "Ryke, close the damn door next time!"

Ryke gives him a middle finger.

Lo is about to retreat indoors. He stays, eyes on us. "Both of you. Your room is right next to Jane's and Sulli's. Remember that tonight before you start doing things. Actually, why don't you two just not do things tonight."

Wasn't dreaming. Lo and whoever else have definitely been talking about the fact that Willow and I are having sex. Maybe because of the whole "blow job" slip-up back in August. Who knows?

Willow's eyes are saucers, skin pale.

"Do things," I say, almost near laughter. "How old are we?"

"Seven years younger than me," Lo says swiftly like he has comebacks on speed dial. "And I was censoring myself for my sister. I could definitely be cruder if you'd like. Would you like that?"

Wow, he's pissy today.

"No," I snap. "Got it. Loud and clear. All of you can have sex, but we're celibate." And I realize my mistake as soon as I say it.

"No, sweetheart, you get to be celibate just like me and Lil," Lo replies with a half-smile and all. That's right—Lily and Lo are not allowed to have sex for the six weeks after Luna was born. Since Luna Hale came into this world at the end of November, Lo still has some time left with just his hand.

"Lo," Willow mutters, "we don't get to see each other that much." Translation: we never usually get to have sex.

Lo cringes like Willow said the untranslated version. "Fine," he concedes sharply.

"We'll be quiet," I tell him. But he's already waving me off with a hand and walking into the house.

Willow and I exchange a look before breaking into laughter. It's cut short when Ryke ascends the stairs, reaching the deck with Coconut jumping excitedly beside him.

His eyes hit Willow. "Dad was just on the phone. He said he's been trying to call you."

The air deadens, and the wind suddenly picks up.

Ryke's brown eyes carry confusion. "Why is he fucking calling you so much?"

Willow shrugs. "We talk every week about school."

I guess that's not a lie. Shit, I hate that she has to lie to them. But I am glad that she's not alone in this secret. She has me.

Ryke rubs his lips. No gloves on. But he hardly looks cold. "You need to be careful, Willow."

She nods. "I know."

His warning stays with me, even after he leaves.

61

Willow Hale

SITTING AGAINST THE FROSTED WINDOWPANE, I READ A HEFTY *Fundamental Accounting Principles* textbook. The next semester starts in January, and I want to get a head start on the reading material. Last semester was tough enough, and my housing issues only makes studying harder.

I spend most days in the student center "quiet zones" and rarely go home. According to upperclassmen, the business courses only get more difficult from here.

Fire roars in the warm, spacious living room. The lake house feels as big as a lodge with vaulted ceilings and balconies that overlook robust leather furniture, wooly rugs, and the stone fireplace.

In the corner, wrapped gifts sit beneath a real fir tree, recently chopped. No ornaments hang on the branches because no one bothered to redecorate. The first fully glammed-out Christmas tree had a hidden nest of spiders.

It was a whole holiday fiasco.

I flip a page and hear the distant cries of a baby.

Must be Luna Hale or Eliot Cobalt, both newborns. The media is rampant with "baby fever" articles about Rose and Lily. Mostly, I think they're trying to determine how many children Rose and Connor will have.

The Cobalts want an *empire*, and right now Rose is pregnant with baby number five. But truthfully, I don't know what constitutes an empire. Five? Six? Fifteen?

I mean…I can't imagine fifteen Cobalt babies. That's…a lot.

Cries grow louder.

From the other side of the window nook, Garrison lifts his head from his laptop. He glances up at the tier of balconies. Hearing the baby wails too. When he drops his head, his eyes meet mine, and his feet rub against my feet. His black wool socks caressing my mustard-yellow ones.

My lips slowly rise. Not much can beat these quiet moments with Garrison Abbey. Sharing company and doing normal everyday things together.

"Do you ever think about babies?" Garrison asks suddenly and abruptly.

"Uh…babies…like the small kind?" Oh God…

What other kind are there, Willow?

Garrison licks his lips, a smile forming. "I mean, we can talk about the *big* babies in the house, but I think Lo has already taken a lot of our time this trip."

I match his smile. "Sorry…I think all functions shutdown at the word *babies* when referring to my life. I'm rebooted now."

"And?" he asks.

"And…" I take a deep breath and nudge my glasses. "I never thought much about them before. I've just been focused on getting into college, paying for college, and now trying to survive college." I close my book and hug the hard binding to my chest, thinking. "But I want the traditional route, I guess. Marriage. Then maybe a baby."

"*A* baby." Garrison emphasizes the singularity of the sentence.

I shrug. "One seems like a good start…or end…or I don't know. What do you think about babies?" Our eyes search each other deeply and eagerly, but my body roasts from head to toe. We rarely discuss *after* I graduate and what lies beyond our early twenties. I still have five semesters left in college, and those upcoming years seem like a millennium.

"Marriage first," he says into a nod. "Then a baby, maybe."

"*A* baby," I repeat his emphasis.

"One," he says, definitive. "Siblings are…" His Adam's apple bobs, swallowing hard.

His brothers.

He's cut all three of them completely out of his life. He never talks to them. Rarely talks *about* them. They're just gone, erased from his world. For good reason. But so much pain remains. Scars on bone buried under muscle and skin.

He lost his brothers.

I found mine.

But I did lose someone, too. "My sister," I say softly, remembering. "I tried calling her this morning." Back in Maine, my family still has a landline home phone.

Garrison frowns. "I thought you were done trying."

I squeeze the textbook harder to my chest. "I guess, now I am," I mutter. "She picked up and told me not to call. She said the holidays are for family and I'm not a part of hers. That if I wanted to talk to our mom, I should call her directly."

But I wanted to talk to Ellie.

My ten-year-old sister.

I've invited her to the lake house for holidays. Lo is her half-brother, but she has no interest in ever knowing him or accepting the olive branches I've held out. Ellie blocked me on social media, and every time I dial my mom, she's short with me. After I say *I love you* at the end of the call, I wait with bated breath just to hear my mom say it back. Sometimes she does.

So there's that.

"Damn," Garrison breathes out, gaze flashing hot. He strokes the side of his foot against mine in comfort. "Your sister still sounds like a brat."

I shake my head. "I deserve it."

"You don't," he says, no hesitation.

I force down the giant lump in my throat, eyes burning. "From Ellie's vantage, I chose a famous brother over her." I blink back raw sentiments. "From anyone's vantage, I chose Lo."

"That's straight bullshit, Willow," Garrison refutes, his heated gaze sinking into mine. He wears his conviction like another tattoo, ink seeping indelibly. "You chose *answers* that your mom wasn't giving you. You chose to reconnect with a brother she kept from you." He leans forward, forearms on his bent knees. "You weren't making a choice between Ellie and Lo. And your mom should be explaining *that* to your little sister—who's eleven-years younger than you. But she won't, and that's fucked up."

I bite my bottom lip, thinking this over. I'm not sure I can release the guilt I feel. I'm not sure I ever will.

Is my mom painting me as a villain to my little sister, so Ellie won't follow after me and leave her all alone in Caribou? Or is my mom just taking a backseat and not helping mend the burnt bridges between her daughters?

It's not my mom's job to heal the pain I've caused by leaving, is it?

That's my burden and my remorse to bear.

Garrison studies my face. "I get it," he says. "There are times during the day that I think maybe it's my fault I didn't try harder for a *better* relationship with my brothers. Because it's easier thinking you had some control in the situation. When in reality, there's *nothing* you or I could do to repair what was already fucking gone. They're gone, Willow. And we have to be okay with that."

My eyes redden, emotions battling to surface.

Garrison places his computer on the floorboards, and I set the textbook behind me. We scoot closer, my left leg dangling off the nook's seat. His right leg does the same, and we bend our other knees. Squeezing close.

Only a sliver of space between us.

I rest my chin on my knee, and I whisper, "She's alive, but sometimes it feels like I'm mourning someone who died."

He presses a kiss to the top of my head and murmurs, "I know."

"No siblings," I say, agreeing with him from before.

His aquamarine eyes fill me up and he nods silently. "But our kid will have plenty of cousins."

Our kid. Hearing him say that pulls a smile out of me. "And they'll be her or his best friends."

"For sure," Garrison nods.

We look around the lake house and listen to the softened baby cries. Those children will be the cousins to our faraway future child.

As our gazes meet, his fingers dip under my soft sweater. His hands slowly skim the bare flesh of my hips. I tingle and light up from the affectionate touch, but this conversation races my pulse.

Wading into new waters with Garrison is like taking a broken flashlight into a cave. It's terrifying, but I trust in both of us to walk in the right direction.

"If you want a baby in your future," Garrison says, "does that mean you want to get married…eventually?"

Marriage…

I elbow up my glasses and hold onto my bent leg, my pulse hammering. I'm afraid we won't be on the same page for this.

"Eventually," I say, and then I blurt out something, wanting to be as honest as humanly possible with Garrison. "Or soon."

He solidifies.

I pale. "I mean, not soon *soon.*"

"You said soon," he rebuts. "You meant soon."

"I meant soon-ish."

He doesn't remove his hands off my bare hips. It's a good sign that I haven't completely scared him off. "What's soon-ish?" he wonders. "Before you're twenty-three?"

Twenty-two is already fast approaching. A little over two months away. And maybe I'll grow older and think that's such a young age to be contemplating marriage and babies.

But I left home at seventeen.

I moved across the world at twenty.

My life has been a series of big challenges, and I've begun to realize that I might not be as adventurous as Daisy Calloway. I might not jump off *literal* bridges, but I have my own adventures. My own big metaphorical plunges into the unknown.

I, Willow Hale, am a risk-taker. A challenge seeker. I see that now. I feel it deep in my bones.

And I want someone with me, always, to face risks together.

I want Garrison. For as long as I can have him.

Forever, I hope.

But I'm not sure he wants those same things: Me. Forever.

Ever since I left Philly, he's opened an escape-door, something to jump out of in case our relationship goes sour. I don't blame him for that, but it's harder to know exactly where his head is at.

"Maybe not *before* I'm twenty-three," I answer Garrison. "I'd still be in school."

He glances at the textbook I set behind me.

I just ask, "Have you thought about marriage before today?"

He shakes his head, and I don't know why but that sends pain rippling down my chest.

Have I dreamed about walking down the aisle towards Garrison? Maybe once or twice lying awake in my dorm with nothing but my thoughts to keep me company. They were just thoughts though—I never went so far as to torture myself by looking up wedding dresses or rings on Pinterest. I'm not such a fool.

Garrison watches me crumple into myself. Head down, fingers grazing the threads of my mustard-yellow sock. "Willow..." My name sounds different in his voice. Almost choked. "Hey, it's not that I don't want to get married. It's just that with everything—I didn't think that far ahead."

"I understand," I say softly.

It's not like I ever thought about *babies* with him before now. Or rather, *a* baby.

His hands rise from my hips to my ribs, as though trying to reach my heart. "I thought you'd break up with me by now," he admits. "And maybe if I was a stronger person, I'd just have broken up with you last December. You deserve someone else who—"

"I deserve you," I snap at him. Pain in my chest radiates everywhere, clawing down my skin, but I'm holding onto his waist now, not letting go. "When will you start believing that?"

He shakes his head, eyes bloodshot. "I don't know." He removes one of his hands from my body to push away the longer strands of hair that've fallen in his eyes. "Maybe I never will, and then what?"

"Then I'll keep reminding you," I say, confident about this future.

He laughs. "Every day? Sounds fucking exhausting for you." He stares me down, straight in the eyes with this raw plea like *just let me go. For your own sake.*

I won't let him push me away.

"The only thing that's exhausting is reading this." I reach back and lift up my textbook. "Who knew accounting could be this dull?"

"That bad, huh?" He removes the other hand off my frame as he steals the book and then flips through the pages. We draw closer, our knees knocking together.

"I'd rather listen to TV static for an hour than read another sentence," I mutter under my breath.

His eyes flit up to me, able to hear my quiet voice.

He'd tell me if he couldn't.

Silence strains as he focuses on the text, flipping more pages. Snowflakes flutter peacefully outside, windowpanes frosted from the cold, and soothing crackling sounds emit from the fireplace. But nothing helps stop the tension that builds around us.

Garrison doesn't look up from the book when he finally speaks. "Maybe you don't realize how bad of a boyfriend I am because this has been your only relationship."

It feels like he yanked out a sword and wedged the blade into my stomach. My face crinkles. So what if my firsts have come later in life?

He's never taken my innocence as naïveté. I'm *not* naïve. I understand that Garrison is my first and only relationship, but I don't need to date other people to know that this is a complicated relationship. Not a bad one.

I can't pull words from my lips. They're stuck in the back of my throat.

He looks up, meeting the hurt in my eyes, but he continues anyway. "I just want to make sure that you get what you're saying—wanting to marry me someday *soon-ish*."

"I obviously don't want to marry you, if you don't want to marry me," I say, those words almost a whisper under my breath, but he's close enough to hear them.

He shakes his head. "Of course, you're all I want, Willow, but that doesn't change things."

"What things?" I ask, my chest on fire.

"I'm the only guy you've ever kissed," Garrison says. "I'm the only guy you've ever slept with. And, fuck, there's a part of me that feels like I'm stealing you from experiencing…from doing…from…" He can't finish. Anguish lances his face.

My hands tremble, and I don't have the book to hold onto, so I hug my arms around myself. Holding on. *Hold on.*

"You'd want me to kiss other guys? To have sex with them?" The thought brings nothing but sickness and a pressure that compounds on my chest.

"Jesus, *no*. The thought of you kissing another guy…" He grimaces. "…I can't even…" His face twists more, and then he reaches for my hand.

I let him take it. He doesn't mention the trembling. He just laces our fingers together. It calms me for a second.

Garrison inhales. "All I'm saying is that I know you think I'm special because I understood that you didn't like to be touched, and I waited… and was patient. But there are other guys who'd do the same. I'm not special. I'm not the only guy who'd fall in love with you."

"Do you honestly believe *I* could fall in love with someone else?" My brows pinch, confused. So fucking confused. "You are special to me, Garrison. How can you not see that? It's not just the touching. It's who you are. Every part of you, even the parts you hate. I love those, too."

He runs his thumb back and forth atop my hand. His eyes pin to mine, carrying more worries. "I can try to see it," he tells me. "But

I need to hear you say the other words, out loud. I just need to hear it, Willow."

"Which ones?" I wonder.

"That you're fine *never* knowing what it'll be like to kiss another man. To have him touch you here." He slides his free hand up my thigh, my leggings feeling thin under his palm. I breathe in, welcoming his touch, only his touch. His fingers are millimeters from my heat, but he stops short. "You'll never know what it's like to have another man's fingers in you. Another man's dick." He says those words without shying, without breaking my gaze.

"Good," I say in response.

"I need to hear you say it," Garrison says. "Please."

"I don't want to know what someone else's lips feel like," I tell him. "I'm happy never knowing what another dick feels like. Looks like. Smells like—"

His lips lift with mine.

I continue, "I don't want someone else's fingers in me. I don't want another set of eyes on my naked body. It literally makes my skin crawl even imagining these things. I only want you, and you're worthy of me. Do you understand that?"

A tear slips down out of his eye, but he brushes it away as quickly as it came. "I'm sor—"

"And you can't be sorry because I'm glad you're making me do this. I'm glad this is happening, okay? We need to *remain* honest with each other. Always."

His chest rises and falls heavily, and this is where we should reunite.

Kiss.

But tension still strains.

"What do you need from me?" Garrison asks, knowing he's wedged an invisible force between us.

"I need you to tell me that you won't leave me because you think you're not good enough," I say. "I need you to believe that you are. And maybe you can't give me that now, but one day."

"I won't ever fucking leave you," he tells me like those words are already cemented down.

But he'll push me away, force me to be the one to leave him. I know this—it's why the second part is so important.

"Do you believe that you're good enough for me?"

"Have I ever believed that?" he counters.

No, I don't think so.

I say, "Maybe you're just forgetting that I'm not as great as you think." I lower my voice. "Not only did I take money from my dad—which I said I'd never do—but I'm lying to Ryke and Lo about it. That's not exactly Girl Scout levels of good."

His lips lift into a big smile.

I pale. "What?"

"You're cute," he tells me. "You think lying to Ryke and Lo is this enormous crime against humanity, but it's fucking normal. People lie. I've done a lot worse. You wanna compare?" He winds an arm around my shoulder, and his eyes ask, *can I?*

I nod.

And he tugs me onto his lap, my legs naturally spreading open and weaving around his waist. I hang onto his shoulders and ask, "How do you know I've never spray painted someone's house? I could've had a rebellious streak back in Maine."

His brows rise. "I would have *definitely* already heard all about that." He tucks a loose strand of my braid behind my ear. "There's no way you wouldn't have gushed about spray painting houses and streaking down the roads."

"I never said anything about streaking." I blush just imagining doing something that brazen.

"I embellished your embellishment."

The fact that we're so different—his past muddled with bad deeds and mine relatively spotless—is what causes most of our friction. Whoever said opposites attract, well, they were right, but they forgot to mention how many strings are weaved and knotted between that attraction.

We're complicated, but as long as we're together, I don't care what we are.

I reroute to the earlier point. "It is a big lie, though," I say softly. Keeping this from Ryke and Lo is difficult, and I don't know what's worse: them finding out Jonathan gave me money to bury the footage of the fight or them finding out I kept it a secret in the first place.

"I know," Garrison nods, not downplaying the situation. "It's a big deal."

February

62

Garrison Abbey

TWO MONTHS PASS IN A BLINK. WILLOW AND I KEEP THE SECRET, and Jonathan isn't brought up much at the Hale house, making it easier.

It's also been two months since I've seen Willow in person, which is starting to get to me. We've talked about marriage and babies and begun to map out a future. Doing that has changed me a little bit. I want what we imagined together. One baby. Marriage. *Soon-ish.*

God, I want it.

But it's not going to happen if we can't see each other for months on end, so I came up with a plan.

And it could go really bad. It's what I know as I wait for 3 p.m. to hit at Cobalt Inc.

No, I'm not quitting. Willow would probably break up with me on the spot if she heard that I quit to move to London.

It's something else, but I'm nervous as hell because if Connor rejects this, then I'm not sure what I'll do. I don't have a plan B.

Maybe I should have a plan B.

"Abbey." Keith struts over and stops at my cubicle. Cobalt Inc. hired him after his internship ended, and Keith, along with his team, was awarded a humongous bonus after their Valentine's marketing push paid off. Some sort of magnet keepsake thing.

I don't really care. My job isn't in the "magnet" sector, so I don't cram my brain with useless shit. But their giant cock-sized bonus is all anyone will fucking talk about. And if he starts yammering on about it, I may just check out early.

"I'm busy," I tell Keith.

"This won't take long." He adjusts his Rolex, a gift from the CEO as part of the big dick bonus. "I heard from Diggy that you have an appointment with Connor at 3 p.m., and I need it."

I narrow my eyes. "Why in the hell does Ryan Diggins like that you all refer to him as *Diggy*?" Ryan is Connor's assistant, and honestly, I don't talk to him much.

"Because it's cool as shit, just like him, and you'd know that if you showed up to any of the company parties." He taps the top of my cubicle wall. "You're missing the point."

"Yeah, totally missed how you want my appointment time," I say, sarcasm on my tongue. "Went right over my head."

He lets out an aggravated noise. "Look, you don't even need to schedule a time to see Connor. You could walk up to him at any point. Hell, you live on his *street*, Abbey. You could knock on his door if you wanted to, and he probably wouldn't think that's weird."

He's right. Connor wouldn't.

But I wanted to do this the professional way. It's a professional matter.

"Sorry, man," I say. "It's not happening."

Keith glances at my mini-fridge. "You still need someone to grab you lunch and dinner from the caf? I've got you covered, no extra charge this time."

His offer almost makes me smile, not because I'm going to take it. But because I don't need it. "Thanks, but no thanks. I actually bring my lunch in to work now."

I make a sub sandwich every morning when I pack Maximoff's snacks for preschool. I took care of it once for Lily and Lo when they were both running late for work, and they've let me do it ever since.

I enjoy helping out, especially since I'm not paying them rent, and Lo would barely accept a check for groceries.

Keith rubs his eyes. "Abbey. There's only a short window of time I have leverage for a raise, and you have one of the only available appointment slots—"

"It's not available," I cut him off. "I have it."

Keith slowly blinks. "I've got blow."

Jesus. "Then you should be going into his office begging not to be fired," I snap. "Connor hates drugs." At least, he doesn't want his employees on them. I would know, I've had to take a fucking drug test every six months since I failed my first one. They've all been negative since.

"I didn't say I use them," Keith whisper-hisses. "But it's good leverage for the assholes who do in here." He says *leverage* and I hear *blackmail.*

I raise my hands. "I don't want a part of your bullshit." There's a reason I enjoy my division existing of one person: *me.*

"Then give me your appointment and I'll be out of your hair," Keith says. "You won't have to talk to me. Otherwise…" He reaches for the empty rolling chair, about to pull the thing over and park his ass next to me. Probably for eternity. Cobalt Inc. is infested with annoyingly persistent type-A pricks.

"*Fine,*" I concede. "Tell Ryan you can have my time."

Keith grins. "You'll need to call Diggy yourself. He doesn't trust anyone in the building." *No shit.*

"Fine," I repeat. "Just leave."

He goes to pat my shoulder like we're bros—I abruptly slide my chair away. "Don'tfuckingtouchme," I snap so caustically and quickly it all slurs together.

His eyes widen. "Shit, sorry." He raises his hands. "Christ." He strolls away from my cubicle, and my pulse beats rapidly and *hard.* Like the Road Runner wields a sledgehammer inside my body.

Get a grip. I run a hand through my hair and grab my phone to call Ryan and take care of this. I'll just have to find another time to talk to Connor. But it has to be today.

LATE EVENING HAS ARRIVED, THE END OF THE WORKDAY, AND I'm on Connor's imperial floor of the high-rise. The CEO is shutting down his computer. Packing up his things.

It's a huge risk to approach him right now. More than one prick has already been reprimanded for trying. I loiter near the glass office, just watching each sorry bastard get rejected. Leaving with their tails between their legs.

And Connor doesn't even yell or raise his voice. He just uses a bunch of words that makes you feel like two pounds of shit.

Still…I approach him.

Heads swing, other high-level employees looking my way. Bodies rotating. I feel more on display than when paparazzi shove cameras in my face.

Connor locks his office door behind him and notices me with a quick glance. He's casual, almost unsurprised that I'm here. Even though I go out of my way to *avoid* him at work.

Before I can say anything, his confident stride is aimed for the elevator. "Let's talk on the way home."

I think that's his way of offering me a ride.

I shake my head. "I drove here—"

"Your car will be fine in the parking deck overnight." He's still walking, brisk but casual. I keep pace beside him.

"You want me to ride in your limo with you?" I'm having a hard time processing this, but I should be able to by now. I'm living with his brother-in-law.

Connor cocks a single brow at me. "You're being impossibly daft today."

I stop short just as he enters the elevator.

He braces a hand on the door, keeping them from closing on me. "You don't want to ride home with me. Fine. But this conversation will have to take place in a home with four children under the age of five. When I say it's extraordinarily loud in there, just remember I'm not the hyperbolic one."

Now he's inviting me to his house…

An older employee passes us, eyeing the interaction. I do something really dumb and look over my shoulder. A handful of employees are craning their necks to watch us, and I'm about to get special treatment. It's fucking obvious.

Right now, I just don't care.

This is for Willow. For us. That matters more to me than whatever anyone else thinks.

I enter the elevator with him. Doors slide shut. On the way to his limo, he talks about his kids—Jane, Charlie, Beckett, and Eliot—like I'm his friend. Happiness flows from every word like these little beings are the center of his whole world, and for a guy like Connor who bars most people from seeing his emotions, it's a privilege that he lets me see this.

It makes it easier for what I'm about to ask.

As soon as we're in the limo, he passes me a water bottle from the cooler. "We should be commuting together," he tells me. "It doesn't make sense for you to drive now that we work the same hours."

"I like my car."

"It's not a matter of like. It's called efficiency." He rests a finger to his temple and looks through me. "Let me give you an example you seem to need. You wouldn't have to make appointments with me if we have extra time to talk on our commute. And without appointment times, you won't have to worry about being hassled during your day."

My face scrunches, not understanding how he knows about my conversation with Keith today. "How did you…?"

Connor arches another brow. "It's my company. I hear everything." He uncaps his own water bottle. "And most of my employees think they're sharks. As soon as Ryan told me you had an appointment today, I knew one of them would try to bite."

I smile, realizing something. "You don't call him Diggy."

"I only use his nickname to his face," Connor says and then studies me like he's adding something up. "You remember Faust?"

Faust…

I couldn't forget that place even if I tried. I lasted a good four months before being kicked out. But that boarding school—that's the same one Connor attended, long before I graced their doors.

"*Fortunately* for me," I say dryly, "Faust is embedded in my brain."

It's an all-boys school. And I mostly hated it for that reason.

I lean my head back and stare up at the limo's ceiling. "You were something like a legend there," I add. "Everyone talked about you." And these were students that didn't even go to school with Connor. Just heard the same old stories passed down.

"I'd ask if they said good things, but I already know that answer," Connor says, confidence laced in arrogance. He sets his water bottle in the cup holder. "You flunked out of Faust for a reason, Garrison."

"Yeah," I snort. "Because I wasn't smart enough." Those guys all spoke three different languages, were tutored in math before they could talk, and had proficiency in at least one musical instrument. They were blue-blooded social climbers with something to prove, and I couldn't hack it.

"No," Connor refutes. "It has nothing to do with intelligence. More than a few idiots stood beside me at graduation." He props an arm on the seat cushion, facing me. "You flunked because you didn't belong there. That school isn't designed to uphold boys who love things other than themselves."

I loved Willow.

I missed Willow.

Every day I was there.

I think about how Faust is a boarding school, cut off from friends and family in the middle of fucking nowhere New York. Most of the guys I met seemed perfectly happy being away. No one missed for anything.

They just wanted for everything. They wanted money and prestige and that billion-dollar glory.

I just wanted my girl.

My best friend, the only friend I came to care about. Who'd turn into the single most important person in my entire life.

It's funny because if I asked Connor what he wanted when he was at Faust, I think I'd know what he'd tell me.

"I wanted it all."

I'm not sure where Connor is going with this, and honestly, I'm too in my head to even stare at his blue eyes. So I divert my gaze to the window.

Lamplight from Philly streets glows softly outside in the dark night.

Connor continues, "Cobalt Inc. isn't Faust. The things I value now are not the things I valued when I was seventeen. You belong at my company."

I know Cobalt Inc. is different than Faust. I don't feel miserable at work. The people are okay. Keith is annoying but harmless. Being around people who are driven and care about their goals is good motivation to keep going. And it's kind of nice seeing the same faces every day.

But I'm going to change that with what I'm about to ask Connor.

I'm going to change everything.

My chest tightens. Maybe Connor knows something is wrong and he's trying to prevent me from quitting. *I won't quit…not unless he says "no."*

The quiet only lasts a couple seconds before I break it. "Before I ask you what I need to ask," I say, caging a breath. "I need to know something."

He waves me on.

"Your kids are cute now, but they're going to get older and not be perfect, you know. So what happens if one of your sons grows up to be something like me: flunks out of two prep schools, inks his body up, smokes and vandalizes houses in your neighborhood?"

Connor doesn't break his gaze from mine, but he's stone-faced, nothing passing through his calm, impassive exterior. And then he says, "I think we already know how that story plays out."

I just shake my head, thoughts spinning.

"You hired me because I can code," I say. "Because I was Willow's boyfriend."

"I hired you because I saw potential," he refutes. "If you believe anything else then you're wrong. Not uncommon. I'm sure it's a natural state that you're learning to live with." He runs a cool hand through his wavy brown hair. "You're in my limo right now because I like you. Despite the fact that you can't seem to enjoy your own company."

Fuck, man.

I rub at my eyes. "I have to ask you something."

He grins a blinding grin that makes me feel the size of Skittle. "So you've already said." His calming gaze softens. "I'm still waiting."

I take a tighter breath. *Let's go, Garrison.* "Willow's everything to me." Her name brings comfort and strength and I continue on. "She's more than a girlfriend. It's like code. She's the script on the program, and I'm nothing but a blank screen without her." I exhale a sharper breath. "And it's not like I haven't learned to be happy on my own in Philly and persevere or whatever. I have. I know I have, but she's still all the way in London. She'll be there for years, and the longer we're apart, the more I get in my head and ruin things. So I just need to see her more." I extend my arm to the limo window. "I can program over there. It's not a problem. I'm just asking for like *one* week every month to telecommute. That's all."

I drop my arm and massage my sweating knuckles, breath like lead in my lungs.

Connor is unreadable, brows arched. Lines crease his forehead, but I don't think they're from confusion.

I feel like shit asking to telecommute not just down the street, but a whole country away. Because I'm asking for more when Connor has already given me everything.

"So you want me to give you a week off every month when I don't even know what you're working on," Connor says. "You do know how that request sounds?"

"It's not one week *off*," I counter quickly. "I'll still be working."

"But I'll have to trust that you're working. If you're not coming into the office, I can't see you on your computer coding every day."

Shit, this is going bad. I rake fingers through my hair. "Look, I know how it sounds."

"Outrageous. Outlandish," Connor says, tilting his head. "And so you also must know that if I grant your request, it's out of nepotism and nothing more—"

"I'm okay with that," I cut him off.

Connor stares at me, still impassively, still unreadable. *Shit.*

I shift uncomfortably on the leather seat. "Until tonight, I thought I got this job out of nepotism," I admit. "It's never stopped me from going to work. It won't stop me from putting forth all my effort." Feeding on that bloated leech one more time won't bother me.

My boss just shakes his head once.

My nerves ratchet to a new degree. "Connor—"

"I won't grant your request," he says calmly, casually, like he's not just ripping apart my entire world. I also zone in on his words.

Won't.

It's not that he *can't.* Because he can. He just doesn't want to.

I look away. Out the window. As pain starts shattering my chest, my ribcage, my fucking heart. *I can't see Willow.*

How long will we be apart? *Forever.* It fucking *feels* like forever.

Unbearable doesn't even cut it. And fuck me, for putting all my hope and desire and utter want into this one thing. Because losing something I never had shouldn't feel this devastating. This *crushing.*

"Garrison," Connor says softly. "Understand that I'm doing this for your own benefit."

That gets to me.

I swing my head and choke on a bitter laugh. "My benefit?" I say in disbelief. "Unless it benefits me to feel *miserable*, then I don't see how this has anything to do with me." I clench my knee with a shaking hand. "You know what. I qu…" I can't finish those words. They're sawed off by something inside of me.

I blink hard, pushing back more emotion.

Connor watches me with tranquility that should calm me but it's setting me on edge. "I'm not trying to push you to quit, Garrison. I don't want that. Neither do you. But if I let you go to London seven days out of the month—*every* month—you will quit."

I don't see how I will. "You don't know that."

He raises his brows. "Four words I don't hear often." His lip lifts. "I know you. I know that you lead with your emotions, not your head. And if you're in London for seven days, you'll email me asking for another day overseas. It'll turn into telecommuting for eight. Then you'll ask for another week. Fourteen days will turn into twenty-one. And then by the end of the year, you'll call me to say that you want to stay there permanently. Because given the choice between Willow and this job, you will choose Willow. So I'm not giving you the choice. I'm allowing you to have both while you still can. And one day, you'll thank me for it."

I grind down on my teeth. Pain leeches everywhere, all doors shutting from me to her. No way there. No escape or passageway.

"You don't trust me to stay seven days in London and come back?" That's what I'm getting from this.

"No, I don't. And if you thought about it more, you might not trust yourself either. Just ask yourself which would be harder: not seeing Willow for months, or having to leave her every three weeks?"

I finally understand what he's saying.

Either way I'm fucked. But at least in one scenario I get to see her. Hold her. Comfort her. But Connor already told me I don't get a choice. He made it for me. That hits me.

"This decision," I say. "It's not from my boss, is it?"

Connor rolls up his sleeves slowly. "No, it's not." He glances my way. Blue eyes hitting mine. "It's from your friend."

The limo rolls towards the gated neighborhood, slowing down. My head is heavy. Spirits dulled. I don't know what to do. How to see Willow more often. How to make this relationship work. If it's even possible anymore. I try one last thing. The good ole *guilt trip*.

"Yeah, and what happens if we break up because we can't see each other?" I ask. "You're going to be an accomplice to that, you know. If you're such a great friend, you could have helped." I feel like utter shit as soon as I say the words. Fuck, why even go there?

Because I'm me.

Because I could.

Connor stares through me like I'm made of glass. "If you break up because you can't see each other, then your relationship is too fragile to last anyway. Blame me, if you'd like. But it will be sorely misdirected."

Fragile.

I feel fucking fragile.

"How do I make us stronger?" I ask him since he seems to have all the fucking answers.

Connor smiles a soft, genuine smile. "First step is believing you already are."

The words roll around in my head for a couple minutes. Until the limo slows to a stop at Loren's house.

There's one more thing I need to ask. One more unanswered question that's going to plague me. "One more thing," I say. "How well do you know Jonathan Hale?"

Connor's expression flatlines, impassive again. "Better than you. Why do you ask?"

I shake my head, already coming up with a roundabout answer. "I just don't know him that well, I guess, and if Willow and I are going to be more serious, I figure I should start trying to." It's not untrue.

Jonathan and I have met briefly at group events—Lo usually invites him—but for the most part I don't interact with Jonathan. I always figured it was because my relationship with Willow was slow and new, but her relationship with her dad was even slower and newer. It never bothered me that she didn't want those two things colliding.

But now that I know Jonathan used to say shit to Lo that my brothers used to say to me…it changes things. I should know my girlfriend's dad better, and I want to make sure he's not going to screw her over with that loan. I can't tell Lo and Ryke about it, so I'm going to try to protect Willow myself—with everything I have.

Connor eyes me. "Jonathan Hale is a person you're better off not knowing. Especially you."

"Why?"

"Because unless you share his last name, you are collateral damage in his life. And you have the most unenviable position."

"What's that?"

"You're dating his only daughter."

THE CALLOWAY SISTERS & THEIR MEN — FAN PAGE

FOLLOWERS: 88K

With Valentine's Day just behind us, it's time for another update on the Calloway Sisters & Their Men! Here's the whereabouts of our favorite flower-named sisters (plus Willow!) and their sexy AF hunks.

The Stokes
Poppy Calloway (34) & Sam Stokes (34)
Daughter: Maria (11)
Update: These two were caught out and about on a romantic Valentine's date night! They did a "sip and paint" at a local studio where paparazzi snapped photos of paint brushes flying at cheeks and arms, purposefully missing that canvas. So adorable! And such a rare sighting for these two who usually keep out of the public eye.

The Cobalts
Rose Calloway (30) & Connor Cobalt (31)
Daughters: Jane (4)
Sons: Charlie & Beckett (2-year-old twins) and Eliot (8-months-old)
Update: Rose and Connor headed to Paris with their entire family for Valentine's. #CoupleGoals. Can you just imagine being a fly on the wall in their private jet?

The Hales

Lily Calloway (28) & Loren Hale (29)

Son: Maximoff (4)

Daughter: Luna (3-months-old)

Update: No photos of Lily and Loren on Valentine's. Boo! But obviously they have good reason, since I'm sure they're staying home to be with the cutest of cute babies – Luna Hale! Don't you love that name?

The Meadows

Daisy Calloway (23) & Ryke Meadows (30)

Daughter: Sullivan (2)

Update: Daisy and Ryke took a motorcycle ride on Valentine's Day, and paparazzi were given the iconic middle finger from Ryke. Check out the gif!

The Unofficial Calloway Sister

Willow Hale (21) & Her Boyfriend – Garrison Abbey (22)

Update: As far as the internet knows, these two didn't see each other on Valentine's. Truthfully, we don't have any photos of them together for like...a whole year. Some sources say they might be broken up. It would be a little odd, if that was the case, since we do know that Garrison still lives with Loren Hale. But stranger things have happened!

What do you think? Are Willow and Garrison still together? Take the poll below!

Love you like Loren loves Lily,

xo Olive

63

Willow Hale

I GLANCE QUICKLY AT MY CELLPHONE, REGRETTING POPPING up the internet notification—or even setting notifications for entertainment headlines. Keeping up with fandoms isn't as fun when my name appears and sends a jolt of anxiety coursing through me.

Only one day has passed since Valentine's, and already, people are speculating that Garrison and I have broken up.

A random poll on a fan site has accumulated *thousands* of entries, and an overwhelming 84% of fans agree that my relationship has failed. And I'm not really surprised a credible magazine linked this fan site as a newsworthy source.

I think back, and I know I used to be the one clicking into polls about the Calloway sisters. Eagerly feeding this machine and rumor mill. Some are fun and harmless. Others cut too deep. And until I was on the receiving end, I never really understood the gravity of those cuts.

Jokes on all of them, though. Garrison and I are 100% still a couple.

But I'm not winning any Best Girlfriend awards this morning. "Maybe the time zones mixed up everything? Are you sure they delivered?" I ask Garrison on the phone while I frantically search the messy common area.

Wine glasses and empty bottles of Sauvignon Blanc make sticky rings on the coffee table, and I toss pillows off a purple thrift store couch, then peek behind the small TV. I already received an un-rate-able, out-of-this-world box of chocolates for Valentine's from Daisy—(half the tin was espresso flavored)—so I don't know why Garrison's gift is missing.

"Nah," he says. "I'm pretty sure they were already sent to your apartment last night—your time. I got an email confirmation, and someone signed off on the delivery. So they have to be there."

I woke up in a cold sweat at 7 a.m. to his text message.

Garrison: did u like the roses? You never said anything about em

My heart sunk to my knees, and I texted back: *what roses?*

And then he called me.

Now I'm sweeping the tiny kitchen for a dozen pink roses and wondering if I should've taken Lo and Ryke's handout.

The offer came early this month.

My brothers flew out to London ASAP—sooner than the visit they planned and booked—after Garrison made an off-handed comment about my flat being unsafe.

I don't blame him for the loose lips. He *lives* with Lo, and he said it just slipped out.

When my famous brothers arrived, the internet went wild.

SPOTTED! Loren Hale & Ryke Meadows in London!

They were trending on Twitter, but they entered my apartment dressed in workout gear—baseball caps, sweatshirts, running pants, and Nikes—appearing more like normal men in their late twenties than billionaire celebrities.

No matter their clothing, they're intimidating. Towering with overprotectiveness as I opened the door. Concern was etched in Lo's sharp gaze and Ryke's hardened jaw.

Lo bulldozed his way in. "Is this the lock?" His glare punctured inanimate objects like the doorknob already accosted me.

"Yeah," I said softly, noticing bodyguards posted up in the apartment hallway.

Ryke was full-on brooding as he sauntered inside the flat, checking on my bedroom door.

"How many people come in here a day?" Lo asked me.

"Um…" I pushed up my glasses. "Besides my roommates, it just depends." *On party nights.* "Maybe like…a dozen…or more."

Lo looked supremely more protective. He put a hand on my shoulder as he rounded my body and motioned for security to check the windows.

All three of my roommates were in class at the time, but Sheetal and Tess texted sad gifs that they missed seeing more of my family.

The living room was still a mess from a party the previous night (one that I avoided), and I'd been trying to clean up. After a short house tour, I swept up potato chip crumbs, and my brothers talked heatedly under their breaths to each other.

Lo came forward, brows cinched with seriousness. "We need to talk." He took the broom out of my hands.

"Okay." I felt really young all of a sudden.

Ryke crossed his arms, eyes darkened.

"You're famous," Lo said flatly, like I'd never been served the fact. "*Severely* famous, Willow." This wasn't the first time his fame had impacted my living situation.

But it's different now that he's an ocean away. He can't bail me out as easily, and I know Lo has always felt responsible for me.

He's my brother.

"You have to remember that," he continued. "Every day, everywhere you go." He sighed out. "For Christ's sake, *you* should have a bodyguard—"

"I don't need one," I protested, worried it'd draw more attention. I can be invisible, but that feels less likely with a muscular shadow following me.

Lo's cheekbones sharpened. "I can't leave you in a situation where you're at risk of kidnap, rape, and *murder.*"

Ryke rolled his eyes. "We can add extra locks, Lo, and a fucking security alarm."

I nodded. "I'd rather just do that..." I trailed off, noticing how Ryke zeroed in on the remnants of the party. Daisy had told him about my roommate problems, so I think he was more fixated on those.

Ryke was popular in college.

The captain of the track team.

Lo was lazy at Penn and skipped class more than he attended.

I know this from what they've told me, not just Wikipedia, but I wonder how they'd be at a collegiate party in their early twenties.

Definitely not like you, Willow. Hiding. In a closet.

"Why do you want to live here?" Lo questioned.

"My lease doesn't end until May."

Ryke frowned and asked, "That's the only reason?"

I wanted to say, *no.* That I've been having a stupendous, heart-warming time living with my friends, but it's been...rocky.

Not just between me and them. Sheetal and Tess blew up at Salvatore after his hookup projectile vomited *everywhere* in the bathroom.

He said that he hired some cleaning service, but they never showed. He left the mess too long, so the three of us ended up mopping puke for two hours.

"Yeah," I said. "That's all that's keeping me here." I looked around. "It's a good location to campus. I can make it work for a while."

Lo and Ryke exchanged a look, and then they offered to cover the cost of me breaking the lease. They'd help me find a new flat ASAP and pay the rent.

I wiped the mist behind my glasses.

Overwhelmed, because their love is unconditional. They'd do just about anything for me, no strings attached.

But I couldn't accept.

It's always been hard to say *yes.*

Yet, I've accepted a worse offer before. The one from our dad that does have stipulations and uncomfortable strings.

It's not pride that stops me from taking money from my brothers. It's something else.

With my decision set, they flew back to Philly after we put in a security system and had dinner together. We hugged, leaving on good terms.

Now I'm racing around the flat in search of missing pink roses, and I can't help but think this wouldn't have happened if I moved.

"It's okay, Willow," Garrison consoles. "They're just flowers. I can send you more."

Palms sweaty, I switch the phone to my other hand. "You put a lot of thought into them though."

"Maybe they'll turn up. Look, don't worry about it."

I turn as Tess exits her room, carrying a khaki satchel with textbooks. Pretty sapphire earrings complement her dark-brown skin, and I'd ask if they're new or from Sheetal, but on her way out, she must see my distress. "Hey, what's happening?"

"Did you see any flowers get delivered?"

Tess shakes her head. "No, I don't think Sheetal did either." She sweeps the wine bottle graveyard. "Ugh, Salvatore left his shit out again?" She sighs, then says, "I meant to tell you, we're doing a charades thing tonight. You should join us. It'll be *really* lowkey."

I shift my weight, hotter all of a sudden.

Their idea of "lowkey" isn't exactly mine. I know because the last "lowkey" flat party involved dares and tequila shots.

"Um..." I hate rejecting their invites. I can tell they feel like they're banishing me to my room.

But I'd rather be there.

I worry the longer I live with Sheetal and Tess, the more likely I'll lose them as friends. I'm the standoffish one, and I know I should make a bigger effort.

It's hard when parties are draining and my bedroom is a foot away with comic books calling out to me.

I thought we could watch *The Flash* together once a week, but no one paid attention to the TV and they always suggest other things when I bring up movies or shows.

My new eulogy: *that anxious turtle, Willow Hale, she should've taken her brothers' offer when she had the chance.*

"It'll be fun," Tess smiles and nudges my arm with her elbow.

I think about it and then nod. "Okay."

Tess high-fives me, and then says she'll see me tonight. She has a huge advertising project that's due later today.

Once she leaves the flat, I put the phone back to my ear. "Did you hear that?"

"Yeah." Garrison sounds tense. "Why'd you accept the invite?"

"I don't want to lose their friendship," I say softly, checking the bathroom for lost flowers.

"I'm gonna be an ass for a second, okay?"

"Okay." I can't help but smile at the warning.

"It feels like you're choosing Tess and Sheetal's friendship over your grades." He knows I'm a firm B and C college student now. "You've tried the whole 'maybe I'll have fun at this party, maybe it'll be different' mantra and you always end up wishing you didn't go. So don't fucking go. If they're your friends, they should understand that."

"They feel bad leaving me out."

"So what?"

I've never really cared about being invited anywhere, and now that I receive invites, I stress about how many I can reject without being alone here in London.

"I think I need to go to this one," I tell him. "I've bailed on them too many times recently." I shut the bathroom door, entering the narrow hall. "Or…I guess I could suggest dinner at Barnaby's?"

That way, they won't care if I retreat to my room early on through charades.

What I've learned: maintaining friendships offline takes work, and I just hope that in the long-run it pays off and gets easier.

"You do have to eat," Garrison says lightly.

I want to smile. It's just harder when I miss him so much. I rub my arm, wishing he was here to draw me into his chest. I just picture my cheek on his heart. And I can almost feel the warmth of his skin. I can almost hear the soft beat.

"Let me know how it goes," Garrison adds.

"I will…" My voice drifts as I glance at an ajar door. *Salvatore's room.* Pink rose petals are strewn around the bed, and a girl's ankle sticks out beneath the sheets.

My stomach drops.

"Willow?" Garrison's voice spikes. "You okay?"

"I found the flowers," I whisper. "I'll call you back." Once we hang up, I take a breath. *Confront them, Willow Hale.*

You can do this.

I step into the room and rap the doorframe. "Hello?"

Under sheets, Salvatore groans awake, stretching an arm, while the hungover girl smashes her face more into the pillow. Ignoring me.

"What is it?" he asks, Italian accent clear.

I push up my glasses. "Those roses belonged to me, and it's okay…it's okay that you signed for them but not if you planned to destroy them and give them to another girl."

He makes a face like I'm delusional. "What are you talking about?"

"My boyfriend sent those roses." I motion to the pink petals surrounding heaps of clothing.

"The card had no name," Salvatore protests.

"Where's the card?"

He points vaguely to the nightstand.

I snatch a square card from plastic wrapping. Near torn condom wrappers.

I read the card:

For my girl,
Hope these make you smile. If a whole
fandom centered on you, I'd be your number
one fan.

Miss you, love you <3 <3 <3

I smile so much that tears brim.

Garrison might not know it, but his love is keeping me afloat here. Every time I think of him and talk to him.

"Sorry," Salvatore says, seeing my reaction and realizing the flowers were mine. "I didn't know." He sounds sincere.

I nod, accepting the apology. Maybe easier than most would, but I'm not here to cause more friction. I just want to survive this semester.

Salvatore sits up, ruffling his hair. "Can I buy you more?"

"No, it's okay."

"Yeah, let me. It's the least I can do." He glances at the sleeping girl, and then he slips out of bed. He's buck-naked.

Oh my God.

I spin on my heels. My back to the naked man.

I saw…I saw his dick.

Salvatore grabs boxer-briefs off the ground.

"Really, Salvatore, I don't need more flowers—"

"It's not a problem, Willow." Before he comes closer, I shuffle out of his room. Putting more distance between us, and for the third time, I tell him firmly that I'm okay and do *not* need more roses. And I quickly dial Garrison and find solace in my bedroom, sinking on the edge of the mattress.

My face is burning in embarrassment.

I'm dead.

I've died. I put a hand to my forehead.

"So what happened?" Garrison asks.

"Uh…I think…" I inhale. "So I kind of saw Salvatore naked and—"

"*What?*" His voice is hot and confused. "How?"

I rehash everything and thank him for the card, but Garrison is understandably stuck on the Salvatore part.

"He's a fucking douchebag, trying to buy you *flowers* when he knows you have a boyfriend. I don't even care if they're replacement flowers—"

"I know," I cut him off in agreement.

Garrison is quiet.

I swallow my mortification. "Garrison?"

"As long as you know that his intentions are fucked…"

"I do." I exhale a deep breath.

He pauses, then asks, "I have the better-looking dick, right?" His serious tone makes me smile.

"Definitely, always."

"Yeah, that's what I thought."

I lower my phone at the sound of another incoming call. "My dad is calling."

"Right now? It's two a.m. here."

"Sometimes he calls late. I think he's lonely and has trouble sleeping."

Garrison sighs, concerned. "You gonna answer?"

"Not right now." I let the call ring out. My dad has still been on my case about an internship. Especially as my second year is coming to an end and the summer is in sight.

I'm afraid unless I follow the path he wants, he'll stop helping me with tuition. He hasn't made that threat yet, but it feels like this underlying truth shoved beneath the rug. He has power over me.

Power that I can't seem to get back.

March

64

Garrison Abbey

TODAY IS GOING TO BE A GOOD DAY. IT'S WHAT I THINK WHEN I wake up. It's the thought I bring with me into the shower.

Good day.

Today.

March 9th.

Tomorrow is Willow's birthday, and a plane ticket rests on my desk. Waiting for me. She has no clue, but I'm taking a red-eye flight tonight. I'll be in breathing distance of Big Ben and the London Eye by tomorrow morning.

And fuck, if I'm not riding on the high.

Beads of water roll down my jaw, shower pouring over me. Heat amasses with gathering steam.

I place a hand on the tiled wall, and with my other, I stroke the length of my dick. Tightening my fist around throbbing veins, my muscles burning, I close my eyes and imagine Willow.

I picture the moment where I wrap my arms around her body. How she buries her head into my chest, her fingers gripping my shirt. Like I'm the safest place she knows.

We hug close for a while, and after a tender, longing kiss, I lift her up around my toned waist. She gasps against the crook of my neck, feeling my hardness against her heat.

I ache to fill her, and she's pleading for me to be closer. *"Inside,"* *she cries in a breathy whimper. "Please, please."*

She's said those words in real life before. Just like that. And remembering them now does a number on me.

I grit down, on fire. I rub myself faster in the steaming shower. Muscles pulling taut in my neck and quads. *Fuuuck.*

In my head, we're magically, suddenly, naked. *Thank you, imagination.* I press her against the wall, ass in my clutch, and I push in between her legs. Warmth wraps around my erection as I nestle deep in Willow.

She hangs on.

We kiss, and I rock and rock.

Our lips break as she lets out soft, breathy noises of pure pleasure.

Fuckfuckfuck. Pressure mounts as blood rushes down south, and I feel like a twelve-year-old boy, coming so quick. That can't happen when I actually see her. *Jesus.*

Cum washes down the drain, and I wash off with soap.

"Garrison!" Loren's voice booms through the bathroom. He bangs on the door with a fist. "When you're done dreaming of my sister, I need to talk to you!"

No idea what that is about, but thank God I came already. If Lo's trying to mess with me, he should have done it five seconds ago.

But really—it's just another day living with Loren Hale.

Oddly, I do love it.

I switch off the shower, grab a towel and quickly tie it around my waist. My soaked hair drips, water sliding down my bare shoulders. I whip the door open, and Lo is just leaning against the wall.

I give him a look. "You're seriously just waiting right there?"

Lo flashes a dry smile. "You have a problem with that? It's not like you were doing anything inappropriate in the shower."

"Since when is rubbing one out illegal in this house?"

Lo grimaces. "It's not. Unless you're thinking about my sister when you do it. Then that has been illegal since the dawn of time."

I raise my brows. "So you want me to think about a different girl while I jack off?"

He glares at me like I'm the one who started this. That was definitely him. "No, Garrison, I want you to bury this conversation into the pits of hell where it belongs."

I readjust my towel on my waist. "It's buried."

"Good. Can you babysit Moffy today?" he asks. "My dad called and wants to do lunch." I already know Lily took Luna to a playdate with Rose's son, Eliot. Both babies. Both adorable but loud as hell.

My head is spinning though, stuck on the fact that Lo doesn't want to bring his own son to Jonathan Hale's house for lunch.

I have to ask. "Is it a work lunch?"

Lo shakes his head and sticks his hands in his pockets. He looks at me like he knows where I'm going. "I love my dad, but the less he's around my kids, the better."

I feel like I need to know Jonathan Hale more than I do. To understand the man that has a grip on my girlfriend's life. Lo and Ryke still have zero clue that he gave Willow money to pay off students. To bury footage of *my* fight.

It happened a year-and-a-half ago, and I forget about it until moments like these. When it bubbles to the surface like molten tar.

My stomach flip-flops.

Lo frowns. "I'll be back in plenty of time for you to catch your flight. You don't have to worry about that."

He knows I'm flying out to see his sister.

"Yeah, no. Of course, I'll babysit."

At that last word, a toddler comes running down the hallway. Arms flailing around him. "UNCLE GARRISON! Did you hear? Did you hear?" Maximoff skids to a stop by his dad. "Mommy said I can go to LEGOLAND!" He bounces on the balls of his feet, and in his happiness, he accidentally flings the Spider-Man toy he's holding. It hits the wall and bounces off.

Lo grins—his eyes sparkling like *that's my son.*

I've never had anyone that brings me that kind of happiness. Not until Willow. Can I even imagine a kid with her?

I don't want to try. Just another thing I can hang onto and lose, right? Anyway, we have to get through this long-distance shit first.

"He's in good hands," I tell Lo as Maximoff picks up the toy. "Take your time." Honestly, babysitting is the one thing I love doing for Lily and Lo. I'm wanted and needed here. And yeah, that feels fucking good.

SO I FEEL LIKE UTTER SHIT.

Literally.

For the past seven hours, I've been sweating so much that I ditched my pull-over *and* T-shirt. The fabric is soaked through.

Maximoff lounges on a beanbag in the living room, munching on a bag of granola bites that belong to Ryke. They taste like dirt, but Moffy seems to like them.

Granola crumbs are *everywhere*. His lap, the beanbag, the rug. And I planned to vacuum before Lily and Lo come home.

But I can't move. I feel like a hundred million pounds, and on top of that, the sound, look, and smell of granola dirt has my stomach in a blender. I fight nausea and bear down on my teeth.

My phone buzzes, and I check the text.

Willow: Birthday plans tomorrow are lowkey, just dessert at Barnaby's with Tess & Sheetal. Wanna Skype later? Let me know a good time for u

She doesn't know I'm coming. But I'll be there. Even if I have to crawl my way to London, *I'll be there.*

Sheetal and Tess, I actually do like. They care about Willow, and they've given me a second chance to make a better first impression. Knowing how much I mean to Willow.

Salvatore is still a dick.

I stare at my phone, fingers hovering over the letters. I have to give her a little bit of a white lie, since it's still a surprise that I'm flying there.

So I send a few *Gilmore Girls* birthday gifs that I made for her, all with Jess and Rory. And I text back: Definitely wanna talk on this big day. Skype me after dessert when u have time *birthday cake emoji*

I cough.

Bad idea. My stomach cramps like someone is wedging a knife into my gut. Fuck, what did I eat? I cringe as another text comes through.

Willow: not that big, only turning 22

I smile through the pain and text her: yeah and we'll be the same age again. Big bold 22.

She texts back a bunch of hearts, and then the front door swings open. My duffel bag is already packed near the stairs, and honestly, I'm ready to go. I could be half-dead on the way to the airport, and I'd still find a way on the plane.

"He do okay?" Lo whispers as he drops keys in a bowl. Eyes pinpoint to his four-year-old.

Maximoff is out. Asleep with granola on his chest.

"He's perfect. Like always," I say. "Hey, I'm gonna head out." I walk past him to grab my duffel.

He frowns. "You're forgetting a shirt." Before I can reply, he adds, "Christ, you look like shit. Garrison—"

"I'm fine," I say, cutting him off and unzipping my bag. I dig through and find a T-shirt. "It's just hot in here." I pull it over my head and stand.

"No, it's not." Lo walks forward, about to reach for my forehead to take my temp. But he stops himself quickly. Quicker than I can flinch. "Please take your temperature. For me. Because I'm betting you're at a hundred-and-one, at least, and it just hurts to look at you." *Awesome.*

"I'm totally fine, man," I say. "I think the turkey in my sandwich this afternoon might have been bad or something." Pain starts jackhammering my stomach, and I suck in a tight breath. "It'll pass."

Lo grimaces. "You'd fly commercial with food poisoning just to see my sister? You're about to spend eight-hours shitting on a cramped airplane *shitter.*"

I don't fucking care. "I'm going." I try to pass, but he steps in front of me. "Lo—"

"Take my jet." He makes a surprised face at himself. "Christ, I sound like Connor."

"Rich and pretentious."

Lo lets out a laugh, a real one. No sarcasm. "Yeah."

"Why's that funny?" I ask.

"Because I've always been rich." Lo can tell that I don't fully get it, and he's not wasting time catching me up to speed. He just says, "If you're going to shit yourself, do it in the comforts of a *private* plane."

I actually laugh now, and the act hurts, pain radiating to my lower back. *Fuuuck.* I suck it down. "Sounds like a plan. See ya."

He walks ahead of me and grabs car keys out of the bowl.

"What are you doing?" I ask, my voice softer.

"Playing Jenga," he says, sarcasm on his lips. "I'm driving you to the goddamn airport. Unless you think you can make it there on your own."

Right now, I feel like I can barely make it to the door. I'll take this handout. As long as it gets me closer to Willow, I'll take whatever I can get.

We drop Maximoff off at Ryke and Daisy's, and then Lo exits the neighborhood. Paparazzi immediately tail us. The sun has set, and darkness clings to the sky. A cameraman hangs out of a Hyundai's window and starts snapping pictures at an excessive rate.

Click click click.

Flash flash flash.

The bright light is blinding in the dark. It's dangerous as fuck. Lo barely blinks, too used to it all, and he keeps both hands tight on the wheel. He'd probably be cursing them out if his kids were in the car.

"Pretty sure there has to be a law against that," I mutter under my breath. I really don't know if there is, but I'm just glad when his bodyguard's security vehicle rides up and blocks the paparazzi van. We ride side-by-side with the Escalade.

Our car bumps over a pothole, and I grimace and try my best not to vomit all over Loren's leather seats.

Fuck.

I have a high pain tolerance, built up over the years, but this is different. A part of me just wants to crawl into the fetal position and cry. Maybe then the pain will stop.

The stabbing in my stomach is a constant companion. The knife goes in and out. In and out and death seems imminent.

I'll die after I see her.

I hang my head. Arms wrapped around my stomach. Lo doesn't talk much as he drives to the airport. But I sense him glancing at me, and he slips out his phone at a stop light to text. Probably checking on his kids.

My head spins, dizzy from the pain and I blow out steady, controlled breaths.

The car starts up again, and when Lo turns the corner, I see the sign to Philly General Hospital. Ambulances pass us, and Lo pulls up to the emergency room.

"No, no, no," I say quickly. "I'm fucking *fi*..." I put my hand over my mouth to stop myself from blowing chunks.

Lo parks and quickly hops out of the car. Not sure when we lost the paparazzi but they're MIA. His bodyguard and another big burly security guy flank him immediately.

"I'm not asking," Lo tells me as he opens my door. "So either you get out of the car, or I carry you out."

I don't have the energy to reply. I'm half here. Half gone to the pain. I barely step onto the pavement before my legs buckle. Someone yells for a wheelchair. It all feels overly dramatic as hell, and I hate it. Too many eyes on me. *Weak shit.* I hear my brothers.

Fuck.

My head is off my shoulders. Up in the clouds. I don't know how I enter the hospital, but someone shoves a blue plastic bag underneath my chin. I vomit.

"Yeah, we're here," Lo says, cell pressed to his ear. "They're bringing him back now…" I lose time and focus. Lo squeezes my shoulder, I think. So I know he's still here with me.

I'm on some hospital bed and the nausea has subsided enough for the pain in my stomach to come back full-force. I'm seconds away from curling into a tiny ball, and when a doctor comes in to check on me, I can't say much but a few moans and grunts.

A nurse starts an IV, and I hear something about *oxy*. Maybe that's just in my head though. Hopeful thinking.

All I know is that I can't die here. Not without seeing her one last time.

Everyone leaves.

That's when it starts getting easier to breathe. Only for some reason, I can only do it through my nose. Otherwise I feel like hurling again.

Lo watches me. "I don't know if you heard—"

I shake my head. I heard jack shit.

"The doctor thinks your appendix might have burst. You're going to have to get a CT scan."

Panic blisters every cell in my body. "And if he's right?"

"It'll have to be removed."

Surgery. Okay, it's alright. It's okay, I convince myself. "How long will that take?" I ask. "I can still make my flight, right? The private plane will wait for me." There's that hope.

Lo tilts his head and looks at me, deeper. "You really love her, huh?"

"Man, I just want to see her," I choke.

Lo rubs the back of his neck and glances nervously to the window. Maybe he feels for me. I don't know. I can't read him. "I want to tell you something…" He shakes his head. "Never mind. I'm not gonna fuck it up. Just lie back and enjoy the narcotics." He waves me off.

I'm confused. But that confusion dies when his bodyguard slips into the room. "Mr. Hale, I just wanted to let you know that the media has been tipped off that you're here with Mr. Abbey."

Great.

Another cherry on top of this motherfucking pie.

Lo nods. "Thanks. I'll get our publicist on it." The bodyguard leaves, and Lo glances to me. "Everything's alright."

It doesn't feel that way.

"Garrison!" Willow calls my name. At least, it sounds like her voice. Faint but recognizable.

Awesome.

I'm hearing her in my head now.

"Garrison!" *What the fuck?*

I look to Lo. He's smiling. Did he hear her too?

With a wince, I pull my body up, my heart thrashing against my chest.

Lo leans out of the doorway. "In here!" he calls out.

And then a second later, I see her.

Brown hair flying out of her messy braid, she bounds close to me and catches my hand in hers. "Garrison, are you okay? Oh my God, you look so pale. And you're burning up." Worry breaches every part of her.

My hand glides to her cheek. "Are you real?" I ask. *How high am I?*

She laughs softly between overcome tears, misting her black-framed glasses. "It was going to be a surprise. My flight was supposed to get in before you even left for the airport. But it got delayed and messed everything up and then Lo texted and said he was taking you to the hospital and I rushed here. And please say something, you look like you're dead. You're not dead, right?" Alarm leeches her voice, and quickly, she takes my pulse.

"I'm so far from dead," I tell her. "And I want to kiss you, but I can't because I've been puking. So can I hold you instead?"

She glances at my IV. "Am I going to mess anything up?"

"No way." I clasp her hip and pull her onto the hospital bed, the same time she crawls next to me.

She's hesitant, scared to hurt me. Eyeing the cords and keeping her body weight off mine.

My lip lifts. I'm so in love with Willow. I tuck her closer to my chest, and she eases more.

"I'm like so fucking jacked up on pain meds right now too. I'm in-de-structable," I say, separating the syllables slowly. Okay, I feel high.

Willow smiles up at me.

I look to Lo. "You knew the whole time? For how long?"

"A month," Lo says. "I can keep a secret." He nods to his sister. "I'll give you two some privacy." He gives me a look. "Only because I know you're not going to kiss." He laughs like his joke is funny. Whatever. I'm not a kid.

"Hey, we don't need chaperones. We're twenty-two!" I yell out to him as he leaves.

"She's twenty-one until tomorrow." His voice tapers off while he walks away.

Willow squeezes my hand in hers, reminding me she's really here. In the flesh.

"It's a weekday," I tell her. "You're missing class."

She nods. "I've asked a few people to take some notes for me. It's all worked out. I'll be here for the rest of the week."

Holy shit.

"Seriously?"

"Seriously."

We're both beyond grinning. My world is lit on fire. Beautiful flames filling my heart. "I thought the universe was trying to tell me something," I say to her. "Getting sick before seeing you."

"Yeah?" she frowns. "Like what?"

"That we're not meant to be together," I laugh, a dry laugh. "And I was ready to choke the universe out to let me get to you."

Willow brushes her finger over my knuckles. "I'm glad you didn't have to do that," she says. "I'm glad I can finally see you."

It should have been me sacrificing time for her, but I bury that guilt. I don't accept it into my life. No more. I'm not going to feel bad for either one of us making time for each other. Because I choose to believe we're stronger than any force in this world. I feel it deeper than I ever have.

No separation will keep us apart. Not really.

We hold each other on the hospital bed, and I dissolve into happiness. "When you leave again," I say, waiting for the pain in those words. But it doesn't come this time. "I just want you to know something."

She lifts her head off my chest to meet my gaze, pushing her glasses up the bridge of her nose.

"Wherever you are, no matter if it's right next to me or a thousand miles away," I say, "I'm tied to you with a thread that can't break. We're connected by something stronger than time or place."

She takes a deep breath, love sweeping around us. "I've felt that for years too, even before I left for London."

"Yeah?" Tears start to crest my eyes.

She wipes the emotion beneath her glasses. "You were there for me when I first moved to Philly, and in a way, it felt like you already hugged me before we even touched."

We breathe in, and I never understood the word *solace* before Willow. But I could lie here next to her, with an inflamed appendix, not saying a thing, and feel that word too deeply.

Solace.

Peace.

We have years left apart, but it's okay. For the first time, I'm truly realizing that nothing can come between us and our love. Not even myself.

I want a career at Cobalt Inc.

I want a future with Willow Hale.

I want it all.

1 YEAR LATER

March

65

Willow Hale

"AM I UNDERDRESSED?" I ASK GARRISON QUIETLY, RIGHT AFTER a suspender-clad hostess seats us at Lola Vine, a cool upscale pizza place in London that I've had my eye on for months. I was so excited about the atmosphere that I forgot to investigate people's clothes off Yelp photos.

I glance down at my thin blue sweater and the unbuttoned plaid flannel I wear on top. And I'm in *jeans*. I could've selected nicer pants.

"Not to me." Garrison scoots closer to the candlelit table. "But if anyone thinks you are, then I am too. We can be underdressed together." He splays a moto jacket on the back of the velvet chair. A black tee molds his toned biceps, but I'm selfishly glad that he's wearing jeans like me.

I smile more, not feeling as out of place.

Garrison adjusts his jacket for another second or two. Giddy energy flutters inside my stomach. I have a lot to be giddy about today.

The biggest one, Garrison is in London. Just seeing my boyfriend makes the weeks of dreaming about him feel real.

And we're on a date. I still can't believe he reserved a table *here*. Every time I wanted to go when he was in town, they'd been booked up for the whole week.

"What do you think so far?" Garrison asks, handing me a leather-bound menu. "As cool as you imagined?"

I realize that I've been staring at him more than the restaurant. Looking around, I soak up my surroundings: orange and purple velvet chairs and booths, swanky curved bar with fancy liquors, a mirrored ceiling, deep red carpet, and rouged drapes.

"Better." I can't stop smiling. "It feels like the Hellfire Club could exist in here." A popular comic book site named ten restaurants that reminded them of the *X-Men* films, and Lola Vine was listed under *X-Men: First Class*. I was shocked a restaurant within distance of my college made the cut.

I wait for Garrison to make a joke like *what's the Hellfire Club?* with mock confusion. After all his time working at Superheroes & Scones, I'm pretty sure he'd remember the clandestine society with Emma Frost as a member.

Garrison nods. "That's good....really good." His aquamarine eyes flit around the packed restaurant. I doubt anyone will recognize us with the lights dimmed to a dark, warm glow.

A waitress brings iced waters, tells us the specials, and leaves to give us time to order.

I peruse Garrison more than the menu. He's acting sort of weird. He keeps scooting his chair closer, perching his elbow on and off the table.

"Is everything okay?" I push up my glasses.

"Yeah, why wouldn't it be?" He takes a hefty swig of water.

I shrug. Maybe I'm overthinking his jitters, but I'd like to think I know him really, *really* well. "I don't know...are you sure nothing's going on?"

He runs a hand through his brown hair. "No, nothing's really going on." He rests his arm on the back of the chair, trying to be more cool and collected.

I mean, he does look cool.

Tattoos on his bicep, hair falling back to his eyes, and bad boy persona like a well-worn cloak—but after all these years, I know better.

Garrison Abbey is *good*.

He just has a bad reputation.

One that's been scrubbed clean by the people who love him most, the ones who gave him another chance, another shot.

I change the topic to movies after we order a margherita pizza and classic pepperoni. "I don't think anything will ever top *Avengers: End Game*." I sip my water.

Garrison is staring off behind me, then blinks to refocus on me. "Yeah, that's a good one. Jake Gyllenhaal killed it as that Mysterio guy."

Wrong movie.

We were talking about *Spider-Man: Far From Home* five minutes ago. I frown and open my mouth, about to ask if he's okay again.

But quickly, he asks, "How'd the meeting with Lily and the attorneys go?"

Lily and the attorneys.

Giddiness returns, and it's weird to think around this time, a whole year ago, I flew to Philly and ran into the hospital. Garrison's appendix was removed. I was still living in the "party" flat. I was worried about my few friendships and my slipping grades.

A lot has happened in a year. While some things have stayed the same.

My lease ended, and I moved into a studio apartment close to campus. No roommates, which has helped boost my grades up to Bs and As.

And with my new place, it's been easier keeping Sheetal and Tess as friends. They've been on-and-off as a couple all year, ever since Tess changed majors to *theatre*. But right now, they're in a "firmly together" stage.

As for Salvatore, I haven't really spoken much to him since I moved out, but we still share a lot of business classes and see each other.

It's awkward, but I prefer awkward over the discomfort and bitter anger I started to feel towards him. Especially how he kept treating Garrison like trash.

Sheetal makes class with Salvatore more bearable. She'll crack jokes before lectures, and the air always feels lighter.

But what Garrison is referencing—Lily and the attorneys—is more recent.

"I figured Lily already told you how it went," I say, since Garrison is still living in her home with Lo and their kids.

"Yeah, but it's not you telling me," Garrison says like hearing me makes all the difference.

My smile tugs higher. "Okay, so it looks like franchising Superheroes & Scones is one-hundred percent a go, and then I pitched the idea of opening up a London branch."

His mouth parts in a little shock. "London?"

I frown, realizing Lily must've left this out. "I didn't go into the franchise meeting thinking London would come out of my mouth, but Lily asked me, *'If you opened up a store, which city would you choose?'*"

He shakes his head, confused. "Why London, though? You could've said…New York City or Pittsburgh."

"I don't know New York or Pittsburgh that well," I say softly. "London has been my home for over two years, and I understand the market and the streets and people. I feel confident I could open a store here, if given the chance."

Garrison gazes at the flickering candle, his thoughts swirling.

I scoot closer now, my pulse haywire. "Even if I open a London branch, Lily said I could be in charge of opening more locations." My voice is too quiet, and in this tender way, he asks me to repeat. So I do, and I add, "She's offering me a job when I graduate. Like a corporate-level, high-paying position that I hope…I hope I can be ready for, but it sounds like a dream…"

Putting my business degree to good use while being surrounded by superheroes and comics every day—I couldn't ask for a better career.

I wait for him to reply, holding my breath. "Garrison?"

"You'll be good at it," he says, certain of this fact. "I know you will be."

"I could suck."

"No." He has so much faith in me that my heart ascends to new levels. "You're smart, Willow, and you're so passionate about business and comics. It makes perfect sense."

I scrutinize the slight dip of his mouth. "But...?" *There has to be a but coming.*

"But what does this mean for us?" He grimaces. "And I feel like a *cock* bringing myself into this and dampening the happiness of your career path."

"It's not dampened," I say with a peeking smile. "And I'd hope you'd think about what this means for us...because I'd rather there be an us to think about, you know?" *Giddiness,* a strange kind of giddy ignites.

Maybe because he's smiling again. "Alright, that's good then." He looks me over, his eyes carrying gentle affection. "What about us? You want to live in London full-time after graduation?"

"I'd rather just fly back every now and then. I know the paparazzi is nuts in Philly, but I miss it there. I miss everyone."

Garrison nods strongly, and I can tell he likes this plan. "It's not that I don't love London," he explains to me. "It's a city that'll always remind me of you. But I love Philly."

I smile. "Me too."

It's where I met my brothers, where I met my best friend Daisy, and where I met my first love who's sitting across from me six years later.

We talk a bit more about my future job. I try not to glance at my phone, but I swear we put our food orders in over forty minutes ago.

I don't care much about the pizza though.

I just like being here with Garrison.

He's gone a little quiet, and he rubs his palms, elbows on the table. He's staring around but his eyes always land on me, almost too much.

I give him a look.

He gives me one. "What?"

I shrug, waiting for him to tell me *something.* But he inhales a tense breath and licks his lips, just looking deeper into me.

I decide to talk. "Do you think they forgot our order?"

He scans the restaurant quickly, then back to me. "It probably takes a while to cook a fresh pizza." He seems disinterested in the food.

"How's lacrosse going?" I ask since he's been playing on a club team. Just for fun on the weekends. He's more resilient and determined than he lets on, or maybe he even realizes. Not a lot of people would return to a sport they have a love-hate relationship with, let alone find enjoyment in the activity again.

"It's good." He nods.

"You've been saying that a lot," I tell him.

He looks confused.

I clarify, "It's *good*, that's *good*, everything's *good*."

"What can I say? I'm a thousand-page thesaurus." His sarcasm is thick, a smile attached.

I want to laugh but my lips draw down. "Really, though, you're starting to worry me. Did something happen—"

"No, I promise, Willow, everything is perfect." His eyes grow far more tender, and he reaches a hand across the table.

I place my palm in his, and his thumb strokes my knuckles, expanding my lungs. His gaze is welling up, just looking at me.

It causes me to tear up. "Why are you staring at me like that?"

"Because I love you, Willow Hale. You're the greatest friend I've ever had, the most beautiful heart I've ever felt, and every morning I wake up, I can only hope to wake to you. Thinking of a single day without you in my life is physical torture." He takes my other hand, careful not to knock over the candle. "There was a time where I didn't even want to live till tomorrow, and now I don't ever want this life with you to end."

Overwhelmed tears roll down my cheeks, emotion that I can't conceal. Emotion that I don't try to hide.

He keeps going, his voice choked, on the verge of crying. "I want to play Street Fighter when we're too old to work the fucking controllers, and I want our kid to beat every high score we set. I want my girl, my greatest friend, to be the mother of my child, and to be my wife."

His wife.

He lets go of my hands, and my palms fly to my mouth.

Garrison.

I watch as he scoots his chair back.

"Garrison?" I croak.

Is he…?

I glance around, but of what I can see in the dim restaurant, no one is filming. People are watching, but no one has cameras out… or phones.

He planned this. He must have.

He planned this for me? For us.

"Willow." He takes a knee in front of my chair.

I'm still in tears, still stunned, and I angle towards him.

Garrison reaches into his back pocket and pulls out a black box. He wipes the wet corners of his eyes and flips the lid. "Will you do the biggest honor of my whole existence and marry me?" His voice trembles.

I cry, pinching my eyes, and I nod and say, "Yes." And then we're in each other's arms. Hugging. He brings me to a stance, to his chest, and our lips meet with so much soul and life and love that I feel like I'm soaring.

When we pull back, he slips a dainty ring on my finger, a diamond on a thin gold band with six tinier diamonds scattered like a vine. It's beautiful, but I don't have the chance to tell him.

Rouged curtains open behind me, and I hear applause and cheering before I see them.

My family.

Lo and Ryke. My dad. And Connor, Rose, Lily, and Daisy. My friends Sheetal and Tess. They're all here. Smiling. Crying.

I'm more overcome with more happiness. Seeing so many faces I love in one room. One place. In London.

I don't let go of Garrison's hand as I greet everyone.

I'm engaged.

To my guy, my greatest friend, to the someday father of my child, to my whole, beautiful future. It's going to be full of him.

PIZZAS ARE SPREAD OUT IN A FANCY, PRIVATE BACKROOM OF Lola Vine, where my family and friends had been hiding and waiting for Garrison to pop the big question.

What I quickly discover: the proposal was *months* in the making. Which means he knew he wanted to marry me months ago.

He asked me to marry him. It's still sinking in.

My face hurts from smiling.

Everyone managed to keep the secret to surprise me, and I still feel light-on-my-toes, floating and butterflies flapping—like I'm seventeen again with Garrison Abbey, about to embark on my first day at Dalton Academy.

And he's next to his car, waiting for me.

The night is winding down, pizzas devoured and a towering meringue pie picked on. I already asked Daisy to be my maid of honor. I blurted it out, and tears streamed down her cheeks as she hugged me. Instantly accepting the role.

Rose and Lily were each other's maids of honor, and Daisy never had a sister place her at the top. But she's number one on my list.

After I say goodbye to Sheetal and Tess, I take a bathroom break with the Calloway sisters, and Garrison and Connor slip into the men's room.

All should be perfectly well and good, but when we return to the backroom to grab coats, the air isn't easygoing or happy like we left it.

Lo and Ryke face our dad, all three on their feet and wielding heated glares and tense postures.

And as their eyes swerve to me, descending upon me with hot intimidation, I know what this has to be about. It's the only thing I can think of that'd elicit this intense reaction.

The lie.

My bad deed.

Years ago, I accepted Jonathan Hale's money to bribe students into deleting video footage of Garrion's fight with Salvatore, and I never told my brothers.

Every butterfly dies in my lungs, wings cut.

Garrison slips an arm around my waist. He's right next to me, but I have a feeling he won't be for long.

Rose is the first to speak. "What's going on?" Her voice is accusatory, like they're harbors of grave news on my celebratory day, and therefore, should be punished.

But it's my fault, for not telling them the truth in the first place.

"We need to talk to our sister," Lo says, his amber eyes still on mine. He seems really upset, and remorse eats at my insides.

Ryke adds, "In private."

I'm frozen, but I try to breathe.

My dad has a hand on his side, standing like he's made of importance and prestige. "If you're not a Hale by blood, you should go wait in the cars. We'll be out in a few minutes."

"I'm not leaving," Garrison retorts. "If this is about Willow—"

"She can talk to you later," Lo interjects. "We won't be that long."

Garrison's eyes fall down to me while Rose and Connor speak rapidly in fiery and smooth French to one another, filling the silence. Daisy and Lily are holding hands, and they exit the backroom first, but not before Daisy mouths to me, *you got this*.

She has no idea what I'm about to face or the truth I withheld, but she's still encouraging me. Still has faith in me. I breathe in, and I look up at Garrison. "I'll be okay."

He studies my expression and my trembling hands that I cup together. His palm glides down my wrist, to my hand, in tender comfort that floods me.

"I can stay," he whispers, and then pauses, our eyes latching like he, too, knows what this is probably about. "I should stay."

My brothers don't want him to. I whisper back, "I think I should do this on my own." I'm anxious by nature, but I'm not as nervous in the company of these three men as I used to be. At the beginning, just being face-to-face with my dad, I could barely hold a drink without water shaking and spilling out.

Ryke and Lo aren't soft, but they love me, and I know they wouldn't hurt me, even when I've hurt them.

Garrison hugs me, then stakes a glare on the room. "I know she's your sister, and your daughter." He looks to my dad. "But just remember I'm going to be her *husband*. So you fuck with her, you're dead to me."

Ryke rolls his eyes. "We're not going to fuck with our sister."

"We get it," Lo tells Garrison. "Skedaddle." He waves him off with two running fingers.

It lightens the air a little, and Garrison leaves the private backroom with one last glance at me, making sure I'm alright.

I nudge up my glasses with a tiny smile.

Connor and Rose reluctantly follow my boyfriend—or I guess, my fiancé. *We're engaged.* And on her way out, Rose grabs her fur coat and squeezes my shoulder with an iron grip.

Now I'm alone with just my older brothers and my dad. I linger awkwardly at one head of the table while they're clustered near the other end. A few half-eaten slices of margherita pizza are left on plates, napkins wadded on the long candlelit surface. Remnants of a happy engagement dinner.

I subconsciously touch the new piece of jewelry on my finger.

And three sets of eyes drop to my engagement ring.

Tension strains the air even more.

Ryke rakes a hand across his unshaven jaw. "Look, we're not going to ruin your fucking engagement. We just want an explanation."

"I want to give one," I say quietly, "but I don't know what you've heard...?"

Lo grips the back of a velvet chair. "Our dad said he gave you *a hundred grand,* so that you could get a bunch of students to delete some video of Garrison sucker-punching another kid. And I get wanting to keep your boyfriend's shitty night out of the press. We've all been there. Too many goddamn times. But out of everyone you could have gone to for help—your first choice was *him*." His brows pinch in hurt and confusion. "I know you've always said you want to do things on your own. You don't want handouts. But what you took was a handout from our dad, and I don't see why you trusted him more than us."

"We would've fucking helped you," Ryke says strongly, gesturing from his chest to Lo's.

I shift my weight, trying to hold their hard and sharp gazes. "I know you would've."

Our dad narrows a jagged-edged look on his sons. "Give her a fucking break. I'm her father. She came to me for help. I *helped* her. You're both blowing this shit out of proportion."

Eyes darkened, Ryke guns him down. "Don't stand there and act like your handouts don't come with selfish fucking *conditions*."

He chokes on a hot breath. "What conditions? All I've ever wanted was for her to go to an Ivy League—not some no-name business school in *London*—but did you hear me complain about it? *No*," our dad snaps. "I applauded and sent her on her way and helped her *stay* there. And then when she called me needing my help again, I did with no questions asked."

Ryke is fuming. "What about the internship with the Nubell family she took last summer? Did she want to do that or did you push her there?"

He pushed me.

I drop my gaze, ashamed.

Nubell cookies are almost as popular as Kraft and Keebler, and I spent the summer running errands for Patrick Nubell, the great-great-grandson of the company. It was a good opportunity, just not the one I really wanted.

I had the chance to intern for a big comic book publishing company in New York. Mostly due to the fact that I was related to Loren Hale, not based on my skill or resumé. I know that, but I still would've accepted.

In the end, I had to decline.

My dad was adamant that I take the Nubell internship. *"I pulled these strings for you, Willow. It wasn't easy."*

"She wanted that internship!" our dad shouts at Ryke. "It was a perfect experience for her future—"

"For the future you want for her!" Ryke yells.

"I want the best for my daughter," he sneers back, eyes like blades. "I want the best for you and Loren. I want the best for my *fucking* children, and you're not going to make me apologize for that!"

"Stop," Lo snaps at them, often having to play peacemaker between his dad and brother. He steps between their rigid builds and focuses on me. "The one thing that just doesn't make sense to me, Willow, is that Ryke and I could've helped you so many times and you said *no* or you didn't ask when you needed it. Not just with burying that video footage, but tuition and even your flat, back when you wanted out of the lease. You didn't let us help you, so why accept our dad's help but not ours?"

Ryke faces me more now, his brows furrowed. He wants this answer too, and I know it's the biggest one.

What changed that made me go to Jonathan and not to them.

Emotion stings my eyes. "I never wanted to burden any of you." I wipe beneath my glasses. "I never wanted to come into your lives taking more than I should. You all know that; I've said as much before. But I needed the money to protect Garrison, and when I had to make a choice to burden a father or a brother, I decided to burden a father." A tear slips out, and I look to Lo. "You've taken care of me since I came to Philly, even before I knew Jonathan was my dad—but you have two children, Lo. You have a son and a daughter, and maybe one day you'll have more babies, and they're going to need your help and your support too. And the way I saw it, I couldn't take from you or Ryke because everything I take could go to your kids."

Their gazes try to soften, and I see their sadness.

"I'm not your child," I continue on. "I'm *his*." I motion to Jonathan. "And he has less on his plate than both of you." He's retired. His sons are grown up and financially independent. It made the most sense.

If they thought I went to our dad because I love him or trust him more, it's almost the opposite.

I love Lo and Ryke and their families too much to ask for more.

Lo's jaw sharpens. "I wish you didn't feel like that." He comes closer as I sniff, and my brother hugs me, a hug that slows my anxious heartbeat.

As we pull back, I wipe my running nose with my knuckles. "You've done everything for me, and it's okay that you let our dad do this."

Lo nods a few times, understanding, but Ryke looks more concerned. He'll always be worried about Jonathan having control over my life. Over Lo's life, too.

But maybe it's good that they both know about the hundred grand. Maybe I should've told them so much sooner. Because the way they turn to our dad, I know they'll never let him dictate where I go or what I do. No matter how many checks he writes.

66

Garrison Abbey

LAST DAY IN LONDON BEFORE WE FLY BACK TO PHILLY, AND I'M still happily engaged to Willow. For a guy who's certifiably *cursed*, that's pretty much all I could ask for, and it's a lot to ask because it's all I want.

I accounted for some drama since I invited her dad to the engagement dinner, so no surprise there. But it's not until his daughter is gone—at a brunch outing with all the Calloway sisters—that he decides to serve his shitty opinions.

And they're all being flung on a gold platter at *me*.

"She hasn't even graduated from college yet or begun a career," Jonathan tells me in his penthouse suite, where he invited his sons, Connor, and me for lunch. "If you thought more about her academics, you would've waited. It's too soon—"

"No, it's not," I retort, leaning backward. My instinct is to draw away from bullshit, not catapult towards a fight.

Connor just went to the bathroom to take a business phone call, but the rest of us are seated at an ornate round table that looks fit for the British royal family, and we have perfect views of the River Thames, Big Ben, and Westminster Abbey.

Willow's dad is loaded. The sheer wealth of this man is literally all around me, and I stare Jonathan Hale down as I add, "Willow and I already agreed to get married *after* she graduates." She has to finish up this semester, and then she'll be a senior.

One year and some months left. That's it.

Piece of cake.

"You're too eager, and you're rushing her," Jonathan criticizes as he dunks a biscuit in coffee. "Give her time."

"Dad," Lo says with the shake of his head.

Ryke glares at their father. "Why are you always speaking for Willow? She's not fucking here, and if she were, we all know she wouldn't agree with you."

Jonathan ignores his son, his eyes on me. "You're not thinking this through, Garrison."

"I am," I snap. "Last time I checked, I have a brain."

"Use it then and let her have a fucking career first. If you're lucky, she'll still be around."

Anger punctures my eyes. He's saying that she might not want to marry me once she's established a career. "Say that in front of Willow," I sneer at Jonathan. He'd never utter half the vile shit he's been spewing if his daughter were around.

He bites into a soggy biscuit.

I can't shut my mouth. "Right." I nod. "You're a gutless fish."

Ryke and Lo go rigid in shock.

And then Jonathan wipes his mouth with a napkin, his eyes lethal as he says, "You're a fucking cunt."

"Hey!" Ryke yells, gripping the table like he could flip it. "For fuck's sake, he's going to be your son-in-law, back the fuck off him."

My hammering pulse is in my ears.

Jonathan stands, zeroing in only on me. "I'm not skirting around you, Garrison, and you should thank me for not patting you on the ass like a goddamn toddler."

I let out a short, sardonic laugh. "Thank you, I'm just so grateful to hear that you think I rushed a proposal *after* I proposed only two days ago."

He rolls his eyes. "You're a petulant child. Grow *up*."

"*Dad*," Lo snarls, and if looks could kill, Jonathan would be butchered in a million serrated pieces by Lo. But likewise, his glare is slaughtering his own son.

I don't want to be on the receiving end of that. It scares the shit out of me, but my brain is shrieking, *fuck him*. "I am grown up. The only one kicking and screaming is you."

He swings his head to me, about to eat me alive. "You ungrateful son of a bitch—"

"Jesus Christ, don't fucking attack him," Lo cuts in, springing to his feet while I stay tilted back in my chair like the degenerate I'm sure Jonathan thinks I am.

Lo blocks his dad from me, and Ryke is standing, sort of between me and his brother. I think in case either of us need him.

Jonathan is seething, glare skewering me. "He said he's a man, Loren, so he should be able to talk to me man-to-man without you coming to his defense." He continues, "Come on, Garrison. You're all grown up, aren't you? Show me."

I grind my teeth, my stomach in knots, and my heated eyes sear the table. I'm shutting down, not wanting deeper in this shit.

I want out.

No part of me wants to prove how big of a man I am. I can't prove shit to him, so what's the fucking point?

I push back, standing up from the table.

Ryke and Lo are speaking to their dad with heat and urgency, but he's not listening to them.

"You're leaving?" Jonathan calls out to me incredulously, like our joust has just begun. He shouts at me as I walk off. "Is that how you'll be with my daughter? When the fight gets hard, you're just going to run away?!"

I will always protect Willow, but I don't need to convince anyone of that.

The hotel elevator is inside the penthouse, and as I reach my escape, Connor exits the bathroom, pocketing his cellphone. His eyes ping to me and then the echoes of Ryke, Lo, and Jonathan's heated argument.

"I leave for five minutes," he says calmly to himself, then sweeps me and then the elevator. "You're going?"

I nod. "To brunch." I'm crashing the girls' thing. Willow won't care.

"Wait here." His soothing voice somehow hypnotizes me to obey. I wait at the elevator, and he disappears. Two seconds later, Ryke and Lo are in his company, their confident strides aimed for the elevator.

I make a confused face.

"We're all going to brunch," Connor informs me, pushing the elevator button. We don't wait long for the doors to slide open, and the four of us file in.

I hang behind them. They're all fucking tall, all towering, and the way they stand like a defensive brick wall—it feels like they're shielding me. Paparazzi might be in the lobby. I think Connor is texting security.

But it's more than that.

Ryke glances back at me. "You okay?"

I can only nod.

Lo looks back next.

Then Connor.

They're all checking on me. And I have to stare at the elevator wall because something pricks my eyes. I blink a few times. Don't fucking cry.

It's okay to cry.

Lo told me that.

It's okay to cry.

I look up at the ceiling, a tear rolling down my jaw. I'm not emotional because of anything Jonathan said.

I'm emotional because I got the three brothers I always wished I had.

Connor, Ryke, and Lo—they protect me all the time. They care about me when they don't have to. These are three brothers that I'd never trade in, never swap out, and even though we're not blood related, I know they're mine.

IN THE MEN'S BATHROOM AT BRUNCH, LO AND I FIND OURSELVES alone, and I end up confessing that I don't know what to do about Jonathan.

"I want to respect him because he's Willow's dad," I say, drying my hands on a paper towel. "But I can't stand him, no offense."

Lo almost laughs. "None taken. I get how he is, man. I grew up with him."

I can't even imagine how he survived that verbal sledgehammer every day. But I don't say it out loud, because I know he'd say the same about me and my brothers.

He leans against the sink. "You know, way back when Lily's sex addiction leaked, he tried to push us into a marriage to save our reputations and those around us."

My brows pinch. "He tried to push you *into* one?"

"Yeah." Lo flashes a bitter smile. "The guilt-trip is heavy, almost enough to make you do things you'd never think you'd do." He stares off and shakes his head, going into a longer explanation about that time in the past.

It makes me feel...not alone.

Like I'm dealing with a cankerous sore that they've all tried to disinfect and rid.

"As much as I love him," Lo says, "he shouldn't have the power to guilt anyone into anything. Not into a marriage and not out of one."

I nod slowly and toss the crumpled towel in the trash. "You think he'll ever lay off me?"

"With my dad, just give it time, and we'll see."

THE CALLOWAY SISTERS & THEIR MEN – FAN PAGE

FOLLOWERS: 201K

If you haven't heard of the *big* news and seen all the adorable pictures circulating GBA News and *Celebrity Crush*, then you're missing out on history. Our gorgeous Calloway sisters and their sexy AF men were in London for Garrison & Willow's engagement! And a little birdie around the inter-webs has revealed that Garrison *surprised* his girlfriend—how cute is that? With everyone except Willow back in Philly, here's a helpful rundown on their whereabouts!

The Stokes
Poppy Calloway (34) & Sam Stokes (34)
Daughter: Maria (12)
Update: Boo, the Stokes are *very* MIA these days. They didn't even show up to London for Willow's big day. It would've been so cool to have a glimpse of preteen Maria!

The Cobalts
Rose Calloway (31) & Connor Cobalt (32)
Daughters: Jane (5)
Sons: Charlie & Beckett (3-year-old twins), Eliot (1), and Tom (11-months-old)
Update: Rumors are floating everywhere about Rose being pregnant again! Whether it's true or not, the Cobalt Empire deserves a confetti-blast congrats for all the lion cubs they're raising. #FamilyGoals. Have

you seen a tighter-knit family? Besides pregnancy possibilities, both Rose and Connor are thriving in their companies. Cobalt Inc.'s stock has risen 31%, and Calloway Couture's boutique was packed last week (pics in the slideshow!)

The Hales
Lily Calloway (29) & Loren Hale (30)
Son: Maximoff (5)
Daughter: Luna (1)
Update: The cutest of the cute! Lily and Lo are back in Philly with their tiny superheroes, and Maximoff *loves* to dress like his Uncle Ryke. He was seen in a cool leather jacket and trying to climb onto Ryke's Ducati. No news about more Hale babies, but fingers crossed!

The Meadows
Daisy Calloway (25) & Ryke Meadows (31)
Daughter: Sullivan (3)
Update: Also back in lovely Philadelphia, Daisy and Ryke are busy, wild bees with summer approaching since Camp Calloway is a tremendous hit! It's sold out for this year and the next. No new photos of Sulli, except some blurry pics after swim lessons with her cousin Maximoff (see below!)

The Unofficial Calloway Sister
Willow Hale (23) & Her Fiancé – Garrison Abbey (23)
Update: Sweet, sweet love! After their epic proposal, Garrison has flown back to Philly, leaving Willow behind as she finishes college in London. No one is sure about *when* the wedding is happening. Some sources are speculating early this year, others think

a lot longer. Until there's clearer info, let us know your favorite Willow & Garrison ship name: #Gillow, #Garlow, or #Wilson. Don't forget to vote in the poll!

Love you like Loren loves Lily,
xo Olive

67

Garrison Abbey

THE PROPOSAL WAS LAST WEEK, AND NOW THAT I'M IN PHILLY, I'm back to doing this thing where I try not to mope while the girl I love is an ocean away. By now, I'd say I'm proficient in the art of being okay with long-distance relationships. Productivity is key or whatever.

That's why I'm at Superheroes & Scones today.

It's weird being back and not being an employee or babysitting Moffy here. I enter the breakroom and ask the store manager where Lily is. Seeing the new face wearing the "manager" nametag reminds me of Maya.

Last I heard, Maya Ahn is still in Portland working for Image Comics.

It was a big deal when she first landed the job. Lily and Willow were really proud.

There was a whole goodbye party when she left the store, and I learned enough Korean to tell her that she'll always know more than me and she's really cool.

She smiled and said shit back in Korean that she knew I wouldn't understand. We laughed, and I hate that I'm remembering all of this—Jesus, I swear every time I walk into Superheroes & Scones, I'm thrown back into these bittersweet, feel-good memories.

The new manager says, "She's in the storage room."

I pop the tab of a Lightning Bolt! energy drink and shove inside. Boxes of merch and comics line the space. Familiarity surrounding me, and I'm honestly trying not to face-plant on Memory Lane.

I find Lily and her two kids pretty easily.

Baggy *Star Wars* tee on and phone close to her ear, Lily looks like she snuck back here for a quiet moment. Which I'm about to interrupt.

Awesome. Looks like I still have Grand Slam worthy timing.

I shut the door with my foot, not bailing.

"Lo," she says into the phone, face flushed, "you didn't tell Garrison, did you?"

"Tell me what?" I stand by an old comic stand in need of serious dusting. *Remember when you dusted the clearance merch with Willow?*

Like yesterday.

Near a life-sized Magneto cutout, Maximoff Hale leaps off a cardboard box and races towards me. "Uncle Garrison!"

The corner of my mouth lifts. Moffy acts like I'm the coolest thing in the room, and we're surrounded by crates of action figures.

The five-year-old rolls up to me, and we do a secret handshake that ends with a fist-bump.

"Never mind," Lily tells me, then listens to her phone call.

"Did you see Luna?" Moffy smiles and points out his one-year-old sister, hiding in a cardboard box. She giggles, glittering eyes peeking out at me.

"Whoa, she's getting smaller and you're getting taller."

"I am?" His smile mushrooms.

I pretend to measure his height with my free hand. "Definitely a centimeter taller than when I last saw you." Which was this morning. I still live with the Hale family.

"You think I'll be as tall as you, Uncle Garrison?" His voice sounds like he's five, but he sometimes acts older, like he's already leveled-up to a preteen in a 90s cult classic movie starring Jonathan Taylor Thomas.

"Way taller." I'm not that short, but his dad is six-two.

"Cool," Maximoff says and stares off in thought.

Lily hangs up her phone, so I walk closer, and Moffy matches my pace. Before she asks why I'm here, I tell her, "I need your help on something."

Lily tickles her daughter in the box, and Luna tugs her mom's finger with another giggle. "What can I do?"

I sip my energy drink and gesture to a few cardboard boxes labeled *The Fourth Degree*. I'm guessing each contain comics slipped in protective plastic. Here, back stock is usually just obscure issues that don't sell or extras to replenish ones that fly off the shelves. I explain, "I need every comic that has Sorin-X. There are too many issues and spin-offs now. Honestly, I don't have time to go through all of them."

I always thought Vic Whistler would continue to be the most popular superhero in *The Fourth Degree* universe. Somehow, Sorin-X surpassed the hero that launched the franchise.

It still blows my mind.

I wait for Lily to ask *why* I'm requesting this shit. She doesn't yet. Instead, Lily picks herself off the floor and glances at her son. "Moffy, there's a little Luna in a box—"

"I got her, Mommy." Maximoff goes to the box and plays with his sister, like babysitting is the equivalent of a trip to Disney.

Weird.

But wholesome.

Honestly, I like being around both.

"They're all in here." Lily guides me to *The Fourth Degree* labeled boxes. "Lo will be here soon, and he might be more help. He's read every issue about a million times."

We tear open a couple boxes and flip through the comic, setting aside any with Sorin-X.

Ones without the character, Lily gingerly slips the issue into its plastic cover. "Are you going to read these?" She motions to the Sorin-X pile.

I place another issue on top. "What else would I be doing with them?"

"I don't know." She squints at me. "You don't really read comics, not like Willow." She notes, "You had no clue who Cypher was when you started working here."

"Yeah, and none of the employees ever let me forget it." I begin to smile, remembering how Willow tried to help me learn factoids about the New Mutants so our co-workers would stop giving me shit. *Six years ago.* I swig my energy drink to swallow down the nostalgia and say, "I've read New Mutants, by the way."

Lily wears a giddy smile. "Because of Willow?" I love how supportive she's always been of me and Willow, especially since she was there at the beginning of it all.

"Yeah, because of Willow." I shake a comic back into the plastic sleeve.

"Which brings everything to Twitter. *Gillow Engagement* has been trending all day, did you see?"

My stomach nosedives, energy drink curdling.

The headlines are pretty generic:

Willow Hale Gets Engaged!
Check out Loren Hale's New Brother-In-Law!

I prepared for press to be all over our ass, but I'm worried the amount of paparazzi interested in us right now could go from "Chaotic Good" to "Chaotic Evil". I'd really love if my fame capped out here.

No more.

Lily continues, "Connor said you both made GBA Entertainment News last night too." I pegged him as a daily C-Span viewer. The guy still reads the *paper.* As in newspaper. Printed. In his hands.

"He watches entertainment news?" I say with cinched brows.

"That was my reaction."

Maybe to check himself out. He is a narcissist.

I flip another comic, recalling other trending Twitter topics. "You also forgot about *Garlow Engagement* and *Wilson Engagement.*"

Fans still can't decide on a ship name, which are dumb anyway. Willow loves ships though and even owns Raisy, Coballoway, and

LiLo merch. She's too kind to play favorites, so she supports all three of our ship names too.

"Does all of this bother you?" Lily asks me. "You and Willow never talk to us about the media presence."

Because *they're* the cause of our fame, and it feels shitty to complain when they've done a lot for us.

I shrug. "Being around you guys, it just comes with the territory, and we both kind of gradually stepped into it." Thank God we weren't thrown into the deep end at the start. If the paparazzi were all over me back then like they are now, I don't think I could handle it.

I tilt a comic upside-down, the panel sort of backwards. Brown hair hangs in my eyes. *Need a haircut.* It's starting to bug the fuck out of me.

My stomach is still in knots. And I know it's not about my hair.

Paparazzi.

Coming home from the engagement in London was pure hell. Fans and media bum-rushed us at the airport, and I could barely see. Barely breathe. Rabid crowds, I've dealt with before, but for maybe the first time, the spotlight was centralized on *me*.

If I think too hard, I can still feel hands scraping down my arms. Tugging my body. Pulling at my shirt, choking me at the collar until Lo's bodyguard shoved them away.

Sickness churns at the thought of that happening again.

But at some point soon, I have to go back to the airport. I have to see Willow.

And next time, Lo, Ryke, Connor, and their security won't be with me.

"Lily...can I ask you something?" I peek over at Moffy, ensuring he's not listening. Last thing I'd want is to scare him about the media. Especially when they're raising their kids to be accustomed to crowds and cameras.

He's climbed into a plushies box with Luna and chats to his sister. She baby-blabbers back.

Lily smiles fondly at her kids, then nods to me. "Sure."

"I just…" I shake my head. *Don't complain.* "Forget it. It's stupid." I chuck a comic aside.

"I bet it's not." She sidles closer.

I stare down at an issue called *Battle of the Extent* and just let it out. "The airport—I don't want to be mobbed like that when I go to London alone." I inhale. "I just…I don't want to be touched like that again."

Lily holds a breath, concerned. "Are you scared to go back to the airport?"

I shrug and then nod.

"I can ride to the airport with you when you need to go, and there's this thing we can do." She explains, "We can drive right up to the private plane and bypass the normal airport entrance?"

When Willow left for London, she did that, but I didn't think the offer would ever be extended to me.

I frown. "We can do that?"

"We've done it before. The airport gives us permission because we cause a lot of disruption. It's safer for us and for everyone else."

"But it's just me…I don't usually fly in a private plane."

"Yeah but you can take our planes alone. We don't mind. We'd want you to."

I'm already shaking my head. "It's too much for just me." I don't know what I expected her to offer—but this feels like the entire world, and I just need…

I don't know.

Air.

"Then I'll send Garth with you," she says, offering me her 24/7 bodyguard for travel. "He's the best. If it's only you, the crowds won't be as bad. I know they won't."

I have a temporary bodyguard that I sometimes use. He's okay, and I know that bodyguards who are *constantly* around the families and assigned to specific people are ten-times better. They're trained for everything. Even kidnappings.

But I don't love the idea of someone following me all day.

Even if they say nothing and just stand there. It's creepy.

Having two bodyguards in the airport would definitely help, so I nod to Lily.

"Have you told Willow?" she asks.

"*No*," I force out, hoping she doesn't tell her either. "If she knew, she'd start flying to Philly to see me instead of the other way around." I lick my dry lips. "Willow gets anxiety when she's stuck in the middle of crowds. I know she'd brave it out for me, but…"

"You want to brave this out for her," she realizes.

I nod more firmly. "Yeah."

Moffy shouts, "I think you're brave, Uncle Garrison!"

I smile weakly and tell Lily, "Your kid is funny."

"Or maybe he's right."

I exhale the heaviness that'd been on my chest. *Yeah, I feel better.* "So I can take Garth when I fly to London?"

"Without a doubt, no take-backs. Cross my heart." She makes an "x" over her heart and adds, "He's pretty much the family bodyguard, and you're our family."

That feels good.

I smile more. "Thanks. I appreciate everything, you know?" Again, she's helping me. Again, she's not even hesitating.

I owe so much to Lily Calloway. For her kindness. For seeing something inside me worth a damn. Because the day I walked in this store, asking for a job—it changed my life.

Lily nods again, a nostalgic smile rising.

We return to the comics, hunting through the boxes for Sorin-X, and she asks me why I need all of them.

Here we go. "I guess I have to ask about it anyway, but you have to promise not to tell the tall one. He's literally throwing hundreds of thousands of dollars at my face. I'm scared shitless he'll shut the entire thing down and fire me if he finds out."

My secret project has been on-going for *three* years. I think he's out of his fucking mind for even letting me code without evidence of what the hell I'm programming.

For all he knows, I could be pissing time away constructing a unicorn farm on Minecraft.

I'm literally a heartbeat away from purging the big secret when the storage door swings open.

Oh shit.

Loren Hale pockets his keys as he enters. He must've just left work at Hale Co. or Halway Comics, and I'm not ready to blow up this project in front of him.

Lily, yeah.

Lo, fucking *no*.

It's complicated.

I chug the rest of my energy drink, watching Moffy and Luna hide in the cardboard box to scare their dad. "Shh," Moffy whispers to Luna and yanks down a flap.

All the while, Lily and Lo embrace.

I do *not* watch their lip-lock. I've seen enough at their house, thank you. When they pull apart, Lo sweeps the storage room and nods to me.

I nod back.

But he's looking for Moffy and Luna. "Where are our kids?" Panic catches in his edged voice but quickly extinguishes as the box giggles and laughs.

I smile.

Lo is an asshole, though, so he layers on fear and panic and yells, "Moffy?! Luna?! Lily, go call 9-1-1 right n—"

"No!" Moffy shrieks, tearing up. He pops out of the box and bolts to his dad. "I'm right here! I'm right here!" He hugs onto Lo's legs, and Lo crouches, hugging his son tight. Acting so relieved to find him.

Savage.

Lily whispers to Lo, but I can't hear, and then Lo assesses Moffy's well-being. "Are you in one piece? Are you okay? Did the aliens get you?"

"What aliens?"

Lo lets out a choked laugh. "You didn't hear about the alien invasion last night? What were you—*sleeping*?"

"Yeah, I like sleep."

"No way, me too."

My smile fades into something else. It's been nice babysitting Moffy and Luna, but seeing Lo interact with his kids just makes me want to be a father.

I want a baby with Willow.

Can't believe I'm at a place where that sounds like walking into a bright horizon. Like the end credits to a movie I want to play all over again.

I tune out a bit—in a *baby* daze—but I'm back at the perfect time. Lily is about to blow up my secret project. I shake my head, trying to get her to shut up.

"We're trying to separate all the ones with Sorin-X. He said…" she trails off, seeing me finally. "What?"

I stifle a groan.

Moffy runs off to play with Tilly Stayzor action figures from *The Fourth Degree* universe.

As Lo drills confusion into me, I decide to go with the moment. "I did have something to ask you."

This isn't about work. I am worried he might say *no,* but I'm not that nervous to actually ask him what I'm about to ask. I figure it seems obvious anyway.

And so I say, "Will you be my best man at my wedding?"

His mouth slowly drops, stunned.

"You've been more of a brother to me than my brothers," I say strongly because this is the fucking truth. "I probably wouldn't be here if it weren't for you…and you." I look to Lily.

I'm not sure I tell them enough how much they mean to me.

How grateful I am and will *always* be.

Lily wipes her gathering tears.

Lo's amber eyes glass. "Of course I'd be your best man."

"Thanks," I say. "Do you think the tall one and the angry one will want to be groomsmen?"

"Connor, without a doubt, and Ryke goes with the flow." Lo laughs. "Christ, if you put him in the back row, he wouldn't even care or take it to heart."

"Okay good." I expel another long breath, until Loren grabs a comic from the growing stack.

He asks, "What's all this for?"

"I don't know," Lily says. "Garrison was just about to tell…"

I'm shaking my head with widened eyes.

She's gaping, brows bunched. "Uhhh…"

I bet she sucks at charades.

Lo glances at me. "Is this about your video game?"

My face falls. "What?" *What the fuck?*

He flashes a half-smile.

I choke out, "How'd you know?" Are there hidden cameras in his house? In my cubicle? What. The. *Fuck.*

"You're working for Connor Cobalt, man. The guy probably has fifteen brains and seven pairs of eyes. You might not know what he's thinking, but he knows what you are." Lo touches his chest. "And he's my best friend. He told me you're working on a game based on a comic book character."

I sway backwards, disbelieving. Connor Cobalt already knows I'm creating a video game on Sorin-X… "And he didn't give a shit? I thought he'd pull the plug on the project."

"He actually likes the idea. So do I."

I'm in another dimension. "What?"

"*I* own the video game rights to *The Fourth Degree* series." Halway Comics is the publisher, duh. "And Belinda and Jackson told me they'd rather eat their left arms than see a thousand people turning the game into a money-making soulless franchise."

Of course I recognize those names. Belinda and Jackson Howell are the young brother-sister duo and artists and writer of *The Fourth Degree* universe.

My head is spinning, but I gather my thoughts fast. "I have most of the technical shit coded, but I'm at the point where storyline is important. That's why I was looking through the comics, but eventually I'd need Belinda and Jackson for the art. I can only code, and what I'm making is classic, indie. I think the game style fits what the comic intended to be."

"I've been mentioning the video game to Belinda and Jackson for a full year," Lo says, "and they're interested. I know they'd work with you. I'll give you their numbers."

My jaw is on the floor.

Speechless.

In shock.

Lo has known for a full year about the video game because of Connor. He's already mentioned the project to the most important people. And they're interested.

My eyes burn, and I think for so long, I didn't believe I should try to chase after what I loved. When other people are faster and smarter, it felt pointless.

It took work to get here, but I know the first step was always belief.

Belief that I could.

Belief that I should.

And yeah...I'm happy I did.

1 YEAR LATER

May

68

Willow Hale

I'M SHAKING.

For someone who likes to be on the outskirts—out of the blazing spotlight—this moment feels way too focused on *me*.

I've already been told I look *lovely* and *divine* and *like a royal goddess* about a billion times. But the extra attention from Lily and Rose only burns my cheeks and spikes my temperature.

With all the wedding planning, the venue was the scariest part to nail down. Do we fly somewhere tropical? Do we marry on the beach? Or do we have a city high-rise wedding like Lily and Lo—though maybe not on a rooftop. Garrison and I couldn't picture ourselves in France like Rose and Connor, or somewhere awe-inspiring like Machu Picchu where Ryke and Daisy tied the knot.

None of that screamed *us*.

We decided on something close to home. Something more simple, quiet, soft, and pretty. A nearby botanical garden had availability, no need to pull strings or flash celebrity cred (Rose offered to do it—but she said we should send Lily since she's the most famous. To which Lily said that she loves me, and she'd proudly fight for my wedding like X-23 with her adamantium claws out. That made me happy.)

Another perk of this botanical garden: the luxury dressing room for the bridal party. The *before* part is going smoothly, I remind myself. While I'm sitting at the vanity, Daisy touches up my makeup. She's pretty skilled in the art of mascara, blush, highlighter, and eye shadow pallets thanks to her modeling days. "I watched the pros do my makeup before runways and stuff," she said when she first unzipped pouches of products. By the Chanel labels alone, I could tell she borrowed a lot of Rose's beauty stash.

I'm thankful for my maid of honor. I didn't have to hire a makeup artist, and one less stranger in this room does wonders for my speeding pulse.

"Your dress is so *you*," Lily swoons over in the corner.

"It's gorgeous," Rose says pointedly. "And flawless."

I touch the lavish fabric of my dress. Beaded floral leaves on a corset top give way to flowing white tulle. 27-yards of tulle to be exact—as Rose told me. Sheer lace applique on the bodice makes the gown feel regal yet simple in a way. It's Rose's design. And Lily is right, it is so *me*.

I cried when Rose handed me the wedding dress last month. She *almost* shed a tear when I asked her to design it. Her hands flung to her eyes like she was commanding the waterworks to stop before they'd even begun. It's about as close to a Rose Calloway Cobalt sob session as you can get.

Rose and Lily continue to praise the dress and then switch to my hair. The praise is sweet, but the attention is a lot.

This isn't just about me. Today is all about me *and* Garrison. Our love, our future—and that notion eases me every few minutes.

Daisy pulls back from applying a shimmery soft rose color to my eyelid. "Alright, we're nearing the end of this magical moment." She looks to her sisters. "Can you two make sure that everyone is seated?"

"Yes, on it!" Lily hops up from the plush armchair like she was given life-or-death instructions. They all wear different styles of a tulle dress in the same powder blue color.

I kind of want to ask if my mom and little sister made it, but I'm too scared of the answer. A part of me already knows what to expect anyway.

Rose stands. "We'll text you updates. Keep your phone on." She shoots Daisy a look. This morning, Daisy came in with a dead battery and had to plug in her phone. Rose—who wants this whole thing to go off without a hitch—was practically hyperventilating.

But I knew who I chose as my maid of honor. In this moment, I *need* Daisy's carefree attitude, not Rose's perfect planning. Daisy's energy is the only thing that will calm me down.

"Maid of honor phone is at seventy-five percent charge." Daisy picks up her phone and waves it playfully. "We're clear for takeoff, Rose."

Rose sucks in a tight breath and then looks to me one final time. "It's going to be perfect, Willow. And if anyone fucks this day up for you, I will murder them myself."

A smile spreads over my face. "Thanks, Rose." Her confidence swims towards me, but I feel my anxiety manifesting itself as a barrier, unwilling to let it touch me.

As soon as Lily and Rose leave, Daisy returns to my eyelids. "Close." She bops my nose with the hard end of the makeup brush.

My smile grows and I shut my eyes, truly relaxing now.

"They can be a lot," Daisy says. "But they mean well."

"They're amazing. Really. I'm the one freaking out."

"It's a big day. You can have as many freak-out sessions as you want."

I try and blow out a measured breath, but pressure still sinks heavy on my chest. It's not even anxiety or fear about marrying Garrison. The idea of spending the rest of my life with him brings only love and happiness to my heart.

It's just…this day.

The wedding. An event where all eyes are on me. *Us,* they'll be on us. I remember what Garrison told me yesterday—as the pre-panic wedding jitters took hold.

"It's not just you out there," Garrison said. "It'll be us. I'll be right next to you, and no one in the crowd will be thinking anything other than *look at those cute kids getting married*—because most of them are either babies and aren't paying attention or they're way older than us. Like ancient farts."

I laughed. "My brothers were talking about how they found gray hairs on their heads the other day."

"See, they're going to need walkers soon."

I smiled more. "Canes and hip replacements."

"Coffin fittings."

"Lo's would be black and green. For Slytherin."

"Naturally."

We were grinning before he hugged me and kissed me, and nothing seemed scary anymore. Even if Lo and Ryke aren't *that* much older than us (six and seven years respectively), they do still see me as their little sister, and they love me a ton—I know they're not going to sit there and judge me if I trip or if I stammer out my vows. They wouldn't care.

Neither would Connor, Daisy, Lily, or Rose.

Still, as the ceremony nears, my pulse hasn't slowed.

"Should we have eloped?" I regret the question as soon as I say it. I shouldn't taint the beauty of today with second-guessing, but then again, only Daisy is here.

She's quick to say, "You and Garrison already banished that idea. You wanted the celebration of it all with the ceremony as a cherry on top."

We considered eloping once. To just express our love to ourselves. Quietly, softly. That still seems peaceful. I think I could've been happy with that too.

But ultimately, we wanted *this*. The special ceremony where we declare our love in front of the people we love most. There aren't many people in attendance. It's an intimate gathering. Skipping to the party or just doing an elopement dinner sounds great—but I'm afraid I'll always feel like I missed a part.

The part where I express how much I love Garrison. Publicly. I've surprised myself by how much I've wanted that, and maybe it's the romantic in me who likes traditional weddings. And I know I'm quiet. I know I don't need to scream for him to *ever* feel or hear my love. I know I can whisper, and to him, that whisper is a bellow from the mountaintops.

But I don't want the fear of public speaking to take anything from me.

So we're doing this. We're having a wedding.

"Yeah, you're right," I breathe out, trying to relax.

"Done," Daisy says. "You can open your eyes now."

I do, and my reflection stares back at me. It's blurry. Go figure. I grab my glasses. Nothing fancy for today. Just a new pair I bought a few months ago with dark rims.

When I put them on, everything is clear. My brown hair cascades over my shoulder in soft waves. Shimmery subtle pink on my eyes looks pretty with the warm blush on my cheeks. Daisy is a miracle worker because I look...stunning.

My lips part. "I look beautiful."

Daisy smiles brighter than the sun, her green eyes on mine through the mirror. "You've always been beautiful. You're just even more radiant today."

I could totally volley that back to her and say, *no*. She's the radiant one, but I believe and *feel* her words. I am Willow Hale. I am radiant.

And I'm about to get married.

My eulogy will change by tomorrow. And I know just what it'll be.

There was that Willow Abbey, how radiant she looked. How in love she was. How beautiful her life has been.

A happy laugh escapes me, and my eyes mist. "Oh crap." I wave a hand at my eyes, trying to stop myself from crying. "I'm gonna mess it up." While I don't care too much about imperfections today, I really don't want to walk down the aisle with mascara streaking my cheeks.

Daisy wafts a magazine towards my face, trying to dry my eyes. "Tears be gone!"

I laugh again.

Daisy smiles. "If Lily said *tears be gone*, it might actually happen. I have a theory she's the most magical of us all."

"I believe that one." We talk about Lily using the *alohomora* spell to get a Pop-Tart to pop out of a toaster faster. Did it work? Kind of.

More than anything, I think it's sweet that Daisy believes her sister is magical.

Daisy sets down the magazine, and when I catch another glimpse of my refection, something heavy weighs my shoulders.

My smile morphs into a frown, and a wave of sadness just... pulverizes me. Tears develop for an entirely different reason.

"Willow," Daisy whispers in concern. "What's wrong?" She plucks a bunch of tissues from a box and passes them to me.

I dab at the corners of my eyes, trying to stop myself from truly crying.

If I dig deep enough, I know where the brunt of my anxiety lies. Where my hurt has been planted like a seed, and it blooms today into an ugly tree right inside my heart.

"I should have tried harder," I whisper. "To contact them. What if they didn't get the invitation and that's why they never RSVP'd?" My mom and Ellie changed their phone numbers, so there was no way to call and invite them to the wedding. A formal invitation by mail was the only way to reach them, but I'm not sure if they still live in the same house.

"I could have driven out to them," I add. "Invited them *in person*." I try not to cry more. "I'm a horrible daughter. Horrible big sister—"

"Hey, you're *none* of those things," Daisy refutes. She puts her hands on my shoulders, gearing me up for an amazing Daisy Meadows pep talk. "It takes two to tango, Willow. Your mom should be the one putting in the *most* effort to bridge this gap. Don't put that on yourself. *Especially* not today."

It's hard not to feel like this is the moment where I finally lose them. Where I shut the door on the idea of a relationship with my mom and sister ever again. Then again, Garrison's family isn't here either. He didn't want them to come, and I understand why.

Maybe it's good that my mom and sister aren't coming too.

There's too much baggage. Too much damage.

For us both.

A knock sounds on the door. "Mommy!"

The door to the dressing room cracks open and a four-year-old bounds in. Her wild brown hair coming undone beneath silver clips, Sullivan Meadows races to her mom's side. I just see a brief glimpse of Poppy, who gives me a short wave and bright smile before closing the door to offer us privacy.

Daisy makes a playful noise. "Well if it isn't the most beautiful mermaid in the whole wide sea."

"Mommy!" Sulli bellows again. "Aunt Poppy says that it's time for me to get the flowers."

"Aunt Poppy is correct on that one." Daisy collects the basket of blue hydrangea petals off another vanity.

"I like your dress, Sulli," I say as I stand, white tulle flowing around my feet.

Sulli spins to me and then *gasps* almost like an imitation of her mom. "Whoa, you're pretty. Like Elsa. No, like *Cinderella*. No, like Ariel!" Sulli goes on to list every single Disney princess. And I mean it, she names every. Single. One.

I'm smiling so much that my cheeks hurt.

Okay, a four-year-old calling me pretty shouldn't make me feel on cloud nine. But seeing as how I've come to realize how *brutally* honest children are, I'm now floating in the sky.

In this moment, I forget about what I've lost, and I focus on what I've found.

Once she finishes her long princess list, I ask Sulli, "You ready?"

She slides her hands down her dusty blue dress. She told me this morning that she was taking her role as flower girl very "seriowously." The mispronunciation of *seriously* made it that much cuter. Even now, she screws on this concentrated face that makes me smile all over again.

"I'm gonna be the bestest flower girl ever, Aunt Willow. Pinky promise." She holds out her pinky to me.

We do a very good pinky tug, and I start yearning. For a little one. For someone that Garrison and I can raise together, and my eyes well up in a newfound feeling. I'm marrying him. We're building a future together.

It's starting to become real.

"But are *you* ready?" Daisy's voice pulls to me, her question directed my way.

I take a deep breath.

"I am."

69

Garrison Abbey

IT'S ABOUT THIS TIME THAT I'D BE CRAVING A SMOKE. A QUICK light just to drown out my nerves. But I gave up smoking around a month ago, and there's not an ounce of regret in my body. I don't want it. I don't need it. Not now.

I'm focused on *today*.

Blooming May flowers envelop the garden like some sort of storybook. Like I'm a prince in a fairytale, and I'd believe it less, if I didn't think Willow was worthy of being a princess. She is. Ten thousand times over. So yeah, maybe that makes me her prince.

Ivy envelops areas that aren't bursting in color. Above us, more ivy, lilacs, soft blue flowers, some vibrant reds cascade off a trellis like a waterfall of florals. Sheer drapes are tied off the trellis and frame the fold-out chairs that face me. Eucalyptus and ivy weave around the chairs and twist up the arch that I stand under.

The garden is small but full of people that love Willow and me.

But most importantly, my family is here.

Loren Hale. Lily. Their little six-year-old who calls me Uncle Garrison but treats me like I'm the coolest guy he's ever known. Moffy has been giving me a thumbs up about every minute. Even if I don't catch his eyes, I can see his little thumb up in the air from my peripheral. Lily bounces their two-year-old on her knee, and Luna giggles softly.

The Hales took me in when I had nowhere to go—they're my family now.

I feel that cemented deeply. Permanently.

And even though Lo is my best man today, he's sitting down with his kids and wife like the rest of my groomsmen. Seeing as how our guest list is small, Willow and I decided to stand at the alter alone. Plus, most of our wedding party have toddlers and babies they need to look after.

Waiting up here for her isn't the easiest thing. My palms sweat, and my eagerness encroaches on stupidity. I'm about a minute away from leaving this whole thing and sprinting inside to see her.

Soft music plays from speakers. *Chill, Garrison.* But the music just reminds me that her dad wanted us to hire a full orchestral quartet. Jonathan Hale can keep his extra bullshit to himself. We chose to have the least number of strangers in this garden as possible.

The only true stranger happens to be a local Justice of the Peace standing a couple feet from me, and he's someone we've met a handful of times before the ceremony today. So yeah, not a "true" stranger. But I wasn't about to ask my boss—Connor Cobalt—to officiate. Lily and Lo already did that, and truth, I don't need that memory.

I like this one.

Where they're all in the audience. In attendance.

Sheetal and Tess, Willow's dad, and even Poppy and Sam are here. They sit in the second row with Maria. Their teenage daughter whispers quietly to a six-year-old Jane Cobalt, keeping an eye on her today. Because the King and Queen have their fucking hands full.

Literally.

Rose cradles a two-month-old Ben to her chest. He just woke up from a nap and looks ready to cry. She glances to her husband, and carefully, they switch children. Connor passes a two-year-old Tom to her, and she gives him Ben.

Just as Ben wails.

Connor is quick to retrieve a bottle from a diaper bag at his feet. Ben quiets as soon as it goes to his lips. Rose exhales in relief, and that makes me smile.

Willow and I knew this wedding wouldn't be perfect. We invited ten kids—over half under the age of five—and that's bound to make this whole thing messy. But we wanted them here. Neither of us had the perfect childhood—we didn't have the kind of love we've seen Lily, Lo, Ryke, Daisy, Connor, and Rose give their children— and it's not just something to admire. It's something we've wanted to surround ourselves around.

So banning these kids from our wedding—not an option.

They're all here. Every one of them.

Plus, watching Connor and Rose reminds me that even the most perfect couple has cracks. That no one is truly always put-together. I mean, come on. Eliot, who turns three tomorrow, has abandoned his seat and currently crawls underneath the chairs, making relatively no noise.

I can't tell if Connor or Rose realize their son is pretending to be a spy. Maybe they're choosing their battles. Maybe they know he'll stay quiet. I don't care much what anyone does.

I'm too busy smiling.

Charlie and Beckett, the three-year-old twins, are quiet next to their Uncle Ryke. Beckett shooshes Charlie whenever his brother makes a loud peep, and they share furtive whispers.

I wonder how a kid with Willow would turn out. Would they be as well-mannered as Beckett or a little terror like Eliot? And fuck, I can't believe *I* even want to bring someone into this world. Knowing what I know about people. About myself.

Curses. All that shit.

But I'd like to think my kid could turn out better than me. More loved than me. And over my dead body will they have siblings.

No fucking way.

There's only one person I could ever envision myself starting a family with, and I get to marry her today. Just as I think it, I see Daisy slip into the garden. She ducks her head, trying to go unnoticed before taking a seat on the open chair beside Ryke.

It's time.

Oh, shit.

My breathing deepens, and I look for help. I look to Lo.

He's smiling like he gets it, and then he gives me a nod. Everything goes calm. Goes still.

Sullivan Meadows appears from the double doors at the end of the aisle. She curtseys before carefully placing blue petals on the ground in a precise line. Ryke beams, while Daisy gives her daughter a wave. I want to smile too, but my whole body is vibrating in anticipation.

Willow. My bride.

We're seconds away from becoming husband and wife. God, I just need to see her.

When Sulli reaches the end of the aisle, she keeps walking forward. And she sprinkles leftover flowers onto my feet. Laughter comes, also with a whistle of approval from her mom—probably so Sulli knows it's okay and doesn't run and hide.

Sulli peers up at me.

And I'm smiling. I hold out my fist.

She bumps knuckles before skipping back to her mom with a grin.

The music changes.

Everyone stands. The adults help some of the kids.

But I don't hear anything anymore. Swedish Hair Metal could be blaring from the speakers, and I wouldn't know.

Willow emerges from the double doors, hair in waves over her shoulder and a white gown sweeping the floor. Her eyes mist behind her glasses—those cute-as-hell glasses—and I almost lose it.

Keep your shit together, Abbey.

I blow out a breath as she walks *quickly* towards me. She pauses suddenly, remembering there's a whole tempo to this thing, and she takes a sudden, deep breath.

I nod.

You've got this, Willow.

Her hands clutch tight to a bundle of flowers. White roses, blue petals, eucalyptus. Don't know all the names of them. Don't really care. I'm mostly just looking at her.

She slowly walks to me. Each step closer might as well take a century. *I've waited years for this.* I've been apart from her for most of it. I can wait a little more.

But it's hard.

And she quickens her pace again. Too cute. I can't stop smiling. She reaches me in record time, and Daisy pops up from her seat to collect Willow's bouquet before sitting down again.

I want to say I'm listening to the officiant. But I'm not.

I don't hear what he says. I'm just watching Willow.

She glances around, trying to soak in everything for a second, before her eyes land on me. She blushes and bites the bottom of her lip.

Yeah, I love you. I hope it's written a thousand times across my face because it's what I feel. And screw it, I mouth the words but end up whispering, "I love you."

Her eyes redden with bubbling, overwhelming affection. Her collarbones rise with a big breath as she whispers back, "I love you."

My hand is in hers, and her fingers curl stronger around mine.

And then I hear, "Willow and Garrison have written vows, and they'd like to share them with you all today. Garrison—" He looks to me.

Right.

I didn't scribble any words on a piece of paper. Some would say I didn't prepare. But I don't need to write down what's already in my heart.

"Willow." My throat swells with raw emotion. "I often wonder what my life would have been like had you never driven over seven hundred miles, alone, from Caribou, Maine to Philadelphia. I try to picture it all the time, but I can never get too far. For one, it hurts. And for another, in every scenario I can come up with, you'd always make that leap. It's just who you are. You're *brave*. The kind of bravery that I dreamt of growing up—" My voice catches on the last word.

Tears glass her gaze, and my eyes sting with surging waterworks. She shakes her head like I'm wrong, but I'm done thinking I'm shit. I know I'm not anymore.

"I admire so much about you, Willow," I say, choked. "But my love for you is more than just admiration. It's built from a friendship we started eight really long years ago in a comic book shop."

That does her in. She wipes at her eyes.

I just let my tears slip down my cheeks.

Yeah, I'm crying.

I don't care.

"From that moment, I knew," I tell her. "There's no one else. There will never be anyone else. Whatever it takes, wherever we are, it's always been you."

Her hold on my hand speaks a million beautiful sentiments, and I don't want to let go. I look to the officiant, and he turns to my bride. "Willow."

She sniffs loudly and rubs at the corners of her eyes, careful not to smear her makeup. "Wow. Okay." She takes a breath and with one hand, slips out a piece of paper. She said she needed to write her vows down to lessen any anxiety, and I'm game for whatever makes Willow more comfortable.

In this moment, I'm not sure I could love her any more than I do. I could burst into a million pieces. I'm honestly shocked I'm still keeping my shit somewhat together.

"When I arrived in Philly, I didn't have any expectations," she says, her voice steady, but the paper trembles in her hand. Her other palm is sweaty in mine, but I squeeze, calming her, and she takes a deeper breath. "I definitely didn't expect to find *you*." Her eyes flit up to mine. "My best friend."

I swallow hard, throat definitely swollen now.

"Some people in this garden believe in fate," she says, and the audience chuckles at that. "And I don't know how else to describe what happened between us. Because I thought in no world would a boy like you ever talk to a girl like me."

It's my turn to shake my head like she's so wrong.

She presses onward. "But you did. And I realized that everything we saw in each other was everything we couldn't see in ourselves. All those good parts. All those loving parts. All those beautiful parts."

Fuck.

I'm crying again.

Her voice trembles with her hands now. "Time. Distance. It has nothing on fate. You have my whole heart, Garrison Abbey." She folds her paper, and then she adds, "You had my heart since that day in the comic book shop."

We're smiling.

We're crying.

"And I'm ready," she says, "for forever with you."

It feels like one of the best days of my life.

It *is* the best day of my life.

The sound of sniffling in the audience and tender *awes* don't steal my gaze off my bride.

The *I dos* are short and sweet, and a stronger feeling starts swelling inside of me. I'm glad we made it here.

I'm glad we never gave up.

Shakily, we exchange rings, and we're holding hands more than letting go.

I do hear the officiant say the word, *kiss.* And tenderly, carefully, I clasp Willow's soft cheek. She clutches onto my arms. Drawing closer, her eyes dance over my features, and I whisper against her lips, "I love you." And we kiss, an overwhelming kiss that brings Willow against my chest. Her fingers rise to the back of my neck, and her heart thumps against mine.

We've been ones and zeroes. Smoke signals written in the sky. Two tin cans tethered by an eternal string.

Now we can add in *husband* and *wife.*

June

70

Garrison Abbey

"OH NO, I'M DYING, I NEED HEALTH—I NEED HEALTH," WILLOW says in panic, punching buttons on a Sega controller with skill.

"Knock over the steel drum—*fuuuck*." I rock back as my health meter depletes to zero. "I just died."

Willow laughs, and then Blaze, her *Streets of Rage* character, kicks ass for another five minutes, gaining health, and not long after that, Blaze perishes too.

We take a food break, and I flip open the pizza box on the floor—where we've thrown down plush blankets, bed pillows, and set up our TV with a few game consoles. Move-in boxes surround us in the large, open space. Sharpie scrawled over the cardboard sides, most labeled *Abbeys – living room* and *Abbeys – kitchen*.

Willow was happy to sell all her textbooks. Not needing to pack any since she *officially* graduated college with a shiny business degree. She'll open up the London branch of Superheroes & Scones soon.

And eventually, Lily wants to hire Willow as the Chief Brand Officer. Which is big.

I'm really proud of everything she's accomplished.

Earlier, we dug into a few boxes to find the N64, so Styrofoam popcorn packaging litters the ground too.

I lost at Diddy Kong Racing like fifteen times in a row.

"You're killing it tonight," I say while tearing into a slice of pepperoni.

Willow smiles, brown hair wet in a messy braid after a shower. "Must be the new place," she says softly, just wearing blue cotton pajamas. "Maybe I'm lucky here."

My lips rise.

Yeah, I like that idea. Our new home together is a place of good fortune for Willow, and me too. It feels that way, at least, and tonight is only our first night here.

She scoops up a cheesy piece of pizza, and I smile at the bathing suit tan lines on her shoulders, visible outside the spaghetti straps of her PJs.

"What?" She nudges up her glasses, seeing me staring.

I lick my lips, feeling my smile expanding. I shake my head at first, but then words come easy. "It just dawned on me that when I look at you, it means that I'm looking at my wife."

She has trouble chewing pizza, her smile uncontrollable. "Stop...I can't..." She laughs.

I laugh.

Willow chokes on the food.

Shit. "You okay?" I place a hand on her back and pass her a water bottle.

She nods repeatedly, then swallows. "Thanks." She sips the water.

I keep my arm around her waist.

We spent our honeymoon in Hawaii. Seven beautiful days under the sun. Hence, our recent tans.

My chest swells. Remembering it all.

Feeling.

Because before that, I married Willow Hale in a small garden wedding, mostly just family attending. Right here in Philadelphia.

The quiet, intimate ceremony on May 31st was perfect, but I think we both loved the honeymoon more. Just us. No crowds, no one to greet or try to please.

Being back home, we've mostly been dealing with the new move. We wanted a place of our own, just not in Philly suburbs.

An industrial factory in Philly was converted into premium lofts about a year ago. Seriously *premium*. A doorman is posted at the entrance, and so far, Barry seems cool.

But living in the city comes with *privacy* issues.

We asked for help testing the "tint" of the massive window in our open living room and kitchen. On the fifteenth floor, we have a pricey view of a cool park and eclectic shops.

Worth the money. I'd rather not stare at a brick wall.

Lo, Connor, and the Calloway sisters came over earlier to determine whether paparazzi could see into our loft from the street.

The verdict: *a little bit.*

A little bit is too much, so we'll need to increase the tint level. Until then, Willow and I hung curtains that are drawn shut.

Willow notices me staring at the shrouded window. "You think if we were Lily and Lo, paparazzi would've taken pics of us by now?"

"For sure." I swallow the crust of my pizza. "Give it a couple days though, and I bet we'll see headlines like: *Newlyweds Move into Coolest Loft Ever.* The article will call me a high school dropout with connections, and you'll be Loren and Ryke's awesome little sister, of course."

"Of course." She smiles into a sip of water and then stares faraway in thought.

"Are you still worried about it?" I gesture to the window. "The media finding us?"

Willow shrugs. "I know it's unavoidable…I guess I'm just scared of what we talked about before." She turns to face me. "Chaotic Evil."

Yeah, we've discussed the probability of our fame piquing to monstrous, catastrophic levels. "We're still at Chaotic Good," I tell my wife—*still love that.* "Media isn't printing any cheating rumors or making up fake scandals. They're just obsessively relishing in our wedding and honeymoon. Next, it'll be our new place."

Willow looks around the loft, all metal and concrete. I can see us living here for a long time.

She agrees, "We haven't been cannibalized. Not yet, but when we have a baby…what if they say that I'm a bad mom or butt into our parenting style?" She's seen the Calloway sisters deal with public criticism raising kids.

Pretty sure they could breathe and the media would say they're not inhaling long enough.

My muscles tighten, just picturing Willow going through that bullshit.

I place a hand on her bare ankle. "Is there more?" I wonder since she intakes a tense breath. "Willow?" My chest hurts.

"I just—I want to not care what happens, if the worst comes, but I've seen so many shippers and fans *turn* on Lily, Rose, and Daisy at a single headline. They go from love to hate with the snap of a finger. It feels like they're Thanos—"

"They're not," I refute, knowing the *Avengers* reference. "They can't 'dust' your universe."

But I won't be the one attacked. I'm a dude. Media and so-called fans harass the girls twenty times more.

So, it's a misogynistic Thanos snap.

Her eyes downcast.

I edge closer, my hand ascending to her calf, and all I'm thinking is that I need to protect my wife from Chaotic Evil. Since we were seventeen, making Willow feel *safe* and at ease in any given situation meant everything to me.

It still does.

Maybe even more now, if that's humanly possible.

"It's just a fear, I guess," she says quietly.

"Hey, your fear is my fear, Willow." My hand travels to her kneecap, and our eyes meet as I tell her, "Fans either don't care about us or they somewhat like us. We're like the underrated gems. I know that could change if we're too overexposed, and maybe we've gotta figure out ways to stay under the radar so no one burns us down."

Fandoms almost always self-implode.

Very few things are loved forever. And we've been sitting inside a beloved thing that's detonated multiple times. Calloway sisters going from *adorned* to *scorned*, back to adorned, then scored and the cycle starts all over again.

Truth: Willow and I haven't even been on Tumblr in months, maybe a solid *year*. If I make gifs, I just send them to her through text.

We'll always love the internet, but our relationship with it has shifted. It had to for our health.

I don't want to stumble on hate posts about Lily or Daisy or Rose. People we love. It sucks the wind out of our sails. Punches a fist through our guts.

Fuck that pain.

We deal with enough already offline.

Willow suggests, "Maybe we shouldn't do interviews on *We Are Calloway* anymore." The critically acclaimed docuseries won an Emmy last year for the fourth season, and we don't make *large* appearances like the core six, but we've done interviews for the show.

We exchange a deeper look. Because I know why she'd propose tossing this out.

I've been quoted *everywhere* after episode twelve aired where I said, *"I married someone much braver than me."*

It's true, but Christ, I didn't expect to become gif sets and video compilations. And yeah, the irony isn't lost on me.

I did the same shit to Ryke for his f-bombs.

Years ago.

Years ago. Time carries my thoughts in a drift.

Knowing what I know now, I wonder if I still would've made the videos. I'm not sure if age has changed me more or just the events and circumstances of my life.

Maybe I'll never really have the answer.

"That's probably the best idea," I nod. "Do you still want to appear on the docuseries, even if we're not doing interviews?" We're often spotted in the background.

"Yeah." She doesn't waver or hesitate. "If we leave Philly where paparazzi is or if we try to avoid cameras, then I feel like we're also avoiding my brothers and Daisy and Lily…Rose." She takes a deep breath. "I never want to subvert the spotlight so much that we draw away from our extended family."

Our extended family.

My eyes burn, but I push back emotion for a second. "Same."

We make a pack to never avoid the media at the cost of our relationships with the Hales, Meadows, and Cobalts.

She smiles more. "You think one day we'll reach Chaotic Neutral? Where we're like flies on the wall to all the madness?"

I stand up. "Let me ask the all-knowing one."

Willow grabs her half-eaten cheesy slice. "You're calling Connor?"

"Uh, *no*. He's still the tall one." We both laugh, and I wash my hands in the sink, then rummage in the game box near the TV.

There it is.

I shake a Magic 8-Ball to Willow. "You ask the question."

She rises to her feet, biting into crust. "Will we be a fly on the wall to all the madness?"

I shake the ball and then steady it, the triangle floating up in the dark-blue dye. I read, "*You may rely on it.*"

Willow is closer, only a foot away from me, and my eyes roam her soft features and the curve of her waist, affection and desire heating my blood. Her eyes travel just as yearningly along the ridges of my abs and the ink along my tanned skin.

I near my wife and she walks backwards to the kitchen, a bashful smile playing at her lips.

I shake the ball as we move. "Will we have a boy, eventually?" I'd rather raise a girl, but I'll be happy no matter what gender.

Her back meets the island counter. "What does it say?"

I press my muscular body up against her soft frame. Her breath shallows, and I whisper, "*Outlook good.*"

Willow holds onto the counter behind her, breastbone rising and falling. "I'm going to ask it something."

"Okay." I run my free hand up her pajama top. Fingertips brushing the flesh along her hips, her ribs.

Love and want flood her brown eyes. "Will Garrison Abbey kiss me?"

I smile and rattle the 8-Ball. "*Reply hazy, try again.*"

She wets her lips, smiling an overwhelmed smile. "Will Garrison kiss me?"

Shaking the ball, I dip my head closer to Willow, our eyes diving deep before I shift them to the results. "*Concentrate and ask again.*"

We laugh.

"Concentrate," I coach.

"Okay, hold on." She shuts her eyes, and in the heady beat, I just look at my girl and our home—and my bright smile conjures tears.

Happiness, it never felt in reach.

But I woke up today, and I love who I am. And I'm forever in love with the girl who fell asleep next to me.

Very softly, eyes still closed, Willow whispers, "Will my husband kiss me?"

I gently cup her cheek and bring my lips to hers. Our tender affection alive and quiet, like a firefly in the summer night.

71

Willow Abbey

MY LIPS STING BENEATH HIS, LIT A BILLION WAYS, AND I WANT more, so much so. But… "I need to wash my hands," I whisper after I pull back.

He already wiped off the pizza grease, but I haven't.

The thought keeps disturbing *the* moment: our new house, a flirty make-out. I've been pulsing between my legs, but the "hand washing request" could've just punctured the sweet and hot mood.

My face is on fire.

Garrison smiles and draws back. "Yeah, go ahead."

I wash my hands in the sink, and I find my phone on the counter, near a liter of Fizz Life. Maybe music will help reset the tone.

I brave a glance back at him. He rests against the island, bare-chested with low-riding drawstring pants. Inked and cool, he waits for me patiently, in no rush. No hurry.

His lip upturns.

Garrison Abbey is my husband.

I realize my eulogy will now say "wife"—I'm someone's wife. *Here lies Willow Abbey, loving wife…*

My pulse races, heart on a tilt-a-whirl, and I dry off my palms and scroll through Spotify for a specific song.

Our marriage reminds me of our wedding, and how we invited my mom and my little sister to the ceremony. Before that, they ended up changing their phone numbers and never gave me their new ones, so it's been harder to stay in contact.

But when they didn't RSVP at all, I knew they'd eradicated me from their lives with more permanence. I don't blame them. My dad was invited to the wedding, and I'm sure my mom didn't want to be anywhere near him.

In the end, Garrison and I both lost our families. He left his, and mine eventually left me. I grieve the loss at times. Like an ocean rising above me, it swells up in random moments. When I see a princess crown in the kid's aisle of a store, reminding me of Ellie.

But I have a lot of love to pull me to the surface. Garrison and I gained another family. Not just with the Calloway sisters, but with each other.

I've never felt more loved than by him and with him. He's my comfort and home.

My lungs are light, and I return to the island with my phone in clean hands.

Garrison clutches my hips and lifts me onto the counter.

I nearly drop the phone, breath caught in my throat, but he steadies my wrist. His other hand travels up my thigh. My legs are split around his waist, so he fits as close as possible against me.

We consume one another by sight alone. Not needing to say much to feel a lot. I click into a song, and as soon as the first few notes play, Garrison smiles more.

Interpol's "Rest My Chemistry"

A few of these lyrics are tattooed on the crease of his forearm and bicep, along with a black skull.

I glance at the Magic 8-Ball beside me on the kitchen surface, then up at him.

"I have another question about our future." I push up my slipping glasses.

He grabs the 8-Ball. "Ask it." We're almost eye-level, his lips skim mine with a light, longing touch.

I hang onto his waist. "Will we always be this happy?"

Our eyes well up. We're finally together in the same city, same house, same room, same bed.

Sharing everything.

A life.

Love.

Garrison stops shaking the 8-Ball and sets the plastic sphere on the counter. "We don't need that to know the answer."

I smile with him. "*Without a doubt,*" I say our answer, my chest elevating with a big breath that we both take.

His forehead touches mine, our mouths an aching distance away. "*It is certain,*" Garrison whispers, and we kiss with slow, yearning passion.

We're twenty-four, but when we're together, I feel blown back. It feels like we're only twenty, then seventeen. Distance, time, miles and hours are intangible, metaphysical things, all woven and jumbled in an invisible tapestry, and like my favorite comic books, the beginning is really the end and the end is just the beginning.

2 YEARS LATER

May

72

Willow Abbey

OH NO. OH NO.

Ohhhh no. "This isn't happening," I whisper under my breath in the pitch-black theater. I feel wetness drip down the side of my leg. *This is happening.*

This is *very much* happening. My pulse speeds and air feels too light in my lungs.

Garrison hears my voice between the crunch of popcorn, but I'm not sure he can see the horror on my face in the dark. He leans closer to whisper, "You okay?"

"Mommy..." Moffy whispers loudly, tapping Lily's shoulder a row in front of him. He's eight, and he tries his best to be quiet and respectful in the theater. "The ground is really wet."

Is it *that* wet? I pick up my feet and realize my sneakers are kind of soaked.

Embarrassment is low thanks to the fact that Lily and Lo bought out the entire movie theater. All of the little kids have been so excited about watching the movie "on the big screen"—and Garrison and I tagged along to partially be babysitters since there are a lot of little hands and feet. But also because I just like spending time with my brothers, the Calloway sisters, Connor, and all their kids.

Technically, the Cobalt children *aren't* related to me like the Meadows and Hale kids, but I consider them my nieces and nephews too.

And I want to believe I just accidentally peed myself. That's better than having to rush out and confront the reality that *this is happening*. Today.

The animated Disney movie keeps playing. It's a screening of *Mulan*, an oldie since the theater is doing a month of animated classics.

What else is classic: *me*, messing up a movie about a princess.

I guess this could be worse. This could've happened in the mall. In front of strangers and glaring florescent *mall* lights.

Lily is holding a one-year-old baby on her lap, and Xander's expressive round eyes can't be torn from the screen, enthralled by the catchy songs and bright colors. Glancing over her shoulder, Lily tries to peer at her oldest son in the dark—just as Garrison switches on his phone's flashlight.

"*Garrison.*" Okay, maybe I am really embarrassed.

His phone illuminates his face first, and I can see the concern morph into a great urgency and worry when he notices the floor.

"Everything okay?" Lily's voice causes a wave of whispers. Mostly from the other adults in the theater.

I take everything back—this is *super* embarrassing. I did not want my water to break in front of Lo, Lily, Rose, and *Connor Cobalt*.

I intake a breath and try to remember this is just human nature. Who cares, right? This is all part of the birthing process. Partly though, I think I'm gripping onto the mortifying feelings, just so I don't panic. *I'm okay. This is happening. You know, birth. It's coming. I'm about to birth a baby.*

I wish I could fast-forward to the part where we hold her. Where we know she's healthy and okay and nothing awful has happened.

And what if I poop during birth?

What if I shit myself?

Those fears are dumb, I know that, but I'd rather just sit in embarrassment than confront my laundry list of fears. I welcome my burning face when I mentally magnify the fact that my water broke and Connor Cobalt and his unflappable (slightly unnerving) face is a few seats down from mine.

What if my bodily fluids drip over there and touches his pristine loafers? I roast inside-out and sink in my seat a little, but my very round belly makes *sinking* difficult.

"Willow?"

Collecting myself, I whisper to Garrison. "My water—"

"I got it." He's already clutching my hand. Already leaning forward to whisper to Lily, "We're going to the hospital."

Garrison calms me, and I take a deeper breath. *He's ready.* I might be scared, but he's prepared for this sudden swerve in our day.

In the dark, I can't make out Lily's expression, but I hear her gasp—and I try to picture her smiling. I hope she's smiling. "It's time?" Excitement radiates from her voice.

"Yeah, we're doing this thing."

My lips lift and heart mushrooms when I hear him say *we*. He's helping me stand. I place a hand on my round belly, a comfy cotton dress molding my frame. Daisy was sure I'd go into labor while I was wearing overalls, my staple item (even before pregnancy).

I rarely wear dresses.

Does that mean today is off? I wish Daisy were here to offer a reassuring theory.

It's fine. Everything will be fine. This'll go smoothly. Everything will be fine. I try to reassure myself while I move. Murmuring continues throughout the rows, and the little kids struggle to keep their voices down.

"What's going on?" Tom asks loudly.

"Is baby Vada coming?" Jane asks.

"Who? Where? What?!" Eliot tries to spring out of his seat, but Connor tugs his son down and refocuses his attention onto the movie.

I slip along the row, glad I just have to make it past Moffy and Jane before I'm at the aisle. Gripping the railing, I inch in slow, careful movements down the theater stairs towards the neon red *exit* sign. Pain cramps my insides in brutal waves. *Contractions.* I blow out a breath like I practiced with Garrison.

"Rose and Connor are staying with the kids. Lily is going to meet us at the hospital after Poppy gets here." Lo's voice is louder behind

I just now see him talking with Garrison. They're keeping ow pace.

Lily is pregnant with Baby #4.

She also just gave birth to Xander back in December. Christmas Day. Mention of Lily reminds me that I am not stuck in an elevator right now. And I still can't believe she went into labor in an *elevator*. Mind blown.

But I don't bring it up to Lo. He's still not over the overwhelming worry that pummeled him that day.

Garrison slips his hand back in mine. "Ready?"

"Yeah," I blow out another breath and cast a glance backwards at the movie screen. *Mulan*. I want my daughter to know she can be a princess and a superhero. She can wear pink or blue or any color in the rainbow or under the sun.

"It'll be a good story," I say in concentrated breaths. "Won't it?"

"Oh for sure," Garrison tells me confidently, but he's supremely focused on my slow pace and my breathing. "You okay?"

I nod, trying not to freak out. "If I had a choice though, we would've been watching *New Mutants*. I always thought...she'd be way more into the...you know, superhero portion of Disney...not the princesses. Not that we've met her. She's not here yet. We don't really know what she'll be like, I guess, but she's wanting to come out during *Mulan*." I'm panicking a little. *I'm about to give birth.*

Is she going to be okay?

Will I poop myself?

Garrison tightens his hold on my clammy hand.

Lo picks up his pace, walking ahead of me. He catches my gaze to say, "She's going to be a little superhero no matter what. Just look at who her parents are."

Warmth fills me, and something more painful. "Ugh. I think she's rebelling at that thought."

"Or she just wants out," Garrison says. "Plus, I'm all for not having a kid who thinks she can jump off shit and fly."

Lo winces. "I hear you on that."

After bursting through the rear emergency exit, we me
Lo's bodyguard at the curb, and I'm grateful for the simplici
hopping in the SUV and letting a driver take me to the hospit
intensifies not even midway into the car ride, and everything
around me.

"How are you feeling?" Garrison asks, his brows knotted a
hand still clasped in mine.

I don't talk.

I'm trying to *breathe*. God, it hurts.

My silence scares Garrison. He leans forward from the backseat,
my brother in the passenger with his bodyguard behind the wheel.

"Hey, can we go any faster?!" Garrison's panic starts panicking
me.

Lo shoots him an edged look. "Take a breath, man."

Garrison glowers. "I am not—and I repeat—I am not having a
kid in a car like Connor and Rose."

Lo reaches over and puts a hand on Garrison's shoulder. I feel
like he's going to give some sage advice, but then he says, "It was a
limo."

He blinks. "Seriously?"

"Garrison, everything will be fine," Lo tries to assure. "Your baby.
Your wife. You. All fine. We're making it there as fast as we can." He
looks to his bodyguard. "Right, Bruno?"

Bruno nods. "I'm going fifteen over."

"There you go," Lo says to Garrison.

My husband slowly leans back.

I want to say *I'm okay*.

Say it.

Try, at least.

I open my mouth to reassure him. To say those two words. *I'm okay*.

"I—aaahhhhh," I groan into a scream and hug myself.

"Lo!" Garrison yells like my brother is inflicting this pain. Garrison
clutches my hand, and I fear I'm cutting off all his circulation, but I
can't stop.

PUTATION 675

et up with
y of just
d. Pain
blurs

d

down, and Lo's face contorts into pure
the obvious. Outside the window,
pers all around us.

ffic.

while I squeeze my eyes closed and breathe.
shoulder and reminds me to tell him if he needs
g. Like what...? He can't actually be preparing for a
SUV?

We're not *that* screwed. We can still reach the hospital.

"A helicopter," Lo deadpans on the phone. "Just go ahead and fly a chopper right onto the Mercedes next to me...bro, we're in *traffic*. I'm not near a goddamn landing pad." He pauses. "I can't run with our sister—she's in labor...the hospital is *ten miles* away...I'm trying!"

I flinch.

Garrison scoots to the front. "*Lo.* You're freaking Willow out."

"Sorry, my brother is trying to come up with amazing solutions." Lo sounds frustrated.

"Tell Ryke to shut up and put the tall one on the line. He's actually delivered a baby." I open an eye and notice Garrison's phone on the seat beside me.

He has WikiHow popped up. The title: *How to deliver a baby.*

No, *no.* I don't want to do this here. Tears crease my eyes, and when Garrison slides back beside me, he sees the waterworks blurring my vision.

"Willow." His voice cracks, and he wipes beneath my fogging glasses.

"I don't want to have the baby here, Garrison." My voice shakes. "She has to wait. I can't do this here. I can't—"

"It's okay. It's okay. We're not doing this here." He cups my face with two hands, and the strength but tenderness in the hold eases my racing pulse and staggered breath. I rub at my wet eyes, and I nod, listening to him repeat the words.

We're not doing this here.

We're going to the hospital.

It'll be okay.

My phone pings, but I don't answer. Garrison says texting. I'm too busy trying to thwart off the pain. I stop w the traffic do nothing.

I just concentrate on breathing.

"Open your eyes, Willow," Garrison murmurs.

I do, and I nearly burst into tears. The SUV is sitting outside th hospital doors. Lo has jumped out to go grab a wheelchair.

"We made it," I cry in happiness and overwhelming relief, hugging onto Garrison.

"We made it." He hugs gently back, and the next part suddenly seems less terrifying.

Quickly, Garrison wheels me into the emergency room and the second he sees a nurse and doctor, he says, "She wants an epidural."

We've planned everything. Down to a science. Except for the fact that I didn't plan on having her two weeks early. Definitely didn't plan on going into labor *during* a Disney movie.

Definitely don't have my emergency duffel bag with me (in case of a long labor).

But I half-panic and half-relax when the nurse says, "It's too late for that."

Don't need that duffel bag then.

Once safely on the hospital bed, a thick layer of sweat clings to my skin and my hair sticks to my forehead. There's not an ounce of me that cares. I don't even care about my bowels. I just want her to be safe and healthy.

Please don't let me mess this up.

My lashes are wet, most are tears from the raw emotion of today. Garrison's the only one here besides the doctor and nurse. Lo went to the waiting room to speak to Lily. She's on her way.

I don't expect Daisy or Ryke to come.

Ever since Winona Meadows came into this world a couple months ago, they've been doting on her like they did Sulli. It's hard 'hich is why they passed on the movie

's Daisy
atching

, vision.

Garrison clutches my hand tighter as my

urgent string. "Hey, look at me."

the tears at the corners of my eyes. "You can do this,"

ut what if…" I trail off, the worst thought popping into my
d.

He waits patiently.

I wince from the pain but say, "What if I'll have to write a eulogy for her before I even have one for myself?" That fear pulverizes me, drowns out the pain with a toxic anxiety.

His face breaks for a second. "Willow. Everything is going right so far. Right, Dr. Jones?" He glances over, and the doctor checks my vitals again—maybe for my peace of mind.

"Right on track," she says cheerfully. "We're just going to need you to push, Willow."

Garrison's eyes stay fixed on me. "I'm right here." He squeezes my hand. "You're my girls. Nothing bad is happening to either of you. I promise. Okay?"

"Okay." Love surges inside me, along with a hearty dose of hope, more powerful than any drug, and after we share a warm, tender kiss—filling my lungs—I know I can do this. I know there is no one else I would want to do this with than him.

And he's here.

We're ready.

And I push. Pain envelops me, but I keep pushing and pushing. Teeth clenching as I try my hardest.

"That's it, Willow," Dr. Jones coaches.

Garrison wipes the sweaty hair off my forehead and adjusts my glasses as they slip awkwardly. I don't stop. I push.

And push.

And push.

And scream.

And I lose time again, but there is an end. And the end is
beginning for this one. Her little cries bring a wave of relief a
She might as well have arrived singing beautiful ballads becau
react like she *is* a singing princess-superhero being.

She's ours.

Our beautiful little squishy baby.

After they cut the umbilical cord and wipe her clean, they rest her
on my chest for warmth. I cup her little head, tears welling up.

I know she will be my one and only.

I'm really happy with that.

"She's perfect," I whisper.

When I look up at Garrison, he's wiping his tear-streaked face. He
keeps nodding and nodding, unable to say much. His reddened eyes
make mine mist even more.

He knows, too.

She's it.

Our one and only.

We spend a good bit of time getting acquainted with Vada Abbey.
She's content, mostly. Her soft cries have turned into loving coos.
Eyes closed and swaddled in a blanket, she relaxes in Garrison's
arms. "Is she supposed to be this good?" I wonder nervously. "Rose,
Lily, and Daisy said that it's okay if she cries a lot, but she's not crying
that much."

"A miracle child," Garrison grins.

I can't help but smile, too. He's not even playing into my anxious
thoughts. I love him that way. I love him all ways.

My body is sore and tired, but I fight everything to watch them
longer. I don't think I can get over how sexy he is holding our baby. I
mean, I've seen him holding babies before (my family now has a lot
of them), but it's different because this baby is ours. Because this is
the one we created together.

of his lip slowly rising. Like he

n my glasses up the bridge of my nose.

says effortlessly, like it's also just a fact, and he
I'm setting his world ablaze. Even though, I'm pretty
more like a hot mess. I'll take the compliment. Pocket it
remember it for later times.

In these quiet moments with our newborn, we keep casting
furtive, loving gazes at each other, then to our baby. For some reason,
I start giggling like I'm seventeen and lovestruck. Garrison's smile
explodes across his face.

I didn't think anything could top our wedding day. But I'm *so* in
love with him. He's my best friend, my husband, the father of my
child—he's my whole present and my whole future.

After some time bathed in pure happiness, another knock sounds
on the door, and the nurse peeks inside. "Ready for visitors?"

Garrison looks to me.

I nod. "Yeah," I say, excited that Lo and Lily will be able to meet
Vada. The nurse shuts the door, leaving quickly.

"You think she'll be into video games?" Garrison muses.

"Most likely. I'm sure she'll try to play them at least." I like
imagining their father-daughter time spent playing *Diddy Kong Racing*
and *Mario Party* together.

Garrison nods, thoughtful about this.

Another knock.

"Come in," I call out.

This time when the door opens, my jaw slowly drops. Tears brim
again. "Daisy?"

She pops into the room like a sprightly fairy that rolled out of
bed. Blonde hair uncombed, no makeup, and sweats. Yet, she still
looks gorgeous. And so, *so* excited.

"You came?" My voice cracks. I'm crying. She's one [...]
that I really wanted to meet Vada. Probably more than [...]
My best friend. But I never thought she'd leave Winona [...]
the hospital. I didn't want to picture a scenario where she [...]
case of the crushed disappointment.

But this—it feels like so much.

"Of course I did," she says like there was never a possib[...]
where she wouldn't. She beelines to the hospital bed and clasps n[...]
hand in hers. "This is one of the most important days of your life.
You thought I would miss this?"

I feel silly thinking it now.

I wipe at my eyes. "Thank you," I say, knowing how much it took
for Daisy to leave her newborn. Even if it's a short time she'll be here
to visit, this was big for her.

She wraps her arms around me in a warm hug. "I heard about the
theater and the traffic. You're amazing. You *did* amazing."

"She is the most amazing," Garrison agrees, giving me a strong
look.

I sniff and wipe snot from my nose before it goes spilling. "Okay, I
really need to stop crying." I laugh at myself, and Daisy laughs with me,
not at me. And the brightness between us lifts me a million feet high.

Daisy plucks some tissues from a box and hands them over.
Then she spins towards Vada in Garrison's arms. "And how is the
teeny-tiny Taurus girl doing?" She steps closer. "Oh, Willow, she's
adorable." Her eyes brighten and glass. "She's really freaking cute."

"Yeah?"

"Definitely more alien than old man."

I laugh. Daisy has a theory that all newborn babies either look like
little aliens from outer space or little wrinkly old men.

"I thought so too," I say softly, watching as Garrison places Vada
in Daisy's arms. My best friend rocks Vada calmly side to side, but
she's already so content and pleased.

"Taurus?" Garrison eyes Daisy. "You already looked up her
zodiac?"

11th are said to be both brilliant and

...ace. "You're telling me that
...ad?"

...ally leaving out the negative. Vada was

...spering something to Vada about her bestie
...nd I know she means Winona. Our daughters will
...ther, and I couldn't be happier to know Vada could
...ave an easy time making a friend. A life-long friend. One
...irth.

When Daisy places our baby back in Garrison's arms, she says, "Of course there's some gloom to balance out the bright parts, but I'm saving that for a different day."

"Nah," Garrison shakes his head. "We should hear it all. How can you even appreciate the good without the bad?"

I smile, love swelling my whole body. From head to toe, I'm floating.

"Alrighty." Daisy nods and smiles over at Vada. "Little Taurus, you will be brilliant, talented, and slightly unstable. Yet, you will be loved by many and you in turn will love deeply."

I'm not sure if those are the exact words from whatever astrology site Daisy consulted, or if she embellished it. I don't care either way.

"Slightly unstable." Garrison is grinning.

I am too.

"Brilliant and talented," I remind him.

He holds her more protectively against his chest. "Not gonna lie, Willow, it sounds like us."

I look at our baby. Our tiny creation. "Welcome to the family, Vada Lauren Abbey."

3 YEARS LATER

September

3

Garrison Abbey

LOFT IN THE CITY IS A HAPPY HOME, NOT JUST FOR WILLOW and me, but now this cute little three-year-old who giggles while eating Fruity Pebbles and who loves mismatched socks. She chose a neon purple sock and a black and teal polka-dot sock today.

Vada is unnaturally patient. Even as I tug her sandy-brown hair with a brush, she swings her legs at the kitchen table, already finished with breakfast. She hums to herself and then slightly winces.

I stop yanking at a knot. "Did that hurt?"

"Yeah," she says. "It's okay though, Daddy. You can keep trying."

If you look up *angelic* in the dictionary, the name *Vada Lauren Abbey* would be printed there. Whatever good thing Willow and I did in our lives, our collective banked luck has befallen upon our daughter. Yeah, I'm biased.

I'm her dad, but seriously, she is patient, kind, and thoughtful.

And she's only three.

Sure, that could all change as she gets older, but these are supposed to be the hardest years, aren't they? Terrible Twos were Terrific Twos. Threes have been a breeze. Give me all the toddler years if they're this good.

I do my best to be gentle with this stupid fucking knot near her ear. She knows Mommy usually does her hair, but Willow is sick with a sinus infection—one that Vada just hurdled over a couple days ago. They were both bed-ridden with stuffy noses, coughs, and headaches.

Vada kept asking why I wasn't sick too. I wanted to say that I'm such an asshole I bet the sinus infection looked at me and said, *nah, he's already plague-ridden, gotta go for the pure ones.*

However, I am not promoting self-loathing in this household, and I'm at a place where I do believe I'm a better person than I once was. It's hard to see my life now and think otherwise.

So I told her that I'm just immune.

She asked what immune meant, and I told her I can't get sick. Which will probably bite me in the ass when I do actually contract a cold in the future. Did I lie to my kid? I don't know. I'm just kind of winging this whole dad thing, and I have to say—I'm not that bad at it. Maybe it's all the babysitting experience or it's just natural for me, but I'm enjoying being a dad to this sweet little girl.

Once I finish her hair, she hops off the chair. "Can we play go-karts now?" She waits expectantly for me to say *sure.*

I check my watch. Shit, we have like fifteen minutes tops before we need to be out the door. She's brushed her teeth. She's dressed in a black shirt and sunflower overalls—the overall phase is purely Vada wanting to wear what Willow wears. Her blue-jean backpack is already filled and zipped.

She's ready. We could leave early.

"Puhleaase," she pleads, melting my heart and part of my resolve to not be late.

"We don't have long. You remember what today is?"

"School with Nony," she says, "but can we...uh, play the go-karts first?" She thinks hard about her words. "We have time!" She brightens like she does think we have time, even if she has no clue what time we really need to leave. "Lots of time, Daddy. Let's go play." She doesn't take my hand and drag me over to the game console and beanbags.

She simply waits.

God, she's such a good kid. I wouldn't say I'm a *softie* necessarily, but I haven't had to be strict with Vada. "We have fifteen minutes. Can you count to fifteen?"

She nods vigorously, then stares at her fingers. "One, toof, three, fifeeth!" She beams.

"Good, okay, go grab your controller and I'll be there in a sec. We don't have long remember, so go fast."

She bolts with a laugh towards the game console. I switch on the TV and put on *Mario Kart* for her. Willow was sad that she doesn't love *Diddy Kong Racing* as much, but at least she enjoys something on the N64 console.

Quickly, I pour coffee in a steaming cup and butter a toasted croissant. Quick glance back—Vada is entranced at the loading screen where NPCs race go-karts on a cow-infested track called Moo Moo Farm. Giving me a second to go check on Willow.

I slip into our bedroom, morning light shining through the curtain. Willow slowly wakes and blows her nose in a tissue. A mountain of tissues fill a trash-bin on her side of the bed.

"Hey, how do you feel?"

She scoots up, and I sit near her thigh. "Stuffy." She sounds worse than yesterday, but she's already seen a doctor and taking medication. "My head doesn't hurt as much."

"That's good. Here, maybe some food will help." I pass her the croissant before the coffee. "You want this or water?"

"Oh coffee." Her eyes widen. "Something warm. I just wanna smell it, really." She cups the mug and sniffs the fumes. "You're the best. I'm sorry I can't help." Willow frowns over at the cracked door. We can hear the theme music to *Mario Kart* from here. "I'm going to miss her first day of pre-K."

"No, you won't."

"I can't get her sick, especially not after she just got over her cough. I thought I'd at least be able to hug her and say goodbye..." She bites into the croissant. "Not that I can see much right now."

I find her glasses on the nightstand. Gently, carefully, I slip them on her face for her—which produces a small smile out of Willow.

"You might not be able to *physically* be there, but you'll be there," I say strongly, then stand off the bed and go to the closet as an idea strikes me. "Hang out with us before we have to go."

"Garrison, I can't—"

"You won't cough on her with this." I dig into the closet and in the back, I find a box of *The Fourth Degree* merch I've been given from working on the Sorin-X game. One of which is an astronaut helmet. "Put this on."

Willow is already crawling out of the bed. Her oversized *Street Fighter* tee reaches her thighs, and she slips her feet into Marvel slippers. The floor of our loft is always cold.

Even stuffy, she sounds elated. "You're a genius."

"Nah, I'm just working for a genius."

She shakes her head like I'm wrong. "You are one, and I think I forgot to say it, but thank you for the breakfast in bed."

I help her fit on the astronaut helmet. "You didn't need to thank me." I can feel her appreciation and love in everything I do. "You're my girl, Willow. I'm always going to take care of you."

Her cheeks flush behind the glass dome of the helmet.

Once we return to the main space of our loft—no divided rooms, just one big open floorplan and big windows looking out at Philly— we head towards the TV.

"Daddy, look, I'm winning!" Vada is still on the loading screen, her gray game controller not hooked up to N64. Before I can tell her good job, she gasps and springs to her feet. "Mommy!!" She stops and gasps. "Are you going to...to space?"

"Not today." Willow taps the glass dome. "This is just so you don't catch Mommy's cough. Don't get too close. You don't want another cough again, do you?"

Vada hesitates because she does want to hug Willow. "Okay..." She sounds reluctant "You want to play, Mommy?" She offers her the controller.

"I'm just gonna watch you beat Daddy."

I smile over at Willow and she smiles back like this is a good day. Even if she feels shitty, even if she couldn't help Vada get ready for pre-K, she's happy, and that makes me really fucking happy.

Vada grins. "I'm gonna try. You ready, Daddy?"

"Five minutes," I tell her.

"Uh-huh. We got lots-a-time." She focuses on the TV. Astronaut Willow lounges on the couch behind us, snuggling beneath a blanket, and as I settled on a beanbag, Vada plops down between my legs.

"Okay, you choose the track, kiddo."

She picks Moo Moo Farm. Of course. I hate this track, but whatever. I'd do anything for her. While she punches buttons, thinking she's playing as Yoshi, I am, in fact, playing as Yoshi and controlling the game. She believes I'm Princess Peach.

Vada careens her whole body to the left as Yoshi turns on the track. "I'm in first. Mommy, you see! I'm in first!"

"Whoa, you're amazing. Keep on racing."

"I am, I am."

When I steal a glimpse back at Willow, I whisper, "She's such a good kid."

"I know…" She smiles softly at Vada. Willow's stuffy voice sounds a little muffed behind the helmet. "I keep waiting for the temper tantrums."

"Same."

"They'll probably come later, right?"

"Teens, yeah," I nod, but I don't know. Maybe not. "What if… what if it's always like this? What if…" I whisper so only my wife can hear—anyway, Vada is hypnotized by Yoshi and flying turtle shells. "…what if we did it…" I stop short of saying *again.*

It feels wrong.

There've been a few moments like today where I've considered, *could we have another kid?* But like now, I always cut myself off. A strange knot forms in my stomach, and Willow can see my wince.

She sits up and leans closer to me. "I've thought about it too.

Because she is so good, but then, I figure, it's just that I love her so much. And I want to duplicate five million of her."

I let out a laugh and I nod, before our gazes fall back to Vada. Willow says exactly what I feel. It's not that I want another kid. It's just that I'm so in love with the one we have.

"I just want her," I realize out loud. It's what I always feel. What I've always *truly* known.

I hear Willow behind me. "Me too."

After Yoshi crosses the finish line in first, Vada asks, "One more race?"

"Time's up. You can't be late for pre-K."

She nods understandingly, and I ask Willow, "Are we sure she's not fifty?"

"I hope she's not stuck in a baby body. That would suck."

"Majorly." I take a seat beside Willow for a quick sec. "Keep your phone on, yeah?" I clutch the glass sides of her helmet. Being physically separated from Willow has never diminished my love for her—it beats just as strongly. "I love you, Willow Abbey. I'll be delivering the three-year-old package to the academic facility in your honor."

Willow grins. "God speed."

I kiss the glass.

She laughs, and as I stand, I'm about to tell Vada to say goodbye to Mommy, but she already jumps up on the couch and clutches the glass helmet like I did.

"I love you, Mommy."

Willow tries not to cry, but her eyes glass. "I love you more, V." She fixes Vada's hair that catches in the hooks of her overalls. "Have fun at school. Be nice to the other students and your teacher."

"I will." With her two little hands on the helmet, Vada leans in and plants a big kiss on the glass.

Willow is a puddle of feelings. Hell, *I'm* a puddle of feelings. Seeing how much my daughter loves her mom and how much Willow loves Vada is like life's greatest fuel, keeping me going.

After Willow gives Vada a quick, loving hug, we're off. Out of the loft. Parking garage, check. Secure Vada in her car seat, check. Drive my Mustang towards pre-K, check.

Get stuck in Philly traffic, *double check*. And I should've seen that coming.

"Shit."

"Uh-oh, Daddy, you said a bad word!"

"Daddy's…not happy about that SUV." Why is he cutting me off? That fuckhead. I change lanes and get stuck behind a red light. I check my mirrors. Is that paparazzi? My pulse hitches, and I grip the steering wheel a little tighter.

They almost never follow me out of the loft. Not unless someone more famous is with me. Like Lo or Lily.

Vada hums to herself, staring out the window. "When can I get a byse?"

"Huh?" I look at her through the rearview mirror.

"A bykse."

She's watching a boy pedal down the sidewalk while his friend skateboards beside him. He does a trick and nearly barrels into a few pedestrians. They shout at him, and he laughs.

What a douchebag. But she's craning her neck to try and see more. This isn't the first time she's asked about bikes. Every time she sees one, she wants on it.

"You mean a *bike*?"

"Yeah, a…*bike*." She tries to enunciate clearer and does a decent job.

"Soon, kiddo," I say. "Let's just get through today."

"Okay." She hums again.

Traffic lets up a little bit, and as I near the pre-K parking lot, I realize that *was* a paparazzi vehicle. But they weren't interested in me or tailing me.

They were tailing the Jeep I park beside. Daisy and Ryke are here with a bouncy, rambunctious Winona. She is hopping up to the curb, her backpack shaped like a Frog.

"Nony!" Vada is already calling, but she's stuck in her car seat.

Bodyguards flank Daisy, Ryke, and their three-year-old daughter like ginormous intimidating shadows. Vada sees them. "When can I get a big man like Nony?"

I unbuckle. "That's a bodyguard." *Not a giant teddy bear.* "And you don't need one, Vada."

Thankfully she doesn't ask why Winona needs one. I'm not sure how to explain the danger levels of fame to my three-year-old.

I'm out of the Mustang, and after I help Vada out of the car seat, I immediately FaceTime Willow.

She answers, back in bed. "Everything okay?"

"Yep. I just wanted you to be here too. Not so far away now, are you?"

"Garrison." Willow pushes up her glasses, eyes misting again. "How does she look?"

"See for yourself." I flip the camera as I take Vada's hand and lead her towards her best friend. Ryke and Daisy are walking their daughter into pre-K ahead of us, and I angle my phone's camera down to Vada who smiles up at me.

"She's so cute," Willow swoons.

"That's 'cause she's mostly you."

"She's half and half."

I disagree. She's like 80% cutie-patootie Willow. And 20% angsty me. I tell her, "We made a cutie."

"We totally did." I hear the smile in her voice. "I'm taking screen-shots."

I grin, loving that she's involved in this part. And these photos, this moment, is for us. We love the internet. Making and posting gifs. Fan forums and edits. But our lives aren't out there for consumption. We're extremely private and trying to raise Vada without the tail of anxiety-inducing paparazzi.

It's not always easy because we do want her to have a relationship with family. People who are famous. But we know how to evade public interest. Because Willow was a fan of the Calloway sisters before she became family.

Because I understand fandoms.

And we know how to be the most uninteresting, *boring* thing on the internet. So I'm confident we'll be able to live a peaceful life out of the public eye.

Once inside the preschool, Vada does the first rebellious thing. She says a quick, "Bye, Daddy!" and she races down the hall to catch up to Winona. Her best friend.

The girls clasp hands and sprint away from us, running up to their teacher.

I stand in shock next to Ryke and Daisy, my phone aimed at our daughters for Willow.

"Fuck," Ryke curses, eyes hardened on the scene. Like his three-year-old is already grown up and doesn't need her mom and dad anymore.

Daisy playfully tips his baseball cap over his eyes. "They're still little. They're just super, magnificent independent girls."

"They're fucking *three*. They don't need to be that independent."

"Ditto," I mention. Shit, I didn't realize this part would be that hard. I want her to come back to me. Am I really going to have to leave her here? I hate school. I hate these walls. I hate this place, but Vada...

"She did so good," Willow says on the phone. "She looks happy."

She does look really, *really* happy. I start smiling. Before Vada slips into the classroom, she turns to glance back down the hall.

She remembers me and waves.

I lift a hand in a stiff wave back, too emotional to be flinging my palm left and right.

"I screen-captured that too," Willow says, emotion in her voice. "It's such a good pic."

"Send it to me."

My phone pings.

Daisy suddenly notices that Willow is on FaceTime with me. "Willow, you feeling any better? Need me to do a chicken noodle soup run? I can be over there in a snap."

I pass Daisy the phone so they can chat.

Ryke goes to speak to the teacher, and I follow to do the same. I'm defaulting to his experience here. And Ryke nods to me in silent greeting. He's never been one for many words outside of *fuck*, but having him here is calming. And cool, really.

I get to raise my kid with his kid.

We share a short smile, and for longer than a second, it feels like I have an older brother with me.

He is my brother-in-law now.

Gratitude suddenly overwhelms me. Yeah, I'm just grateful—to have found this family I wish I always had. A family my daughter will always know.

There is nothing cooler than that.

10 YEARS LATER

EPILOGUE

Garrison Abbey

DIRT TRACKS, BICYCLE TIRES, AND A FAMILIAR ANNOUNCEMENT projected over a rowdy audience, "riders ready…watch the gates"—I smile, taking it all in.

Summer.

I've lived through thirty-nine summers, and before I met my wife, before those long drawn-out summer days in a comic book store, the few hot months out of school were hell.

I hated every summer.

My brothers were home more, and I'd do anything and everything to stay away.

Now, I hunger for the summer days, for the sticky heat and dirt under my soles. And I know with certainty—at thirty-nine—that I've loved more summers than I've hated.

Standing behind a wooden fence, I'm among the noisy crowd who cheer on racers. Sun beats on an outdoor BMX track, a little bit outside of Baltimore.

I run my palm back and forth over my head, hair buzzed short. I prefer nothing in my eyes. Not needing to hide anymore.

I haven't for a long time.

My parents never tried to reconnect. Not even when I was in my early twenties and first left. They released me from their household like a crow who flew through the window and found its way out.

I never had to attempt to pull away twice or a third time. Once was all it took. And I'm grateful for that.

All three of my brothers ended up working for our father's tech company. I never see them. Never speak to them, and like my parents, they're gone from my world.

"Let's go! Let's go!" people shout from the sidelines, pumping up the teen racers as they catch air over dirt hills and skid along the curves of berm turns. Pedaling towards the finish line.

I drop my left arm, while my right arm remains loosely draped over my wife's shoulder. And I smile as my eyes graze Willow and her fingers that are laced with my hand.

My gaze keeps traveling across the event. Competitors in full-face helmets, visors, and long-sleeved jerseys line up with their BMX bikes and wait for their *moto*, what Lo still calls a "heat" even after the tall one corrected him a hundred times.

Loren Hale is still *that* guy.

The corner of my mouth rises, and I glance down the fence. Where Lo has his arms around Lily while they watch the race. Lo is smiling, and in a quiet beat, he catches my gaze and we exchange something pure and happy.

Something I think only guys like me and him can ever truly understand. How long it's been and how far we've come. To peace around us and to peace with ourselves.

I nod.

He nods back.

Jonathan Hale died twelve years ago after his many years of alcohol abuse finally caught up to him. He started laying off me after my kid was born. And by the time he passed away, we were on better terms.

Close by Lily and Lo, Rose spritzes water on her neck and collar. Connor says something to his wife, inaudible over the crowds. She glares up at him. He grins down at her.

My office is still inside Cobalt Inc.—so that weird back and forth between Connor and Rose is too commonplace.

Willow always thought they'd have like eleven children. Enough to fill out a football team. They didn't end up with *that* many. But all the Cobalts are at the BMX track today, and their *seven* kids make up a large portion of our group.

An empire.

Literally the media calls them the *Cobalt Empire*, and Willow and Lily own too much Cobalt Empire merch. I love the T-shirts and water bottles. Hate the snow globes.

"Oh…no, I'm out of storage," Willow says beside me, and I glance back as she untangles our hands and quickly tries to free up storage on the DSLR camera strapped around her neck.

Keeping my arm splayed over her shoulder, I use my other hand to hold the camera and help Willow.

Daisy notices the dilemma after Ryke drops her on her feet. He had her upside-down. Even after all these years, Ryke is a beast. Physically able to climb any mountain and also toss his wife over his shoulder. Paparazzi aren't allowed in the event, but I bet their telephoto lenses captured that shot.

Media loves a flirty *Raisy*.

"I still have the video camera." Daisy holds up a newer digital camcorder, Velcro-ed to her hand. "We won't miss a thing."

Everyone also has cellphones. No matter what, the competition will be recorded a billion times over by the core six.

Willow smiles at Daisy, who smiles brightly back, and they let me fix the DSLR. My eyes skim the women as they talk and laugh.

Their friendship has only strengthened through the years. Even as work pulls everyone away at times. Willow is the Chief Brand Officer for Superheroes & Scones, and every now and then, we'll return to London. We always make a point to time meetups with Tess and Sheetal. They live in Atlanta, but they visit Sheetal's family in Liverpool about twice a year.

We went to their wedding in London.

And currently, Tess is an actress on a medical TV drama that we tape every Tuesday night, and Sheetal is a producer on the same show.

I click into the camera settings. Two clicks later and the *no storage* warning sign disappears. "Got it."

Willow grins up at me. Rising on her toes, we kiss and she whispers, "Thanks."

My lips upturn more, and I cup the back of her neck in tender affection. "Anytime, anywhere." Still, to this day, my heart belongs to Willow.

At the sound of a familiar whistle, my gaze drifts. Near us, twenty-two-year-old Jane Cobalt has two fingers in her mouth, whistling the way her Aunt Daisy taught her.

Bright smile, freckled cheeks—Jane cheers on other teens, basically strangers, while we wait for the next moto.

She's smart. Like genius intellect. In a minute flat, she calculated the points needed for the top ten racers to qualify for the Grand Nationals in Tulsa.

And I thought I was good with numbers.

While Jane lives in Philly, she's been seen out with some douchey bro. Connor acts like it's not the worst thing in the world, but I see how his face twitches whenever Lo and Ryke bring up the subject. Connor has run about ten different background checks on the guy and was even a heartbeat away from asking me to hack into the bro's computer.

I don't blame him.

Jane is severely famous.

The five oldest kids are.

I glance over my shoulder at our tent. Coolers surround pop-up chairs under the shade. Maximoff Hale has a few bottles of Ziff in arm, on his way back to everyone. Athletic, kind-hearted, unwavering confidence is in his entire demeanor.

I feel fucking old. Because next month, he'll turn twenty-two, and I look at him and still see the little kid I'd babysit.

The one who made me feel alive when being away from Willow seemed like certain death.

His thick brown hair is dyed lighter and blows in the wind.

Moffy smiles as he stops beside me. "Is it time yet?"

"Should be next." As he passes a blue flavored Ziff to Willow and limeade to me, I notice a wet piece of paper in his hand. "What's that?"

He makes a face and stuffs the paper in his back pocket. "A guy gave me his number." His eyes briefly flit towards a group of twenty-something racers before landing on me. "I didn't want to reject him in from of his friends."

I glance between the smiling guy and Moffy, a lot more coolly than his dad would be. Lo has no chill when it comes to his kids and dating. "You're not interested?"

He shakes his head. "He's cute, but…" Moffy stares off in thought. He's bi and considered a top "eligible bachelor" in the nation. He's never been in a serious relationship, and I think whoever ends up with Moffy will probably need to be tough as hell.

As new riders reach the gate, we all face the track.

Willow squeezes my hand in excitement and then starts snapping pictures.

"Let's go!"

"You got this!"

Everyone shouts around me.

I cup my hands around my mouth and yell, "Ride smart! Stay sharp!" My pulse ratchets up.

USA's BMX East Coast Nationals has been in full swing. Day three, and my kid already raced six motos to qualify for this Main.

Every time I watch my thirteen-year-old, I'm fucking nervous. It's not a safe sport, and we've already dealt with a broken arm at age six. Lost control of the bike during a district championship.

Crowds cheer, "Come on! Let's go!"

Eight competitors grip their handlebars. My thirteen-year-old among them. In the blue and black jersey and full-face helmet.

Let's go.

I keep my arm over Willow.

"Set yourselves," the announcer calls out. "Riders ready…watch the gates." *Beep beep beep.* The gates drop, and I hold my breath as tires descend on dirt track. Speeding and flying over hills.

I clap and yell, and when the last lap comes, Willow grips my shoulder.

Our kid is in third and shooting for first.

"Wait, wait…" Willow says and then we wince when two competitors pass at the turn.

Shit.

We see the standing.

Sixth place.

"Good race!" I shout and clap. This year, our thirteen-year-old came in first at the East Conference Championships and needed to place fourth at this event to have enough points to attend Grand Nationals.

Have to wait till next year.

Willow and I meet the competitors at the end of the track.

"Awesome job," I say with a hug and tap of the helmet. "You did great out there."

"Except I *screwed* that turn."

"You'll get it next time," Willow encourages with a loving smile.

And then our kid grips the helmet with two gloved hands. Taking it off and shaking out a loose sandy-brown braid.

Our daughter smiles a gap-toothed smile like she won the race, even when she lost. "I did better than last year, faster start out the gate."

"Yeah, for sure," Willow says, passing her a water bottle.

"Thanks, Mom." She takes a swig. "So I can go to Arcadia Galactica tomorrow, right?"

I lift my brows. "You're still grounded, Vada."

"Aw, come on." Her voice is light, knowing she shouldn't get a reprieve for biking after dark. A rule she constantly breaks. We still live in the city, in the same Philly loft.

Vada is brave like her mom. And she's also nonconfrontational, in a way like me. I rest easy knowing she walks away from fights.

"Next week," Willow reminds her, "you can always go then, unless you get grounded aga—"

"I won't," she says quickly, walking her bike back to the tent with us. "I'm having Pac-Man withdrawals like so bad." Her aquamarine eyes flit to me. "Literally, Dad."

I hate that game. She knows I hate that game, and honestly, I can't believe my kid loves playing for hours upon *hours*. Vada pulverized Willow's high score when she was four, and not because her mom is bad. Willow is fucking good at that one.

While we keep walking, Vada talks and smiles over the pics that her mom captured.

They both laugh.

And my chest rises in a light breath. In happiness.

Vada Lauren Abbey was born from love, and we named her *Vada* after the character in the movie *My Girl*. Lauren after the guy who changed our lives.

As soon as we enter the tent, Vada is rushed by family, by her cousins, three of which are girls around her age—and also her best friends. They pour ice water over her head. Laughing. Congratulating.

I extend my arm back around Willow, sharing a gentle smile with my wife. Summers are my favorite part of the year, always full of family.

And with this family, these people who protect and love without question, sixth place can feel like first.

VIDEO GAME REVIEWS

Sorin-X 5

Overview: 9.5 IGN.com, 5/5 Trusted Reviews, 94% Metacritic

Developer: Abbey Game Studios
Publisher: Cobalt Electronics
Creator: Garrison Abbey
Director: Garrison Abbey
Designer: Garrison Abbey
Programmer: Garrison Abbey
Writer(s): Garrison Abbey, Jasmine Lang
Artist(s): Belinda Howell, Jackson Howell
Composer: Anya Rhodes
Series: *Sorin-X*

SALES: *Sorin-X 5* sold 1.6 million copies within 24-hours of release and sold through its 15 million first-run shipment order to retailers.

AWARDS: *Sorin-X 5* received high critical praise and gaming awards from publications, including awards from GamesHighlight and Game eVolution. It also won the Game of the Year for innovative gameplay and story, and the *Sorin-X* series continues to dominate the gaming landscape. Working under a small team with an emphasis on originality and character-connection, the creator has been lauded since the first iteration of the game fourteen years ago. Garrison Abbey is considered one of the greatest video game creators in modern history.

READING GUIDE

Willow & Garrison are first introduced as side characters in the *Addicted/Calloway Sisters Series*. Timelines overlap between those books and *Bad Reputation*. In order to read both stories together, we've created a helpful guide on the next page.

Note: Willow makes a small appearance in *Addicted for Now*, but she has a much more significant role in *Addicted After All*.

Addicted/Calloway Sisters Series Reading Order
1. Addicted to You
2. Ricochet
3. Addicted for Now
4. Kiss the Sky
5. Hothouse Flower
6. Thrive
7. Addicted After All **(*Bad Reputation* Read Along Starts Here!)**
8. Fuel the Fire
9. Long Way Down
10. Some Kind of Perfect

THE COMPLETE READING GUIDE
Addicted + Calloway Sisters + Bad Rep

Some chapters from Bad Reputation overlap with chapters from the Addicted/Calloway Sisters Series where they're the same scene but written from Willow or Garrison's POVs. In most instances, we recommend reading the Addicted/Calloway Sisters Series chapters first, and this is reflected in the reading guide.

ACKNOWLEDGEMENTS
from Whatever It Takes

Pizza, comic books, video games, pop culture references (hello, *Gilmore Girls* and *One Tree Hill*)—this book is a bowl of nostalgia that we've absolutely *loved* writing and experiencing together. Whatever It Takes has always been this overwhelming passion project of ours, and to be able to return to Willow & Garrison's love story (as they were first side characters in the Addicted series) and give them *more* is what dreams are made of.

Their romance and journey isn't over yet, but we have amazing people to thank for making Whatever It Takes possible.

To our superhero mom, thank you for being our Rose Calloway, our fierce supporter when we're doubting ourselves. You always come in the clutch when we need you, and this book wouldn't be nearly as sparkly without your touch. We love you like Garrison loves pizza!

To our agent Kimberly Brower, thank you for helping Garrison & Willow's story become audiobooks! It's a dream to be able to hear their romance come to life.

To Jenn, Lanie, and Shea, thank you so much for believing in us and helping us shout about Willow & Garrison from the rooftops of the world. We're the luckiest twins to be able to know you three and that you still love our books and characters after all these years. We love you like family.

To patrons, this book wouldn't have been possible without you. *Thankyouthankyouthankyou.* We're able to keep writing full-time because of you, and you're a huge reason why we were able to return to side characters like Willow & Garrison and take time to write their stories.

And finally, thank you to the Fizzle Force and to you, dear reader, for finishing this book in its entirety. We're incredibly grateful that you've taken the time to read our words when so many books exist, and we hope that you've enjoyed spending your day with comic-book-loving, video game and TV-obsessed geeks.

More is on the way! Next up is *Wherever You Are*, the conclusion to the duet, and hold onto your pizza slices, it might be a bumpy ride!

SPECIAL THANKS
from Wherever You Are

The biggest thanks to our mom for continuing to be in our corner and putting up with our intense deadlines. We love you to the moon and back. When we call, you're there. No questions asked. We always say you're our very own Rose Calloway, and it's never been more true. From the bottom of our hearts, thankyouthankyouthankyou.

xoxo Krista & Becca

CPSIA information can be obtained
at www.ICGtesting.com
Printed in the USA
LVHW041647010223
738416LV00001B/12

7